# The Count of Monte Cristo

## ALEXANDRE DUMAS

ABRIDGED

DOVER PUBLICATIONS
GARDEN CITY, NEW YORK

*Bibliographical Note*

This Dover edition, first published in 2007, is a republication of a standard abridged edition.

*International Standard Book Number*

*ISBN-13: 978-0-486-45643-0*
*ISBN-10: 0-486-45643-9*

Manufactured in the United States of America
45643914    2023
www.doverpublications.com

# Contents

# Contents

# The Count of Monte Cristo

# CHAPTER I

## MARSEILLES—THE ARRIVAL

On the 24th of February, 1815, the watch-tower of Notre-Dame de la Garde signalled the arrival of the three-master *Pharaon*, from Smyrna, Trieste, and Naples.

The usual crowd of curious spectators immediately filled the quay of Fort Saint-Jean, for at Marseilles the arrival of a ship is always a great event, especially when that ship, as was the case with the *Pharaon*, has been built, rigged, and laden in the dockyard of old Phocaea and belongs to a shipowner of their own town.

Meanwhile the vessel drew on, and was approaching the harbour under topsails, jib, and foresail, but so slowly and with such an air of melancholy that the spectators, always ready to sense misfortune, began to ask one another what ill-luck had overtaken those on board. However, those experienced in navigation soon saw that if there had been any ill-luck, the ship had not been the sufferer, for she advanced in perfect condition and under skilful handling; the anchor was ready to be dropped, the bowsprit shrouds loose. Beside the pilot, who was steering the *Pharaon* through the narrow entrance to the port, there stood a young man, quick of gesture and keen of eye, who watched every movement of the ship while repeating each of the pilot's orders.

The vague anxiety that prevailed among the crowd affected one of the spectators so much that he could not wait until the ship reached the port; jumping into a small boat, he ordered the boatman to row him alongside the *Pharaon*, which he reached opposite the creek of La Réserve.

On seeing this man approach, the young sailor left his post beside the pilot, and, hat in hand, leant over the ship's bulwarks. He was a tall, lithe young man of about twenty years of age, with fine dark eyes and hair as black as ebony; his whole manner bespoke that air of calm resolution peculiar to those who, from their childhood, have been accustomed to face danger.

1

"Ah, is that you, Dantès!" cried the man in the boat. "You are looking pretty gloomy on board. What has happened?"

"A great misfortune, Monsieur Morrel," replied the young man, "a great misfortune, especially for me! We lost our brave Captain Leclère off Civita Vecchia."

"What happened to him?" asked the shipowner. "What has happened to our worthy captain?"

"He died of brain-fever in dreadful agony. Alas, monsieur, the whole thing was most unexpected. After a long conversation with the harbour-master, Captain Leclère left Naples in a great state of agitation. In twenty-four hours he was in high fever, and died three days afterwards. We performed the usual burial service. He is now at rest off the Isle of El Giglio, sewn up in his hammock, with a thirty-six-pounder shot at his head and another at his heels. We have brought home his sword and his cross of honour to his widow. But was it worth his while," added the young man, with a sad smile, "to wage war against the English for ten long years only to die in his bed like everybody else?"

"Well, well, Monsieur Edmond," replied the owner, who appeared more comforted with every moment, "we are all mortal, and the old must make way for the young, otherwise there would be no promotion. And the cargo ...?"

"Is all safe and sound, Monsieur Morrel, take my word for it. It has been a voyage that will bring you in a good twenty-five thousand francs!"

As they were just past the Round Tower the young man shouted out: "Ready there! Lower topsails, foresail, and jib!"

The order was executed as promptly as on board a man-of-war.

"Lower away! and brail all!"

At this last order, all the sails were lowered and the ship moved on almost imperceptibly.

"And now, Monsieur Morrel," said Dantès, "here is your purser, Monsieur Danglars, coming out of his cabin. If you will step on board he will furnish you with every particular. I must look after the anchoring and dress the ship in mourning."

The owner did not wait to be invited twice. He seized a rope which Dantès flung to him, and, with an agility that would have done credit to a sailor, climbed up the ladder attached to the side of the ship, while the young man, returning to his duty, left the conversation to the individual whom he had announced under the name of Danglars, and who now came toward the owner. He was a man of twenty-five or twenty-six, of unprepossessing countenance, obsequious to his superiors, insolent to his subordinates; and besides the fact that he was the purser—and pursers are always unpopular on board—he was personally as much disliked by the crew as Edmond Dantès was beloved by them.

"Well, Monsieur Morrel," said Danglars, "you have heard of the misfortune that has befallen us?"

"Yes, yes, poor Captain Leclère! He was a brave and honest man!" "And a first-rate seaman, grown old between sky and ocean, as a man should be who is entrusted with the interests of so important a firm as that of Morrel and Son," replied Danglars.

"But," replied the owner, watching Dantès at his work, "it seems to me that a sailor need not be so old to understand his business; our friend Edmond seems to understand it thoroughly, and to require no instructions from anyone."

"Yes," said Danglars, casting a look of hatred on Dantès, "yes, he is young, and youth is never lacking in self-confidence. The captain was hardly dead when, without consulting anyone, he assumed command of the ship, and was the cause of our losing a day and a half off the Isle of Elba instead of making direct for Marseilles."

"As captain's mate, it was his duty to take command, but he acted wrongly in losing a day and a half off Elba unless the ship was in need of repair."

"The ship was as right as I am and as I hope you are, Monsieur Morrel; it was nothing more than a whim on his part, and a fancy for going ashore, that caused the delay off Elba."

"Dantès," called the owner, turning toward the young man, "just step this way, will you?"

"One moment, monsieur," he replied, "and I shall be with you." Then turning to the crew, he called out: "Let go!"

The anchor was instantly dropped and the chain ran out with a great rattle. In spite of the pilot's presence Dantès remained at his post until this last task was accomplished, and then he added: "Lower the flag and pennant to half-mast and slope the yards!"

"You see," said Danglars, "he already imagines himself captain."

"And so he is," said his companion. "Why should we not give him the post? I know he is young, but he seems to be an able and thoroughly experienced seaman."

A cloud passed over Danglars' brow.

"Your pardon, Monsieur Morrel," said Dantès, approaching. "Now that the boat is anchored, I am at your service. I believe you called me."

Danglars retreated a step or two.

"I wished to know the reason of the delay off Elba."

"I am unaware of the reason, monsieur; I only followed the last instructions of Captain Leclère, who, when dying, gave me a packet for the Maréchal Bertrand."

"And did you see the Maréchal?"

"Yes."

Morrel glanced around him and then drew Dantès on one side.

"How is the Emperor?" he asked eagerly.

"Very well, so far as I could see. He came into the Maréchal's room while I was there."

"Did you speak to him?"

"It was he who spoke to me, monsieur," said Dantès, smiling. "He asked me some questions about the ship, about the time of her departure for Marseilles, the route she had followed and the cargo she carried. I believe that had she been empty and I the master, he would have bought her; but I told him I was only the mate and that the ship belonged to the firm of Morrel and Son. 'Ah, ah,' said he. 'I know the firm. The Morrels have all been shipowners for generations, and there was a Morrel who served in the same regiment with me when I was garrisoned at Valance.'"

"Quite true! Quite true!" Monsieur Morrel exclaimed, delighted. "It was Policar Morrel, my uncle, who afterwards became a captain. Dantès, you must tell my uncle that the Emperor still remembers him and you will see tears of joy in the old soldier's eyes. Well, well!" he added, giving Dantès a friendly tap on the shoulder, "you were quite right in carrying out Captain Leclère's instructions and putting in at the Isle of Elba, though if it were known that you delivered a packet to the Maréchal and talked with the Emperor you might get into trouble."

"How so?" said Dantès. "I don't even know what the packet contained, and the Emperor merely made such inquiries as he would of any newcomer. But excuse me, monsieur, for one moment, here are the medical and customs officers coming on board."

As the young man departed Danglars approached.

"Well," said he, "it would seem that he has given you good reasons for dropping anchor off Porto Ferrajo?"

"Most satisfactory ones, dear Monsieur Danglars."

"So much the better," replied the purser, "for it is never pleasant to see a comrade neglect his duty."

"Dantès certainly did his, and there is nothing more to be said on the matter. It was Captain Leclère who ordered him to call at Elba."

"Talking of Captain Leclère, hasn't Dantès given you a letter from him?"

"No, was there one for me?"

"I think that, in addition to the packet, Captain Leclère gave him a letter."

"What packet do you mean, Danglars?"

"The one Dantès delivered at Porto Ferrajo."

"How do you know that he had a packet for Porto Ferrajo?"

Danglars turned red.

"I was passing the captain's door, which was ajar, and saw him give Dantès the packet and the letter."

"He has not mentioned a letter to me, but if he has one I have no doubt he will give it to me."

"Then, Monsieur Morrel, pray don't mention it to Dantès. Perhaps I am mistaken."

Just then the young man returned and Danglars retreated as before.

"Well, Dantès, have you finished now?"

"Yes, monsieur."

"Then you can come and dine with us?"

"I beg you to excuse me, Monsieur Morrel. I owe my first visit to my father. All the same, I greatly appreciate the honour you pay me."

"You are quite right, Dantès. I know you are a good son."

"And do you know if my father is quite well?" he asked with some hesitation.

"Oh, I believe so, my dear Edmond, but I have not seen him lately. At any rate I am sure that he has not wanted for anything during your absence."

Dantès smiled. "My father is proud, monsieur, and even had he been in want of everything, I doubt whether he would have asked anything of anybody except God."

"Well, then, after this first visit has been paid, may we count on you?"

"Once more I must ask you to excuse me, Monsieur Morrel. There is yet another visit which I am most anxious to pay."

"True, Dantès; I had forgotten that there is at the Catalans some one who is awaiting you with as much impatience as your father—the fair Mercédès."

Dantès smiled.

"Well! well!" said the shipowner. "Now I understand why she came to me three times for news of the *Pharaon*. Upon my word, Edmond, you are to be envied: she is a handsome girl. But don't let me keep you any longer. You have looked after my affairs so well that it is but your due that you should now have time to look after your own. Are you in need of money?"

"No, thank you, monsieur, I have all my pay from the voyage; that is nearly three months' salary."

"You are a careful fellow, Edmond."

"Say rather that I have a poor father."

"Yes, yes, I know you are a good son. Off you go to your father. I too have a son, and I should be very angry with anyone who kept him away from me after a three months' voyage."

"I have your leave, monsieur?" said the young man, saluting.

"Yes, if you have nothing more to say to me. By the way, before Captain Leclère died, did he not give you a letter for me?"

"He was unable to write, monsieur. But that reminds me, I shall have to ask you for a fortnight's leave."

"To get married?"

"First of all, and then for a journey to Paris."

"Very well, take what time you need. It will take us quite six weeks to unload the cargo, and we shall not be ready to put to sea again for another three months. But you must be back in three months, for the *Pharaon* cannot sail without her captain," he added, patting the young sailor on the back.

"Without her captain, did you say?" cried Dantès, his eyes sparkling with joy. "Oh! if you really mean that, monsieur, you are touching on my fondest hopes. Is it really your intention to make me captain of the *Pharaon?*"

"If it depended on me alone, my dear Dantès, I should give you my hand saying, 'It is settled,' but I have a partner, and you know the Italian proverb, *Chi ha compagne ha padrone.* But half the battle is won since you already have my vote. Leave it to me to get my partner's for you. Now, off you go; I shall remain here awhile and go over the accounts with Danglars. By the by, were you satisfied with him on the voyage?"

"That depends on what you mean by that question. If you mean as comrade I must say no, for I do not think he has been my friend ever since the day I was foolish enough to propose to him that we should stop for ten minutes at the Isle of Monte Cristo to settle a little dispute. I never ought to have made the suggestion, and he was quite right in refusing. If you mean as purser I have nothing to say against him, and I think you will be satisfied with the way in which he has discharged his duties."

Thereupon the young sailor jumped into the boat, seated himself in the stern and ordered the oarsmen to put him ashore at the Cannebière. With a smile on his lips M. Morrel glanced after him till he saw him jump ashore. There he was immediately lost in the motley crowd that, from five o'clock in the morning until nine o'clock in the evening, collects in that famous street of the Cannebière, of which the modern Phocaeans are so proud that they say in all seriousness, and with that peculiar accent which lends so much character to what they say, "If Paris owned the Cannebière she would be a little Marseilles."

On turning round the shipowner saw Danglars standing behind him. The latter, who appeared to be awaiting his orders, was in reality, like him, following the movements of the young sailor. But how different was the expression in the eyes of each of these two men as they gazed after Dantès' retreating figure!

## CHAPTER II

## FATHER AND SON

LET us leave Danglars struggling with his feeling of hatred and trying to whisper some evil insinuation against his comrade into their master's ear, and let us follow Dantès, who, after having run along the Cannebière, turned down the Rue Noailles. Here he entered a small house situated to the left of the Allées de Meilhan, ran up the four flights of dark stairs, and, trembling with excitement, stopped before a half-open door which revealed the interior of the little room.

It was the room which Dantès' father inhabited.

The news of the *Pharaon's* arrival had not yet reached the old man, who was mounted on a chair, and, with a hand trembling with old age, was busy staking some nasturtiums that, intermingled with clematis, climbed up the trellis before his window. Suddenly he felt an arm thrown round him, and a well-known voice called out:

"Father, my dear old Dad!"

With a cry of joy the old man turned round and saw his son; pale and visibly trembling he threw his arms round him.

"What ails you, Father?" the young man anxiously inquired. "Are you ill?"

"No, no! my dear Edmond . . . my boy . . . my son . . . not at all, but I was not expecting you, and the joy at suddenly seeing you again has given me rather a shock."

"Well, calm yourself, Father, it is really I. They say that joy never harms anyone, so I came in without warning. I have come back and we are going to be happy together."

"That's right, my boy," replied the old man, "but in what way are we going to be happy? You are not going to leave me any more? Come, now, tell me how you have fared."

"May God forgive me that I should rejoice in good fortune brought about by another's death! Goodness knows, I never sought it. It has happened and I have not the strength to regret it. Our good old Captain Leclère is dead, Father, and it is probable that with Monsieur Morrel's assistance I shall take his place. Do you understand, Father? A captain at twenty, with a salary of a hundred louis, besides a share in the profits! Isn't it really more than a poor sailor like me could hope for?"

"Yes, my son, yes, it certainly is," said the old man.

"With my first pay I shall buy you a little house with a garden where you can plant your clematis, your nasturtiums, and your honeysuckle. But, Father, what *is* the matter? You don't look well."

"It is nothing, it will soon pass," said the old man; but his strength failed him and he fell backward.

"This will never do!" exclaimed the youth. "A glass of wine will soon put you right. Tell me where you keep it," he continued, opening one cupboard after another.

"It is useless to look for it," said the old man. "There is no wine."

"What! no wine?" said the young man, turning pale and looking first at the old man's sunken and pallid cheeks and then at the bare cupboards. "No wine? Have you been in want of money, Father?"

"I have not wanted for anything now that you are here," said the old man.

"Yet," stammered Edmond, wiping the perspiration from his brow, "yet when I went away three months ago I left you two hundred francs."

"True enough, but you forgot a little debt you owed to our neighbour Caderousse. He reminded me of it, and told me that if I did not pay it for you he would go to Monsieur Morrel for the money. Fearing that might do you harm, I paid it for you."

"But," cried Dantès, "I owed Caderousse a hundred and forty francs. Do you mean to say that you paid him that sum out of the two hundred francs I left you?"

The old man nodded.

"So that you have lived for three months on sixty francs?"

"You know that I require very little."

"May God forgive me!" cried Edmond, throwing himself on his knees before his father.

"Nay, nay!" said the old man, with a quiet smile. "Now that you are with me again the past is all forgotten and all is well."

"Yes," said the young man, "here I am with a little money in my pockets and a good future before me. Here, Father, take some money, take some and send for something good to eat and drink." So saying, he emptied the contents of his pockets on to the table—a dozen pieces of gold, five or six crowns, and some smaller coins.

His father's face brightened. "Whose is that?" said he.

"Mine . . .yours . . . ours! Take some, buy some provisions and be happy, for we shall have some more to-morrow."

"Gently, gently," said the old man, smiling. "If you don't mind, I shall spend your money warily. If people see me buying too many things at a time, they will think I have had to wait for your return before buying them. But hush! here comes some one; it is Caderousse, who has no doubt heard of your arrival, and has come to welcome you home."

At that moment Caderousse entered. He was a man of five- or six-and-twenty, with a mass of black hair. He carried in his hand a piece of cloth which, in his capacity of tailor, he was going to turn into a coat-lining.

"So you have come back, Edmond?" he said with a strong Marseilles accent, and with a broad smile that disclosed teeth as white as ivory.

"Yes, as you perceive, neighbour Caderousse, and ready to serve you in any way," Dantès answered, but ill concealing his coldness by these civil words.

"Thank you. Happily I am not in need of anything; it is sometimes others who have need of my assistance." Dantès made a slight movement. "I don't mean that for you, boy; I lent you money and you returned it. That was but a neighbourly action and we are now quits."

"We are never quits with those who oblige us," said Dantès, "when we no longer owe them money we owe them gratitude."

"Why speak of it? What is past is gone and done with. Let us talk of your happy return. It would appear that you have had a stroke of luck and are already well in Monsieur Morrel's good books."

"Monsieur Morrel has always been very kind to me."

"In that case you were wrong to refuse to dine with him."

"What! refuse to dine with him!" exclaimed old Dantès. "So he asked you to dinner, did he?"

"Yes, Father," returned Edmond, with a smile, "because, you know, I wanted to come to you as soon as possible."

"I don't suppose your dear kind Monsieur Morrel was overpleased at that," said Caderousse, "and of course when a man aims at being captain he mustn't offend his employer. You should butter him up a bit."

"Oh! I hope to be captain without doing that," replied Dantès.

"Capital! That will please your old friends, and I know some one who won't be sorry to hear it."

"Do you mean Mercédès?" said the old man.

"Yes," Edmond replied. "And now that I have seen you, Father, and assured myself that you are well and want for nothing, I will ask your permission to leave for a time. I am anxious to see Mercédès."

"Go, my son, go," said old Dantès. "And may God bless you in your wife as He has blessed me in my son."

Edmond took leave of his father, nodded to Caderousse, and went out. Caderousse waited a few minutes, and then he also descended the stairs and joined Danglars, who had been waiting for him at the corner of the Rue Senac.

"Well," said Danglars, "did you see him?"

"I have just left him," said Caderousse.

"Did he speak of his hopes of becoming captain?"

"He spoke as if it were quite settled."

"Patience," said Danglars; "it seems to me he is in too much of a hurry."

"But I believe Monsieur Morrel has even promised him the captaincy."

"Pooh!" said Danglars, "he is not captain yet! Is he still in love with the beautiful Catalan?"

"Head over ears! He has just gone to see her, but if I am not greatly mistaken there is a storm brewing in that direction."

"What do you mean?"

"I do not know anything for certain, but I have seen things which make me think that the future captain will not have it all his own way up at the Vieilles-Infirmeries."

"What have you seen?"

"Every time that Mercédès has come to town lately, she has been accompanied by a tall, gay young Catalan with black eyes and red complexion who seems very attentive to her, and whom she addresses as cousin."

"Really! And do you think he is making love to her?"

"I suppose so. What else would a man of twenty-one be doing with a beautiful young girl of seventeen?"

"And you say Dantès has gone to the Catalans?"

"He left before me."

"Let us go in the same direction; we can turn in at La Réserve and await events over a glass of wine."


## CHAPTER III

## THE CATALANS

ABOUT a hundred paces from the spot where the two friends were sitting sipping their wine the village of the Catalans rose behind a bare hill, exposed to the fierce sun and swept by the biting north-west wind.

One day a mysterious colony set out from Spain and landed on the narrow strip of land which they inhabit to this very day. No one knew whence they came or what tongue they spoke. One of their chiefs who could speak a little Provençal solicited from the commune of Marseilles the bare and barren promontory on which they, like the sailors of ancient times, had run their boats ashore. Their request was granted, and three months later, around the twelve or fifteen boats which had brought these Bohemians from the sea, there arose a little village.

This is the same village that we see to-day constructed in an odd and picturesque fashion, half Moorish and half Spanish, inhabited by the descendants of these people and speaking the language of their fathers. For three or four centuries they remained faithful to the little promontory on which they had settled like a flight of sea-birds. They did not mix with the inhabitants of Marseilles, but intermarried amongst their own folk and preserved the customs and costumes of their original country just as they preserved its language.

We would ask our readers to follow us along the only street of this little hamlet and enter with us one of its tiny houses. A young and beautiful girl, with hair as black as jet and eyes of the velvety softness of the gazelle, was standing leaning against the wall. Three steps away a young man of about twenty years of age was sitting tilting his chair and leaning his elbow on an old worm-eaten piece of furniture. He was looking at the girl with an air which betrayed both vexation and uneasiness; his eyes questioned her, but the girl's firm and steady gaze checked him.

"Mercédès," said the young man, "Easter is nearly round again, and it is just the right time for a wedding. Give me an answer, do!"

"I have answered you a hundred times, Fernand. I really think you must be your own enemy that you should ask me again. I have never encouraged you in your hopes, Fernand; you cannot reproach me with one coquettish look. I have always said to you: 'I am fond of you as a brother, but never ask anything more of me. My heart belongs to another.' Haven't I always told you that, Fernand?"

"Yes, I know, Mercédès. I know that you have always been cruelly frank with me."

"Fernand," Mercédès answered, shaking her head, "a woman becomes a bad housekeeper and cannot even be sure of remaining a good wife when she loves another than her husband. Be satisfied with my friendship, for, I repeat it once more, this is all I can promise you."

Fernand rose from his seat, walked round the room, and returned to Mercédès, standing before her with scowling brows.

"Tell me once more, Mercédès; is this your final answer?"

"I love Edmond Dantès," the girl answered coldly, "and none other shall be my husband."

"You will always love him?"

"As long as I live."

Fernand bowed his head in defeat, heaved a sigh resembling a groan, and then, suddenly raising his head, hissed between his clenched teeth:

"But if he is dead?"

"If he is dead I too shall die."

"But if he forgets you?"

"Mercédès!" cried a gladsome voice outside the door, "Mercédès!"

"Ah!" the girl exclaimed, blushing with joy and love, "you see he has not forgotten me since here he is!"

And she ran toward the door which she opened, calling:

"Here, Edmond, here I am!"

Fernand, pale and trembling, recoiled like a wayfarer at the sight of a snake, and, finding a chair, sat down on it.

Edmond and Mercédès fell into each other's arms. The fierce Marseilles sun which penetrated the room through the open door covered them with a flood of light. At first they saw nothing around them. Their intense happiness isolated them from the rest of the world. Suddenly Edmond became aware of the gloomy countenance of Fernand peering out of the shadows, pale and menacing, and instinctively the young man put his hand to the knife at his belt.

"I beg your pardon," said Dantès, "I did not perceive that there were three of us here." Then, turning to Mercédès, he asked, "Who is this gentleman?"

"He will be your best friend, Dantès, for he is my friend. He is my cousin Fernand, the man whom, after you, I love best in the world. Don't you recognize him?"

"Ah, so it is!" Edmond said, and, still keeping Mercédès' hand clasped in one of his, he held the other one out in all friendliness to the Catalan. Instead, however, of responding to this show of cordiality Fernand remained mute and motionless as a statue. Edmond cast an inquiring glance at the agitated and trembling Mercédès, and then at Fernand, who stood there gloomy and forbidding.

This glance told him all, and his brow became suffused with anger. "I did not hasten thus to your side to find an enemy here, Mercédès."

"An enemy?" Mercédès cried, with an angry look at her cousin. "An enemy in my house, did you say, Edmond? You have no enemy here. Fernand, my brother, is not your enemy. He will grasp your hand in token of devoted friendship."

So saying, Mercédès fixed the young Catalan with an imperious look, and, as though mesmerized, he slowly approached Edmond and held out his hand. Like a powerless though furious wave his hatred had broken against the ascendency which this girl exercised over him.

But no sooner had he touched Dantès' hand than he felt he had done all that was within his power; he turned tail and fled out of the house.

"Oh!" he cried out, running along like one demented and tearing his hair. "How can I get rid of this fellow? Poor, wretched fool that I am!"

"Hey, Fernand, where are you running to?" a voice called out.

The young man suddenly stopped, turned round, and perceived Caderousse seated at a table in an arbour of a tavern with Danglars.

"Why don't you join us?" said Caderousse. "Are you in such a hurry that you cannot wait to pass the time of the day with your friends?"

"Especially when those friends have got a full bottle before them," Danglars added.

Ferdinad friend of
Dantes

Fernand looked at the two men as though dazed, and answered not a word. Then he wiped away the perspiration that was coursing down his face, and slowly entered the arbour. The cool shade of the place seemed to restore him to calmness and brought a feeling of relief to his exhausted body. He uttered a groan that was almost a sob, and let his head fall on to his arms crossed on the table.

"Shall I tell you what you look like, Fernand?" said Caderousse, opening the conversation with that frank brutality which the lower classes show when their curiosity gets the upper hand of them. "You look like a rejected lover!" And he accompanied his little jest with a coarse laugh.

"What are you saying?" said Danglars. "A man of his good looks is never unlucky in love. You've made a bad shot this time, Caderousse!"

"Not at all. Just listen to his sighs. Come, Fernand, raise your head and give us an answer. It is not polite to give no reply when friends inquire about your health."

"I am quite well," said Fernand without raising his head.

"Ah, you see, Danglars," Caderousse said, winking at his friend. "This is how the land lies. Fernand, whom you see here and who is one of the bravest and best of the Catalans, to say nothing of being one of the best fishermen in Marseilles, is in love with a pretty girl called Mercédès; unfortunately, however, this fair damsel appears to be in love with the mate of the *Pharaon*, and as the *Pharaon* put into port to-day . . . well, you understand."

"No, I don't understand."

"Poor Fernand has been given his *congé*, that's all."

"And what about it?" said Fernand, raising his head and looking at Caderousse as if he would vent his anger on him. Mercédès is tied to no man, and is free to love anyone she likes, isn't she?"

"Of course, if you take it like that, it is quite a different matter, but I thought you were a Catalan, and I have always been told that a Catalan is not a man to be supplanted by a rival; it has even been said that Fernand is terrible in his vengeance."

"Poor fellow!" Danglars exclaimed, pretending to feel a great pity for the young man. "You see, he did not expect Dantès to return in this way without giving any warning. Perhaps he thought him dead or even faithless."

"When is the wedding to take place?" asked Caderousse, on whom the fumes of the wine were beginning to take effect.

"The date is not yet fixed," Fernand mumbled.

"No, but it will be, as surely as Dantès will be captain of the *Pharaon*, eh, Danglars?"

Danglars started at this unexpected attack, and, turning toward Caderousse, scrutinized his face to try to detect whether this blow had been premeditated; he could read nothing, however, but envy on that drink-besotted face.

"Ah, well," said he, filling the glasses, "let us drink to Captain Edmond Dantès, husband of the beautiful Catalan!"

Caderousse raised his glass to his mouth with a trembling hand and emptied it at one gulp. Fernand took his glass and dashed it to the ground.

"Look there!" hiccoughed Caderousse. "What do I see on the top of the hill yonder near the Catalans? You have better sight than I, Fernand, come and look. I believe my sight is beginning to fail me, and you know wine is treacherous. I seem to see two lovers walking side by side and clasping hands. Heaven forgive us! They have no idea we can see them, for they are actually kissing!"

Danglars did not lose one agonized expression on Fernand's face.

"Do you know them, Monsieur Fernand?" he asked.

"Yes," the latter answered in a husky voice. "It is Monsieur Edmond and Mademoiselle Mercédès."

"You don't mean to say so!" said Caderousse. "Fancy my not recognizing them! Hallo, Dantès! hallo, fair damsel! Come here and tell us when the wedding is to be, for Monsieur Fernand is so obstinate that he won't say a word."

"Be quiet!" said Danglars, pretending to restrain Caderousse, who, with the tenacity of a drunkard, was leaning out of the arbour. "Try to stand up straight and leave the lovers to their love-making. Now, look at Fernand, he at any rate has got some sense."

Danglars looked first at the one and then at the other of the two men: the one intoxicated with drink, the other mad with love.

"I shall not get any further with these two fools," he murmured. "Dantès will certainly carry the day; he will marry that fair damsel, become captain, and have the laugh over us, unless . . ."—a livid smile was seen to pass over his lips—"unless I set to work."

"Hallo," Caderousse continued to call out, half out of his seat and banging on the table, "hi there! Edmond, don't you recognize your friends, or are you too proud to speak to them?"

"No, my dear fellow, I am not proud, but I am in love, and I believe love is more apt to make one blind than pride is."

"Bravo! a good excuse!" Caderousse said. "Good day, Madame Dantès!"

Mercédès curtsied gravely and said: "That is not yet my name, and in my country it is looked upon as bringing bad luck when a girl is given her sweetheart's name before he has become her husband. Call me Mercédès, if you please."

"I suppose your wedding will take place at once, Monsieur Dantès?" said Danglars, bowing to the young couple.

"As soon as possible, Monsieur Danglars. All the preliminaries will be arranged with my father to-day, and to-morrow or the day after at the latest we shall give the betrothal feast at La Réserve here, at which we hope to see all our friends. You are invited, Monsieur Danglars, as also you, Caderousse, and you, of course, Fernand."

Fernand opened his mouth in answer, but his voice died in his throat and he could not say a single word.

"The preliminaries to-day . . . to-morrow the betrothal feast . . . to be sure, you are in a great hurry, captain."

"Danglars," Edmond said smiling, "I repeat what Mercédès said to Caderousse just now. Do not give me the title that does not yet belong to me. It brings bad luck."

"I beg your pardon. I simply said that you seemed to be in a great hurry. Why, there's plenty of time. The _Pharaon_ won't put out to sea for another three months."  *Ship name*

"One is always in a hurry to be happy, Monsieur Danglars, for when one has been suffering for a long time it is difficult to believe in one's good fortune. But it is not selfishness alone that prompts me to press this matter. I have to go to Paris."

"You are going on business?"

"Not on my own account. I have a last commission of Captain Leclère's to execute. You understand, Danglars, it is sacred. But you can put your mind at rest. I shall go straight there and back again."

"Yes, yes, I understand," said Danglars aloud. Then to himself he said: "To Paris? No doubt to deliver the letter the Maréchal gave him. Better and better! This letter has given me an excellent idea. Ah, Dantès, my friend, you are not yet entered in the _Pharaon's_ log book as number one." Then, turning to Edmond, who was moving away, he called out, _"Bon voyage!"_

"Thank you," Edmond replied, turning round and giving him a friendly nod.

Then the two lovers went on their way, peaceful and happy, like two of the elect on their way to Heaven, while the three men continued their interesting conversation.

## CHAPTER IV

# THE BETROTHAL FEAST

THE next day was gloriously fine. The sun rose red and resplendent, its first rays tinting the fleecy clouds with many delicate and brilliant hues. The festive board had been prepared in a large room at La Réserve, with whose arbour we are already acquainted. Although the meal was fixed for noon, the tavern had been filled with impatient guests since eleven o'clock. They consisted chiefly of some of the favoured sailors of the *Pharaon*, and several soldier friends of Dantès'. In order to do honour to the happy couple they had all donned their finest clothes. To crown all, M. Morrel had determined to favour the occasion with his presence, and on his arrival he was greeted with hearty cheers from the sailors of the *Pharaon*. Their owner's presence was to them a confirmation of the report that Dantès was to be their captain, and, as he was popular with them all, they wished to show their owner, by this means, their appreciation of the fact that by a stroke of good luck his choice coincided with their wishes on the subject. Danglars and Caderousse were immediately dispatched to inform the bridegroom of the arrival of this important personage whose entrance had caused such a sensation, and to bid him make haste.

They had barely gone a hundred yards when they perceived the small bridal party approaching. It was composed of the betrothed pair, four maids in attendance on the bride, and Dantès father, who walked beside Mercédès. Fernand walked behind, wearing an evil smile.

Neither Edmond nor Mercédès noticed this evil smile. They were so happy that they had eyes only for each other, and for the beautiful blue sky whence they hoped would come a blessing on their union.

Having acquitted themselves of their errand, the two ambassadors shook hands amicably with Edmond; and while Danglars took his place beside Fernand Caderousse joined old Dantès, who was the object of general attention as he walked along, supporting himself on his curiously carved stick. He was attired in his best black suit, adorned with large steel buttons beautifully cut in facets. His thin but still vigorous legs were arrayed in a pair of beautifully embroidered stockings, which had obviously been smuggled from England. Long blue and white streamers flowed from his three-cornered hat.

Dantès himself was simply clad. As he belonged to the mercantile marine his uniform was half military and half civilian, and, with his good-looking face radiant with joy and happiness, a more perfect specimen of manly beauty could scarcely be imagined.

As the bridal party came in sight of La Réserve M. Morrel advanced to meet them, followed by the soldiers and sailors and other guests. Dantès at once withdrew his arm from that of his betrothed and placed Mercédès' arm respectfully in that of his patron. The shipowner and the blushing girl then led the way up the wooden steps to the room where the feast was prepared. For fully five minutes the boards creaked and groaned under the unwonted pressure of the many steps.

No sooner were they seated than the dishes were handed round. Arles sausages, brown of meat and piquant of flavour, lobsters and prawns in brilliant red shells, sea-urchins whose prickly exteriors resemble chestnuts just fallen from the trees, cockles esteemed by the epicure of the South as surpassing the oyster of the North, in fact every delicacy which the sea washes up on the sandy beach, and which the fishermen call sea-fruit.

"What a silent party!" old Dantès remarked as he caught a whiff of the fragrant yellow wine that old Pamphile himself had just put before Mercédès. "Who would think there are thirty light-hearted and merry people assembled here!"

"A husband is not always light-hearted," Caderousse replied.

"The fact is," said Dantès, "at the present moment I am too happy to be gay. If that is what you mean by your remark, neighbour Caderousse, you are quite right. Joy has that peculiar effect that at times it oppresses us just as much as grief."

Danglars looked at Fernand, whose impressionable nature was keenly alive to every emotion.

"Well, I never!" said he; "are you anticipating trouble? It seems to me you have everything you can desire."

"That is just what alarms me," said Dantès. "I cannot help thinking it is not man's lot to attain happiness so easily. Good fortune is like the palaces of the enchanted isles, the gates of which were guarded by dragons. Happiness could only be obtained by overcoming these dragons, and I, I know not how I have deserved the honour of becoming Mercédès' husband."

"Husband?" said Caderousse, laughing. "Nay, captain, not yet. Act towards her as if you were husband, and you will see how she will like it."

Mercédès blushed, but made no reply. Fernand grew very restless: he started at every sound, and from time to time wiped away the perspiration that gathered on his brow like large drops of rain, the precursors of a storm.

"Upon my word, neighbour Caderousse, it is hardly worth while taking notice of such a little slip on my part," Dantès said. "'Tis true that Mercédès is not yet my wife, but . . . " here he pulled out his watch—"she will be in an hour and a half. Yes, my friends, thanks to the influence of Monsieur Morrel, to whom, after my father, I owe all I possess, every difficulty has been removed. We have got a special licence, and at half-past two the Mayor of Marseilles will be awaiting us at the Hôtel de Ville. As it has just struck a quarter-past one I think I am quite right in saying that in another hour and thirty minutes Mercédès will have changed her name to Madame Dantès."

Fernand closed his eyes, for they gave him a burning pain; he leant against the table to save himself from falling, but in spite of his effort he could not restrain a groan, which, however, was lost amid the noisy congratulations of the company.

"This feast, then, is not in honour of your betrothal, as we supposed, but is your wedding breakfast?"

"Not at all," said Dantès. "I leave for Paris to-morrow morning. Four days to go, four days to return, one day to execute my commission, and I shall be back again on the first of March. We will have our real wedding breakfast the very next day."

At this moment Danglars noticed that Fernand, on whom he had kept an observant eye and who was seated at the window overlooking the street, suddenly opened his haggard eyes, rose with a convulsive movement and staggered back on to his seat. Almost at the same moment a confused noise was heard on the stairs. The tread of heavy steps and the hubbub of many voices, together with the clanking of swords and military accoutrements, drowned the merry voices of the bridal party. The laughter died away. An ominous silence fell on all as the noise drew nearer, and when three peremptory knocks resounded on the door, they looked at each other with uneasy glances.

"Open in the name of the law!" cried a peremptory voice. There was no answer.

The door opened, and a police commissary entered, followed by four armed soldiers and a corporal.

"What is all this about?" the shipowner asked, advancing toward the commissary, whom he knew. "I fear there must be some mistake."

"If there is a mistake, Monsieur Morrel," the commissary replied, "you may rest assured that it will be promptly put right. In the meantime I am the bearer of a warrant for arrest, and, though I regret the task assigned me, it must nevertheless be carried out. Which of you gentlemen answers to the name of Edmond Dantès?"

Every eye was turned on the young man as he stepped forward, obviously agitated, but with great dignity of bearing, and said:

"I do, monsieur. What do you want of me?"

"Edmond Dantès, I arrest you in the name of the law."

"You arrest me?" said Dantès, changing colour. "Why, I pray?"

"I know not, monsieur. Your first examination will give you all information on that score."

Resistance was useless, but old Dantès did not comprehend this. There are certain things the heart of a father or a mother will never understand. He threw himself at the officer's feet and begged and implored, but his tears and supplications were of no avail.

"There is no call for alarm, monsieur," the commissary said at last, touched by the old man's despair. "Perhaps your son has but neglected to carry out some customs formality or health regulation, in which case he will probably be released as soon as he has given the desired information."

In the meantime Dantès, with a smile on his face, had shaken hands with all his friends and had surrendered himself to the officer, saying: "Do not be alarmed. You may depend on it there is some mistake which will probably be cleared up even before I reach the prison."

"To be sure. I am ready to vouch for your innocence," Danglars said as he joined the group round the prisoner.

Dantès descended the stairs preceded by the police officer and surrounded by soldiers. A carriage stood at the door. He got in followed by two soldiers and the commissary. The door was shut, and the carriage took the road back to Marseilles.

"Good-bye, Edmond, oh, my Edmond! Good-bye!" Mercédès called out, leaning over the balcony.

The prisoner heard these last words sobbed from his sweetheart's breast, and, putting his head out of the window, simply called out: "*Au revoir*, my Mercédès!"

The carriage then disappeared round the corner of Fort Saint-Nicolas.

"Await me here," M. Morrell said to the rest of the party. "I shall take the first carriage I can find to take me to Marseilles, and shall bring you back news."

"Yes, do go," they all cried out. "Go, and come back with all possible speed."

The guests, who had been making merry but a short time before, now gave way to a feeling of terror. They feverishly discussed the arrest from every point of view. Danglars was loud in his assertion that it was merely a trifling case of suspected smuggling: the customs officials had been aboard the *Pharaon* during their absence and something had aroused their suspicion: M. the purser was sure of it. But Mercédès felt, rather than knew, that the arrest had some deeper significance. She suddenly gave way to a wild fit of sobbing.

"Come, come, my child, do not give up hope," said old Dantès, hardly knowing what he was saying.

"Hope!" repeated Danglars.

Fernand also tried to repeat this word of comfort, but it seemed to choke him; his lips moved but no word came from them.

"A carriage! A carriage!" cried one of the guests, who had stayed on the balcony on the look-out. "It is Monsieur Morrel. Cheer up! He is no doubt bringing us good news."

Mercédès and the old father rushed out to the door to meet the shipowner. The latter entered, looking very grave.

"My friends," he said, with a gloomy shake of the head, "it is a far more serious matter than we supposed."

"Oh, Monsieur Morrel," Mercédès exclaimed, "I know he is innocent!"

"I also believe in his innocence," replied the shipowner, "but he is accused of being an agent of the Bonapartist faction!"

Those of my readers who are well acquainted with the period of my story must be aware of the gravity of such an announcement. Consternation and dismay were written on the faces of the assembled guests as the party silently and sadly broke up.

Fernand, who had now become the horror-stricken girl's only protector, led her home, while some of Edmond's friends took charge of the broken-hearted father; and it was soon rumoured in the town that Dantès had been arrested as a Bonapartist agent.

"Would you have believed it, Danglars?" M. Morrel asked as he hastened to the town with his purser and Caderousse in the hopes of receiving direct news of Edmond through his acquaintance, M. de Villefort, the Deputy of the Procureur du Roi.

"Why, monsieur, you may perhaps remember I told you that Dantès anchored off the Isle of Elba without any apparent reason. I had my suspicions at the time."      *Napolean*

"Did you mention these suspicions to anyone but myself?"

"God forbid," exclaimed Danglars; and then in a low whisper he added: "You know, monsieur, that on account of your uncle who served under the old Government and does not attempt to hide his feelings, you are also suspected of sympathizing with Napoleon; so if I mentioned my suspicions, I should be afraid of injuring not only Edmond, but you also. There are certain things it is the duty of a subordinate to tell his master, but to conceal from every one else."

"Quite right, Danglars. You are a good fellow. I had not forgotten your interests in the event of poor Dantès becoming captain."

"In what respect, monsieur?"

"I asked Dantès to give me his opinion of you and to say whether he would have any objection to your retaining your post, for it seemed to me that I had noticed a certain coolness between you two of late."

"What answer did he give you?"

"He merely referred to some personal grievance he had against you, but said that any person who enjoyed his master's confidence was also sure of his."

"The hypocrite!" Danglars muttered.

"Poor Dantès!" said Caderousse. "He's the right sort, and that's a fact."

"Quite agreed," said M. Morrel, "but in the meantime the *Pharaon* is captainless."

"We cannot put to sea for another three months," Danglars added, "and it is to be hoped that Dantès will be released before then."

"No doubt, but in the meantime . . . ?"

"I am at your service. You know that I am as capable of managing a ship as the most experienced captain. Then when Dantès comes out of prison, he can take his post and I will resume mine."

"Thanks, Danglars, that would be a way out of the difficulty. I therefore authorize you to assume command of the *Pharaon* and superintend the loading of the cargo. No matter what misfortune befalls any one of us, we cannot let business suffer." So saying, he proceeded in the direction of the law courts.

"So far everything is succeeding wonderfully," Danglars said to himself. "I am already temporary captain, and if that fool of a Caderousse can be persuaded to hold his tongue, I shall soon have the job for good and all."

## CHAPTER V

## THE DEPUTY PROCUREUR DU ROI

IN one of the old mansions built by Puget in the Rue du Grand Cours, opposite the fountain of the Medusa, another betrothal feast was being celebrated on the same day, and at the same hour, as that which took place in the humble inn. There was, however, a great difference in the company present. Instead of members of the working class and soldiers and sailors, there was to be seen the flower of Marseilles society: former magistrates, who had resigned their office under the usurper's reign, old officers who had deserted their posts to join Condé's army, young men in whom their families had kindled a hatred for the man whom five years of exile were to convert into a martyr and fifteen years of restoration into a demi-god.

The guests were still at table. Their heated and excitable conversation betrayed the passions of the period, passions which in the South had been so much more terrible and unrestrained during the past five years, since religious hatred had been added to political hatred. The Emperor, king of the Isle of Elba after having held sovereign sway over one half of the world, now reigning over five or six thousand souls after having heard "Long live Napoleon" uttered by a hundred and twenty million subjects, and in ten different languages—the Emperor was regarded as a man that was lost to the throne of France for ever. The magistrates recounted political blunders, the military officers discussed Moscow and Leipzig, the ladies aired their views on his divorce from Josephine. It was not in the downfall of the man that these royalists rejoiced and gloried, but rather in the annihilation of the principle, for it seemed to them that they were awakening from a dreadful nightmare and were about to enter upon a new life.

An old man, the Marquis of Saint-Méran, wearing the cross of Saint-Louis, rose and proposed the health of King Louis XVIII. The toast, recalling the exiled but peace-loving King of France, elicited an enthusiastic and almost poetic response; glasses were raised after the English fashion, and the ladies, taking their bouquets from their dresses, strewed the table with flowers.

"Ah," said the Marquise de Saint-Méran, a woman with a forbidding eye, thin lips, and an aristocratic and elegant bearing despite her fifty years, "if those revolutionists were here who drove us out of our old castles, which they bought for a mere song, and in which we left them to conspire against each other during the Reign of Terror, they would have to own that true devotion was on our side. We attached ourselves to a crumbling monarchy; they, on the contrary, worshipped the rising sun and made their fortunes, while we lost all we possessed. They would be compelled to own that our king was truly Louis the Well-beloved to us, while their usurper has never been more to them than Napoleon the Accursed! Don't you agree with me, de Villefort?"

"What did you say, madame? I must crave your pardon. I was not listening to the conversation."

"Leave the young people alone," interposed the old gentleman who had proposed the toast. "They are thinking of their approaching wedding, and naturally they have more interesting subjects of conversation than politics."

"I am sorry, Mother," said a beautiful, fair-haired girl with eyes of velvet floating in a pool of mother-o'-pearl. "I will give up Monsieur de Villefort to you, for I have been monopolizing him for some few minutes. Monsieur de Villefort, my mother is speaking to you."

"I am at your service, madame, if you would be kind enough to repeat your question," M. de Villefort said.

"You are forgiven, Renée," said the Marquise with a smile of tenderness that one hardly expected to see on that dry hard face. "I was saying, Villefort, that the Bonapartists had neither our conviction, nor our enthusiasm, nor our devotion."

"No, madame, but they had fanaticism to take the place of all those other virtues. Napoleon is the Mahomet of the West to all those plebeian but highly ambitious people; he is not only a legislator and a master, he is a type, the personification of equality."

"Equality?" exclaimed the Marquise. "Napoleon the personification of equality! Do you know, Villefort, that what you say has a very strong revolutionary flavour? But I excuse you; one cannot expect the son of a Girondin to be quite free from a spice of the old leaven."

A deep crimson suffused the countenance of Villefort.

"It is true that my father was a Girondin, madame, but he did not vote for the King's death. My father was an equal sufferer with yourself during the Reign of Terror, and he well-nigh lost his head on the same scaffold which saw your father's head fall."

"True," said the Marquise, "but they would have mounted the scaffold for reasons diametrically opposed, the proof being that whereas my family have all adhered to the exiled princes, your father lost no time in rallying to the new government, and that after Citizen Noirtier had been a Girondin, Count Noirtier became a senator."

"Mother," said Renée, "you know we agreed not to discuss such painful reminiscences any more."

"I quite agree with Mademoiselle de Saint-Méran," de Villefort replied. "For my own part, I have discarded not only the views, but also the name of my father. My father has been, and possibly still is, a Bonapartist and bears the name of Noirtier. I am a royalist and style myself de Villefort."

"Well said, Villefort!" the Marquis replied. "I have always urged the Marquise to forget the past, but I have never been able to prevail upon her to do so. I hope you will be more fortunate than I."

"Very well, then," the Marquise rejoined. "Let it be agreed that we forget the past. But, Villefort, should a conspirator fall into your hands, remember that there will be so many more eyes watching you since it is known that you come of a family which is perhaps in league with the conspirators."

"Alas, madame," Villefort replied, "my profession and especially the times in which we live compel me to be severe. I have already had several political prosecutions which have given me the opportunity of proving my convictions. Unfortunately we have not yet done with such offenders."

"Don't you think so?" the Marquise inquired.

"I am afraid not. Napoleon on the Isle of Elba is very near to France; his presence there, almost in view of our coasts, stimulates the hopes of his partisans."

At this moment a servant entered and whispered something into his ear. Villefort, excusing himself, left the table, returning a few minutes later.

"Renée," he said, as he looked tenderly on his betrothed, "who would have a lawyer for her husband? I have no moment to call my own. I am even called away from my betrothal feast."

"Why are you called away?" the girl asked anxiously.

"Alas! if I am to believe what they tell me, I have to deal with a grave charge which may very well lead to the scaffold."

"How dreadful!" cried Renée, turning pale.

"It appears that a little Bonapartist plot has been discovered," Villefort continued. "Here is the letter of denunciation," and he read as follows:

"The Procureur du Roi is hereby informed by a friend to the throne and to religion that a certain Edmond Dantès, mate on the *Pharaon*, which arrived this morning from Smyrna after having touched at Naples and Porto Ferrajo, has been entrusted by Murat with a letter for the usurper, and by the usurper with a letter for the Bonapartist party in Paris. Corroboration of this crime can be found on arresting him, for the said letter will be found either on him, or at his father's house, or in his cabin on board the *Pharaon*."

"But," Renée said, "this letter is addressed to the Procureur du Roi and not to you, and is, moreover, anonymous."

"You are right, but the Procureur du Roi is absent, so the letter has been handed to his secretary, who has been instructed to open all correspondence. On opening this one, he sent for me and, not finding me, gave orders for the man's arrest."

"Then the culprit is already arrested?" the Marquis said.

"You mean the accused person," Renée made answer. Then, turning to Villefort, "Where is the unfortunate man?"

"He is at my house."

"Then away, my dear boy," said the Marquis, "do not neglect your duty in order to stay with us. Go where the King's service calls you."

## CHAPTER VI

## THE EXAMINATION

VILLEFORT had no sooner left the room than he discarded his jaunty manner and assumed the grave air of a man called upon to decide upon the life of his fellow-man. In reality, however, apart from the line of politics which his father had adopted, and which might influence his future if he did not separate himself altogether from him, Gérard de Villefort was at this moment as happy as it is given to any man to be. Already rich, and, although only twenty-seven years of age, occupying a high position on the bench, he was about to marry a young and beautiful girl, whom he loved, not passionately, it is true, but with calculation as befits a future Procureur du Roi; for in addition to her beauty, which was remarkable, Mademoiselle de Saint-Méran, his betrothed, belonged to one of the most influential families of the period, and furthermore had a dowry of fifty thousand crowns, besides the prospect of inheriting another half-million.

At the door he met the commissary of police, who was waiting for him. The sight of this man brought him from his seventh heaven down to earth; he composed his face and, advancing toward the officer, said: "Here I am, monsieur. I have read the letter. You were quite right in arresting this man. Now give me all the information you have discovered about him and the conspiracy."

"As yet we know nothing about the conspiracy, monsieur; all the papers found on the man have been sealed and placed on your desk. You have seen by the letter denouncing him that the prisoner is a certain Edmond Dantès, first mate of the three-master *Pharaon,* trading in cotton with Alexandria and Smyrna, and belonging to Morrel and Son of Marseilles."

"Did he serve in the navy before he joined the mercantile marine?"

"Oh, no, monsieur, he is too young. He is only nineteen or twenty at the most."

At this moment, just as Villefort had arrived at the corner of the Rue des Conseils, a man, who seemed to be waiting for him, approached. It was M. Morrel.

"Ah, Monsieur de Villefort," he cried, "I am very fortunate in meeting you. A most extraordinary and unaccountable mistake has been made: the mate of my ship, a certain Edmond Dantès, has just been arrested."

"I know," Villefort made answer, "and I am on my way to examine him."

"Oh, monsieur!" M. Morrel continued, carried away by his friendship for the young man, "you do not know the accused, but I do. He is the gentlest and most trustworthy man imaginable, and I don't hesitate to say he is the best seaman in the whole mercantile service. Oh, Monsieur de Villefort, with all my heart I commend him to your kindly consideration."

"You may rest assured, monsieur, that you will not have appealed to me in vain if the prisoner is innocent, but if, on the contrary, he is guilty—we live in a difficult age, monsieur, when it would be a fatal thing to be lenient—in that case I shall be compelled to do my duty."

As he had just arrived at his own house beside the law courts, he entered with a lordly air, after having saluted with icy politeness the unhappy shipowner who stood petrified on the spot where Villefort had left him.

The antechamber was full of gendarmes and policemen, and in their midst stood the prisoner, carefully guarded.

Villefort crossed the room, threw a glance at Dantès, and, after taking a packet of papers from one of the gendarmes, disappeared. His first impression of the young man was favourable, but he had been warned so often against trusting first impulses that he applied the maxim to the term impression, forgetting the difference between the two words. He therefore stifled the feelings of pity that were uppermost in his heart, assumed the expression which he reserved for important occasions, and sat down at his desk with a frown on his brow.

"Bring in the prisoner."

An instant later Dantès was before him. Saluting his judge with an easy politeness, he looked round for a seat as if he were in M. Morrel's drawing-room.

"Who are you, and what is your name?" asked Villefort, as he fingered the papers which he had received from the police officer on his entry.

"My name is Edmond Dantès," replied the young man calmly. "I am mate of the *Pharaon* owned by Messrs Morrel and Son."

"Your age?" continued Villefort.

"Nineteen."

"What were you doing when you were arrested?"

"I was at my betrothal breakfast, monsieur," the young man said, and his voice trembled slightly as he thought of the contrast between those happy moments and the painful ordeal he was now undergoing.

"You were at your betrothal feast?" the Deputy said, shuddering in spite of himself.

"Yes, monsieur, I am about to marry a woman I have loved for three years."

Villefort, impassive though he usually was, was struck with this coincidence; and the passionate voice of Dantès, who had been seized in the midst of his happiness, touched a sympathetic chord in his own heart. He also was about to be married, he also was happy, and his happiness had been interrupted in order that he might kill the happiness of another.

"Now I want all the information in your possession," he said. "Have you served under the usurper?"

"I was about to be drafted into the marines when he fell."

"I have been told you have extreme political views," said Villefort, who had never been told anything of the kind but was not sorry to put forward the statement in the form of an accusation.

"Extreme political views, monsieur? Alas! I am almost ashamed to say it, but I have never had what one calls a view; I am barely nineteen years of age, as I have already had the honour to tell you. I know nothing, for I am not destined to play any great *rôle* in life. The little I am and ever shall be, if I am given the position I desire, I owe to Monsieur Morrel. My opinions, I do not say political, but private, are limited to these three sentiments: I love my father, I respect Monsieur Morrel, and I adore Mercédès. That, monsieur, is all I have to tell you. You see for yourself that it is not very interesting."

As Dantès spoke, Villefort looked at his genial and frank countenance, and, with his experience of crime and criminals, he recognized that every word Dantès spoke convinced him of his innocence. In spite of Villefort's severity, Edmond had not once expressed in his looks, his words, or his gestures anything but kindness and respect for his interrogator.

"This is indeed a charming young man," Villefort said to himself, but aloud he said: "Have you any enemies?"

"Enemies, monsieur? My position is happily not important enough to make me any enemies. As regards my character, I am perhaps too hasty, but I always try to curb my temper in my dealings with my subordinates. I have ten or twelve sailors under me: if you ask them, monsieur, you will find that they love and respect me, not as a father, for I am too young, but as an elder brother."

"Perhaps you have no enemies, but you may have aroused feelings of jealousy. At the early age of nineteen you are about to receive a captaincy, you are going to marry a beautiful girl who loves you; these two pieces of good fortune may have been the cause of envy."

"You are right. No doubt you understand men better than I do, and possibly it is so, but if any of my friends cherish any such envious feelings towards me, I would rather not know lest my friendship should turn to hatred."

"You are wrong, you should always strive to see clearly around you, and indeed, you seem such a worthy young man that I am going to depart from the ordinary rule by showing you the denunciation which has brought you before me. Here is the paper. Do you recognize the writing?"

So saying, Villefort took the letter from his pocket and handed it to Dantès. Dantès looked at it and read it. His brow darkened as he said:

"No, monsieur, I do not know this writing. It is disguised and yet it is very plainly written. At any rate it is a clever hand that wrote it. I am very lucky," he continued, looking at Villefort with an expression of gratitude, "in having you to examine me, for there can be no doubt that this envious person is indeed my enemy."

And the light that shone in the young man's eyes as he said this revealed to Villefort how much energy and deep feeling lay concealed beneath his apparent gentleness.

"Very well, then," said the Deputy, "answer me quite frankly, not as a prisoner before his judge, but as a man in a false position to another man who has his interest a heart. What truth is there in this anonymous accusation?"

"It is partly true and partly false, monsieur. Here is the plain truth. I swear it by my honour as a sailor, by my love for Mercédès, and by my father's life! When we left Naples, Captain Leclère fell ill of brain-fever; as we had no doctor on board and as he would not put in at any port, since he was very anxious to reach Elba, he became so very ill that towards the end of the third day, feeling that he was dying, he called me to him. 'My dear Dantès,' he said, 'swear to me on your honour that you will do what I bid you, for it is a matter of the utmost importance.'

"'I swear it, captain,' I said.

"'After my death the command of the ship devolves upon you as mate; take command, head for the Isle of Elba, go ashore at Porto Ferrajo, ask for the Maréchal and give him this letter. You may be given another letter and be entrusted with a mission. That mission was to have been mine, Dantès, but you will carry it out in my stead and get all the glory of it.'

"'I shall carry out your instructions, captain, but perhaps I shall not be admitted into the Maréchal's presence as easily as you think.'

"Here is a ring which will give you admittance and remove all difficulties."

"He then gave me a ring. It was only just in time. Two hours later he was delirious and the next day he died."

"What did you do then?"

"What I was bound to do, and what every one would have done in my place. In any circumstances the requests of a dying man are sacred, but with a sailor a superior's request is an order that has to be carried out. So I headed for Elba, where I arrived the next day. I gave orders for everybody to remain on board while I went ashore alone. The ring gained admittance for me to the Maréchal's presence. He asked me about poor Captain Leclère's death and gave me a letter which he charged me to deliver in person at an address in Paris. I gave him my promise in accordance with the last request of my captain. I landed here, rapidly settled all the ship's business, and hastened to my betrothed, whom I found more beautiful and loving than ever. Finally, monsieur, I was partaking of my betrothal breakfast, was to have been married in an hour, and was counting on going to Paris to-morrow, when, owing to this denunciation, which you seem to treat as lightly as I do, I was arrested."

"I believe you have told me the truth," was Villefort's answer, "and if you have been guilty it is through imprudence, an imprudence justified by your captain's orders. Hand me the letter that was given you at Elba, give me your word of honour that you will appear directly you are summoned to do so, and you may rejoin your friends."

"I am free, monsieur!" Dantès cried out, overcome with joy.

"Certainly, but first give me the letter."

"It must be in front of you, monsieur. It was taken along with my other papers, and I recognize some of them in that bundle."

"Wait a moment," the Deputy said as Dantès was taking his hat and gloves. "To whom was it addressed?"

"To Monsieur Noirtier, Rue Coq Héron, Paris."

These words fell on Villefort's ears with the rapidity and unexpectedness of a thunderbolt. He sank into his chair from which he had risen to reach the packet of letters, drew the fatal letter from the bundle and glanced over it with a look of inexpressible terror.

"Monsieur Noirtier, Rue Coq Héron, number thirteen," he murmured, growing paler and paler. "Have you shown this letter to anyone?"

"To no one, monsieur, on my honour!"

Villefort's brow darkened more and more. When he had finished reading the letter his head fell into his hands, and he remained thus for a moment quite overcome. After a while he composed himself and said:

"You say you do not know the contents of this letter?"

"On my honour, monsieur, I am in complete ignorance of its contents."

Dantès waited for the next question, but no question came. Villefort again sank into his chair, passed his hand over his brow dripping with perspiration, and read the letter for the third time.

"Oh! if he should know the contents of this letter!" he murmured, "and if he ever gets to know that Noirtier is the father of Villefort I am lost, lost for ever!"

Villefort made a violent effort to pull himself together, and said in as steady a voice as possible:

"I cannot set you at liberty at once as I had hoped. I must first consult the Juge d'Instruction. You see how I have tried to help you, but I must detain you as a prisoner for some time longer. I will make that time as short as possible. The principal charge against you has to do with this letter, and you see——" Villefort went to the fire, threw the letter into the flames, and remained watching it until it was reduced to ashes.

"You see," he continued, "I have destroyed it."

"Oh, monsieur," Dantès exclaimed, "you are more than just, you are kindness itself!"

Duties saved
by more police
officer

"But listen," Villefort went on, "after what I have done you feel you can have confidence in me, don't you? I only wish to advise you. I shall keep you here until this evening. Possibly some one else will come to examine you: in that event, repeat all that you have told me, but say not a word about this letter."

"I promise, monsieur."

"You understand," he continued, "the letter is destroyed, and you and I alone know of its existence; should you be questioned about it, firmly deny all knowledge of it, and you are saved."

Villefort rang and the commissary entered. The Deputy whispered a few words into his ear, and the officer nodded in answer.

"Follow the commissary!" Villefort said to Dantès.

Dantès bowed, cast a look of gratitude at Villefort, and did as he was bid.

The door was hardly closed when Villefort's strength failed him, and he sank half fainting into his chair.

After a few moments he muttered to himself: "Alas! alas! if the Procureur du Roi had been here, if the Juge d'Instruction had been called instead of me, I should have been lost! This little bit of paper would have spelt my ruin. Oh! Father, Father, will you always stand in the way of my happiness in this world, and must I eternally fight against your past!"

Suddenly an unexpected light appeared to flash across his mind, illuminating his whole face; a smile played around his drawn mouth, and his haggard eyes became fixed as though arrested by a thought.

"The very thing!" he said. "Yes, this letter which was to have spelt my ruin will probably make my fortune. Quick to work, Villefort!"

And after having assured himself that the prisoner had left the antechamber, the Deputy hastened to the house of his betrothed.

## CHAPTER VII

## THE CHÂTEAU D'IF

As he passed through the antechamber, the commissary of police made a sign to two gendarmes, who instantly placed themselves on either side of Dantès; a door communicating with the law courts was opened; they passed down one of those long, dark passages which make all those who enter them give an involuntary shudder.

In the same way as Villefort's chambers communicated with the law courts, the law courts communicated with the prison, that sombre edifice overlooking the clock-tower of the Accoules. They wound their way along the passage and at last they came to a door; the commissary knocked on it thrice with an iron knocker, and it seemed to Dantès as if each blow had been aimed at his heart. The door was opened, the gendarmes gave their hesitating prisoner a push forward, Dantès crossed the formidable threshold, and the door closed behind him with a loud bang. He now breathed a different air, a thick and mephitic air. He was in a prison.

His cell was clean enough, though it was barred and bolted, and its appearance did not fill him with any dread. Why should it? The words of the Deputy, who seemed to show so much interest in him, rang in his ears like a sweet promise of hope.

It was four o'clock when Dantès was taken to his cell, and, as it was the first of March, the prisoner soon found himself in utter darkness. With loss of sight, his hearing became more acute: at the least sound he rose quickly and advanced toward the door in the firm conviction that they had come to set him free; but the noise died away in another direction and Dantès sank back onto his stool.

At last, about ten o'clock, when Dantès was beginning to lose all hope, he heard steps approaching his door. A key was turned in the lock, the bolts creaked, the massive oak door swung open, and a dazzling light from two torches flooded the cell.

By the light of these torches, Dantès saw the glittering swords and carbines of four gendarmes.

"Have you come to fetch me?" Dantès asked.

"Yes," was the answer of one of the men.

"By order of the Deputy?"     Dutes freed

"I should say so!"

"Very well," said Dantès, "I am ready to follow you."

In the belief that they came at the Deputy's orders, Dantès, relieved of all apprehension, calmly stepped forward and placed himself in their midst. A police van was waiting at the door, the coachman was on the box, and a police officer was seated beside him. The door of the carriage was opened and Dantès was pushed in. He had neither the power nor the intention to resist and he found himself in an instant seated between two gendarmes, the other two taking their places opposite, and the heavy van lumbered away.

The prisoner glanced at the windows: they were grated. He had but changed his prison; only this one moved and was conveying him he knew not whither. Through the grating, the bars of which were so close that there was barely a hand's-breadth between them, Dantès recognized the Rue Casserie, and saw that they were passing along the Rue Saint-Laurent and the Rue Taramis toward the quay. Soon he saw the lights of the Consigne before him. The van stopped, the officer got down from the box, and opened the locked door with his key; whereupon Dantès stepped out and was immediately surrounded by the four gendarmes, who led him along a path lined with soldiers to a boat which a customs-house officer held by a chain near the quay. The soldiers looked at Dantès with vacant curiosity. He was given a place in the stern of the boat and was again surrounded by the four gendarmes, whilst the officer stationed himself at the bows. The boat was shoved off, four oarsmen plied their oars vigorously, and soon Dantès found himself in what they call the Frioul, that is, outside the harbour.

His first feeling on finding himself once more in the open air was one of joy, for did it not mean freedom? But the whole proceeding was incomprehensible to him.

"Whither are you taking me?" he asked.

"You will know soon enough."

"But . . ."

"We are forbidden to give you any explanation."

Dantès knew from experience that it was useless to question a sub-ordinate who had been forbidden to answer any questions, and he remained silent.

As he sat there, the most fantastic thoughts passed through his mind. It was not possible to undertake a long voyage in such a small boat, so perhaps they were going to take him a short distance from the coast and tell him he was free; they had not attempted to handcuff him, which he considered a good augury; besides, had not the Deputy, who had been so kind to him, told him that, provided he did not mention the fatal name of Noirtier, he had nothing to fear? Had not de Villefort destroyed the dangerous letter in his presence, the letter which was the only evidence they had against him?

He waited in silence and deep in thought. With that far-away look in his eyes peculiar to sailors, he tried to pierce the depths of the night. Leaving Ratonneau Island with its lighthouse on their right, and keep-ing close to the coast, they arrived opposite the Catalan creek. It was here that Mercédès lived, and now and then he imagined he saw the indistinct and vague form of a woman outlined on the dark shore.

Why did a presentiment not warn her that the man she loved was but a hundred yards away from her? If he gave a shout, she could hear him. A false shame restrained him, however. What would these men say if he called out like a madman?

In spite of the repugnance he felt at putting fresh questions to the gendarmes, he turned to the one nearest him and said:

"Comrade, I adjure you on your honour as a soldier to have pity on me and answer! I am Captain Dantès, an honest and loyal Frenchman, though accused of treason. Whither are you taking me? Tell me, and on my honour as a sailor, I will submit to my fate."

The gendarme scratched his ear and looked at his comrade. The latter made a motion with his head which seemed to say: "I can't see any harm in telling him now"; and the gendarme, turning to Dantès, replied:

"You are a native of Marseilles and a sailor, and yet you ask us where we are heading for?"

"Yes, for on my honour I do not know."

"Have you no idea?"

"None at all."

"Impossible!"

"I swear it by all that I hold most sacred! Tell me, I entreat you!"

"Unless you are blind or have never been outside the port of Marseilles, you must know. Look round you."

Dantès got up and quite naturally looked in the direction the boat was moving. Before him, at a distance of a hundred fathoms, rose the black, steep rock on which stood the frowning Château d'If.

This strange pile, this prison whose very name spelt terror, this fortress around which Marseilles had woven its legends for the past three hundred years, rising up so suddenly before Dantès, had the effect on him that the sight of a scaffold must have on a condemned man.

"My God!" he cried, "the Château d'If! Why are we going there?"

The gendarme smiled.

"You cannot be taking me there to imprison me?" Dantès went on. "The Château d'If is a State prison, and is only used for important political offenders. I have committed no crime. Are there any judges or magistrates at the Château d'If?"

"As far as I know there are a governor, some gaolers, a garrison, and some good thick walls."

"Are you trying to make out that I am to be imprisoned there? What about Monsieur Villefort's promise?"

"I don't know anything about Monsieur Villefort's promise; all I know is that we are going to the Château d'If."

Quick as lightning Dantès sprang to his feet and tried to hurl himself into the sea, but four stout arms caught him before even his feet left the bottom boards of the boat. With a howl of rage he fell back. The next moment a sudden impact shook the boat from stem to stern and Dantès realized that they had arrived. His guardians forced him to land, and dragged him to the steps that led to the gate of the fortress, the police officer following him with fixed bayonet.

Dantès made no useless resistance; his slow movements were caused by inertia rather than opposition—he was dazed, and reeled like a drunken man. He saw more soldiers stationed along the slope, he felt the steps which forced him to raise his feet, he perceived that he passed under a door, and that this door closed behind him, but all his actions were mechanical and he saw as through a mist; he could distinguish nothing. He did not even see the ocean, that cause of heartbreaking despair to the prisoners who look on that wide expanse of water with the awful conviction that they are powerless to cross it.

There was a moment's halt, during which he tried to collect his thoughts. He looked around him; he was in a square courtyard enclosed by four high walls; the slow and measured tread of the sentinels was heard, and each time they passed before the light which shone from within the château he saw the gleam of their musket-barrels.

They waited here about ten minutes, evidently for orders. At last a voice called out:

"Where is the prisoner?"

"Here," one of the gendarmes replied.

"Let him follow me. I will take him to his cell."

"Go!" said the gendarme, giving Dantès a push.

The prisoner followed his guide who led him into a subterranean room whose bare and reeking walls seemed as though impregnated with tears. A sort of lamp, standing on a stool, the wick swimming in fetid oil, illumined the shiny walls of this terrible abode, and revealed to Dantès the features of his guide, an under-gaoler, ill-clad and of a low type.

"Here is your cell for to-night," he said. "It is late and the governor is in bed. To-morrow, when he has read the instructions regarding you, he may change your cell. In the meantime here is some bread, there is some water in the pitcher over there and some straw in the corner yonder. That is all a prisoner requires. Good night."

Before Dantès could think of an answer, before he had noticed where the gaoler had placed the bread and the pitcher of water, or looked at the corner where lay the straw for his bed, the fellow had taken the lamp and locked the door behind him, leaving his prisoner to the darkness and silence of the gaol.

When the first rays of the sun had brought some light into the den, the gaoler returned with the information that Dantès was not to change his cell. An iron hand seemed to have nailed him to the spot where he stood the night before; he was motionless with his eyes fixed on the ground. Thus he had stood the whole night long without sleep. The gaoler advanced; Dantès did not appear to see him. He tapped him on the shoulder; Dantès shuddered and shook his head.

"Have you not slept?" asked the gaoler.

"I do not know," was Dantès reply.

The gaoler stared at him in astonishment.

"Are you not hungry?"

"I do not know," Dantès still made answer.

"Do you want anything?"        *to be freed*

"I want to see the governor."

The gaoler shrugged his shoulders and went out.

Dantès gazed after him, stretched out his hands toward the half-open door, but the door was closed upon him.

Then his whole frame was shaken with one mighty sob. The tears which choked him streamed down his cheeks; he beat his forehead against the ground; he remained a long time in prayer, and, while reviewing his past life, asked himself what crime he had committed at his tender age to merit such a cruel punishment.

The day passed thus. He scarcely touched his bread or water. At times he would sit absorbed in thought, at other times he would walk round and round his cell like a wild animal in a cage.

The next morning the gaoler again made his appearance.

"Well," he said, "are you more reasonable to-day than you were yesterday?"

Dantès made no reply.

"Come, now, don't lose heart! Is there anything I can do for you?"

"I want to speak to the governor."

"I have already told you that is impossible," the gaoler answered impatiently.

"Why is it impossible?"

"Because the rules of the prison do not allow it."

"Then what is allowed here?"

"Better food if you pay for it, a walk in the courtyard, and sometimes books."

"I don't want any books, neither do I want to walk in the courtyard, and I find my food good enough. I only desire one thing and that is to see the governor."

"If you keep on bothering me with that every time I come, I shall not bring you any more food."

"Well, then," said Dantès, "I shall die of starvation, that's all about it."

"Now, look here!" said the gaoler, "don't go on brooding over the impossible in this way, or you will go mad before the end of a fortnight."

"Do you think so?" was the reply.

"I am sure of it. Madness always begins like that. We have an instance of it here. There was an abbé in this cell before you came: it was through his unceasingly offering a million francs to the governor if he would set him free that his brain was turned."

"Listen, I am not an abbé, neither am I mad, though I may be before long; unfortunately I am at present in full possession of my senses. Now I too have a proposal to make. I can't offer you a million francs for the simple reason that I have not so much to give you, but I offer you a hundred crowns if, the next time you go to Marseilles, you will go to the Catalans and give a letter to a girl named Mercédès . . . not even a letter, just a couple of lines."

"If I were to take that letter and were found out I should lose my place which is worth a thousand francs a year in addition to my food, so you see I should be a fool to risk a thousand francs for three hundred."

"Very well," said Dantès, "but remember this. If you refuse to take my letter to Mercédès or at least to tell her that I am here, I shall one day hide behind the door and, as you enter, break your head with this stool."

"Threats!" the gaoler called out, retreating a step and placing himself on the defensive. "You are certainly going mad. The abbé commenced like that. In three days you will be raving mad. Luckily we have dungeons at the Château d'If."

Dantès picked up the stool and swung it round his head.

"That's enough! that's enough!" the gaoler exclaimed. "Since you insist on it, I will go and tell the governor."

"That's something like!" said Dantès, putting the stool down and sitting on it with bent head and haggard eyes as though he were really losing his senses.

The gaoler went out and returned a few minutes later with four soldiers and a corporal.

"The governor's orders are that the prisoner shall be taken to the dungeon. We must put madmen with madmen."

The four soldiers seized Dantès, who fell into a kind of coma and followed them without resistance. He descended fifteen steps, the door of the dungeon was opened, and he entered mumbling, "He is right, they must put madmen with madmen."

## CHAPTER VIII

# VILLEFORT AND MERCÉDÈS

As we have said, Villefort hastened back to the Rue du Grand Cours, and on entering the house of Madame de Saint-Méran found the guests he had left at table seated in the salon at their coffee. Renée with the rest of the company was anxiously awaiting him, and he was received with a universal fire of exclamations.

"Hallo, decapitator, guardian of the State, Brutus," said one. "Tell us your news!"

"Are we threatened with a new Reign of Terror?" asked another.

"Has the Corsican Ogre broken loose?" cried a third.

"Marquise," Villefort said, advancing toward his future mother-in-law. "I have come to ask you kindly to excuse my abrupt departure... Monsieur le Marquis, would you honour me with a few moments' private conversation?"

"Is it really so serious as all that?" the Marquis asked, noticing the dark cloud that had gathered on Villefort's brow.

"It is so serious that I must take leave of you for a few days."

"You are going away?" Renée cried, unable to conceal the emotion she felt at this unexpected news.

"Alas! mademoiselle, I am obliged to do so."

"Where are you going?" the Marquise asked.

"That is a State secret, madame, but if you have any commissions for Paris a friend of mine is going there to-night."

Every one looked at him.

"You wish to speak to me," asked the Marquis.

"Yes, let us go into your study."

The Marquis took Villefort's arm and they left the room together.

"Well, and what has happened?"

"An affair which I consider to be of a very grave nature and which necessitates my immediate departure for Paris. Will you give me a letter to the King?"

"To the King? But I dare not take upon myself to write to His Majesty."

"I do not ask you to write the letter. I want you to ask Monsieur de Salvieux to do so. He must give me a letter which will enable me to gain His Majesty's presence without all the formalities attendant on the request for an audience which would only lose precious time."

"If it is so urgent, my dear Villefort, go and pack your things and I will make de Salvieux write the letter."

"Do not lose any time, I must start in a quarter of an hour."

So saying, Villefort ran out, but at the door he bethought himself that the sight of the Deputy of the Procureur du Roi running through the streets would be enough to disturb the general peace of the town, so he resumed his ordinary magisterial pace.

At his door he perceived in the shadow a white spectre waiting for him, erect and motionless. It was Mercédès. Having no news of Edmond, she had come in person to inquire the reason of her lover's arrest.

As Villefort drew near, she moved from the wall against which she had been leaning and barred his way. Dantès had spoken to the Deputy of his betrothed and he now he recognized her at once. He was astonished at her beauty and dignity, and when she asked him what had become of him whom she loved he felt as though he were the culprit and she his judge.

"The man you speak of," he said abruptly, "is a criminal, and I can do nothing for him."

A great sob escaped Mercédès' lips, and when Villefort tried to pass by she again stopped him.

"But tell me at least where he is," she said, "so that I may learn whether he is alive or dead."

"I know not," was the answer, "he has passed out of my hands."

Embarrassed by the straight look she gave him, as also by her entreaties, he pushed by her and entered his house, locking the door after him as though to shut out all sadness. But sadness is not banished so easily. Like the wounded hero of Virgil he carried the arrow in his wound. He had no sooner entered his room than his legs gave way under him; he heaved a deep sigh, which was more like a sob, and sank into his chair. For a moment the man was in doubt. He had often passed sentence of death, but the condemned men who owed their execution to his crushing eloquence had not caused him the slightest compunction, for they had been guilty, or at all events Villefort had believed them to be so. But if at this moment the fair Mercédès had entered and had said to him: "In the name of Almighty God, Who watches over us and is our judge, give me back my lover," he would have given way and, in spite of the risk to himself, his icy-cold hand would have signed the order for Dantès' release. But no voice broke the stillness, the door opened only to admit Villefort's valet, who came to tell him that his carriage was at the door.

Poor Mercédès had returned to the Catalans followed by Fernand. Grief-stricken and desperate, she threw herself on her bed. Fernand, kneeling by her side, took her hand, which she did not attempt to withdraw, and covered it with kisses: but she was oblivious to it all.

So passed the night. The lamp went out when the oil was consumed. Mercédès was no more aware of the darkness than she had been of the light. Day broke but she heeded it not. Grief had made her blind to all but Edmond.

M. Morrel did not give up hope: he had learnt of Dantès' imprisonment and had gone to all his friends and all the influential men of the town, but it was already reported that Dantès had been arrested as a Bonapartist, and since even the most sanguine looked upon any attempt of Napoleon's to remount the throne as impossible he met with nothing but coldness, fear, or refusals, and returned home in despair.

Caderousse was restless and uneasy, but instead of trying to do something to help Dantès he had shut himself up in his house with two bottles of wine.

Danglars alone felt no pang of remorse or restlessness: he was even happy, for had he not avenged himself on an enemy and assured for himself the position on board the *Pharaon* he was in danger of losing? He was one of those calculating men who are born with a pen behind their ears and an ink-pot in place of a heart. He went to bed at the usual hour and slept peacefully.

## CHAPTER IX

## THE LITTLE CABINET OF THE TUILERIES

WE will now leave Villefort travelling with all speed to Paris and pass into the little cabinet of the Tuileries with its arched windows, which is so well known as being the favourite cabinet of Napoleon, Louis XVIII, and Louis-Philippe.

There, seated at a walnut table which he had brought from Hartwell, and to which he was greatly attached, King Louis XVIII was listlessly listening to a grey-haired, well-groomed, aristocratic-looking man of fifty or fifty-two years of age, and was at the same time making notes on the margin of a volume of Gryphius' edition of *Horace,* an edition full of inaccuracies but nevertheless much valued, from which His Majesty drew many of his wise, philosophical observations.

"What did you say?" the King inquired.

"That I am somewhat harassed, Sire."

"Really? What carking care is on your mind, my dear Blacas?"

"Sire, I have every reason to believe that a storm is brewing in the South."

"Well, my dear Duke," Louis XVIII replied, "I believe that you are misinformed, for I know for certain that the weather is very fine in that quarter."

Intellectual as he was, Louis XVIII was very fond of a pleasant jest.

"Sire," M. de Blacas continued, "if only to ease the mind of a faithful servant, could Your Majesty not send to Languedoc, Provence, and Dauphiné some trustworthy men who would report on the feeling in these three provinces?"

"*Canimus surdis,*" answered the King, continuing his annotations.

"Sire," the courtier laughingly replied, "as you appear to understand the hemistich of the poet of Venusia, it is only fitting that Your Majesty should believe in the good feeling of France; nevertheless I do not think I am quite wrong in fearing some desperate attempt."

"By whom?"

"By Bonaparte, or at any rate his party."

"My dear Blacas," replied the King, "your alarms prevent me from working."

"And your feeling of security, Sire, prevents me from sleeping."

"Wait, my dear Duke, wait a moment. I have a happy note on *pastor quum traheret*; you can continue afterwards."

There was a moment's silence during which Louis XVIII wrote in as minute a handwriting as possible a note on the margin of his *Horace*, which having finished, he said, rising with the satisfied air of a man who thinks he has an idea of his own because he has commented on the idea of another, "Continue, my dear Duke, I am listening."

"Sire," Blacas said, for one moment hoping to use Villefort to his own advantage. "I must tell you that these are not mere meaningless rumours and idle tales that disquiet me. A man of strong common sense, meriting all my confidence and charged by me to watch over the South"—the Duke uttered these last words hesitatingly—"has arrived in all haste to bring me the news that a great danger threatens the King. I came without delay to you, Sire."

"*Mala ducis avi domum,*" Louis XVIII continued, still making his notes. "Ah, here is Monsieur Dandré. You did say Monsieur Dandré?" he asked of the chamberlain, who had just announced the Minister of Police.

"Yes, Sire, Baron Dandré."

"You have just come at the right moment," said Louis. "Come in, Baron, and tell the Duke your latest news of Monsieur Bonaparte. Do not conceal anything, no matter how serious. Is the Isle of Elba a volcano from which will issue a bloody, death-bringing war? *Bella, horrida bella?*"

M. Dandré balanced himself gracefully on the back of a chair on which he was leaning his hands, and said:

"Has Your Majesty been pleased to peruse yesterday's report?"

"Yes, yes, but give the Duke the contents of the report; tell him exactly what the usurper is doing on his island."

"Monsieur," said the Baron to the Duke, "all His Majesty's faithful servants have good reason to rejoice at the latest news that has reached us from Elba. Bonaparte . . ."

M. Dandré looked at Louis who, busily engaged in writing a note, did not even raise his head.

"Bonaparte is bored to distraction," continued the Baron. "He spends whole days watching his miners at work at Porto Longone. Moreover, we have ascertained that it will not be very long before the usurper is quite insane. His brain is giving way. One moment he is weeping bitterly, the next laughing boisterously. At other times he will spend hours on the shore throwing pebbles into the water, and if he succeeds in making five or six ducks and drakes he is as pleased with himself as if he had won another Marengo or a second Austerlitz. You must agree with me that these are sure signs of insanity."

"Or else signs of wisdom, monsieur," smiled Louis. "The great captains of olden times amused themselves by casting pebbles into the sea; see Plutarch's *Life of Scipio Africanus*. Well, Blacas," the King continued triumphantly, "what do you say to that?"

"I say, Sire, that either the Minister of Police is mistaken or else I am; but as this would be impossible for a Minister of Police who has the safe custody of Your Majesty in his keeping, it is probably I who am under a wrong impression. Nevertheless, Sire, I would question before Your Majesty the gentleman of whom I spoke just now; in fact, I beg Your Majesty to do him this honour."

"Most willingly, Duke. Under your auspices, I will receive whom you will, but I must receive him armed to the teeth. Have you a later report than this one, Dandré? This one is dated February the twentieth and to-day is March the third."

"No, Sire, I am expecting one hourly. I have been out since early morning and it is possible that one has arrived during my absence."

"Then hie you to your office and do not forget that I am waiting for you."

"I go, Sire, and shall be gone but ten minutes."

"In the meantime, Sire," said Monsieur de Blacas, "I will fetch my messenger. He has covered two hundred and twenty leagues in barely three days."

"Why all this unnecessary fatigue and anxiety when we have the telegraph which takes but three or four hours!"

"Ah, Sire, that is poor recompense for Monsieur de Villefort, who has come all that distance with such haste to communicate to Your Majesty some valuable information."

"Monsieur de Villefort?" exclaimed the King. "Is that the messenger's name?"

"Yes, Sire. I thought the name was unknown to Your Majesty."

"Not at all, not at all, Blacas. He is a serious-minded and intellectual young man, and above all he is ambitious. Added to that his father's name is Noirtier!"

"Noirtier the Girondin? Noirtier the Senator?"

"The very same."

"And Your Majesty has employed the son of such a man?"

"Blacas, my dear friend, you are very slow of understanding. I told you that Villefort was ambitious; he would sacrifice everything to gain his end, even his father. Go and fetch him."

When Blacas returned with Villefort, the King said:

"The Duke of Blacas tells me you have some important information. Give me full details, if you please, and above all begin at the beginning. I like order in all things."

"Sire," Villefort answered, "I will give Your Majesty a faithful report. I have come to Paris with all speed to inform Your Majesty that, in the exercise of my duties, I have discovered a conspiracy; not one of those everyday, meaningless, vulgar plots of the lower classes of our people, but a veritable tempest which threatens Your Majesty's very throne, Sire, the usurper has manned three vessels; he meditates some attack, senseless perhaps, yet it may have terrible consequences. By this time he will have left Elba, bound for I know not whither. He will most probably attempt to land either at Naples or on the coast of Tuscany, or even in France. Your Majesty is aware that the lord of the Isle of Elba has maintained relations with Italy and France?"

"Yes, monsieur, I know," replied the King, greatly agitated, "and lately we have been informed of Bonapartist meetings in the Rue Saint-Jacques. Whence have you your details?"

"Sire, I have them from a man whom I have been watching for some time past, and for whose arrest I gave orders the day before my departure from Marseilles. He is a turbulent sailor whom I suspected of Bonapartism, and he has been secretly to Elba. There he saw the Grand Maréchal, who entrusted him with a verbal mission to a Bonapartist in Paris, whose name he would not disclose; the nature of the mission was to prepare the adherents of Bonaparte for a return—note, Sire, these are the man's very words—for a return which must take place very shortly."

"Where is this man?"

"In prison, Sire."

"Do you think the thing is serious?"

"Sire, I fear it is more than a mere plot, it is a conspiracy."

"In these days it is easy to plan a conspiracy," the King answered, smiling, "but it is difficult to carry it out for the simple reason that, being recently re-established on the throne of our ancestors, we have our eyes at once on the past, the present, and the future. If Bonaparte landed at Naples, the whole coalition would be at his heels before he reached Piombino; if he landed in Tuscany, he would be in a hostile country; whereas if he landed in France he would have but a handful of men and we should soon overpower him."

At this moment the Minister of Police entered, pale and trembling and with a scared look.

CHAPTER X

# THE OGRE

On perceiving the Minister's agitated demeanour, Louis violently pushed back the table at which he had been sitting. "Why, Baron," he cried, "what is your trouble? You appear completely upset! Is your agitation in any way connected with the report given by Monsieur Blacas and confirmed by Monsieur de Villefort?" "Sire . . ." stammered the Baron. "Well . . . go on," replied Louis.

The Minister of Police was about to throw himself in despair at the King's feet, but the latter drew back a step and knitting his brows, said: "Well, are you going to speak? I command you to give me your news!"

"Sire, the usurper left Elba on February the twenty-eighth and disembarked on March the first in France, at a little port near Antibes in the Gulf of Juan."

"The usurper disembarked in France near Antibes in the Gulf of Juan, two hundred and fifty leagues from Paris on March the first and you only report it to me on March the third?"

Louis XVIII made a movement of indescribable anger and alarm and drew himself up straight as if a sudden blow had struck him both mentally and physically.

"In France!" he cried. "The usurper in France! Is he marching on Paris?"

"Sire, I know not. The dispatch only states that he has landed and the route he has taken," was the Police Minister's answer.

"How did you get the dispatch?"

The Minister bowed his head while a deep colour suffused his cheeks.

"By telegraph, Sire."

Louis XVIII took a step forward and crossed his arms as Napoleon would have done.

"So," he said, turning pale with anger, "seven allied armies overthrew that man; a miracle of God placed me on the throne of my fathers after an exile of twenty-five years, during which time I studied, probed, analysed the men and affairs of this France that was promised me, so that when I had attained my desires the power I held in my hand should burst and break me! What our enemies say of us is only too true. We have learnt nothing and forgotten nothing! If I had been betrayed like him, some consolation would be left to me; but to be surrounded by men whom I have raised to high dignities, who were to watch over me with more care than over themselves, who before my time were nothing, and who, when I have gone, will again be nothing and will probably perish through their own inability and ineptitude! Oh, cruel fate! Oh, I would sooner mount the scaffold of my brother Louis the Sixteenth than thus be forced down the steps of the Tuileries by ridicule! You do not know what ridicule is in France, yet you ought to know. And now, messieurs," he continued, turning toward M. de Blacas and the Police Minister, "I have no further need of you. The War Minister alone can help now." Then suddenly turning to Baron Dandré, he asked: "What further news have you in regard to the Rue Saint-Jacques affair?"

"Sire," the Minister of Police replied, "I was about to give Your Majesty the latest information on the matter when Your Majesty's attention was attracted towards this other terrible catastrophe; now these facts will not interest Your Majesty."

"On the contrary, monsieur, on the contrary. It seems to me that this affair may have some direct connexion with the other, and the death of General Quesnel will perhaps put us on the direct track of a great internal conspiracy."

Villefort shuddered at the name of General Quesnel.

"In fact, Sire," the Minister of Police continued, "everything goes to show that his death was not due to suicide as was at first believed, but was the work of some assassin. Apparently General Quesnel left the precincts of a Bonapartist Club and disappeared. An unknown man had called on him in the morning and arranged a meeting in the Rue Saint-Jacques."

While the Minister was telling his story, Villefort, who seemed to hang on his very words, turned alternately red and pale.

The King turned to him. "Do you not share my opinion, Monsieur de Villefort, that Quesnel, who was believed to be attached to the usurper though he was in reality entirely loyal to me, was the victim of a Bonapartist trap?"

"It is very probable, Sire, but have you no further information?"

"We are on the track of the man who made the appointment with him. We have his description. He is a man of fifty to fifty-two years of age, has brown hair, dark eyes with bushy eyebrows, and wears a moustache. He was dressed in a blue coat, and in his buttonhole wore the rosette of an Officer of the Legion of Honour. Yesterday a man answering to this description was followed but was lost sight of at the corner of the Rue de la Jussienne and the Rue Coq Héron."

Villefort leaned against the back of a chair; his legs seemed to be giving way under him, but when he heard that the unknown man had escaped his pursuers he breathed again.

"Seek this man out!" said the King to the Police Minister, "for if,

as everything leads me to suppose, General Quesnel, who would have
been so useful to us now, has been the victim of a murder, I will have
his assassins severely punished, be they Bonapartists or not. I will not
detain you longer, Baron. Monsieur de Villefort, you must be fatigued
after your long journey; go and rest. You are putting up at your
father's house, no doubt?"

Villefort seemed on the point of fainting.

"No, Your Majesty," he said, "I am staying at the Hôtel de Madrid,
in the Rue de Tournon."

"But you will see him?"

"I think not, Sire."

"Ah! of course," said Louis XVIII, smiling in a manner which
showed that all these questions had been put to him with a motive. "I
was forgetting that you are not on good terms with Monsieur
Noirtier. Another sacrifice to the royal cause, for which you shall be
recompensed." The King detached the cross of the Legion of Honour
which he usually wore on his blue coat and giving it to Villefort said:
"In the meantime take this cross."

Villefort's eyes filled with tears of joy and pride. He took the cross
and kissed it.

## CHAPTER XI

## THE HUNDRED DAYS

EVENTS followed one another very rapidly. Every one knows the history of the famous return from Elba, a return which, unexampled as
it was in the past, will probably remain unimitated in the future.

Louis XVIII made but a feeble attempt to parry the blow. The
monarchy which he had but ill reconstructed trembled on its insecure
foundation, and a wave of the Emperor's hand brought down with a
crash the whole edifice that was naught but an unsightly mass of
ancient prejudices and new ideas. Villefort therefore gained nothing
from the King but a gratitude which was not only useless but dangerous at the present time, and the cross of the Legion of Honour,
which he had the prudence not to display.

Napoleon would, doubtless, have dismissed Villefort but for the
protection of Noirtier, who was all-powerful at the Court of the
Hundred Days; the Procureur du Roi alone was deprived of his office,
being under suspicion of lukewarm support of Bonaparte.

Meanwhile the imperial power had hardly been re-established, the
Emperor had hardly re-entered the Tuileries and issued his numerous

and divergent orders from that little cabinet into which we have introduced our readers, and on the table of which he found Louis XVIII's snuff-box, still open and half full, when the flames of civil war, always smouldering in the South, began to light up Marseilles, and the populace seemed like to indulge in acts of violence against the royalists of the town in place of the shouts and insults with which they hitherto had greeted them whenever they ventured abroad.

Villefort retained his post, but his marriage was postponed until happier times. If the Emperor remained on the throne, Gérard would require a different alliance and his father undertook to find this for him; if, on the contrary, a second Restoration brought back Louis XVIII, the influence of M. de Saint-Méran and himself would be strengthened and the marriage would be more suitable than ever.

As for Dantès, he remained a prisoner; hidden away in the depths of his dungeon he was ignorant of the downfall of Louis XVIII's throne and the re-establishment of Napoleon.

Twice during this short revival of the Empire, which was called the Hundred Days, had M. Morrel renewed his appeal for the liberation of Dantès, and each time Villefort had quietened him with promises and hopes. Finally there was Waterloo. Morrel did not present himself before Villefort any more; he realized he had done all that was humanly possible for his young friend and that to make any further attempts under this second restoration would be to compromise himself unnecessarily.

When Louis XVIII remounted the throne, Villefort successfully petitioned for the post of Procureur du Roi at Toulouse, and a fortnight later he married Mademoiselle de Saint-Méran.

When Napoleon returned to France, Danglars understood the full significance of the blow he had struck at Dantès; his denunciation had been given some sort of justification and he called this extraordinary coincidence the Hand of Providence. But when Napoleon reached Paris and his voice was once more heard, imperious and powerful, Danglars grew afraid. Dantès might return any day with full information on the cause of his arrest and eager for vengeance. He, therefore, informed M. Morrel of his desire to leave the merchant service and obtained a recommendation from him to a Spanish merchant. He went to Madrid and was heard of no more for a long time.

Fernand, on the other hand, could not understand anything. Dantès was absent and that was all he cared about. What had happened to him? He did not know, neither did he care.

In the meantime the Empire made a last appeal to her soldiers, and every man, capable of bearing arms, rushed to obey the far-reaching voice of his Emperor. Fernand left Mercédès and joined up with the

others, but the gloomy and terrible thought preyed upon his mind that
Dantès might return now that his back was turned and marry her
whom he loved. His devotion to Mercédès, the pity he pretended to
have for her in her sorrow, the care with which he anticipated her least
desire, had produced the effect that outward signs of devotion always
produce on generous hearts: Mercédès had always been fond of him as
a friend and this affection was now increased by a feeling of gratitude.
Fernand therefore went off to the army with hope in his heart, and
Mercédès was now left alone. She could be seen, bathed in tears, wandering incessantly round the little village of the Catalans: at times she
would stand under the fierce midday sun as motionless and dumb as
a statue with her eyes fixed on Marseilles; at other times she would sit
on the beach listening to the moaning of the sea, as eternal as her
grief, and ask herself whether it would not be better to leap down
into the abyss below than to suffer this cruel alternative of a hopeless
suspense. She did not lack the courage to do this deed; it was her religion that came to her aid and saved her from suicide.   *Mercedes*
    As for old Dantès, he had now lost all hope. Five months after he
had been separated from his son, and almost at the very hour at which
he had been arrested, the old man breathed his last in Mercédès' arms.
M. Morrel paid the expenses of the funeral and the small debts the old
man had incurred during his last illness. It required more than benev-
olence to do this, it required courage. The South was aflame, and to
help the father of a Bonapartist as dangerous as Dantès, even though
he were on his deathbed, was a crime.


## CHAPTER XII

# NUMBERS 34 AND 27

DANTÈS passed through all the various stages of misery that affect a
forgotten and forsaken prisoner in his cell. First there was pride born
of hope and a consciousness of his innocence; next, he was so reduced
that he began to doubt his innocence; finally his pride gave way to
entreaty, yet it was not God he prayed to, for that is the last resource,
but man. The wretched and miserable should turn to their Saviour
first, yet they do not hope in Him until all other hope is exhausted.
    Dantès begged to be taken from his dungeon and placed in another
one, even though that were deeper and darker. Even a change for the
worse would be welcome and would give him a few days' distraction.
He entreated his gaolers to let him go for a walk, to give him books,
anything to while away the time. One day he entreated his gaoler to

ask for a companion for him. The gaoler passed the request of prisoner No. 34 to the proper quarter, but the governor, being as prudent as a politician, imagined that Dantès would stir up the prisoners to mutiny, weave some plot, or make an attempt to escape, so he refused.

Dantès had now exhausted all human resources and turned toward God. All the pious thoughts which are sown broadcast in the human field and which are gleaned by the victims of a cruel fate came to comfort him; he recalled the prayers taught him by his mother and discovered in them a hidden meaning hitherto unknown to him. To the happy and prosperous man prayer is but a meaningless jumble of words until grief comes to explain to the unfortunate wretch the sublime language which is our means of communication with God.

In spite of his prayers, however, Dantès still remained a prisoner.

His gloom gave way to wrath. He began to roar out blasphemies which made even his gaoler recoil with horror, and dashed himself in a paroxysm of fury against the walls of the prison. Then there recurred to his mind the informer's letter which Villefort had shown him. Each line of it was reflected on the walls in fiery letters. He told himself it was the hatred of men and not the vengeance of God that had thrust him into this dark abyss. He doomed these unknown men to the most cruel torments his fiery imagination was capable of conjuring up, but, even so, the most awful of these torments seemed to him too mild and too short for them, for after the torment would come death, and in death they would find, if not repose, at all events that insensibility which so nearly resembles repose.

Sometimes he said to himself: "When I was still a man, strong and free, commanding other men, I have seen the heavens open, the sea rage and foam, the storm rise in a patch of sky and like a gigantic eagle beat the two horizons with its wings. Then I felt that my ship was but a weak refuge from the tempest, for did it not shiver and shake like a feather in the hand of a giant? Soon the sight of the sharp rocks, coupled with the frightful noise of the waves, announced to me that death was near, and death terrified me. I exerted all my efforts to escape it, and I combined all my man's strength with all my sailor's skill in that terrible fight against God! For to me life was happy then, and to escape from the jaws of death was to return to happiness. I had no use for death; I loathed the thought of sleeping my last sleep on a bed of hard rocks and seaweed, or of serving after my death as food for gulls and vultures, I who was made in the image of God! Now, however, it is quite a different matter. I have lost all that bound me to life; now death smiles on me as a nurse smiles on the child she is about to rock to sleep; now welcome death!"

No sooner had this idea taken possession of the unhappy young

man than he became more calm and resigned; he felt more contented
with his hard bed and black bread, ate less, slept not at all, and almost
found his miserable existence supportable, for could he not cast it off
at will as one casts off old clothes?

There were two ways of dying open to him. One was quite simple;
it was only a question of tying his handkerchief to a bar of the window and hanging himself. The other way was by starving himself.
Hanging seemed to him a disgraceful thing, so he decided upon the
second course.

Nearly four years had passed since he had taken this resolution; at
the end of the second year he ceased to count the days.

Dantès had said to himself, "I will die," and had chosen his mode
of death; he had weighed the matter well, but, being afraid he might
go back on his resolution, he had sworn to himself that he would
starve himself to death. "When the gaoler brings me my food in the
morning and evening," he said to himself, "I shall throw it through
the window and he will think I have eaten it." He kept his word. At
first he threw it away with pleasure, then with deliberation, and finally
with regret. It was only the remembrance of his oath that gave him
the strength to carry out this dreadful purpose. The food which he
had once loathed, hunger now made pleasant to the eye and delicious
to the smell. At times he would hold his plate in his hand for an hour,
his eyes fixed on the morsel of putrid meat or tainted fish and the
black and mouldy bread. It was the last instincts of life struggling
within him and breaking down his resolution. At length came the day
when he had no longer the strength to raise himself to throw his supper away. The next day he could no longer see and scarcely hear; the
gaoler thought he was seriously ill. All at once, toward nine in the
evening, just as he was hoping that death would come soon, Dantès
heard a dull sound on the wall against which he was lying.

So many loathsome animals had made their noises in his cell that
little by little he had grown accustomed to them and did not let them
disturb his sleep. This time, however, whether it was that his senses had
become intensified by his long abstinence, or that the noise was louder
or more significant than usual, Edmond raised his head to hear better.
And what he heard was an even scraping noise as though caused by
an enormous claw, a powerful tooth, or the pressure of some sharp
instrument on the stone. Though weakened, the young man's brain
seized on the idea that is ever present to the mind of a prisoner: liberty. The noise lasted for about three hours, then Edmond heard the
sound of something crumbling away and all was silence again.

Some hours later the scraping was continued again, but this time
louder and nearer. Edmond's interest was aroused, and the noise

seemed almost like a companion to him. "As it continues even in daylight," he thought to himself, "it must be some unfortunate prisoner
trying to escape. Oh, if I were only near and could help him! But I
must ascertain this. I have only to knock on the wall and if it is an
ordinary workman, he will instantly cease working and will endeavour to discover who it is that knocks, and why he knocks; and then,
as his work is lawful, he will soon resume it. If, on the contrary, it is a
prisoner, the noise I make will alarm him; he will be afraid of being
discovered; he will cease his work and only resume it at night when
he believes every one to be in bed and asleep."

Edmond went to a corner of the cell, detached a stone that had
become loosened with the damp, and knocked three times on the
wall, just where the sound had been loudest. At the first knock the
noise stopped as if by magic. Edmond listened intently all through that
day but there was complete silence. "It is a prisoner," Dantès said with
inexpressible joy.

Three days—seventy-two deadly hours—passed without a repeti-
tion of the noise. One evening, however, after the gaoler had paid his
last visit, Dantès, who had his ear to the wall, thought he heard an
almost imperceptible sound. He moved away, paced round the cell
several times to calm himself, and then returned to the same spot.
There could be no doubt about it: something was happening on the
other side of the wall. The prisoner had recognized the danger of his
previous tactics and had substituted the crowbar for the chisel.

Encouraged by this discovery, Edmond resolved to help the untiring worker. He looked round for some object he could use as a tool,
but could discover nothing. He had no knife or sharp instrument; the
only iron in the cell was that at the windows, and he had already
proved the impossibility of moving the bars.

He had but one resource, and this was to break his pitcher and use one
of the jagged fragments. Accordingly he dashed the pitcher to the
ground and, choosing two or three of the sharp, broken bits, hid them
under his bed; the others he left scattered about the floor. The breaking
of the jug was such a natural accident that it would cause no suspicion.

He had the whole night to work in, but, groping about in the dark,
he did not make much headway, and he soon found that he blunted
his instrument against the hard stone. He laid down his tool and
waited for the morning. Hope had given him patience.

All night long he listened to the unknown miner at his subterranean work. Day came, the gaoler entered. Dantès told him the
pitcher had fallen from his hands as he was drinking out of it the previous evening. The gaoler went grumblingly to fetch another one
without even taking the trouble to pick up the bits of the old one.

The grinding of the lock in the door which had always caused Dantès a pang now gave him inexpressible joy. He listened for the last of the dying footsteps and then, hastily moving his bed away, he saw by the faint ray of light that penetrated his cell, how useless had been his work of the previous night in attacking the hard stone instead of the plaster surrounding it.

The damp had rendered the plaster friable, and Dantès' heart beat with joy when he saw it break off in little bits: they were but tiny atoms, it is true, but within half an hour he had scraped away nearly a handful. A mathematician would have calculated that if he worked like that for about two years, and if he did not encounter a rock, he might succeed in excavating a passage two feet square and twenty feet deep.

In three days he managed, with untold precautions, to lay bare a stone. The wall was made of ashlars, for the greater solidity of which a freestone had been placed at intervals. It was one of these freestones which Dantès had now laid bare, and which he must now dislodge. He used his nails, but they were useless tools; the fragments of the pitcher broke whenever he tried to make them do the duty of a crowbar. After an hour of useless toil, he paused, his forehead bathed in perspiration. Was he to be thus stopped at the beginning, and must he wait, inert and useless, while his neighbour, who was perhaps growing weary, should accomplish all?

Suddenly an idea occurred to him. He stood up smiling; the perspiration on his forehead dried.

The gaoler always brought him his soup in a tin saucepan with an iron handle. It was this iron handle he longed for, and he would have given ten years of his life to get it. The contents of the saucepan were always poured into Dantès' plate; this he ate with his wooden spoon and washed his plate in readiness for the next day.

On the evening in question Dantès placed his plate on the floor, half-way between the door and the table. When the gaoler entered, he stepped on it and broke it to pieces. This time the gaoler could not blame Dantès; it is true he should not have left his plate on the floor, but then, the gaoler should have looked where he was going. He contented himself with grumbling and looked around for some other vessel for Dantès' soup.

"Leave the saucepan," the prisoner said, "you can take it again when you bring me my breakfast in the morning."

This advice suited the gaoler as it spared him the necessity of going up and down the many steps again. He left the saucepan.

Dantès was trembling with delight. He ate his soup and meat hastily, and then, after waiting an hour to make sure the gaoler would not change his mind, he set himself to the task of dislodging the freestone, using the saucepan handle as a lever. At the end of an hour he had extricated the stone, leaving a hole of more than a foot and a half in diameter. Dantès collected all the plaster very carefully, carried it into the corners of the cell and, with a piece of broken earthenware, scraped some of the grey earth from the floor and strewed it over the plaster. He continued to work all night and at dawn of day replaced the stone, pushed the bed up against the wall, and lay down to sleep.

His breakfast consisted of a piece of bread which the gaoler placed on the table.

"Aren't you going to bring me another plate?" Dantès asked.

"No, you break everything. First of all there was your pitcher, then you made me break your plate. You can keep the saucepan now and your soup will be poured into that."

Dantès lifted up his eyes to Heaven, joined his hands under the coverlet, and said a prayer of thanks. The piece of iron which had been left him created in him a feeling of gratitude toward God stronger than any he had felt for the greatest blessings in past years.

He worked all day unremittingly; thanks to his new instrument he had scraped out more than ten handfuls of broken stone, plaster, and cement by the end of the day. He continued working all through the night, but after two or three hours he encountered an obstacle. The iron did not grip any more, it simply slid off a smooth surface. He touched the obstacle with his hand and soon recognized it as a beam. It crossed, or rather blocked the hole that Dantès had commenced. It now meant that he had to dig either above or below it.

"Oh, my God! my God!" he cried, "I prayed so fervently that I hoped Thou hadst heard my prayer. My God! after having deprived me of my liberty! after having deprived me of the peace of death, oh, my God! and after calling me back to existence, have pity on me, oh, my God! and let me not die of despair!"

"Who speaks of God and of despair in the same breath?" said a voice that seemed to come from under the ground and sounded sepulchral to the young man. His hair stood on end and he drew back.

"Ah," he murmured, "I hear a man's voice!"

Edmond had not heard any man's voice but that of his gaoler for the past four or five years, and to a prisoner a gaoler is not a man; he is but a living door added to his oaken door; he is but a bar of flesh added to his bar of iron.

"In Heaven's name," Dantès cried out, "speak once more, though the sound of your voice frightened me. Who are you?"

"And who are you?" the voice asked.

"An unhappy prisoner," replied Dantès, who had no difficulty in answering this question.

"What nationality?"

"French."

"Your name?"

"Edmond Dantès."

"Your profession?"

"A sailor."

"How long have you been here?"

"Since February twenty-eighth, eighteen-fifteen."

"Your crime?"

"I am innocent of any crime."

"But what are you accused of?"

"Of having conspired in favour of the Emperor's return."

"What? The Emperor's return? Is the Emperor, then, no longer on the throne?"

"He abdicated at Fontainebleau in eighteen-fourteen and was banished to the Isle of Elba. How long have you been here that you do not know this?"

"Since eighteen-eleven."

Edmond shuddered. This man had been in prison four years longer than himself.

"Dig no more," the voice continued, speaking quicker, "tell me only at what height your hole is."

"On a level with the floor."

"How is it concealed?"

"It is behind my bed."

"Where does your room lead to?"

"To the passage."

"And the passage?"

"To the courtyard."

"Alas! alas!" muttered the voice.

"Oh, my God! What is the matter?" Dantès cried out.

"Only that I have made a mistake, that the inaccuracy of my plans has misled me, that the lack of a compass has ruined all, that one wrong line on my plan is equivalent to fifteen feet, and that what I believed to be the wall of the fortress is the wall you have been digging!"

"But in any case the fortress would only give you access to the sea."

"That is what I desired."

"And if you had succeeded?"

"I should have thrown myself into the sea, swum to one of the islands round the Château d'If, or even to the shore, and then I should have been saved. Now all is lost. Fill in your hole again very carefully, work no more and wait till you hear from me again."

"Tell me at least who you are."

"I am—I am number twenty-seven."

"Ah! you surely mistrust me," cried Dantès. "I swear by the living God that I will not betray you. Do not forsake me! You will not leave me alone any more, will you? Come to me or else let me come to you. We will escape together, and if we cannot escape we will talk together, you of those you love, and I of those I love. You must love some one."

"I am all alone in the world."

"Then you will learn to love me. If you are young, I shall be your companion: if you are old, I shall be your son. I have a father who must be seventy years of age if he is still alive. I love but him and a girl named Mercédès. I know that my father has not forgotten me, but who knows whether she still thinks of me! I will love you as I loved my father."

"So be it," said the prisoner. "Farewell till to-morrow."

From this moment Dantès' happiness knew no bounds; he was not going to be alone any more, and perhaps he might even gain his freedom; anyway, even if he remained a prisoner, he would have a companion, and captivity shared with another is but half captivity. He walked up and down his cell all day long, his heart beating wildly with joy. At moments it almost seemed to choke him. At the least sound he heard he sprang to the door. Once or twice he was seized with the fear that they would separate him from this man whom he knew not, but whom he already loved as a friend.

Night came. Dantès thought his neighbour would take advantage of the silence and the darkness to renew conversation with him, but he was mistaken; the night passed without a single sound breaking in upon his feverish waiting. But the next morning, after the gaoler had been, he heard three knocks at equal intervals. He threw himself upon his knees:

"Is that you?" he said. "Here I am."

"Has your gaoler gone?" inquired the voice.

"Yes," replied Dantès, "and he will not come again till this evening, so we have got twelve full hours of freedom."

"I can set to work, then?"

"Oh, yes, yes, without delay. This very instant, I beg of you."

The piece of earth on which Dantès was leaning suddenly gave way; he threw himself back, and a mass of earth and loose stones crumbled into a hole which opened up just beneath the aperture he himself had made; then from the bottom of this hole, of which he could not gauge the depth, he saw a head appear, then a pair of shoulders, and finally the body of a man who crept with great agility out of the hole just made.

## CHAPTER XIII

## AN ITALIAN SCHOLAR

DANTÈS threw himself into the arms of his new friend, for whom he had waited so impatiently and so long, and drew him toward the window that the little light that penetrated into his cell might reveal his features.

His new-found friend was short, with hair blanched with suffering rather than age. His keen, penetrating eyes were almost hidden beneath thick grey eyebrows, and his beard, which was still back, reached down to his chest. His thin face, furrowed with deep lines, and the bold outlines of his characteristic features revealed a man who was more accustomed to exercise his mental faculties than his physical strength. Large drops of perspiration stood on his brow, and as for his garments, it was impossible to distinguish their original form, for they were in rags.

He appeared at least sixty-five years of age, but the agility of his movements seemed to imply that this aged appearance was due to long captivity. He received the young man's enthusiastic outbursts with a certain pleasure; his icy soul seemed to gather warmth for an instant and to melt in the contact with this ardent youth. He thanked him with much feeling for his cordiality, though his disappointment had been very bitter at finding another dungeon where he had hoped to find liberty.

"Now let us see whether we can conceal from the eyes of your gaolers all traces of my entrance," said the newcomer; and, stooping down to the aperture, he lifted the stone with the greatest ease, in spite of its weight, and fitted it into the hole.

"This stone has been removed very carelessly," he said, shaking his head. "Hadn't you any tools?"

"Have you any?" Dantès asked with astonishment.

"I made some. With the exception of a file, I have all I need: chisel, pincers, crow-bar."

"Oh, I should like to see these products of your patience and industry."

"Well, to begin with, here is my chisel."

And he showed Dantès a sharp, strong blade with a handle of beech-wood.

"How did you make that?" asked Dantès.

"Out of one of the clamps of my bed. I have hollowed out the passage, a distance of about fifty feet, with this instrument. To think that all my work has been in vain! There is now no means of escape. God's will be done!"

Dantès looked with astonishment mingled with admiration at this man, who renounced with such philosophy a hope cherished for so long.

"Now," Dantès said, "will you tell me who you are?"

"Yes, if it interests you." Then he continued sadly: "I am the Abbé Faria, a prisoner in the Château d'If since eighteen-eleven, and previously imprisoned in the fortress of Fenestrella for three years. In the year eighteen-eleven I was transferred from Piedmont to France. It was then that I learned that the god of destiny, who at that time seemed subservient to Napoleon's every wish, had given him a son, and that while still in its cradle the child had been named King of Rome. Little did I think then that this superman would be overthrown."

"But why are you here at all?"

"Because in eighteen-seven I meditated the very scheme that Napoleon tried to realize in eighteen-eleven; because like Machiavelli I desired Italy to be one great, strong, and compact empire, instead of a nest of petty principalities each with its weak and despotic ruler; because I thought I had found my Caesar Borgia in a crowned fool, who pretended to share my views so as the better to betray me. It was the scheme of Alexander the Sixth and Clement the Seventh; it will never materialize now, for their attempt was fruitless, and not even Napoleon has accomplished it. There is no doubt, Italy is an accursed country."

For a moment Dantès stood motionless and mute.

"Then you abandon all hope of escaping?" he said at last.

"I realize that it is impossible, and that it is tantamount to revolting against God to attempt what is contrary to His designs."

"Why despair? Why not start afresh?"

"Start afresh! Ah! you little know how I have toiled. Do you know that it took me four years to make my tools? Do you know that for the past two years I have been scraping and digging out earth as hard as granite? I have had to move stones that I once thought it impossible to loosen. I have spent whole days in these titanic efforts, and there were times when I was overjoyed if by night-time I had scraped away a square inch of the cement that age had made as hard as the stones themselves. I have had to pierce the wall of a staircase so that I could deposit all my stones and earth in its well. And I thought I had almost finished my task, and felt I had just enough strength left to accomplish it, when I found that all my plans were frustrated. I assure you, I have known very few successful attempts to escape. Only those have been crowned with success which were planned and worked out with infinite patience. We shall do best now to wait till some unforeseen occurrence gives us the opportunity of making our escape. When such an opportunity occurs, we will seize it."

"You could well wait," Dantès said with a sigh. "Your work occupied every minute of your time, and when you could not work, you had your hope in a brighter future to console you."

"I accomplished other things besides all this."

"What did you do?"

"I wrote or studied."

"Who gave you paper, pens, and ink?"

"No one," said the abbé, "I made them myself."

Dantès looked at the man with admiration; only he could scarcely credit all he told him. Faria noticed this shade of doubt on the young man's face and said:

"When you come to my cell, I will show you an entire volume entitled *Treatise on the Possibility of a General Monarchy in Italy*, which is the result of the thoughts, reflections, and researches of my whole life; ideas which I have worked out in the shadow of the Colosseum at Rome, at the foot of Saint Mark's Column at Venice, or on the banks of the Arno at Florence."

"Do you mean to say you have written it?"

"On two shirts. I have invented a preparation by means of which linen is rendered as smooth and glossy as parchment. I also made some excellent quills which every one would prefer to the ordinary ones if once they were known. I made them from the cartilage of the head of those enormous whiting they sometimes give us on fast-days. Formerly there must have been a fireplace in my cell which was doubtless closed up some time before I came. It must have been used for very many years, for the interior was coated with soot. I dissolved some soot in a portion of the wine they bring me every Sunday, and my ink was made. For notes to which I wished to draw special attention, I pricked my fingers and wrote with my blood."

"When can I see all this?" Dantès asked.

"As soon as you like."

"Let it be at once, then!" the young man exclaimed.

"Then follow me."

So saying the abbé re-entered the subterranean passage and disappeared. Dantès followed and found himself at the far end of the passage, into which the abbé's door opened. Here the passage became narrower; indeed there was scarcely room for a man to crawl through on his hands and knees. The abbé's room was paved; it had been by raising one of the flag-stones in the darkest corner of the room that he had commenced the laborious task of which Dantès witnessed the completion.

As soon as he entered the cell, the young man examined it very carefully, but at first sight it presented nothing out of the ordinary.

"And now I am very anxious to see your treasures," Dantès said.

The abbé went toward the fireplace, removed a stone which was formerly the hearthstone, and which hid a fairly deep cavity.

"What do you wish to see first?"

"Show me your work on the Monarchy of Italy."

Faria took from his cupboard three or four rolls of linen four inches wide and eighteen long which were folded like papyrus leaves. These strips of linen were numbered and covered with writing.

"Here you have the whole of it," he said, "I put the word *finis* at the bottom of the seventy-eighth strip just a week ago. I have used for it two of my shirts and all the handkerchiefs I had. If ever I gain my liberty and can find a publisher in Italy who will publish it, my reputation is made."

He then showed Dantès the quills he had made; the penknife of which he was particularly proud and which he had made out of an old iron candle-stick; the ink, the matches, the sulphur which he had obtained by feigning a skin disease; the rope-ladder, the material for which he had obtained by unravelling the ends of his sheets; and finally the needle. On seeing these ingenious products of an intelligent and highly developed brain, Dantès became thoughtful, and it occurred to him that the man might be able to clear up the mystery surrounding his own misfortune which he himself had been unable to fathom.

"What are you thinking of?" the abbé asked with a smile, seeing his companion's pensiveness, and attributing it to inexpressible admiration.

"I was thinking that though you have related to me the events of your life, yet you know nothing of mine."

"Your life, young man, is far too short to contain anything of importance."

"Nevertheless it contains a very great misfortune," said Dantès, "a misfortune that I do not deserve, and I would rather attribute the authorship of it to mankind and no longer blaspheme God as I have hitherto done."

"Tell me your story, then."

Dantès then related what he called the story of his life, consisting of a voyage to India, two or three voyages to the East, and finally his last voyage, the death of Captain Leclère, the package confided to him for the Grand Maréchal, the letter given him by the latter addressed to a certain M. Noirtier. Then he went on to tell his friend of his arrival at Marseilles, his interview with his father, his love for Mercédès, his betrothal feast, his arrest, his examination, his temporary imprisonment in the Law Courts, and finally his permanent imprisonment in the Château d'If. After this he knew nothing more, not even how long he had been a prisoner. When Dantès had finished his story, the abbé sat silent, deep in thought. After a time he said: "There is a maxim with a very deep meaning which says: 'If you wish to discover the author of a crime, endeavour to find out in the first place who would derive advantage from the crime committed.' You were about to be nominated captain and also to marry a beautiful girl, were you not?"

"That is true."

"Was it to anyone's interest that you should not be appointed captain of the *Pharaon?* And again, was it to anyone's interest that you should not marry Mercédès? Answer the first question first; order is the key to all problems."

"I was very popular on board. If the sailors could have chosen their chief, I am sure they would have chosen me. There was only one person who had any reason to wish me ill; I quarrelled with him some time ago and challenged him to a duel, but he refused."

"Now we are coming to the point. What was this man's name?"

"Danglars, the purser of the ship."

"Had you been appointed captain, would you have retained him as such?"

"Not if it had depended on me, for I thought I had noticed some inaccuracies in his accounts."

"Good. Now who was present at your last conversation with Captain Leclère?"

"No one; we were alone."

"Could anyone have overheard your conversation?"

"Yes, the door was open, and . . . wait . . . yes, it is true, Danglars passed at the very moment Captain Leclère was handing me the package for the Grand Maréchal."

"Better still. Now we are on the right track. Did you take anyone ashore when you put in at the Isle of Elba?"

"No one at all."

"What did you do with the letter the Grand Maréchal gave you?"

"I put it in my portfolio."

"Had you your portfolio with you then? How could a portfolio large enough to contain an official letter find room in a sailor's pocket?"

"My portfolio was on board."

"So you did not put the letter into the portfolio until you returned to the ship?"

"No."

"What did you do with the letter from the time you left Porto Ferrajo till you reached the ship?"

"I carried it in my hand."

"So that when you went on board, every one could see that you carried a letter?"

"Yes."

"Danglars as well?"

"Yes; Danglars as well as the others."

"Now listen to me and try to recall all the incidents. Do you remember how the denunciation was phrased?"

"Oh, yes, I read it over three times and each word is engraved on my memory." And he repeated it word for word.

The abbé shrugged his shoulders. "It is as clear as daylight," he said. "You must have a very noble heart and simple mind that you had not your suspicions from the very outset."

"Do you really think so?" Dantès exclaimed. "Such infamy is not possible!"

"How did Danglars usually write?"

"He had a good, round hand."

"How was the anonymous letter written?"

"With a backward slant."

The abbé smiled. "I suppose it was a disguised hand?"

"It was too bold to be disguised."

The abbé took one of his quills and wrote the first two or three lines of the denunciation on a piece of prepared linen. Dantès stood aghast and looked at the abbé in terror, and exclaimed: "How extraordinarily alike the two writings are!"

"The simple explanation is that the denunciation was written with the left hand. I have noticed that whereas handwritings written with the right hand vary, those written with the left hand are nearly always alike. Now let us pass to the second question. Was it to anyone's interest that you should not marry Mercédès?"

"Yes, there was a young man who loved her, a young Catalan named Fernand."

"Do you think he would be capable of writing the letter?"

"No, he would rather have stuck his knife into me. Besides, he was ignorant of the details stated in the denunciation. I had not mentioned them to anyone."

"Stay a moment. Did Danglars know Fernand?"

"No. Oh, yes, I remember now. On the eve of my betrothal, I saw them together in old Pamphile's tavern. Danglars was friendly and jocular, but Fernand looked pale and agitated. A tailor, named Caderousse, whom I know very well, was with them. He was quite drunk though."

"Do you want to know something else?" asked the abbé laughing.

"Yes, since you seem to be able to fathom every mystery. Tell me why I was only submitted to one examination, and why I was condemned without trial."

"This is a more serious matter," was the reply. "What we have just done for your two friends is mere child's play by comparison. You must give me the most precise details. Who examined you?"

"The Deputy."

"Did you tell him everything?"

"Yes, everything."

"Did his manner towards you change at all in the course of the examination?"

"He certainly did appear disturbed when he read the compromising letter. He seemed quite upset at my misfortune."

"Are you quite sure he was so perturbed on your account?"

"At any rate he gave me one great proof of his sympathy. He burnt the letter, my one incriminating document, before my very eyes."

"Ah! This man may have been a greater scoundrel than you imagine. The Deputy's conduct was too sublime to be natural. To whom was the letter addressed?"

"To Monsieur Noirtier, thirteen, Rue Coq Héron, Paris."

"Can you think of any selfish motive the Deputy might have had in destroying the letter?"

"I do not know of any, but he may have had some reason, for he made me promise two or three times that, in my own interest, I would not speak to anyone of the letter, and he made me swear that I would not utter the name of the person to whom it was addressed."

"Noirtier?" the abbé repeated. "Noirtier? . . . I knew a Noirtier at the Court of the old Queen of Etruria, a man who was a Girondist during the Revolution. What was the Deputy's name?"

"De Villefort."

The abbé burst into loud laughter. Dantès looked at him in stupefaction. "What is the matter?" he said.

"Only that I have a clear and complete understanding of everything now. Poor blind young man! This Noirtier was no other than the Deputy's father."

"His father?" Dantès cried out.

"Yes, his father, who styles himself Noirtier de Villefort," the abbé replied.

Dantès now began to see clearly, and many details which had been incomprehensible to him up to this moment now began to assume their real significance. Villefort's change of demeanour during the examination, the burning of the letter, the exacted oath, the magistrate's almost supplicating voice which seemed to implore rather than to threaten, all passed through his mind. A cry broke from his lips and he staggered like a drunken man; then rushing toward the opening which led to his cell, he called out: "I must be alone to think this over."

Reaching his cell he fell on his bed, and here the turnkey found him in the evening, motionless, his eyes staring into space, his features drawn.

During these hours of meditation, which had passed like so many seconds, he had formed a terrible resolution and taken a fearful oath.

At length a voice roused him from his reverie; it was the voice of Faria, who had come to invite Dantès to have his supper with him. The young man followed him. His face had lost that drawn look it had worn, and instead there was a determined, almost radiant expression which clearly denoted that he had taken a resolution. The abbé looked at him attentively.

"I almost regret having helped you in your researches and having told you what I did," he said.

"Why?"

"Because I have instilled into your heart a feeling that previously held no place there—vengeance."

Dantès smiled and said: "Let us speak of something else."

The abbé looked at him again and shook his head sadly; but he did what his companion asked him and spoke of other matters.

Dantès listened to his words with admiring attention. At first he spoke of things and ideas of which the young man had no comprehension until later on; like the aurora borealis which lights the navigator of the northern seas on his way, he showed the young man new landscapes and horizons illuminated by fantastic lights, and Dantès realized what happiness it would bring to an intelligent being to follow this exalted mind to those moral, philosophical, or social heights to which he was wont to soar.

"You must impart to me a little of your knowledge," Dantès said, "otherwise an ignoramus like myself will only be a bore to you. I am sure that you must prefer solitude to a companion without education such as I am. If you do what I ask, I promise to speak no more of escaping."

"Alas, my good friend," said the abbé smiling, "human knowledge is very limited, and when I have taught you mathematics, physics, history, and the three or four living languages I speak, you will know all that I know. It will not take more than two years to give you the knowledge I possess."

"Two years?" exclaimed Dantès. "Do you really think you can teach me all these things in two years? What will you teach me first? I am anxious to begin. I am thirsting for knowledge."

That selfsame evening the two prisoners drew up a plan for the younger man's education and began to put it into execution the next day. Dantès had a prodigious memory and a great facility for assimilation. The mathematical turn of his mind gave him aptitude for all kinds of calculation, while the sense of poetry that is in every sailor gave life to dryness of figures and severity of lines.

Whether it was that the distraction afforded him by his study had taken the place of liberty, or because he adhered strictly to the promise given to the abbé, he made no further reference to escaping, and the days passed rapidly, each day adding to his store of knowledge. At the end of the year he was a different man. Dantès noticed, however, that in spite of his companionship, the Abbé Faria seemed to lose some of his animation with each succeeding day. It seemed as though there was something on his mind. At times he would become wrapt in thought, sigh unconsciously, then suddenly rise and, with his arms crossed over his breast, gloomily pace his cell. One day, all at once, he ceased his incessant wandering and exclaimed: "If only there were no sentry!"

"Have you found a means of escape then?" asked Dantès excitedly.

"Yes, provided that the sentry in the gallery is both deaf and blind."

"He shall be deaf and he shall be blind," answered the young man in such a determined way that it frightened the abbé.

"No! No!" he cried out. "I will have no bloodshed."

Dantès wanted to pursue the subject, but the abbé shook his head and refused to answer any more questions. Three months passed.

"Are you strong?" the abbé one day asked Dantès.

Without replying Dantès picked up the chisel, bent it into the shape of a horse-shoe and straightened it out again.

"Will you promise not to kill the sentry except as a last resource?"

"Yes, on my honour."

"Then we may accomplish our task," was the reply.

"How long will it be before we can accomplish it?"

"At least a year."

"Shall we begin at once?"

"Without any delay. Here is my plan."

The abbé showed Dantès a drawing he had made. It was a plan of his own cell, that of Dantès, and the passage joining them. In the middle of this passage they would bore a tunnel, like those used in mines. This tunnel would lead the prisoners under the gallery where the sentry was on duty; arrived there, a large excavation would be made by loosening one of the flagstones with which the floor of the gallery was paved; at a given moment the stone would give way under the soldier's weight and he would disappear into the excavation below. Dantès would throw himself upon him before he had recovered from the shock of the fall and while he was still unable to defend himself. He would gag and blindfold him, and then the two prisoners would jump through one of the windows, climb down the outside wall by means of the rope-ladder the abbé had made, and they would be saved!

Dantès clapped his hands, and his eyes shone with joy. It was such a simple plan that it was bound to succeed.

That same day the two miners commenced operations with renewed vigour after their long rest.

At the end of fifteen months the hole was made, the excavation was completed under the gallery, and the two prisoners could distinctly hear the measured tread of the sentry. They were obliged to wait for a dark, moonless night for the success of their plans, and their one fear was that the flagstone might give way under the soldier's heavy tread sooner than they desired. To guard against this, they decided to prop the stone up with a kind of beam they had found in the foundations. Dantès was busy putting it into position when he suddenly heard the abbé cry out in pain. He rushed to him and found him standing in the middle of the room, his face ghastly pale, his hands clenched, and the perspiration streaming down his forehead.

"Good heavens!" cried Dantès. "Whatever has happened? What ails you?"

"Quick! quick!" the abbé replied. "Listen to me."

Dantès looked at Faria's livid face. His eyes had deep lines under them, his lips were white, and his very hair seemed to stand on end.

"Oh! What is the matter with you?" Dantès cried terror-stricken.

"All is over with me! A terrible disease, it may even be mortal, is about to attack me. I feel it coming. I was seized with it the year before my imprisonment. There is only one remedy for it. Run quickly to my cell and raise the foot of my bed. It is hollow, and you will find in it a little glass bottle half filled with a red liquid. Bring it to me. No, I might be found here; help me back to my cell while I still have the strength. Who knows what may happen while the attack lasts?"

In a flash Dantès realized that his hopes of escape were now dashed to the ground; nevertheless he did not lose his head. He crept into the tunnel dragging his luckless companion after him, and with infinite trouble helped him to his cell and placed him on the bed.

"Thank you," the abbé said, trembling in every limb as though he had just stepped out of freezing water. "I am seized with a cataleptic fit. It may be that I shall not move or make a sound; on the other hand, I may stiffen, foam at the mouth and shriek. Try not to let them hear me, for if they do, they might change my cell and we should be separated for ever. When you see me motionless, cold, and to all appearances dead, then and not until then force my teeth apart with the knife, and pour eight to ten drops of the liquid down my throat and I shall perhaps revive."

"Perhaps?" exclaimed Dantès, grief-stricken.

"Help! Help!" the abbé cried. "I am . . . I am dy——"

The attack was so sudden and so violent that the unfortunate prisoner was unable to finish the word. His features became distorted, his eyes dilated, his mouth twisted, his cheeks took on a purple hue; he struggled, foamed at the mouth, moaned and groaned. This lasted for two hours, then stretching himself out in a last convulsion, he became livid and lay as inert as a block of wood, whiter and colder than marble, more crushed than a reed trampled underfoot.

Edmond waited until life seemed to have departed from the abbé's body and he apparently lay cold in death; then, taking the knife, with great difficulty he forced the blade between the clenched teeth. He carefully poured ten drops of the red liquid down his friend's throat and waited.

An hour elapsed and still the abbé made not the slightest movement. Dantès began to fear he had waited too long before administering the remedy, and stood anxiously gazing at him. At last a faint colour spread over his cheeks, his eyes, which had remained open in a fixed stare, now began to see, a slight sigh escaped his lips, and he began to move.

"He is saved! he is saved!" Dantès exclaimed.

The abbé could not yet speak, but he pointed with visible anxiety toward the door. Dantès listened and heard the gaoler's footsteps. He jumped up, darted toward the opening which he entered, replacing the flagstone after him, and regained his cell.

An instant later the gaoler entered and, as usual, found his prisoner sitting on his bed.

Scarcely had he turned his back, scarcely had the sound of his footsteps in the passage outside died away, when Dantès, too anxious to eat anything, hastened back to the abbé's cell by the same way he had come a few seconds before. Faria had regained consciousness, but he was still lying stretched on his bed helpless and inert.

"I little thought I should see you again," he said.

"Why?" asked the young man. "Did you think you were going to die?"

"No, but everything is ready for your flight, and I thought you would go."

"Without you?" he exclaimed. "Did you really think I was capable of such a base action?"

"I see now that I was mistaken. But, alas! I feel very weak and worn."

"Take courage, your strength will return," said Dantès, seating himself on the bedside and taking the abbé's hands.

Faria shook his head.

"My first fit lasted but half an hour, leaving only a feeling of hunger; I could even get up alone. To-day, I can move neither my right leg nor my arm; my head feels heavy, which proves a rush of blood to the brain. The third attack will leave me entirely paralysed or else it will kill me."

"No, no, I assure you, you will not die. When you have your third attack, if you have one, you will be at liberty."

"My friend," the old man said, "you are mistaken. The attack I have just had has condemned me to perpetual imprisonment. Before fleeing, one must be able to walk."

"Well then, we will wait a week, a month, two months if necessary; during that time you will regain your strength. All is ready for our escape, we have but to choose the day and hour. The day you feel strong enough to swim, we will put our plan into execution."

"I shall swim no more," Faria said. "My arm is paralysed not for one day only, but for ever. Raise it yourself and you will soon know by the weight of it."

The young man did as he was bid and the arm fell back heavy and lifeless.

"You are convinced now, I expect," Faria said. "Believe me, I know what I am saying; I have thought about it unceasingly ever since I had the first attack. I have been expecting this, for it runs in the family. My father, as well as my grandfather, died after the third attack. The physician who prepared this medicine for me has predicted the same fate for me."

"The physician has made a mistake," Dantès cried out. "As for your paralysis, that will not trouble me in the least. I shall swim the sea with you on my shoulders."

"My son," the abbé said, "you are a sailor and a swimmer, and should therefore know that a man could not possibly make more than fifty strokes with such a load on his back. I shall stay here till the hour of my deliverance has struck, the hour of my death. But you, my son, flee, escape! You are young, lithe, strong; trouble not about me . . . I give you back your word!"

"Very well," said Dantès, "in that case I shall stay here too!" Rising and solemnly stretching one hand over the old man, he said: "By all that I deem most holy, I swear that I shall not leave you till death takes one of us!"

Faria looked up at this noble-minded, simple young man, and read in the expression on his face, now animated by a feeling of pure devotion, the sincerity of his affection and the loyalty of his oath.

"So be it," said the sick man, "I accept. Thank you." Then holding out to him his hand, he said: "It may be that you will be rewarded for this unselfish devotion, but as I cannot leave, and you will not, we must fill in the tunnel under the gallery. The soldier might notice that that particular spot is hollow and call the inspector's attention to it. We should then be found out and separated. Go and do it at once; unfortunately I cannot help you. Spend the whole night on the task if necessary, and come to me again in the morning after the gaoler has made his visit. I shall have something important to tell you."

Dantès took the abbé's hand and was rewarded with a smile. With a feeling of deep respect, the young man then left his old friend in obedience to his wishes.

## CHAPTER XIV

## THE TREASURE

THE next morning when Dantès entered the cell of his friend in captivity, he found him sitting up with a resigned expression on his face. In the ray of light which entered his cell by the narrow window, he held in his left hand, the only one he could use now, a piece of paper which, from being continuously rolled up very tightly, had taken on a cylindrical shape. Without saying a word, he showed it to Dantès.

"What is this?" the young man asked.

"Look at it well," the abbé said, smiling. "This paper, my friend— I can tell you everything now for I have tried you—this piece of paper is my treasure, half of which belongs to you from this day forward."

"Your treasure?" Dantès stammered.

Faria smiled.

"Yes," he said. "You are a noble-hearted lad, Dantès, but I know by the way you shuddered and turned pale what is passing in your mind. This treasure really exists, and though it has not been my lot to possess it, you will one day be the owner of it all."

"My friend, your attack has tired you, will you not rest a little?" said Dantès. "If you wish, I will listen to your story to-morrow; to-day I only want to nurse you back to health, nothing more. Besides," he continued, "a treasure is not a very pressing matter for us just now, is it?"

"Very pressing, indeed," replied the old man. "How do we know that I shall not be seized with the third attack to-morrow or the day after? Remember that then all will be over. Yes, it is true. I have often thought with bitter joy of these riches, which are vast enough to make the fortunes of ten families, and which my persecutors will never enjoy. This has been my vengeance, and in the despair of my captivity I have lived on it during the long nights spent in my dungeon. But now that I have forgiven them all, for love of you, now that I see you full of youth and with a bright future before you, now that I think of all the happiness which will result to you from this disclosure, I tremble at any delay in securing to one so worthy as you the possession of such an enormous buried treasure."

Edmond turned away with a deep sigh.

"You persist in your incredulity, Edmond," Faria continued. "I see you must have proofs. Well, then, read this paper which I have not shown to anyone until now."

"I will not vex him," Dantès said to himself, and, taking the paper, half of which was missing, having, no doubt, been burnt by accident, he read:

> This treasure which may amount to two . . .
> Roman crowns in the farthest cor . . .
> of the secret opening which . . .
> declare belongs to him as . . .
> heir . . .
> *April 25, 1498*

"Well?" said Faria when the young man had finished reading.

"I see nothing here but broken lines and disjointed words; fire has made it unintelligible."

"That may be so to you who are reading it for the first time, but not to me who have toiled over it for many a long night, and reconstructed each phrase and completed each thought."

"Do you think you have discovered the whole meaning?"

"I am sure of it, but you shall judge for yourself presently. First of all let me relate the story of the piece of paper."

"Hush!" exclaimed Dantès, "I hear footsteps . . . some one is coming . . . I am going . . . Good-bye."

Dantès was very glad thus to escape a story and explanation which would only confirm his fear that the attack of catalepsy had deprived his friend of his reason. He stayed in his room all day in order to postpone the terrible moment when he would be quite satisfied that the abbé was mad. But when evening drew on and Dantès still did not make his appearance, not even after the gaoler had paid his customary visit, Faria tried to cover the space between his cell and that of his friend. Edmond shuddered when he heard the painful efforts he made to drag himself along; his leg was lifeless and he could no longer use his arm. Edmond was compelled to assist him, for alone he would never have been able to get through the narrow opening that led to Dantès' cell.

"Here I am, obstinately resolved on pursuing you," he said with a kindly smile. "You thought to escape my munificence, but it is useless. Now listen to me."

Edmond realized that he had to comply, so he placed the old man on the bed while he seated himself on the stool.

"You know already," the abbé began, "that I was the secretary and intimate friend of Cardinal Spada, the last prince of that name. It is to this worthy lord that I owe all the happiness of my life. He was not rich, although the riches of his family were proverbial, and he lived on the reputation of his wealth. His palace was my paradise. I taught his nephews but they died, and when he was alone in the world, I made some return for all he had done for me during ten years by absolute devotion to his every wish.

"The Cardinal's house held no secrets for me. I often saw Monsignor examining some old books and eagerly searching among family manuscripts. One day when I reproached him with the uselessness of working thus for whole nights together, which alone could account for his low spirits, he looked at me and, smiling bitterly, opened a book which was a history of Rome. There in the twentieth chapter of the *Life of Pope Alexander the Sixth,* I read the following lines which I shall never forget:

"'The great wars of the Romagna were ended. Caesar Borgia, who had made his conquest, had need of money with which to buy the whole of Italy. The Pope, too, had need of money to rid himself of Louis the Twelfth, King of France, who was still a formidable foe in spite of his recent defeats. It was necessary, therefore, to make some profitable speculation, which was no easy matter in Italy at that time owing to her impoverished and exhausted condition.'

"His Holiness had an idea. He decided to create two new cardinals. By choosing two of the greatest and, above all, richest personages in Rome he would make a very profitable speculation. First of all he could hold up for sale the splendid appointments and offices these two cardinals already held, and besides, he expected to realize a large sum by the sale of the two hats.

"There was still a third factor which we shall come to presently.

"The Pope and Caesar Borgia found the desired prospective cardinals, in John Rospigliosi, who alone held four of the highest titles of the Holy See, and Caesar Spada, one of the noblest and richest Romans. They both appreciated such high favour from the Pope for they were both ambitious. Caesar soon found purchasers for their appointments. The result was that Rospigliosi and Spada paid for the honour of being made cardinals, and eight other persons paid for the honour of holding the late appointments of the newly created cardinals. Eight hundred thousand crowns passed into the coffers of the speculators.

"It is now time we touched upon the third part of the speculation. The Pope having overwhelmed Rospigliosi and Spada with favours, having conferred on them the insignia of a cardinalate and feeling sure that they must have realized their fortunes to enable them to pay their very material debt of gratitude and to establish themselves at Rome, he and Caesar Borgia invited the two Cardinals to dinner.

"There now arose a dispute between the Holy Father and his son. Caesar Borgia thought that use might be made of one of those expedients which were always at the disposal of his intimate friends. There was first of all the famous key with which certain people were asked to open a particular cupboard. The key was furnished with a small iron point, due to negligence on the part of the maker. When bringing pressure to bear on this key, for the lock was a difficult one, the person would prick himself with this point and the next day he would die. Then there was the ring with the lion's head which Caesar placed on his finger when he shook hands with certain people. The lion bit the favoured hand and at the end of twenty-four hours this bite proved mortal.

"Caesar proposed to his father that they should send the cardinals to open the cupboard, or else shake each one heartily by the hand; but Alexander the Sixth replied:

"Do not let us begrudge these two worthy cardinals a dinner. Something tells me we shall get our money back. Besides, you forget that an attack of indigestion declares itself immediately, whereas the results of a prick or bite do not manifest themselves for a day or two.'

"Caesar gave way to this reasoning and the two cardinals were invited to dinner. The table was laid in a vineyard belonging to the Pope near San Pietro in Vincoli, a charming residence of which the Cardinals had often heard.

"Rospigliosi, overwhelmed with his new dignity, made all preparations for this new favour. Spada, being a prudent man who only loved his nephew, a hopeful young captain, took paper and pen and wrote his will. He then sent a message to his nephew to meet him near the vineyard, but apparently the messenger did not find him.

"Spada left for the vineyard near San Pietro in Vincoli at about two o'clock; the Pope was awaiting him. The first person Spada saw was his nephew, in full dress, the recipient of marked attentions from Caesar Borgia. Spada turned pale as Caesar cast on him a look full of irony, which seemed to say that he had foreseen everything and had seen to it that the trap was well laid.

"They went into dinner. Spada had only been able to ask his nephew whether he had received his message. The nephew answered that he had not. He understood what was meant by this question but it was too late. He had just drunk a glass of excellent wine which the

Pope's butler had set aside for him. Spada was liberally supplied from another bottle, and an hour later the physician declared they had both been poisoned through eating mushrooms. Spada died on the threshold of the vineyard, his nephew expired at his door while making a sign to his wife which she did not understand.

"Caesar and the Pope hastened to lay their hands on the heritage on the pretext that they were seeking for the dead man's papers. But the sole heritage was a piece of paper on which were written the words:

"'I bequeath to my dearly beloved nephew my coffers and my books, amongst which he will find my gold-cornered breviary, and I desire him to keep them in memory of his affectionate uncle.'

"Spada's would-be heirs searched everywhere, admired the breviary, laid hands on the furniture, and were filled with astonishment that Spada, the rich man, was in reality the most worthless of uncles: there were no treasures unless one reckoned the works of science in the library and the laboratories. There was nothing more. Caesar and his father searched and examined, rummaged amongst the papers, investigated everything, but nothing could they find, or at any rate very little: about a thousand crowns' worth of plate and about the same value in ready money. Yet, before dying, the nephew had had time to say to his wife:

"'Look among my uncle's papers; there is a will.'

"She searched even more energetically than the august heirs had done but all was in vain. There was nothing more than two palaces and a vineyard; and as at that period real property was of very little value, palaces and vineyards remained in the family as unworthy of the rapacity of the Pope and his son.

"Months and years rolled on. Alexander the Sixth was poisoned; Caesar was poisoned at the same time, but escaped death by shedding his skin like a snake, assuming a new cuticle on which the poison left spots like those on a tiger's skin. Compelled to leave Rome, he was killed in a nocturnal brawl almost forgotten by history.

"After the death of the Pope and the exile of the son, it was generally supposed that the Spada family would resume their splendour of the Cardinal's time, but it was not the case. They continued to live in doubtful comfort, and a mystery veiled the whole affair. It was noised abroad that Caesar, who was more politic than his father, had taken the fortunes of the two Cardinals from under his father's nose.

"Do you find my story very stupid?" Faria suddenly asked his companion with a smile.

"Oh, no, my friend," returned Dantès, "on the contrary. It is as though I were reading a most interesting narrative. Pray continue."

"I will. Spada's family accustomed themselves to living in obscurity and the years rolled on. Some of the descendants were soldiers, others diplomats, some entered the church, others became bankers. Some of them grew rich, while others lost all their fortunes. I come now to the last of the family, the Count Spada to whom I acted as secretary.

"I felt sure that neither the Cardinal's relations nor Borgia had profited by his fortune, and that it had remained ownerless in the bowels of the earth guarded by some genie. I searched and ransacked everything and everywhere; thousands of times did I add up the income and expenditure of the family for the past three hundred years, but it was all in vain. I remained ignorant and Count Spada remained poor.

"My patron died. He bequeathed to me his library, composed of five thousand books, his breviary, which had remained in the family and had been handed down from father to son, and in addition a thousand Roman crowns with the request that I should have anniversary masses said for the repose of his soul, draw up a genealogical tree, and write a history of his family. All this I carried out most scrupulously.

"In eighteen-seven, a month before my arrest, and fifteen days after Count Spada's death, on December the twenty-fifth—you will understand presently why the date of this memorable day became fixed in my memory—I was reading for the thousandth time the papers I was putting in order, for the palace had been sold to a stranger and I was leaving Rome to settle at Florence, taking with me what money I possessed, my library, and the famous breviary, when, tired with my assiduous study and rendered drowsy by the heavy dinner I had partaken of, my head fell in my hands and I dropped off to sleep. This was at three o'clock in the afternoon.

"I awoke as the clock was striking six to find that I was in complete darkness. I rang for a servant to bring me a light, but as no one came I resolved to help myself. Taking the candle in one hand, I groped about with the other for a piece of paper which I intended to light at the last flame flickering in the hearth. However, fearing that in the dark I might take a valuable piece of paper, I hesitated, but suddenly recollected that I had seen in the famous breviary which lay on the table beside me, an old piece of paper, yellow with age, which had probably served as a bookmark and had been kept in the same place for centuries by the different owners. I found this useless piece of paper and, putting it into the dying flame, lighted it.

"But as the flames devoured the paper I held between my fingers, I saw yellowish characters appear, as if by magic; an unholy terror seized me. I crushed the paper in my hand and choked the flame. Then I lighted the candle and with inexpressible emotion opened out the crumpled paper. I recognized that a mysterious, sympathetic ink had traced these characters which could only become apparent when placed in contact with heat. A little more than one-third of the paper had been consumed by the flames. It was the very paper you read this morning; read it again, Dantès, and then I will give you the missing words to make the sense complete."

So saying, Faria gave Dantès the paper, and he read this time with great eagerness the following words which had been written with an ink of the colour of rust:

This 25th day of April 1498, be ...
Alexander VI, and fearing that, not ...
he may desire to become my heir, and re ...
and Bentiviglio, who were poisoned, ...
my sole heir, that I have bu ...
and has visited with me—that is, in ...
isle of Monte Cristo—all I pos ...
els, diamonds, gems that alone ...
may amount to about two mil ...
will find on raising the twentieth ro ...
creek to the East in a straight line. Two open ...
in these caves; the treasure is in the farthest cor ...
which treasure I bequeath to him and leave en ...
sole heir.

CAES ...

*April 25, 1498*

"Now," continued the abbé, "read this other paper." And he gave Dantès a second piece containing the other half of the broken sentences.

... ing invited to dinner by His Holiness
... content to make me pay for my hat
... serve for me the fate of Cardinals Crapara
... I declare to my nephew, Guido Spada,
... ried in a spot he knows
... the caves of the small
... sess in ingots, gold, money, jew-
... I know the existence of this treasure, which
... lion Roman crowns, and which he
... ck from the small
... ings have been made
... ner of the second,
... tire to him as my
... AR † SPADA

Faria watched him attentively.
When he saw that Dantès had read the last line, he said:

"Now place the two fragments together and judge for yourself."
Dantès obeyed and read as follows:

> This 25th day of April 1498, being invited to dinner by His
> Holiness Alexander VI, and fearing that, not content to make me
> pay for my hat, he may desire to become my heir, and reserve for
> me the fate of Cardinals Crapara and Bentiviglio, who were poi-
> soned, I declare to my nephew, Guido Spada, my sole heir, that I
> have buried in a spot he knows and has visited with me—that is, in
> the caves of the small isle of Monte Cristo—all I possess in ingots,
> gold, money, jewels, diamonds, gems; that alone I know the exis-
> tence of this treasure, which may amount to about two million
> Roman crowns, and which he will find on raising the twentieth
> rock from the small creek to the East in a straight line. Two open-
> ings have been made in these caves; the treasure is in the farthest
> corner of the second, which treasure I bequeath to him and leave
> entire to him as my sole heir.
>
> CAESAR † SPADA
>
> *April 25, 1498*

"Well! Do you understand it now?" Faria asked.

"Then it is the declaration of Cardinal Spada and the will so long
sought for?" Dantès asked with incredulity.

"Yes, and a thousand times yes."

"Who reconstructed it in this way?"

"I did. With the assistance of the half of the will I had rescued, I
worked out the rest by measuring the length of the lines with that of
the paper, and by fathoming the missing words by means of those
already in my possession, just as in a vault one is guided by a ray of
light that enters from above."

"And what did you do when you thought you had solved the mysterious script?"

"I made up my mind to leave Rome at once, which I did, taking
with me the beginning of my big work on the unity of the Kingdom
of Italy. The imperial police, however, had been watching me for
some time past, and my sudden departure aroused their suspicions. I
was arrested just as I was about to embark at Piombino."

"Now, my dear friend," Faria continued, looking at Dantès with an
almost paternal expression, "you know as much as I do; if we ever
escape together half of my treasure is yours; if I die here and you
escape alone, the whole of it belongs to you."

"But is there not a more legitimate owner to this treasure than ourselves?" asked Dantès hesitatingly.

"No, none whatever. You can make your mind easy on that score.

The family is completely extinct and, besides, the last Count Spada made me his heir; in bequeathing the breviary to me, he bequeathed to me all that it contained. No, if we lay our hands on this fortune, we can enjoy it without any compunction."

"And you say this treasure consists of . . ."

"Two million Roman crowns and about thirteen millions of money in French coin."

Edmond thought he was dreaming: he wavered between incredulity and joy.

"I have kept this a secret from you for so long," Faria continued, "simply because I wanted to give you proofs, and also because I thought to give you a surprise. Had we escaped before my attack, I should have taken you to Monte Cristo, but now," he added with a sigh, "it will be you who will take me. Well, Dantès, are you not going to thank me?"

"This treasure belongs to you alone, my friend, and I have no right to it," Dantès replied. "I am not even related to you."

"You are my son, Dantès," exclaimed the old man. "You are the child of my captivity. My profession condemned me to celibacy, but God has sent you to console the man who could not be a father, and the prisoner who could not be a free man."

Faria held out his one remaining arm to the young man, who threw himself round his neck and burst into tears.

## CHAPTER XV

## THE THIRD ATTACK

Now that this treasure, which had been the object of the abbé's meditations for so long, could give future happiness to him whom he truly loved as a son, it had redoubled its value in his eyes; daily would he expatiate on the amount, holding forth to Dantès on the good a man could do to his friends in modern times with a fortune of thirteen or fourteen millions. Dantès' face would darken, for the oath of vengeance he had taken would come into his mind, and he was occupied with the thought of how much harm a man could do to his enemies in modern times with a fortune of thirteen or fourteen millions.

The abbé did not know the Isle of Monte Cristo, which was situated twenty-five miles from Pianosa between Corsica and Elba, but Dantès had often passed it and had once landed there. He drew a plan of the island and Faria advised him as to the best means to adopt to recover the treasure. He had kept silent about it for all these many long years, but now it became a daily topic of conversation between the two. Fearing that the will might one day be mislaid or lost, he made Dantès learn it by heart until he knew it word for word. Then he destroyed the second part in the firm conviction that, even if the first part were discovered and seized, nobody could understand its meaning. Sometimes Faria would spend whole hours giving Dantès instructions what to do against the time he should be a free man. Once free he was not to lose an hour, not even a minute, before setting out for Monte Cristo; he was to remain alone on the island under some pretext or other, and as soon as he was alone endeavour to discover the marvellous caves and search the spot designated in the will.

In the meantime the hours passed, if not rapidly, at least not unendurably. One night Edmond woke suddenly and thought he heard some one calling him. He opened his eyes and tried to penetrate the darkness. He heard his name, or rather a plaintive voice trying to articulate his name. He raised himself in his bed and listened, his anxiety bringing great beads of perspiration to his forehead. There could be no doubt, the voice came from his companion's cell.

"Great God!" he murmured. "Could it be?"

He moved his bed, drew the stone away, and rushed to his friend's cell. There by the flickering light of the lamp he beheld the old man clinging to his bedside. His features were drawn with the horrible symptoms which Edmond already knew, and which had filled him with such terror the first time he saw them.

"Ah! my friend," Faria said resignedly, "you understand, don't you? There is no need to explain anything. Think only of yourself now, think only how to make your captivity supportable and your escape possible. It would take you years to achieve unaided what I have done here. In any case, you need have no fear that my cell will remain empty for any length of time; another unfortunate wretch will soon take my place and you will be to him an angel of salvation. He may be young, strong, and patient like yourself, and may even help you to escape, whereas I have only been an obstacle. You will no longer have a half-dead body fettered to you to paralyse your every movement. God is decidedly doing you a good turn at last. He is giving you more than He is taking away, and it is quite time for me to die."

Edmond could only wring his hands and exclaim: "Oh, my friend, my dearest friend, don't talk like that any more! I saved you once and I will save you a second time." And raising the foot of the bed, he took the phial, which was still one-third full of the red liquid.

"See," he said, "there is still some of this saving draught. Tell me quickly what I am to do this time. Have you any fresh instructions? Speak, my friend, I am all attention."

"There is no hope," Faria replied, shaking his head.

"Oh, yes, yes!" exclaimed Dantès, "I tell you, I shall save you!"

"Try then if you like! Do as you did the first time, but do not wait so long. If I do not revive after you have administered twelve drops, pour the remaining contents of the phial down my throat. Now, carry me to my bed. I can no longer stand."

Edmond took the old man in his arms and placed him on his bed.

"And now, my dear boy," said Faria, "sole consolation of my miserable life, whom Heaven sent to me somewhat late in life, yet sent me an invaluable gift for which I am most thankful, at this moment when I must leave you, I wish you all the happiness and prosperity you desire. My son, I give you my blessing."

A violent shock checked the old man's speech. Dantès raised his head; he saw his friend's eyes all flecked with crimson as though a flow of blood had surged up from his chest to his forehead.

"Farewell! farewell!" the old man murmured, clasping the young man's hand convulsively. "Farewell! Forget not Monte Cristo!"

And with these words he fell back on to his bed.

The attack was terrible: convulsed limbs, swollen eyelids, foam mingled with blood, a rigid body, was all that remained on this bed of agony in place of the intelligent being that had been there but an instant before.

Dantès took the lamp, placed it on a ledge formed by a stone at the head of the bed, whence its flickering light cast a strange and weird reflection on the contorted features and inert, stiff body. With staring eyes, he anxiously awaited the propitious moment for administering the saving draught. When he thought the moment had come, he took the knife, forced apart the teeth, which offered less resistance than on the previous occasion, counted ten drops one after the other and waited: the phial still contained double that quantity.

He waited ten minutes, a quarter of an hour, half an hour, and still there was no sign of movement. Trembling in every limb, his hair on end, his forehead bathed in perspiration, he counted the seconds by the beatings of his heart. Then he thought it was time to make the last desperate attempt. He placed the phial to Faria's purple lips—his jaws had remained wide apart—and poured the rest of the liquid down his throat. A violent trembling seized the old man's limbs, his eyes opened and were frightful to behold, he heaved a sigh that sounded like a scream, and then his trembling body gradually reverted to its former rigidity. The face assumed a livid hue, and the light faded out of the wide-open eyes.

It was six o'clock in the morning; day began to dawn and its yet feeble gleam invaded the cell, putting to shame the dying light of the lamp. Weird reflections were cast over the face of the corpse, giving it from time to time a lifelike appearance. As long as this struggle between night and day lasted, Dantès still doubted, but as soon as the day held its own, he knew that he was alone with a corpse.

Then an overmastering terror seized him; he dared press no more the hand that hung down from the bed: he dared look no more on those vacant and staring eyes which he endeavoured in vain to close several times, for they opened again each time. He extinguished the lamp, hid it carefully and fled from the cell, replacing the stone behind him as carefully as he could.

It was time he went, too, for the gaoler was coming. Dantès was seized with an indescribable impatience to know what would happen in his unfortunate friend's cell; he, therefore, went into the subterranean passage where he arrived in time to hear the turnkey calling for assistance.

Other turnkeys soon arrived; then was heard the tread of soldiers, heavy and measured even when off duty; behind them came the governor.

Edmond heard the bed creaking; he heard too the voice of the governor, who ordered water to be thrown on the face of the dead man, and then, as this did not revive him, sent to summon the doctor.

The governor left the cell, and some words of compassion, mingled with coarse jokes and laughter, reached Dantès' ears.

"Perhaps," said one, "as he is a man of the church, they will go to some expense on his account."

"Then he will have the honour of the sack," said another.

Edmond listened and did not lose a word of the conversation, though he could not comprehend very much of it. Soon the voices ceased and it seemed to him they had all left the cell. Still he dared not yet go back; it was possible they had left some turnkeys to watch by the dead man.

At the end of an hour or so he heard a faint noise which gradually increased. It was the governor coming back with the doctor and several officials.

The doctor declared the prisoner dead and diagnosed the cause of death. There was more coming and going and a few seconds later, a sound like the rubbing together of sacking reached Dantès' ears. The bed creaked, a heavy step like that of a man lifting a weight resounded on the floor, then the bed creaked again under the weight placed on it.

"To-night, then," Dantès heard the governor say.

"Will there be a Mass?" asked one of the officials.

"That is impossible," replied the governor, "the chaplain asked me yesterday for leave to go to Hyères for a week. The poor abbé should not have been in such a hurry, and then he would have had his requiem."

In the meantime the body was being laid out.

"At what o'clock to-night?" asked one of the turnkeys.

"Between ten and eleven."

"Shall we watch by the corpse?"

"Whatever for? Lock the door as though he were alive; nothing more is needed."

The footsteps died away, the voices became gradually less distinct, the grating noise of the lock and the creaking of the bolts were heard, and then a silence more penetrating than solitude, the silence of death, prevailed, striking its icy chill through the young man's whole frame.

Then he slowly raised the stone with his head and cast a swift glance round the room. It was empty. Dantès entered.

## CHAPTER XVI

# THE CEMETERY OF THE CHÂTEAU D'IF

ON the bed, at full length, faintly lighted by a dim ray that entered through the window, Dantès saw a sack of coarse cloth, under the ample folds of which he could distinctly discern a long, stiff form: it was Faria's shroud. All was over then. Dantès was separated from his old friend. Faria, the helpful, kind companion, to whom he had become so attached, to whom he owed so much, existed now but in his memory. He sat on the edge of the bed and became a prey to deep and bitter melancholy.

Alone! He was quite alone once more! Alone! No longer to see, to hear the voice of, the only human being that attached him to life! Would it not be better to seek his Maker, as Faria had done, to learn the mystery of life even at the risk of passing through the dismal gates of suffering?

The idea of suicide which had been dispelled by his friend and which he himself had forgotten in his presence, rose again before him like a phantom beside Faria's corpse.

"If I could only die," he said, "I should go where he has gone. But how am I to die? It is quite simple," said he with a smile. "I will stay here, throw myself on the first one who enters, strangle him and then I shall be guillotined."

Dantès, however, recoiled from such an infamous death, and swiftly passed from despair to an ardent desire for life and liberty. "Die? Oh, no!" he cried out, "it would hardly have been worth while to live, to suffer so much and then to die now. No, I desire to live, to fight to the end. I wish to reconquer the happiness that has been taken from me.

Before I die, I have my executioners to punish, and possibly also some friends, to recompense. Yet they will forget me here and I shall only leave this dungeon in the same way that Faria has done."

As he uttered these words, Edmond stood stock-still, with eyes fixed like a man struck by a sudden and terrifying idea.

"Oh, who has given me this thought?" he murmured. "My God, comes this from Thee? Since it is only the dead who go free from here, I must take the place of the dead!"

Without giving himself time to reconsider his decision, and as though he would not give reflection time to destroy his desperate resolution, he leaned over the hideous sack, slit it open with the knife Faria had made, took the dead body out, carried it to his own cell, and placed it on his bed, put round the head the piece of rag he always wore, covered it with the bed-clothes, kissed for the last time the ice-cold forehead, endeavoured to shut the rebellious eyes, which were still open, and stared so horribly, and turned the head to the wall so that, when the gaoler brought his evening meal, he would think he had gone to bed as he often did. Then he returned to the other cell, took the needle and thread from the cupboard, flung off his rags that the men might feel naked flesh under the sacking, slipped into the sack, placed himself in the same position as the corpse, and sewed the sack up again from the inside. If, by any chance, the gaolers had entered then, they would have heard the beating of his heart.

Now this is what Dantès intended doing. If the grave-diggers discovered that they were carrying a live body instead of a dead one, he would give them no time for thought. He would slit the sack open with his knife from top to bottom, jump out, and, taking advantage of their terror, escape; if they tried to stop him, he would use his knife. If they took him to the cemetery and placed him in a grave, he would allow himself to be covered with earth; then, as it was night, as soon as the grave-diggers had turned their backs, he would cut his way through the soft earth and escape; he hoped the weight would not be too heavy for him to raise.

He had eaten nothing since the previous evening, but he had not thought of his hunger in the morning, neither did he think of it now. His position was much too precarious to allow him time for any thought but that of flight.

At last, toward the time appointed by the governor, he heard footsteps on the staircase. He realized that the moment had come, he summoned all his courage and held his breath.

The door was opened, a subdued light reached his eyes. Through the sacking that covered him he saw two shadows approach the bed. There was a third one at the door holding a lantern in his hand. Each of the two men who had approached the bed took the sack by one of its two extremities.

"He is very heavy for such a thin old man," said one of them as he raised the head.

"They say that each year adds half a pound to the weight of one's bones," said the other, taking the feet.

They carried away the sham corpse on the bier. Edmond made himself rigid. The procession, lighted by the man with the lantern, descended the stairs. All at once Dantès felt the cold, fresh night air and the sharp north-west wind, and the sensation filled him at once with joy and with anguish.

The men went about twenty yards, then stopped and dropped the bier on to the ground. One of them went away, and Dantès heard his footsteps on the stones.

"Where am I?" he asked himself.

"He is by no means a light load, you know," said the man who had remained behind, seating himself on the edge of the bier.

Dantès' impulse was to make his escape, but, fortunately, he did not attempt it. He heard one of the men draw near and drop a heavy object on the ground; at the same moment a cord was tied round his feet, cutting into his flesh.

"Well, have you made the knot?" one of the men asked.

"Yes, and it is well made. I can answer for that."

"Let's on, then."

The bier was lifted once more, and the procession proceeded. The noise of the waves breaking against the rocks on which the Château is built sounded more distinctly to Dantès with each step they took.

"Wretched weather!" said one of the men, "the sea will not be very inviting to-night."

"Yes, the abbé runs a great risk of getting wet," said the other, and they burst out laughing.

Dantès could not understand the jest, nevertheless his hair began to stand on end.

"Here we are at last!"

"No, farther on, farther on! You know the last one was dashed on the rocks and the next day the governor called us a couple of lazy rascals."

They went another five yards, and then Dantès felt them take him by the head and feet and swing him to and fro.

"One! Two! Three!"

With the last word, Dantès felt himself flung into space. He passed through the air like a wounded bird falling, falling, ever falling with a rapidity which turned his heart to ice. At last—though it seemed to him like an eternity of time—there came a terrific splash; and as he dropped like an arrow into the icy cold water he uttered a scream which was immediately choked by his immersion.

Dantès had been flung into the sea, into whose depths he was being dragged down by a cannon-ball tied to his feet.

The sea is the cemetery of the Château d'If.

## CHAPTER XVII

# THE ISLE OF TIBOULEN

THOUGH stunned and almost suffocated, Dantès had yet the presence of mind to hold his breath and, as he grasped the open knife in his right hand ready for any emergency, he rapidly ripped open the sack, extricated his arm and then his head; but in spite of his efforts to raise the cannon ball, he still felt himself being dragged down and down. He bent his back into an arch in his endeavour to reach the cord that bound his legs, and, after a desperate struggle, he severed it at the very moment when he felt that suffocation was getting the upper hand of him. He kicked out vigorously and rose unhampered to the surface, while the cannon ball dragged to the unknown depths the sacking which had so nearly become his shroud.

Dantès merely paused to take a deep breath and then he dived again to avoid being seen. When he rose the second time, he was already fifty yards from the spot where he had been thrown into the sea. He saw above him a black and tempestuous sky; before him was the vast expanse of dark, surging waters; while behind him, more gloomy than the sea and more sombre than the sky, rose the granite giant like some menacing phantom, whose dark summit appeared to Dantès like an arm stretched out to seize its prey. He had always been reckoned the best swimmer in Marseilles, and he was now anxious to rise to the surface to try his strength against the waves. To his joy he found that his enforced inaction had not in any way impaired his strength and agility, and he felt he could still master the element in which he had so often sported when a boy.

An hour passed. Exalted by the feeling of liberty, Dantès continued to cleave the waves in what he reckoned should be a direct line for the Isle of Tiboulen. Suddenly it seemed to him that the sky, which was already black, was becoming blacker than ever, and that a thick, heavy cloud was rolling down on him. At the same time he felt a violent pain in his knee. With the incalculable rapidity of imagination, he thought it was a shot that had struck him, and he expected every moment to hear the report. But there was no sound. He stretched out his hand and encountered an obstacle; he drew his leg up and felt land; he then saw what it was he had mistaken for a cloud. Twenty yards from him rose a mass of strangely formed rocks looking like an immense fire petrified at the moment of its most violent combustion: it was the Isle of Tiboulen.

Dantès rose, advanced a few steps and with a prayer of gratitude on his lips, stretched himself out on the jagged rocks which seemed to him more restful and comfortable than the softest bed he had ever slept on. Then, in spite of the wind and storm, in spite of the rain that began to fall, worn out with fatigue as he was, he fell into the delicious sleep of a man whose body becomes torpid but whose mind remains alert in the consciousness of unexpected happiness.

For an hour he slept thus, and was awakened by the roar of a tremendous clap of thunder. A flash of lightning that seemed to open the heavens to the very throne of God, illuminated all around, and by its light he saw about a quarter of a mile away, between the Isle of Lemaire and Cap Croisille, a small fishing boat borne along by the wind, and riding like a phantom on the top of a wave only to disappear in the abyss below. A second later it appeared on the crest of another wave advancing with terrifying rapidity. By the light of another flash, he saw four men clinging to the masts and rigging; a fifth was clinging to the broken rudder. Then he heard a terrific crash followed by agonizing cries. As he clung to his rock like a limpet, another flash revealed to him the little boat smashed to pieces and, amongst the wreckage, heads with despairing faces, and arms stretched heavenward. Then all was dark again. There was nothing left but tempest.

By degrees the wind abated; the huge grey clouds rolled toward the west. Shortly afterward a long, reddish streak was seen along the horizon; the waves leaped and frolicked, and a sudden light played on their foamy crests, turning them into golden plumes. Daylight had come.

It must have been five o'clock in the morning; the sea continued to grow calm. "In two or three hours," Dantès said to himself, "the turnkeys will enter my cell, find the dead body of my poor friend, recognize him, seek me in vain, and give the alarm. Then they will find the aperture and the passage; they will question the men who flung me into the sea and who must have heard the cry I uttered. Boats filled with armed soldiers will immediately give chase to the wretched fugitive who, they know, cannot be far off. The cannon will warn the whole coast that no one shall give shelter to a naked, famished wanderer. The spies and police of Marseilles will be notified, and they will beat the coast while the Governor of the Château d'If beats the sea. And what will become of me pursued by land and by sea? I am hungry and cold and have even lost my knife. I am at the mercy of the first peasant who cares to hand me over to the police for the reward of twenty francs. Oh God! my God! Thou knowest I have suffered to excess; help me now that I cannot help myself!"

As Dantès finished this fervent prayer that was torn from his exhausted and anguished heart, he saw appearing on the horizon what he recognized as a Genoese *tartan* coming from Marseilles.

"To think that I could join this vessel in half an hour if it were not for the fear of being questioned, recognized as a fugitive, and taken back to Marseilles," said Dantès to himself. "What am I to do? What can I say? What story can I invent which might sound credible? I might pass as one of the sailors wrecked last night." So saying he turned his gaze toward the wreck and gave a sudden start. There, caught on a point of rock, he perceived the cap of one of the shipwrecked sailors, and close by still floated some of the planks of the unfortunate vessel.

Dantès soon thought out a plan and as quickly put it into action. He dived into the sea, swam toward the cap, placed it on his head, seized one of the timbers, and turning back, struck out in a direction which would cut the course the vessel must take.

The boat changed her course, steering toward him, and Dantès saw that they made ready to lower a boat. He summoned all his strength to swim toward it, but his arms began to stiffen, his legs lost their flexibility, and his movements became heavy and difficult. Breath was failing him. A wave that he had not the strength to surmount, passed over his head, covering him with foam. Then he saw and heard nothing more.

When he opened his eyes again, Dantès found himself on the deck of the *tartan*; a sailor was rubbing his limbs with a woollen cloth, another was holding a gourd to his mouth, and a third, who was the master of the vessel, was looking at him with that feeling of pity which is uppermost in the hearts of most people when face to face with a misfortune which they escaped yesterday, and of which they may be the victim to-morrow.

"Who are you?" the skipper asked in bad French.

"I am a Maltese sailor," replied Dantès in equally bad Italian. "We were coming from Syracuse laden with wine and grain. We were caught in a storm last night off Cape Morgion, and we were wrecked on the rocks you see yonder."

"Where have you come from?"

"From those rocks over there. Fortunately for me I was able to cling to them, but our poor captain and my three companions were drowned. I believe I am the sole survivor. I saw your ship, and I risked swimming towards you. Thank you," he continued, "you have saved my life. I was lost when one of your sailors caught hold of my hair."

"It was I," said a sailor with a frank and open face, encircled by long black whiskers. "It was time, too, for you were sinking."

"Yes," said Dantès, holding out his hand to him. "I know, and I thank you once more."

"Lord! but you nearly frightened me," the sailor replied. "You looked more like a brigand than an honest man with your beard six inches long and your hair a foot in length."

Dantès suddenly recollected that neither his hair nor his beard had been cut all the time that he had been at the Château d'If.

"Once when I was in danger," he said, "I made a vow to the Madonna of Piedigrotta not to cut my hair or beard for ten years. The time is up this very day, and I nearly celebrated the event by being drowned."

"Now, what are we going to do with you?" asked the skipper.

"Alas! do with me what you will," replied Dantès. "The bark I sailed in is lost, my captain is dead, and I nearly shared the same fate. Fortunately I am a good sailor. Leave me at the first port you touch at, and I shall be sure to find employment in some merchantman."

"Take the helm and let us see how you frame."

The young man did as he was bid. Ascertaining by a slight pressure that the vessel answered to the rudder, he saw that, without being a first-rate sailer, she was yet tolerably obedient.

"Man the lee-braces," he cried.

The four seamen, who composed the crew, obeyed, whilst the skipper looked on.

"Haul away!"

They obeyed.

"Belay!"

This order was also executed, and, instead of tacking about, the vessel made straight for the Isle of Rion, leaving it about twenty fathoms to starboard.

"Bravo!" said the captain.

"Bravo!" repeated the sailors.

And they all regarded with astonishment this man whose eye had recovered an intelligence and his body a vigour they were far from suspecting him to possess.

"You see," said Dantès, handing over the tiller to the helmsman, "I shall be of some use to you, at any rate during the voyage. If you do not want me at Leghorn, you can leave me there and with the first wages I earn, I will pay you for my food and for the clothes you lend me."

"Very well," said the captain. "We can fix things up if you are not too exacting."

"Give me what you give the others," returned Dantès.

"Hallo! What's the matter at the Château d'If?" exclaimed the captain.

A small white cloud crowned the summit of the bastion of the Château d'If. At the same moment, the faint report of a gun was heard. The sailors all looked at one another.

"A prisoner has escaped from the Château d'If, and they are firing the alarm gun," said Dantès calmly.

"What is the day of the month?" he presently asked of Jacopo, the sailor who had saved him and who now sat beside him.

"The twenty-eighth of February."

"What year?"

"Have you forgotten that you ask such a question?"

"I was so frightened last night," replied Dantès, with a smile, "that I have almost lost my memory. What year is it?"

"The year eighteen-twenty-nine," returned Jacopo.

It was fourteen years to the very day since Dantès' arrest. He was nineteen when he entered the Château d'If; he was thirty-three when he escaped.

A sad smile passed over his lips. He wondered what had become of Mercédès, who must now believe him dead. Then his eyes flashed with hatred as he thought of the three men to whom he owed so long and cruel a captivity. Against Danglars, Fernand, and Villefort he renewed the oath of implacable vengeance which he had vowed in his dungeon.

This oath was no longer a vain threat, for the fastest sailer in the Mediterranean could never have overhauled the little *tartan,* which, with all sails set, was scudding before the wind in the direction of Leghorn.

Dantès had not been a day on board before he realized who the people were with whom he was sailing. With his experience of the ways of seafaring men it was not difficult to guess that the *Jeune Amélie*—for such was the name of the Genoese *tartan*—was a smuggler. The skipper had received Dantès on board with a certain amount of misgiving. He was well known to all the customs officers of the coast, and as there was between these worthies and himself an interchange of the most cunning stratagems, he had at first thought that Dantès might be an emissary of the excise authorities, who had employed this ingenious means of penetrating some of the secrets of his trade. The skilful manner in which Dantès had manœuvred the little bark, however, had entirely reassured him, and when he saw the light smoke floating like a plume above the bastion of the Château d'If and heard the distant report, it occurred to him for an instant that he had on board his vessel one for whom, as for the arrivals and departings of kings, they accord a salute of guns. This made him less uneasy, it must be owned, than if the new-comer had been a custom-house officer, but even this latter supposition disappeared like the first, when he beheld the perfect tranquillity of his recruit.

Edmond thus had the advantage of knowing what the skipper was, without the skipper knowing what he was; and, however much the old sailor and his crew tried to pump him, they extracted nothing more from him: he gave accurate descriptions of Naples and Malta, which he knew equally as well as Marseilles, and persisted stoutly in his first statement. Thus, subtle as he was, the Genoese was duped by Edmond, whose gentle demeanour, nautical skill, and admirable dissimulation stood him in good stead. Moreover, it is possible that the Genoese was one of those shrewd persons who know nothing but what they should know, and believe nothing but what it suits them to believe. Such was the position when they reached Leghorn.

As Dantès had landed at Leghorn very many times before, he knew a barber in the Via San Fernando and went straight there to have his hair and beard cut, for his comrades believed his vow was now fulfilled.

When the operation was concluded and Edmond's chin was smooth and his hair reduced to the fashionable length, he asked for a mirror. He was now, as we have said, thirty-three years of age, and the fourteen years' imprisonment had worked a great change in his features.

When he first went to the Château d'If his face was the round, smiling, cheerful face of a happy young man whose early years had passed smoothly, and who looked forward to his future in the light of his past. All this was now changed.

His oval face had lengthened; his smiling mouth had assumed the firm and determined lines indicative of resolution; his eyebrows had become arched beneath a single pensive wrinkle; his eyes had a look of deep sadness in them, and at times gloomy fires of misanthropy and hatred would sparkle in their depths; his skin, hidden from the light of day and the rays of the sun for so long, had assumed the pale and soft colour which, when the face is encircled with black hair, makes the aristocratic beauty of the North. The deep learning he had acquired was reflected on his face in an expression of intelligent self-confidence; in addition, though naturally tall, he had acquired the healthy vigour of a body continuously concentrating all its force within itself.

The elegance of his wiry, slender form had given way to the solidity of a round, muscular figure. His voice, too, had undergone a change. The continuous prayers, sobs, and imprecations had given it at times a strangely soft intonation, while at others it was gruff and almost hoarse. Moreover, his eyes, having been accustomed to twilight and darkness, had acquired the peculiar faculty of distinguishing objects in the dark, like those of the hyena and the wolf.

Edmond smiled when he saw himself: it was impossible that even his best friend, if he had any friends left, would recognize him: he did not even recognize himself.

The skipper of the *Jeune Amélie*, who was most anxious to keep amongst his crew such a valuable man as Dantès, offered to re-engage him, but Dantès had other plans in view, and would only accept for three months.

The *Jeune Amélie* had a very active crew ready to obey their master's orders, and he was accustomed to losing no time. He had barely been at Leghorn a week when the rounded sides of his vessel were stacked with printed muslins and prohibited cottons, English powders and tobacco, on which the excise authorities had forgotten to affix their seal. He had to get all this out of Leghorn free of duty and land it on the shores of Corsica, whence certain speculators undertook to transmit the cargo to France.

They put off, and Dantès was once more sailing the blue ocean, which he had seen so often in his dreams while in confinement.

The next morning when the captain went on deck, which he always did at a very early hour, he found Dantès leaning over the bulwarks and gazing with a strange expression on his face at a pile of granite rocks that the rising sun had tingled a rosy hue: it was the Isle of Monte Cristo. The *Jeune Amélie* left it about three-quarters of a league to starboard and kept to her course for Corsica.

Fortunately Dantès had learnt to wait: he had waited fourteen years for his liberty. Now that he was free he could easily wait six months or a year for his treasure. Besides, was not this treasure chimerical? Born in the diseased brain of poor Abbé Faria, had it not died with him? It is true Cardinal Spada's letter was singularly convincing, and Dantès repeated it word for word from beginning to end: he had not forgotten a single syllable of it.

Two months and a half passed in similar trips, and he had become a skilful a coaster as he had been a hardy sailor. He had struck up an acquaintance with all the smugglers on the coast, and had learned all the masonic signs by which these semi-pirates recognize each other. He had passed and repassed his Isle of Monte Cristo twenty times, but had never once found an opportunity of going ashore. He therefore made up his mind that immediately after the termination of his engagement with the skipper of the *Jeune Amélie*, he would hire a small bark on his own account (he was able to do so for he had picked up a hundred piastres or so on his different voyages), and under some pretext or other make for the Isle of Monte Cristo.

Once there he would be free to make his researches, perhaps not entirely free, for he was fully aware that he would be spied upon by those who accompanied him. But in this world one must risk something.

Dantès was trying to solve the problem when one evening the skipper, who placed great confidence in him and was very anxious to keep him in his service, took him by his arm and led him to a tavern in the Via del Oglio, where the aristocrats of the Leghorn smugglers were wont to congregate.

It was here they discussed the affairs of the coast. This time a matter of great importance was debated: it concerned a ship laden with Turkish carpets, materials from the Levant, and cashmere shawls. They would have to find some neutral ground where an exchange could be made, and then endeavour to land the goods on the coast of France. The prize-money would be enormous, and if they succeeded it would mean fifty to sixty piastres for each one of the crew. The skipper proposed the Isle of Monte Cristo as a suitable place for discharging the cargo. Trembling with joy, Dantès got up to hide his emotion and paced round the smoky tavern where all the known languages of the world are mixed into a *lingua franca*. When he joined the skipper again, it was already decided that they should touch at Monte Cristo, and that they should start on the expedition the following evening. When Edmond was consulted, he gave it as his opinion that the island afforded every possible security, and that if enterprises were to succeed, they should be carried out quickly.

Nothing was changed in the programme: they were to weigh anchor the next evening and, given a good sea and a favourable wind, they hoped to be in the waters of the neutral island by the evening of the following day.

## CHAPTER XVIII

## THE ISLE OF MONTE CRISTO

AT seven o'clock the next evening all was ready, at ten minutes past seven they rounded the lighthouse just as the beacon was kindled. The sea was calm with a fresh wind blowing from the south-east; they sailed under a sky of azure where God was also lighting up his lanterns, each one of which is a world.

The vessel skimmed merrily over the water under full sail: there was not a rag of cloth that was not bellied in the wind.

The Isle of Monte Cristo loomed large on the horizon.

Toward five o'clock they saw a complete view of the island. They could see the smallest objects, thanks to the clearness of atmosphere peculiar to the light that is shed by the rays of the sun at sunset. Edmond gazed and gazed on this mass of rocks, which was tinged with all the colours of twilight, from bright pink to deep blue; at times his face would become a deep red, and a blue mist passed before his eyes. Never did gamester, whose whole fortune was staked on one throw of the dice, experience the anguish that Dantès felt.

Night came. They landed at ten o'clock. The *Jeune Amélie* was first at the rendezvous. Nothwithstanding his usual self-restraint, Dantès could control himself no longer: he jumped on to the shore and, like Brutus, he would have kissed the earth if he had dared. It was already dark night, but at eleven o'clock the moon rose over the ocean, silvering every little ripple, and, as she ascended, began to play on the mass of rocks casting white cascades of light on this second Pelion.

Dantès' every thought was concentrated on finding Spada's grotto. It was useless to search for it during the night, so he put off all investigations until the next day. Besides, a signal hoisted half a league out at sea, to which the *Jeune Amélie* immediately answered with a similar signal, indicated that it was time to set to work.

The late-comer, reassured by the signal that all was well, soon came in sight, silent and pale as a phantom, and cast anchor within a cable's length of the shore. Then the work of unloading began. While working, Dantès continually reflected upon the shout of joy which one word of his would draw from the throats of all these men if he were to express aloud the thought that was incessantly in his mind. But far from revealing his precious secret, he feared he had already said too much, and that he had, by his comings and goings and his repeated questions, minute observations, and continual preoccupation, aroused suspicion.

This was not the case, however, and when he took a gun and some powder and shot the next day, and manifested a desire to go and shoot some of the numerous wild kids they could see jumping from rock to rock, they attributed his proposed excursion to nothing more than a love of sport or a desire for solitude.

Thus Dantès who, three months previously, had desired nothing more than liberty, was now no longer satisfied with that alone and aspired after riches. He started forth. Lost to view between two walls of rock, he followed a path hollowed out by continuous torrents and which, in all probability, no human foot had ever trodden before. He approached the spot where he supposed the grottoes to be situated. Following the coast and examining the most minute objects with serious attention, he thought he noticed on several rocks incisions that had been made by man.

Time which casts its mantle of moss on all things material, and its mantle of oblivion on all things moral, seemed to have respected these marks, which were made with a certain regularity, no doubt to indicate some trail; now and then, however, they disappeared beneath tufts of myrtle which grew in large clusters laden with flowers, and beneath parasitical lichen. Then Edmond was obliged to raise the branches or remove the moss to find the marks which were to lead him to this labyrinth. The marks had filled him with new hope. Surely it must have been the Cardinal who had traced them, so that in the event of a catastrophe, which even he had not foreseen would be so complete, they would serve as a guide to his nephew. This isolated spot was a most appropriate place for burying a treasure. But had these unfaithful signs not already attracted the attention of other eyes than those for which they were meant? Or had the isle of gloomy marvels faithfully kept its precious secret?

About sixty yards from the harbour, it seemed to Dantès, who was still hidden from his companions by the inequalities of the ground, that the incisions ceased. There was no grotto! A large round rock, perched on a solid base seemed the only goal to which they led. He thought that, instead of having arrived at the end, he was perhaps only at the beginning, so he turned round and retraced his steps.

In the meantime his companions were preparing breakfast and when it was ready they fired a shot as a signal. Edmond at once came running toward them. Just as they were all watching him jumping like a chamois from rock to rock, his foot gave way under him. They saw him stagger at the edge of a rock and disappear. They all rushed toward him with one bound, for, in spite of his superiority, they all loved him. They found him lying bleeding and half conscious. They forced some rum down his throat, and this remedy, which had been so beneficial to him before, had the same good effect on him now. Edmond opened his eyes, complained of a sharp pain in his knee, a feeling of heaviness in his head, and unbearable pain in his back. They wanted to carry him to the beach, but, directly they touched him, he declared, with groans, that he had not the strength. The old skipper urged Dantès to rise, for he was obliged to leave in the morning to deposit his cargo on the frontiers of Piedmont and France, between Nice and Fréjus. Edmond made a superhuman effort to comply with his wishes, but, turning very white, he fell back each time with a moan.

"He has broken his back," the skipper said in a low voice. "No matter, we will not forsake him. Let us carry him on board."

But Dantès declared that he would sooner die where he was than bear the agonizing pain that the slightest movement caused him.

"Very well," said the skipper, "come what may, it shall not be said that we have deserted such a good shipmate as you. We will not leave till this evening." This proposal was a cause of great astonishment to the sailors, though no one opposed it. Dantès, however, would not allow such a serious violation of the rules of discipline on his behalf. "No," he said, "I have been clumsy and it is only right that I should pay the penalty. Leave me a supply of biscuit, a gun, some powder and shot for killing some kids or maybe to use in my own defence, also a pickaxe so that I can make myself some sort of shelter in case you should be delayed in returning to fetch me."

"But you will die of hunger," replied the skipper. "We cannot leave you like this, and on the other hand we cannot stay."

"Leave me! Go!" Dantès cried out.

Nothing could shake Dantès' determination to remain and to remain alone. The smugglers gave him all he had asked for and left him. He dragged himself cautiously to the top of a rock which afforded him full view of the sea, whence he watched the *tartan* making ready to sail; he saw her weigh anchor and, balancing herself as gracefully as a gull ere it takes wing, put out to sea.

At the end of an hour she had completely disappeared from his view, and rising, more agile and light of limb than the kids jumping about these rugged rocks among the myrtle- and mastic-trees, Dantès took his gun in one hand, the pickaxe in the other, and ran toward the rock on which the incisions terminated.

"Now," he exclaimed, thinking of the story of the Arabian fisherman which Faria had related to him. "Now, open, Sesame!"

## CHAPTER XIX

## THE TREASURE CAVE

THE sun had run about a third of his course, sending his warm and invigorating rays full on the rocks which seemed almost insensible to their warmth. The monotonous and continuous chirp of thousands of grasshoppers invisible in the heath could be heard; the leaves of the myrtles and olive-trees waved and shook in the wind, sending forth an almost metallic sound. With every step Edmond took on the warm granite he sent scurrying away numerous lizards bright as emeralds. In the distance wild goats were to be seen jumping from crag to crag. In a word, the island was inhabited and very much alive. Yet Dantès felt quite alone under God's blue sky. He felt an indescribable sensation akin to fear; a distrust of daylight which, even in the desert, gives us the feeling that inquisitive eyes are following us. The feeling was so strong in him that no sooner had he commenced his task than he stopped, laid down his pickaxe, picked up his gun and, climbing to the top of the highest rock, gazed all around him. But he could see neither man nor ship; nothing but the blue sky overhead and the azure sea below. Reassured, he descended rapidly, but at the same time cautiously, fearing an accident similar to the one he had so cleverly simulated.

As we have already said, Dantès traced the marks on the rocks back the other way, and found that they led to a kind of small creek hidden away like the bath of a nymph of ancient days; the creek was wide enough at its mouth and deep enough in the centre to allow a small ship to enter and lie concealed there. Then, as he followed the clue that had been so skilfully handled by Faria to guide him through the labyrinth of probabilities, he came to the conclusion that Cardinal Spada, in order to avoid being seen, must first have landed in this little creek, where he hid his small bark, followed the path indicated by the incisions, and finally buried his treasure at the extreme end.

This supposition had brought Dantès to the circular rock. There was only one thing that perplexed him and upset his whole theory. How could this rock, at least several tons in weight, have been hoisted on to its base without the employment of considerable force?

Suddenly an idea occurred to Dantès. Instead of having been lifted, thought he, it has been lowered. And he jumped on to the rock to find its original resting place. He soon perceived that a slope had been formed; the rock had slid along until it stopped in its present position, another medium-sized rock serving as a wedge. Stones and pebbles had been carefully placed to conceal every sign of an orifice. This piece of masonry had been covered over with earth, grass, and moss which had taken seed there, myrtle- and mastic-bushes had taken root, and the old rock appeared fixed to the ground.

Dantès raised the earth carefully, and detected, or thought he did, the whole of this ingenious artifice. But, he reflected, the rock was too firmly wedged and too heavy for any one man to move, were he Hercules himself. What means could he employ? He looked around for something, and his eye suddenly lighted upon the powder-horn his friends had left him. He smiled: this infernal invention would serve his purpose.

By means of his pickaxe, Dantès then cut an opening between the upper and the lower rocks and filled it with powder. Then he shredded his handkerchief, rubbed it in the powder, and thus had a match. Directly he had set a light to it, he withdrew.

The explosion was instantaneous. The upper rock was lifted from its base by the terrific force, while the lower one was blown to pieces. Thousands of trembling insects scuttled away and a long snake, the guardian of this mysterious cave, crawled away on its blue belly and disappeared.

Dantès returned to the spot. The upper rock was hanging with scarcely any support over the cliff. The intrepid treasure-hunter walked round it, chose the loosest spot and inserting his lever into one of the crevices, like Sisyphus, he strained every muscle in his attack on the huge mass.

The rock, already shaken by the explosion, tottered; Dantès redoubled his efforts. He looked like one of the Titans uprooting the mountains in their war against the father of the gods. At last the rock yielded and rolled headlong into the sea. It had uncovered a circular place revealing an iron ring set in the middle of a square-shaped flagstone. Dantès uttered a cry of joy and astonishment. Never had a first attempt been crowned with such splendid success. He would fain have continued his task, but his legs trembled so uncontrollably, his heart beat so violently, and his eyes became so dim, that he was compelled to pause awhile. He did not wait long, however. Passing his lever through the ring, he lifted with all his might; the flagstone yielded and revealed a kind of staircase which went deeper and deeper into an increasingly dark grotto.

Dantès descended, murmuring the supreme word of human philosophy: 'Perhaps.' But, instead of the darkness and the thick and mephitic air he had expected to find, he saw a soft and bluish light. The air and light filtered not only through the aperture just made but also through some cracks in the rocks which were invisible from without, while from the inside Dantès could see the blue of the sky.

After having been for a few seconds in the cave, the atmosphere of which was warm rather than damp, fragrant rather than fetid, Dantès' eyes, accustomed as they were to the dark, could penetrate into its furthermost corners; it was of granite, the facets of which sparkled like diamonds.

"Alas!" said Dantès with a smile, "these are no doubt the only treasures the Cardinal has left!"

Suddenly he thought of the words of the will which he knew by heart: "In the farthest corner of the second cave." He had only gained admittance to the first cave and must now find the entrance to the second one, which must naturally penetrate farther into the interior of the island. He examined the stones and sounded the wall where he supposed the opening would be—no doubt disguised for precaution's sake. The pickaxe resounded for an instant with a thick echo which caused the perspiration to stand in great beads on Dantès' forehead;

but at length it appeared to the persevering miner that one portion of the granite wall gave forth a hollower and deeper sound. He scanned this part eagerly and recognized with a perception that probably no one but a prisoner possesses, that there must be an opening there. He struck it again with more vigour. This time he noticed something peculiar. As he struck the wall, a sort of stucco fell to the ground laying bare soft white stone. The opening in the rock had been closed with stones of a different kind; these had been covered with stucco, and on this the colour and sparkle of the granite had been imitated.

Dantès struck into the wall with the sharp end of his pick, which penetrated about an inch. Here then was the spot where he must dig.

As yet he had had no food, but this was not the moment to eat. He swallowed a mouthful of rum and again attacked his work somewhat strengthened. He took up his pickaxe, and after several strokes with it he perceived that the stones were not cemented, but simply placed one on top of the other and covered with stucco. He pushed the point of his pick into one of the interstices, pressed on the handle, and to his joy one of the stones fell at his feet. The opening thus made was large enough to admit him, and so he was able to pass from the first grotto into the second. It was lower, darker and more uncanny than the first: the air, which only entered by the aperture he had just made, had that fetid smell Dantès had expected to find in the first. He gave the exterior air time to replace this foul air and then he entered.

To the left of the aperture there was a dark and gloomy corner. As we have already mentioned, however, there was no darkness for the eyes of Dantès. He looked round the second grotto; like the first one it was empty! The treasure, if it existed, was buried in the dark corner yonder. Dantès' hour of anguish had arrived. To dig through two feet of earth was all that remained to him between supreme joy and bottomless despair. He approached the corner and, as though seized by a sudden resolution, set to work on the soil with all his might. At the fifth or sixth stroke it sounded as though the pickaxe had encountered some iron substance. Never did funeral knell or alarm bell produce such an effect on its hearer. Had Dantès found nothing, he could not have become more deadly pale. He plunged his pick into the earth a little to one side of this spot and encountered resistance but not the same sound.

"It is a wooden chest bound with iron," he said.

In a very short time he had cleared a space about three feet long and two wide, and, by the light of the torch he had improvised, he recognized an oak chest bound with wrought iron. In the middle of the lid on a silver plate which the earth had left untarnished, were engraved the arms of the Spada family, namely, a sword on an oval

shield like that of the Italians, and surmounted by a cardinal's hat.
Dantès easily recognized them. Faria had drawn them for him time
and again. There could now be no doubt that the treasure was there;
no one would have taken such precautions for an empty chest.

Edmond laid bare the chest in very little time and saw appearing bit
by bit the centre lock placed between two padlocks and the handles
at each end, all carved as things were carved at that period when art
lent beauty to the basest of metals.

Dantès took the chest by the handles and tried to lift it, but that was
quite impossible. He tried to open it: it was locked. He inserted the
sharp end of his pickaxe between the chest and the lid and burst it
open. The chest was uncovered!

The chest was divided into three compartments. In the first shone
bright red gold crown pieces. In the second unpolished ingots
arranged in order, their only attraction being their weight and value.
In the third compartment, which was but half full, Dantès took up
whole handfuls of diamonds, pearls, and rubies, which as they fell
through his fingers in a sparkling cascade gave forth the sound of hail
beating against the window-panes.

After he had touched, fingered, buried his trembling hands in the
gold and precious stones, Edmond rose and rushed through the caves
like a man seized with a frenzy. He leapt on to a rock whence he could
behold the sea. He was alone, quite alone with these incalculable,
unheard-of, fabulous riches which all belonged to him! Was he awake
or was it all a dream? Could he possibly be face to face with reality?
He wanted to see his gold, yet he felt he had not the strength to look
at it. For a moment he pressed his head in his hands as though to prevent his senses from leaving him; then he rushed wildly about the
island, terrifying the wild goats and scaring the seagulls with his shouts
and gesticulations. Finally he returned, still with doubt in his mind,
rushed from the first grotto into the second, and found himself in
presence of his mine of gold and diamonds.

This time he fell on his knees, murmuring a prayer that was intelligi-
ble to God alone. He soon became calmer and happier, and began to
believe in his good fortune. He began to count his treasures; there were
a thousand ingots of gold, each weighing two or three pounds; he piled
up twenty-five thousand gold crowns, each one of which he valued at
twenty-four francs of the present currency, and which bore the effigy of
Pope Alexander VI or his predecessors: yet this did not constitute one-
half of the contents of the compartment. He measured out ten handfuls
of pearls, precious stones, and diamonds, many of which were mounted
by the best goldsmiths of the period and were valuable on account of
their remarkable workmanship in addition to their intrinsic worth.

This night was for Edmond one of those delicious yet terrible nights, of which this man of astounding emotions had already spent two or three in his lifetime.

## CHAPTER XX

## THE STRANGER

DAY broke. Dantès had long been waiting for it with wide open eyes. He rose with the first streak of daylight, climbed the highest peak of the island, as on the previous evening, and explored his surroundings. As on the previous evening also, silence reigned supreme.

Edmond descended, raised the stone, filled his pockets with precious stones, replaced the lid on the chest, covered it with earth which he carefully stamped down, and sprinkled some sand over it so as to make this spot look like the rest of the ground. Then he left the cave, replacing the stone after him, and effaced all traces of his steps for some distance round the grotto. He now longed with impatience for his companions' return, for in truth he could not waste his time in Monte Cristo looking at his gold and diamonds like a dragon guarding a useless treasure. He must return into the world and take the rank, influence, and power in society bestowed by riches only, the first and greatest force at man's disposal.

The smugglers returned on the sixth day. Dantès recognized the *Jeune Amélie* from a distance and dragged himself to the port. When his comrades landed, he assured them that he was better, though still suffering, and listened to an account of their adventures.

He displayed the most admirable self-possession; he did not even smile at the enumeration of the gains he would have derived had he been able to leave the island. As the *Jeune Amélie* had only come to Monte Cristo to fetch him, he embarked the same evening and went with the skipper to Leghorn. Arrived at Leghorn, he sought out a Jew to whom he sold four of his smallest diamonds for five thousand francs each. The Jew might have wondered how it came about that a sailor was in possession of such valuable jewels, but he asked no questions and made a profit of one thousand francs on each one of them.

The next day Dantès bought a small, fully equipped bark for one of his comrades, on condition that he should set out at once for Marseilles for news of Mercédès and old Dantès and rejoin him at Monte Cristo. He accounted for his sudden wealth by saying that on his arrival at Leghorn he found that a very rich uncle had died, leaving him sole heir to the whole of his fortune. Dantès' superior education made this story plausible, and no one doubted his word.

As the period of his engagement on board the *Jeune Amélie* had now expired, Dantès took leave of the captain, who tried in vain to retain him in his service, and of his comrades, giving each one of them a handsome present. He then set sail for Genoa.

Here he bought a small yacht. It had been built for an Englishman for forty thousand francs; Dantès offered sixty thousand on condition that it should be delivered to him at once. He ordered a secret cupboard containing three secret compartments to be made in the cabin at the head of his bunk. This was finished the next day, and two hours later a crowd of curious sightseers was speculating on the destination of a vessel which put out from Genoa with a crew of one man, who said he preferred to sail alone. His destination, of course, was the Isle of Monte Cristo, where he arrived at the end of the second day. His yacht was an excellent sailer and had done the distance in thirty-eight hours. Instead of landing at the customary landing-place, Dantès cast anchor in the little creek.

The island was deserted; no one seemed to have been on it since he left. He made straight for his treasure, and found everything just as he had left it. The next day he carried his enormous fortune to his yacht and locked it up in the three compartments of his secret cupboard.

He had to wait eight weary days before his comrade returned from Marseilles, which time he spent in sailing his yacht round the island. When his comrade arrived, he had a sad reply to each of the two questions put to him. His father was dead and Mercédès had disappeared.

Edmond heard these tidings with apparent calm, though he expressed a desire to be left alone and sprang on shore. Two hours later he reappeared and set sail for Marseilles. He had quite expected to hear of his father's death, but what had become of Mercédès?

A glance at himself in a mirror at Leghorn had reassured him that he ran no risk of being recognized; besides, he had now at his disposal every means of disguising himself. One fine morning, therefore, he boldly entered the port of Marseilles and stopped opposite the spot where, on that memorable, fatal evening, he had set out for the Château d'If.

It was not without a tremor that he saw a gendarme accompanied by the quarantine officer come on board, but with the perfect self-command he had acquired, Dantès presented an English passport which he had bought at Leghorn, and this permit being more respected in France than any other, he was allowed to land without let or hindrance. That same evening he stepped forth on to the Cannebière alone, unknown, as it were a stranger in a strange land.

## CHAPTER XXI

# THE PONT DU GARD INN

SUCH of my readers as have, like me, made a walking tour through the south of France, may perchance have noticed midway between the town of Beaucaire and the village of Bellegarde a small roadside inn, in front of which hung, creaking and flapping in the wind, an iron shield bearing a grotesque representation of the Pont du Gard.

The little inn had been occupied for the last seven or eight years by no other than Dantès' old acquaintance Gaspard Caderousse. He was standing, as was his wont, at his place of observation before the door, his eyes wandering listlessly from a small patch of grass, where some hens were scratching for food, to the deserted road leading from north to south, when suddenly he descried the dim outline of a man on horseback approaching from Bellegarde at that easy amble which betokens the best of understanding between horse and rider. The rider was a priest robed in black and wearing a three-cornered hat in spite of the scorching sun, which was then at its zenith.

Arrived at the door of the inn, he halted. It would have been difficult to say whether it was the horse that stopped the man or the man that stopped the horse. In any case the man dismounted, and, dragging the animal after him by the bridle, tied it to a dilapidated shutter.

Caderousse advanced, all bows and smiles.

"Are you not Monsieur Caderousse?" asked the priest in a strong Italian accent.

"Yes, monsieur," replied the innkeeper. "That is my name. Gaspard Caderousse, at your service. Can I not offer you some refreshment, Monsieur l'Abbé?"

"Certainly, give me a bottle of your best wine and afterward, with your permission, we will resume our conversation."

When mine host reappeared after a few minutes' absence he found the abbé sitting on a stool with his elbows on the table; he placed a bottle of wine and a glass before him.

"Are we alone?" asked the abbé.

"Oh, yes, all alone or nearly so, for my wife doesn't count as she is always ailing."

"First of all I must convince myself that you are really he whom I seek. In the year eighteen-fourteen or fifteen did you know a sailor named Dantès?"

"Dantès? I should think I did! Poor Edmond! Why, he was one of my best friends," exclaimed Caderousse. "What has become of poor

Edmond, monsieur? Do you know him? Is he still living? Is he free? Is he happy?"

"He died a prisoner, more wretched and more miserable than any prisoner lying in chains in the prison at Toulon."

The deep red of Caderousse's face gave way to a ghastly paleness. He turned aside, and the abbé saw him wipe away a tear with a corner of the handkerchief tied round his head.

"Poor fellow!" Caderousse murmured.

"You seem to have been very fond of this boy?"

"I was indeed," answered Caderousse, "though I have it on my conscience that at one time I envied him his happiness. But I swear to you, Monsieur l'Abbé, I swear it on my honour, that since then I have deeply deplored his lot."

There was a moment's silence during which the abbé's fixed gaze did not cease to examine the agitated features of the innkeeper.

"Did you know the poor lad?" continued Caderousse.

"I was called to his bedside to administer to him the last consolation of his religion. What is so very strange about it all," the abbé continued, "is that on his death-bed, Dantès swore by the crucifix that he was entirely ignorant of the cause of his imprisonment. He besought me, therefore, to clear up the mystery of his misfortune, which he had never been able to explain himself and, if his memory had been sullied, to remove the tarnish from his name."

The abbé's eyes were fixed on Caderousse's countenance and seemed to penetrate to his very soul.

"A rich Englishman," continued the abbé, "his companion in misfortune for a time, but released at the second Restoration, owned a diamond of very great value. On leaving the prison he wished to give his companion a token of his gratitude for the kind and brotherly way he had nursed him through an illness, and gave him the diamond. When on his deathbed, Dantès said to me: 'I had three good friends and a sweetheart, and I am sure they have deeply regretted my misfortune. One of these good friends was named Caderousse.'"

Caderousse could not repress a shudder.

"'Another one,'" the abbé went on without appearing to notice Caderousse's emotion, "'was named Danglars: the third one,' he said, 'also loved me though he was my rival, and his name was Fernand; the name of my betrothed was . . .' I do not remember the name of his betrothed."

"Mercédès," said Caderousse.

"Oh, yes, that was it," replied the abbé with a repressed sigh. Mercédès it was. 'Go to Marseilles,' Dantès said, 'and sell this diamond. The money obtained for it divides into five parts and give an equal share to each of these good friends, the only beings on earth who have loved me.'"

"Why into five parts?" exclaimed Caderousse. "You only named four persons."

"Because I hear that the fifth person is dead. The fifth share was for Dantès' father."

"Alas! it is only too true!" said Caderousse, deeply moved by the contending passions that were aroused in him. "The old man died less than a year after his son disappeared."

"What did he die of?"

"I believe the doctors called his disease gastric enteritis, but those who knew him say that he died of grief, and I, who practically saw him die, say that he died of . . ."

Caderousse hesitated.

"Died of what?" the priest asked anxiously.

"Why, of hunger . . ."

"Of hunger?" the abbé cried, jumping up. "Do you say of hunger? Why, the vilest animals are not allowed to starve. The dogs wandering about the streets find a compassionate hand to throw them a piece of bread, and a man, a Christian, has died of hunger amidst men who also call themselves Christians! Is it possible? No, it cannot be!"

"It is as I have said," replied Caderousse.

"But," continued the priest, "was the unhappy old man so completely forsaken by every one that he died such a death?"

"It was not became Mercédès or Monsieur Morrel had forsaken him," replied Caderousse. "The poor old man took a strong dislike to this same Fernand whom Dantès named as one of his friends," he added with an ironical smile.

"Was he not a friend then?" asked the abbé.

"Can a man be a friend to him whose wife he covets? Dantès was so large-hearted that he called them all his friends. Poor Edmond!"

"Do you know in what way Fernand wronged Dantès?"

"No one better than I."

"Will you not tell me?"

"What good would it do?"

"Then you would prefer me to give these men who, you say, are false and faithless friends, a reward intended for faithful friendship?"

"You are right," said Caderousse. "Besides, what would poor Edmond's legacy be to them now? No more than a drop of water in the mighty ocean!"

"How so, have they become rich and mighty?"

"Then you do not know their history?"

"No, tell it to me."

Caderousse appeared to reflect for an instant. "No," he said. "It would take too long."

"You may please yourself, my friend," said the abbé with an air of complete indifference. "I respect your scruples and admire your sentiment. We will let the matter drop. I will sell the diamond."

So saying he took the diamond out of his pocket and let the light play on it right in front of Caderousse.

"Oh, what a magnificent diamond!" exclaimed the latter in a voice almost hoarse with emotion. "It must be worth at least fifty thousand francs."

"Remember it is your wish that I divide the money amongst all four of you," the abbé said calmly, replacing the diamond in the pocket of his cassock. "Now, be kind enough to give me the address of Edmond's friends, so that I may carry out his last wishes."

The perspiration stood out in big drops on Caderousse's forehead; he saw the abbé rise and go toward the door as if he wished to ascertain that his horse was all right; afterward he returned and asked:

"Well, what have you decided to do?"

"To tell you everything," was the innkeeper's reply.

"I really believe that is the best thing you can do," replied the priest, "not because I am anxious to know what you wish to conceal from me, but simply because it will be much better if you can help me to distribute the legacy as the testator would have desired. Begin; I am all attention."

Caderousse went to the door and closed it, and, by the say of greater precaution, shot the bolt. The priest chose a seat in a corner where he could listen at his ease and where he would have his back to the light while the narrator would have the light full on his face. There he sat, his head bent, his hands joined, or rather clenched, ready to listen with all attention. Caderousse took a stool and sat in front of him and began his story.

## CHAPTER XXII

## CADEROUSSE'S STORY

IT is a very sad story, monsieur," said Caderousse shaking his head. "I dare say you already know the beginning."

"Yes, Edmond told me everything up to the moment of his arrest. He himself knew nothing except what touched him personally, for he never again set eyes on any of the five people I mentioned just now, nor did he ever hear their names mentioned."

"Well, directly after Dantès' arrest in the middle of his betrothal feast, Monsieur Morrel left to obtain further information. The news he brought us was very sad. The old father returned to the house alone, and, with tears streaming from his eyes, folded up his wedding clothes. He spent the whole night pacing up and down his room and did not go to bed at all, for my room was beneath his, and I heard him walking about the whole night long. I must say, I did not sleep either; I was too upset at the old man's grief, and every step he took caused me as much pain as if he had actually trampled on me.

"The next day Mercédès went to Marseilles to implore Monsieur de Villefort's protection, but in vain. She paid the old man a visit at the same time. When she saw him so miserable and grief-stricken, she wanted to take him with her to her cottage to look after him, but the old man refused.

"'No,' said he, 'I will not leave the house. My poor son loves me more than anyone else, and, if he is let out of prison, he will come to see me first of all. What would he say if I were not there to welcome him?'

"I was at the window listening to all this, for I was very anxious that Mercédès should persuade the old man to go with her; the sound of his footsteps overhead gave me not a second's rest."

"Didn't you go to the old man yourself and try to console him?" the priest asked.

"Ah! monsieur! One can only console those who will let themselves be consoled, and he would not," was Caderousse's reply. "He became more and more lonely with each succeeding day. Mercédès and Monsieur Morrel often came to see him, but they always found his door shut, and, though I knew he was at home, he never opened it to them. One day, contrary to custom, he received Mercédès, and when the poor girl, herself desperate and hopeless, tried to comfort him, he said:

"'Believe me, my daughter, he is dead. Instead of our waiting for him, it is he who awaits us. I am very glad that I am the elder, as I shall therefore be the first to see him again.'

"However good and kind-hearted one may be, you can quite understand that one soon ceases to visit those that depress one, and thus came about that poor old Dantès was left entirely alone. Now I only saw strangers go to his room from time to time, and these came out with suspicious-looking bundles: little by little he was selling all he possessed to eke out his miserable existence. At length he had nothing left but his few clothes.

"During the next three days I heard the old man pacing the floor as usual, but on the fourth day, there wasn't a sound to be heard. I ventured to go up to him. The door was locked, but I peeped through the keyhole and saw him so pale and haggard-looking that I felt sure he must be very ill. I sent word to Monsieur Morrel and myself ran for Mercédès. Neither of them wasted any time in coming. Monsieur Morrel brought with him a doctor, who diagnosed gastric enteritis and put his patient on diet.

"Mercédès came again and saw such a change in the old man that, as before, she wanted to have him moved to her own cottage. Monsieur Morrel was also of the opinion that this would be best, and wanted to move him by force, but he protested so violently that they were afraid to do so. Mercédès remained at the bedside. Monsieur Morrel went away, making a sign to Mercédès that he had left a purse on the mantelshelf. Nevertheless, taking advantage of the doctor's instructions, the old man would eat nothing. Finally after nine days' despair and fasting, the old man died, cursing those who had caused all this misery. His last words to Mercédès were: 'If you see my Edmond again, tell him I died blessing him.'"

The abbé rose, and twice paced round the room, pressing his trembling hand to his parched throat.

"And you believe that he died of . . ."

"Of hunger, monsieur, pure starvation," said Caderousse. "I am as certain of it as that we two are Christians."

"A sad, sad tragedy!" said the priest, and his voice was hoarse with emotion.

"All the more sad," said Caderousse, "because it was none of God's doing but the work of those men."

"Let me know about those men," said the abbé, "and remember you have bound yourself to tell me everything. Who are the men who caused the son to die of despair and the father of hunger?"

"Two men who were jealous of him, the one through love and the other through ambition. Their names are Fernand and Danglars."

"In what way did they show this jealousy?"

"They denounced Edmond as a Bonapartist agent."

"Which of the two denounced him? Who was the real culprit?"

"Both were guilty. The letter was written on the day before the betrothal feast. It was Danglars who wrote it with his left hand, it was Fernand who posted it."

"And yet you did not protest against such infamy?" said the abbé. "Then you are their accomplice."

"They both made me drink so excessively, monsieur, that I was no longer responsible for my actions. I only saw through a mist. I said all that a man is capable of saying when in such a state, but they both told me that they were only playing a harmless joke which would carry no consequences with it."

"But the next day you saw what consequences it had, yet you said nothing, though you were present when he was arrested."

"Yes, monsieur, I was there and I tried to speak. I wanted to say all I knew, but Danglars prevented me. I will own that I stood in fear of the political state of things at that time, and I let myself be overruled. I kept silence. It was cowardly, I know, but it was not criminal."

"I understand. You just let things take their course."

"Yes, monsieur," was Caderousse's rejoinder, "and I regret it night and day. I often ask pardon of God for it, I assure you, especially as this action, the only one I have to reproach myself with during the whole of my lifetime, is no doubt the cause of my adversity. I am paying the penalty for one moment's selfishness."

With these words Caderousse bowed his head with all the signs of a true penitent. There followed a short silence; the abbé got up and paced the room in deep thought. At length he returned to his place and sat down, saying: "You have mentioned a Monsieur Morrel two or three times. Who was he?"

"He was the owner of the *Pharaon.*"

"What part did he play in this sad affair?"

"The part of an honest, courageous, and affectionate man, monsieur. Twenty times did he intercede for Dantès. When the Emperor returned, he wrote, entreated, and threatened, with the result that during the Second Restoration, he was persecuted as a Bonapartist. As I told you before, he came again and again to Dantès' father to persuade him to live with him in his house, and, as I also mentioned, the day before the old man's death, he left on the mantelshelf a purse which contained sufficient money to pay off his debts and to defray the expenses of the funeral. Thus the poor old man was enabled to die as he had lived, without doing wrong to anyone. I have still got the purse; it is a red silk one."

"If Monsieur Morrel is still alive, he must be enjoying God's blessing: he must be rich and happy."

Caderousse smiled bitterly. "Yes, as happy as I am," was the answer. "He stands on the brink of poverty, and, what is more, of dishonour. After twenty-five years' work, after having gained the most honoured place in the business world of Marseilles, Monsieur Morrel is utterly ruined. He has lost five ships during the last two years, has had to bear the brunt of the bankruptcy of three large firms, and his only hope is now in the *Pharaon,* the very ship that poor Dantès commanded, which is expected from the Indies with a cargo of cochineal and indigo. If this ship goes down like the others, all is lost."

"Has the unfortunate man a wife and children?"

"Yes, he has a wife who is behaving like a saint through all this trouble; he has a daughter who was to have married the man she loves, but his family will not allow him to marry the daughter of a bankrupt; and he has a son, a lieutenant in the army. But you may well understand that this only increases the wretched man's grief instead of alleviating it. If he were alone, he would blow out his brains and there would be an end to it."

"It is terrible," murmured the priest.

"It is thus that God rewards virtue, monsieur. Just look at me. I have never done a wrong action apart from the one I related to you a moment ago, yet I live in poverty, while Fernand and Danglars are rolling in wealth. Everything they have touched has turned into gold, whereas everything I have done has gone all wrong."

"Danglars was the more guilty of the two, the instigator, was he not? What has become of him?"

"He left Marseilles and, upon the recommendation of Monsieur Morrel, who was unaware of his crime, he became cashier in a Spanish bank. During the war with Spain, he was employed in the commissariat of the French army and made a fortune. Then he speculated with his money and quadrupled his capital. He married his banker's daughter and was left a widower after a short time; then he married a widow, the daughter of the chamberlain who is in great favour at Court. He became a millionaire and was made a Baron. Thus he is now Baron Danglars, owns a large house in the Rue du Mont Blanc, has ten horses in his stable, six footmen in his antechamber, and I don't know how many millions in his coffers."

"But how could Fernand, a poor fisherman, make a fortune? He had neither resources nor education. I must own this surpasses my comprehension."

"It is beyond the comprehension of every one. There must be some strange secret in his life of which we are all ignorant. It is all very mysterious. A few days before the Restoration, Fernand was called up for conscription. The Bourbons left him in peace at the Catalans, but when Napoleon returned, an extraordinary muster was decreed and Fernand was compelled to join up. I also joined up, but as I was older and had just married, I was only sent to the coast. Fernand was enrolled in a fighting unit, reached the frontier, and took part in the battle of Ligny.

"The night following the battle, he was on sentry duty outside the door of a general who was in secret communication with the enemy and who intended going over to the English that very night. He suggested that Fernand should accompany him. To this Fernand agreed, and, deserting his post, followed the general.

"This would have meant a court-martial for Fernand if Napoleon had remained on the throne, but to the Bourbons it only served him as a recommendation. He returned to France with the epaulette of a sub-lieutenant and, as he still enjoyed the protection of the general, who stood in high favour, he was promoted captain during the

Spanish war in eighteen-twenty-three; that is to say, at the time when Danglars was first launching forth in speculation. Fernand was a Spaniard, so he was sent to Madrid to inquire into the feeling existing among his compatriots. While there he met Danglars, who became very friendly with him, promised his general support amongst the Royalists of the capital and the provinces, obtained promises for himself, and on his side made pledges. He led his regiment along paths known only to himself in gorges guarded by Royalists, and in short rendered such services during that short campaign that after the fall of Trocadero, he was promoted colonel and received the cross of an Officer of the Legion of Honour."

"Fate! Fate!" murmured the abbé.

"Yes, but that is not all. When the Spanish war was ended, Fernand's career was checked by the long period of peace which seemed likely to prevail throughout Europe. Greece alone had risen against Turkey and had just commenced her war of independence. All eyes were turned towards Athens, and it became the fashion to pity and support the Greeks. Fernand sought and obtained permission to serve in Greece, but his name was still retained on the army list.

"Some time later it was stated that the Count of Morcerf, which was the name he now bore, had entered the service of Ali Pasha with the rank of Instructor-General. Ali Pasha was killed, as you know, but before he died, he recompensed Fernand for his services by leaving him a considerable sum of money. Fernand returned to France, where his rank of lieutenant-general was confirmed, and to-day he owns a magnificent house at Paris in the Rue du Helder, number twenty-seven."

The abbé opened his mouth as though to speak, hesitated for a moment, then, with a great effort, said: "What about Mercédès? They tell me she has disappeared."

"Disappeared?" said Caderousse. "Yes, as the sun disappears only to rise with more splendour the next day."

"Has she also made her fortune then?" asked the abbé with an ironical smile.

"Mercédès is at present one of the grandest ladies in Paris. At first she was utterly overcome by the blow which had robbed her of her Edmond. I have already told you how she importuned Villefort with entreaties, and have also touched upon her devoted care for Dantès' father. In the midst of her despair she was assailed by another trouble, the departure of Fernand, of whose crime she was unaware and whom she regarded as a brother.

"Mercédès was alone and uncared for. She spent three months weeping and sorrowing. No news of Edmond and none of Fernand, with nothing to distract her but an old man dying of despair.

"One evening after she had been sitting all day at the crossroads leading to Marseilles and the Catalans, as was her wont, she returned home more depressed than ever. Neither her lover nor her friend had returned along either of these two roads, neither had she any news of them.

"Suddenly she seemed to recognize a step behind her and turned round anxiously. The door opened, and Fernand entered in the uniform of a sub-lieutenant. It was only the half of what she was grieving for, but it was a portion of her past life restored to her. She seized Fernand's hands in an ecstasy of joy. This he took for love, whereas it was nothing more than joy at being no longer alone in the world, and at seeing a friend again after so many long hours of solitary sadness. Then you must remember she had never hated Fernand, she simply did not love him. Another one owned Mercédès' heart, and he was absent . . . he had disappeared . . . perhaps he was dead. At this last thought, Mercédès always burst into tears and wrung her hands in anguish; but, whereas she had always rejected the idea when suggested by some one else, the same thought now began to prey on her mind, and old Dantès incessantly said to her: 'Our Edmond is dead, for, if he were not, he would have come back to us.'

"The old man died. Had he lived, in all probability Mercédès would never have become the wife of another; he would have been there to reproach her with her infidelity. Fernand realized that fact. As soon as he heard that the old man was dead, he returned. This time he was a lieutenant. The first time he returned he had not spoken of love; the second time he reminded her that he loved her. Mercédès asked for six months in which to await and bewail Edmond."

"Well, that made eighteen months in all," said the abbé with a bitter smile. "What more could the most adored lover ask?" Then he murmured the words of the English poet: "'Frailty, thy name is woman!'"

"Six months later," continued Caderousse, "the wedding took place in the Church des Accoules."

"The very church in which she was to have married Edmond," murmured the abbé. "The bridegroom was changed, that was all."

"So Mercédès was married," continued Caderousse, "but although to all appearances she was calm, she was nevertheless well nigh fainting when she passed La Réserve where, eighteen months previously, she had celebrated her betrothal with him whom she still loved, which she would have realized herself had she dared to probe to the depths of her heart."

"Did you see Mercédès again?" asked the priest.

"Yes, during the Spanish war at Perpignan where Fernand had left her; she was attending to the education of her son."

The abbé started. "Her son, did you say?"

"Yes," was Caderousse's reply, "little Albert's education."

"But I am sure Edmond told me she was the daughter of a simple fisherman and that, though she was beautiful, she was uneducated. Had she taken a course of instruction that she was able to teach her son?" "Oh!" exclaimed Caderousse. "Did he know his sweetheart so little? If crowns were bestowed upon beauty and intelligence, Mercédès would now be a queen. Her fortune was growing, and she grew with it. She learnt drawing, music, everything. Personally I think she did all this simply to distract her mind, to help her to forget; she crammed so much knowledge into her head to alleviate the weight in her heart. I must tell you everything as it is," continued Caderousse. "Her fortune and honours have no doubt afforded her some consolation; she is rich, she is a Countess, and yet . . ." Caderousse hesitated.

"Yet what?" asked the abbé.

"Yet I am sure she is not happy."

"Do you know what has happened to Monsieur de Villefort and what part he played in Edmond's misfortune?"

"No, I only know that some time after he had him arrested he married Mademoiselle de Saint-Méran and shortly afterwards left Marseilles. No doubt Dame Fortune has smiled upon him, too; no doubt like Danglars he is rich, and like Fernand covered with honours, while I alone, you understand, have remained poor, miserable, and forsaken by all."

"You are mistaken, my friend," said the abbé. "There are times when God's justice tarries for a while and it appears to us that we are forgotten by Him, but the time always comes when we find it is not so, and here is the proof."

With these words the abbé took the diamond from his pocket and handed it to Caderousse.

"Here, my friend," he said. "Take this, it is yours."

"What! For me alone!" exclaimed Caderousse. "Ah, monsieur, do not jest with me!"

"The diamond was to be divided amongst Edmond's friends. He had but one friend, therefore it cannot be divided. Take the diamond and sell it; it is worthy fifty thousand francs, a sum which will, I trust, suffice to relieve you of your poverty."

"Oh, monsieur, do not play with the happiness or despair of a man!" said Caderousse, putting out one hand timidly, while with the other he wiped away the perspiration that gathered in big drops on his forehead.

"I know what happiness means as I also know what despair means, and I should never play with either of these feelings. Take the diamond, but in exchange . . ."

Caderousse already had his hand on the diamond, but at these last words he hastily withdrew it.

The abbé smiled.

"In exchange," continued he, "give me the red silk purse Monsieur Morrel left on the mantelshelf in old Dantès' room."

More and more astonished, Caderousse went to a large oak cupboard, opened it, and, taking out a long purse of faded red silk on two copper rings, once gilt, he handed it to the priest.

The abbé took it and gave the diamond in exchange.

"You are verily a man of God, monsieur!" exclaimed Caderousse. "No one knew Dantès gave you the diamond, and you could easily have kept it."

The abbé rose and took his hat and gloves, unbarred the door, mounted his horse, and, saying good-bye to Caderousse, who was most effusive in his farewells, started off by the road he had come.

## CHAPTER XXIII

## THE PRISON REGISTER

THE day following the events just recorded, a man of about thirty or thirty-two years of age, clad in a bright blue coat, nankeen trousers, and a white waistcoat, and having both the appearance and the accent of an Englishman, presented himself before the Mayor of Marseilles.

"Monsieur," said he, "I am head clerk of the firm of Thomson and French, of Rome. We have had business connexions with Morrel and Son, of Marseilles, for the last ten years involving a hundred thousand francs or so of our money. As reports are current that the firm is faced with ruin, we are beginning to feel somewhat anxious, so I have come from Rome for the sole purpose of obtaining some information from you in regard to the firm."

"I know well enough, monsieur, that misfortune seems to have dogged Monsieur Morrel for the past four or five years," replied the Mayor. "He has lost five ships one after the other, and has suffered badly through the bankruptcy of three or four firms, but though I am his creditor to the extent of some ten thousand francs, it is not my place to give you any information on the state of his finances. If you ask me in my capacity as Mayor what I think of Monsieur Morrel, I can but answer that he is as honest as it is possible for man to be, and that up to the present he has fulfilled his engagements with absolute punctuality. That is all I can tell you, monsieur. If you wish to know more, apply to Monsieur de Boville, Inspector of Prisons, Rue de Noailles, number fifteen. I believe he has two hundred thousand francs invested with the firm, and if there are really any grounds for apprehension you will doubtless find him better informed on the subject than I am."

The Englishman appeared to appreciate this great delicacy on the part of the Mayor, bade him good morning, and, with that gait peculiar to the sons of Great Britain, set off for the street mentioned.

M. de Boville was in his office. With the coolness of his race, the Englishman put almost the same question to him as he had put to the Mayor.

"Unfortunately your fears are only too well founded, monsieur," exclaimed M. de Boville, "and you see before you a ruined man. I have two hundred thousand francs in that firm and they were to constitute the dowry of my daughter, who is to be married in a fortnight. One hundred thousand francs of this sum was redeemable on the fifteenth of this month, and another hundred thousand francs on the fifteenth of next month. I notified Monsieur Morrel of the fact that I desired to have the payment punctually made, and here he comes hardly an hour back and tells me that if his ship, the *Pharaon,* does not return by the fifteenth, he will find it impossible to effect the payment. It looks very much like bankruptcy."

"Then, monsieur, you fear for your money?"

"I consider it as good as lost."

"Well, then, I will buy it from you."

"You will? But at an enormous discount, I presume."

"No, for two hundred thousand francs. Our firm does not conduct business in that way," he added with a smile. "What is more, I will pay you cash down."

The Englishman took from his pocket a bundle of banknotes amounting to about double for the sum M. de Boville was fearful of losing. An expression of joy lit up M. de Boville's face, but he restrained his feelings and said: "I must warn you, monsieur, that in all probability, you will not get six per cent. of that sum."

"That has nothing to do with me," was the reply. "It is the affair of Thomson and French for whom I am acting. It may be that it is to their interest to hasten the ruin of a rival firm. What I do know, monsieur, is that I am ready to hand over this sum in exchange for a deed of assignment; all I require of you is a commission."

"That is but just, monsieur!" exclaimed M. de Boville. "The commission is generally one and a half. Do you want two . . . three . . . five . . . per cent., or even more? You have only to say the word."

"I am like my firm, monsieur," replied the Englishman with a smile. "I do not conduct business on those lines. My commission is something entirely different. You are the Inspector of Prisons, are you not?"

"I have been for the last fourteen years and more."

"Do you keep a register of entrances and dismissals?"

"Of course."

"Are there any notes in the register pertaining to the different prisoners?"

"Each prisoner has his *dossier.*"

"Well, monsieur, I was educated at Rome by a poor old abbé who suddenly disappeared. Later I learned that he had been detained in the Château d'If, and I should like to have some details in regard to his death."

"What was his name?"

"The Abbé Faria."

"Oh, yes, I remember him perfectly. He died last February."

"You have a good memory, monsieur."

"I remember this case because the poor fellow's death was accompanied by a very peculiar circumstance. The abbé's dungeon was about forty-five or fifty feet from that of a Bonapartist agent, one of those who had greatly contributed to the return of the usurper in eighteen-fifteen. He was a very determined and dangerous man."

"Really?" said the Englishman.

"Yes," was the reply. "I had an opportunity of seeing this man myself in eighteen-sixteen or seventeen. We could only go down to his dungeon accompanied by a file of soldiers. He made a deep impression on me, and I shall never forget his face."

The Englishman gave the ghost of a smile.

"Edmond Dantès was the man's name," continued the inspector, "and he must have either procured some tools or else made some, for a passage was found by means of which the two prisoners communicated with one another."

"The passage was doubtless made with a view to escape?"

"Exactly, but unfortunately for the prisoners, the abbé was seized with an attack of epilepsy and died."

"I understand; that must have put an end to their plans."

"As far as the dead man was concerned, it certainly did, but not for the one who lived. On the contrary, Dantès saw a means of effecting his escape more easily. He doubtless thought that the prisoners who die in the Château d'If are buried in an ordinary cemetery, so he carried the corpse into his own cell and took its place in the sack in which it had been sewn up, and waited for the burial. The Chateau d'If has no cemetery, however. The dead are simply thrown into the sea with a cannon ball attached to their feet."

"Is that really so?" exclaimed the Englishman.

"Yes, monsieur," continued the inspector. "You may imagine the fugitive's astonishment when he felt himself being hurled down the rocks. I should like to have seen his face at that moment."

"That would have been somewhat difficult."

"Never mind," said M. de Boville, whom the certainty of getting his two hundred thousand francs had put into a good humour. "Never mind, I can imagine it." And he burst out laughing.

"I can also imagine it," said the Englishman, with a forced laugh. "So I suppose the fugitive was drowned. But if he was, no doubt some official report must have been made on the occurrence."

"Oh, yes, a death certificate was made out. You see, his relatives, if he had any, might be interested to know whether he was dead or alive. Would you like to see what documents we have relating to the poor abbé?"

"It would give me great pleasure," replied his companion.

"Let us go to my office then."

And they both passed into the office of M. de Boville. Everything was in perfect order; each register had its number, each *dossier* had its file. The inspector gave the Englishman his easy-chair, set before him the register and the *dossier* relating to the Château d'If, and let him look through them at his leisure, while he himself sat in a corner of the room and read his paper.

The Englishman had no difficulty in find the *dossier* relating to the Abbé Faria. It appeared as though the story which the inspector had related greatly interested him, for, after having perused the first documents, he turned over the leaves until he reached the deposition respecting Edmond Dantès. There he found everything arranged in due order—the denunciation, the examination, Morrel's petition, Monsieur de Villefort's marginal notes. He folded up the denunciation noiselessly and put it into his pocket, read the examination, and noted that the name of Noirtier was not mentioned in it; perused, too, the application dated the 10th of April, 1815, in which Morrel, on the Deputy's advice, exaggerated with the best intentions (for Napoleon was then on the throne) the services Dantès had rendered to the imperial cause—services which Villefort's certificate rendered incontestable. Then he saw through it all. The petition to Napoleon, kept back by Villefort, had become under the Second Restoration, a terrible weapon against him in the hands of the Procureur du Roi. On searching further he was no longer astonished to find in the register the following remarks placed in brackets against his name:

EDMOND DANTÈS  {  An inveterate Bonapartist; took an active part in the return from the Isle of Elba. To be kept in solitary confinement and under strict supervision.

He compared the writing of the bracketed remarks with that of the certificate placed beneath Morrel's petition and felt convinced that they were both in the same handwriting: they were both written by Villefort.

"Thanks!" said the Englishman, closing the register with much noise. "I have all I want; now it is my turn to perform my promise. Give me a simple assignment of your credit; acknowledge therein receipt of the cash, and I will hand you over the money."

He rose, gave his seat at the desk to M. de Boville, who took it without ceremony, and drew up the required assignment, while the Englishman counted out the banknotes on the ledge of the filing-cabinet.

## CHAPTER XXIV

## MORREL AND SON

ANYONE who had left Marseilles a few years back knowing the interior workings of the firm of Morrel and Son and returned at this period would have noted a great change. Instead of the animation, comfort, and happiness that seem to radiate from a prosperous house, instead of the merry faces seen from behind the window curtains, of the busy clerks hurrying to and fro with their pens behind their ears, instead of the yard filled with bales of goods and echoing with the shouts and laughter of the porters, he would at once have perceived a certain sadness and a gloomy listlessness. The corridor was deserted and the yard empty; of the numerous employees who formerly filled the office two only remained: the one a young man of twenty-three or twenty-four, named Emmanuel who was in love with Morrel's daughter and had stayed with the firm in spite of his relatives' efforts to get him to resign; the other an old one-eyed cashier, called Coclès, a nickname which had been given him by the young people who used to throng this buzzing hive, now almost uninhabited, and which had so completely taken the place of his real name that in all probability he would now not have answered to the latter.

Coclès had remained in M. Morrel's service, and a singular change had been effected in his position. He had been raised to the rank of cashier, and at the same time lowered to that of servant. Nevertheless, it was the same good, patient Coclès, inflexible where arithmetic was concerned, the only point on which he would stand his ground against the whole world; if need be, even against M. Morrel himself. Nothing had yet occurred to shake Coclès' belief in the firm; last month's payments had been effected with rigorous punctuality. Coclès had detected an error of seventy centimes made by M. Morrel to his own disadvantage, and the same day he had brought the money to his chief who took it and, with a sad smile, dropped it into the almost empty drawer, saying: "Thanks, Coclès, you are a pearl among cashiers."

No man could have been happier than Coclès was at hearing his master speak thus, for praise from M. Morrel, the pearl of all honest men of Marseilles, counted more with Coclès than a gift of fifty crowns.

M. Morrel had spent many a cruel hour since the end of the month. To enable him to meet his liabilities he had been obliged to gather in all his resources, and, fearing lest a rumour of his difficulties should be spread about the town of Marseilles when it was known that he had had recourse to such extremities, he had himself gone to the Fair at Beaucaire to sell some of his wife's and daughter's jewellery and some of his silverware. By means of this sacrifice the honour of the firm had been preserved, but funds were now exhausted. Following the reports that had been noised abroad, credit was no longer to be had, and M. Morrel's only hope of meeting the payment of a hundred thousand francs, due to M. Boville on the 15th of that month and the hundred thousand due on the 15th of the following month, lay in the return of the *Pharaon*. He had news of her departure from another ship that had weighed anchor at the same time and had arrived safely in port. This was more than a fortnight ago, and yet there was still no further news of the *Pharaon*.

Such was the state of affairs when the representative of Thomson and French of Rome called on M. Morrel. Emmanuel received him. Every fresh face was a new cause of alarm to the young man, for it suggested yet one more anxious creditor come to question the head of the firm, and he was ever desirous of sparing his employer an embarrassing interview. He now questioned the newcomer, but the stranger would have nothing to do with M. Emmanuel and wished to see M. Morrel in person. Emannuel rose with a sigh, and, summoning Coclès, bade him conduct the stranger to M. Morrel.

Coclès walked in front and the stranger followed. On the staircase they met a pretty girl of sixteen or seventeen who looked at the stranger with an uneasy expression.

"Is Monsieur Morrel in his office, Mademoiselle Julie?" asked the cashier.

"Yes, at least I think so," answered the girl hesitatingly. "Go first and see whether my father is there, Coclès, and announce the gentleman."

"It would be useless to announce me, mademoiselle," replied the Englishman; "Monsieur Morrel does not know my name. All that this good man can say is that I am the head clerk of Messrs Thomson and French of Rome, with whom your father has business connexions."

The girl turned pale, and passed downstairs, while Coclès and the Englishman went up.

On seeing the stranger enter his office, M. Morrel closed the ledger he had before him, rose and offered him a chair. Fourteen years had worked a great change in the worthy merchant, who, but thirty-six at the beginning of this story, was now nearing fifty. His hair had turned white, anxiety and worry had ploughed deep furrows on his brows, and the look in his eyes, once so firm and staunch, had now become vague and irresolute.

The Englishman looked at him with a feeling of curiosity mingled with interest.

"You wished to speak with me, monsieur?" said Morrel, becoming embarrassed under the stranger's steady gaze.

"Yes, monsieur. Messrs Thomson and French of Rome have to pay three or four hundred thousand francs in France during the course of the present month and the next, and, knowing your strict promptitude in regard to payments, they have collected all the bills bearing your signature and have charged me to collect the money from you as it falls due, and to make appropriate use of the money."

M. Morrel heaved a deep sigh, and passed his hand over his sweat-bedewed forehead.

"You hold bills signed by me, monsieur?" asked Morrel.

"Yes, monsieur, for a considerable sum. But first of all," he continued, taking a bundle of papers from his pocket, "I have here an assignment for two hundred thousand francs, made over to our firm by Monsieur de Boville, the Inspector of Prisons. Do you acknowledge this debt?"

"Yes, monsieur. He invested the money with me at four and a half per cent. nearly five years ago, half of it being redeemable on the fifteenth of the present month, and the other half on the fifteenth of the coming month."

"Just so; then I have here thirty-two thousand five hundred francs payable at the end of the month; these are bills signed by you and assigned to our firm by the holders."

"I recognize them," said Morrel, whose face became red with shame at the thought that for the first time in his life he would in all probability not be able to honour his signature. "Is that all?" "No, monsieur. I have these bills for the end of the month assigned to us by Pascal and Wild and Turner of Marseilles—about fifty-five thousand francs in all, making a total of two hundred and eighty-seven thousand five hundred francs."

What M. Morrel suffered during this enumeration is impossible to describe.

"Two hundred and eighty-seven thousand five hundred francs," he repeated automatically.

"Yes, monsieur," replied the Englishman. "But," he continued after a moment's silence, "I will not conceal from you, Monsieur Morrel, that though I am fully aware of your blameless probity up to the present, public report is rife in Marseilles that you are not in a position to meet your obligations."

At this almost brutal frankness Morrel turned pale.

"Up to the present, monsieur," said he, "and it is more than twenty-four years since I took over the directorship of the firm from my father, who had himself managed it for thirty-five years—until now not one bill signed by Morrel and Son has ever been presented for payment that has not been duly honoured."

"I am fully aware of that," replied the Englishman, "but as one man of honour to another, tell me quite frankly, shall you pay these with the same exactitude?"

Morrel started and looked at this man who spoke to him with more assurance than he had hitherto shown.

"To questions put with such frankness," said he, "a straightforward answer must be given. Yes, monsieur, I shall pay if, as I hope, my ship arrives safely, for its arrival will restore to me the credit which one stroke of ill-fortune after another has deprived me of. But should, by some ill-chance, this, my last resource, the *Pharaon*, fail me, I fear, monsieur, I shall be compelled to suspend payment."

"The *Pharaon* is your last hope, then?"

"Absolutely the last. And," he continued, "her delay is not natural. She left Calcutta on February the fifth and should have been here more than a month ago."

"What is that?" exclaimed the Englishman, listening intently. "What is the meaning of this noise?"

"Oh, heavens!" cried Morrel, turning a ghastly colour. "What fresh disaster is this?"

In truth, there was much noise on the staircase. People were running hither and thither, and now and then a cry of distress was heard.

Morrel rose to open the door, but his strength failed him and he sank into his chair. The two men sat facing each other: Morrel was trembling in every limb, while the stranger was looking at him with an expression of profound pity. The noise ceased, but, nevertheless, it was apparent that Morrel was simply awaiting events; the hubbub was not without reason and would naturally have its sequel.

The stranger thought he heard several people come up the stairs quietly and stop on the landing. A key was inserted in the lock of the first door, which creaked on its hinges. Julie entered, her cheeks bathed with tears. Supporting himself on the arm of his chair, Morrel rose unsteadily. He wanted to speak, but his voice failed him.

"Oh, Father! Father!" exclaimed the girl clasping her hands. "Forgive your daughter for being the bearer of bad news. Father, be brave!"

Morrel turned deadly pale. "So the *Pharaon* is lost?" he asked in a choked voice.

The girl made no answer, but she nodded her head and fell into his arms.

"And the crew?"

"Saved!" said the young girl. "Saved by the Bordeaux vessel that has just entered the port."

"Thank God!" said he. "At least Thou strikest me alone!"

Scarcely had he uttered these words when Mme Morrel came in sobbing, followed by Emmanuel. Standing in the background were to be seen the stalwart forms of seven or eight half-naked sailors. The Englishman started at sight of these men; he took a step toward them, but then restrained himself and withdrew to the farthest and darkest corner of the room.

Mme Morrel seated herself in a chair and took her husband's hand in hers, whilst Julie still lay with her head on her father's shoulder. Emmanuel remained in the middle of the room like a link between the Morrel family and the sailors at the door.

"How did it happen?" asked Morrel.

"Draw nearer, Penelon," said the young man, "and relate all that happened."

An old sailor, bronzed by tropical suns, advanced, twirling the remains of a hat in his hand.

"Good day, my friend," said the shipowner, unable to refrain from smiling through his tears. "What has become of your captain?"

"The captain, monsieur, has stayed behind sick at Palma, but there is nothing serious the matter, and, God willing, you will see him here in a few days as well as you or I."

"I am glad of that. Now, Penelon, say what you have to say."

Penelon rolled his quid of tobacco from his left to his right cheek, put his hand before his mouth, turned round and shot a long jet of dark saliva into the antechamber; then he drew nearer and, with arms akimbo, said:

"Well, then, Monsieur Morrel, we were somewhere between Cape Blanc and Cape Boyador, sailing along with a good south-south-westerly breeze, after dawdling along under eight days' calm, when Captain Gaumard comes up to me—I must explain that I was at the helm—and says: 'Daddy Penelon, what do you make of those clouds rising on the horizon?'

"I was just looking at them myself. 'What do I make of them, captain? I think they are rising faster than they have any business to do, and they are too black for clouds that mean no mischief.'

"'I think so too,' says the captain, 'and I am going to be prepared. We have too much canvas for the gale we shall have in a very short time.'

"'A gale,' says I. 'He who bets that what we are going to have is a gale will get more than he bargained for. We are in for a downright good hurricane, or I know nothing about it.'

"You could see the wind coming just as you can see the dust at Montredon; luckily, it had some one to deal with it who had met it before.

"'All hands take in two reefs in the topsails,' bawls the captain. 'Let go the bowlines, brace to, lower the top-gallant sails, haul out the reef-tackles on the yards!'

"Well, after being tossed about for twelve hours, we sprung a leak. 'Penelon,' says the captain to me, 'I believe we are sinking. Give me the helm and go down to the hold.'

"I gave him the helm and went down. We had already shipped three feet of water. I came up again, crying out: 'To the pumps! To the pumps!' But it was too late. We all set to work, but the faster we pumped, the more water she seemed to take.

"'Well, since we are sinking,' says I, 'let us sink. One can die but once!'

"'Is that the example you set, Master Penelon?' says the captain. 'Just wait a bit!'

"He went to his cabin and fetched a brace of pistols.

"'I will blow the brains out of the first man who leaves the pumps!' he bellows out.

"There is nothing like common sense to put courage into a man," continued the sailor, "especially as by that time the wind had abated and the sea gone down. Still the water continued to rise, not much it is true, about two inches an hour. Nevertheless it rose. Two inches an hour does not seem much, but in twelve hours that is no less than twenty-four inches, and twenty-four inches are two feet. Two feet added to the three we had before made five. When a ship has got five feet of water inside her, she is as much good as a man with the dropsy. "'Come along now,' says the captain. 'We have had enough of this. We have done what we could to save the ship, now we must try to save ourselves. To the boats, boys, as quick as you can!'

"You see, Monsieur Morrel," continued Penelon, "we loved the *Pharaon* well enough, but, much as a sailor may love his ship, he loves his life more. We required no second telling, especially as the boat seemed to moan and call out to us: 'Get along, save your lives!' And the poor *Pharaon* told no lie, we literally felt her sink under our feet. We had the boat out in a trice, with eight of us in it.

"The captain was the last to leave the ship, or rather he would not leave her, so I takes hold of him and throws him down to my comrades, and then I jumps down after him. We were only just in time, for I had no sooner jumped into the boat than the deck burst with a noise like the broadside of a man-of-war. Ten minutes later she pitched forward, then she pitched the other way, and finally began to spin round like a dog after its tail. Then it was good-bye to the *Pharaon!*

"As for us, we were three days without food or drink. We had already spoken about drawing lots as to which of us should serve as food for the others, when we sighted the *Gironde*. We made signals to her, she sighted us, made towards us, put out her boat, and took us on board. There now, Monsieur Morrel, that is exactly how it all happened, on my word of honour as a sailor. Speak up, you others, and say whether it is the truth."

A general murmur of assent indicated that the narrator had their votes as to the verity of the subject and the picturesqueness of the details.

"Well done, my friends," said M. Morrel; "you are good fellows. I felt sure I had nothing to blame for what has happened but my own bad luck. It is God's will and not man's doing! Let us submit to the will of God. Now, what pay is due to you?"

"Oh, don't let us speak of that, Monsieur Morrel."

"On the contrary, we must," said the shipowner with a sad smile.

"Well, then, there is three months' pay due to us."

"Coclès, pay each of these good men two hundred francs. At another time," continued M. Morrel, "I should have added: 'Give each one an extra two hundred!' But times are hard, my friends, and the little bit of money I have left does not belong to me. Excuse me, therefore, and don't think any the worse of me for that."

Penelon was visibly and deeply moved, and, turning toward his comrades, he exchanged a few words with them.

"As far as that goes, Monsieur Morrel," said he, rolling his quid to the other side of his mouth and shooting a second jet of saliva into the antechamber, "as far as that goes, my shipmates and I say that for the time being fifty francs is quite enough for us, and that we will wait for the rest."

"Thank you, my friends, thank you," M. Morrel exclaimed, deeply touched. "You are dear, good fellows. Take the money though, and if you find another employer, enter his service. You are free to do so. I have no more ships and therefore have no further use for sailors."

"You have no more ships?" said Penelon. "Well, then, you will build some, and we will wait. A spell of short commons won't hurt us, thank Heaven!"

"I have no money to build other ships, Penelon," said the shipowner with a sad smile, "so I cannot accept your offer, much as I appreciate it."

"If you have no money, you surely shall not pay us; like the *Pharaon,* we can go under bare poles."

"Enough, enough, my friends!" said Morrel, choking with emotion. "Leave me, I beg you. We will see each other again at a happier time. Emmanuel," he continued, "accompany them and see to it that my wishes are carried out."

He made a sign to Coclès, who went on in front, followed by the sailors and finally by Emmanuel.

"Now," said the shipowner to his wife and daughter, "leave me awhile. I wish to speak with this gentleman."

The two ladies looked at the stranger, whom they had entirely forgotten, and withdrew. When going out, however, the girl cast an entreating look on the Englishman, to which he responded with a smile, such as one would hardly expect to see on those stern features. The two men were left alone.

"Well, monsieur," said Morrel, sinking into his chair. "You have seen and heard all. I have nothing further to tell you."

"Yes, monsieur, I have learnt that you are the victim of fresh misfortune, as unmerited as the rest. This has only confirmed my desire to render you a service. I am one of your principal creditors, am I not?"

"In any case, you are in possession of the bills that will fall due first."

"Would you like the date of payment prolonged?"

"It would certainly save my honour and consequently my life."

"How long do you ask?"

Morrel hesitated a moment and then he said: "Three months. But do you think Messrs Thomson and French . . ."

"Do not worry about that. I will take all responsibility upon myself. To-day is the fifth of June. Renew these bills up to the fifth of

September, and at eleven o'clock" (at that moment the clock struck eleven) "on the fifth of September, I shall present myself."

"I shall await you, monsieur," said Morrel, "and you will be paid, or else I shall be dead."

These last words were said in such a low voice that the stranger did not hear them.

The bills were renewed and the old ones destroyed so that the unfortunate shipowner was given another three months in which to gather together his last resources.

The Englishman received his thanks with the coldness peculiar to his race and bade farewell to Morrel, who, calling down blessings on him, accompanied him to the door.

On the stairs he met Julie. She pretended to be going down, but in reality she was waiting for him.

"Oh, monsieur!" she exclaimed clasping her hands.

"Mademoiselle," said the stranger, "one day you will receive a letter signed Sinbad the Sailor. Do exactly what the letter bids you to do, no matter how extraordinary the instructions may appear. Will you promise me to do this?"

"I promise."

"Very good, then. Farewell, mademoiselle, always remain as good and virtuous as you are now, and I am sure God will reward you by giving you Emmanuel as your husband."

Julie uttered a faint exclamation and blushed like a rose, while the stranger nodded a farewell and went on his way.

In the yard he met Penelon, who had a roll of a hundred francs in each hand, and seemed as though he could not make up his mind to keep them.

"Come along with me, my friend," the Englishman said to him. "I should like to have a word with you."

## CHAPTER XXV

## THE FIFTH OF SEPTEMBER

THE extension of time granted by Messrs Thomson and French's agent, at a time when Morrel least expected it, seemed to the poor shipowner like one of those returns to good fortune which announce to man that fate has at last become weary of spending her fury on him. The same day he related to his daughter, his wife, and Emmanuel all that had occurred, and a ray of hope, one might almost say of peace, once more entered their hearts.

Unfortunately, however, Morel had other engagements than those with Thomson and French, who had shown themselves so considerate toward him, and, as he has said, one had correspondents only in business, and not friends. Any bill signed by Morel was presented with the most scrupulous exactitude, and, thanks to the extension granted by the Englishman, each one was paid by Coclès at sight. Coclès therefore maintained his prophetic calmness and his hope in a better future. Morel alone realized with terror that if he had to repay 100,000 francs to de Boville on the 15th as also the 32,500 francs which would fall due on the 30th, he would be a ruined man. He spent the next three months in strenuous efforts to gather in all his outstanding resources.

Thomson and French's agent had been seen no more at Marseilles. He disappeared a couple of days after his visit to M. Morrel, and, as he had had nothing to do with anyone except the Mayor, the Inspector of Prisons, and M. Morrel, his sojourn there had left no other trace than the different memories these three people had retained of him.

August rolled by in untiring and unsuccessful attempts on the part of Morrel to renew his old credit or to open up fresh ones. Then he remembered Danglars, who was now a millionaire and could save Morrel without taking a penny from his pocket by guaranteeing a loan; but there are times when one feels a repugnance one cannot master, and Morrel had delayed as long as possible before having recourse to this. His feeling of repugnance was justified, for he returned from Paris borne down by the humiliation of a refusal. Yet he uttered no complaint and spoke no harsh word. He embraced his weeping wife and daughter, shook hands with Emmanuel, and closeted himself in his office with Coclès.

When he appeared for dinner, he was outwardly quite calm. This apparent calmness, however, alarmed his wife and daughter more than the deepest dejection would have done. Emmanual tried to reassure them, but his eloquence failed him. He was too well acquainted with the business of the firm not to realize that a terrible catastrophe was pending for the Morrel family.

Night came. The two women watched, hoping that when Morrel left his office he would rejoin them, but they heard him pass by their door, stepping very lightly, no doubt lest they should hear and call him. They heard him go to his room and lock the door.

Mme Morrel sent her daughter to bed, and an hour later, taking off her shoes, she crept down the landing and peeped through the keyhole to see what her husband was doing. She saw a retreating figure on the landing. It was Julie, who, being anxious, had anticipated her mother.

"He is writing," she said to her mother. They understood each other without speaking. Mme Morrel stooped down to the keyhole. Morrel was indeed writing. The terrible idea flashed across her mind that he was making his will. It made her shudder, yet she had strength enough to say nothing.

Two days passed. On the morning of the 5th of September Morrel came down, calm as usual, but agitation of the previous days had left its mark on his pale and careworn face. He was more affectionate toward his wife and daughter than he had ever been; he gazed fondly on the poor child and embraced her again and again. When he left the room Julie made as if to accompany him; but he pushed her back gently, saying:

"Stay with your mother."

Julie tried to insist.

"I wish it!" said Morrel.

It was the first time Morrel had ever said "I wish it" to his daughter, but he said it in a tone of such paternal fondness that Julie dared not advance a step. She remained rooted to the spot, and spake never a word.

An instant later the door opened again. Julie felt two strong arms about her and a mouth pressing a kiss on her forehead. She looked up with an exclamation of joy: "Maximilian! my brother!"

At these words Mme Morrel sprang up, and, running toward her son, threw herself in his arms.

"Mother, what has happened?" said the young man, looking alternately at Mme Morrel and her daughter. "Your letter made me feel very anxious, so I hastened to you."

"Julie, go and tell your father that Maximilian has come," said Mme Morrel, making a sign to the young man.

The girl hastened to obey, but, on the first stair, she met a young man with a letter in his hand.

"Are you not Mademoiselle Julie Morrel?" he said with a very pronounced Italian accent.

"Yes, monsieur," stammered Julie. "What do you wish of me? I do not know you."

"Read this letter," said the man handing her a note.

The girl snatched the note from his hands, opened it hastily, and read:

> Go this moment to No. 15 Allées de Meilhan, ask the porter for the key to the room on the fifth floor. Enter the room, take a red silk purse that is on the corner of the mantelshelf and give it to your father. It is important that he should have it before eleven o'clock.

You promised me blind obedience, and I now remind you of that
promise.

                                               SINBAD THE SAILOR

Julie uttered an exclamation of joy, yet even in her joy she felt a certain uneasiness. Was there nothing to fear? Was this not all a trap that
had been laid for her? She hesitated and decided to ask advice, but a
strange feeling urged her to apply to Emmanuel rather than to her
brother or her mother. She told him all that had happened the day
Thomson and French's agent came to see her father, repeated the
promise she had made, and showed him the letter.

"You must go, mademoiselle," Emmanuel said, "and I shall go with
you."

"Then it is your opinion, Emmanuel," said the girl with some misgiving, "that I should carry out these instructions?"

"Listen," he said. "To-day is the fifth of September, and at eleven
o'clock your father must pay out nearly three hundred thousand
francs, whereas he does not possess fifteen thousand."

"What will happen then?"

"If your father has not found some one to come to his aid by eleven
o'clock, he will be obliged by twelve o'clock to declare himself
bankrupt."

"Come along then, come!" cried Julie, pulling Emmanuel after her.

In the meantime Mme Morrel had told her son everything. He
knew that after his father's successive misfortunes all expenditure in
the house had been rigidly cut down, but he was unaware that matters had come to such a pass. He was horrorstruck.

Then he suddenly rushed out of the room and ran upstairs, expecting to find his father in the office, but he received no answer to his
repeated knocks. As he was waiting at the door, however, his father
came from his bedroom. He uttered a cry of surprise on seeing
Maximilian; he did not know of his arrival. He stood where he was,
pressing with his left hand something he was trying to conceal under
his coat. Maximilian ran down the stairs quickly and threw himself
round his father's neck. Suddenly he drew back, and stood there as
pale as death.

"Father," said he, "why have you a brace of pistols under your coat?"

"Ah, I feared as much," murmured Morrel.

"Father! Father!" cried the young man. "In God's name, why have
you got those weapons?"

"Maximilian, you are a man and a man of honour," replied Morrel,
looking at his son with a fixed stare. "Come with me and I will tell you."

With a firm step Morrel went up to his office followed by Maximilian in great agitation. Morrel closed the door behind his son, then crossing the antechamber, went to his desk, placed the pistols on a corner of the table and pointed to an open ledger. This ledger gave an exact statement of his affairs.

"Read that," said Morrel.

The young man read, and for a moment was quite overcome. Morrel did not speak. What could he have said in face of the damning figures?

"In half an hour, then," said Maximilian in a grim voice, "our name will be dishonoured."

"Blood washes out dishonour!" said Morrel.

"You are right, Father. I understand."

Morrel was about to throw himself on his knees before his son, but Maximilian caught him in his arms and for a moment these two noble hearts beat one against the other.

"You know it is not my fault?" said Morrel.

Maximilian smiled. "I know, Father, that you are the most honourable man I have ever known!"

"Good, my son; enough is said. Now go and rejoin your mother and sister."

"Father," said the young man, kneeling down, "bless me!"

Morrel seized his son's head between his two hands and, pressing his lips to it again and again, said: "Yes, yes, I bless you in my own name and in the name of three generations of irreproachable men. See to it, my son, that our name shall not be dishonoured. Work, fight zealously and courageously; see that you, your mother and sister, expend only what is strictly necessary so that the sacred trust I leave to you of repaying my debts of honour may be speedily fulfilled. Think how glorious the day will be, how grand and solemn, when you can restore all, and when, sitting at this same desk, you will say: 'My father died because he could not do what I am doing to-day, but he died in peace and at rest because he knew he could put his faith in me.'"

"Oh, Father, Father!" cried the young man. "If only you could live!"

"I should be looked upon as a man who has broken his word and failed in his engagements. If I lived you would be ashamed of my name. When I am dead, you will raise your head and say "I am the son of him who killed himself because, for the first time in his life, he was unable to keep his word.' Now," continued Morrel, "leave me alone and keep your mother away. Once more, farewell. Go, go, I need to be alone. You will find my will in the desk in my room."

When his son had gone Morrel sank into his chair and looked up at the clock. He had only seven minutes left and the hand seemed to move round with incredible rapidity. The pistols were loaded; stretching out his hand, he seized one, murmuring his daughter's name. Putting the weapon down again, he took up his pen to write a few words. It occurred to him he might have been more affectionate in his farewell to his beloved daughter. Then he turned to the clock again; he no longer counted by minutes, but by seconds. Taking the weapon once more, he opened his mouth with his eyes on the clock. The noise he made in cocking the pistol sent a shiver through him: a cold perspiration broke out on his forehead and he was seized by a mortal anguish.

He heard the outer door creak on its hinges. The inner door opened. The clock was about to strike eleven. Morrel did not turn round.

He put the pistol to his mouth. . . . Suddenly he heard a cry. . . . It was his daughter's voice. He turned round and saw Julie. The pistol dropped from his hands.

"Father!" cried the girl out of breath and overcome with joy. "You are saved! You are saved!"

She threw herself into his arms, at the same time holding out to him a red silk purse.

"Saved, my child?" said he. "What do you mean?"

"Yes, saved! See here!"

Morrel started at sight of the purse, for he had a faint recollection that it had once belonged to him. He took it in his hand. At one end it held the receipted bill for 287,500 francs, at the other a diamond as big as a nut, with these two words written on a piece of parchment attached to it:

JULIE'S DOWRY

Morrel passed his hand across his brow: he thought he must be dreaming. At the same moment the clock struck eleven.

"Explain, my child," said he. "Where did you find this purse?"

"On the corner of the mantelshelf of a miserable little room on the fifth floor of number fifteen, Allées de Meilhan."

"But this purse is not yours!"

Julie showed her father the letter she had received that morning.

Just then Emmanuel came rushing in full of excitement and joy.

"The *Pharaon!*" cried he. "The *Pharaon!*"

"What? The *Pharaon?* Are you mad, Emmanuel? You know quite well she is lost."

Then in came Maximilian. "Father, how could you say the *Pharaon* was lost? The look-out has just signalled her, and she is putting into port."

"If that is the case, my friends," said his father, "it must be a miracle. Let us go and see, but God have pity on us if it is a false report."

They all went out and on the stairs met Mme Morrel, who had not dared to go into the office. They were soon on the Cannebière, where a large crowd was gathered. All made way for Morrel, and every voice was calling out: "The *Pharaon!* The *Pharaon!*"

True enough, though wonderful to relate, there, in front of the St. Jean tower, was a ship with the words "*Pharaon* (Morrel and Son, Marseilles)" in white letters on her stern; she was the exact counterpart of the other *Pharaon,* and also carried a cargo of indigo and cochineal. She was casting her anchor with all sails brailed. On the deck Captain Gaumard was issuing orders.

As Morrel and his son were embracing each other on the quayside amid the applause of the onlookers, a man whose face was half hidden by a black beard and who had been watching the scene from behind a sentry-box, muttered to himself: "Be happy, noble heart. May you be blessed for all the good you have done and will do hereafter!" And with a smile of joy he left his hiding-place without being observed, descended the steps to the water, and called out three times: "Jacopo! Jacopo! Jacopo!"

A shallop came alongside, took him on board, and conveyed him to a beautifully rigged yacht. He jumped on deck with the nimbleness of a sailor, and from thence once more gazed on the happy scene on the quay.

"Now, farewell to kindness, humanity, gratitude," said he. "Farewell to all the sentiments which rejoice the heart. I have played the part of Providence in recompensing the good, may the god of vengeance now permit me to punish the wicked!"

Muttering these words, he made a sign, and the yacht immediately put out to sea.

## CHAPTER XXVI

## ROMAN BANDITS

TOWARD the beginning of the year 1838 two young men belonging to the best society of Paris were staying at Florence: one was Viscount Albert de Morcerf and the other Baron Franz d'Épinay. They had decided to spend the Carnival together at Rome, and Franz, who had lived in Italy for more than four years, was to be his friend's cicerone.

As it is no small matter to spend the carnival at Rome, especially when you have no great desire to sleep in the Piazza del Popolo or the Campo Vaccino, they wrote to Signor Pastrini, the proprietor of the Hôtel de Londres to ask him to reserve a comfortable suite for them.

On the Saturday evening before the Carnival they arrived in

Rome. The suite reserved for them consisted of two small bedrooms and a sitting-room. The bedrooms overlooked the street, a fact which Pastrini commented upon as a priceless advantage. The remaining rooms on that floor were let to an immensely rich gentleman who was supposed to be either a Sicilian or a Maltese, the proprietor was not quite sure which.

"That is all very well, Pastrini," said Franz, "but we want some supper at once, and also a carriage for to-morrow and the following days."

"You shall have supper instantly, signore, but as for the carriage . . . we will do all we can to procure one for you, and that is all I can say."

"Then we shall harness the horses to mine; it is a little the worse for the journey but that doesn't matter."

"You will not find any horses," said Pastrini.

Albert looked at Franz with the expression of a man who has been given an incomprehensible answer.

"Do you understand that, Franz? No horses! Then surely we can have post horses?"

"They were hired out a month ago, and there are now none left but those absolutely necessary for the postal service."

"What do you say to that?" asked Franz.

"What I say is that when a thing surpasses my comprehension, I cease to think about it at all. Supper ready, Pastrini?"

"Yes, Excellency."

"Well, then, let us go and have it."

"But what about the carriage and horses?"

"Make your mind easy about that, my friend, they will come by themselves. It is only a question of price."

And with that admirable philosophy which believes nothing impossible to a full purse and a well-lined pocket-book, Morcerf supped, went to bed, and dreamed he was racing all over Rome in a carriage and six.

The next morning Franz was the first to wake and immediately rang the bell. The tinkling had not yet ceased when mine host appeared.

"Well, Excellency," said he triumphantly, "I was quite right not to promise you anything yesterday. You are too late; there is not a single carriage to be had in Rome, in any case not for the last three days of the carnival."

"Well, I don't think much of your Eternal City!"

"That is to say, Excellency, there are no more carriages to be had from Sunday morning till Tuesday evening, but until Sunday you can have fifty if you wish," replied Pastrini, anxious to preserve the dignity of the capital of the Christian world in the eyes of his guests.

"Ah, that is something," said Albert. "To-day is Thursday. Who knows what good things will come our way by Sunday?"

"Ten to twelve thousand trippers to make it more difficult than ever!" was Franz's reply.

"My friend, let us enjoy the present and give no thought to the evils of the future."

"I presume we can at least have a window?" asked Franz.

"Where?"

"Overlooking the Corso, naturally!"

"Impossible! Absolutely out of the question!" exclaimed Pastrini. "There was only one left on the fifth floor of the Doria Palace and that has been taken by a Russian Prince for twenty sequins a day."

The two friends looked at each other astounded.

"In that case," said Franz to Albert, "we had better go to Venice for the Carnival. Even if we don't find a carriage there, we shall be sure to find a gondola."

"No fear," cried Albert, "I have made up my mind to see the Carnival at Rome, and see it I will, even if I have to go about on stilts."

"Do Your Excellencies still wish for a carriage until Sunday?"

"What do you think?" said Albert. "Do you imagine we are going to run about the streets of Rome on foot like lawyers' clerks?"

"I will hasten to execute Your Excellencies' orders," said Pastrini. "I will do my best, and I hope you may be satisfied. At what time do you wish the carriage?"

"In an hour."

"Very well, Excellency. In an hour it shall be at the door."

When Albert and Franz descended an hour later, the carriage was there.

"Where do Your Excellencies wish to go?" asked the cicerone.

"To St. Peter's, of course, and then on to the Colosseum," said Albert.

Albert did not know, however, that it takes a day to see St. Peter's and a month to study it. Suddenly the two friends noticed that the day was drawing to a close. Franz took out his watch—it was half-past four.

They immediately returned to the hotel. At the door Franz ordered the coachman to be ready again at eight. He wanted to show Albert the Colosseum by moonlight, as he had seen St. Peter's by daylight. They were to leave by the Porta del Popolo, follow the outer walls, and return by the Porta San Giovanni.

When they had finished their dinner the innkeeper appeared before them.

"I hear," he said, "that you have ordered the carriage for eight o'clock and that you propose visiting the Colosseum?"

"You have heard aright."

"Is it also true that you intend to start from the Porta del Popolo, then to follow the outer walls, and to return by the Porta San Giovanni?"

"Those were my very words."

"Your itinerary is impossible, or to say the least very dangerous."

"Dangerous! Why?"

"Because of the bandit, Luigi Vampa."

"Prick up your ears, Albert! Here's a bandit for you at last!"

"Well, and what has that to do with my orders to the coachman to leave by the Porta del Popolo and return by the Porta San Giovanni?"

"Simply that you may leave by the one, but I very much doubt whether you will return by the other, and because, as soon as night falls, one is not safe fifty yards from the gates."

"Here's a great adventure for us, old man," said Albert, turning to Franz. "We will fill our carriage with pistols, blunderbuses, and double-barrelled guns. Instead of Luigi Vampa holding us up, will hold him up. We will take him to Rome and present him to His Holiness the Pope, who will ask us what recompense we desire for such great service. We shall merely ask for a carriage and pair. Then we shall have a carriage for the Carnival and, what is more, the Roman people will in all probability give expression to their gratitude by crowning us in the Capitol and proclaiming us the saviours of their country."

"Your Excellency knows that it is not customary to defend oneself when attacked by bandits."

"What!" cried Albert, whose courage revolted at the idea of letting himself be robbed without making any resistance. "It is not customary, did you say?"

"No, for it would be useless. What would you do against a dozen bandits suddenly springing out at you from a ditch, a ruin, or an aqueduct, with their guns levelled at your head?"

Albert poured himself out a glass of Lachryma Christi, which he drank in sips, muttering unintelligibly to himself all the time.

"Well, Signor Pastrini," said Franz, "now that my companion has cooled down and you can appreciate our peaceful intentions, tell us who this Luigi Vampa is. Is he a shepherd or a nobleman? Is he young or old? Tall or short? Describe him to us, so that if by any chance we should meet him we shall recognize him."

"I knew Luigi Vampa when he was a mere boy. He was a shepherd on a farm belonging to the Count de San Felice. He is now about twenty-two years of age and is of medium height. When hardly more than a youth, he killed the captain of a gang of bandits and himself became their captain. I fell into his hands once when going from Ferentino to Alatri. Luckily for me he remembered me and not only set me free without making me pay a ransom, but also made me a present of a beautiful watch."

"What do you think of Luigi Vampa now, old man?" said Franz, turning to his friend.

"I say that he is a myth and that he has never existed."

"Do you say he still carries on his business in the outskirts of Rome?"

"Yes, and with a boldness unequalled by any before him."

"What is his procedure in regard to foreigners?"

"Oh, that is quite simple. According to the distance from the town he gives them eight, twelve, or twenty-four hours wherein to pay their ransom; after this time has elapsed, he grants an hour's grace. If he has not received the money by the sixtieth minute of that hour, he blows out his prisoner's brains with one shot, or thrusts a dagger into his heart, and the matter is ended."

"What do you think about it?" Franz asked his companion. "Are you still inclined to go to the Colosseum by the outer Boulevards?"

"Certainly, if the route is picturesque," was the reply.

Nine o'clock struck and the door opened to admit the coachman. "Excellencies," said he, "your carriage is waiting."

"To the Colosseum then!" said Franz.

"By the Porta del Popolo, Your Excellencies, or through the streets?"

"Through the streets; most certainly through the streets!" cried Franz.

"Really, my dear friend, I thought you were braver than that," said Albert, rising and lighting his third cigar.

The two young men went down the stairs and entered the carriage.

## CHAPTER XXVII

## THE APPARITION

FRANZ arranged the route in such a way that Albert might reach the Colosseum without passing a single ancient ruin, so that nothing should attract his eye till the Colosseum itself burst upon him in all its gigantic proportions. They therefore followed the Via Sistina, cut across in front of Santa Maria Maggiore, and drove along the Via Urbana and by San Pietro in Vincoli until they came to the Via del Colosseo.

When they arrived at the sombre-looking and gigantic Colosseum the long, pale rays of the moon were pouring through the gaping apertures in its massive walls.

The carriage stopped a few yards from the Meta Sudans. The coachman opened the door of the carriage, whereupon the two

young men leapt out and found themselves face to face with a
cicerone who seemed to have sprung from nowhere.

Franz had already visited the Colosseum some ten times. His companion, however, had never set foot in it before, and it must be said to
his credit that, in spite of the ignorant prattle of his guide, he was
deeply impressed. And, indeed, no one who has not beheld it can have
any idea of the majesty of a ruin such as this, with its proportions
magnified by the mysterious clearness of a southern moon which
darts forth rays that are like the phantasy of an Eastern twilight.

Scarcely had Franz, the pensive one, gone a hundred yards under
the inner portals, however, when he left Albert to his guide, who
would not renounce his prescriptive right to show him all around the
Lions' Den, the Loggia of the Gladiators, the Podium of the Caesars.
Ascending a half-dilapidated staircase, Franz seated himself in the
shadow of a column facing a niche which gave him an all-embracing
view of the gigantic dimensions of this majestic ruin.

He had been sitting thus for about a quarter of an hour when he
seemed to hear a stone rolling down the staircase opposite the one by
which he had ascended. It was no strange matter for a stone, loosened
by age, to break away, but it seemed to Franz that this stone had been
displaced by the pressure of a human foot, and that the sound of a
muffled footstep reached his ears.

He was not mistaken; a moment later a man appeared, and from the
hesitating manner in which he came up the last few steps and stopped
at the top, apparently listening, it was obvious he had come for some
particular purpose and was expecting to meet some one.

Instinctively Franz withdrew behind his column.

The individual whose mysterious arrival had attracted his attention
stood partly in the shadow of the ruins, so that Franz was unable to
distinguish his features, although the details of his dress were plainly
discernible. He wore a large, dark-brown cloak, one end of which was
thrown over his left shoulder in such a way as to hide the lower part
of his face, while a broad-brimmed hat concealed the upper part.

He had been standing there for some minutes and began to show
visible signs of impatience, when another man appeared.

"I crave your pardon for keeping you waiting, Excellency," said he
with a Roman accent. "I am, however, but a few minutes late; it has just
struck ten by the clock on Saint John Lateran. I have just come from
the Castle of Saint Angelo and had great difficulty in seeing Beppo."

"Who is Beppo?"

"Beppo is employed in the prison, and I pay him a small fee every
year for information as to what is going on in His Holiness's Palace."

"Ha ha! I see you are a prudent man."

"Why, just so, Excellency! One never knows what may happen. One day I may be entrapped like poor Peppino and shall also be in need of a rat to gnaw the cords that keep me a prisoner."

"To come to the point, what news did you glean?"

"There will be two executions on Tuesday at two o'clock, as is customary in Rome at the commencement of all great festivals. One of the condemned men will be *mazzolato*. He is a worthless wretch who has murdered the priest that brought him up and therefore deserves no pity. The other one will be *decapitato*, and he, Your Excellency, is no other than poor Peppino."

"What can you expect, my dear friend? You have struck such terror into the pontifical government and the neighbouring kingdoms, that they are going to make an example of him."

"But Peppino does not even belong to my gang. He is a poor shepherd whose only crime consisted in supplying us with provisions."

"Which certainly made him your accomplice. But mark the consideration that is being shown him. Instead of clubbing him to death, as they will do to you if they ever get hold of you, they content themselves with merely guillotining him."

"I am in the mood to do anything and everything to prevent the execution of this poor wretch who has got himself into trouble by doing me a service. *Per la Madonna!* I should be a coward if I did not do something for the poor fellow!"

"What do you intend doing?"

"I shall place a score of men round the scaffold and the moment they bring him out I shall give the signal, and, with daggers drawn, my men and I will throw ourselves on the guard and carry off their prisoner."

"That seems to me very risky. I veritably believe my plan is better than yours."

"What is your plan, Excellency?"

"I shall give ten thousand piastres to a friend of mine who will arrange to have Peppino's execution delayed until next year. In the course of the year I shall give another ten thousand piastres to some one else I know, by which means his escape from prison shall be effected."

"Are you sure of success?"

"I shall do more with my gold than you and your people will do with all your daggers, pistols, carbines, and blunderbusses. Leave it to me."

"Splendid! We will, however, keep ourselves in readiness in case your plan should fail."

"Certainly do so if you like, but you can count on the reprieve."

"How shall we know whether you have been successful?"

"That is easily arranged. I have hired the three last windows of the Café Ruspoli. If I obtain the reprieve, the two corner windows will be draped in yellow damask, while the centre one will be hung with white damask, having a large red cross marked upon it."

"Excellent! But who will bring the reprieve?"

"Send me one of your men disguised as a friar, and I will give it to him. His dress will give him access to the foot of the scaffold. There he can give the bull to the officer in charge, who will hand it to the executioner. In the meantime, however, I would advise you to let Peppino know lest he should die of fright or go mad, which would mean that we had gone to unnecessary expenditure on his behalf."

"If you save Peppino, Excellency, you may count not only on my devotion to you but on my absolute obedience."

"Be careful what you say, my friend. I may remind you of that one day! Sh . . . I hear a noise. It is unnecessary for us to be seen together. All these guides are spies and they might recognize you, and, though I appreciate your friendship, I fear my reputation would suffer if they knew we were on such a friendly footing."

"Farewell, then, Excellency, I rely on you as you may rely on me."

With these words the last speaker disappeared down the stairs, while the other, covering himself more closely with his cloak, almost touched Franz as he descended to the arena by the outer steps.

Just then Franz heard his name echoing through the vaults. It was Albert calling him. Ten minutes later the two were rumbling along toward the hotel, and Franz was listening in a very indifferent and distracted manner to the learned dissertations Albert made, in the style of Pliny and Calpurnius, on the iron-pointed nets used to prevent the ferocious beasts from springing on the spectators. He let him talk on without interruption; he wanted to be alone to think undisturbed over what had happened.

The next day Franz had several letters to write and left Albert to his own devices. Albert made the most of his time; he took his letters of introduction to their addresses, and received invitations for every evening. He also achieved the great feat of seeing all Rome in one day, and spent the evening at the opera. Moreover, by the time he reached his hotel he had solved the carriage question. When the two friends were smoking their last cigar in their sitting-room before retiring for the night, Albert suddenly said:

"I have arranged a little surprise for you. You know how impossible it is to procure a carriage. Well, I have a wonderful idea."

Franz looked at his friend as though he had no great confidence in his imagination.

"We cannot get a carriage and horses, but what about a wagon and a pair of oxen?"

Franz stared, and a smile of amused interest played about his lips.

"Yes, a wagon and a yoke of oxen. We will have the wagon decorated and we will dress ourselves up as Neapolitan harvesters, and represent a living picture after the magnificent painting by Leopold Robert."

"Bravo!" exclaimed Franz. "For once you have hit upon a capital idea. Have you told anyone about it?"

"I have told our host. When I came in, I sent for him and explained to him all that I should require. He assured me that it would be quite easy to obtain everything. I wanted to have the oxen's horns decorated, but he told me it would take three days to do it, so we must do without this superfluity."

"Where is our host now?"

"Gone out in search of our things."

As he spoke, the door opened, and their landlord put his head in.

"*Permesso?*" said he.

"Certainly," Franz replied.

"Well, have you found the wagon and oxen for us?" said Albert.

"I have done better than that," he replied in a very self-satisfied manner. "Your Excellencies are aware that the Count of Monte Cristo is on the same floor as yourself. Hearing of the dilemma in which you are placed, he offers you two seats in his carriage and two seats at his window in the Palazzo Ruspoli."

Albert and Franz exchanged looks.

"But can we accept this offer from a stranger, a man we do not even know?" asked Albert.

"It seems to me," said Franz to Albert, "that if this man is as well-mannered as our host says he is, he would have conveyed his invitation to us in some other way, either in writing or——"

At this instant there was a knock at the door.

"Come in," said Franz.

A servant wearing a very smart livery made his appearance.

"From the Count of Monte Cristo to Monsieur Franz d'Épinay and the Viscount Albert de Morcerf," said he, handing two cards to the host, who gave them to the young men.

"The Count of Monte Cristo asks permission to call upon you to-morrow morning," continued the servant. "He will be honoured to know what hour is convenient to you."

"Upon my word, there is nothing to find fault with here," said Albert to Franz. "Everything is as it should be."

"Tell the Count that, on the contrary, we shall do ourselves the honour of calling upon him."

The servant withdrew.

"That is what I should call assaulting us with politeness," said Albert.

"Signor Pastrini, your Count of Monte Cristo is a very gentlemanly fellow."

"You accept his offer then?"

"Of course we do," replied Albert. "Nevertheless, I must own that I regret the wagon and the harvesters, and if it were not for the window at the Palazzo Ruspoli to compensate us for our loss, I think I should revert to my first idea. What about you, Franz?"

"The window in the Palazzo Ruspoli is the deciding point with me, too."

In truth, the offer of two seats in the Palazzo Ruspoli reminded Franz of the conversation he had overheard in the ruins of the Colosseum, when the man in the cloak undertook to obtain the condemned man's reprieve. Were he and the Count one and the same person? He would doubtless recognize him, and then nothing would deter him from satisfying his curiosity regarding him.

The next morning Franz woke up at eight o'clock, and, as soon as he was dressed, sent for the landlord, who presented himself with his usual obsequiousness.

"Signor Pastrini," said Franz, "is there not an execution to-day?"

"There is, Your Excellency; but if you ask me because you wish to have a window, it is too late."

"No, that is not the reason," replied Franz. "What I want to know is how many condemned men there are, their names, and the nature of their punishment."

"What a bit of good luck, Your Excellency! They have just brought me the *tavolette*."

"What are the *tavolette?*"

"They are wooden tablets put up at the corners of the streets on the evening before an execution, giving the names of the condemned men, the reason of their condemnation, and the nature of their punishment. The purpose of the notice is to invite the faithful to pray to God that He may grant the culprits sincere repentance."

"I should like to read one of the *tavolette,*" said Franz.

"Nothing could be easier," said the landlord, opening the door, "I have had one put on the landing." Taking the *tavoletta* from the wall, he handed it to Franz. A literal translation of the wording on the tablet is as follows:

It is hereby made known to all that the following will be executed in the Piazza del Popolo by order of the Rota Tribunal on Tuesday, the 22nd of February, the first day of Carnival: Andrea Rondolo, accused of the murder of the highly honoured and venerable priest Don Cesare Terlini, canon at the church of St. John Lateran, and Peppino, *alias* Rocca Priori, accused of complicity with the detestable bandit Luigi Vampa and other members of his gang.

The first-named shall be *mazzolato,* the latter shall be *decapitato.*

All charitable souls are hereby entreated to pray God to grant these two unfortunates the grace of sincere repentance.

This was exactly what Franz had heard the previous evening in the ruins of the Colosseum.

Time was passing, however; it was nine o'clock, and Franz was just going to waken Albert when, to his great astonishment, he came out of his room fully dressed.

"Well, now that we are ready, do you think we could go and pay our respects to the Count of Monte Cristo?" Franz inquired of his host.

"Certainly," was the reply. "The Count of Monte Cristo is an early riser and I feel sure he has been up these two hours."

"Then you do not think we shall be committing an act of indiscretion if we call on him now?"

"I am sure we should not."

"Then, Albert, if you are ready, let us go and thank our neighbour for his courtesy."

They had only to cross the landing; the landlord preceded them and rang the bell. A servant opened the door.

"*I signori francesi,*" said the landlord.

The servant bowed and invited them to enter.

They were conducted through two rooms, more luxuriously furnished than they had thought possible in Pastrini's hotel, and were then shown into a very elegant sitting-room. A Turkey carpet covered the parquet floor, and the most comfortably upholstered settees and chairs seemed to invite one to their soft, well-sprung seats and slanting backs. Magnificent paintings intermingled with glorious war trophies decorated the walls, while rich tapestried curtains hung before the door.

"If Your Excellencies will take a seat," said the servant, "I will let the Count know you are here." And he disappeared through one of the doors.

As the door opened, the sound of a *guzla* reached the ears of the two friends but was immediately lost; the door, being closed almost as soon as it was opened, merely permitted one swell of harmony to penetrate the room.

Franz and Albert looked at one another and then at the furniture, pictures, and trophies. On closer inspection it all appeared to them even more magnificent than at first.

"Well, what do you think of it all?" Franz asked his friend.

"Upon my word, I think our neighbour must be some stockbroker who has speculated on the fall of Spanish funds; or else some prince travelling incognito."

"Hush! hush! that is what we are now going to find out, for here he comes."

As he finished speaking the sound of a door turning on its hinges was heard, and almost immediately the tapestry was drawn aside to admit the owner of all these riches.

Albert advanced toward him, but Franz remained glued to his seat. He who entered was no other than the cloaked man of the Colosseum.

## CHAPTER XXVIII

## THE CARNIVAL AT ROME

MESSIEURS," said the Count of Monte Cristo as he entered, "pray accept my excuses for allowing myself to be forestalled, but I feared I might disturb you if I called on you at an early hour. Besides, you advised me you were coming, and I held myself at your disposal."

"Franz and I owe you a thousand thanks, Count," said Albert. "You have truly extricated us from a great dilemma."

"Indeed!" returned the Count motioning the two young men to be seated on a settee, "it is only that idiot Pastrini's fault that you were not relieved of your anxiety sooner. As soon as I learnt that I could be of use to you, I eagerly seized the opportunity of paying you my respects."

The two young men bowed. Franz had not yet found anything to say; he was still undecided whether this was the same man he had seen at the Colosseum. He determined, therefore, to turn the conversation to a subject which might possibly throw light on the situation.

"You have offered us seats in your carriage, Count," said he, "as well as at your window in the Palazzo Ruspoli! Could you now tell us where we can obtain a view of the Piazza del Popolo?"

"Yes, I believe there is to be an execution in the Piazza del Popolo, is there not?" said the Count in a casual tone.

"That is so," replied Franz, delighted to see that the Count was at last coming to the point he wished.

"Just one moment, I believe I told my steward to attend to this yesterday. Perhaps I can be of service to you in this matter also."

He put out his hand toward the bell-rope and pulled it three times. The Count's steward immediately appeared.

"Signor Bertuccio," said the Count, "have you procured a window overlooking the Piazza del Popolo, as I instructed you to do?"

"Yes, Excellency," replied the steward, "but it was very late."

"What!" said the Count frowning, "did I not tell you that I wanted one?"

"And Your Excellency has one, the one which had been let to Prince Lobanieff, but I had to pay a hundred . . ."

"That will do, that will do, Signor Bertuccio! spare these gentlemen such domestic details. You have procured a window and that is all I want to know. Give the coachman the address and hold yourself in readiness on the staircase to conduct us thither. You may go."

The steward bowed and was about to retire when the Count said: "Ah! be good enough to ask Signor Pastrini if he has received the *tavolette* and if he will send me the programme of the execution."

"It is unnecessary," said Franz, taking his notebook from his pocket, "I have seen the tablets and copied them here."

"Very well. In that case I require nothing more; you can retire. Let me know when breakfast is ready." Then turning to Albert and Franz he said: "You will, I hope, do me the honour of staying to breakfast with me."

"Nay, Count, that would really be abusing your hospitality," replied Albert.

"Not at all. On the contrary, you will give me great pleasure, and perhaps one of you, or even both, will return the compliment one day in Paris. Signor Bertuccio, have covers laid for three."

He took the notebook out of Franz's hand.

"We were saying," he continued in the same tone in which he would have read a gossipy newspaper paragraph, "that 'the following will be executed on the Piazza del Popolo by order of the Rota Tribunal on Tuesday, the twenty-second of February, the first day of the Carnival; Andrea Rondolo, accused of the murder of the highly honoured and venerable priest Don Cesare Terlini, Canon of the Church of Saint John Lateran, and Peppino, *alias* Rocca Priori, accused of complicity with the detestable bandit, Luigi Vampa, and the other members of his gang.

"'The first-named shall be *mazzolato,* the latter shall be *decapitato.*

"'All charitable souls are hereby entreated to pray God to grant these two unfortunates the grace of sincere repentance.' Hm! 'The first-named shall be *mazzolato,* the latter shall be *decapitato.*' Quite right," continued the Count, "this is how it was arranged first, but since yesterday, I think, some change has been made in the order of the ceremony."

"Really!" said Franz.

"Yes, I spent yesterday evening with Cardinal Rospigliosi, and there was question of one of the two condemned men being reprieved."

"Andrea Rondolo?" asked Franz.

"No," the Count answered carelessly, "the other one" (he glanced at the notebook as if to recall the name), "Peppino, *alias* Rocca Priori. It will deprive you of seeing a man guillotined, but there is still the *mazzolata*, which is an extraordinary and interesting form of punishment when you see it for the first time, and even for the second time. You asked me for a seat at my window. Well, you shall have it. But let us first sit down to table, for they are just coming to inform us that breakfast is ready."

And in truth a servant opened one of the four doors saying:

*"Al suo commodo."*

They all rose and passed into the dining-room.

At the end of the breakfast Franz took out his watch.

"Well," said the Count, "what are you doing?"

"Excuse us, Count," said Franz, "but we have a thousand and one things to attend to."

"What things?"

"We have no disguises, and they cannot be dispensed with to-day."

"Do not concern yourself about that. As far as I know, we have a private room in the Piazza del Popolo; I will have any costumes you desire sent there, and we can change into our disguises on the spot."

"After the execution?" said Franz.

"After, during, or before, just as you like."

"In front of the scaffold?"

"The scaffold is part of the festival."

"Count, upon reflection, I shall content myself with accepting a seat in your carriage and in the window of the Palazzo Ruspoli, but I leave you free to dispose of my seat in the window of the Piazza del Popolo, though I appreciate your courtesy."

"But I warn you, you will miss a very curious sight," was the Count's reply.

"You will tell me all about it," replied Franz, "and I am convinced that the recital from your lips will make almost as great an impression on me as the sight itself. More than once have I wished to witness an execution, but have never been able to make up my mind to it. I should very much like to pass through the Corso," continued he. "Would that be possible?"

"It would on foot, but not in a carriage."

"Well, then, I shall go on foot."

"Is it necessary for you to go down the Corso?"

"Yes, I want to see something."

"In that case the carriage can wait for us at the Piazza del Popolo. I shall be quite pleased to go along the Corso myself to see whether some orders I have given have been executed."

"Excellency," said the servant opening the door, "a man in the habit of a friar wishes to speak with you."

"Ah, yes, I know what he wants," said the Count. "If you will go into the salon, you will find some excellent Havana cigars on the centre table. I will rejoin you in a minute."

The two young men rose and went out by one door while the Count, after renewing his apologies, left by the other.

"Well, what do you think of the Count of Monte Cristo?" asked Franz of his friend.

"What do I think of him?" said Albert, obviously astonished that his companion should ask him such a question. "I think he is a charming man who does the honours of his table to perfection; a man who has seen much, studied much, and thought much; who, like Brutus, belongs to the school of the Stoics, and who possesses most excellent cigars," he added appreciatively, sending out a whiff of smoke which rose to the ceiling in spirals.

That was Albert's opinion of the Count, and as Franz knew that he prided himself on forming an opinion of men and things only after mature reflection, he did not attempt to change his own opinion of him.

"But did you notice how attentively he looked at you?"

"At me?"

"Yes."

Albert thought for a moment.

"Ah, that is not surprising," he said with a sigh. "I have been away from Paris for nearly a year, and my clothes must have become old-fashioned. The Count probably thinks I come from the provinces; undeceive him, old man, and the first opportunity you have, tell him that this is not the case."

Franz smiled, and an instant later the Count returned.

"Here I am, messieurs," he said, "and entirely at your service. I have given the necessary orders; the carriage will go to the Piazza del Popolo, and we shall go down the Corso if you really wish to. Take some of those cigars, Monsieur de Morcerf."

"By Jove, I shall be delighted," said Albert, "for your Italian cigars are awful. When you come to Paris, I shall return all this hospitality."

"I will not refuse; I hope to go there some day and, with your permission, I shall pay you a visit. Come along, messieurs, we have no time to lose; it is half-past twelve. Let us be off."

All three went out together and, passing the Piazza di Spagna, went along the Via Frattina which led them straight to the Fiano and Ruspoli Palaces. Franz's whole attention was directed to the windows of the Palazzo Ruspoli; he had not forgotten the signal agreed upon by the cloaked man and his mysterious companion.

"Which are your windows?" he asked the Count as naturally as he could.

"The last three," replied the Count with a carelessness which was quite unaffected, for he could not guess the reason of the question.

Franz rapidly looked up at the three windows. The side windows were draped with yellow damask and the centre one with white damask having a red cross on it. The man in the cloak had kept his word, and there was no doubt that the cloaked man and the Count were one and the same person.

By this time the Carnival had begun in real earnest. Picture the wide and beautiful Corso lined from end to end with tall palaces with their balconies tapestried and their windows draped, and at these windows and balconies three hundred thousand spectators, Romans, Italians, and strangers from every part of the world: aristocrats by birth side by side with the aristocrats by wealth and genius; charming women who, succumbing to the influence of the spectacle, bent over the balconies or leaned out of the windows showering confetti on the carriages and catching bouquets hurled up at them in return; the air thickened with sweetmeats thrown down and flowers thrown up; in the streets a gay, untiring, mad crowd in fantastic costumes: gigantic cabbages walking about, buffalo heads bellowing on human bodies, dogs walking on their hind legs. In the midst of all this a mask is raised revealing, as in Callot's dream of the temptation of St. Antony, a beautiful face that one follows only to be separated from it by these troops of demons such as one meets in one's dreams; picture all this to yourself, and you have a faint idea of the Carnival at Rome.

When they had driven round for the second time, the Count stopped the carriage and asked his companions' permission to quit them, leaving his carriage at their disposal. Franz looked up; they were opposite the Palazzo Ruspoli. At the centre window, the one hung with white damask with a red cross, was a blue domino.

"Messieurs," said the Count, jumping out, "when you are tired of being actors and wish to become spectators, you know you have seats at my windows. In the meantime, my coachman, my window, and my servants are at your disposal."

Franz thanked the Count for his kind offer; Albert, however, was busy coquetting with a carriageful of Roman peasants who had taken their stand near the Count's carriage, and was throwing bouquets at them.

Unfortunately for him the line of carriages drove on, and while he went toward the Piazza del Popolo, the carriage that had attracted his attention moved on toward the Palazzo di Venezia.

In spite of Albert's hopes he could boast of no other adventure that day than that he had passed the carriage with the Roman peasants two or three times. Once, whether by accident or intentionally, his mask fell off. He took his remaining bouquets and threw them into the carriage.

One of the charming ladies whom Albert suspected to be disguised in the coquettish peasant's costume was doubtless touched by this gallantry, for, when the friends' carriage passed the next time, she threw him a bouquet of violets. Albert seized it and put it victoriously into his buttonhole, while the carriage continued its triumphant course.

"Well!" said Franz, "here is the beginning of an adventure."

"Laugh as much as you like," said Albert. "I think you are right though, anyway I shall not let this bouquet go!"

"I should think not indeed, it is a token of gratitude."

The Count of Monte Cristo had given definite orders that his carriage should be at their disposal for the remaining days of the Carnival, and they were to make use of it without fear of trespassing too much on his kindness. The young men decided to take advantage of the Count's courtesy, and the next afternoon, having replaced their costume of the previous evening, which was somewhat the worse for the numerous combats they had engaged in, by a Roman peasant's attire, they gave orders for the horses to be harnessed. With a sentimental touch, Albert slipped the bouquet of faded violets in his buttonhole. They started forth and hastened toward the Corso by the Via Vittoria.

When they were going round the Corso for the second time, a bouquet of fresh violets was thrown into the carriage from one filled with pierrettes, from which it was quite clear to Albert that the *contadine* of the previous evening had also changed their costumes, and that, whether by chance or whether both parties had been prompted by a similar sentiment, he was now wearing their costume and they were wearing his.

Albert put the fresh flowers into his buttonhole, but kept the faded ones in his hand, and when he again met the carriage he put it amorously to his lips, which appeared to afford great amusement, not only to the one who had thrown it but also to her gay companions.

The day was no less animated than the previous evening; it is even probable that a keen observer would have noted more noise and gaiety. Once the two friends saw the Count at his window, but when they next passed he had disappeared. Needless to say, the flirtation between Albert and the pierrette with the violets lasted the whole day.

When they returned home in the evening Franz found a letter

awaiting him from the Ambassador informing him that he would have the honour of being received by His Holiness on the morrow. At each previous visit to Rome he had solicited and had been granted the same honour, and, moved by a religious feeling as much as by gratitude, he did not wish to leave the capital of the Christian world without paying his respectful homage at the feet of one of the successors of St. Peter who has been such a rare example of all virtues. There was, therefore, no question of the Carnival for him that day; for, in spite of his simplicity and kindness, the grandeur of the noble and holy old man whom they called Gregory XVI was such that one was always filled with awe and respectful emotion at the thought of kneeling before him.

On leaving the Vatican Franz went straight to the hotel, carefully avoiding the Corso. He had brought away with him a treasure of pious thoughts, and he felt it would be profanation to go near the mad gaiety of the *mascherata* for some little time.

At ten minutes past five Albert entered overjoyed. The pierrette had reassured her peasant's costume, and, as she passed his carriage, had raised her mask. She was charming to behold.

Franz congratulated Albert, who received his congratulations with the air of a man conscious that they were merited. He had recognized, by certain unmistakable signs, that his fair incognita belonged to the aristocracy, and had made up his mind to write to her the next day.

Though given no details, Franz noticed that Albert had something to ask him, but hesitated to formulate the request. He insisted upon it, however, declaring beforehand that he was willing to make any sacrifice for his pleasure. Albert's reluctance to tell his friend his secret lasted just as long as politeness demanded, and then he confessed to Franz that he would do him a great favour by permitting him to go in the carriage alone the next day, for he attributed to Franz's absence the extreme kindness of the fair *contadina* in raising her mask.

Franz was not so selfish as to stand in Albert's way in the case of an adventure that promised to prove so agreeable to his curiosity and so flattering to his vanity. He felt assured that his friend would duly blurt out to him all that happened; and as a similar piece of good fortune had never fallen to his share during the three years that he had travelled in Italy, Franz was by no means sorry to learn what was the proper thing to do on such an occasion. He therefore promised Albert that he would be quite pleased to witness the Carnival on the morrow from the windows of the Ruspoli Palace.

The next morning he saw Albert pass and repass. He held an enormous bouquet, which he, doubtless, meant to make the bearer of his amorous epistle. This probability was changed into certainty when

Franz saw the bouquet, a beautiful bunch of white camellias, in the hands of a charming pierrette dressed in rose-coloured satin. The evening was no longer joy but ecstasy. Albert did not doubt that the fair unknown would reply in the same manner; nor was he mistaken, for the next evening saw him enter, triumphantly waving a folded paper he held by the corner.

"Well," said he, "what did I tell you?"

"She has answered you?" asked Franz.

"Read!"

Franz took the letter and read:

> At seven o'clock on Tuesday evening, descend from your carriage opposite the Via dei Pontefici, and follow the Roman peasant who snatches your *moccoletto* from you. When you arrive at the first step of the church of St. Giacomo, be sure to fasten a knot of rose-coloured ribbons to the shoulder of your pierrot's costume so that you will be recognized. Until then you will not see me. Constancy and discretion.

"Well?" asked he, when Franz had finished reading. "What do you think of that?"

"I think that the adventure is looking decidedly interesting."

"If my unknown be as amiable as she is beautiful," said Albert, "I shall stay at Rome for at least six weeks. I adore Rome and I have always had a great taste for archaeology."

"Yes, to be sure, two or three more such adventures and I do not despair of seeing you a member of the Academy!"

At length Tuesday, the last and most tumultuous day of the Carnival arrived, the day on which the theatres open at ten o'clock in the morning and Lent begins at eight in the evening; the day when all those who, through lack of money or enthusiasm, have not taken part in the Carnival before, let themselves be drawn into the orgy and gaiety and contribute to the general noise and excitement. From two o'clock till five, Franz and Albert followed in the line of carriages, exchanging handfuls of confetti with other carriages and pedestrians, who crowded about the horses' feet and the carriage-wheels without a single accident, a single dispute, or a single fight.

Albert was triumphant in his pierrot costume with a knot of rose-coloured ribbons falling from his shoulder almost to the ground.

As the day advanced, the tumult became greater. On the pavement, in the carriages, at the windows, there was not one silent tongue, not one idle hand. It was in truth a human storm composed of a thunder of shouts and a hail of sweetmeats, flowers, eggs, oranges, and nosegays. At three o'clock the sound of rockets let off in the Piazza del Popolo and at the Palazzo di Venezia (heard but dimly amid the din and confusion), announced that the races were about to begin. Like the *moccoli,* the races are one of the episodes peculiar to the last days of Carnival. At the sound of the rockets, the carriages instantly broke the ranks and retired by the nearest by-streets.

The pedestrians ranged themselves against the walls; the trampling of horses and the clashing of steel was heard. A detachment of carabineers, fifteen abreast, galloped up the Corso to clear it for *barberi.* Almost instantly, in the midst of a tremendous and general outcry, seven or eight horses, excited by the shouts of three thousand spectators, passed by with lightning speed. Then three cannons were fired to indicate that number three had won, whereupon the carriages moved on again toward the Corso, surging down all the streets, like torrents which, pent up for a while, flow back more rapidly than ever into the parent river; and the immense stream again continued its course between its two granite banks.

A new source of noise and movement was given to the crowd when the *moccoletti* appeared on the scene. These are candles which vary in size from the pascal taper to the rushlight, and which awaken in the actors of the great scene which terminates the Carnival two opposed ideas—the first is how to keep their own *moccoletto* alight, and the second how to extinguish those of the others.

Night was rapidly approaching, and already at the cry of "*Moccoletti!*" repeated by the shrill voices of a thousand vendors, two or three stars began to twinkle amidst the crowd. It was a signal. At the end of ten minutes fifty thousand lights were glittering. It seemed like a dance of Jack-o'-lanterns. It is impossible to form any idea of it without having seen it. Imagine all the stars come down from the sky and mingling in a wild dance on the face of the earth, the whole accompanied by cries never heard in any other part of the world! Irrespective of class, the mad revellers blow, extinguish, relight. Had old Aeolus appeared at this moment, he would have been proclaimed king of the *moccoli,* and Aquilo the heir presumptive to the crown.

This flaming frolic continued for two hours; the Corso was light as day; the features of the spectators on the third and fourth storeys were visible. Every five minutes Albert took out his watch; at length it pointed to seven. The two friends were at that moment in the Via dei Pontefici. Albert sprang out of the carriage, *moccoletto* in hand. Two or three masks strove to tear it from him or extinguish it, but, being a neat boxer, Albert sent them sprawling one after the other, and continued his course toward the church of St. Giacomo. The steps were crowded with curious and masked revellers striving to snatch the torches from each other's hands. Franz watched Albert's progress and saw him put his foot on the first step; a masked lady wearing the well-known peasant's costume instantly stretched out her hand and, without meeting with any resistance, snatched the *moccoletto* from him.

Franz was too far away to hear the words that passed between them, but they must have been friendly, for he saw them go away together arm in arm. He watched them for some time making their way through the crowd, but lost sight of them in the Via Macello. Suddenly the bell sounded signalling the close of Carnival, and at the same moment all the *moccoletti* were extinguished as if by magic. It was just as though one tremendous gust of wind had risen, carrying everything before it, and Franz found himself in complete darkness.

The shouts ceased just as suddenly as though the strong wind had not only blown out the lights, but had also carried all the noise with it. No sound was heard save the rolling of carriages taking the revellers to their homes; no lights were to be seen save those at a few isolated windows. The Carnival was over.

## CHAPTER XXIX

## THE CATACOMBS OF ST. SEBASTIAN

IN his whole life Franz had never experienced such a sudden change of impressions, such a swift transition from jollity to sadness as at that moment. It was as though Rome had been changed by the magic breath of some demon of darkness into a vast tomb. It so chanced, too, that the moon was on the wane and would not rise until about eleven o'clock, which added to the intensity of the darkness. The streets the young man traversed were, therefore, plunged into blackest obscurity. He had not far to go, however, and at the end of ten minutes his carriage, or rather the Count's, stopped before the Hôtel de Londres.

Dinner was waiting, but as Albert had said he did not expect to be in so soon, Franz sat down to table without him.

At eleven o'clock Albert had not come back. Franz put on his coat and went out, telling his host that he was spending the evening at the Duke of Bracciano's.

The Duke of Bracciano's house was at that time one of the most charming in Rome; his wife, who was one of the last descendants of the Colonnas, did the honours in the most perfect style, and the parties she gave attained European celebrity. Franz and Albert had brought letters of introduction to them, and the Duke's first question was as to what had become of Albert. Franz replied that he had left him when they were extinguishing the *moccoletti* and had lost sight of him in the Via Macello.

"Do you know where he went to?" asked the Duke.

"Not exactly, but I believe there was some question of a rendezvous."

"Good heavens!" cried the Duke. "It is a bad day, or rather night, to be out late. You know Rome better than he does and should not have let him go."

"I should just as easily have stopped number three of the *barberi* that won the race to-day. Besides, what could happen to him?"

"Who knows! It is a very dark night and the Tiber is very close to the Via Macello."

Franz felt a shudder run down his back when he observed that the Duke was as uneasy in his mind as he himself was.

"I left word at the hotel that I had the honour of spending the evening with you, Duke," he said, "and that they were to inform me directly he returned."

"Wait a moment; I believe one of my servants is looking for you."

The Duke was not mistaken; on observing Franz, the servant came up to him.

"Excellency," said he, "the proprietor of the Hôtel de Londres has sent to inform you that a man is waiting for you there with a letter from Viscount Morcerf."

"A letter from the Viscount!" cried Franz. "Where is the messenger?"

"He went away directly he saw me come into the ball-room to find you."

Franz took his hat and hastened away. As he neared the hotel, he saw a man standing in the middle of the road and did not doubt he was Albert's messenger. He went up to him, and said:

"Have you not brought me a letter from Viscount Morcerf?"

"What is Your Excellency's name?"

"Baron Franz d'Épinay."

"Then the letter is addressed to Your Excellency."

"Is there an answer?" asked Franz, taking the letter.

"Your friend hopes so!"

Franz went in and, as soon as his candle was lit, unfolded the paper. The letter was written in Albert's handwriting and signed by him. Franz read it twice before he could comprehend the contents, which were as follows:

DEAR FRANZ,

Directly you receive this, be good enough to take my letter of credit from my portfolio in the drawer of the writing-desk and add

yours to it should it not be enough. Hasten to Torlonia's and draw
out at once four thousand piastres, which give to bearer. It is urgent
that this sum of money should be sent to me without delay.
I will say no more, for I count on you as you would count on
me.

Yours ever,

ALBERT DE MORCERF

P.S.—I now believe in Italian bandits.

Beneath these lines the following words were written in a strange
hand:

Se alle sei della mattina le quattro mile piastre non sono nelle mie
mani, alle sette il conte Albeto avrà cessato di vivere.[1]

LUIGI VAMPA

This second signature explained all to Franz. Albert had fallen into
the hands of the famous chief of *banditti* in whose existence he had
for so long refused to believe.

There was no time to lose. He hastened to the desk, opened it,
found the portfolio in the drawer and in the portfolio the letter of
credit: it was made out for six thousand piastres, but Albert had already
spent three thousand. Franz had no letter of credit; as he lived at
Florence and had come to Rome for but seven or eight days, he had
only taken a hundred louis with him, and of these he had not more
than fifty left.

Seven or eight hundred piastres were therefore lacking to make up
the requisite sum, but in such circumstances Franz could always be
sure that Messrs Torlonia would oblige him. He was about to return
to the Bracciano Palace without the loss of time, when a bright idea
occurred to him; he would appeal to the Count of Monte Cristo.

The Count was in a small room which was surrounded by divans
which Franz had not yet seen.

"Well, what good wind blows you here at this hour?" said he. "Have
you come to ask me to supper? That would indeed by very kind of you."

"No, I have come to speak to you of a very serious matter. Are we
alone?"

The Count went to the door and returned. "Quite alone," said he.

Franz gave him Albert's letter. "Read that," said he.

---

[1] If the four thousand piastres are not in my hands by six in the morning, Count
Albert will have ceased to exist at seven o'clock.

The Count read it.

"What do you say to that," asked Franz.

"Have you the money he demands?"

"Yes, all but eight hundred piastres."

The Count went to his desk, opened a drawer filled with gold, and said:

"I hope you will not offend me by applying to anyone but me."

"You see that, on the contrary, I have come straight to you."

"Thank you. Take what you please."

"Is it absolutely necessary to send the money to Luigi Vampa?" asked the young man, looking fixedly at the Count.

"Judge for yourself. The postscript is explicit."

"I have an idea that if you took the trouble to reflect, you would find an easier way out of it," said Franz.

"How so?" returned the Count with surprise.

"I am sure that if we went together to Luigi Vampa, he would not refuse you Albert's freedom."

"What influence can I possibly have over a bandit?"

"Have you not just rendered him one of those services that are never forgotten?"

"What is that?"

"Have you not saved Peppino's life?"

"Who told you that?"

"No matter. I know it."

The Count knit his brows and remained silent a moment.

"And if I were to seek Vampa, would you accompany me?"

"If my society would not be disagreeable."

"Very well, then. It is a lovely night, and a drive in the outskirts of Rome will do us both good. Where is the man who brought this letter?"

"In the street."

"We must learn where we are going to. I will call him in."

The Count went to the window and whistled in a particular manner. The man left the cover of the wall and advanced into the centre of the street.

"*Salite!*" said the Count in the same tone in which he would have given an order to a servant. The messenger obeyed without the least hesitation, with alacrity rather, and, coming up the steps at a bound, entered the hotel; five seconds later he was at the door.

"Ah! it is you, Peppino," said the Count.

Instead of answering, Peppino threw himself on his knees and, seizing the Count's hands, covered them with kisses.

"You have not forgotten that I saved your life then!"

"No, Excellency, and I shall never forget it!" returned Peppino in a tone of profound gratitude.

"Never? That is a long time; but it is something that you believe so. Rise and answer me."

Peppino glanced anxiously at Franz.

"Oh, you may speak before His Excellency," said the Count, "he is one of my friends—permit me to give you this title," continued the Count in French, "it is necessary so as to give this man confidence."

"Good," returned Peppino, "I am ready to answer any questions Your Excellency may address to me."

"How did Viscount Albert fall into Luigi's hands?"

"Excellency, the Frenchman's carriage several times passed the one in which Teresa was driving. The Frenchman threw her a bouquet; Teresa returned the compliment; of course with the consent of the chief, who was in the carriage."

"What!" cried Franz. "Was it Luigi Vampa in the carriage with the Roman peasants?"

"It was he who drove, disguised as a coachman. The Frenchman took off his mask, and Teresa, with the chief's consent, did the same. The Frenchman asked for a rendezvous; Teresa gave him one, but instead of Teresa it was Beppo on the steps of the church of San Giacomo."

"What?" exclaimed Franz. "The peasant girl who snatched his *moccoletto* from him . . . ?"

"Was a lad of fifteen," replied Peppino. "But it was no shame on your friend to have been deceived. Beppo has taken in many more."

"And Beppo led him outside the walls?" asked the Count.

"Exactly so. A carriage was waiting at the end of Via Macello. Beppo got in and invited the Frenchman to follow him, and he did not wait to be asked twice. Beppo told him he was going to take him to a villa a league from Rome; the Frenchman assured him he would follow him to the ends of the world. When they were about two hundred yards outside the gates, the Frenchman became somewhat too familiar, so Beppo put a brace of pistols to his head; the coachman pulled up and did likewise. At the same time four of the band, who were concealed on the banks of the Almo, dashed up to the carriage doors. The Frenchman tried to defend himself and indeed nearly strangled Beppo, but he was powerless against five armed men and was forced to give in. They made him get out and walk along the bank of the river, and thus brought him to Teresa and Luigi, who were waiting for him in the catacombs of Saint Sebastian."

"Well, this seems quite a likely story," said the Count, turning to Franz. "What do you say to it?"

"Why, that I should think it very funny if it had happened to anyone but Albert."

"He is in a very picturesque spot. Do you know the catacombs of Saint Sebastian?"

"I have never been there, though I have often wanted to go."

"Well, here is an opportunity ready to hand and, it would be difficult to find a better one."

The Count rang, and a footman appeared.

"Order out the carriage," he said, "and remove the pistols which are in the holsters. You need not awaken the coachman. Ali will drive."

In a very short time the noise of wheels was heard and, the carriage stopped at the door. The Count took out his watch. "Half-past twelve," he said. "If we started at five o'clock, we should be in time, but the delay might cause your friend an uneasy night, so we had better go with all speed to rescue him from the hands of the brigands. Are you still resolved to accompany me?"

"More determined than ever."

"Well then, come along."

Franz and the Count went downstairs accompanied by Peppino and found the carriage at the door with Ali on the box. Franz and the Count got in, Peppino placed himself beside Ali, and they set off at a rapid pace. At the St. Sebastian gate the porter raised objections, but the Count of Monte Cristo produced an authorization from the Governor of Rome to leave or enter the city at any hour of the day or night; the portcullis was therefore raised, the porter had a louis for his trouble, and they went on their way. The road which the carriage now traversed was the ancient Appian Way, with its border of tombs. By the light of the moon which was now rising, Franz imagined from time to time that he saw a sentry emerge from behind a ruin and at a sign from Peppino disappear again.

A short time before they reached the Circus of Caracalla the carriage stopped; Peppino opened the door, and the Count and Franz alighted.

"We shall be there in about ten minutes," said the Count to his companion.

Taking Peppino aside, he gave him some instructions in a low voice, and Peppino went away, taking with him a torch they had brought with them in the well of the carriage.

Five minutes elapsed, during which time Franz saw a shepherd advance along a narrow path in between the irregularities of the ground and then disappear in the tall red grass that looked like the bristling mane of some gigantic lion.

"Now, let us follow him," said the Count. They went along the same path which, after about a hundred yards, led them down a sharp incline to the bottom of a little valley. There they perceived two men talking together in a sheltered nook. One of these men was Peppino, the other was a man on sentry-duty. Franz and the Count advanced, and the bandit saluted.

"Excellency," said Peppino, addressing the Count, "have the goodness to follow me; the opening to the catacombs is but two yards from here."

"Very well," said the Count, "lead the way."

And there behind a clump of bushes in the midst of several rocks an opening presented itself which was hardly large enough for a man to pass through. Peppino was the first to creep through the crack, but had not gone many steps before the subterranean passage suddenly widened. He stopped, lighted his torch, and looked round to ascertain whether the others were following him. Franz and the Count were still compelled to stoop, and there was only just sufficient width to allow them to walk two abreast. They had proceeded about fifty yards in this manner when the cry: "Who goes there?" brought them to a standstill. At the same time, they saw the light of their torch reflected on the barrel of a carbine in the darkness beyond.

"A friend," said Peppino, and, advancing alone, he said a few words in an undertone to the sentry, who, like the first, saluted and signed to the nocturnal visitors to continue their way.

Behind the sentry there were some twenty steps. Franz and the Count went down them and found themselves in front of the cross-roads of a burial place. Five roads diverged like the rays of a star, and the sides of the walls, hollowed out into niches in the shape of coffins, indicated that they had at last come to the catacombs. In one of these cavities, of which it was impossible to discover the size, some rays of light were visible. The Count placed his hand on Franz's shoulder and said: "Would you like to see a bandit camp at rest?"

"I should indeed," was Franz's reply.

"Come with me, then; Peppino, put out the torch!"

Peppino obeyed, and they were in complete darkness. They proceeded in silence, the Count guiding Franz as if he possessed the peculiar faculty of seeing in the dark. Three arches confronted them, the centre one forming a door. On one side these arches opened on to the corridor in which Franz and the Count were standing, and on the other into a large square room entirely surrounded by niches similar to those already mentioned. In the centre of this room were four stones, which had formerly served as an altar, as was evident from the cross which still surmounted them. A lamp, placed at the base of a pillar, lighted with a pale and flickering flame the singular scene which presented itself to the eyes of the two visitors concealed in the shadow. A man was seated reading, with his elbow on the column and his back to the arches, through which the newcomers watched him. This was the chief of the band, Luigi Vampa. Around him, grouped according to fancy, could be seen some twenty brigands lying in their mantles or with their backs against one of the stone seats which ran all around the Columbarium; each one had his carbine within reach. Down below, silent, scarcely visible, and like a shadow, was a sentry, who was walking up and down before a kind of opening. When the Count thought Franz had gazed long enough on this picturesque tableau, he raised his finger to his lips to warn him to be quiet, and, ascending the three steps which led from the corridor to the Columbarium, entered the room by the centre arch, and advanced toward Vampa, who was so intent on the book before him that he did not hear the sound of his footsteps.

"Who goes there?" cried the sentry, who was on the alert and saw by the light of the lamp a growing shadow approaching his chief.

At this cry Vampa rose quickly, at the same time taking a pistol from his belt. In a moment twenty bandits were on their feet with their carbines levelled at the Count.

"Well," said he in a perfectly calm voice, and without moving a muscle, "well, my dear Vampa, it appears to me that you receive your friends with a great deal of ceremony!"

"Ground arms!" shouted the chief with a commanding sweep of one hand, whilst with the other he respectfully took off his hat. Then, turning to the singular person who was watching this scene, he said: "Excuse me, Count, but I was far from expecting the honour of a visit from you and did not recognize you."

"It seems that your memory is equally short in everything, Vampa," said the Count, "and that, not only do you forget people's faces, but also the conditions you make with them."

"What conditions have I forgotten, Count?" inquired the bandit with the air of a man who, having committed an error, is anxious to repair it.

"Was it not agreed," asked the Count, "that not only my person but that of my friends, should be respected by you?"

"And how have I broke faith, Your Excellency?"

"You have this evening carried off and conveyed hither the Viscount Albert de Morcerf. Well," continued the Count, in a tone which made Franz shudder, "this young gentleman is one of my friends, this young gentleman is staying in the same hotel as myself, this young gentleman has done the Corso for a week in my carriage, and yet, I repeat to you, you have carried him off and conveyed him hither, and," added the Count, taking a letter from his pocket, "you have set a ransom on him as if he were just anybody."

"Why didn't some of you tell me all this?" inquired the brigand chief, turning toward his men, who all retreated before his look. "Why have you allowed me to fail thus in my word toward a gentleman like the Count who has all our lives in his hands? By heavens! if I thought that one of you knew that the gentleman was a friend of His Excellency's, I would blow his brains out with my own hand!"

"You see," said the Count, turning toward Franz, "I told you there was some mistake."

"Are you not alone?" asked Vampa with uneasiness.

"I am with the person to whom this letter was addressed, and to whom I desired to prove that Luigi Vampa was a man of his word. Come, Your Excellency, here is Luigi Vampa, who will himself express to you his regret at the mistake he has made."

Franz approached; the chief advanced several steps toward him.

"Your Excellency is right welcome," he said to him. "You heard what the Count just said and also my reply; let me add that I would not have had such a thing happen, not even for the four thousand piastres at which I had fixed your friend's ransom."

"But where is the Viscount?" said Franz, looking round anxiously.

"Nothing has happened to him, I hope?" asked the Count with a frown.

"The prisoner is there," replied Vampa, pointing to the recess in front of which the bandit sentry was on guard, "and I will go myself and tell him he is free."

The chief went toward the place he had pointed out as Albert's prison, and Franz and the Count followed. Vampa drew back a bolt and pushed open a door.

By the gleam of a lamp Albert was seen wrapped up in a cloak which one of the bandits had lent him, lying in a corner of the room in profound slumber.

"Well, I never!" said the Count, smiling in his own peculiar way. "That is not so bad for a man who is to be shot at seven o'clock to-morrow morning!"

Vampa looked at Albert in admiration. "You are right, Count," he said, "this must be one of your friends."

Then, going up to Albert, he touched him on the shoulder, saying: "Will Your Excellency please to awaken?"

Albert stretched out his arms, rubbed his eyes, and said: "Ah, is that you, captain? Well, you might have let me sleep. I was having such a delightful dream. I was dancing the galop at the Duke's with the Countess G——"

Then he drew from his pocket his watch, which he had kept by him that he might see how the time sped.

"Half-past one only!" said he. "Why the devil do you rouse me at this hour?"

"To tell you that you are free, Excellency! A gentleman to whom I can refuse nothing has come to command your liberty."

"Come here?"

"Yes, here."

"Really, that's very kind of him!"

Albert looked round and perceived Franz.

"What! is it you, Franz, who have been so friendly . . . ?"

"No, not I, but our friend the Count of Monte Cristo."

"You, Count?" said Albert gaily, the while arranging his neck-band and cuffs. "You are really a most valuable friend, and I hope you will consider me as eternally obliged to you, in the first place for the carriage and now for this service!" And he put out his hand; the Count shuddered as he gave his own, but he gave it nevertheless.

The bandit gazed on this scene with amazement; he was evidently accustomed to see his prisoners grovel before him, yet here was one whose gay spirits never faltered, even for one moment. As for Franz, he was delighted at the way in which Albert had maintained the honour of his country, even in the presence of death.

"If you make haste, Albert," he said, "we shall still have time to finish the night at the Duke's. You can continue your interrupted galop, so that you will owe no ill-will to Signor Luigi, who has, indeed, acted like a gentleman throughout this whole affair."

"Quite right, we may reach the Palazzo by two o'clock. Signor Luigi," continued Albert, "is there any formality to fulfil before I take leave of Your Excellency?"

"None, signore," replied the bandit. "You are as free as the air."

"Well, then, a happy and merry life to you! Come, messieurs, come! Ah! excuse me! May I?" And he lighted a cigar at a torch which one of the bandits was holding. "Now, Count," he continued, "let us make all possible speed. I am most anxious to finish my evening at the Duke of Bracciano's."

They found the carriage where they had left it. The Count said a word to Ali, and the horses went off at a great speed.

It was just two o'clock by Albert's watch when the two friends entered the ball-room.

Their return made quite a stir, but, as they entered together, all uneasiness on Albert's account was instantly dispelled.

"Madame, you were kind enough to promise me a galop," said Viscount Morcerf, advancing toward the Countess, "I am rather late in claiming this gracious promise, but my friend here, whose truthful character you well know, will assure you the delay was through no fault of mine."

At this moment the music struck up for a waltz, and Albert put his arm round the Countess's waist and disappeared with her in the whirl of dancers. Franz in the meanwhile was pondering over the peculiar shudder that shook the Count of Monte Cristo's whole frame when he had been, in some sort, compelled to give his hand to Albert.

On rising the next morning, Albert's first thought was to pay a visit to the Count. He had thanked him in the evening, it is true, but it seemed to him it was not too much to thank a man twice for a service such as the Count had rendered him.

The Count of Monte Cristo attracted Franz, yet filled him with terror, and he would not let Albert go alone. They were shown into the salon, where the Count joined them five minutes later.

Albert advanced toward him, saying: "Permit me, Count, to say to you this morning what I expressed so badly yesterday evening. Never shall I forget the way in which you came to my assistance, nor the fact that I practically owe you my life."

"My dear fellow," replied the Count smiling, "you are exaggerating your obligations towards me. You are indebted to me for a small economy of some twenty thousand francs in your travelling budget, and that is all; it is scarcely worth mentioning. On the other hand," he added, "permit me to congratulate you on your admirable coolness and indifference in the face of danger."

"Oh! tut, tut!" said Albert. "I tried to imagine I had had a quarrel resulting in a duel, and I wanted to show these bandits that though duels are fought in nearly every country of the world, it is only the French who fight with a smile on their lips. This, however, in no way lessens my obligations towards you, and I have come to ask you whether I, my friends, or my acquaintances cannot serve you in any way. My father, the Count of Morcerf, who is of Spanish origin, holds a high position both in France and in Spain, and he and all who love me will be only too pleased to be of any service to you."

"I will own that I expected your offer, Monsieur de Morcerf," said the Count, "and I accept it wholeheartedly. I had already decided to ask you a great favour. I have never yet been to Paris. I do not know it at all. I should probably have undertaken this indispensable journey long ago, had I known some one to introduce me into Paris society. Your offer has decided me. When I go to France, my dear Monsieur de Morcerf" (the Count accompanied these words with a peculiar smile), "will you undertake to introduce me to the society of the capital, where I shall be as complete a stranger as though I came from Huron or Cochin China?"

"It would give me great pleasure to do so," replied Albert. "You can depend on me and mine to do all in our power for you."

"I accept your offer," said the Count, "for I assure you I have only been waiting for just such an opportunity to realize a hope I have had in view for some time past."

"When do you propose going?"

"When shall you be there yourself?"

"Oh, I shall be there in a fortnight or three weeks at the latest."

"Very well," said the Count, "I will give you three months, which would be allowing a wide margin." Then examining a calendar that was hanging near the mirror, he continued: "To-day is the twenty-first of February. Will it suit you if I call on you on the twenty-first of May at half-past ten in the morning?"

"Splendid!" said Albert, "breakfast will be ready."

"Where do you live?"

"Rue du Helder, number twenty-seven."

"Very well," said the Count. He took his notebook from his pocket and wrote: "Rue du Helder, number twenty-seven, May the twenty-first at 10.30 A.M." "And now," said he, replacing his notebook, "you may rely on me. The hand of your timepiece will not be more accurate than I shall be."

"Shall I see you again before I leave?" Albert asked.

"That depends upon when you leave."

"I leave at five o'clock to-morrow evening."

"In that case I must bid you farewell. I have to go to Naples on business, and shall not be back until Saturday or Sunday. What about you, Baron?" the Count asked Franz. "Are you leaving Rome too?"

"Yes, I am going to Venice. I intend staying in Italy for another year or two."

"We shall not see you in Paris, then?"

"I regret that I shall not have that pleasure."

"Well then, I wish you a safe journey, messieurs," said the Count to the two friends shaking hands with them both.

It was the first time Franz had touched this man's hand, and he felt a shudder go through him, for his hand was as cold as a corpse.

"It is quite understood then," said Albert, "that on your honour, you will visit me at number twenty-seven, Rue du Helder, at ten-thirty on the morning of the twenty-first of May, is it not?"

"At ten-thirty on the morning of the twenty-first of May," repeated the Count.

Upon this the two young men took their leave of the Count and went to their own quarters.

"What is the matter with you?" Albert asked Franz. "You have a somewhat worried look!"

"I must own," said Franz, "that the Count is a peculiar man, and I feel very uneasy about the appointment he has made with you in Paris."

"Uneasy about our appointment! Really, my dear Franz, you must be mad!" exclaimed Albert.

"Whether I am mad or not, that's what I feel about it," said Franz.

## CHAPTER XXX

## THE GUESTS

IN the house in the Rue du Helder, to which Albert de Morcerf had invited the Count of Monte Cristo, great preparations were being made on the morning of the twenty-first of May to do honour to the guest.

Albert de Morcerf's house was at the corner of a large courtyard opposite another building set apart for the servants' quarters. Only two of the windows faced the street; three others overlooked the court-yard, and two at the back overlooked the garden. Between the court and the garden was the spacious and fashionable residence of the Count and Countess of Morcerf, built in the unsightly Imperial style. A high wall ran the whole length of the property facing the street, and was surmounted at intervals by vases, and divided in the middle by a large wrought-iron gate, with gilt scrollings, which served as a carriage entrance; while pedestrians passed in and out of the building through a small door next to the porter's lodge.

In the choice of a house for Albert it was easy to discern the deli-cate foresight of a mother, who, while not wishing to be separated from her son, realized that a young man of the Viscount's age needed entire liberty. On the other hand, the intelligent egotism of a young man enchanted with the free and easy life of an only son who had been thoroughly pampered could also be recognized.

On the morning of the appointed day the young man was sitting in a small salon on the ground floor. A valet entered. He had in one hand a bundle of newspapers, which he deposited on a table, and in the other a packet of letters, which he gave to his young master.

Albert glanced carelessly at the different missives, selected two per-fumed envelopes which were written in a small, neat handwriting, opened them and pursued their contents with a certain amount of attention.

"How did these letters come?" he asked.

"The one came by post, and the other one was brought by Madame Danglars' valet."

"Inform Madame Danglars that I accept the seat she offers me in her box. Wait a moment . . . some time during the day tell Rosa that when I leave the Opera, I will sup with her as she asks. Take her six bottles of assorted wines, Cyprus, sherry, and Malaga, and a barrel of Ostend oysters; get the oysters from Borel's, and be sure to tell him they are for me."

"What time do you wish breakfast, monsieur?"

"What time is it now?"

"A quarter to ten."

"Very well, have it ready punctually by half-past. By the way, is the Countess up yet?"

"If the Viscount wishes, I will inquire."

"Do—and ask her for one of her liqueur cellarets, mine is incomplete; tell her also that I shall have the honour of calling on her at about three o'clock, and that I ask permission to introduce some one to her."

The valet left the room. Albert threw himself on the divan, opened two or three newspapers, looked at the theatre page, turned up his nose on perceiving that an opera and not a ballet was to be given, looked in vain amongst the advertisements for a toothpowder of which he had heard, and finally threw down one after the other the three leading papers of Paris, muttering between his yawns: "Really these newspapers become more and more boring every day!"

Just then a carriage drew up at the door, and a moment later the valet announced M. Lucien Debray. A tall, fair young man with a pale face, clear grey eyes, and thin, compressed lips, wearing a blue suit with chased gold buttons, a white necktie, and tortoise-shell eyeglasses on a fine silk cord, entered the room with a semi-official air, without a smile and without saying a word.

"Good morning, Lucien! Good morning!" said Albert. "What punctuality! Did I say punctuality? Why, I expected you last, and you have arrived at five minutes to ten, whereas the time fixed was half-past ten. It is really marvellous!"

"Monsieur Beauchamp," announced the servant.

"Come in, come in! you wielder of the terrible pen!" said Albert, rising and advancing to meet the young man. "Here is Debray, who detests you and will not read your works. Anyhow, that is what he says."

"Quite right too, for I criticize his works without even knowing what he does," said Beauchamp. "Good morning." Then, turning to Albert, he asked: "What sort of people are you expecting for breakfast?"

"A gentleman and a diplomat," was the reply.

"That means waiting another two hours for the gentleman and about three hours for the diplomat."

"Nonsense, Beauchamp," said Albert, "we shall sit down to breakfast punctually at half-past ten. In the meantime, follow Debray's good example and taste my sherry and biscuits."

"Well, then, I will stay. I must do something to distract my thoughts this morning."

"Monsieur de Château-Renaud! Monsieur Maximilian Morrel!" said the valet, announcing two fresh guests.

"Now we are all here and can go into breakfast," said Beauchamp. "If I remember rightly, you only expected two more guests."

"Morrel?" Albert murmured, surprised. "Morrel? Who is that?"

But before he had finished speaking, Monsieur de Château-Renaud, a handsome young man of thirty, and a gentleman to his fingertips, took Albert by the arm, saying:

"Allow me to introduce to you Monsieur Maximilian Morrel, Captain of Spahis, my friend and, what is more, my saviour. Salute my hero, Viscount!"

So saying, he stepped to one side and disclosed to the view of all present the tall and noble-looking young man with the wide brow, penetrating eyes and black moustache, whom our readers will remember having seen at Marseilles in circumstances sufficiently dramatic to prevent his being forgotten. A handsome uniform, partly French and partly Oriental, set off to perfection his broad chest decorated with the cross of the Legion of Honour, and showed up his graceful and stalwart figure. The young officer bowed with easy politeness. Being strong, he was graceful in his every movement.

"The Baron of Château-Renaud knew what pleasure it would give me, monsieur, to make your acquaintance," said Albert courteously. "You are his friend, be mine too."

"Well said!" remarked Château-Renaud, "and I hope that, given the occasion, he will do as much for you, Viscount, as he has done for me."

"What has he done for you?"

"Oh, nothing worth mentioning!" said Morrel. "My friend is exaggerating."

"What? Not worth mentioning!" said Château-Renaud. "Is life, then, not worth mentioning? Upon my word, that is rather too philosophical, my dear Morrel."

"It is evident from all this that Captain Morrel saved your life. Tell us all about it," said Beauchamp.

"Beauchamp, old fellow, you know I am dying of hunger," said Debray. "Don't begin any of your stories now."

"Well, that won't prevent us from sitting down to table," replied Beauchamp. "Château-Renaud can tell us the story while we are at breakfast."

"Messieurs," said Albert, "it is not yet a quarter-past ten, and you know I am expecting another guest."

"Well, then, as we cannot yet go into breakfast," said Debray, "pour yourself out a glass of sherry as we have done, and tell us what took place."

"You all know that I had a fancy for a trip to Africa," began Château-Renaud. "Being unwilling to let such talents as mine lie dormant, I decided to try upon the Arabs some new pistols that had been given me. I therefore embarked for Oran, whence I reached Constantine, arriving in time to witness the raising of the siege. I retreated with the others, and withstood the rain during the day and the snow at night fairly well for forty-eight hours. On the morning of the third day, my horse died of the cold, poor beast! My horse now being dead, I was compelled to make my retreat on foot. Six Arabs rushed upon me at a gallop to cut off my head. I dropped two of them with two shots of my gun and two more with my pistol; but there were still two more, and I was disarmed. One of the Arabs caught hold of me by the hair—that is why I now wear it short, for one never knows what may happen—the other one put his yataghan to my throat, and I already felt the cold point of the steel when this gentleman, whom you see here, charged down upon them, killed with a shot of his pistol the one who held me by the hair, and with his sword severed the head of the other who was making ready to cut my throat. He had set himself the task of saving a man on that particular day, and chance chose me to be that man. When I am rich, I shall have a statue of Chance made by Klagmann or Marochetti."

"It was the fifth of September," said Morrel smiling, "the anniversary of the day on which my father was miraculously saved. Every year I celebrate the day as far as possible by some action——"

"The story Monsieur Morrel is alluding to is a most interesting one," continued Château-Renaud, "and he will tell it you when he knows you better. To-day let us fill our stomachs and not our memories. What time are you having breakfast, Albert?"

"At half-past ten."

"To the minute?" asked Debray, taking out his watch.

"You must give me five minutes' grace," said Morcerf, "for I am expecting a saviour too."

"Whose saviour?"

"Mine, to be sure," replied Morcerf. "Do you think I cannot be saved, too, and that is only Arabs who cut off heads? Our breakfast is a philanthropic one, and we shall have at table two benefactors of humanity, at least I hope so."

"Do you think he is likely to be punctual?" asked Debray.

"Everything is possible with him."

"Well, with the five minutes' grace, we have only ten left."

"I will profit by them to tell you something about my guest. I was at Rome last Carnival."

"We know that," said Beauchamp.

"Yes, but what you don't know is that I was carried off by bandits."

"There are no bandits!" exclaimed Debrary.

"Indeed there are, and ugly fellows too, or rather I should say fine ones, for I found them frightfully handsome. To continue, the brigands carried me off to a very gloomy spot called the Catacombs of Saint Sebastian. I was told I was their prisoner subject to a ransom, a mere trifle of four thousand Roman crowns. Unfortunately I had no more than one thousand five hundred. I was at the end of my journey and my credit was exhausted, so I wrote to Franz. Oh, yes, Franz was there too, and you can ask him whether I am telling you the absolute truth or not. Well, I wrote to Franz that if he did not come with the four thousand crowns by six o'clock, I should have gone to join the blessed saints and glorious martyrs by ten minutes past. And I can assure you that Monsieur Luigi Vampa (that is the name of the chief of the bandits) would have kept most scrupulously to his word."

"But Franz did arrive with the four thousand crowns?" said Château-Renaud. "A man bearing the name of Franz d'Épinay or Albert de Morcerf is certainly not at a loss for a sum of that amount!"

"No, he simply came accompanied by the guest whom I hope to introduce to you in a few minutes. He said two words in the chief's ear, and I was free!"

"I suppose they even apologized for having kidnapped you?" said Beauchamp.

"Just so," was the reply.

"Why, this man is a second Ariosto!"

"No, he is nothing more nor less than the Count of Monte Cristo!"

"There is no Count of Monte Cristo!" said Debray.

"I do not think there is," added Château-Renaud with the air of a man who has got the whole of European nobility at his fingertips. "Does anyone know of a Count of Monte Cristo anywhere?"

"Perhaps he comes from the Holy Land," said Beauchamp. "One of his ancestors most likely owned Calvary just as the Mortemart owned the Dead Sea."

"Pardon me, messieurs, but I think I can help you out of the dilemma," said Maximilian. "Monte Cristo is a small island I have often heard mentioned by my father's old sailors. It is a grain of sand in the middle of the Mediterranean, an atom in the infinite."

"You are quite right," said Albert, "and the man I speak of is lord and master of this grain of sand, this atom. He has doubtless purchased his title of Count somewhere in Tuscany."

"There is no Count of Monte Cristo," exclaimed Debray. "There is half-past ten striking!"

"Confess that you have had a nightmare, and let's go in to breakfast."

The sound of the clock had hardly died away, however, when the door opened and the valet announced:

"His Excellency the Count of Monte Cristo!"

All those present started involuntarily, thus showing the impression Albert's recital had made on them. Albert himself was seized with a sudden emotion. They had not heard the carriage in the street nor any steps in the antechamber; even the door had been opened noiselessly.

The Count appeared on the threshold dressed with the utmost simplicity, yet the most exacting dandy could not have found fault with his attire. He advanced smiling into the centre of the room and went straight up to Albert who shook his hand warmly.

"Punctuality is the politeness of kings," said Monte Cristo, "at any rate according to one of our sovereigns, but in spite of their good will, travellers cannot always achieve it. I trust, however, that you will accept my goodwill, Count, and pardon me the two or three seconds by which I have failed in keeping our appointment. Five hundred leagues are not made without some trouble, especially in France where it is apparently forbidden to beat the postilions."

"I was just announcing your visit to some of my friends whom I have invited to do honour to the promise you were good enough to make me, and whom I now have the pleasure of introducing to you. They are the Count of Château-Renaud, who traces his nobility back to the twelve peers and whose ancestors had a seat at the Round Table; Monsieur Lucien Debray, private secretary to the Minister of the Interior; Monsieur Beauchamp, a formidable journalist and the terror of the French Government; and Monsieur Maximilian Morrel, Captain of Spahis."

On hearing this latter name the Count, who had till now bowed courteously, but almost with the proverbial coldness and formality of the English, involuntarily took a step forward, and a slight tinge of red spread over his pale cheek.

"You wear the uniform of the new conquerors, monsieur," he said. "It is a handsome uniform."

One could not have said what caused the Count's voice to vibrate so deeply or why his eye, usually so calm and limpid, now shone as though against his will.

"Have you never seen our Africans, Count?" Albert asked.

"Never!" replied the Count, who had gained complete possession over himself once more.

"Beneath this uniform beats one of the bravest and noblest hearts of the army."

"Oh, Monsieur de Morcerf!" interrupted Morrel.

"Let me speak, Captain. We have just heard tell of such an heroic action on his part," continued Albert, "that though I see him to-day for the first time, I ask his permission to introduce him to you as my friend."

At these words there was again discernible in Monte Cristo that strange fixed stare, that furtive flush, and that slight trembling of the eyelids which in him denoted emotion.

"You have a noble heart!" said he.

"Messieurs," said Albert, "breakfast is ready. Count, permit me to show you the way."

They passed into the dining-room in silence.

The Count was, it soon became apparent, a most moderate eater and drinker. Albert remarked this and expressed his fear that at the outset Parisian life might be distasteful to the traveller in the most material, but at the same time the most essential point.

"If you knew me better," said the Count smiling, "you would not worry about such an almost humiliating matter in regard to a traveller like myself, who has lived successively on macaroni at Naples, polenta at Madrid, olla podrida at Valencia, pilau at Constantinople, karrick in India, and swallows' nests in China. Cooking does not enter into the calculations of a cosmopolitan like myself. I eat whatever is set before me, only I eat very little. To-day, however, when you reproach me with moderation, I have a good appetite, for I have not eaten since yesterday morning."

"Not since yesterday morning?" the guests exclaimed. "You have not eaten for twenty-four hours?"

"No, I was compelled to deviate from my route to get some information at Nîmes, which made me a little late, so I would not wait for anything."

"So you ate in your carriage?" said Morcerf.

"No, I slept as I always do when I am bored and have not the courage to amuse myself, or when I am hungry and have not the desire to eat."

"Can you then command sleep at will?" asked Morrel.

"More or less. I have an infallible recipe."

"That would be an excellent thing for us Africans, who have not always enough to eat and rarely enough to drink," said Morrel.

"That may be," said Monte Cristo. "Unfortunately, however, my recipe, which is excellent for a man like myself who leads an exceptional life, would be very dangerous when administered to an army, which might not wake when it was needed."

"But do you always carry this drug about with you?" asked Beauchamp, who, being a journalist, was very incredulous.

"Always," replied Monte Cristo.

"Would you mind if I asked to see one of these precious pills?" continued Beauchamp, hoping to take him at a disadvantage.

"Not at all," replied the Count, and he took from his pocket a wonderful *bonbonnière* scooped out of a single emerald and closed by means of a gold screw, which, being turned, gave passage to a small round object of a greenish colour and about the size of a pea. The pill had an acrid and penetrating odour. There were four or five of them in the emerald, which was large enough to contain a dozen.

The *bonbonnière* passed from one guest to another, but it was to examine the wonderful emerald rather than to see the pills.

"It is a magnificent emerald, and the largest I have ever seen, though my mother has some remarkable family jewels," said Château-Renaud.

"I had three like that one," returned Monte Cristo. "I gave one of them to the Grand Seigneur, who has had it mounted on his sword, and the second to His Holiness the Pope, who has had it set in his tiara opposite one that is very similar, but not quite so magnificent, which was given to his predecessor, Pius the Seventh, by the Emperor Napoleon. I have kept the third one for myself, and have had it hollowed out. This has certainly reduced its value by one-half, but has made it more adapted to the use I wished to make of it."

Every one looked at Monte Cristo in astonishment. He spoke so simply that it was evident he either was telling the truth or was mad.

"What did the two sovereigns give you in exchange for your magnificent gift?" asked Debray.

"The Grand Seigneur gave me a woman's freedom; His Holiness the life of a man."

"Was it not Peppino you saved?" exclaimed Morcerf. "Was it not in his favour that you made use of your right to a pardon?"

"Perhaps," said Monte Cristo smiling.

"You have no idea, Count, what pleasure it gives me to hear you talk thus," said Morcerf. "I had spoken of you to my friends as a fabulous man, a magician out of the *Arabian Nights,* a sorcerer of the Middle Ages, but Parisians are so subtle in paradoxes that they think the most incontestable truths are but flights of the imagination when such truths do not enter into their daily routine. For instance, they contest the existence of the bandits of the Roman Campagna or the Pontine Marshes. Pray tell them yourself, Count, that I was kidnapped by these bandits and that in all probability, without your generous intervention, I should to-day be awaiting the eternal resurrection in the Catacombs of Saint Sebastian instead of inviting them to breakfast in my humble little house in the Rue du Helder."

"Tut, tut! You promised me never to speak of that trifle," said Monte Cristo.

"If I relate all that I know," said Morcerf, "will you promise to tell what I do not know?"

"That is only fair," replied Monte Cristo.

"Well, then, I will relate my story, though my pride must inevitably suffer thereby," began Albert. "For three days I thought I was the object of the attentions of a masked lady whom I took to be the descendant of Tullia or Poppaea, whereas I was but being lured on by the coquetry of a *contadina;* you will note I say *contadina* to avoid using the word peasant. All I know is that, fool that I was, I mistook for this *contadina* a young bandit of fifteen or sixteen with a beardless chin and slim figure. Just as I was taking the liberty of imprinting a kiss on his chaste shoulder, he put his pistol to my throat and with the aid of seven or eight of his companions, led or rather dragged me to the depths of the Catacombs of Saint Sebastian. Here I was informed that if by six o'clock the next morning I had not produced a ransom of four thousand crowns, I should have ceased to exist by a quarter-past six. The letter is still to be seen and is in Franz's possession, signed by me and with a postscript by Luigi Vampa. If you doubt my word, I will write to Franz, who will have the signature legalized. That is all I know. What I do not know, Count, is how you contrived to instil such great respect into the Roman bandits, who have respect for so little. I will own that both Franz and I were lost in admiration."

"I have known this famous Vampa for more than ten years," said the Count. "When he was quite young and still a shepherd, I once gave him a gold coin for showing me my way. To be under no obligation to me, he gave me a poniard carved by himself which you must have seen in my collection of arms. Later on, whether it was that he had forgotten this little exchange of presents which should have sealed our friendship or whether it was that he did not recognize me, I know not, but he tried to kidnap me. I, however, captured him together with twelve of his men. I could have delivered him up to Roman justice, which is somewhat expeditious, but I did not do so. I set him and his men free."

"On condition that he should sin no more!" said the journalist laughing. "It delights me to see that they have kept their word so conscientiously."

"No, Monsieur Beauchamp, on the simple condition that they should always respect me and mine. And," continued the Count, "I will appeal to these gentlemen, how could I have left my host in the hands of these terrible bandits, as you are pleased to call them? Besides, you know I had a motive in saving you. I thought you might be useful in introducing me into Parisian society when I visited France. No doubt you thought this but a vague plan on my part, but to-day you see you are faced with the stern reality and must submit to it under pain of breaking your word."

"And I shall keep my word," said Morcerf, "but I fear you will be greatly disillusioned, accustomed as you are to mountains, picturesque surroundings, and fantastic horizons, whereas France is such a prosaic country and Paris such a civilized city. There is but one service I can render you, my dear Count, and in regard to that, I place myself entirely at your disposal. I can introduce you myself or get my friends to introduce you everywhere. You have really no need of anyone though. With your name, your fortune, and your talented mind"— Monte Cristo bowed with a somewhat ironical smile—"you can present yourself everywhere and will be well received. I can, therefore, only serve you in one way. If my knowledge of Parisian customs, of what is comfortable, and of our shops can be of any use to you, I can assist you in finding a suitable establishment. I will not offer to share my apartments with you, as I shared yours at Rome, for, except for myself, you would not see a shadow here, unless it were the shadow of a woman."

"Ah, the reservation of a family man! May I congratulate you on your coming happiness?"

"It is nothing more than a project, Count."

"And he who says project means accomplishment," retorted Debray.

"Not at all!" said Morcerf. "My father is anxious it should be so, and I hope soon to introduce to you, if not my wife, at least my future wife, Mademoiselle Eugénie Danglars."

"Eugénie Danglars!" exclaimed Monte Cristo. "One moment . . . Is not her father Baron Danglars?"

"Yes, a newly created Baron."

"What does that matter so long as he has rendered a service to the State which merits such a distinction?" was Monte Cristo's reply.

"He has rendered the State very signal services," said Beauchamp. "Though a Liberal in opinions, in eighteen-twenty-nine he effected a loan of six millions for King Charles the Tenth, who made him a Baron and Commander of the Legion of Honour. Now he wears the ribbon, not in his waistcoat pocket as one would imagine, but in full view in the buttonhole of his coat."

"Oh, Beauchamp, Beauchamp," said Morcerf, smiling. "Keep that for the *Corsaire* and the *Charivari,* but spare my future father-in-law in my presence." Then, turning to Monte Cristo, he said: "You mentioned the Baron's name just now as though you knew him?"

"I do not know him," said Monte Cristo, carelessly, "but in all probability I shall not be long in making his acquaintance, since I have a credit opened with him through Richard and Blount of London, Arstein and Eskeles of Vienna, and Thomson and French of Rome."

As he pronounced these last two names, Monte Cristo stole a glance at Maximilian Morrel, and if he expected to startle him, he was not disappointed. The young man started as though he had had an electric shock.

"Thomson and French?" said he. "Do you know that firm?"

"They are my bankers in Rome," said the Count calmly. "Can I exert my influence with them on your behalf?"

"You might, perhaps, be able to help us in inquiries which have up to the present been ineffective. Some years back, these bankers rendered a great service to our firm, and for some reason have always denied having done so."

"I am at your orders," replied Monte Cristo.

"But in speaking of Monsieur Danglars, we have altogether strayed from the subject of our conversation," said Maximilian. "We were talking about a suitable house for the Count of Monte Cristo. I should like to offer him a suite in a charming little house in the Pompadour style which my sister has taken in the Rue Meslay."

"You have a sister?" asked Monte Cristo.

"Yes, and an excellent one."

"Married?"

"For the past nine years."

"Happy?"

"As happy as it is permitted to a human creature to be," replied Maximilian. "She is married to a man she loves, who remained faithful to us in our bad fortune, Emmanuel Herbault. I live with them when I am on furlough," continued Maximilian, "and my brother-in-law Emmanuel and I will be only too pleased to place ourselves at your disposal, Count."

"Thank you, Monsieur Morrel, thank you very much. I shall be most happy if you will introduce me to your brother-in-law and your sister, but I cannot accept your kind offer of a suite in your sister's house as my accommodation is already provided for."

"What? Are you going to put up at an hotel?" exclaimed Morcerf. "You will not be very comfortable."

"I have decided to have my own house at Paris. I sent my valet on in advance, and he will have bought a house and furnished it ere this. He arrived here a week ago, and will have scoured the town with the instinct a sporting dog alone possesses. He knows all my whims, my likes, and my needs, and will have arranged everything to my liking. He knew I was to arrive at ten o'clock this morning, and was waiting for me at the Barrière de Fontainebleau from nine o'clock, and gave me this piece of paper. It is my new address. Read it for yourself."

So saying, Monte Cristo passed Albert a piece of paper.

"Number thirty, Champs Élysées," read Morcerf.

The young men stared at one another. They did not know whether Monte Cristo was joking; there was such an air of simplicity about every word he uttered in spite of its originality, that it was impossible to believe he was not speaking the truth. Besides, why should he lie?

"We must content ourselves with doing the Count any little service within our power," said Beauchamp. "In my capacity of journalist, I will give him access to all the theatres of Paris."

"Thank you, monsieur," said the Count smiling. "I have already instructed my steward to take a box for me at every theatre. You know my steward, Monsieur de Morcerf?"

"Is it by any chance that worthy Signor Bertuccio, who understands the hiring of windows so well?"

"The very same; you saw him the day you honoured me by breakfasting with me. He is a very good man and has been a soldier and a smuggler, and in fact has tried his hand at everything possible. I would not even say that he has not been mixed up with the police for some trifling stabbing affair."

"Then you have your household complete," said Château-Renaud, "you have a house in the Champs Élysées, servants and stewards. All you want now is a mistress."

"I have something better than that. I have a slave. You take your mistresses from the Opera House, the Vaudeville, the Music Halls, but I bought mine at Constantinople. She cost me dear, but I have nothing to fear so far as she is concerned."

"But you forget that we are 'Franks by name and frank by nature,' as King Charles said, and that the moment she steps on French soil your slave becomes free," said Debray.

"Who will tell her that?" asked Monte Cristo.

"Why, the first person who sees her."

"She speaks nothing but Romaic."

"That is a different matter, but shall we not at least see her? Or have you eunuchs as well as mutes?"

"Oh, dear no," said Monte Cristo. "I do not carry Orientalism so far as that. Everybody around me is at liberty to leave me, and on leaving me will have no further need of me or anyone else. It may be that is the reason why they do not leave me."

They had long since passed to dessert and cigars.

"My dear Albert, it is half-past twelve," said Debray rising. "Your guest is charming, but you know the best of friends must part. I must return to my office. Are you coming, Morrel?"

"As soon as I have handed the Count my card. He has promised to pay us a visit at fourteen, Rue Meslay."

"Rest assured that I shall not forget," said the Count with a bow.

Maximilian Morrel left with the Baron of Château-Renaud, leaving Monte Cristo alone with Morcerf.

## CHAPTER XXXI

## THE PRESENTATION

WHEN Albert was alone with Monte Cristo, he said: "Permit me to commence my office of cicerone by showing you my bachelor quarters. Accustomed as you are to the palaces of Italy, it will be interesting for you to note in what a small space a young man of Paris can live, and not feel that he is too badly off in regard to accommodation."

Albert conducted the Count to his study, which was his favourite room.

Monte Cristo was a worthy appreciator of all the things Albert had collected here: old cabinets, Japanese porcelain, Oriental stuffs, Venetian glass, weapons of all countries of the world; everything was familiar to him, and he recognized at a glance their date and country of origin. Morcerf had expected to be the guide, whereas it was he who, under the Count's guidance, followed a course of archaeology, mineralogy, and natural history. He led his guest into the salon, which was filled with works of modern artists; there were landscapes by Dupré, Arabian horsemen by Delacroix, water colours by Boulanger, paintings by Diaz, drawings by Decamps—in a word, all that modern art can give in exchange and as recompense for the art lost and gone with ages long since past.

Albert expected to have something new to show the traveller this time at least, but, to his surprise, without looking for the signatures, many of which were only initials, the Count at once named the author of every picture in such a manner that it was easy to see that each name was not only known to him, but that each style had been appreciated and studied.

From the salon they passed into the bed-chamber. It was a model of good taste and simple elegance. One portrait only, signed Leopold Robert, loomed forth from an unpolished gilt frame.

It was this portrait that first of all attracted the Count's attention, for he took three rapid steps across the room and suddenly stopped in front of it. It was the portrait of a young woman of about five- or six-and-twenty, with a dark complexion, eyes which glowed beneath languishing eyelids. She wore the picturesque costume of a Catalan fisherwoman, a red and black bodice, and had golden pins stuck in her hair. She was looking at the sea, and her beautiful profile was outlined against the two-fold azure of sky and ocean.

"This is a beautiful woman you have here, Viscount," said Monte Cristo in a perfectly calm voice, "and her dress, doubtless a ball dress, suits her charmingly."

"That," said Albert, "is my mother's portrait. She had it painted six or eight years ago, during the Count's absence. Doubtless she thought to give him a pleasant surprise upon his return, but, strange to say, he did not like the portrait, and could never get over his antipathy to it. Between ourselves, I must tell you that Monsieur de Morcerf is one of the most hard working peers at the Luxembourg, and as a general is renowned for theory, but is an indifferent connoisseur of works of art. It is not so with my mother who paints remarkably well, and who, esteeming such a work too good to part with altogether, gave it to me to hang up in my room where it would be less exposed to Monsieur de Morcerf's displeasure. Forgive my talking so much on family matters, but as I shall have the honour of introducing you to the Count, I tell you this lest you should praise this portrait before him. The portrait seems to have a malign influence, for my mother rarely comes to the room without looking at it, and still more rarely does she look at it without weeping. The appearance of this portrait in the house is, however, the only contention between my mother and father who are still as united to-day, after more than twenty years of married life, as they were on their wedding day. And now that you have seen all my treasures, will you accompany me to Monsieur de Morcerf, to whom I wrote from Rome giving an account of the service you rendered

me and announcing your visit? I may say that both the Count and
the Countess are anxious to tender you their thanks. Look upon
this visit as an initiation into Paris life, a life of formalities, visits, and
introductions."

Monte Cristo bowed without replying. He accepted the proposal
without enthusiasm and without regret as one of those society conventions which every gentleman looks upon as a duty. Albert called
his valet and ordered him to announce to M. and Mme de Morcerf
the arrival of the Count of Monte Cristo. On entering the salon they
found themselves face to face with Monsieur de Morcerf himself.

He was a man of forty to forty-five years of age, but he appeared at
least fifty, and his black moustache and eyebrows contrasted strangely
with his almost white hair which was cut short in the military fashion. He was dressed in civilian clothes and wore in his buttonhole the
ribbons indicating the different orders to which he belonged.

"Father," said the young man, "I have the honour to introduce to
you the Count of Monte Cristo, the generous friend I had the good
fortune to meet in the difficult circumstances with which you are
acquainted."

"You are welcome amongst us," said the Count of Morcerf with a
smile. "In preserving the life of our only heir, you have rendered our
house a service which solicits our eternal gratitude."

So saying, the Count of Morcerf gave Monte Cristo an armchair,
while he seated himself opposite the window.

In taking the chair indicated to him, Monte Cristo arranged himself in such a manner as to be hidden in the shadow of the large velvet curtains whence he could read on the careworn features of the
Count a whole history of secret griefs in each one of the wrinkles
time had imprinted there.

"The Countess was at her toilet when your visit was announced,"
said Morcerf, "she will join us here in ten minutes or so."

"It is a great honour for me," said Monte Cristo, "that on the very
day of my arrival at Paris I should be brought into contact with a man
whose merits equal his reputation, and on whom Dame Fortune, acting with equity for once, has never ceased to smile. But has she not
on the Mitidja Plains or the Atlas Mountains still the baton of a mar-
shal to offer you?"

"I have left the service, monsieur," said Morcerf, turning somewhat
red. "Created a peer at the Restoration, I served during the first campaign under Maréchal de Bourmont; I was therefore entitled to a
higher rank, and who knows what would have happened had the elder
branch remained on the throne! But the July revolution was apparently glorious enough to permit of ingratitude; and it was, indeed,

inappreciative of any service that did not date from the imperial period. I, therefore, tendered my resignation. I have hung up my sword and have flung myself into politics. I devote myself to industry and study the useful arts. I was anxious to do so during the twenty years I was in the army, but had not the time."

"Such are the ideas that render your nation superior to all others," replied Monte Cristo. "A gentleman of high birth, in possession of a large fortune, you were content to gain your promotion as an obscure soldier. Then after becoming a general, a peer of France, a commander of the Legion of Honour, you are willing to go through another apprenticeship with no other prospects, no other reward than that one day you will serve your fellow-creatures. Really, Count, this is most praiseworthy; it is even more than that, it is sublime."

"If I were not afraid of wearing you, Count," continued the General, obviously charmed with Monte Cristo's manners, "I would have taken you to the Chamber with me; to-day's debate will be very interesting to such as do not know our modern senators."

"I should be most grateful to you, Count, if you would renew this invitation another time. I have been flattered with the hope of an introduction to the Countess to-day, and I will wait for her."

"Ah, here is my mother!" exclaimed Albert.

And in truth, as Monte Cristo turned round, he saw Mme de Morcerf, pale and motionless, on the threshold of the door. As Monte Cristo turned toward her, she let fall her arm which, for some reason, she had been resting against the gilt door-post. She had been standing there for some seconds, and had overheard the last words of the conversation.

Monte Cristo rose and bowed low to the Countess, who curtsied ceremoniously without saying a word.

"Whatever ails you, madame?" said the Count. "Perhaps the heat of this room is too much for you?"

"Are you ill, Mother?" exclaimed the Viscount, rushing toward Mercédès.

She thanked them both with a smile. "No," said she. "It has upset me a little to see for the first time him without whose intervention we should now be in tears and mourning. Monsieur, it is to you that I owe my son's life," she continued, advancing with queenly majesty, "and I bless you for this kindness. I am also grateful to you for giving me the opportunity of thanking you as I have blessed you, that is from the bottom of my heart."

"Madame, the Count and yourself reward me too generously for a very simple action. To save a man and thereby to spare a father's agony and a mother's feelings is not to do a noble deed, it is but an act of humanity."

These words were uttered with the most exquisite softness and politeness.

"It is very fortunate for my son, Count, that he has found such a friend," replied Madame de Morcerf, "and I thank God that it is so." And Mercédès raised her beautiful eyes to Heaven with an expression of such infinite gratitude that the Count fancied he saw two tears trembling in them.

M. de Morcerf went up to her. "Madame, I have already made my excuses to the Count," said he. "The session opened at two o'clock; it is now three, and I have to speak."

"Go along, then, I will try to make up to the Count for your absence" said the Countess in the same tone of deep feeling. "Will you do us the honour, Count, of spending the rest of the day with us?" she continued, turning to Monte Cristo.

"Believe me, Countess, no one could appreciate your kind offer more than I do, but I stepped out of my travelling-carriage at your door this morning and know not yet where or how my residence is provided for. I know it is but a slight cause for uneasiness, yet it is quite appreciable."

"Then we shall have this pleasure another time. Promise us that at least."

Monte Cristo bowed without replying, but his gesture might well have been taken for assent.

"Then I will not detain you longer," said the Countess. "I would not have my gratitude become indiscreet or importunate."

Monte Cristo bowed once more and took his leave. A carriage was waiting for him at the door.

The illustrious traveller sprang into it, the door was closed behind him, and the horses went off at a gallop, yet not so quickly that the Count did not notice an almost imperceptible movement which fluttered the curtain in the salon where he had just left Madame de Morcerf.

When Albert returned to his mother he found her reclining in a deep velvet armchair in her boudoir.

"What is this name Monte Cristo?" asked the Countess when the servant had gone out. "Is it a family name, the name of an estate, or simply a title?"

"I think it is nothing more than a title. The Count has bought an island in the Tuscan Archipelago. Otherwise he lays no claim to nobility and calls himself a 'Count of Chance,' though the general opinion in Rome is that he is a very great lord."

"He has excellent manners," said the Countess, "at least so far as I could judge during the few moments he was here."

The Countess was pensive for a moment, then after a short pause, she said: "I am addressing a question to you, Albert, as your mother. You have seen Monsieur de Monte Cristo at home. You are perspicacious, know the ways of the world, and are more tactful than most men of your age. Do you think the Count is really what he appears to be?"

"And what is that?"

"You said it yourself a minute ago, a great lord."

"I told you, Mother, that he was considered as such."

"But what do you think of him yourself, Albert?"

"I must own, I do not quite know what to make of him; I believe he is a Maltese."

"I am not questioning you about his origin but about himself."

"Ah! that is a totally different matter. I have seen so many strange traits in him that if you wish me to say what I think, I must say that I consider him as a man whom misfortune has branded; a derelict, as it were, of some old family, who, disinherited of his patrimony, has found one by dint of his own venturesome genius which places him above the rules of society. Monte Cristo is an island in the middle of the Mediterranean, without inhabitants or garrison, the resort of smugglers of every nationality and of pirates from every country. Who knows whether these worthy industrialists do not pay their lord for his protection?"

"Possibly," said the Countess, deep in thought.

"What does it matter," replied the young man, "whether he be a smuggler or not? Now that you have seen him, Mother, you must agree that the Count of Monte Cristo is a remarkable man who will create quite a sensation in Paris."

"Has this man any friendship for you, Albert?" she asked with a nervous shudder.

"I believe so, Mother."

"And you . . . are you fond of him?"

"I like him in spite of Franz d'Épinay, who always tries to convince me that he is a being returned from the other world."

There was a strange terror in the Countess's voice as she said:

"Albert, I have always put you on your guard against new acquaintances. Now you are a man and capable of giving me advice. Nevertheless, I repeat to you: be prudent, Albert."

"Yet, if this advice is to be profitable, Mother, I must know in advance what I am to guard against. The Count does not gamble, he drinks nothing but water coloured with a little Spanish wine; he is said to be so rich that, without making himself a laughing-stock, he could not borrow money from me. What, then, have I to fear from him?"

"You are right," said the Countess, "my fears are stupid; especially when directed against a man who has saved your life. By the way, did

your father receive him nicely, Albert? It is important that we should
not receive him like a mere stranger. Your father is sometimes preoccupied, his business worries him, and it may be that unintentionally ..."

"My father was perfect, Mother," Albert broke in, "what is more,
he seemed greatly flattered by two or three clever and appropriate
compliments the Count paid him with such ease that he might have
known him for thirty years. They parted the best of friends."

The Countess did not answer. She was so deeply absorbed in her
own thoughts that her eyes gradually closed. The young man stood
before her, looking down on her with filial affection, which is more
tender and loving in children whose mother is still young and beautiful; then, seeing her close her eyes, he listened for a moment to her
peaceful breathing and tiptoed out of the room.

## CHAPTER XXXII

## UNLIMITED CREDIT

THE next day, toward two o'clock in the afternoon, a carriage drawn
by two magnificent English horses drew up before Monte Cristo's
door. In it sat a man dressed in a blue coat with silk buttons of the
same colour, a white waistcoat over which passed a heavy gold chain,
and brown trousers; his hair was jet black, and descended so far over
his forehead that it hardly looked natural, for it formed too great a
contrast with the deep furrows left uncovered. In short, he was a man
of some fifty to fifty-five years of age who tried to appear forty. He
put his head through the door of the carriage, on which a coronet was
painted, and sent the groom to ask whether the Count of Monte
Cristo was at home.

The groom tapped at the porter's window and asked: "Does the
Count of Monte Cristo live here?"

"His Excellency does live here, but he is engaged," replied the
porter.

"In that case, here is the card of my master, Baron Danglars. Hand
it to the Count of Monte Cristo and tell him that my master stopped
on his way to the Chamber in order to have the honour of seeing the
Count."

"I never speak to His Excellency," replied the porter. "The valet
will deliver the message."

The groom returned to the carriage, and, somewhat crestfallen at
the rebuke he had just received, gave his master the porter's answer.

"Oh, the man whom they call Excellency is a prince then, to

whom only the valet has the right to speak. Never mind! since he has a credit on my bank, I shall see him when he wants money."

Then throwing himself back in his carriage, he called out to his coachman in a voice that could be heard at the other side of the street: "To the Chamber of Deputies!"

The Count had been informed of this visit, and had had time to examine the Baron from behind a window-blind.

"He's decidedly an ugly brute," he said with a gesture of disgust. "At the very first sight of the man anyone can recognize in him the snake by his flat forehead, the vulture by his protruding cranium, and the buzzard by his sharp beak!"

"Ali!" he cried, striking once on the copper gong. Ali appeared. "Call Bertuccio!" said he. Bertuccio instantly made his appearance.

"Your Excellency sent for me?" said the steward.

"Yes!" said the Count. "Did you see the horses that just now drew up before my door?"

"Certainly, Excellency, and very beautiful they were too."

"How comes it," said Monte Cristo frowning, "that, when I instructed you to obtain for me the best horses to be had in Paris, there are in the town two other horses outside my stables as good as mine?"

"The horses you mention were not for sale, Count," said Bertuccio.

Monte Cristo shrugged his shoulders.

"Do you not know, steward, that everything is for sale to him who cares to pay the price?"

"Monsieur Danglars paid sixteen thousand francs for them, Count!"

"Well, then, offer him thirty-two thousand; he is a banker, and a banker never loses the opportunity of doubling his capital."

"Do you mean that seriously?" asked Bertuccio.

Monte Cristo looked at the steward as one astonished that he should dare to ask such a question.

"I have a call to make this evening," said he. "I wish to have these horses harnessed to my carriage."

Bertuccio retired bowing. He stopped near the door and said: "At what time does Your Excellency propose paying this call?"

"At five o'clock," replied the Count.

"May I point out to Your Excellency that it is now two o'clock," the steward ventured to remark.

"I know," was Monte Cristo's sole reply.

At five o'clock the Count sounded his gong three times. One stroke summoned Ali, two Baptistin, and three strokes Bertuccio. The steward entered.

"My horses!" said the Count.

"They've been put in, Excellency," was Bertuccio's reply.

The Count went down and saw the much-coveted horses of Danglars harnessed to his own carriage.

"They are really beautiful," he said. "You did well to buy them, though you were late in doing so."

"Excellency, I had considerable difficulty in getting them," said Bertuccio. "They have cost a great deal of money."

"Are the horses less beautiful for that?" asked the Count, shrugging his shoulders.

"If Your Excellency is satisfied, all is well," said Bertuccio. "Where is Your Excellency going?"

"To Baron Danglars', Rue de la Chaussée d'Antin."

Arrived at the Baron's residence the Count was ushered into that nobleman's presence.

"Have I the honour of addressing Monsieur de Monte Cristo?"

"And I of addressing Baron Danglars, Chevalier of the Legion of Honour and member of the Chamber of Deputies?" said the Count.

Monte Cristo repeated all the titles he had read on the Baron's card. Danglars felt the thrust and bit his lips.

"I have received a letter of advice from Messrs Thomson and French," he said.

"I am delighted to hear it, Baron; I am delighted. It will not be necessary to introduce myself, which is always embarrassing. You say you have received a letter of advice?"

"Yes, but I must confess I do not quite understand its meaning," said Danglars. "The letter . . . I have it with me, I think . . ." He searched in his pocket. "Yes, here it is. This letter opened credit on my bank to the Count of Monte Cristo for an unlimited sum."

"Well, Baron, what is there incomprehensible in that?"

"Nothing, monsieur, but the word unlimited."

"And is that word unknown in France?"

"Oh, no, monsieur, it is quite all right in regard to syntax, but not quite so from a banker's point of view."

"Is the banking firm of Thomson and French not sound, do you think, Baron?" asked Monte Cristo as naively as possible. "That would be a nice thing, to be sure. I have some property deposited with them."

"Oh, they are perfectly sound," replied Danglars with an almost mocking smile, "but the meaning of the word unlimited in connexion with finances is so vague . . . And what is vague is doubtful, and in doubt, says the wise man, there is danger."

"In other words," replied Monte Cristo, "if Thomson and French are inclined to commit a folly, Danglars' bank is not going to follow suit. No doubt Messrs Thomson and French do not need to consider figures in their operations, but Monsieur Danglars has a limit to his. As he said just now, he is a wise man."

"No one has ever questioned my capital, monsieur," replied the banker proudly.

"Then obviously I am the first one to do so."

"How so?"

"The explanations you demand of me, monsieur, which certainly appear to imply hesitation . . ."

"Why, then, monsieur, I will try to make myself clear by asking you to name the amount for which you expect to draw on me," continued Danglars after a moment's silence.

"But I have asked for unlimited credit because I am uncertain of the amount I shall require," replied Monte Cristo, determined not to lose an inch of ground.

The banker thought the moment had come for him to take the upper hand; he flung himself back in the armchair and with a slow, arrogant smile on his lips, said: "Do not fear to ask, monsieur; you will then be convinced that the resources of the firm of Danglars, limited though they may be, are sufficient to meet the highest demands, even though you asked for a million . . ."

"What did you say?"

"I said a million," repeated Danglars with the audacity of stupidity.

"What should I do with a million?" said the Count. "Good heavens! I should not have opened an account for such a trifling sum. Why, I always carry a million in my pocket-book or my suit-case." And he took from his small card-case two Treasury bills of five hundred thousand francs each.

A man of Danglars' type requires to be overwhelmed, not merely pin-pricked, and this blow had its effect. The banker was simply stunned. He stared at Monte Cristo in a stupefied manner, his eyes starting out of his head.

"Come, now, own that you mistrust Messrs Thomson and French. I expected this, and, though I am not very businesslike, I came forearmed. Here are two other letters of credit similar to the one addressed to you; one is from Arstein and Eskeles of Vienna on Baron Rothschild, the other is from Baring Bros. of London on Monsieur Lafitte. You have only to say the word, and I will relieve you of all anxiety by presenting my letter of credit to one or the other of these two firms."

That was enough; Danglars was vanquished. Trembling visibly, he took the letters from London and Germany that the Count held out to him, opened them, verified the authenticity of the signatures with a care that would have been insulting to Monte Cristo had they not served to mislead the banker.

"Here are three signatures which are worth many millions," said Danglars, rising as though to pay homage to the power of gold personified in the man before him. "Three unlimited credits on our banking firms. Excuse me, Count, though I am no longer mistrustful, I cannot help being astonished."

"But nothing can astonish a banking establishment like yours," said Monte Cristo with a great show of politeness. "You can send me some money, then, I suppose?"

"Speak, Count, I am at your service."

"Well, since we understand each other and you no longer mistrust me . . . I am not presuming too much in saying this, am I? Let us fix on a general sum for the first year; six millions, for example."

"Very well, let it be six millions," replied Danglars hoarsely.

"If I require more," said Monte Cristo carelessly, "we can add to it, but I do not expect to stay in Paris more than a year, and I don't suppose I shall exceed that sum in a year. Anyway, we shall see. To begin with, will you please send me to-morrow five hundred thousand francs, half in gold and half in notes? I shall be at home until noon, but should I have to go out, I will leave the receipt with my steward."

"You shall have the money at ten o'clock in the morning, Count." The Count rose.

"I must confess to you, Count," said Danglars, "I thought I was well informed on all the large fortunes of Europe, and yet, I must own, that though yours appears to be very considerable, I had no knowledge of it. Is it of recent date?"

"No, monsieur; on the contrary, it is of very long standing," replied Monte Cristo. "It is a kind of family treasure which it was forbidden to touch. The interest has gone on accumulating and has trebled the capital. The period fixed by the testator only expired a few years ago, so your ignorance of the matter was quite natural. You will know more about it, though, in a short time."

The Count accompanied his words with one of those pale smiles that struck such terror into the heart of Franz d'Épinay.

"If you would allow me, Count, I should like to introduce you to Baroness Danglars. Excuse my haste, but a client like you almost forms part of the family."

Monte Cristo bowed as a sign that he accepted the proferred honour. The financier rang the bell, and a footman in a brilliant livery appeared.

"Is the Baroness at home?" asked Danglars.

"Yes, Monsieur le Baron," replied the footman.

"Is she alone?"

"No, Monsieur le Baron, Monsieur Debray is with her."

Danglars nodded his head, then turning to the Count, he said: "Monsieur Debray is an old friend of ours and private secretary to the Minister of the Interior. As for my wife, she belongs to an ancient family and lowered herself in marrying me. She was Mademoiselle de Servières, and when I married her she was a widow after the death of her first husband, Colonel the Marquis de Nargonne."

"I have not the honour of knowing Madame Danglars, but I have already met Monsieur Lucien Debray."

"Really? Where?"

"At the house of Monsieur de Morcerf."

"Ah, you know the little Viscount then?"

"We were together at Rome during the Carnival."

"It is true," said Danglars. "Have I not heard something about a strange adventure with bandits in the ruins? He had a most miraculous escape! I believe he told my daughter and wife something about it when he returned from Italy."

"The Baroness awaits your pleasure, messieurs!" said the footman, who had been to inquire of his mistress whether she would receive visitors.

"I will go on in front to show you the way" said Danglars, bowing.

"And I will follow you!"

## CHAPTER XXXIII

## THE PAIR OF DAPPLED GREYS

Mme Danglars, whose beauty was quite remarkable in spite of her thirty-six years, was at the piano, a little masterpiece of inlay, while Lucien Debray was seated at a work-table turning over the pages of an album. Before the Count's arrival, Lucien had had time to relate many particulars regarding him to Mme Danglars, and her curiosity, being aroused by the old stories related by Morcerf, was brought to its highest pitch by the details told her by Lucien. In consequence she received the Baron with a smile, which was her custom, while the Count received a ceremonious but at the same time graceful curtsey in acknowledgment of his bow.

"Baroness, permit me to present to you the Count of Monte Cristo, who has been most warmly recommended to me by my correspondents at Rome," said Danglars. "I will only add one fact which will make him a favourite among the ladies: he intends staying in Paris for a year, and during that time he proposes spending six millions; that sounds promising for a series of balls, dinners, and supper parties, and I hope the Count will not forget us, as we shall not forget him in the small parties we give."

Though the introduction was so vulgar in its flattery, it is such a rare event that a man comes to Paris to spend a princely fortune that Mme Danglars gave the Count a look which was not devoid of interest.

"You have come at a very bad season," said she. "Paris is detestable in summer. There are no more balls, receptions, or parties. The Italian opera is at London, the French opera is everywhere except at Paris; there remain for our sole entertainment a third-rate race-meeting or two on the Champs de Mars or at Satory."

At this moment Baroness Danglars' confidential maid entered and, approaching her mistress, whispered something into her ear.

Madame Danglars turned pale.

"Impossible!" said she.

"It is nevertheless the truth, madame," replied the maid.

Madame turned to her husband: "Is this true, monsieur, what my maid tells me?"

"What has she told you, madame?" asked Danglars, visibly agitated.

"She tells me that when my coachman went to put my horses to the carriage, they were gone from the stables. What does this signify, may I ask?"

"Madame, listen to me," said Danglars.

"I will certainly listen to you, for I am curious to know what you have to tell me. I will ask these gentlemen to be our judge. Messieurs," continued she, "Danglars has ten horses in his stables, two of these, the handsomest in Paris, belong to me. You know my dappled greys, Monsieur Debray. I have promised to lend Madame de Villefort my carriage to go to the Bois to-morrow, and now my horses are gone! I suppose monsieur has found some means of making a few thousands of francs on them and has sold them. What a money-grasping lot speculators are!"

Just then Debray, who was looking out of the window, suddenly exclaimed: "By Jove! surely those are your very horses in the Count's carriage!"

"My dappled greys?" cried out Madame Danglars, rushing to the window. "Yes, those are mine indeed!"

Danglars was astounded.

"Is it possible?" said Monte Cristo, affecting astonishment.

"It is incredible!" said the banker.

Danglars looked so pale and discomfited that the Count almost had pity on him. The banker foresaw a disastrous scene in the near future; the Baroness's frowning brow predicted a storm. Debray saw the gathering clouds and, on pretext of an appointment, took his leave, while Monte Cristo, not wishing to mar the advantages he hoped he had gained by staying any longer, bowed to Mme Danglars and withdrew, leaving the Baron to his wife's anger.

"All is well!" thought Monte Cristo. "I have achieved my object. The domestic peace of this family is now in my hands, and with one action I am going to win the gratitude of both the Baron and the Baroness. What a stroke of luck! But with all this," he added, "I have not been introduced to Mademoiselle Eugénie, whose acquaintance I am very anxious to make. Never mind," he continued with that peculiar smile of his, "I am in Paris with plenty of time before me . . . That can be left for a later date." With this reflection, he stepped into his carriage and returned to his house.

Two hours later Mme Danglars received a charming letter from the Count of Monte Cristo, in which he wrote that he did not wish to make his entrance into Paris society by causing annoyance to a beautiful woman, and entreated her to take back her horses. The horses were sent back wearing the same harness as in the morning, but in the centre of each rosette which adorned the sides of their heads, there was a diamond. Danglars also received a letter. The Count asked his permission to satisfy a millionaire's whim, and requested him to excuse the Eastern fashion adopted in returning the horses.

In the evening Monte Cristo went to his country-house at Auteuil accompanied by Ali.

Toward three o'clock next day, Ali, summoned by a stroke on the gong, entered the Count's study.

"Ali, you have often spoken to me of your skill in throwing the lasso," said the Count.

Ali drew himself up proudly and nodded assent.

"Good! You could stop a bull with your lasso?"

Ali nodded assent.

"A tiger?"

Another nod.

"A lion?"

Ali pretended to throw the lasso and imitated the choked roar of a lion.

"I understand," said Monte Cristo. "You have hunted lions."

Ali nodded his head proudly.

"But could you stop two runaway horses?"

Ali smiled.

"Well then, listen," said Monte Cristo. "In a few minutes a carriage will come along drawn by two runaway horses, the same dappled greys that I had yesterday. Even at the risk of being run over, you must stop these horses before my door."

Ali went out into the street and traced a line on the pavement before the door. Then the Nubian seated himself on the stone that formed the angle of the house and the road and began smoking his chibouque, while Monte Cristo returned to his study.

Toward five o'clock, however, when the Count expected the arrival of the carriage, he began to manifest distinct signs of impatience; he paced a room overlooking the road, stopped at intervals to listen, and from time to time approached the window, through which he could see Ali blowing out puffs of smoke with a regularity which indicated that he was quite absorbed in his important occupation.

Suddenly a distant rumbling was heard which drew nearer with lightning rapidity; then a carriage appeared, the coachman vainly striving to restrain the wild, infuriated horses who were bounding along at a mad speed.

In the carriage a young lady and a child of seven or eight years were lying in each other's embrace; their terror had deprived them of all power to utter a sound. A stone under the wheel or any other impediment would have sufficed to upset the creaking carriage. It kept to the middle of the road, and the cries of the terrified spectators could be heard as it flew along.

Suddenly Ali laid down his chibouque, took the lasso from his pocket and threw it, catching the forelegs of the near horse in a triple coil; he suffered himself to be dragged along three or four yards, by which time the tightening of the lasso so hampered the horse that it fell on the pole which it snapped, thus paralysing the efforts the other horse made to pursue its mad course. The coachman took advantage of this short respite to jump down from his box, but Ali had already seized the nostrils of the other horse in his iron grip, and the animal, snorting with pain, sank down beside its companion.

All this took no more time than it takes a bullet to hit its mark. It was nevertheless sufficient for a man, followed by several servants, to rush out from the house opposite which the accident had happened. As soon as the coachman opened the door of the carriage, he lifted out the lady who was clinging to the cushion with one hand, while with the other she pressed to her bosom her fainting son. Monte Cristo carried them both into the salon and, placing them on a sofa, said:

"You have nothing more to fear, madame, you are safe!"

The lady soon came round, and pointed to her son with a look which was more eloquent than all entreaties. The child, indeed, was still unconscious.

"I understand, madame," said the Count, examining the child, "but you need not be alarmed, the child has received no injury. It is only fear that has rendered him unconscious."

"Are you only telling me this to still my anxiety? Look how pale he is. My son! My child! My Edward! Answer your mother! Oh, monsieur, send for a doctor! I will give my fortune to him who restores my son to me!"

Monte Cristo opened a casket and took out a flagon of Bohemian glass incrusted with gold, containing a blood-red liquid, a single drop of which he placed on the child's lips. Though still pale, the child immediately opened his eyes. On seeing this, the mother was beside herself with joy.

"Where am I?" she cried out, "and to whom do I owe so much happiness after such a cruel trial?"

"Madame, you are under the roof of a man who esteems himself most fortunate at having been able to spare you any pain," said Monte Cristo.

"It is all the fault of my wretched inquisitiveness!" said the lady. "All Paris talked of Madame Danglars' magnificent horses, and I was foolish enough to want to try them."

"Is it possible?" exclaimed the Count with admirably feigned surprise. "Do these horses belong to the Baroness?"

"Yes, monsieur, do you know her?"

"I have that honour, and I feel a double joy at having been the means of saving you from the danger that threatened you, for you might have attributed the accident to me. I bought these horses from the Baron yesterday, but the Baroness appeared to regret their loss so deeply that I sent them back with the request that she would accept them from me."

"Then you must be the Count of Monte Cristo of whom Hermine spoke so much yesterday."

"That is so, madame."

"And I, monsieur, am Madame Héloïse de Villefort."

The Count bowed as though he heard a name completely unknown to him.

"How grateful Monsieur de Villefort will be," continued Héloïse. "He owes both our lives to you; you have restored to him his wife and his son. If it had not been for your brave servant, this dear child and myself would certainly have been killed."

"Alas, madame, I still shudder at the thought of your danger!"

"I hope you will permit me to give your servant the just reward for his devotion."

"Madame, I beg of you not to spoil Ali either by praise or by reward," replied the Count. "Ali is my slave; in saving your life, he served me, and it is his duty to serve me."

"But he risked his life!" said Madame de Villefort, who was strangely impressed by the Count's masterful tone.

"I saved his life, madame, consequently it belongs to me," replied Monte Cristo.

Madame de Villefort made no reply. Perhaps she was thinking about this man who made such a strong impression on everybody who set eyes on him.

During this momentary silence, the Count had leisure to examine the child whom his mother was covering with kisses. He was small and slender; his skin was of that whiteness generally found with auburn-haired children, yet a mass of rebellious black hair covered his rounded forehead. It fell on to his shoulders, encircling his face and redoubling the vivacity of his eyes which were so expressive of sly malice and childish naughtiness. His mouth was large, and his lips, which had scarcely regained their colour, were thin; the features of this child of eight were those of a boy of twelve or more. His first movement was to wriggle himself free from his mother's arms, and to open the casket from which the Count had taken the phial of elixir. With the air of a child accustomed to satisfy his every whim and without asking anyone's permission, he began to unstopper the phials.

"Don't touch anything there, sonny," said the Count sharply. "Some of those liquids are dangerous, not only to taste but even to inhale."

Madame de Villefort turned pale and, seizing her son's arm, drew him toward her. Her fears calmed, she immediately cast on the casket a fleeting but expressive glance, which did not escape the Count's notice.

"Do you reside here?" Madame de Villefort inquired as she rose to take her leave.

"No, madame," replied the Count. "This is only a little country house I have just bought. I reside at number thirty Champs Élysées. But I see that you have quite recovered and are desirous of returning home. I have just given orders for the same horses to be put to my carriage, and Ali will have the honour of driving you home, while your coachman stays here to repair the damage."

"I dare not go with the same horses!" said Madame de Villefort.

"Oh, you will see, madame, that in Ali's hands they will be as gentle as lambs," was Monte Cristo's reply.

Indeed, Ali had already tackled the horses that had only with difficulty been set on their legs again. He held in his hand a sponge soaked in aromatic vinegar with which he rubbed away the sweat and foam that covered their heads and nostrils. Almost immediately they began to breathe loudly and to tremble violently; this lasted several seconds. Then in the midst of a large crowd which the news of the accident had gathered before the house, Ali harnessed the horses to the Count's brougham, took the reins, mounted the box, and to the utter astonishment of those spectators who had beheld these same horses bolting like a whirlwind, he was compelled to use his whip vigorously to make them move. Even then they went at such a slow trot that it took nearly two hours to reach the Faubourg Saint-Honoré where Madame de Villefort lived.

## CHAPTER XXXIV

## HAYDEE

MY readers will remember that the new, or rather old, acquaintances of the Count of Monte Cristo were Maximilian, Julie, and Emmanuel. He had promised Maximilian that he would call at the house in the Rue Meslay, and the day had now come. Anticipation of the visit he was about to make, of the few happy moments he was about to spend, of the fleeting glimpse of paradise in the hell to which he had voluntarily engaged himself, brought a charming expression of serenity to Monte Cristo's countenance, and his face was radiant with a joy rarely depicted there.

It was midday and the Count had set apart one hour to be spent with Haydee. It seemed as though he sensed that his crushed spirit needed to be prepared for gentle emotions as other spirits have to be prepared for violent ones.

The young Greek occupied a suite separated from the Count's. It was furnished entirely in the Oriental style; the floors were covered with thick Turkey carpets, rich brocades hung suspended from the walls, and in each room there was a large and spacious divan with piles of cushions, which could be placed according to the fancy of those that used them.

The Greek girl was in the room at the far end of her suite. She was reclining on the floor on cushions of blue satin with her back against the divan; one softly rounded arm encircled her head, and between her lips she had the coral tube in which was set the flexible pipe of a narghile. Her dress was that of a woman of Epirus: white satin trousers embroidered with pink roses displayed two small child-like feet, which might have been taken for Parian marble had they not been playing with two little slippers with curling toes embroidered with gold and pearls, a long white-and-blue-striped vest with long sleeves ornamented with loops of silver and buttons of pearl, and on her head was a small gold cap embroidered with pearls which she wore tilted to one side; from under the cap, on the side where it was tilted up, fell a beautiful natural rose of a deep crimson hue mingling with her hair, which was of such a deep black that it appeared almost blue.

The beauty of her face was the perfect Grecian type, with large black eyes of the softness of velvet, straight nose, coral lips, and pearly teeth. To complete the picture she had all the charm and freshness of young womanhood, for Haydee had seen no more than nineteen or twenty summers.

When Monte Cristo entered, she raised herself on her elbow and, welcoming him with a smile, held out her hand to him.

"Why do you ask permission to see me?" she said in the sonorous language of the daughters of Sparta and Athens. "Are you my master no longer? Have I ceased to be your slave?"

Monte Cristo smiled as he replied: "Haydee, we are in France, you know, so you are free!"

"Free to do what?" asked the girl.

"Free to leave me!"

"To leave you! Why should I leave you?"

"How do I know? We shall see people . . ."

"I do not wish to see anyone."

"Should you meet amongst the handsome young men one who pleases you, I should not be so unjust . . ."

"I have never yet seen a man more handsome than you, and I have never loved anyone but my father and you."

"Poor child!" said Monte Cristo. "That is only because you have scarcely spoken to anyone but your father and me."

"What need have I to converse with others? My father called me his joy, you call me your love, and both of you have called me your child."

"Do you remember your father, Haydee?"

The girl smiled. "He is here and here," said she, pointing to her eyes and her heart.

"And where am I?" Monte Cristo asked with a smile.

"You? Why, you are everywhere!"

Monte Cristo took her hand to kiss it, but the simple child withdrew it and offered her cheek.

"Listen to me, Haydee," said the Count. "You know that you are free. You are your own mistress. You may still wear your national costume or discard it according to your inclination; you may stay here if and when you wish, and go out if and when you wish. There will always be a carriage in readiness for you. Ali and Myrta will accompany you everywhere and will be at your command. There is but one thing I ask of you."

"Speak!"

"Disclose not the secret of your birth, say not a word in regard to your past; on no occasion mention the name of your illustrious father or of your poor mother."

"I have already told you, my lord, that I will not see anyone."

"Listen, Haydee, it may be that this seclusion, which is customary in the East, will be impossible in Paris. Continue to learn all you can of our Northern countries as you did at Rome, Florence, and Madrid; such knowledge will always stand you in good stead whether you continue to live here or return to the East."

The slave girl raised her large tear-bedewed eyes to the Count, and said: "You mean to say whether *we* return to the East, do you not, my lord?"

"Yes, child, you know I shall never leave you. The tree does not forsake the flower, it is the flower that forsakes the tree."

"My lord, I shall never leave you," said Haydee. "I could not live without you."

"Poor child! I shall be old in ten years, and you will still be young."

"My father had a long white beard but that did not prevent my loving him. My father was sixty years of age, but to me he was more handsome than all the young men I saw."

"Do you think you will be able to settle down here?"

"Shall I see you?"

"Every day."

"Then what do you fear for me?"

"I fear you may grow weary."

"That cannot be, my lord, for in the morning I shall be occupied with the thought that you will be coming to see me, and in the evening I shall dwell on the memories of your visit. Besides, when I am alone, I have much to occupy my mind. I summon up mighty pictures of the past, vast horizons with Pindus and Olympia in the distance. Then again, my heart is filled with three great sentiments—sadness, love, and gratitude—and with these as companions it is impossible to grow weary."

"You are a worthy daughter of Epirus, Haydee, full of grace and poetry. It is easily seen that you are descended from that family of goddesses born in your own country. Rest assured, my daughter, I will not permit your youth to be lost, for if you love me as a father, I love you as my child."

"You are mistaken, my lord, I did not love my father as I love you. The love I bear you is quite different. My father is dead, yet I am not dead; whereas if you die I die."

With a smile of exquisite tenderness the Count held out his hand to her; she pressed her lips to it as she always did.

The Count was now fully prepared for his interview with Morrel and his family, and took his leave of Haydee, murmuring these lines of Pindar:

> Youth is the flower of which love is the fruit;
> Happy the gatherer who picks it after watching it slowly mature.

In accordance with his orders the carriage was ready. He stepped in and sped along at his usual high speed.

## CHAPTER XXXV

## THE MORREL FAMILY

THE Count arrived at No. 14 Rue Meslay in a very few minutes. Coclès opened the door, and Baptistin, springing from the box, asked if M. and Mme Hebault and M. Maximilian Morrel were at home to the Count of Monte Cristo.

"To the Count of Monte Cristo!" cried Maximilian, throwing away his cigar and hastening toward his visitor. "I should think we are at home to him! A thousand thanks, Count, for having kept your promise."

The young officer shook the Count's hand so cordially that there could be no doubt as to the sincerity of his feelings.

"Come along," said Maximilian, "I will announce you myself. My sister is in the garden plucking the dead roses; my brother is within five yards of her reading his two papers, for wherever Madame Herbault is, Monsieur Herbault will be found within a radius of four yards and vice versa."

At the sound of their steps, a young woman of twenty to twenty-five, dressed in a morning gown, raised her head from the rose-bush which she was carefully trimming.

It was no other than Julie, who, as Thomson and French's representative had predicted, had become Mme Emmanuel Herbault. She uttered a cry of surprise on seeing the stranger. Maximilian began to laugh. "Don't upset yourself, Julie," said he. "The Count has only been in Paris two or three days, and knows what a householder of the Marais has to do, and if he does not, you will show him."

"It is most unkind of my brother to bring you thus, but he never has any regard for his poor sister's vanity. Penelon! Penelon! . . ."

An old man who was digging a bed of Bengal roses stuck his spade into the ground and approached, cap in hand, the while striving to hide a quid of tobacco he had just put into his mouth. A few silvery strands mingled with his thick hair, while his bronzed face and bold keen eye betrayed the old sailor, tanned by tropical suns and many a tempestuous sea.

"I believe you hailed me, Mademoiselle Julie," he said. Penelon had retained the habit of calling his master's daughter "Mademoiselle Julie," and could never accustom himself to addressing her as "Madame Herbault."

"Penelon, go and inform Monsieur Emmanuel of this gentleman's arrival."

Then, turning to Monte Cristo, she said:

"You will permit me to leave you for a few minutes? In the meantime Maximilian will take you into the salon."

Without waiting for a reply she disappeared behind a clump of trees, and regained the house by a side entrance.

The salon was impregnated with the scent of sweet-smelling flowers massed together in a huge Japanese vase. Julie, appropriately dressed and her hair coquettishly arranged (she had accomplished this feat in ten minutes), was waiting to receive the Count.

The birds could be heard chirping in a neighbouring aviary; the laburnum and acacia trees spread their branches so close to the window that the clusters of bloom almost formed a border to the blue velvet curtains. Everything in this little retreat breathed peaceful tranquillity, from the song of the birds to the smiles of its owners. From the moment the Count entered, he sensed the atmosphere of happiness; he stood silent and pensive, forgetting that the others were waiting for him to continue the conversation which had been interrupted during the exchange of salutations.

He suddenly became aware of this almost embarrassing silence and, tearing himself away from his dreams with a great effort, he said:

"Pray excuse my emotion, madame. It must astonish you who are accustomed to the peace and happiness I find here, but it is so unusual for me to find contentment expressed on a human face, that I cannot grow weary of looking at you and your husband."

"We are very happy, monsieur," replied Julie, "but we have gone through long and bitter suffering, and there are few people who have bought their happiness at such a high price."

The Count's face manifested great curiosity.

"It is a family history, Count," said Maximilian. "The humble little picture would have no interest for you who are accustomed to the misfortunes of the illustrious and the joys of the rich. We have known bitter suffering."

"And did God send you consolation in your sorrow as He does to all?" asked Monte Cristo.

"Yes, Count, we can truly say that He did," replied Julie. "He did for us what He only does for His elect: He sent us one of His angels."

The Count's cheeks became scarlet, and he coughed in order to have an excuse for hiding his emotion behind his handkerchief.

"Those who are born in a gilt cradle and have never wanted for anything, do not know what happiness life contains," said Emmanuel, "just as they do not appreciate to the full a clear sky who have never entrusted their lives to the mercy of four planks on the raging sea."

Monte Cristo got up and, without replying, for he feared the tremulousness of his voice would betray his emotion, began to pace round the room.

"Our magnificence makes you smile!" said Maximilian, who was watching Monte Cristo.

"Not at all," replied Monte Cristo, deathly pale and pressing one hand to his heart to still its throbbings, while with the other he pointed to a glass case under which lay a silk purse carefully placed on a black velvet cushion. "I was only wondering what could be the use of this purse containing what looks like a piece of paper at one end and a fairly valuable diamond at the other."

"That is the most precious of our family treasures, Count."

"The diamond is, indeed, quite a good one."

"My brother was not alluding to the value of the stone, though it has been estimated at a hundred thousand francs; what he meant was that the articles contained in that purse are the relics of the angel I mentioned just now."

"Forgive me, madame, I did not mean to be indiscreet. I could not understand the meaning of the purse, and will ask for no explanation."

"Indiscreet, did you say? On the contrary we are grateful to you for giving us an opportunity to open our hearts on the subject. If we wished to make a secret of the noble action which that purse reminds us of, we should not expose it thus to view. We would rather make it known to everyone, so that our benefactor may be compelled to betray his presence by his emotion."

"Really!" said Monte Cristo in a stifled voice.

"This has touched the hand of a man who saved my father from death, all of us from ruin, and our name from dishonour," said Maximilian, raising the glass case and devoutly kissing the silk purse. "It has touched the hand of one whose merit it is that, though we were doomed to misery and mourning, others now express their wonder at our happiness. This letter," continued Maximilian, taking the piece of paper from the purse and handing it to the Count, "this letter was written by him on a day when my father had taken a desperate resolution, and the diamond was given by our unknown benefactor to my sister as her dowry."

Monte Cristo opened the letter and read it with an indescribably happy expression. As our readers will know, it was the note addressed to Julie and signed "Sinbad the Sailor."

"I have not given up hope of one day kissing that hand as I kiss the purse it has touched," said Julie. "Four years ago, Penelon, the gallant tar you saw in the garden with a spade, was at Trieste; on the quay he saw an Englishman on the point of boarding a yacht; he recognized him as the man who came to see my father on the fifth of June, eighteen-twenty-nine, and who wrote this note on the fifth of September. He assures me it was he, but he dared not speak to him."

"An Englishman?" asked Monte Cristo, deep in thought and feeling most uneasy every time Julie looked at him. "An Englishman, did you say?"

"Yes," replied Morrel, "an Englishman who introduced himself to us as the representative of Messrs Thomson and French of Rome. That is why you saw me start the other day when you mentioned that they were your bankers. As we have said, all this happened in eighteen-twenty-nine. For pity's sake, Count, tell us, do you know this Englishman?"

"What was his name?" asked Monte Cristo.

"He left no name but the one he signed at the bottom of the letter 'Sinbad the Sailor,'" said Julie, looking at the Count very closely.

"Which is evidently only a pseudonym," said Monte Cristo. Then, remarking that Julie was eyeing him more closely than ever and was trying to detect some resemblance in his voice, he continued: "Was this man not about my height, perhaps a little taller and somewhat thinner; his neck imprisoned in a high cravat; his coat closely buttoned up; and hadn't he the habit of constantly taking out his pencil?"

"You know him then?" exclaimed Julie, her eyes sparkling with joy.

"No, I am only guessing," said Monte Cristo. "I knew a Lord Wilmore who was continually doing things of this kind."

"Sister, sister, remember what father so often told us," interposed Morrel. "He always said it was not an Englishman who had done us this good turn."

Monte Cristo started. "What did your father tell you?" he asked.

"My father regarded the deed as a miracle. He believed that a benefactor had come from his tomb to help us. It was a touching superstition, Count, and, though I could not credit it myself, I would not destroy his faith in it. How often in his dreams did he not mutter the name of a dear friend who was lost to him for ever! On his deathbed, when his mind had been given that lucidity that the near approach of death brings with it, this thought which had till then only been a superstition, became a conviction. The last words he spoke were: 'Maximilian, it was Edmond Dantès!'"

At these words, the Count, who had been gradually changing colour, became alarmingly pale. The blood rushed from his head, and he could not speak for a few seconds. He took out his watch as though he had forgotten the time, picked up his hat, took a hurried and embarrassed leave of Mme Herbault and, pressing the hands of Emmanuel and Maximilian, said: "Permit me to renew my visit from time to time, madame. I have spent a happy hour with you and am very grateful for the kind way in which you have received me. This is the first time for many years that I have given way to my feelings." With that he strode rapidly out of the room.

"What a peculiar man this Count of Monte Cristo is," said Emmanuel.

"He certainly is," replied Maximilian, "but I believe he is very noble-hearted, and I am sure he likes us."

"As for me," said Julie, "his voice went to my heart, and two or three times it occurred to me that I had heard it before."

## CHAPTER XXXVI

## TOXICOLOGY

THE Count of Monte Cristo had arrived at Mme de Villefort's door, and the mere mention of his name had set the whole house in confusion.

Mme de Villefort was in the salon when the Count was announced, and immediately sent for her son to come and renew his thanks to the Count. Edward had heard of nothing but this great personage for the last two days, and hastened to obey the summons, not through obedience to his mother, nor yet because he wanted to thank the Count, but from sheer curiosity and in the hope that he might fire off one of his saucy jokes which always elicited from his mother the remark: "The bad boy! but I must really overlook it, he is so clever!"

After the first formalities were exchanged, the Count inquired after M. de Villefort.

"My husband is dining with the Chancellor," replied Mme de Villefort. "He has only just left, and I am sure he will greatly regret that he has been deprived of the pleasure of seeing you. Where is your sister Valentine?" said Mme de Villefort, turning to Edward. "Send some one for her, so that I may introduce her to the Count."

"You have also a daughter, madame?" asked the Count. "She must be quite a young child."

"It is Monsieur de Villefort's daughter by his first marriage, and a pretty, well-grown girl she is, too."

"But melancholy," interrupted Edward, who, wishing to have a plume for his hat, was pulling feathers out of the tail of a parrot that screeched with pain.

Mme de Villefort merely said: "Be quiet, Edward! This young madcap is quite right, nevertheless, and is only repeating what he has, unfortunately, often heard me say. In spite of all we do to distract her, Mademoiselle Villefort is of a melancholy and taciturn disposition, which often mars her beauty. Why is she not coming, Edward? Go and see what is keeping her so long."

"They are looking for her where she is not to be found."

"Where are they looking for her?"

"In Grandpa Noirtier's room."

"Where is she, then? If you know, tell me."

"She is under the large chestnut-tree," continued the mischievous boy as, notwithstanding his mother's expostulations, he presented live flies to the parrot, who appeared to relish them.

Mme de Villefort stretched out her hand to ring for the maid to tell her where Valentine was to be found, when the girl herself entered. She certainly looked sad, and on closer inspection the traces of tears were to be seen in her eyes. She was a tall, slim girl of nineteen, with bright chestnut hair and deep blue eyes; her whole deportment was languid but stamped with the elegance which had characterized her mother. Her white and slender hands, her pearly neck and blushing cheek, gave her at first sight the aspect of one of those beautiful Englishwomen who have been rather poetically compared to swans admiring themselves.

On seeing beside her mother the stranger of whom she had already heard so much, she curtsied with such grace that the Count was more struck with her than ever. He stood up at once.

"My stepdaughter, Mademoiselle de Villefort," said Mme de Villefort.

"And the Count of Monte Cristo, King of China, Emperor of Cochin China," said the young imp, casting a sly look at his sister.

"Have I not had the honour of seeing both you and mademoiselle somewhere?" asked the Count, looking first at Madame de Villefort and then at Valentine. "It occurred to me just now that I had, and when I saw mademoiselle enter, her face seemed to throw some light on the confused remembrance, if you will excuse the remark."

"It is hardly likely, Count. Mademoiselle de Villefort does not like society, and we rarely go out."

"It is not in society that I have met you, mademoiselle, and the charming little rogue. I shall remember in a moment, stay . . ."

The Count put his hand to his forehead as though to concentrate his thoughts.

"No . . . it was abroad. It was . . . I do not quite know where, but it seems to me that this recollection is connected with a beautiful sunny sky and some religious feast . . . mademoiselle had some flowers in her hand, and the boy was chasing a peacock, while you, madame, were under a vine-arbour . . . Help me out, madame, does nothing I have told you bring back anything to your mind?"

"No, nothing," replied Mme de Villefort, "and it seems to me, Count, that if I had met you anywhere, I should not have forgotten you."

"Perhaps the Count saw us in Italy," said Valentine timidly.

"That, indeed, is possible," said Monte Cristo. "Have you travelled in Italy, mademoiselle?"

"My stepmother and I went there two years ago. The doctors feared for my chest and prescribed Naples air for me. We stayed at Bologna, Perugia, and Rome."

"You are right, mademoiselle," exclaimed Monte Cristo as though this simple indication had sufficed to freshen his memory. "It was at Perugia on the Feast of Corpus Christi in a garden of the Hôtel de la Poste that we chanced to meet, you, madame, mademoiselle, the boy, and myself. Yes, I remember having had the pleasure of seeing you there."

"I remember Perugia perfectly, also the Hôtel de la Poste and the feast you mention," said Mme de Villefort, "but though I have taxed my memory, I am ashamed to say, I do not recollect having seen you."

"Strangely enough, I do not recollect it either," remarked Valentine, raising her beautiful eyes to the Count.

"I remember," said Edward.

"I will assist you, madame," resumed the Count. "It was a baking hot day; you were waiting for your carriage, which had been delayed in consequence of the feast-day celebrations, mademoiselle went down the garden while your son was chasing the bird; you stayed in the arbour. Do you not remember sitting on a stone bench there, talking for a long time with some one?"

"It is true," said the lady, turning a deep red. "I recollect now. I was conversing with a gentleman in a long woollen mantle . . . I believe he was a doctor."

"Exactly so. I was that man. I had been staying at that hotel for the past fortnight and had cured my valet of a fever and my host of the jaundice, so that I was looked upon as a great doctor. We talked for a long time on different topics. I do not recollect all the details of our conversation, but I do remember that, sharing the general erroneous opinion about me, you consulted me about your daughter's health."

At this moment the clock struck six.

"It is six o'clock," said Mme de Villefort, obviously agitated. "Will you go and see whether your grandfather is ready for his dinner, Valentine?"

Valentine rose and, bowing to the Count, left the room without saying a word.

"Was it on my account that you sent Mademoiselle Valentine away?" asked the Count when Valentine had gone.

"Not at all," was the quick reply. "It is the hour when we give Monsieur de Noirtier the miserable repast which supports his wretched existence. You are aware, monsieur, of the deplorable condition of Monsieur de Villefort's father?"

"Yes, madame. He is paralysed, I think?"

"He is, alas! The poor old man has lost all power of movement; his mind alone is active in this poor human machine, and even that is weak and flickering like a lamp waiting to be extinguished. Excuse me for worrying you with our domestic troubles. I interrupted you when you were telling me that you were a skilful doctor."

"I did not say that, madame," replied the Count with a smile. "Quite the contrary. I have studied chemistry because, having decided to live chiefly in the East, I wished to follow the example of King Mithridates."

"*Mithridates, rex Ponticus,*" said the young scamp, cutting up some illustrations in a magnificent album; "that was the one who breakfasted every morning off a cup of poison with cream."

"Edward, you naughty child!" Mme de Villefort cried out, snatching the mutilated book from her son's hands. "You are unbearable and only make yourself a nuisance. Leave us and go along to your sister in your grandfather's room."

"The album!" said Edward.

"What do you mean?"

"I want the album!"

"Why have you cut up the drawings?"

"Because it amused me!"

"Leave us! Go!"

"I shan't go until you have given me the album!" said the child, settling himself down in a big armchair, true to his habit of never yielding.

"Here it is! Now leave us in peace!" said Mme de Villefort.

She gave Edward the book, and he went out.

"Allow me to observe, madame," said the Count good-naturedly, "that you are very severe with your mischievous child."

"It is sometimes necessary," replied Mme de Villefort with all the firmness of a mother.

"He was reciting his Cornelius Nepos when he spoke of King

Mithridates," said the Count, "and you interrupted a quotation which proves that his tutor has not lost time with him; in fact that your son is advanced for his age."

"The fact is, Count," replied the mother, pleasantly flattered, "that he is very quick, and can learn all he wants to. He has only one fault: he is very self-willed. But do you really think Mithridates took such precautions and that they were efficacious?"

"I believe it so firmly that I myself have taken these precautions so as not to be poisoned at Naples, Palermo, and Smyrna, that is to say, in the three cases when, without these precautions, I should have lost my life."

"Did you find this means successful?"

"Perfectly."

"It is true. I recollect that you told me something about it at Perugia."

"Really?" said the Count with well-feigned surprise. "I do not remember."

"I asked you whether poisons acted with the same force with Northerners as with Southerners, and you informed me that the cold, lymphatic temperament of the Northerners did not offer the same aptitude as the rich and energetic nature of the Southerners."

"It is true," said Monte Cristo, "I have seen Russians devour vegetable substances without being in the least indisposed, which would have infallibly killed a Neapolitan or an Arab."

"Then do you think the result would be more certain with us than in the East, and that, in the midst of our fog and rain, a man would become more easily accustomed to this progressive absorption of poison than he would do in a warm climate?"

"Certainly. It must be understood, however, that he would only become immune from the particular poison to which he had accustomed himself."

"I quite understand that. But tell me, how would you accustom yourself, or rather how did you accustom yourself?"

"It is quite easy. Supposing you knew beforehand what poison was going to be administered to you, supposing this poison were brucine, for instance——"

"Brucine is extracted from the *Brucea ferruginea*, is it not?" inquired Mme de Villefort.

"Just so. Well, then, supposing the poison were brucine," resumed the Count, "and that you took a milligramme the first day, two milligrammes the second day, and so on progressively. Well, at the end of ten days you would have taken a centigramme; at the end of twenty days, by increasing this by another milligramme, you would have taken another three centigrammes; that is to say, a dose you would absorb without suffering inconvenience, but which would be extremely dangerous for any other person who had not taken the same precautions as yourself. Well, then, at the end of a month you would have killed the person who drank the water out of the same carafe as yourself; yet, except for a slight indisposition, you would have no other indication that there was poisonous substance mixed with the water."

"Do you know of any other antidote?"

"I do not."

Mme de Villefort sat pensive. After a short silence she said:

"It is very fortunate that such substances can only be prepared by chemists, otherwise one-half of the world would be poisoning the other."

"By chemists or those who dabble in chemistry," replied Monte Cristo carelessly.

"And then no matter how scientifically planned a crime may be, it is still a crime," said Mme de Villefort, tearing herself from her thoughts with an effort, "and though it may escape human investigation, it cannot escape the eye of God. Yes, there is conscience to grapple with," continued Mme de Villefort in a voice broken with emotion and stifling a sigh.

"It is fortunate that we still have some conscience left, otherwise we should be very unhappy," said Monte Cristo. "After any vigorous action it is conscience that saves us, for it furnishes us with a thousand and one excuses of which we alone are judges, and however excellent these reasons may be to lull us to sleep, before a tribunal they would most likely avail us little in preserving our lives. Take, for instance, Lady Macbeth. She found an excellent servant in her conscience, for she wanted a throne, not for her husband but for her son. Ah, maternal love is a great virtue and such a powerful motive that it excuses much. But for her conscience, Lady Macbeth would have been very unhappy after Duncan's death."

"Do you know, Count, that you are a terrible reasoner," said Mme de Villefort after a moment's silence, "and that you view the world through very dark spectacles! Is it by regarding humanity through alembics and retorts that you have formed your opinion? You are right; you are a great chemist, and the elixir you administered to my son which brought him back to life so rapidly . . ."

"Oh! madame," said Monte Cristo, "one drop of the elixir sufficed to call the dying child back to life, but three drops would have forced the blood to his lungs in such a manner as to produce palpitations of the heart; six would have arrested respiration and caused a much more serious syncope; ten would have killed him! You may remember, madame, how eagerly I snatched from him the phials that he so imprudently touched."

"Is it such a terrible poison then?"

"Good gracious, no! First of all let us admit that the word poison does not exist, since poisons are used in medicines and, according to the manner in which they are administered, become health-giving remedies."

"What is your elixir then?"

"A scientific preparation of my friend, the Abbé Adelmonte, who taught me the use of it."

"It must be an excellent antispasmodic," observed Mme de Villefort.

"A perfect one, madame. You saw for yourself. I frequently make use of it; with all possible prudence of course," he added with a laugh.

"I should think so," replied Mme de Villefort in the same tone. "As for me, who am so nervous and prone to fainting, I need a Doctor Adelmonte to invent for me some means of breathing freely to relieve me of my fear that I shall suffocate one of these days. In the meantime, as it is difficult to obtain it in France, and as your abbé will not feel inclined to make a journey to Paris on my account, I must content myself with Monsieur Planche's antispasmodics."

"But I have the pleasure of offering it to you," said Monte Cristo, rising.

"Oh, Count!"

"Only remember one thing. In small doses it is a remedy, in large doses it is a poison! One drop will restore life as you have witnessed, five or six will inevitably kill and all the more terribly that, even when diluted in a glass of wine, it in no way changes the flavour. But I will say no more, madame. It is almost as if I were advising you."

The clock struck half-past six, and a friend of Mme de Villefort's, who was dining with her, was announced.

"If I had the pleasure of seeing you for the third or fourth time, Count, instead of the second, if I had the honour of being your friend instead of simply having the pleasure of being under an obligation to you, I should insist on keeping you for dinner, and I should not let myself be daunted by a first refusal."

"A thousand thanks, madame," replied Monte Cristo, "but I have an engagement which I cannot avoid. I have promised to take to the Opera a Grecian princess of my acquaintance, who has never yet seen Grand Opera and is relying on me to escort her."

"I will not detain you then, but do not forget my recipe."

"Most assuredly not, madame, for that would mean forgetting the hour's conversation I have just had with you, and that would be impossible."

Monte Cristo bowed and went out.

Mme de Villefort remained standing, wrapt in thought.
"He is a strange man," said she, "and I could almost believe his baptismal name is Adelmonte."

As for Monte Cristo, the results had far surpassed all expectations. "Here is fruitful soil," said he to himself as he went away. "I am convinced that the seed I have sown has not fallen on barren ground."

Next morning, faithful to his promise, he sent the prescription Mme de Villefort had requested.

## CHAPTER XXXVII

## THE RISE AND FALL OF STOCKS

SOME days later, Albert de Morcerf called on the Count of Monte Cristo at his house in the Champs Élysées, which had already assumed that palace-like appearance that the Count, thanks to his immense fortune, always gave even to his temporary residences.

Albert was accompanied by Lucien Debray. The Count attributed this visit to a twofold sentiment of curiosity, the larger share of which emanated from the Rue de la Chaussée d'Antin. It was obvious that Mme Danglars, being unable to view with her own eyes the home of the man who gave away horses worth thirty thousand francs, and who went to the opera accompanied by a slave wearing a million's worth of diamonds, had sent her deputy to gather what information he could. Notwithstanding, the Count did not appear to suspect the slightest connexion between Lucien's visit and the Baroness's curiosity.

"You are in constant communication with Baron Danglars?" he inquired of Albert de Morcerf.

"Oh, yes, you know what I told you."

"It still holds good then?"

"It is quite a settled affair," interposed Lucien, and, doubtless thinking that this remark was all he was called upon to make, he put his tortoiseshell lorgnette to his eye and, with the gold top of his stick in his mouth, began to pace round the room examining the different pictures and weapons.

"Is Mademoiselle Eugénie pretty?" asked Monte Cristo. "I seem to remember that is her name."

"Very pretty, or rather beautiful," replied Albert, "but it is a beauty I do not appreciate. I am an undeserving fellow! Mademoiselle Danglars is too rich for me. Her riches frighten me."

"That's a fine reason to give!" said Monte Cristo. "Are you not rich yourself?"

"My father has an income of some fifty thousand francs, and will probably give me ten or twelve thousand when I marry. But there is something besides that."

"I must own I can hardly understand your objections to such a beautiful and rich young woman," replied the Count.

"Even if there are any objections, they are not all on my side."

"Who raises objections then? I think you told me your father was in favour of the marriage."

"My mother objects to it, and she has a very prudent and penetrating eye. She does not smile on this union; for some reason she has a prejudice against the Danglars family."

"Ah, that is quite comprehensible," said the Count in a somewhat strained tone of voice. "The Countess of Morcerf, who is distinction, aristocracy, and refinement personified, is somewhat disinclined to touch the thick, clumsy hand of a plebeian; that is only natural."

"I really do not know whether that is the reason," said Albert. "What I do know is that, if this marriage is concluded, it will make her unhappy. It would be too great a disappointment to my father if I did not marry Mademoiselle Danglars. And yet I would rather quarrel with the Count than cause my mother pain."

Monte Cristo turned away, apparently agitated.

"What are you doing there?" said he to Debray, who was seated in a deep armchair at the other end of the room with a pencil in one hand and notebook in the other. "Are you making a sketch of that Poussin?"

"I?" said he calmly; "a sketch! No, I am doing something very different. I am doing some arithmetic."

"Arithmetic?"

"Yes, and it concerns you indirectly, Morcerf. I was reckoning what the firm of Danglars have gained by the last rise in Hayti stock; they have risen from two hundred and six to four hundred and nine in three days, and the wise banker bought a large amount at two hundred and six. He must have gained three hundred thousand francs."

"That is not his best deal," said Morcerf. "Didn't he make a million this year with his Spanish bonds?"

"Yes, but the Haytis are quite a different matter. Yesterday Monsieur Danglars sold them at four hundred and six and pocketed three hundred thousand francs; had he waited until to-day when the bonds fell to two hundred and five, he would have lost twenty-five thousand francs instead of making three hundred thousand."

"But why have the bonds fallen from four hundred and nine to two hundred and five?" asked Monte Cristo. "Pardon my question, but I am very ignorant of all these tricks on the Exchange."

"Because one piece of news follows the other and there is great dissimilarity between them," replied Albert with a laugh. "What? Does Monsieur Danglars speculate at the risk of losing or gaining three hundred thousand francs a day? He must be enormously rich!"

"It is not he who speculates," exclaimed Lucien energetically. "It is Madame Danglars. She is very daring."

"But you should stop her," said Morcerf with a smile. "You have common sense enough to know how little one can rely on *communiqués*, for you are at their very source."

"How should I be able to stop her when her husband has not yet succeeded in doing so? You know the Baroness. No one has any influence over her. She does just what she pleases."

"If I were in your place, I should cure her," said Albert. "You would be doing a kind action to her future son-in-law."

"How would you set about it?"

"It would be perfectly easy. I should teach her a lesson. Your position as Minister's secretary gives you great power over telegraphic dispatches. You never open your mouth to speak but stockbrokers take down every word you say. Make her lose a hundred thousand francs and she will soon be more careful."

"I don't understand," stammered Lucien.

"Nevertheless it is quite comprehensible," replied the young man simply. "One fine morning tell her something stupendous, a telegraphic communication that you alone could know, for example, that Henry the Fourth was seen yesterday at Gabrielle's. That would cause the bonds to rise, she would speculate and would certainly lose when Beauchamp wrote in his journal the following day: 'The news circulated by some well-informed person that King Henry the Fourth was seen at Gabrielle's the day before yesterday is absolutely without foundation; King Henry the Fourth has not left the Pont Neuf.'"

Lucien gave a forced laugh. Monte Cristo, to all appearances quite indifferent to the conversation, had not lost one word of it, and his quick perception had detected a hidden secret in the private secretary's embarrassment.

In fact Lucien was so embarrassed, though Albert did not perceive it, that he cut short his visit. He evidently felt ill at ease. When the Count accompanied him to the door, he said something to him in a low voice to which he replied: "I accept with pleasure, Count."

The Count returned to young Morcerf, and said: "Do you not think that, on reflection, you were wrong to speak as you did of your mother-in-law before Monsieur Debray?"

"Not so fast, Count," said Morcerf. "I pray, do not give her that title so prematurely."

"Without any exaggeration, is your mother really so greatly opposed to this marriage?"

"To such an extent that the Baroness rarely comes to the house, and so far as I know, my mother has not visited Madame Danglars twice in her whole life."

"Then I am emboldened to speak openly to you," said the Count. "Monsieur Danglars is my banker; Monsieur de Villefort has overwhelmed me with politeness in return for a service which a casual piece of good fortune enabled me to render him. I predict from this an avalanche of dinners and parties. Now, in order to forestall them, and if it be agreeable to you, I propose inviting Monsieur and Madame Danglars and Monsieur and Madame de Villefort to my country house in Auteuil. If I were to invite you and the Count and Countess of Morcerf to this dinner, it would give it the air of a matrimonial rendezvous, or at least, Madame de Mercerf would look upon it in that light, especially if Baron Danglars did me the honour of bringing his daughter. In that case I should incur your mother's displeasure, and that I do not wish; on the contrary (pray tell her this whenever the occasion arises), I desire to occupy a prominent place in her esteem."

"I thank you sincerely for having been so candid with me, Count, and I gratefully accept the exclusion you propose. You say you desire my mother's good opinion of you; I assure you it is already yours to a very large extent."

"Do you think so?" said Monte Cristo interestedly.

"I am sure of it; we talked of you for an hour after you left us the other day. But to return to what we were saying. If my mother knew of this consideration on your part, and I will venture to tell her, I am sure she would be most grateful to you; it is true that my father will be equally furious."

The Count laughed.

"But I think your father will not be the only angry one," he said to Morcerf. "Monsieur and Madame Danglars will think me a very ill-mannered person. They know that I am on an intimate footing with you, that you are in fact one of my oldest Paris acquaintances, yet they will not find you at my house. They will certainly ask me why I did not invite you. Be sure to provide yourself with some prior engagement with a semblance of probability, and communicate the fact to me in writing. You know that with bankers nothing but a written document is valid."

"I will do better than that," said Albert. "My mother is anxious to go to the seaside. For which day is your dinner fixed?"

"Saturday."

"This is Tuesday. Well, we will leave to-morrow evening, and the day after we shall be at Tréport. Do you know, Count, you have a charming way of setting people at their ease."

"Indeed, you give me credit for more than I deserve; I only wish to do what would be agreeable to you."

"That is settled, then. Now will you show yourself a true friend and come and dine with me? We shall be a small party, only yourself, my mother and I. You have scarcely seen my mother; you will have an opportunity of making her closer acquaintance. She is a remarkable woman, and I only regret there does not exist another about twenty years younger like her. In that case I assure you there would very soon be a Countess and a Viscountess of Morcerf."

"A thousand thanks," said the Count. "Your invitation is most kind, and I regret exceedingly that it is not in my power to accept it. I am not so free as you suppose; on the contrary, I have a most important engagement."

"Take care! You showed me just now how one could creditably refuse an unwelcome invitation. I require proofs. I am not a banker like Monsieur Danglars, but, I assure you, I am as incredulous as he."

"I will give you a proof," said the Count as he rang the bell.

"Humph!" said Morcerf. "This is the second time you have refused to dine with my mother; it is evidently done deliberately."

Monte Cristo started. "You do not mean that," said he. "Besides, here comes my proof."

Baptistin entered and remained standing at the door.

"Baptistin," said the Count, "what did I tell you this morning when I called you into my study?"

"To close the door against visitors as soon as the clock struck five," replied the valet.

"What then?"

"You further told me to admit no one but Major Bartolomeo Cavalcanti and his son."

"You hear: Major Cavalcanti, a man who ranks amongst the most ancient nobility of Italy, whose name Dante has celebrated in the tenth canto of the *Inferno*; you remember it, don't you? Then there is his son, a charming young man of about your own age, Viscount, and bearing the same title as yourself, who is making his debut into Paris society aided by his father's millions. The Major will bring his son, the *contino,* as we say in Italy, with him this evening; he wishes to confide him to my care. If he prove himself worthy of it, I will do what I can for him; you will assist me, will you not?"

"Most certainly. This Major Cavalcanti is an old friend of yours?"

"By no means. I met him several times at Florence, Bologna, and

Lucca, and he has now communicated to me that he has arrived here.
I shall give him a good dinner; he will confide his son to my care; I
shall promise to watch over him; I shall let him follow in whatever
path his folly may lead him, and then I shall have done my part."

"Splendid! I see you are a valuable mentor," said Albert. "Good-bye.
We shall be back on Sunday. By the way, I have received news of Franz."

"Have you? Is he still enjoying himself in Italy?"

"I believe so, and he greatly regrets your absence. He says you were
the sun of Rome, and that without you all appears dark and cloudy; I
am not sure that he does not go so far as to say that it rains."

"He is a charming young man," said Monte Cristo, "and I have
always felt a lively interest in him. He is the son of General d'Épinay,
I think."

"Yes, he is."

"The same who was so shamefully assassinated in eighteen-fifteen?"

"By the Bonapartists."

"That's it. Really, I like him extremely. Is there not a matrimonial
engagement contemplated for him, too?"

"Yes, he is to marry Mademoiselle de Villefort."

"Indeed!"

"And you know I am to marry Mademoiselle Danglars," said
Albert laughing.

"You smile? Why?"

"I smile because there seems to me to be as much sympathy for that
marriage as there is for my own. But really, my dear Count, we are
talking as much of women as they do of us; it is unpardonable."

Albert rose.

"Give my compliments to your illustrious visitor, Cavalcanti," he
continued, "and if by any chance he should be desirous of finding a
wife for his son who is very rich, of very noble birth on her mother's
side, and a Baroness in right of her father, I will help you to find one."

And with a laugh Albert departed.

## CHAPTER XXXVIII

## PYRAMUS AND THISBE

OUR readers must permit us to conduct them to the enclosure surrounding Monsieur de Villefort's house, and, behind the gate half
hidden by wide-spreading chestnut-trees, we shall find some persons
of our acquaintance.

Maximilian was the first to arrive. With his eyes close to the fence he was watching for a shadow among the trees at the bottom of the garden, and listening for a footfall on the gravel paths.

At length the desired sound was heard, but instead of one shadow there were two. Valentine had been delayed by a visit from Mme Danglars and Eugénie which had lasted longer than she had anticipated; but that she might not fail to keep her appointment with Maximilian, she had proposed to Mlle Danglars that they should take a walk in the garden, which would enable her to show Maximilian that the delay was not caused by any fault of hers.

With the intuitive perception of a lover, the young man understood the circumstances and was greatly relieved. Besides, without coming within speaking distance, Valentine led her companion where Maximilian could see her go by, and each time she passed near him a look, unperceived by her companion, said to him: "Have patience, my friend, you see it is none of my doing."

And Maximilian was patient and spent his time appreciating the contrast between the two young girls: the one fair-haired, with languid eyes and a tall figure, slightly bent like a beautiful weeping willow; the other dark-haired, with fiery eyes and a figure as upright as a poplar. Needless to say, the comparison between these two opposed natures was all in Valentine's favour, at least in the opinion of the young man.

At the end of half an hour, the girls disappeared, and an instant later Valentine returned alone. She ran up to the gate.

"Good evening, Valentine," said a voice.

"Good evening, Maximilian. I have kept you waiting, but you saw the reason."

"Yes, I recognized Mademoiselle Danglars. I did not know you were so intimate with her."

"Who told you we were intimate?"

"No one, but the manner in which you walked and talked rather suggested it. You looked like two schoolgirls exchanging confidences."

"We were in fact exchanging confidences," returned Valentine. "She was telling me how repugnant to her was the idea of a marriage with Monsieur de Morcerf, and I confessed to her how unhappy I was at the thought of marrying Monsieur d'Épinay. In speaking of the man I cannot love, I thought of the man I love. She told me that she detests the idea of marriage, that her greatest joy would be to lead a free and independent life, and that she almost wished her father would lose his fortune so that she could become an artist like her friend, Mademoiselle Louise d'Armilly. But let us talk of ourselves and not of her, for we have not more than ten minutes together."

"Why, what has happened, Valentine, that you must leave me so soon?"

"I do not know. Madame de Villefort told me to go to her room as she had something to communicate to me which influences a part of my fortune. Ah, well! let them take the whole of my fortune, I am too rich. When they have taken it, perhaps they will leave me in peace. You would love me just as much if I were poor, would you not, Maximilian?"

"I shall always love you. What should I care about wealth or poverty so long as my Valentine was near me, and I was sure no one could take her from me! But do you not fear the communication may be in connexion with your approaching marriage?"

"I do not think so."

"In any case, listen to me, Valentine, and do not be afraid, for as long as I live, I will never belong to another."

"Do you think you make me happy by telling me that, Maximilian?"

"Forgive me, dear, for being such a churl. What I wanted to tell you is that the other day I met Monsieur de Morcerf who, as you know, is Monsieur Franz's friend. He had received a letter from him intimating his early return."

Valentine turned pale and leaned against the gate for support.

"Can it be that?" she cried. "But no, such a communication would not come from Madame de Villefort."

"Why not?"

"Because . . . I scarcely know why . . . but though she does not oppose my proposed marriage openly, Madame de Villefort seems to be against it."

"Is that so? Then I think I almost love Madame de Villefort!"

"Do not be in such a hurry, Maximilian," said Valentine with a sad smile.

"If she is averse to this marriage, let the engagement be broken off, and then perhaps she would lend her ear to some other proposal."

"Do not lay any hopes on that, Maximilian, it is not the husband my stepmother objects to, it is marriage itself."

"You don't mean to say so! But if she has such a strong aversion to marriage, why did she herself marry?"

"You do not understand. A year ago, when I spoke of entering a convent, though she felt it her duty to make certain comments, she accepted my proposal with joy. Even my father consented—at her instigation, I am sure. It was my poor grandfather kept me back! Maximilian, you can have no idea of the expression in the eyes of the old man, who loves no one but me, and (may God forgive me if I am wrong) who is loved by no one but me. If you knew how he looked at me when he heard of my resolution! What reproach there was in those dear eyes and despair in the uncomplaining tears that chased each other down his lifeless cheeks! Oh, Maximilian, I felt such remorse that I threw myself at his feet exclaiming: 'Forgive me. Oh, forgive me, Grandfather! Let them do with me what they will, I will never leave you!' He just raised his eyes to Heaven! I can suffer much! That look recompensed me in advance for all I shall suffer."

"Dearest Valentine! You are an angel, and I am sure I do not know in what way I have merited your love. But tell me, how could it be to Madame de Villefort's interest that you should not marry?"

"Did I not tell you just now that I was rich, too rich? I have an income of nearly fifty thousand francs from my father; my grandfather and grandmother, the Marquis and Marquise of Saint-Méran, will leave me a similar amount; Monsieur Noirtier obviously intends to make me his sole heir. By comparison with me, therefore, my brother Edward, who will inherit no fortune from his mother, is poor. Madame de Villefort's love for this child amounts to adoration, and if I had taken the veil, all my fortune would have descended to my father, and would ultimately have reverted to her son."

"How strange that such a young and beautiful woman should be so avaricious!"

"It is not for herself she wants the money; it is for her son, and what you consider a vice is almost a virtue from the point of view of maternal love."

"But why not give up part of your fortune to her son?"

"How could I propose such a thing, especially to a woman who continually speaks of her disinterestedness?"

"Valentine, my love is sacred to me, and, this being so, I have covered it with the veil of respect and locked the door to my heart. No one knows of its existence there, for I have confided in no one. Will you permit me to speak of this love to a friend?"

Valentine started. "To a friend?" said she. "Oh, to hear you speak thus makes me shudder. Who is this friend?"

"Valentine, have you never felt for anyone an irresistible sympathy so that, though you meet this person for the first time, you feel you have known him long since?"

"I have."

"Well, then, this is the feeling I had the first time I saw this extraordinary man, who has, I hear, the power to prophesy."

"Then," said the girl sadly, "let me know him that I may learn from him whether I shall be loved sufficiently to compensate me for all I have suffered."

"Poor girl! You know him already. It is he who saved the life of your stepmother and her son."

"The Count of Monte Cristo!"

"It is he."

"Oh, he can never be my friend!" exclaimed Valentine. "He is too much the friend of Madame de Villefort ever to be mine."

"The Count your stepmother's friend, Valentine? That cannot be! I am sure you must be mistaken."

"If you but knew! It is no longer Edward who rules in the house, it is the Count. Courted by my stepmother who sees in him the essence of human knowledge; admired, mark well, Maximilian, admired by my father, who says he has never heard the most elevated ideas expressed so eloquently; idolized by Edward, who, despite his fear of the Count's large black eyes, runs to him as soon as he arrives and forces his hand open, where he always finds some fascinating toy. Monte Cristo is not in my father's or my stepmother's house, he is in his own house."

"Valentine, you are mistaken, I assure you!"

"If it were otherwise, he would have honoured me at least with one of those smiles, of which you think so much. On the contrary, he sees me unhappy, but he realizes that I can be of no use to him, so he does not pay any attention to me. Quite frankly, I am not a woman to be treated with contempt in this manner without any reason for it. You yourself have told me as much. Forgive me, Maximilian," she continued on seeing the impression her words were producing on Maximilian. "I am a wicked girl, and am saying things about this man that I did not know existed in my heart. Alas, I see that I have pained you! If only I could take your hand to ask your forgiveness! I desire nothing better than to be convinced. Tell me, what has this Count done for you?"

"I must confess that question rather embarrasses me. He has done nothing that I can definitely mention. My friendship for him is as unaccountable as his is for me. A secret voice warns me that there is something more than chance in this unlooked-for reciprocity of friendship. You will laugh at me, I know, but ever since I have known him the absurd idea possesses me that everything good that befalls me comes from him! Yet I have lived for thirty years without feeling the need of this friendship. I will give you an example of his consideration for me. He has invited me to dinner on Saturday, which is quite natural in view of our present relations. But what have I learned since? Your mother and father are also invited. I shall meet them, and who knows what will be the issue of such a meeting? In appearance this is a perfectly simple circumstance, I know; nevertheless I see in it something that astonishes me and fills me with a strange hope. I cannot help thinking that this extraordinary man, who divines all things, has arranged this meeting with some aim in view. I assure you there are times when I try to read in his eyes whether he has not even guessed my love for you."

"My dear," said Valentine, "I should take you for a visionary, and should really fear for your reason if I were to listen to many more such arguments from you. No, no, believe me, apart from you, there is no one in this world to whom I can turn for help and support but my grandfather, who is not much more than alive, and my poor mother, of whom there is nothing left but a shadow."

"I feel that you are right, Valentine, from a logical point of view, but your sweet voice, which at other times possesses so much power over me, cannot convince me to-day."

"Neither can you convince me," said Valentine, "and I will confess that if you have no other proofs to give me . . ."

"But I have," interrupted Maximilian, "though I am compelled to own that it sounds even more absurd than the first one. Look through the palings and you will see tied to that tree yonder the horse that brought me here."

"What a beautiful animal!" exclaimed Valentine. "Why did you not bring him up to the gate? I should have spoken to him, and he would have understood me!"

"As you see, it is really a very valuable animal," Maximilian continued. "You also know that my income is limited, and I am what one would call a careful man. I went to a horsedealer's and saw this magnificent animal that I have called Médéah. On asking the price, I was told four thousand five hundred francs. As you can imagine I admired it no longer but, I must confess, I left with a heavy heart. I had a few friends at my house that evening, and they proposed a game of *bouillotte*. As we were seating ourselves at the table, the Count of Monte Cristo arrived. He took his seat, we played, and I won. I hardly dare tell you how much: it was five thousand francs! We parted at midnight. I could contain myself no longer; I took a cab and drove to the horsedealer's and, filled with feverish excitement, rang the bell. The man who opened the door to me must have taken me for a madman. I rushed through to the stable. Oh, joy! There was Médéah calmly eating his hay. I took a saddle and bridle and put them on him; then, placing the four thousand five hundred francs in the astonished dealer's hand, I leapt on to Médéah's back and spent the night riding in the Champs Élysées. I saw a light in the Count's window, and I seemed to see his shadow behind the curtain. Now, I am perfectly certain the Count knew how badly I wanted that horse, and that he intentionally lost at cards so that I might win."

"Dearest Maximilian, you are becoming so fanciful that I verily believe you will not love me any more. A man who lives in such a world of poetry will grow weary of a monotonous passion such as ours. But listen, they are calling me. Do you hear?"

"Oh, Valentine, give me your little finger through the gate that I may kiss it!"

"Maximilian, we said we would be to each other as two voices, two shadows."

"As you wish, Valentine."

"Will it make you happy if I do what you ask?"

"Oh, yes!"

Valentine jumped on to a bench and passed her whole hand, not her little finger, through the grating.

Maximilian uttered a cry of joy and, springing forward, seized the beloved hand and imprinted on it a long and impassioned kiss; but the little hand slipped out of his almost immediately, and the young man heard his beloved running toward the house, frightened perhaps at her own sensations.

## CHAPTER XXXIX

## M. NOIRTIER DE VILLEFORT

THIS is what happened in the house of the Procureur du Roi after the departure of Mme Danglars and her daughter, and while the foregoing conversation was taking place.

M. de Villefort entered his father's room followed by Mme de Villefort. After saluting the old man and dismissing Barrois, his old servant, they seated themselves on either side of the old gentleman.

M. Noirtier was sitting in his wheel-chair, to which he was carried every morning and left there until the evening. Sight and hearing were the only two senses that, like two solitary sparks, animated this poor human body that was so near the grave. His hair was white and long, reaching down to his shoulders, while his eyes were black, overshadowed by black eyebrows, and, as is generally the case when one organ is used to the exclusion of the others; in these eyes were concentrated all the activity, skill, strength, and intelligence which had formerly characterized his whole body and mind. It is true that the gesture of the arm, the sound of the voice, the attitude of the body were now lacking, but his masterful eye supplied their place. He commanded with his eyes and thanked with his eyes; he was a corpse with living eyes, and nothing was more terrifying than when, in this face of marble, they were lit up in fiery anger or sparkled with joy. There were only three persons who understood the language of the poor paralytic—Villefort, Valentine, and the old servant. As Villefort rarely saw his father, however, and even then did not take any pains to understand him, all the old man's happiness centered upon his grand-daughter, and by force of devotion, love, and patience, she had learned to read all his thoughts by his look. To this dumb language, unintelligible to all others, she replied by throwing her whole soul into her voice and the expression of her countenance. In this manner animated dialogues took place between the granddaughter and this mere lump of clay, now nearly turned to dust, which constituted the body of a man still in possession of an immense fund of knowledge and most extraordinary perception, together with a will as powerful as it is possible for a mind to possess which is encumbered by a body over which it has lost the power of compelling obedience.

His servant had been with him for twenty-five years and was so perfectly acquainted with his master's habits that Noirtier rarely had to ask for anything.

"Do not be astonished, monsieur," Villefort began, "that Valentine is not with us or that I have dismissed Barrois, for our interview is one which could not take place before a young girl or a servant. Madame de Villefort and I have a communication to make which we feel sure will be agreeable to you. We are going to marry Valentine."

A wax figure could not have evinced more indifference on hearing this intelligence than did M. Noirtier.

"The marriage will take place within three months," continued Villefort.

The old man's eyes were still expressionless.

Mme de Villefort then took her part in the conversation, and added: "We thought this news would be of interest to you, monsieur, for Valentine has always appeared to be the object of your affection. It now only remains for us to tell you the name of the young man for whom she is destined. It is one of the most desirable connexions Valentine could aspire to; he has a fortune, a good name, and her future happiness is guaranteed by the good qualities and tastes of him for whom we have destined her. His name is not unknown to you, for the young man in question is Monsieur Franz de Quesnel, Baron d'Épinay."

During his wife's discourse, Villefort fixed his eyes upon the old man with greater attention than ever. When the name of Franz d'Épinay was uttered, Noirtier's eyes, whose every expression was comprehensible to his son, quivered like lips trying to speak, and sent forth a lightning dart. The Procureur du Roi was well aware of the reports formerly current of public enmity between his own father and Franz's father, and he understood Noirtier's agitation and anger. Feigning not to perceive either, however, he resumed the conversation where his wife had left off.

"It is important, monsieur," he said, "that Valentine, who is about to enter upon her nineteenth year, should finally be settled in life. Nevertheless, we have not forgotten you in our discussions on the matter and have ascertained that the future husband of Valentine will consent, not to live with you, as that might be embarrassing for a young couple, but that you live with them. In this way you and Valentine, who are so greatly attached to one another, will not be separated, and you will not need to make any change in your mode of living. The only difference will be that you will have two children to take care of you instead of one."

Noirtier's look was one of fury. It was evident that something desperate was passing through the old man's mind and that there rose to his throat a cry of anger and grief which, being unable to find vent in utterance, was choking him, for his face became purple and his lips blue.

"This marriage," continued Mme de Villefort, "is acceptable to Monsieur d'Épinay and his family, which, by the way, only consists of an uncle and aunt. His mother died in giving him birth, and his father was assassinated in eighteen-fifteen, that is to say, when the child was barely two years of age. He has, therefore, only his own wishes to consult."

"That assassination was most mysterious," continued Villefort, "and the perpetrators are still unknown, although suspicion has fallen on many."

Noirtier made such an effort to speak that his lips expanded into a weird kind of smile.

"Now the real criminals," continued Villefort, "those who are conscious of having committed the crime and upon whose heads the justice of man may fall during their lifetime and the justice of God after their death, would be only too happy if they had, like us, a daughter to offer to Monsieur Franz d'Épinay to allay all appearances of suspicion."

Noirtier composed his feelings with a mastery one would not have supposed existed in that shattered frame.

"I understand," his look said to Villefort, and this look expressed at once a feeling of profound contempt and intelligent anger. Villefort read in it all that it contained, but merely shrugged his shoulders in reply, and made a sign to his wife to take her leave.

"I will leave you now," she said. "May I send Edward to pay his respects to you?"

It had been arranged that the old man should express assent by closing his eyes, refusal by blinking several times, a desire for something by casting a look heavenward. If he wanted Valentine, he only closed his right eye, if Barrois the left.

At Mme de Villefort's proposal he blinked vigorously. Vexed at this

refusal, Mme de Villefort bit her lips as she said: "Would you like me
to send Valentine, then?"

"Yes," signed the old man, shutting his right eye tightly.

M. and Mme de Villefort bowed and left the room, giving orders
for Valentine to be summoned. She had, however, already been
warned that her presence would be required in her grandfather's room
during the day. Still flushed with emotion, she entered as soon as her
parents had left. One glance at her grandfather told her how much he
was suffering, and that he had a great deal to communicate to her.

"Grandpapa dear, what has happened?" she exclaimed. "Have they
vexed you? Are you angry?"

"Yes," said he closing his eyes.

"With whom are you angry? Is it with my father? No. With
Madame de Villefort? No. With me?"

The old man made a sign of assent.

"With me?" repeated Valentine astonished. "What have I done,
dear Grandpapa? I have not seen you the whole day. Has anyone been
speaking against me?"

"Yes," said the old man, closing his eyes with emphasis.

"Let me think. I assure you, Grandpapa . . . Ah! Monsieur and
Madame de Villefort have been here. They must have said something
to annoy you? What is it? How you frighten me! Oh, dear, what can
they have said?" She thought for a moment. "I have it," she said, lowering her voice and drawing closer to the old man. "Did they perhaps
speak of my marriage?"

"Yes," replied the angry look.

"I understand. Are you afraid I shall forsake you and that my marriage will make me forgetful of you?"

"No," was the answer.

"Did they tell you that Monsieur d'Épinay agrees that we shall all
live together?"

"Yes."

"Then why are you angry?"

The old man's eyes beamed with an expression of gentle affection.

"I understand," said Valentine. "It is because you love me."

The old man made a sign of assent.

"Are you afraid I shall be unhappy?"

"Yes."

"Do you not like Franz?"

His eyes repeated three or four times: "No, no, no."

"Then you are very grieved?"

"Yes."

"Well, listen," said Valentine, throwing herself on her knees and putting her arms round his neck. "I am grieved, too, for I do not love Monsieur Franz d'Épinay. If only you could help me! If only we could frustrate their plans! But you are powerless against them, though your mind is so active and your will so firm."

As she said these words, there was such a look of deep cunning in Noirtier's eyes, that the girl thought she read these words therein: "You are mistaken, I can still do much for you."

Noirtier raised his eyes heavenward. It was the sign agreed upon between Valentine and himself whenever he wanted anything.

"What do you wish, Grandpapa?" She then recited all the letters of the alphabet until she came to N, all the while watching his eyes with a smile on her face. When she came to N he signalled assent.

"Then what you desire begins with the letter N. Now, let me see what you can want that begins with the letter N. Na . . . ne . . . ni . . . no . . ."

"Yes, yes, yes," said the old man's eyes.

Valentine fetched a dictionary, which she placed on a desk before Noirtier. She opened it, and, as soon as she saw that his eyes were fixed on its pages, she ran her fingers quickly up and down the columns. All the practice she had had during the six years since M. Noirtier first fell into this pitiable state had made her expert at detecting his wishes in this manner, and she guessed his thoughts as quickly as though he himself had been able to seek for what he wanted.

At the word 'Notary' the old man made a sign for her to stop.

"You wish me to send for a notary?" asked Valentine.

"Yes."

"Do you wish to have the notary at once?"

"Yes."

"Then he shall be sent for immediately."

Valentine rang the bell, and told the servant to request M. and Mme de Villefort to come to M. Noirtier.

"Are you satisfied now?" Valentine asked. "Yes, I am sure you are. But it was not easy to discover what you wanted, was it?"

And the maiden smiled at her grandfather as though he had been a child.


## CHAPTER XL

## THE WILL

THREE-QUARTERS of an hour later, Barrois returned bringing the notary with him.

"You were sent for by Monsieur Noirtier, whom you see here," said

Villefort after the first salutations were over. "He is paralysed and has lost the use of his voice and limbs, and we ourselves have great difficulty in understanding his thoughts."

Noirtier cast on Valentine an appealing look which was at once so earnest and imperative that she answered immediately: "Monsieur, I understand all that my grandfather wishes to say."

"That is true, absolutely true," said Barrois, "and it is what I told the gentleman as we walked along."

"Permit me," said the notary, turning first to Villefort and then to Valentine, "permit me to state that the case in question is just one of those in which a public official like myself cannot proceed to act without due consideration, as he might incur serious responsibility. The first thing necessary to render a document valid is that the notary is absolutely convinced that he has faithfully interpreted the wishes of the person dictating them. Now, I cannot be sure of the approbation or disapprobation of a client who cannot speak, and, as owing to his loss of speech the object of his desire or repugnance cannot be clearly proved to me, my services here would be more than useless and cannot be exercised legally."

The notary prepared to retire. An almost imperceptible smile of triumph was expressed on Villefort's lips, but Noirtier looked at Valentine with such an expression of grief that she arrested the departure of the notary.

"The language I speak with my grandfather, monsieur," said she, "is easily learnt, and in a very few minutes I can teach you to understand it almost as well as I do myself. By the help of two signs, you can be absolutely certain that my grandfather is still in full possession of all his mental faculties. Being deprived of power of speech and motion, Monsieur Noirtier closes his eyes when he wishes to signify 'yes,' and blinks when he means 'no.' You now know quite enough to enable you to converse with Monsieur Noirtier; try."

Noirtier gave Valentine such a look of love and gratitude that it was comprehended by the notary himself.

"Have you heard and understood what your granddaughter was telling me, monsieur?" the notary asked.

Noirtier closed his eyes gently and after a second opened them again.

"And you approve of what she said—that is, that the signs she mentioned are really those by means of which you are accustomed to convey your thoughts to others?"

"Yes."

"It was you who sent for me?"

"Yes."

"And you do not wish me to go away without carrying out your original intention?"

The old man blinked violently.

"Well, monsieur," said Valentine, "do you understand now? Will your conscience be at rest in regard to this matter? I can discover and explain to you my grandfather's thoughts so completely as to put an end to any doubts and fears you may have. I have now been six years with Monsieur Noirtier, and let him tell you if, during that time, he has ever entertained a thought which he was unable to make me understand."

"No," signalled the old man.

"Let us try what we can do then," said the notary. "Do you accept this young lady as your interpreter, Monsieur Noirtier?"

"Yes."

"What do you require of me, monsieur? What document do you wish me to draw up?"

Valentine named all the letters of the alphabet until she came to W. At this letter Noirtier's eloquent eyes notified that she was to stop.

"It is very evident that it is the letter W Monsieur Noirtier wants," the notary said.

"Wait," said Valentine, and, turning to her grandfather, she repeated: "Wa . . . we . . . wi . . ."

Her grandfather stopped her at the last syllable.

Valentine then took the dictionary, and the notary watched her whilst she turned over the pages. She passed her finger slowly down the columns, and when she came to the word 'Will' Monsieur Noirtier's eyes bade her stop.

"Will!" cried the notary. "It is very evident that monsieur desires to make his will"

"Yes, yes, yes!" motioned the invalid.

"Really, monsieur," interposed Villefort, "you must allow that this is most extraordinary; for I cannot see how the will is to be drawn up without Valentine's intervention and she may, perhaps, be considered as too much interested in its contents to allow of her being a suitable interpreter of the obscure and ill-defined wishes of her grandfather."

"No, no, no!" replied the eyes of the paralytic.

"What! Do you mean to say that Valentine is not interested in your will?" said Villefort.

"No."

"What appeared to me so impossible an hour ago has now become quite easy and practicable," said the notary, whose interest had been greatly excited. "This will be a perfectly valid will, provided it be read in the presence of seven witnesses approved by the testator, and sealed by the notary in the presence of the witnesses. In order to make the instrument incontestable, I shall give it the greatest possible authenticity. One of my colleagues will help me, and, contrary to custom, will assist in the dictation of the instrument. Are you satisfied, monsieur?" continued the notary, addressing M. Noirtier.

"Yes," looked the invalid, his eyes beaming with delight that his meaning had been so well understood.

"What is he going to do?" thought Villefort, whose position demanded so much reserve, though he was longing to know what were his father's intentions. He left the room to give orders to send for another notary, but Barrois, who had heard all that passed, had guessed his master's wishes and had already gone to fetch one. The Procureur du Roi called his wife up.

In the course of a quarter of an hour every one had assembled in the paralytic's room, and the second notary had also arrived. A few words sufficed for a mutual understanding between the two officers of the law. They read to Noirtier the formal copy of a will in order to give him an idea of the terms in which such documents are generally couched; then, to test the intelligence of the testator, the first notary, turning toward him, said:

"When an individual makes his will, it is generally in favour or in prejudice of some person."

"Yes."

"Have you an exact idea of the amount of your fortune?"

"Yes."

"Your fortune exceeds three hundred thousand francs, does it not?"

Noirtier made a sign that it did.

"Do you possess four hundred thousand francs?" inquired the notary.

Noirtier's eyes remained unmoved.

"Five hundred thousand?"

There was still no movement.

"Six hundred—seven hundred—nine hundred thousand?"

Noirtier stopped him at the last-named sum.

"You are then in possession of nine hundred thousand francs?" asked the notary.

"Yes."

"In scrip?"

"Yes."

"The scrip is in your own hands?"

The look which Noirtier cast on Barrois sent the old servant out of the room, and he presently returned, bringing a small casket.

"Do you permit us to open the casket?" asked the notary.

Noirtier gave his assent.

They opened it and found nine hundred thousand francs in bank scrip.

The first notary examined each note and handed them all to his colleague. The total amount was found to be as M. Noirtier stated.

"It is all as he said; it is very evident that his mind has retained its full force and vigour." Then, turning toward the paralytic, he said: "You possess nine hundred thousand francs of capital, which, according to the manner in which you have invested it, should bring in an income of forty thousand francs?"

"Yes."

"Is it, then, to Mademoiselle Valentine de Villefort that you leave these nine hundred thousand francs?" demanded the notary, thinking that he had but to insert this clause, though he must first wait for Noirtier's assent, which needed to be given before all the witnesses of this singular scene.

Valentine had stepped back with eyes cast down and was weeping silently. The old man looked at her for a moment with an expression of the deepest tenderness; then, turning toward the notary, he blinked in a most emphatic manner.

"What!" said the notary. "Do you intend making Mademoiselle Valentine de Villefort your residuary legatee?"

"No."

"You are not making any mistake, are you?" said the notary. "You really mean to say no?"

"No, no."

Valentine raised her head; she was astonished not so much at the fact that she was disinherited as that she should have provoked the feeling which generally dictates such actions. Noirtier, however, looked at her so lovingly that she exclaimed:

"Oh, Grandpapa! I see now that it is only your fortune of which you deprive me; you still leave me your love."

The old man's declaration that Valentine was not the destined inheritor of his fortune had raised hopes in Mme de Villefort; she approached the invalid and said:

"Then, doubtless, dear Monsieur Noirtier, you desire to leave your fortune to your grandson, Edward de Villefort?"

The blinking of the eyes was terrible in its vigour and expressed a feeling almost amounting to hatred.

"No!" said the notary. "Then perhaps to your son, Monsieur de Villefort?"

"No."

The two notaries looked at each other in mute astonishment and inquiry. Villefort and his wife both flushed a deep crimson, the one from shame, the other from anger.

"What have we all done, then, dear Grandpapa?:" said Valentine. "Do you not love us any more?"

Noirtier fixed his intelligent eyes on Valentine's hand.

"My hand?" said she. "Ah, I understand, I understand. It is my marriage you mean, is it not, dear Grandpapa?"

"Yes, yes, yes!" the paralytic repeated three times, and each time he raised his eyelids his eyes gleamed angrily.

"You are angry with us all on account of this marriage, are you not?"

"Yes."

"Really this is too absurd!" exclaimed Villefort.

"Excuse me, monsieur," said the notary, "but it is, on the contrary, very logical and I quite follow his train of thought."

"You do not wish me to marry Monsieur Franz d'Épinay?" observed Valentine.

"I do not wish it!" said her grandfather's eyes.

"And you disinherit your granddaughter," continued the notary, "because she has contracted an engagement contrary to your wishes?"

"Yes."

There was profound silence. The two notaries entered into consultation; Valentine, her hands clasped, looked at her grandfather with a smile of intense gratitude, and Villefort bit his thin lips in suppressed anger, whilst Mme de Villefort could not succeed in repressing an inward feeling of joy which, in spite of herself, was depicted on her whole countenance.

"But I consider that I am the best judge of the propriety of the marriage in question," said Villefort, who was the first to break the silence. "I alone possess the right to dispose of my daughter's hand. It is my wish that she should marry Monsieur Franz d'Épinay—and marry him she shall!"

Valentine sank into a chair, weeping.

"How do you intend disposing of your fortune, monsieur, in the event of Mademoiselle de Villefort marrying Monsieur Franz?" said the notary. "You will, of course, dispose of it in some way or other?"

"Yes."

"In favour of some member of your family?"

"No."

"Do you intend devoting it to charitable purposes, then?"

"Yes."

"But you are aware that the law does not allow a son to be entirely deprived of his patrimony?" said the notary.

"Yes."

"Then you only intend to dispose of that part of your fortune which the law allows you to subtract from your son's inheritance?"

Noirtier made no answer.

"Do you still wish to dispose of all?"

"Yes."

"But they will contest the will after your death!"

"No."

"My father knows me," replied Villefort. "He is quite sure that his wishes will be held sacred by me; besides, he understands that, in my position, I cannot plead against the poor."

Noirtier's eyes beamed triumphantly.

"What have you decided on, monsieur?" asked the notary of Villefort.

"Nothing; it is a resolution which my father has taken, and I know he never changes his mind. I am quite resigned. These nine hundred thousand francs will pass from the family to enrich some hospital; but I shall not yield to the whims of an old man, and I shall therefore act according to the dictates of my conscience."

Having said this, Villefort quitted the room with his wife, leaving his father at liberty to do what he pleased.

The same day the will was drawn up, the witnesses were brought forward, it was approved by the old man, sealed in the presence of all, and given into the charge of M. Deschamps, the family notary.

## CHAPTER XLI

## THE TELEGRAPH

ON returning to their own apartments, M. and Mme de Villefort learned that the Count of Monte Cristo, who had come to pay them a visit, had, during their absence, been shown into the salon where he was awaiting them. Mme de Villefort was too agitated to see him at once and retired to her bedroom, while her husband, being more self-possessed, went straight into the salon. But though he was able to master his feelings and compose his features, he could not dispel the cloud that shadowed his brow, and the Count, who received him with a radiant smile, noticed his gloomy and preoccupied manner.

"What on earth is the matter, Monsieur de Villefort?" said Monte Cristo after the first compliments were exchanged. "Have you just been drawing up some capital indictment?"

"No, Count," said he, trying to smile, "this time I am the victim. It is I who have lost my case, and fate, obstinacy, and madness have been the counsel for the prosecution."

"What do you mean?" asked the Count, with well-feigned interest. "Have you really met with some serious misfortune?"

"Oh, it is not worth mentioning," said he, with a calmness that betokened bitterness. "It is nothing, only a loss of money."

"Loss of money is, indeed, somewhat insignificant to a man with a fortune such as you possess, and to a mind as elevated and philosophical as yours is."

"It is, however, not the loss of the money that grieves me, though after all nine hundred thousand francs is worthy of regret, and annoyance at its loss is quite comprehensible. What hurts me is the ill-will manifested by fate, chance, fatality, or whatever the designation of the power may be that has dealt this blow. My hopes of a fortune are dashed to the ground, and perhaps even my daughter's future blasted by the whims of an old man who has sunk into second childhood."

"Nine hundred thousand francs, did you say?" exclaimed the Count. "That is certainly a sum of money that even a philosopher might regret. Who has caused you this annoyance?"

"My father, of whom I spoke to you."

"My dear," said Mme de Villefort, who had just entered the room, "perhaps you are exaggerating the evil."

"Madame," said the Count, bowing.

Mme de Villefort acknowledged the salutation with one of her most gracious smiles.

"What is this Monsieur de Villefort has just been telling me?" asked Monte Cristo. "What an incomprehensible misfortune!"

"Incomprehensible! That is the very word," exclaimed Villefort, shrugging his shoulders. "A whim born of old age!"

"Is there no means of making him revoke his decision?"

"There is," was Mme de Villefort's reply. "It is even in my husband's power to have the will changed in Valentine's favour instead of its being to her prejudice."

"My dear," said Villefort in answer to his wife, "it is distasteful to me to play the patriarch in my own house; I have never believed that the fate of the universe depended upon a word from my lips. Nevertheless my opinions must be respected in my family, and the insanity of an old man and the caprices of a child shall not be allowed to frustrate a project I have entertained for so many years. The Baron d'Épinay was my friend, as you know, and an alliance with his son is most desirable and appropriate."

"Notwithstanding your father's wishes?" asked Madame de Villefort, opening a new line of attack. "That is a very serious matter."

Though pretending not to listen, the Count did not lose a word of the conversation.

"I may say that I have always entertained the highest respect for my father, madame. To-day, however, I must refuse to acknowledge intelligence in an old man who vents his anger on a son because of his hatred for the father. I shall continue to entertain the highest respect for Monsieur Noirtier. I shall submit uncomplainingly to the pecuniary loss, but I shall remain adamant in my determination. I shall, therefore, bestow my daughter's hand on Baron Franz d'Épinay because in my opinion this marriage is appropriate and honourable and, finally, because I shall marry my daughter to whom I choose."

"But it seems to me," said Monte Cristo after a moment's silence, "and I crave your pardon for what I am about to say, it seems to me that if Monsieur Noirtier disinherits Mademoiselle de Villefort because she wishes to marry a young man whose father he detested, he cannot have the same cause for complaint against this dear child Edward."

"You are right, Count. Is it not atrociously unjust?" cried Mme de Villefort in tones impossible to describe. "Poor Edward is just as much Monsieur Noirtier's grandchild as Valentine is, and yet if she were not going to marry Monsieur Franz she would inherit all his riches. Edward bears the family name, yet, even though she be disinherited by her grandfather, she will be three times as rich as he!"

Having thrust his dart, the Count merely listened and said nothing.

"We will not entertain you longer with our family troubles, Count," said M. de Villefort. "It is quite true that my patrimony will swell the coffers of the poor, who are the truly rich. My father has frustrated my legitimate hope, without any reason whatsoever, nevertheless I have acted as a man of intelligence and feeling. I have promised Monsieur d'Épinay the income accruing from this sum, and he shall have it, though I have to suffer the cruellest privations in consequence."

When M. de Villefort had finished speaking, the Count rose to depart.

"Are you leaving us, Count?" said Mme de Villefort.

"I am obliged to, madame. I only came to remind you of your promise for Saturday. You will come?"

"Did you think we should forget it?"

"You are too kind, madame. Now you must allow me to take leave of you. I am going, merely as a looker-on, you understand, to see something that has given me food for many long hours' thought."

"What is that?"

"The telegraph. There, my secret is out!"

"The telegraph!" repeated Mme de Villefort.

"Yes, indeed. On a hillock at the end of the road I have sometimes seen these black, accommodating arms shining in the sun like so many spiders' legs, and I assure you they have always filled me with deep emotion, for I thought of the strange signs cleaving the air with such precision, conveying the unknown thoughts of one man seated at his table three hundred leagues distant to another man at another table at the other end of the line; that these signs sped through the grey clouds or blue sky solely at the will of the all-powerful operator. Then I began to think of genii, sylphs, gnomes, in short of occult powers until I laughed aloud. Nevertheless I never felt any desire to see at close quarters these fat, white-bellied insects with their long, slender legs, for I feared I might find under their stone-like wings some stiff and pedantic little human genius puffed out with science or sorcery. One fine morning, however, I discovered that the operator of every telegraph was a poor wretch earning a miserable pittance of twelve thousand francs, who spent his whole day not in observing the sky as the astronomer does, not in watching the water as the fisherman does, nor yet in studying the landscape as the dreamer does, but in watching that other white-bellied black-legged insect, his correspondent, placed at some four or five leagues from him. Then I was seized with a strange desire to see this living chrysalis at close quarters, and to be present at the little comedy he plays for the benefit of his fellow chrysalis by pulling one piece of tape after another. I will tell you my impressions on Saturday."

The Count of Monte Cristo hereupon took his departure. That same evening the following telegram was read in the *Messager:*

> King Don Carlos has escaped the vigilance exercised over him at Burgos and has returned to Spain across the Catalonian frontier. Barcelona has risen in his favour.

All that evening nothing was talked about but Danglars' foresight in selling his shares, and his luck as a speculator in having lost but five hundred thousand francs by the deal.

The next day the following paragraph was read in the *Moniteur:*

> The report published in yesterday's *Messager* of the flight of Don Carlos and the revolt of Barcelona is devoid of all foundation. King Don Carlos has not left Burgos, and perfect peace reigns in the Peninsula. A telegraphic sign improperly interpreted owing to the fog gave rise to this error.

Shares rose to double the price to which they had fallen, so that, with what he had actually lost and what he had failed to gain, it meant a difference of a million francs to Danglars.

## CHAPTER XLII

# THE DINNER

AT first sight the exterior of Monte Cristo's house at Auteuil presented nothing magnificent, nothing of what one would have expected of a house chosen for such a grand personage as the Count of Monte Cristo. But no sooner was the door opened than the scene was changed. Monsieur Bertuccio had certainly surpassed himself in the taste he had displayed in furnishing the house and in the rapidity with which the work had been executed. Just as formerly the Duke of Antin in one single night had an avenue of trees hewn down which obstructed Louis XIV's view, so M. Bertuccio in three days had an entirely bare yard planted with beautiful poplars and sycamores which gave shade to the whole of the house. Instead of the flagstones, overgrown with grass, there extended a lawn which had only been laid down that morning and now looked like a vast carpet, upon which still glistened the water with which it had been sprinkled.

But then the Count himself had given all instructions; he had drawn up for Bertuccio a plan indicating the number and position of the trees to be planted, and the shape and extent of the lawn that was to succeed the flagstones.

That which best manifested the ability of the steward and the profound science of the master, the one in serving and the other in being served, was that this house, which had been deserted for twenty years and had appeared sad and gloomy on the previous evening, impregnated as it was with the insipid smell of decay, had with its return to life become permeated with its master's favourite perfumes and had been given the system of lighting especially favoured by him. Directly he arrived the Count had his books and weapons at hand; his eyes rested upon his favourite pictures; in the hall he was welcomed by his dogs, whose caresses he loved, and his birds, in whose songs he rejoiced; throughout the whole house, suddenly awakened from its long sleep like the Sleeping Beauty's castle in the wood, there burst forth life, song, and gaiety.

Servants were merrily moving hither and thither across the fine courtyard; those belonging to the kitchens were skipping down the staircase, but yesterday repaired, as though they had always inhabited the house; others filled the coach-houses, where the carriages were each numbered and each one had its allotted place, as though they had been installed there for the last fifty years; in the stables the horses at the mangers were whinnying to the grooms, who spoke to them with considerably more respect than many a servant does to his master.

The library was divided into two parts and contained about two thousand books; one complete section was devoted to modern novels, and even the one that had only been published the day before was to be seen in its place, proudly displaying its red and gold binding. On the other side of the house, and matching the library, was a conservatory with exotic plants displayed in large Japanese pots, which were at once wonderful to behold and most pleasing in perfume, and in the middle of the conservatory there was a billiard-table which looked as if it had been abandoned but an hour ago by players who had left the balls on the cloth.

At five precisely the Count arrived, followed by Ali. Bertuccio was awaiting his arrival with impatience mingled with anxiety; he hoped for praise, yet he feared frowns.

Monte Cristo alighted from his carriage in the courtyard, went over the whole house, and strolled through the garden in silence, and without giving the least sign of approval or disapproval. When he came to his bedroom, however, he pointed to a little piece of furniture in rosewood, saying: "The only use you can make of that is for my gloves."

"If Your Excellency will open the drawer, he will find gloves in it," said Bertuccio, delighted.

In the various cupboards and drawers about the room the Count found everything for his personal use: bottles of all kinds, cigars, jewellery.

"Good!" said he, and so real was the influence of this man on all around him, that M. Bertuccio withdrew greatly elated.

At six o'clock sharp a horse was heard pawing the ground before the front door. It was our friend the Captain's horse, Médéah. Monte Cristo awaited Morrel on the steps, a smile on his lips.

"I am the first, I know," Morrel called out to him. "I have done it on purpose so as to have you to myself for a minute before the others came. Julie and Emmanuel sent you all kinds of messages. It is truly magnificent here! But are you sure your servants will take good care of my horse?"

"You need not worry about that, my dear Maximilian. They understand horses."

"He will want rubbing down. If you knew at what a pace I came—like the wind!"

"I should say so, too, with a horse that cost five thousand francs!" said Monte Cristo in the tone a father might adopt toward his son.

"Do you regret it?" said Morrel with his frank smile.

"Good gracious, no!" replied the Count. "I should only regret it if the horse were no good."

"He is so good that I have outdistanced Monsieur de Château-

Renaud, the greatest expert in France, and Monsieur Debray, who rides the Minister's Arabs; at their heels are Baroness Danglars' horses, which always do their six leagues an hour."

"They are following you then?" asked the Count.

"See, here they are!"

Indeed at that moment a carriage drawn by a sweating pair of bays, and two gentlemen on winded horses arrived at the gate, which opened before them. The carriage drove round and stopped at the steps, followed by the two riders. Debray instantly dismounted and opened the carriage door. He offered his hand to the Baroness, who, in alighting, made a sign to Debray which passed unnoticed by all except Monte Cristo. Nothing ever escaped the Count's eye, and he perceived a note slipped almost imperceptibly, and with an ease indicating practice, from the Baroness's hand into that of the Minister's secretary.

The Baroness was followed by the banker, looking as pale as though he had issued from the grave instead of his carriage. Madame Danglars threw a rapid and inquiring glance around her, embracing in her view the courtyard, the peristyle, and the front of the house. Monte Cristo showed her two immense Chinese porcelain jars on which was intertwined marine vegetation, the size and beauty of which denoted that it could but be the work of nature herself. The Baronness expressed great admiration.

"Why, that would hold a chestnut tree from the Tuileries," she said. "How did they manage to bake such enormous jars?"

"Oh, madame, that is a question we manufacturers of statuettes and fine glass cannot answer. It is the work of another age, that of the genii of the earth and sea."

"What do you mean by that? To what period do these jars belong?"

"I know not; I have heard it said, however, that the Emperor of China had an oven built for the purpose. In this oven twelve jars were baked, one after the other, like the one you see here. Two were broken by the fierceness of the fire, the other ten were sunk three hundred fathoms deep into the sea. As though it knew what was demanded of it, the sea threw over them its weeds, encircled them with coral, and encrusted them with shells: the whole being cemented by two hundred years' submersion in the depths; for the Emperor who made this experiment was carried away by a revolution, and left nothing but a document stating that the jars had been baked and let down into the sea. At the end of two hundred years this document was found, and it was decided to raise the vases. Special diving apparatus was made, and divers descended into the depths of the bay where they had been cast. Of the ten, however, but three were recovered, the others had been shattered and scattered by the waves. I like these vases, and at times my mind conjures up the unshapely, terrifying, and mysterious monsters, such as have been seen by divers only, which have cast their dull, cold, wondering gaze into the depths of the jars, wherein myriads of fish have slept finding refuge there from the pursuit of their enemies."

In the meantime Danglars, caring little for curiosities, had been mechanically plucking one blossom after another from a magnificent orange-tree; when tired of that tree, he turned his attention to a cactus which, being of a less easygoing character, pricked him outrageously. He rubbed his eyes with a shudder as though awakening from a dream.

"Major Bartolomeo Cavalcanti! The Viscount Andrea Cavalcanti!" announced Baptistin.

A black satin stock, fresh from the maker's hands, a well-trimmed beard and grey moustache, a bold eye, a major's uniform decorated with three stars and five crosses, in short the irreproachable bearing of an old soldier, such was the appearance of Bartolomeo Cavalcanti, the tender father. Close beside him, in brand new clothes, and with a smile upon his lips, came Viscount Andrea Cavalcanti, the respectful son.

The three young men chatted together; their eyes wandered from the father to the son and from the very nature of things rested longer on the latter, whom they began criticizing.

"Cavalcanti!" said Debray.

"A fine name, to be sure," said Morrel.

"You are right," said Château-Renaud. "These Italians have a fine name, but they are badly dressed."

"You are difficult to please," added Debray. "Their clothes are very well cut and are quite new."

"That is precisely where they are at fault. This gentleman looks as though he were dressed for the first time in his life."

"Who are they?" Danglars inquired of Monte Cristo.

"You heard . . . the Cavalcantis."

"That tells me their name, but nothing further."

"I had forgotten that you do not know Italian nobility: to speak of the Cavalcantis is the same as speaking of a princely race."

"Any fortune?" asked the banker.

"A fabulous one."

"What do they do?"

"They try to get through their fortune, but cannot succeed. From what they told me when they called on me the other day, I gather that they intend opening a credit account with your bank. I have invited them to-day on your account. I will introduce you to them."

"They appear to speak very good French."

"The son was educated at a college in the South, at Marseilles or some-where in that district, I believe. You will find him most enthusiastic."

"On what subject?" inquired the Baroness.

"On the subject of French women, madame. He is quite decided to find a wife for himself in Paris."

"That is a fine idea," said Danglars, shrugging his shoulders.

"The Baron is very grim to-day," said Monte Cristo to Mme Danglars. "Do they by any chance wish to make him a Minister?"

"Not so far as I know. I am more inclined to think he has been speculating and has lost money; now he does not know whom to blame for it."

"Monsieur and Madame de Villefort!" announced Baptistin.

Five minutes later the two doors of the salon opened; Bertuccio appeared and announced in a loud voice:

"Dinner is served, Your Excellency!"

Monte Cristo offered his arm to Mme de Villefort.

"Monsieur de Villefort," said he, "will you escort Baroness Danglars?"

Villefort did as he was requested, and they all passed into the dining-room.

The repast was magnificent. Monte Cristo had endeavoured to deviate from the uniformity observed at all such Paris dinners, and his object was to satisfy the curiosity rather than the appetites of his guests. It was an Oriental feast he offered them, but such as one would attribute to Arabian fairies. Every kind of delicious fruit that the four quarters of the globe can send to fill Europe's cornucopia was piled pyramid-like in Chinese vases and Japanese bowls. Rare birds in all their brilliant plumage, monstrous fish on silver dishes, every wine of the Archipelago, Asia Minor, and the Cape, in decanters of every weird shape the sight of which seemed to add to the flavour, passed like one of Apicius' reviews before one of his guests.

Monte Cristo noticed the general amazement and began to laugh and jest about it.

"My friends, you will no doubt admit," said he, "that, arrived at a cer-tain degree of fortune, the superfluous takes the place of the necessary, and, as you ladies will admit, arrived at a certain degree of exaltation, the ideal takes the place of the real. Now to continue this argument, what is marvellous? That which we do not comprehend. What is truly desir-able? That which we cannot have. Now to see things I cannot under-stand, to procure things impossible of possession, such is the plan of my life. I can realize it by two means: money and will. For instance, I expend as much perseverance in the pursuit of a whim as you, Monsieur Danglars, would expend in constructing a new railway line, as you,

Monsieur de Villefort, in condemning a man to death, as you, Monsieur Debray, in pacifying a kingdom, as you, Monsieur de Château-Renaud, in pleasing a lady, and you, Morrel, in taming a horse that no one can ride. Thus, for example, you see these two fish. One was born fifty leagues from St Petersburg, the other five leagues from Naples. Do you not find it amusing to unite them on the same table?"

"What are these two fish?" asked Danglars.

"Monsieur de Château-Renaud, who has lived in Russia, will tell you the name of the one, and Major Cavalcanti, who is an Italian, will tell you the name of the other," said Monte Cristo.

"This one is a sterlet, I believe," said Château-Renaud.

"Capital!"

"And if I mistake not," said Cavalcanti, "this one is a lamprey."

"Just so. Now, Monsieur Danglars, ask these two gentlemen where these fish are found."

"Sterlets are only found in the Volga," said Château-Renaud.

"And I know that the Lake of Fusaro alone supplies lampreys of this size."

"Exactly so. One comes from the Volga, the other from the Lake of Fusaro."

"Impossible!" the guests exclaimed unanimously.

"You see, this is precisely what affords me amusement. I am like Nero: *cupitor impossibilium*. At the present moment it is amusing you, too, and the reason why these fish, which, I dare say, are in reality not such good eating as perch or a salmon, seem exquisite is that in your opinion it was impossible to procure them. Yet here they are."

"How did you have them brought to Paris?"

"Nothing simpler. They were each brought in a large cask, the one lined with reeds and river weeds, the other with rushes and other lake plants: these were placed in a waggon built specially for them. Here the sterlet lived twelve days and the lamprey eight. Both of them were alive when my cook took them out of the casks to kill them, the former in milk and the latter in wine. You do not believe me, Monsieur Danglars?"

"At any rate I doubt it," replied Danglars, with a heavy smile.

"Baptistin, send for the other sterlet and lamprey," said Monte Cristo. "You know, those that came in the other casks and are still alive."

Danglars opened his eyes in amazement; the rest of the company clapped their hands.

Four servants brought in two casks decorated with marine plants, in each of which was panting a fish similar to those on the table.

"But why are there two of each kind?" asked Danglars.

"Because one of them might have died," replied Monte Cristo simply.

"You are really a wonderful man," said Danglars. "Philosophers may well say it is superb to be rich."

"Above all to have ideas," said Mme Danglars.

"Oh, do not give me credit for this one, madame. It is an idea that was much esteemed by the Romans, and Pliny relates that they sent relays of slaves from Ostia to Rome who carried on their heads fish of the species he calls *mullus,* which, from the description he gives, is probably the goldfish. It was considered a luxury to have them alive, and an amusing sight to see them die; when dying they changed colour two or thee times and, like the fading rainbow, they passed through all the prismatic shades; then they were sent to the kitchens. Their agony formed part of their merit. If they were not seen alive, they were despised when dead."

"Yes, but it is only seven or eight leagues from Ostia to Rome!"

"Quite true," said Monte Cristo. "But where would be the merit of living eighteen hundred years after Lucullus if we did not go one better than he?"

The two Cavalcantis opened their enormous eyes wide, but they had the good sense not to say a word.

"This is all very amusing," said Chateau-Renaud, "but I must confess that what I admire most is the wonderful promptitude with which you are served. Is it not true, Count, that you only bought this house five or six days ago?"

"Certainly not longer."

"Well, I am sure it has undergone complete transformation in a week for, if I mistake not, it had quite a different entrance and the yard was paved and empty, whereas what formerly was the yard is to-day a magnificent lawn bordered by trees which look a hundred years old."

"Why not? I like grass and shade," said Monte Cristo.

"In four days!" said Morrel. "It is marvellous!"

The evening wore on. Mme de Villefort expressed her desire to return to Paris, which Mme Danglars did not dare to do, notwithstanding her obvious uneasiness.

At his wife's request M. de Villefort was the first to give the signal for departure, and offered Mme Danglars a seat in his landau. As for M. Danglars he was so absorbed in a most interesting conversation on industry with M. Cavalcanti, that he did not pay any attention to what was going on around him. More and more delighted with the Major, he offered him a seat in his carriage.

Andrea Cavalcanti found his tilbury awaiting him at the gate, and the groom, fitted out in an exaggeration of the prevailing English fashion, was standing on the tips of his high boots, holding the head of the enormous iron-grey horse.

Andrea had not spoken much during dinner, but afterward he had been seized upon by M. Danglars, who, after a rapid glance at the stiff-necked old Major and his timid son, and taking into consideration the hospitality of the Count, had come to the conclusion that he was face to face with some nabob come to Paris to put the final polish on his society education.

He had noticed with indescribable satisfaction the enormous diamond which shone on the Major's little finger, and after dinner, of course on pretext of business and travels, he questioned the father and son on their mode of living, and both the father and the son had been most charming and affable.

He was, therefore, greatly pleased when Cavalcanti said: "To-morrow, monsieur, I shall have the honour of calling on you on business matters."

"And I shall be happy to receive you," was Danglars' reply, and he further proposed that he should accompany him to his hotel if it would not be depriving him too much of his son's company.

Cavalcanti replied that for some time past his son had been accustomed to living independently of him; he had his own horses and carriages, and, as they had not come to the Count's house together, it would offer them no difficulty to leave separately. The Major had already seated himself in Danglars' carriage, and the banker took his place beside him, more and more charmed with the ideas of order and economy of this man who, notwithstanding, gave his son fifty thousand francs a year, which meant an income of five or six hundred thousand francs.

As for Andrea, in order to look grand, he began by reprimanding his groom because instead of driving up to the steps he had waited at the gate, thus giving him the fatigue of walking thirty yards to reach his tilbury. The groom received the scolding with humility, and, taking the bit in his left hand to keep back the impatient horse that was pawing the ground, with his right hand he gave the reins to Andrea.

## CHAPTER XLIII

## A CONJUGAL SCENE

AT the Place Louis XV the three young men separated. Debray drove on till he reached the house of M. Danglars, arriving there just as M. de Villefort's landau drove up to the door with Mme Danglars. Debray was the first to enter the courtyard, and, with the air of a man on a familiar footing at the house, he threw the bridle to a footman and handed the Baroness from the carriage and into the house.

At the door of her room, the Baroness met Mlle Cornélie, her confidential maid. "What is my daughter doing?" she asked her. "She practised the whole evening and then went to bed," replied Mlle Cornélie.

"I seem to hear her at the piano now."

"That is Mademoiselle Louise d'Armilly, who is playing to Mademoiselle Danglars while she is in bed."

"Very well," said Mme Danglars, "come and undress me." They entered the bedroom. Debray stretched himself out on a large settee, and Mme Danglars went into her dressing-room with Mlle Cornélie.

"My dear Monsieur Lucien," said Mme Danglars through the door, "you are always complaining that Eugénie does not do you the honour of addressing a word to you."

"I am not the only one to make such complaints, madame," said Lucien, playing with the Baroness's little dog, which, recognizing him as a friend of the house, was making a great fuss of him. "I believe I heard Morcerf tell you the other day that he could not get a single word out of his betrothed."

"It is true," said Mme Danglars, "but I think all that will change, and one of these days you will see Eugénie at your office."

"At my office?"

"That is to say, at the Minister's office."

"What for?"

"To ask for an engagement at the Opera House. Really, I have never known such an infatuation for music: it is ridiculous in a society girl."

Debray smiled as he said: "Well, let her come with your consent and the Baron's, and we will try to give her an engagement in accordance with her merits."

"You may go, Cornélie," said Mme Danglars, "I do not need you any more."

Cornélie disappeared, and an instant later Mme Danglars emerged from her dressing-room and seated herself beside Debray. She began to caress the little spaniel in a thoughtful mood. Lucien looked at her for a moment in silence.

"Tell me frankly, Hermine," he said presently, "what is it that is annoying you?"

"Nothing," replied the Baroness.

Suddenly the door opened and M. Danglars entered. "Good evening, madame," said he. "Good evening, Monsieur Debray!"

The Baroness no doubt thought that this unexpected visit signified a desire to repair the sharp words he had uttered during the day.

Assuming a dignified air, she turned to Lucien and, without answering her husband, said: "Read something to me, Monsieur Debray." "Excuse me," said the Baron. "You will tire yourself if you stay up so late, Baroness; it is eleven o'clock and Monsieur has far to go."

Debray was dumbfounded, for, though Danglars' tone was perfectly calm and polite, he seemed to detect in it a certain determination to do his own will that evening and not his wife's. The Baroness was equally surprised and showed it by a look which would no doubt have given her husband food for thought if he had not been busy reading the closing prices of shares in the paper. The haughty look was entirely lost on him.

"Monsieur Lucien," said the Baroness, "I assure you I have not the least inclination for sleep. I have much to tell you this evening, and you shall listen to me though you go to sleep standing."

"At your service, madame," replied Lucien phlegmatically.

"My dear Monsieur Debray, don't ruin a good night's rest by staying here and listening to Madame Danglars' follies to-night," said M. Danglars; "you can hear them just as well to-morrow. Besides, I claim to-night for myself, and, with your permission, I propose to talk over some important business matters with my wife."

This time the blow was struck with such directness that Lucien and the Baroness were staggered. They exchanged looks as though each was asking the other for help in the face of such intrusion, but the irresistible power of the master of the house prevailed and he gained the ascendancy.

"Don't think I am turning you out, my dear Debray," continued Danglars. "Not in the least! Unforeseen circumstances oblige me to demand this interview of madame to-night; it is such an unusual occurrence that I am sure you will bear me no illwill."

Debray stammered out a few words, bowed and left the room.

"Do you know, monsieur," said the Baroness when Lucien had gone, "you are really making progress? As a rule you are merely churlish, to-night you are brutal."

"That is because I am in a worse temper to-night than usual," replied Danglars.

"What is your bad temper to me?" replied the Baroness, irritated at her husband's impassiveness. "What have I to do with it?"

"I have just lost seven hundred thousand francs in the Spanish loan."

"And do you wish to make me responsible for your losses?" asked the Baroness with a sneer. "Is it my fault that you have lost seven hundred thousand francs?"

"In any case it is not mine."

"Once and for all, monsieur, I will not have you talk money with me," returned the Baroness sharply. "It is a language I learnt neither with my parents nor in my first husband's house. The jingling of crowns being counted and re-counted is odious to me, and there is nothing but the sound of your voice that I dislike more."

"That is really strange!" replied Danglars. "I always thought you took the greatest interest in my affairs!"

"I should like you to show me on what occasion."

"Oh! that's easily done. Last February you were the first to tell me of the Hayti bonds. You dreamt that a ship had entered the harbour at Havre, bringing the news that a payment which had been looked on as lost was about to be effected. I know how clear-sighted your dreams are. On the quiet I bought up all the bonds of the Hayti debt I could lay my hands on, and made four hundred thousand francs, of which I conscientiously paid you one hundred thousand. You spent it as you wished, but that was your affair.

"In March there was talk of a railway concession. Three companies presented themselves, each offering equal securities. You told me that your instinct—and though you pretend to know nothing about speculation I consider, on the contrary, that you have a very clear comprehension of certain affairs—well, you said your instinct told you that the privilege would be given to a so-called Southern Company. I instantly subscribed two-thirds of the company's shares and made a million out of the deal. I gave you two hundred and fifty thousand francs for pin-money. What have you done with it?"

"But what are you driving at, monsieur?" cried the Baroness, trembling with anger and impatience.

"Have patience, madame, I am coming to it. In April you dined with the Minister. The conversation turned upon Spain, and you heard some secret information. There was talk of the expulsion of Don Carlos. I bought some Spanish bonds. Your information was correct, and I made six hundred thousand francs the day Charles the Fifth crossed the Bidassoa. Of these six hundred thousand francs you had fifty thousand crowns. They were yours, and you disposed of them according to your fancy. I do not ask you to account for the money, but it is none the less true that you have received five hundred thousand francs this year.

"Then three days ago you talked politics with Monsieur Debray, and you gathered from his words that Don Carlos had returned to Spain. I sold out, the news was spread, and a panic ensued. I did not sell the bonds, I gave them away. The next day it transpired that the news was false, but it cost me seven hundred thousand francs."

"Well?"

"Well, since I give you a quarter of my profits, it is only right you should give me a quarter of what I lose. The quarter of seven hundred thousand francs is one hundred and seventy-five thousand francs!"

"That is ridiculous, and really I do not see why you should bring Debray's name into this affair."

"Simply because if you don't happen to have the hundred and seventy-five thousand francs I claim, you have lent it to your friends, and Monsieur Debray is one of them!"

"For shame!"

"No gesticulations, screams, or modern drama, if you please, madame, otherwise I shall be compelled to tell you that I can see Monsieur Debray having the laugh of you over the five hundred thousand francs you have handed to him this year, and priding himself on the fact that he has finally found that which the most skilful gamblers have never discovered, that is a game in which he wins without risking a stake and is no loser when he loses."

The Baroness was boiling with rage.

"You wretch!" said she. "You are worse than despicable!"

"But I note with pleasure, madame, that you are not far behind me in that respect."

"You would insult me now?"

"You are right: let us look facts in the face and reason coolly. I have never interfered in your affairs, except for your good; treat me in the same way. You suggest that my cash-box is no concern of yours. Be it so. Do as you like with your own, but do not fill or empty mine. Besides, how do I know that this is not a political trick, that the Minister, enraged at seeing me in the Opposition and jealous of the popular sympathy I enjoy, is not conspiring with Monsieur Debray to ruin me?"

"As though that were likely!"

"Why not? Whoever has heard before of such an almost impossible thing as false telegraphic news? Yet in the last two telegrams, some signs were interpreted quite differently. It was done on purpose for me, I am sure of it. Monsieur Debray has made me lose seven hundred thousand francs; let him bear his share of the loss and we will continue business together; otherwise, let him declare himself bankrupt for the hundred and seventy-five thousand francs and then do what all bankrupts do—disappear. He is quite a charming man, I know, when his news is correct, but when it is not, there are fifty others in the world better than he."

Mme Danglars was simply overwhelmed, but she made a supreme

effort to reply to this last attack. She sank into a chair, thinking of the strange chain of misfortunes that had befallen them one after another. Danglars did not even look at her, though she did her best to faint. Without saying another word, he opened the door and went into his room; when Mme Danglars recovered from her semi-faint she thought she must have had a bad dream.

## CHAPTER XLIV

## MATRIMONIAL PLANS

THE day following this scene, M. Debray's carriage did not make its appearance at the customary hour to pay a little visit to Mme Danglars on his way to the office. She, therefore, ordered her carriage to be brought round and went out. This was only what Danglars expected. He gave instructions that he should be informed directly Madame returned, but when two o'clock struck and she was not yet back, he went to the Chamber and put his name down to speak against the Budget.

From midday until two o'clock Danglars stayed in his office deciphering telegrams and heaping figure upon figure till he became increasingly depressed. Among other visits he received one from Major Cavalcanti, who, as stiff and exact as ever, presented himself precisely at the hour named the previous evening to transact his business with the banker. On leaving the Chamber, where he had shown marked signs of agitation during the sitting and had been more bitter than usual against the Ministry, Danglars once more entered his carriage and told the coachman to drive him to No. 30 Avenue des Champs Élysées.

Monte Cristo was at home, but he was engaged with some one and asked Danglars to wait a moment in the salon. While the banker was waiting, the door opened, and a man in priest's garb entered. He was evidently more familiar with the house than the Baron for, instead of waiting, he merely bowed and passing into the other room disappeared. A minute later the door through which the priest had entered reopened, and Monte Cristo made his appearance.

"Pray, excuse me, Baron," said he, "but one of my good friends, Abbé Busoni, whom you may have seen pass by, has just arrived in Paris. It is a long time since we saw each other, and I could not make up my mind to leave him at once. I trust you will find the motive good enough to forgive my keeping you waiting. But what ails you, Baron? You look quite careworn; really, you alarm me. A careworn capitalist is like a comet, he presages some great misfortune to the world."

"Ill-luck has been dogging my steps for the last few days," said Danglars, "and I receive nothing but bad news."

"Did you really lose by that affair in Spain?"

"Assuredly. Seven hundred thousand francs out of my pocket, that is all!"

"How could an old hand like you make such a mistake?"

"Oh, it was all my wife's fault. She dreamed Don Carlos had returned to Spain, and she believes in dreams. She says it is magnetism and assures me that what she dreams is bound to come true. But do you mean to say you have not heard of this affair? It created such a stir."

"I certainly heard something about it, but I was ignorant of the details. I know so little about the Exchange."

"You do not speculate then?"

"How could I? It gives me quite enough to do to regulate my income, and if I were to speculate I should be compelled to employ an agent and cashier in addition to my steward. But in regard to this Spanish affair, I believe it was not only the Baroness who dreamed of Don Carlos' return. Did not the newspapers say something about it?"

"Do you believe all the newspapers say?"

"Oh, dear, no. But I thought that the *Messager* was an exceptionally reliable paper, and that the news it published was telegraphic and therefore true."

"That is just what is so inexplicable."

"So you have lost about seventeen hundred thousand francs this month?"

"About that."

"Have you ever reflected on the fact that seven times seventeen hundred thousand francs makes about twelve millions? Be careful, my dear Monsieur Danglars! Be on your guard!"

"What a bad calculator you are!" exclaimed Danglars, calling to his assistance all his philosophy and art of dissimulation. "Money has flowed into my coffers from other successful speculations. I have lost a battle here and there, but my Indian navy will have taken some galleons, my Mexican pioneers will have discovered some mine."

"Very good, very good! The wound is still there, however, and will reopen at the first loss."

"No, it will not, for I tread on sure ground," continued Danglars in the idle language of the mountebank crying out his wares. "Three governments must fall before I am involved in difficulties."

Then turning the conversation into other channels he added: "Tell me what I am to do for Monsieur Cavalcanti."

"Give him money, of course, if he has a letter of credit and you think the signature good."

"The signature is good enough. He came to me this morning with a bill for forty thousand francs payable at sight, signed by Busoni, and sent by you to me with your endorsement. Naturally I immediately counted him out the forty banknotes."

Monte Cristo nodded in token of approval.

"But that is not all," continued Danglars. "He has also opened a credit account for his son."

"May I ask how much he allows the young man?"

"Five thousand francs a month."

"Sixty thousand francs a year! I thought as much," said Monte Cristo, shrugging his shoulders. "How niggardly these Cavalcantis are! What does he expect a young man to do with five thousand francs a month?"

"But of course if the young man needs a few thousand more . . ."

"Do not advance anything. His father will never pay you. You do not know what misers these ultra-millionaires are! Keep to the terms of the letter."

"Do you mistrust this Cavalcanti then?"

"I? I would give him ten millions on his signature."

"Yet how simple he is! I should have taken him for nothing more than a Major. The young man is better, though."

"Yes, a little nervous perhaps, but on the whole quite presentable. He has apparently been travelling with a very severe tutor and has never been to Paris before."

"All Italians of high standing marry amongst themselves, do they not?" asked Danglars carelessly. "They like to unite their fortunes, I believe."

"I believe they do as a rule, but Cavalcanti is an eccentric man who never does as others do. I am convinced he has sent his son to France to choose a wife."

"Do you really think so?"

"I am sure of it."

"The boy is sure to marry a Bavarian or a Peruvian princess; he will want a crown or an Eldorado."

"No, the great lords from beyond the Alps frequently marry into plain families. Are you thinking of finding a wife for Andrea, my dear Monsieur Danglars, that you ask so many questions?"

"It would not be a bad speculation, I fancy, and after all I am a speculator."

"You are not thinking of Mademoiselle Danglars, I presume? I thought she was engaged to Albert."

"Monsieur Morcerf and I have certainly discussed this marriage, but Madame de Morcerf and Albert . . ."

"You are not going to tell me it would not be a good match?"

"Oh, I think Mademoiselle Danglars is as good as Monsieur de Morcerf."

"Mademoiselle will have a good dowry, no doubt, especially if the telegraph does not play any more tricks. But then Albert has a good name."

"I like mine as well!" said Danglars.

"Your name is certainly popular, and it gives distinction to the title that was intended to distinguish it. At the same time you have too much intelligence not to realize that according to prejudices, which are too deeply rooted to be exterminated, a patent of nobility which dates back five centuries confers greater lustre than that which only dates back twenty years."

"That is precisely the reason why I should prefer Monsieur Cavalcanti to Monsieur Albert de Morcerf," responded Danglars with a smile he attempted to make sardonic.

"Still, I should not think the Morcerfs would yield preference to the Cavalcantis," said Monte Cristo.

"The Morcerfs . . . See here, Count, you are a gentleman, are you not?"

"I hope so."

"And you understand something about heraldry?"

"A little."

"Well, look at my coat-of-arms; it is worth more than Morcerf's, for, though I may not be a Baron by birth, I do at least keep to my own name, whereas Morcerf is not his name at all."

"Do you really mean that?"

"I have been made a Baron, so I actually am one; he has given himself the title of Count, therefore he is not one at all."

"Impossible!"

"Monsieur de Morcerf and I have been friends, or rather acquaintances, for the last thirty years. As you know, I make good use of my coat-of-arms, and I do so for the simple reason that I never forget whence I sprang."

"Which shows either great pride or great humility," said Monte Cristo.

"When I was a clerk, Morcerf was but a simple fisherman."

"What was his name?"

"Fernand Mondego."

"Are you sure of that?"

"Good gracious, he has sold me enough fish for me to know his name."

"Then why are you letting his son marry your daughter?"

"Because as Fernand and Danglars are both upstarts, have both been given a title of nobility and become rich, there is a great similarity between them except for one thing that has been said about him which has never been said about me."

"What is that?"

"Nothing."

"I understand! What you have just told me has brought back to my mind that I have heard his name in Greece."

"In connexion with the Ali Pasha affair?"

"Just so."

"That is a mystery I would give much to discover," replied Danglars.

"It would not be difficult. No doubt you have correspondents in Greece, perhaps at Janina?"

"I have them everywhere."

"Why not write to your correspondent at Janina and ask him what part a certain Frenchman named Fernand played in the Ali Tebelin affair?"

"You are right!" exclaimed Danglars, rising quickly. "I will write this very day."

"And if you receive any scandalous news . . ."

"I will let you know."

"I should be much obliged."

Danglars rushed out of the room and leaped into his carriage.

## CHAPTER XLV

## A SUMMER BALL

SCARCELY had M. Danglars left the Count of Monte Cristo to write in all haste to his correspondent at Janina when Albert de Morcerf was announced. The Count received him with his habitual smile. It was a strange thing, but nobody ever seemed to advance a step in that man's favour. Those who attempted to force a way into his heart encountered an impassible wall.

Morcerf ran toward him with open arms, but as soon as he drew near, he dropped them in spite of the Count's friendly smile, and did no more than put out his hand. The Count merely touched the tips of his fingers as he always did.

"Here I am, Count. What is the news?"

"News! You ask that question of me, a stranger?"

"Of course. I mean have you done anything for me?"

"Did you ask me to do anything for you?" asked the Count, feigning uneasiness.

"Oh, nonsense!" said Albert. "Don't pretend to be so indifferent. They say that one mind can communicate with another through space. When I was at Tréport I felt that you were either working for me or thinking of me"

"That is possible," said Monte Cristo. "As a matter of fact, I have been thinking of you. Monsieur Danglars dined with me."

"I know that. Was it not to avoid meeting him that my mother and I left town for a few days?"

"But Monsieur Cavalcanti also dined with me."

"Your Italian prince?"

"That is an exaggeration. Monsieur Andrea only styles himself Viscount."

"Styles himself, do you say?"

"Yes, I said styles himself."

"Is he not a viscount then?"

"How do I know? He gives himself the title, I give it him, everybody does, which is the same as if he actually was a viscount."

"What a strange man you are! So Monsieur Danglars dined here with your Viscount Andrea Cavalcanti?"

"With Viscount Andrea Cavalcanti, the Marquis his father, Madame Danglars, Monsieur and Madame de Villefort, all charming people, then Monsieur Debray, Maximilian Morrel, and ... let me see ... oh, yes, and Monsieur de Château-Renaud."

"Did they speak of me?"

"Not a word."

"More's the pity."

"Why? It seems to me you would prefer them to forget you."

"My dear Count, if they did not speak of me, it only means that they thought all the more of me. Truly, I am an unlucky fellow."

"What does that matter since Mademoiselle Danglars was not amongst the number? Ah, it is true though, she might have been thinking of you at home."

"I have no fear of that; at any rate, if she was, it was in the same way in which I think of her."

"What touching sympathy! Do you really hate each other?"

"I think Mademoiselle Danglars would make a charming mistress, but as a wife ...!"

"Is that the way you think of your future spouse?" said Monte Cristo, laughing.

"It is a little unkind, perhaps, but true none the less. Since this dream cannot be realized, I shrink from the idea of Mademoiselle Danglars becoming my wife; that is to say, living with me, thinking, singing in my company, composing her verses and music by my side, my whole life long! One can always leave a mistress, but a wife . . . Deuce take it! that is a different matter, you must live with her perpetually."

"You are difficult to please, Viscount."

"I am, for I so often crave for the impossible."

"What is that?"

"To find a wife such as my father found."

"So your father was one of the few fortunate ones?" said he.

"You know my opinion of my mother. She is an angel sent from Heaven. She is still beautiful, quick-witted, sweeter than ever. I have just been to Tréport with her. Most sons would look upon that as an irksome filial duty or an act of condescension on their part, but I assure you, Count, the four days I spent alone with my mother were more restful, more peaceful, and more poetic than if I had been accompanied by Queen Mab or Titania."

"That is perfection indeed! Anyone hearing you speak thus will take the vow of celibacy!"

"The reason why I do not care about marrying Mademoiselle Danglars is that I know a perfect woman. This is the reason why my joy will be indescribable the day she realises that I am but a piteous atom with scarcely as many hundred thousand francs as she has millions!"

"Let things take their course. Perhaps everything will come as you wish. But tell me, do you seriously wish to break off your engagement?"

"I would give a hundred thousand francs to do so."

"Then make yourself quite happy. Monsieur Danglars would give twice that much to attain the same end."

"That is almost too good to be true," replied Albert. Yet as he spoke an almost imperceptible cloud passed over his brow, and he asked: "Has Monsieur Danglars any reason?"

"Ah, here comes your proud and selfish nature to the fore! Well, well, I have once again found a man ready to hack at another's self-respect with a hatchet, but, who cries out when his own is pricked with a pin."

"Not at all, but I think Monsieur Danglars . . ."

"Should be charmed with you! Well, Monsieur Danglars has such execrably bad taste that he is still more charmed with someone else."

"With whom?"

"How should I know? Look around you, judge for yourself, and profit by the inferences you draw."

"All right. I think I understand. Listen, my mother . . . no, not my mother, my father is thinking of giving a ball."

"At this time of the year?"

"Summer balls are fashionable. You see those who remain in Paris in the month of July are the real Parisians. Will you convey our invitation to the Messieurs Cavalcanti?"

"When is the ball to take place?"

"On Saturday."

"Monsieur Cavalcanti Senior will have left Paris by then."

"But Monsieur Cavalcanti Junior will be here. Will you bring him along with you?"

"I do not know him. I never saw him till two or three days ago, and I cannot hold myself responsible for him."

"But you receive him at your house."

"That is quite a different matter. He was recommended to me by a worthy abbé who may himself be mistaken in him. Invite him yourself, if you like, but do not ask me to introduce him. If he marries Mademoiselle Danglars later on, you will accuse me of interfering and challenge me to a duel. Besides, I do not know whether I shall go to your ball myself."

"Why not?"

"In the first place because you have not yet invited me."

"I have come for that express purpose."

"That is very kind of you. I may, however, still be compelled to refuse."

"When I tell you that my mother specially asks you to come, I am sure you will brush aside all obstacles."

"The Countess of Morcerf asks me?" inquired Monte Cristo with a start.

"I can assure you, Count, Madame de Morcerf speaks freely to me, and if you have not been stirred by a sympathetic impulse during the last four days, it must be that you have no response in you, for we have talked incessantly of you. May we expect you on Saturday?"

"You may, since Madame de Morcerf expressly invites me."

"You are very kind."

"Will Monsieur Danglars be there?"

"Oh, yes, he has been invited. My father has seen to that. We shall also try to persuade Monsieur de Villefort to come, but have not much hope of success. Do you dance, Count?"

"No, I do not, but I enjoy watching others. Does your mother dance?"

"No, never. You can entertain her. She is very anxious to have a talk with you."

"Really?"

"On my word of honour. Do you know, you are the first person in whom my mother has manifested such curiosity."

Albert rose and took his hat; the Count accompanied him to the door.

"I have to reproach myself with having been somewhat indiscreet," he said, stopping at the top of the steps. "I should not have spoken to you about Monsieur Danglars."

"On the contrary, continue speaking about him, now and always, so long as it is in the same strain."

"That's all right then. By the way, when does Monsieur d'Épinay arrive?"

"In five or six days at the latest."

"And when is he to be married?"

"As soon as Monsieur and Madame de Saint-Méran arrive."

"Bring him to see me when he comes. Though you always say I do not like him, I shall be very glad to see him."

"Your orders shall be obeyed, Count."

"Good-bye!"

"Until Saturday. That is quite certain?"

"I have given you my promise."

It was in the warmest days of June when, in due course of time, the Saturday arrived on which M. de Morcerf's ball was to take place. It was ten o'clock in the evening. From the rooms on the ground floor might be heard the sounds of music and the whirl of the waltz and galop, while brilliant light streamed through the interstices of the venetian blinds. At that moment the garden was only occupied by some ten servants, who were preparing the supper-tables. The paths had already been illuminated by brilliant coloured lanterns, and a mass of choice flowers and numberless candles helped to decorate the sumptuous supper-tables.

No sooner had the Countess returned to the salon after giving her final orders than the guests began to arrive, drawn thither by the charming hospitality of the Countess more than by the distinguished position of the Count. Mme Danglars came, not only beautiful in person but radiantly splendid. Albert went up to her and, paying her well-merited compliments on her toilette; offered her his arm and conducted her to a seat. Albert looked around him.

"You are looking for my daughter?" said the Baroness with a smile.

"I confess I am," responded Albert. "Could you have been so cruel as not to bring her?"

"Now don't get excited; she met Mademoiselle de Villefort and will be here presently. Look, there they come, both of them wearing white, one with a bouquet of roses and the other with myosotis. But tell me . . ."

"What do you wish to know, madame?"

"Is the Count of Monte Cristo not coming this evening?"

"Seventeen!" said Albert.

"What do you mean?"

"Only that you are the seventeenth person who has put that same question to me," replied Albert laughing. "He is doing well . . . I congratulate him."

"Have you answered every one as you have answered me?"

"Oh, to be sure, I have not yet replied to your question. Do not fear, madame, we shall have the privilege of enjoying the company of the lion of the day."

"Were you at the Opera yesterday? He was there."

"No, I did not go. Did the eccentric man do anything original?"

"Does he ever do anything else? Elssler was dancing in *le Diable Boiteux,* and the Greek Princess was in raptures. After the *cachucha,* he threw the dancer a bouquet in between the flowers of which there was a magnificent ring; when she appeared again in the third act, she did honour to the gift by wearing it on her little finger. But leave me here now and go and pay your respects to Madame de Villefort. I can see she is longing to have a talk with you."

Albert bowed and went toward Mme de Villefort, who was about to say something when Albert interrupted her.

"I am sure I know what you are going to ask me," he said.

"What is it?"

"Whether the Count of Monte Cristo is coming."

"Not at all. I was not even thinking of him just then. I wanted to ask you whether you had received news of Franz."

"I had a letter from him yesterday. He was then leaving for Paris."

"That's good. Now what about the Count?"

"The Count is coming right enough."

Just then a handsome young man with keen eyes, black hair, and a glossy moustache bowed respectfully to Mme de Villefort. Albert held out his hand to him.

"Madame, I have the honour of presenting to you Monsieur Maximilian Morrel, Captain of Spahis, one of our best and bravest officers."

"I had the pleasure of meeting this gentleman at Auteuil, at the Count of Monte Cristo's," replied Mme de Villefort, turning away with marked coldness.

This remark, and above all the tone in which it was said, chilled the heart of poor Morrel. There was a recompense in store for him, however. Turning round he perceived near the door a beautiful figure all in white, whose large blue eyes were fixed on him without any apparent expression, whilst the bouquet of myosotis slowly rose to her lips.

Morrel understood the salutation so well that, with the same expressionless look in his eyes, he raised his handkerchief to his mouth. These two living statues, whose hearts beat so violently under their apparently marble-like forms yet were separated from one another by the whole length of the room, forgot themselves for a moment, or rather for a moment forgot everybody and everything in their mute contemplation of one another. They might have remained lost in one another much longer without anyone noticing their obliviousness to all things around them had not the Count of Monte Cristo just entered. As we have already remarked, the Count seemed to exercise a fascination, whether artificial or natural, which attracted general attention wherever he went; it was certainly not his black coat, irreproachable in cut but perfectly plain and devoid of all trimmings, that attracted attention; nor was it his white unembroidered waistcoat, nor his trousers displaying a perfectly shaped foot. It was rather his pale face and black wavy hair, his calm and serene expression, his deep-set, melancholy eyes and his delicately chiselled mouth, which so easily expressed excessive disdain, that drew all eyes toward him.

There may have been men who were more handsome than he, but there were certainly none who were more significant, if we may use the expression. Everything about the Count seemed to have its meaning and value, for the habit of profitable thinking had given an incomparable ease and firmness to his features, to the expression of his face, and to his slightest gesture. Yet the world is so strange that all this would have been passed by unheeded, if it had not been complemented by a mysterious story gilded over by an immense fortune.

However that may be, the Count was the cynosure of every eye as he advanced, exchanging bows on his way, to where Mme de Morcerf was standing before a flower-laden mantelshelf. She had seen his entrance in a mirror placed opposite the door and was prepared to receive him. She turned toward him with a serene smile just as he was bowing to her. No doubt she thought the Count would speak to her, while he on the other hand thought she was about to address him. They both remained silent, therefore, apparently feeling that banalities were out of place between them, so after exchanging salutations, Monte Cristo went in search of Albert.

"Have you seen my mother?" was Albert's first remark.

"I have just had the pleasure," said the Count, "but I have not yet seen your father."

"He is talking politics with a small group of great celebrities."

Just then the Count felt his arm pressed; he turned round to find himself face to face with Danglars.

"Ah, it is you, Baron," said he.

"Why do you call me Baron?" returned Danglars. "You know quite well I care nothing for my title. I am not like you in that respect, Viscount; you lay great value on your title, do you not?"

"Certainly I do," replied Albert, "for if I were not a viscount, I should be nothing at all, whereas, while sacrificing your title of Baron, you would still be a millionaire."

"Which appears to me the finest title in existence," replied Danglars.

"Unfortunately," said Monte Cristo, "the title of millionaire does not always last one's lifetime as does that of Baron, Peer of France, or Academician: as a proof you have only to consider the case of the millionaires Francke and Polmann, of Frankfort, who have just become bankrupt."

"Is that really the case?" asked Danglars, turning pale.

"Indeed it is. I received the news this evening by courier. I had about a million deposited with them, but, having been warned in time, I demanded its withdrawal some four weeks ago."

"Good heavens! They have drawn on me for two hundred thousand francs!"

"Well, you are warned."

"But the warning has come too late," said Danglars. "I have honoured their signature."

"Ah, well," said the Count, "that's another two hundred thousand francs gone to join . . ."

"Hush, do not mention such things before Monsieur Cavalcanti," added the banker, turning his head toward the young man with a smile.

In the meantime the heat in the room had become excessive. Footmen went round with trays laden with fruit and ices. Monte Cristo wiped with his handkerchief the perspiration that had gathered on his forehead, nevertheless he stepped back when the tray passed before him and would not take refreshment.

Mme de Morcerf did not lose sight of Monte Cristo. She saw him refuse to take anything from the tray and even noticed his movement as he withdrew from it.

"Albert," said she, "have you noticed that the Count will not accept an invitation to dine with your father?"

"But he breakfasted with me," said Albert, "in fact it was at that breakfast that he was first introduced into our society."

"That is not your father's house. I have been watching him tonight, he has not taken anything."

"The Count is very temperate."

Mercédès smiled sadly.

"Go to him, Albert," said she, "and, the next time a waiter goes round, persuade him to take something."

"Why, Mother?"

"Because I ask you, Albert."

Albert kissed his mother's hand, and went to do her bidding. Another tray was handed round; Mercédès saw how Albert tried to persuade the Count, how he himself took an ice from the tray and presented it to him, only to meet with an obstinate refusal.

Albert rejoined his mother; she was very pale.

"Well, you see he refused?" said she.

"Yes, but why need that worry you?"

"You know, women are singular creatures, Albert. It would give me pleasure to see him take something, even though it were nothing more than a bit of pomegranate. It may be that he is not yet reconciled to the French way of living, or that he would prefer something else."

"Oh, dear no, I have seen him eat of everything in Italy. No doubt he does not feel inclined this evening."

"Then again, he may not feel the heat as much as we do, since he has always lived in hot climates."

"I do not think that is so," said Albert, "he complained just now of feeling almost suffocated, and asked why the venetian blinds were not opened as well as the windows."

"Ah! It will give me the means of ascertaining whether or not his abstinence is deliberate."

She left the room, and an instant later the venetian blinds were opened, permitting a view through the jasmine and clematis that overhung the windows of the lantern-illuminated garden. Dancers, players, and talkers all uttered an exclamation of joy; everybody inhaled with delight the air that flowed in.

At the same moment Mercédès returned, even paler than before, but with a determined look on her face which was characteristic of her in certain circumstances. She went straight up to the group of gentlemen round her husband, and said: "Do not detain these gentlemen here; if they are not playing I have no doubt they would prefer to take the fresh air in the garden rather than stay in this suffocating room."

"But, madame, we will not go into the garden alone!" said a gallant old general.

Very well, I will set the example," said Mercédès, and turning to Monte Cristo, she added: "Will you give me your arm, Count!"

The Count was staggered at these simple words; he looked at Mercédès. It was but a momentary glance, but the Count put so many thoughts into that one look that it seemed to Mercédès it lasted a century. He offered the Countess his arm; she laid her delicate hand gently on it, and together they went into the garden, followed by some twenty of the guests. With her companion, Mme de Morcerf passed under an archway of lime-trees leading to a conservatory.

"Did you not find it too hot in the room?" said she.

"Yes, madame, but it was an excellent idea of yours to open the windows and venetian blinds."

As he said the last words he felt Mercédès's arm tremble.

"Maybe you feel cold, though, in that thin dress with no other wrap than a thin gauze scarf?" said he.

"Do you know whither I am taking you?" said Mercédès without answering Monte Cristo's question.

"No, madame, but, as you see, I make no resistance."

"To the conservatory at the end of this path."

The Count looked at Mercédès as if he was about to ask her a question, but she went on her way without saying another word, and the Count also remained silent.

They reached the building resplendent with magnificent fruit of every kind. The Countess left the Count's side, and went over to a vine-stock to pluck a bunch of Muscatel grapes. "Take these, Count," said she with such a sad smile that one could almost see the tears springing up into her eyes. "I know our French grapes cannot compare with yours of Sicily and Cyprus, but you must make allowances for our poor Northern sun."

The Count bowed and drew back a step.

"Do you refuse?" said Mercédès in a tremulous voice.

"I must ask you to excuse me, madame, I never eat Muscatel grapes."

With a sigh Mercédès dropped the grapes. A magnificent peach, warmed by the artificial heat of the conservatory, was hanging against an adjoining wall. Mercédès plucked it.

"Take this peach, then."

The Count again refused.

"What, again!" she exclaimed in so plaintive a tone that one felt she was stifling a sob. "Really, Count, you pain me."

A long silence ensued; like the grapes, the peach rolled to the ground.

"There is a touching Arabian custom, Count," Mercédès said at last, looking at Monte Cristo supplicatingly, "which makes eternal friends of those who share bread and salt under the same roof."

"I know it, madame, but we are in France and not in Arabia, and in France eternal friendships are as rare as the beautiful custom you just mentioned."

"But we are friends, are we not?" said the Countess breathlessly, with her eyes fixed on Monte Cristo, whose arm she convulsively clasped between her two hands.

"Certainly we are friends, madame," he replied, "in any case, why should we not be?"

His tone was so different from what Mercédès desired that she turned away to give vent to a sigh resembling a groan.

"Thank you!" was all she said; she began to walk on, and they went all round the garden without uttering another word. After about ten minutes' silence, she suddenly said: "Is it true that you have seen much, travelled far, and suffered deeply?"

"I have suffered deeply, madame," answered Monte Cristo.

"But now you are happy?"

"Doubtless," replied the Count, "since no one hears me complain."

"And has your present happiness softened your heart?"

"My present happiness equals my past misery," said the Count.

"Are you not married?" asked the Countess.

"I, married!" exclaimed Monte Cristo shuddering, "who could have told you that?"

"No one told me you were, but you have frequently been seen at the Opera with a young and lovely person."

"She is a slave whom I bought at Constantinople, madame, the daughter of a prince. Having no one else to love in the world, I have adopted her as my daughter."

"You live alone, then?"

"I do."

"You have no sister, no son, no father?"

"I have no one."

"How can you live thus, with no one to attach you to life?"

"It is not my fault, madame. At Malta, I loved a young girl, and was on the point of marrying her when war came and carried me away, as in a whirlpool. I thought she loved me well enough to wait for me, even to remain faithful to my memory. When I returned she was married. Most men who have passed thirty have the same tale to tell, but perhaps my heart was weaker than that of others, and in consequence I suffered more than they would have done in my place. That's all."

The Countess stopped for a moment, as if gasping for breath. "Yes," she said, "and you have still preserved this love in your heart—one can only love once—and have you ever seen her again?"

"Never!"

"Never?"

"I have never returned to the country where she lived."

"At Malta?"

"Yes, at Malta."

"She is now at Malta, then?"

"I think so."

"And have you forgiven her for all she has made you suffer?"

"Yes, I have forgiven her."

"But only her. Do you still hate those who separated you?"

The Countess placed herself before Monte Cristo, still holding in her hand a portion of the fragrant grapes.

"Take some," she said.

"I never eat Muscatel grapes, madame," replied Monte Cristo as if the subject had not been mentioned before.

The Countess flung the grapes into the nearest thicket, with a gesture of despair.

"Inflexible man!" she murmured.

Monte Cristo remained as unmoved as if the reproach had not been addressed to him. At this moment Albert ran up to them.

"Oh, Mother!" he exclaimed, "such a misfortune has happened!"

"What has happened?" asked the Countess, as though awaking from a dream to the realities of life. "A misfortune, did you say? Indeed, it is little more than I should expect!"

"Monsieur de Villefort has come to fetch his wife and daughter."

"Why?"

"Madame de Saint-Méran has just arrived in Paris, bringing the news of Monsieur de Saint-Méran's death, which occurred at the first stage after he left Marseilles. Madame de Villefort was in very good spirits when her husband came, and could neither understand nor believe in such misfortune. At the first words, however, Mademoiselle Valentine guessed the whole truth, notwithstanding all her father's precautions; the blow struck her like a thunderbolt, and she fell down senseless."

"How was Monsieur de Saint-Méran related to Mademoiselle Valentine?" asked the Count.

"He was her maternal grandfather. He was coming here to hasten her marriage with Franz."

"Indeed!"

"Franz is reprieved then! Why is Monsieur de Saint-Méran not grandfather to Mademoiselle Danglars too?"

"Albert! Albert!" said Mme de Morcerf, in a tone of mild reproof, "what are you saying? Ah! Count, he esteems you so highly, tell him he has spoken amiss."

So saying she took two or three steps forward. Monte Cristo glanced after her with such a pensive expression, at the same time so full of affectionate admiration, that she retraced her steps. Taking his hand and that of her son, she joined them together, saying: "We are friends, are we not?"

"Oh, madame, I do not presume to call myself your friend, but at all times I am your most respectful servant."

## CHAPTER XLVI

## MME DE SAINT-MÉRAN

VALENTINE found her grandmother in bed; silent caresses, heartrending sobs, broken sighs, and burning tears were the sole recountable details of the distressing interview, at which Mme de Villefort was present, leaning on her husband's arm, and manifesting, outwardly at least, great sympathy for the poor widow.

After a few moments she whispered to her husband: "I think it would be better for me to retire, for the sight of me still appears to distress your mother-in-law."

Mme de Saint-Méran heard her and whispered to Valentine: "Yes, yes, let her go, but do you stay with me."

Mme de Villefort went out and Valentine remained alone with her grandmother, for the Procureur du Roi, dismayed at the sudden death, had followed his wife.

At last, worn out with grief, Mme de Saint-Méran succumbed to her fatigue and fell into a feverish sleep. Valentine placed a small table within her reach and on it a decanter of orangeade, her usual beverage, and, leaving her bedside, went to see old Noirtier. She went up to the old man and kissed him. He looked at her with such tenderness that she again burst into tears.

"Yes, yes, I understand," she said. "You wish to convey to me that I have still a good grandfather, do you not?"

He intimated that such was his meaning.

"Happily I have," returned Valentine. "Otherwise what would become of me?"

It was one o'clock in the morning. Barrois, who wished to go to bed himself, remarked that after such a distressing evening every one had need of rest. M. Noirtier would have liked to say that all the repose he needed was to be found in his granddaughter's presence, but he bade her good-night, for grief and fatigue had made her look quite ill.

When Valentine went to see her grandmother the next day she found her still in bed; the fever had not abated, on the contrary, the old Marquise's eyes were lit up with a dull fire and she was prone to great nervous irritability.

"Oh, Grandmama, are you feeling worse?" exclaimed Valentine on perceiving all these symptoms.

"No, child, but I was impatiently waiting for you to fetch your father to me."

"My father?" inquired Valentine uneasily.

"Yes, I wish to speak to him."

Valentine did not dare oppose her grandmother's wish, and an instant later Villefort entered.

"You wrote me, monsieur, concerning this child's marriage," said Mme de Saint-Méran, coming straight to the point as though afraid she had not much time left.

"Yes, madame," replied Villefort. "The matter has already been settled."

"Is not the name of your future son-in-law Monsieur Franz d'Épinay?"

"Yes, madame."

"Is he the son of General d'Épinay, who belonged to our party and was assassinated a few days before the usurper returned from Elba?"

"The very same."

"Is he not opposed to this alliance with the granddaughter of a Jacobin?"

"Our civil dissensions are now happily dispelled," said Villefort. "Monsieur d'Épinay was little more than a child when his father died. He hardly knows Monsieur Noirtier and will greet him, if not with pleasure, at least with unconcern."

"Is it a desirable match?"

"In every respect. He is one of the most gentlemanly young men I know."

Valentine remained silent throughout this conversation.

"Then, monsieur, you must hasten on the marriage, for I have not much longer to live," said Mme de Saint-Méran after a few seconds' reflection.

"You, madame?" "You, Grandmama?" cried Monsieur de Villefort and Valentine simultaneously.

"I know what I am saying," returned the Marquise. "You must hasten on the arrangements so that the poor motherless child may at least have a grandmother to bless her marriage. I am all that is left to her of dear Renée, whom you appear so soon to have forgotten."

"But, Grandmama, consider decorum—our recent mourning. Would you have me begin my married life under such sad auspices?"

"Nay, I tell you I am going to die, and before dying I wish to see your husband. I wish to bid him make my child happy, to read in his eyes whether he intends to obey me. In short, I must know him," continued the grandmother with a terrifying expression in her eyes, "so that I may arise from the depths of my grave to seek him out if he is not all he should be."

"Madame, you must dispel such feverish ideas that are almost akin to madness," said Villefort. "When once the dead are laid in their graves, they remain there never to rise again."

"And I tell you, monsieur, it is not as you think. Last night my sleep was sorely troubled. It seemed as though my soul were already hovering over my body; my eyes, which I tried to open, closed against my will; and, what will appear impossible, above all to you, monsieur, with my eyes shut I saw in yonder dark corner, where there is a door leading to Madame de Villefort's dressing-room, I tell you I saw a white figure enter noiselessly."

Valentine screamed.

"It was the fever acting on you, madame," said Villefort.

"Doubt my word if it pleases you, but I am sure of what I say. I saw a white figure, and, as if God feared I should discredit the testimony of my senses, I heard my tumbler move—the same one that is now on the table."

"But it was a dream, Grandmama!"

"So far was it from being a dream that I stretched out my hand towards the bell, but as I did so the shadow disappeared and my maid entered with a light. Phantoms are visible only to those who are intended to see them. It was my husband's spirit. If my husband's spirit can come to me, why would not mine appear to guard my granddaughter? It seems to me there is an even stronger tie between us."

"Madame, do not give way to such gloomy thoughts," said Villefort, deeply affected in spite of himself. "You will live long with us, happy, loved, and honoured, and we will help you to forget . . ."

"Never, never, never!" said the Marquise. "When does Monsieur d'Épinay return?"

"We expect him any moment."

"It is well; as soon as he arrives, let me know. We must lose no time. Then I also wish to see a notary that I may be assured that all our property reverts to Valentine."

"Ah, my Grandmother!" murmured Valentine, pressing her lips to her grandmother's burning brow, "do you wish to kill me? Oh, how feverish you are! It is a doctor we must send for, not a notary."

"A doctor?" she said, shrugging her shoulders, "I am not ill; I am thirsty—nothing more."

"What are you drinking, Grandmama?"

"The same as usual, my dear, orangeade. Give me my glass, Valentine."

Valentine poured the orangeade into a glass and gave it to her grandmother, though not without a feeling of dread, for it was the same glass she declared the shadow had touched. The Marquise drained the glass at a single draught, and then, turning over on her pillow, repeated: "The notary! the notary!"

M. de Villefort left the room, and Valentine seated herself at her grandmother's bedside.

Two hours passed thus, during which Mme de Saint-Méran was in a restless, feverish sleep. At last the notary arrived. He was announced in a very low voice, nevertheless Mme de Saint-Méran heard and raised herself on her pillows.

"Go, Valentine, go," she said, "and leave me alone with this gentleman."

Valentine kissed her grandmother and left the room with her handkerchief to her eyes. At the door she met the valet who told her the doctor was waiting in the salon. She instantly went down.

"Oh! dear Monsieur d'Avrigny, we have been waiting for you with such impatience."

"Who is ill, dear child?" said he. "Not your father or Madame de Villefort?"

"It is my grandmother who needs your services. You know the calamity that has befallen us."

"I know nothing," said M. d'Avrigny.

"Alas!" said Valentine, choking back her tears, "my grandfather is dead."

"Monsieur de Saint-Méran?"

"Yes."

"Suddenly?"

"From an apoplectic stroke."

"An apoplectic stroke?" repeated the doctor.

"Yes! and my poor grandmother fancies that her husband, whom she never left, is calling her, and that she must go and join him. Oh! Monsieur d'Avrigny, I beseech you, do something for her!"

"Where is she?"

"In her room with the notary."

"And Monsieur Noirtier?"

"Just as he was, perfectly clear in his mind but still incapable of moving or speaking."

"And the same love for you—eh, my dear child!"

"Yes," said Valentine, "he is very fond of me."

"Who does not love you?"

Valentine smiled sadly.

"What are your grandmother's symptoms?"

"An extremely nervous excitement and an unnatural restlessness.

This morning, in her sleep, she fancied that her soul was hovering over her body, which she saw asleep. It must have been delirium! She fancies, too, that she saw a phantom enter her chamber, and even heard the noise it made in touching her glass."

"It is singular," said the doctor. "I was not aware that Madame de Saint-Méran was subject to such hallucinations."

"It is the first time I ever saw her thus," said Valentine, "and this morning she frightened me so that I thought she was mad, and even my father, who you know is a strong-minded man, appeared deeply impressed."

"We will go and see," said the doctor. "What you tell me seems very strange."

The notary came downstairs, and Valentine was informed her grandmother was alone.

"Go upstairs," she said to the doctor.

"And you?"

"Oh, I dare not. She forbade my sending for you, and I am agitated, feverish, unwell. I will go and take a turn in the garden to compose myself."

The doctor pressed Valentine's hand, and, while he visited her grandmother, she went into the garden. We need not say which was her favourite walk. After remaining for a short time in the flower garden surrounding the house, and gathering a rose to place in her waist or hair, she turned into the dark avenue which led to the bench, from thence to the gate. As she advanced she fancied she heard a voice pronounce her name. She stopped astonished, then the voice reached her ear more distinctly, and she recognized it to be the voice of Maximilian.

## CHAPTER XLVII

## THE PROMISE

IT was indeed Maximilian Morrel. He had been in despair since the previous day. With the instinct of a lover, he had divined that with the arrival of Mme de Saint-Méran, and the death of the Marquis, some change would take place in the Villefort household which would touch his love for Valentine.

Valentine had not expected to see Morrel, for it was not his usual hour, and it was only pure chance or, better still, a happy sympathy that took her into the garden. When she appeared, Morrel called her, and she ran to the gate.

"You here, at this hour!" she said.

"Yes, my poor dear," replied Morrel. "I have come to bring and to hear bad tidings."

"This is indeed a house of mourning," said Valentine. "Speak, Maximilian, yet in truth my cup of sorrow seems full to overflowing."

"Dear Valentine, listen, I entreat you," said Morrel endeavouring to conceal his emotion. "I have something grave to tell you. When are you to be married?"

"I will conceal nothing from you, Maximilian," said Valentine. "This morning the subject was introduced, and my grandmother, in whom I had hoped to find a sure support, not only declares herself favourable to the marriage, but is so anxious for it that the day after Monsieur d'Épinay arrives the contract will be signed."

A sob of anguish was wrung from the young man's breast, and he looked long and mournfully at his beloved.

"Alas!" he whispered, "it is terrible thus to hear the woman you love calmly say: 'The time of your execution is fixed, and will take place in a few hours; it had to be, and I will do nothing to prevent it!' Monsieur d'Épinay arrived this morning!"

Valentine uttered a cry.

"And now, Valentine, answer me, and remember that my life or death depends on your answer. What do you intend doing?"

Valentine hung her head; she was overwhelmed.

"This is not the first time we have reflected on our present grave and critical position. It is not now the moment to give way to useless sorrow; leave that to those who delight in suffering, and wallow in their grief. There are such people, but those who feel in themselves the desire to fight against their bitter lot must not lose one precious moment. Are you prepared to fight against our ill-fortune, Valentine? Tell me, for this is what I have come to ask you."

Valentine trembled visibly, and stared at Maximilian with wide-open eyes. The idea of opposing her grandmother, her father, in short, her whole family, had never occurred to her.

"What is this you bid me do, Maximilian?" asked Valentine. "How could I oppose my father's orders and my dying grandmother's wish! It is impossible!"

Morrel started.

"You are too noble-hearted not to understand me, and your very silence is proof that you do. I fight! God preserve me from it! No, I need all my strength to hold back my tears. Never could I grieve my father or disturb the last moments of my grandmother!"

"You are right," said Morrel phlegmatically.

"How you say that!" cried Valentine in a hurt voice.

"I speak as one full of admiration for you, mademoiselle."

"Mademoiselle!" exclaimed Valentine. "Mademoiselle?—how selfish! He sees me in despair and pretends he cannot understand my point of view!"

"On the contrary, I understand you perfectly. You do not wish to thwart your father or disobey the Marquise, so you will sign the contract to-morrow which will bind you to your husband."

"How can I do otherwise?"

"It is no good appealing to me, mademoiselle, for I am not a competent judge. My selfishness will blind me," Morrel continued, and his toneless voice and clenched hands showed his increasing exasperation.

"What would you have proposed, had you found me willing to comply with your wishes? Ah! Maximilian, tell me what you advise!"

"Do you mean that seriously?"

"Certainly I do, and, if your advice is good, I shall follow it. You know how I love you."

"Valentine, give me your hand in token that you forgive me my anger," said Morrel. "I am utterly distraught, and for the past hour the most extravagant ideas have been running through my head. Follow me, Valentine. I will take you to my sister, who is worthy to be your sister also. We will embark for Algiers . . . England . . . America . . . Or, if you prefer, we can go together to some province until our friends have persuaded your family to reconciliation."

Valentine shook her head.

"Then you will submit to your fate whatever it may be, without even attempting to oppose it?"

"Even if it spelt death!"

"I repeat once more, Valentine, you are quite right. Indeed, it is I who am mad and you are but giving me a proof that passion blinds the most balanced minds. Fortunate are you that you can reason dispassionately. It is, therefore, an understood thing that to-morrow you will be irrevocably promised to Franz d'Épinay, not by the theatrical formality invented to bind a couple together which is called the signing of the contract, but by your own free will."

Morrel said these words with perfect calmness. Valentine looked at him for a moment with her large searching eyes, at the same time endeavouring to conceal from him the grief that struggled in her heart.

"And what are you going to do?" she asked.

"I shall have the honour of bidding you farewell, mademoiselle, calling on God to make your life so happy and contented that there may be no place for me even in your memory. He will hear my prayers for He sees to the bottom of my heart. Farewell, Valentine, farewell!" continued he, bowing.

"Where are you going?" cried the distracted girl, thrusting her hand through the gate and seizing Maximilian's coat. Her own agitated feelings told her that her lover's calmness could not be real. "Where are you going?"

The young man gave a sad smile.

"Oh! speak, speak! I entreat you!" said Valentine.

"Has your resolution changed, Valentine?"

"It cannot change, unhappy man! You know it cannot!" cried she.

"Then farewell, Valentine!"

Valentine shook the gate with a strength she had not thought herself capable of, and as Morrel was going away pushed her two hands through, and, clasping them, called out:

"Maximilian, come here; I wish it."

Maximilian drew near with his sweet smile, and had it not been for his pallor, one would have thought that nothing unusual had taken place.

"Listen to me, my dear, my adored Valentine," said he in a solemn voice. "People like us who have never harboured a thought for which we had reason to blush before the world, our parents or God, people like ourselves can read one another's heart like an open book. I have never been romantic, and I shall not be a melancholy hero. However, without words, protestations, or vows, I have laid my life in your hands. You fail me, and, I repeat once more, you are quite right in acting thus; nevertheless in losing you I lose part of my life. The moment you part from me, Valentine, I am alone in the world. My sister is happy with her husband; her husband is only my brother-in-law, that is to say, a man who is attached to me solely by social laws; no one on earth has any further need of my useless existence. This is what I shall do: I shall wait until you are actually married, for I will not lose the smallest of one of those unexpected chances fate sometimes holds in store for us. After all, Monsieur Franz might die, a thunderbolt might fall on the altar as you approach it; everything appears possible to the condemned man, to whom a miracle becomes an everyday occurrence when it is a question of saving his life. I shall therefore wait until the very last moment, and when my fate is sealed, and my misery beyond all hope and remedy, I shall write a confidential letter to my brother-in-law, another one to the prefect of police, to notify him of my design; then, in a corner of some wood, in a ditch, or on the bank of some river, I shall blow out my brains, as certainly as I am the son of the most honest man who ever breathed in France."

A convulsive trembling shook Valentine in every limb; she relaxed her hold of the gate, her arms fell to her sides, and two large tears rolled down her cheeks.

The young man stood before her gloomy and resolute.

"Oh! my God . . . ! Promise me, Maximilian, that you will not take your life!" she cried.

"I promise you I will not," said Maximilian. "But what does that matter to you? You will have done your duty and your conscience will be at rest."

Valentine fell on her knees, pressing her hand to her breaking heart.

"Maximilian, my friend, my brother on earth, my real husband before Heaven," she cried, "I entreat you, do as I am going to do— live in suffering; one day, perhaps, we shall be united."

"Farewell!" repeated Morrel.

"My God," said Valentine, raising her two hands to Heaven with a sublime expression on her face. "Thou seest I have done my utmost to remain a dutiful daughter. I have begged, entreated, implored. He has heeded neither my entreaties, nor my supplications, nor my tears . . . I would rather die of shame than of remorse," she continued, wiping away her tears and resuming her air of determination. "You shall live, Maximilian, and I shall belong to no other than you! When shall it be? At once? Speak, command, I will obey."

Morrel had already gone several steps; he returned on hearing these words, and pale with joy, his heart beating tumultuously, he held his two hands through the gate to Valentine, and said:

"Valentine, my beloved, you must not speak to me thus; better let me die. Why should I win you by force if you love me as I love you? Is it for pity that you compel me to live? Then I would rather die!"

"'Tis too true!" murmured Valentine to herself, "who but he loves me? Who but he has consoled me in all my sorrow? In whom but in him do my hopes lie, and to whom but to him can I fly when in trouble? He is my all! Yes, you are right, Maximilian, I will follow you. I will leave my father's home, leave all! Ungrateful girl that I am!" she cried, sobbing. "Yes, I will leave all, even my grandfather whom I had nearly forgotten!"

"No, you shall not leave him," said Maximilian. "You say that your grandfather likes me. Very well, then, before you flee, tell him all; his consent will be your justification before God. As soon as we are married, he shall come to us: instead of one child, he will have two children. Oh, Valentine, instead of our present hopelessness, nought but happiness is in store for you and me. But if they disregard your entreaties, Valentine," he continued, "if your father and Madame de Saint-Méran insist on sending for Monsieur d'Épinay to-morrow to sign the contract . . ."

"You have my word, Maximilian."

"Instead of signing . . ."

"I shall flee with you, but until then, Morrel, let us not tempt Providence. We will see each other no more: it is a marvel, almost a miracle one might say, that we have not been discovered before. If it were found out, and if they learned how we see each other, our last resource would be gone. In the meantime I will write to you. I hate this marriage, Maximilian, as much as you do."

"Thank you, my beloved Valentine," Morrel replied. "Then all is settled. As soon as I know the time, I will hasten here. You will climb the wall with my help and then all will be easy. A carriage will be awaiting us at the gate which will take us to my sister's."

"So be it! Good-bye!" said Valentine, tearing herself away. *"Au revoir!"*

"You will be sure to write to me?"

"Yes."

"Thank you, my beloved wife. *Au revoir!"*

Morrel stayed, listening, till the sound of her footsteps on the gravel had died away, then he raised his eyes heavenward with an ineffable smile of gratitude that such supreme love should be given him.

The young man returned home and waited the whole of that evening and the next day without receiving any news. Toward ten o'clock of the third day, however, he received by post a note which he knew was from Valentine, although he had never before seen her handwriting. The note read as follows:

> Tears, supplications, entreaties have been of no avail. I went to the church of St Philip du Roule yesterday and for two hours prayed most fervently. But God appears as unfeeling as man is and the signing of the contract is fixed for this evening at nine o'clock. I have but one heart and can give my hand to one person only: both my hand and my heart are yours, Maximilian.
>
> I shall see you this evening at the gate at a quarter to nine.
>
> Your wife,
>
> VALENTINE DE VILLEFORT
>
> P.S.—I think they are keeping it a secret from Grandpapa Noirtier that the contract is to be signed to-morrow.

Not satisfied with the information Valentine had given him, Morrel went in search of the notary, who confirmed the fact that the signing of the contract had been fixed for nine o'clock that evening.

Maximilian had made all arrangements for the elopement. Two ladders were hidden in the clover near the garden; a cabriolet, which was to take Maximilian to the gate, was in readiness. No servants would accompany him, and the lanterns would not be lit till they reached the first bend of the road.

From time to time a shudder passed through Morrel's whole frame as he thought of the moment when he would assist Valentine in her descent from the top of the wall, and when he would clasp in his arms the trembling form of her whose finger tips he had as yet hardly ventured to kiss.

In the afternoon, when the hour drew near, Morrel felt the necessity of being alone. He shut himself up in his room and attempted to read, but his eyes passed over the pages without understanding what he was reading, and in the end he flung the book from him. At last the hour arrived. The horse and cabriolet were concealed behind some ruins where Maximilian was accustomed to hide.

The day gradually drew to its close, and the bushes in the garden became nothing but indistinct masses. Morrel came out of his hiding-place, and, with beating heart, looked through the hole in the paling. There was no one to be seen. The clock struck nine . . . half-past nine . . . ten! In the darkness he searched in vain for the white dress, in the stillness he waited in vain for the sound of footsteps. Then one idea took possession of his mind: she had been coming to him, but her strength had failed her and she had fallen in a faint on one of the garden paths. He ventured to call her name, and he seemed to hear an inarticulate moan in response. He scaled the wall and jumped down on the other side. Distracted and half mad with anxiety, he decided to risk everything and anything in order to ascertain if and what misfortune had befallen Valentine. He reached the outskirts of the clump of trees and was just about to cross the open flower-garden with all possible speed when a distant voice, borne upon the wind, reached his ear.

He retreated a step and stood motionless, concealed, hidden among the trees. He made up his mind that if Valentine was alone, he would warn her of his presence; if she was accompanied, he would at least see her and know whether she was safe and well.

Just then the moon escaped from behind a cloud and by its light Morrel saw Villefort on the steps followed by a man in black garb. They descended the steps and approached the clump of trees where Morrel was hiding, and he soon recognized the other gentleman as Doctor d'Avrigny. After a short time, their footsteps ceased to crunch the gravel, and the following conversation reached his ears:

"Oh, Doctor, the hand of God is heavy upon us! What a terrible death! What a blow! Seek not to console me, for alas, the wound is too deep and too fresh. Dead! dead!"

A cold perspiration broke out on Maximilian's forehead, and his teeth chattered. Who was dead in that house that Villefort himself called accursed?

"I have not brought you here to console you, quite the contrary," said the doctor, in a voice that added to the young man's terror.

"What do you mean?" asked the Procureur du Roi alarmed.

"What I mean is, that behind the misfortune that has just befallen you, there is perhaps a much greater one. Are we quite alone?"

"Yes, quite alone. But why such precautions?"

"I have a terrible secret to confide in you," said the doctor.

"Let us sit down."

Villefort sank on to a bench. The doctor stood in front of him, one hand on his shoulder. Petrified with fear, Morrel put one hand to his head, and pressed the other to his heart to stop the beatings, lest they should be heard.

"Speak, Doctor, I am listening," said Villefort. "Strike your blow. I am prepared for all."

"Madame de Saint-Méran had attained a great age, it is true, but she was in excellent health."

Morrel began to breathe freely again.

"Grief has killed her," said Villefort, "yes, Doctor, grief! After living with the Marquis for more than forty years!"

"It is not grief, my dear Villefort," said the doctor. "Grief does kill, though very rarely, but not in a day, not in an hour, nor yet in ten minutes."

Villefort made no reply; he just raised his bowed head, and looked at the doctor with staring eyes.

"Were you present during the death agony?" asked Doctor d'Avrigny.

"Certainly," replied the Procureur du Roi, "you yourself whispered to me not to go away."

"Did you note the symptoms of the disease to which Madame de Saint-Méran succumbed?"

"Perfectly. Madame de Saint-Méran had three successive attacks at intervals of a few minutes, each one worse than the other. When you arrived, she had been gasping for breath for some few minutes; then she had a fit which I took for a simple nervous attack. I did not actually become alarmed till I saw her raise herself on her bed, and her limbs and neck stiffen. Then I saw by your face that it was more serious than I had supposed. When the attack was over, I sought your eyes, but you did not look at me. You were feeling her pulse, counting her respirations, and the second attack seized her before you had turned round. This was more terrible than the first, the same twitching of the nerves, the mouth contracted and purple in colour. At the end of the third attack she died. At the very first attack I saw signs of tetanus; you confirmed my opinion."

"Yes, in the hearing of everybody," replied the doctor, "but now we are alone."

"My God! What are you going to tell me?"

"That the symptoms of tetanus and poisoning by vegetable matter are absolutely identical!"

M. de Villefort sprang up, then after a moment sank on to the bench again.

"My God! Doctor," said he, "do you realize what you are telling me?"

Morrel knew not whether he was awake or dreaming.

"I know both the significance of my statement and the character of the man to whom I make it."

"Do you speak to me as magistrate or as friend?" asked Villefort.

"At this moment as friend only; the similarity of tetanus and poisoning by vegetable matter is so great that I should hesitate to sign the statement I have just made. I therefore repeat once more, I speak not to the magistrate but to the friend, and to the friend I declare that during the three-quarters of an hour the agony lasted, I watched the convulsions and the death struggle of Madame de Saint-Méran, and my firm conviction is that she died of poisoning, and what is more, I can name the poison that killed her."

"Oh, Doctor! Doctor!"

"All the symptoms were there; sleep disturbed by nervous tremors, excitement of the brain followed by torpor. Madame de Saint-Méran has succumbed to a large dose of brucine or strychnine, which has doubtless been administered to her by mistake."

Villefort seized the doctor's hands.

"It is impossible!" he said. "Am I dreaming? Surely I must be. It is terrible to hear such things from a man like you! For pity's sake, Doctor, tell me you have been mistaken!"

"Did anyone see Madame de Saint-Méran besides myself?"

"No one."

"Has any prescription been made up at the chemist's that has not been shown me?"

"None."

"Had Madame de Saint-Méran any enemies?"

"I do not know of any."

"Would her death be to anyone's interest?"

"No, no, surely not! My daughter is her sole heiress, Valentine alone ... Oh, if such a thought came into my heart, I should stab that heart to punish it for having harboured such a thought if only for one moment."

"God forbid that I should accuse anyone," exclaimed M. d'Avrigny.

"I speak of an accident, a mistake, you understand. But whether accident or mistake, the fact remains and is appealing to my conscience, which compels me to speak to you. Make inquiries."

"Of whom? How? About what?"

"Is it not possible that Barrois, the old servant, has made a mistake and given Madame de Saint-Méran a potion prepared for his master?"

"But how could a potion prepared for my father kill Madame de Saint-Méran?"

"Nothing more simple. You know that in the case of certain diseases poison becomes a remedy. Paralysis is one of these cases. I have been giving Monsieur Noirtier brucine for the past three months, and in his last prescription I ordered six grains, a quantity that would be perfectly safe for one whose paralysed organs have gradually become accustomed to it, whereas it would be sufficient to kill anyone else."

"But there is no communication between Monsieur Noirtier's room and that of Madame de Saint-Méran, and Barrois never went near my mother-in-law."

"It is through carelessness that this has happened; watch your servants; if it is the work of hatred, watch your enemies. In the meantime let us bury this terrible secret in the depths of our hearts. Keep constant watch, for it may be that it will not end here. Make active investigations and seek out the culprit, and if you should find him, I shall say to you: 'You are a magistrate, do as you will.'"

"Oh, thank you, Doctor, thank you!" said Villefort with indescribable joy. "Never have I had better friend than you."

Fearing lest d'Avrigny might think better of his decision, he rose and ran into the house. The doctor also went away.

As though he had need of air, Morrel immediately put his head out of the bushes, and the moon shining on his face gave him the appearance of a ghost.

"I have been protected in a wonderful yet terrible way," said he. "Valentine, my poor Valentine! how will she bear so much sorrow!"

As though in answer, he seemed to hear a sob coming from one of the open windows of the house, and he thought he heard his name called by a shadow at the window. He rushed out of his hiding-place, and, at the risk of being seen and of frightening Valentine, and thus causing some exclamation to escape her lips which would lead to discovery, he crossed the flower-garden, which looked like a large white lake in the moonlight, reached the steps, ran up them quickly, and pushed open the door, which offered no resistance. The description of the house Valentine had given him now stood him in good stead, and the thick carpets deadened his tread. He reached the top of the stairs without any accident; a half-open door, from which issued a stream of light, and the sound of a sob indicated to him which direction to take. Pushing open the door, he entered the room.

In an alcove, under a white sheet, lay the corpse, more terrifying than ever to Morrel since chance had revealed to him the secret concerning the dead woman. Beside the bed knelt Valentine, her hands stretched out in front of her and her whole frame shaking with sobs. The moon shining through the open blinds made pale the light of the lamp, and cast a sepulchral hue over this picture of desolation. Morrel was not of a pious or impressionable nature, but to see Valentine suffering and weeping was almost more than he could endure in silence. With a deep sigh he murmured her name, and the tear-stained face buried in the velvet of the armchair was slowly raised and turned toward him. Valentine manifested no astonishment at seeing him.

"How came you here?" she asked. "Alas! I should say you are welcome, but that Death has opened the doors of this house to you!"

"Valentine, I have been waiting there since half-past eight," said Morrel in a trembling voice. "Such anxiety was tearing at my heart when you did not come that I scaled the wall and . . ."

"But we shall be lost if you are found here!" said Valentine in a voice devoid of all fear or anger.

"Forgive me," replied Morrel in the same tone. "I will go at once."

"No, you cannot go out either by the front door or the garden gate. There is only one safe way open to you and that is through my grandfather's room. Follow me!"

"Have you thought what that means?"

"I have thought long since. He is the only friend I have in the world and we both have need of him. Come!"

Valentine crossed the corridor and went down a small staircase which led to Noirtier's room. She entered; Morrel followed her on tiptoe.

Still in his chair, Noirtier was listening for the least sound. He had been informed by his old servant of all that had happened and was now watching the door with eager eyes. He saw Valentine, and his eyes brightened. There was something grave and solemn about the girl's whole attitude which struck the old man, and his eyes looked on her questioningly.

"Dear Grandpapa," she said, "you know that Grandmama Saint-Méran died an hour ago, and now I have no one but you in the whole world to love me."

An expression of infinite tenderness shone in the old man's eyes.

"Thus to you alone can I confide all my sorrows and hopes."

The old man made a sign of assent.

Valentine took Maximilian by the hand. "Then look well at this gentleman," said she.

Somewhat astonished, the paralytic fixed his scrutinizing gaze on Morrel.

"This is Maximilian Morrel," said she, "the son of an honest merchant at Marseilles, of whom you have doubtless heard."

"Yes," was the answer.

"It is an irreproachable name, and Maximilian is in a fair way to making it a glorious one, for, though but thirty years of age, he is Captain of Spahis and an Officer of the Legion of Honour."

The old man made a sign that he recollected him.

Valentine threw herself on her knees before the old man, saying: "Grandpapa, I love him and will belong to no other. If they force me to marry another, I shall die or kill myself."

The paralytic's eyes expressed a wealth of tumultuous thoughts.

"You like Monsieur Maximilian Morrel, do you not, Grandfather?" asked Valentine.

"Yes," was the old man's motionless reply.

"Will you protect us, then, who are your children, against my father's will?"

Noirtier fixed his intelligent gaze on Morrel as though to say: "That depends."

Maximilian understood him.

"Mademoiselle, you have a sacred duty to fulfil in your grandmother's room. Will you permit me to have a few minutes' conversation with Monsieur Noirtier?"

"Yes, yes, that is right," said the old man's eyes. Then he looked at Valentine with an expression of anxiety.

"You wonder how he will understand you, Grandpapa? Have no fear; we have spoken of you so often that he knows quite well how I converse with you." Then turning to Maximilian with a smile that was adorable, though overshadowed by great sadness, she said: "He knows all that I know."

Valentine rose and kissed her grandfather tenderly, and, taking leave of Morrel, sorrowfully left the two men together.

Then, to show that he was in Valentine's confidence and knew all their secrets, Morrel took the dictionary, a pen and some paper and placed them on the table near the lamp.

"First of all, monsieur," said he, "permit me to tell you who I am, how deeply I love Valentine, and what plans I entertain in regard to her."

"I am listening," said Noirtier's eyes.

It was an imposing sight to behold this old man, to all appearances a useless mass, now become the sole protector and support of two young handsome lovers just entering upon life. Imprinted on his face was a noble and remarkably austere expression which filled Morrel with awe. He related how he had become acquainted with Valentine, how he had learned to love her, and how in her unhappiness and solitude Valentine had welcomed his offer of devotion; he gave full information regarding his birth and position, and more than once when he questioned the paralytic's eye, it said to him: "That is well! Continue!"

Then Morrel related to him how they had intended to flee together that very night. When he had finished speaking, Noirtier closed and opened his eyes several times which, as we know, was his manner of expressing negation.

"No?" said Morrel. "You disapprove of my plan?"

"Yes, I do disapprove of it."

"But then, what am I to do?" asked Morrel. "Madame de Saint-Méran's last words were to the effect that her grandchild's marriage should not be delayed. Am I to allow it to take place?"

Noirtier remained motionless.

"I understand you," said Morrel. "I am to wait. But we shall be lost if we delay. Alone Valentine is powerless, and she will be compelled to submit like a child. It was little short of miraculous the way I gained admittance to this house to learn what was happening, and was permitted to enter your room; but I cannot reasonably expect the fates to be so kind to me again. Believe me, there is no other course for me to take. Do you give Mademoiselle Valentine permission to entrust herself to my honour?"

"No!" looked the old man.

"Whence will help come to us then; are we to seek it in chance?"

"No."

"In you?"

"Yes."

"Do you fully comprehend what I ask, monsieur? Forgive my importunity, but my life depends upon your answer. Is our salvation to come from you?"

"Yes."

"You are sure?"

"Yes."

"You can answer for it?"

"Yes."

There was so much determination in the look that gave this answer that it was impossible to doubt his will, even if one could not credit his power.

"Oh, thank you, thank you a hundred times. But unless a miracle restore to you your speech and power of movement, how can you, chained to your chair, mute and motionless, how can you prevent this marriage?"

A smile illumined the old man's face—a weird smile in the eyes alone, while the rest of his face was impassive.

"You say I must wait?" asked the young man.

"Yes."

"But the contract?"

Again the same smile.

"Do you mean to say that it will not be signed?"

"I do," said Noirtier.

"The contract will not be signed!" exclaimed Morrel. "Forgive me, but I cannot help doubting such happiness. Will the contract really not be signed?"

"No," said the paralytic.

Whether it was said that Noirtier understood the young man's decision, or whether he had not complete confidence in his docility, he looked steadily at him.

"What do you wish, monsieur?" asked Morrel. "Do you wish me to renew my promise to do nothing?"

Noirtier's eyes remained on him in a fixed and firm stare, as though he wished to say that a promise was not sufficient; then they wandered from the face to the hand.

"Do you wish me to swear it?" asked Maximilian.

"Yes," motioned the old man with great solemnity.

Morrel understood that the old man attached great importance to an oath. He held up his hand: "On my honour," said he, "I swear to await your decision before acting in any way against Monsieur d'Épinay."

"That is right," said the old man with his eyes.

"Do you wish me to retire now, monsieur?" asked Morrel.

"Yes."

"Without seeing Mademoiselle Valentine again?"

"Yes."

Morrel made a sign that he was ready to obey. "Now, monsieur, will you permit your grandson to embrace you as your granddaughter did just now?"

There was no mistaking the expression in Noirtier's eyes.

The young man pressed his lips to the old man's forehead, on the same spot where the girl had imprinted her kiss. Then he bowed again and retired.

He found the old servant waiting for him on the landing. Valentine had given him all instructions. He took Morrel along a dark corridor which led to a small door opening on to the garden. Once in the garden, Morrel soon scaled the wall, and by means of his ladder reached the field where his cabriolet was waiting for him. He jumped in, and worn out by so many emotions, though feeling more at peace, he reached his home toward midnight, threw himself on his bed, and fell into a deep, dreamless sleep.

## CHAPTER XLVIII

## MINUTES OF THE PROCEEDINGS

No sooner were the Marquis and Marquise laid to rest together in the family vault than M. de Villefort thought about putting into execution the Marquise's last wishes. He sent a message to Valentine to request her to be in the salon in half an hour, as he was expecting M. d'Épinay, his two witnesses, and the notary.

This unexpected news created a great stir throughout the house. Mme de Villefort could scarcely believe it, and Valentine was thunderstruck. She looked round her, as though seeking for help, and would have gone to her grandfather, but on the stairs she met M. de Villefort, who, taking her arm, conducted her to the salon. In the hall she met Barrois, and threw him a despairing look. A moment later Mme de Villefort with her son Edward joined them. It was evident the young woman shared the family grief, for she was pallid, and looked terribly fatigued.

She sat down with Edward on her knees, and from time to time convulsively caught him to her breast. Soon the rumbling of two carriages was heard. The notary alighted from one, and Franz and his friends from the other.

Every one was now united in the salon. Valentine was so pale that one could trace the blue veins round her eyes and down her cheeks.

After arranging his papers on the table in true lawyer-like fashion, the notary seated himself in an armchair, and taking off his eyeglasses turned to Franz. "Are you Monsieur Franz de Quesnel, Baron d'Épinay?" he asked, though he knew perfectly well that he was.

"Yes, monsieur," replied Franz.

The notary bowed. "I must warn you, monsieur," he continued, "on Monsieur de Villefort's behalf, that your projected marriage with mademoiselle has effected a change in Monsieur Noirtier's designs toward his granddaughter, and that he has disinherited her entirely. I will add, however, that the testator has no right to will away the whole of his fortune. In doing so he has made the will contestable and liable to be declared null and void."

"That is right," said Villefort, "but I should like to warn Monsieur d'Épinay that never in my lifetime shall the will be contested, for my position does not permit of the slightest scandal."

"I greatly regret that this point should have been raised in Mademoiselle Valentine's presence," said Franz. "I have never asked the amount of her fortune, which, reduced though it may be, is still considerably larger than mine. What my family seeks in this alliance with Mademoiselle de Villefort is prestige, what I seek is happiness."

Valentine made a slight movement in acknowledgment, while two large tears rolled down her cheeks.

"Apart from the disappointment to your hopes, which is due solely to Monsieur Noirtier's weakness of mind," said Villefort, addressing his future son-in-law, "this unexpected will contains nothing that adversely affects you. What displeases my father is not that Mademoiselle de Villefort is about to marry you, but that she marries at all; a union with any other would have caused him the same grief. Old age is selfish, monsieur. Mademoiselle de Villefort has been a faithful companion to Monsieur de Noirtier: this will be impossible when once she is Baroness d'Épinay.

"My father's sad condition prevents our speaking to him of serious affairs, which the weakness of his mind would not permit him to understand, and I am perfectly convinced that while grasping the fact that his granddaughter is to be married, Monsieur Noirtier has even forgotten the name of the man who is to be his grandson."

Scarcely had M. de Villefort finished these words, which Franz acknowledged with a bow, when the door opened and Barrois appeared.

"Messieurs," said he, in a voice strangely firm for a servant speaking to his masters on such a solemn occasion, "messieurs, Monsieur Noirtier de Villefort desires to have speech with Monsieur Franz de Quesnel, Baron d'Épinay, immediately."

That there might be no mistake made in the person, he also, like the notary, gave Franz his full title.

Villefort started; Mme de Villefort let her son slip from her knees; Valentine rose as white and silent as a statue. The notary looked at Villefort.

"It is impossible!" said the Procureur du Roi. "Monsieur d'Épinay cannot leave the room for the moment. Tell Monsieur Noirtier that what he asks cannot be."

"In that case Monsieur Noirtier warns you, messieurs, that he will have himself carried into the salon," replied Barrois.

Astonishment knew no bounds. A smile appeared on Mme de Villefort's face. Valentine instinctively raised her eyes to the ceiling to thank her God in Heaven.

"Valentine, please go and see what this new whim of your grandfather's is," said Villefort.

Valentine jumped up to obey, but M. de Villefort changed his mind. "Wait," said he, "I will accompany you."

"Excuse me, monsieur," spoke Franz, "it seems to me that since Monsieur Noirtier has sent for me it is only right that I should do as he desires; besides, I shall be happy to pay him my respects, as I have not yet had the opportunity of doing so."

"I beg you, monsieur, do not give yourself so much trouble," said Villefort with visible uneasiness.

"Pardon me, monsieur," said Franz in a determined tone, "I will not miss this opportunity of showing Monsieur Noirtier that he does wrong to harbour bad feeling towards me, and that I am decided to overcome it by my devotedness."

With these words he rose and followed Valentine, who was running downstairs with the joy of a shipwrecked mariner who has touched rock. M. de Villefort followed them.

Noirtier was waiting, dressed in black, and seated in his chair. When the three persons he expected to see had entered his room, he looked at the door, and his valet immediately closed it.

Villefort went up to Noirtier.

"Here is Monsieur Franz d'Épinay," said he, "you sent for him; he has granted your wish. We have long desired this interview, and I hope it will prove to you that your opposition to this marriage is ill-founded."

Noirtier's sole answer was a look which made the blood run cold in Villefort's veins. He made a sign to Valentine to approach.

With her usual alertness in conversing with her grandfather, she very quickly understood him to signify the word 'Key.' Then she consulted the paralytic's eyes, which were fixed on the drawer of a little chest placed between the windows. She opened it, and found therein a key.

The paralytic made a sign that that was what he wanted, and then his eyes rested on a writing-desk which had been forgotten for years and which was believed to contain nothing but useless papers.

"Do you wish me to open the desk?" asked Valentine.

"Yes," signaled the old man.

"Do you wish me to open the drawers?"

"Yes."

"The middle one?"

"Yes."

Valentine opened it and took out a bundle of papers.

"Is this what you want, Grandpapa?" said she.

"No."

She took out all the papers, one after the other, till there were no more left in the drawer.

"The drawer is empty now," said she.

Noirtier's eyes were fixed on the dictionary.

"Very well," said Valentine, "I understand you," and she repeated the letters of the alphabet; at S Noirtier stopped her. She opened the dictionary and found the word 'Secret.' Noirtier looked at the door by which his servant had gone out.

"Do you wish me to call Barrois?" Valentine said.

"Yes."

She did as he bade her.

Villefort was becoming more and more impatient during this conversation, and Franz was stupefied with amazement.

The old servant entered.

"Barrois," began Valentine, "my grandfather desired me to take a key from this chest and open his desk. There is a secret drawer which you apparently understand; open it."

Barrois looked at his master.

"Obey!" said Noirtier's intelligent eyes.

Barrois obeyed and took out the false bottom, revealing a bundle of papers tied together with a black ribbon.

"Is this what you wish, monsieur?" asked Barrois.

"Yes."

"Shall I give the papers to Monsieur de Villefort?"

"No."

"To Monsieur Franz d'Épinay?"

"Yes."

Amazed, Franz advanced a step and took the papers from Barrois. Casting a glance over the envelope, he read:

"To be given, after my death, to General Durand; who shall bequeath the packet to his son with an injunction to preserve it as containing a paper of the utmost importance."

"And what do you wish me to do with this paper, monsieur?" asked Franz.

"He doubtless wishes you to keep it, sealed as it is," said the Procureur du Roi.

"No, no!" replied Noirtier vigorously.

"Perhaps you wish Monsieur Franz to read it?" said Valentine.

"Yes," was the reply.

"Then let us be seated," said Villefort impatiently, "for it will take some time."

Villefort sat down, but Valentine remained standing beside her grandfather, leaning against his chair, while Franz stood before him. He held the mysterious document in his hand; he unsealed the envelope, and complete silence reigned in the room as he read:

"Extract from the Minutes of a Sitting of the Bonapartist Club in Rue Saint-Jacques, held on February the fifth, eighteen-fifteen."

"The undersigned, Louis-Jacques Beaurepaire, Lieutenant-Colonel of Artillery. Étienne Duchampy, Brigadier-General, and and Claude Lecharpal, Director of Waterways and Forests, hereby declare that on February the fourth, eighteen-fifteen, a letter arrived from the Isle of Elba recommending to the goodwill and confidence of the members of the Bonapartist Club one General Flavien de Quesnel who, having served the Emperor from eighteen-four to eighteen-fifteen, was supposed to be most devoted to the Napoleonic dynasty notwithstanding the title of Baron that Louis the Eighteenth had conferred on him, together with his estate of Épinay.

"In consequence thereof, a note was dispatched to General de Quesnel inviting him to attend the meeting the next day, the fifth. The note gave neither the name of the road nor the number of the house where the meeting was to be held, neither did it bear any signature, but it informed the General that, if he were ready at nine o'clock, some one would call for him.

"The meeting lasted from nine o'clock in the evening until midnight.

"At nine o'clock the President of the club presented himself. The General was ready. The President told him that one of the conditions of his introduction into the club was that he should be for ever ignorant of the place of the meeting and that he should allow himself to be blindfolded, at the same time swearing on oath that he would not attempt to raise the bandage.

"General de Quesnel accepted these conditions, and gave his word of honour not to attempt to see whither he was being conducted.

"The General ordered his carriage, but the President told him it was impossible to use it as it would not be worth while blindfolding the master if the coachman were permitted to know through which streets they passed.

"'What shall we do then?' asked the General.

"'I have my own carriage,' said the President.

"'Are you so sure of your coachman that you can trust him with a secret you cannot confide in mine?'

"'Our coachman is a member of the club,' said the President, 'we shall be driven by a State Councillor.'

"'Then we run the risk of being upset,' said the General laughing.

"We record this joke as a proof that the General was in no way forced to attend the meeting, but on the contrary came of his own free will.

"As soon as they were in the carriage, the President reminded the General of his promise to suffer himself to be blindfolded and he made no objection to this act of formality. On the way, the President thought he saw the General endeavour to see under his bandage and reminded him of his oath.

"'Ah! just so,' said the General.

"The carriage drew up at a passage leading to the Rue Saint-Jacques. The General alighted, leaning on the arm of the President, whom he took for an ordinary member of the club. They crossed the passage, went up some stairs, and entered the conference room. The sitting was in progress. The members of the club, apprised of the introduction that was to take place, were in full complement. The General was invited to remove his bandage, which he instantly did, and appeared extremely astonished to find such a large number of acquaintances in a society of whose existence he had had no idea. They questioned him as to his sentiments, but he merely answered that the letters from the Isle of Elba must have given them full information on that score."

Franz stopped short, saying: "My father was a Royalist; it was unnecessary to question him regarding his views, they were well known."

"Hence my acquaintance with your father, dear Monsieur Franz," said Monsieur Villefort. "A similarity of views soon draws people together."

"Read on," said the old man's eyes.

Franz continued:

"The President then requested the General to express himself more explicitly. Monsieur de Quesnel replied that he first of all wished to know what they wanted of him. He was made acquainted with the contents of the letter from the Isle of Elba which recommended him to the members of the club as a man on whose assistance they might rely. One paragraph was entirely devoted to the probable return of Napoleon from Elba and gave promise of another letter with further details upon the arrival of the *Pharaon*, a ship belonging to Morrel of Marseilles, whose captain was a loyal adherent of the Emperor's. While the letter was being read, the General, on whom they thought they could rely as on a brother, gave visible signs of discontent and repugnance. When they had finished, he stood silent with knit brows.

"'Well, what have you to say to this letter, General?' the President asked.

"'What I say is, that the vows of fealty made to Louis the Eighteenth are still too fresh to be violated in favour of the ex-Emperor.'

"This answer was too plain to permit of any doubt as to his views.

"'General,' said the President, 'for us there is no King Louis the Eighteenth any more than there is an ex-Emperor. For us there is but His Majesty the Emperor and King, who was driven out of France, his kingdom, ten months ago by violence and treason!'

"'Pardon, messieurs,' returned the General, 'maybe there is no King Louis the Eighteenth for you, but there is for me; it was he who created me Baron and Maréchal, and I shall never forget that I owe these two titles to his happy return to France.'

"'Be careful what you say, monsieur,' said the President in a very grave tone as he rose from his seat. 'Your words clearly denote that they were mistaken about you in the Isle of Elba and that they have also misled us. The communication made to you was inspired by the confidence they placed in you, a sentiment which does you honour. We have been acting under a misapprehension; for the sake of promotion and a title, you have thrown in your lot with the new Government, a Government we would overthrow. We will not force you to give us your assistance; we do not enroll anyone against his will or conscience, but we would compel you to act like a man of honour, even though you do not feel that way disposed.

"'What you call acting like a man of honour is presumably knowing of your conspiracy and not revealing it. I call that being your accomplice. You see, I am more frank than you are.'"

"Poor father!" Franz broke in again. "Now I understand why they assassinated you!"

Valentine subconsciously looked at Franz; the young man was actually beautiful in his filial enthusiasm. Villefort paced up and down behind him. Noirtier watched the expression on each face, while he himself preserved his dignified and severe attitude.

Franz took up the manuscript and continued:

"'You were not brought by force into the midst of our assembly, monsieur,' continued the President, 'you were invited; it was suggested you should be blindfolded, and you accepted. When you acceded to these two requests, you knew perfectly well we were not interested in securing the throne to Louis the Eighteenth, otherwise we should not have taken such precautions. Now, you understand, it would be too convenient for you to put on a mask to aid you in learning the secret of others and then have nothing further to do than remove the mask to ruin those who put their trust in you. No, no, you must tell us quite frankly whether you stand for the king of the moment who is now reigning, or for His Majesty the Emperor.'

"'I am a Royalist,' was the General's reply. 'I have taken the oath of allegiance to Louis the Eighteenth, and I shall abide by my oath.'

"These words were followed by a general murmur, and it was evident that a large number of the members of the club were discussing the propriety of making Monsieur d'Épinay repent of his foolish words.

"The President stood up, and, calling for silence, said: 'You are too serious-minded and too sensible, monsieur, not to understand the consequences of our present position. Your candour dictates to us what conditions to make. You will swear on your honour to reveal nothing of what you have heard.'

"The General put his hand to his sword and cried out: 'If you speak of honour, begin by not ignoring its laws and impose nothing by violence.'

"'And I would advise you, General, not to touch your sword,' continued the President with a calmness that was perhaps more terrible than the General's anger.

"The General glanced round him, and the look in his eyes betrayed signs of uneasiness. Nevertheless, summoning all his courage, he said without flinching: 'I will not swear.'

"'Then, monsieur, you shall die!' replied the President calmly.

"Monsieur d'Épinay turned very pale; he looked round him once more and perceived that several of the members were whispering together and getting their arms from under their cloaks.

"'You need fear nothing as yet, General,' said the President. 'You are amongst men of honour who will employ every means to convince you before having recourse to the last extremity. At the same time, however, as you yourself said, you are amongst conspirators. You are in possession of their secret and must restore it to them.'

"An ominous silence ensued, and, as the General still made no reply, the President called out to the doorkeeper: 'Shut the doors!'

"Again there was a deathlike silence. Then the General advanced and, making a violent effort, said: 'I have a son and must think of him when surrounded by assassins.'

"'One man always has the right to offer insult to fifty, General, it is the privilege of weakness,' said the head of the assembly gallantly; 'nevertheless, you act wrongly in using this privilege. It were best to take the oath instead of heaping insults upon our members.'

"'Once more dominated by the superiority of the President, the General hesitated an instant; finally he advanced to the presidential desk and asked: 'What is the formula?'

"'The formula is this: I swear on my honour never to reveal to any-one what I have seen and heard between nine and ten o'clock of the evening of February the fifth, eighteen-fifteen, and I hereby declare that, if I violate my oath, it is only just that my life shall pay forfeit.'

"The General was so affected by a nervous shivering for a few seconds that he was unable to reply. Finally overcoming his obvious repugnance, he took the oath demanded of him, but in such a low and inaudible voice that several of the members insisted that it should be repeated louder and more distinctly. This the General did.

"'Now I should like to retire,' said the General. 'Am I at liberty to do so?'

"The President rose, appointed three members of the assembly to accompany him, and after having blindfolded the General stepped into the carriage with him. In addition to the three members was the coachman who had driven them before. The other members of the club dispersed in silence.

"'Where would you like us to take you?' asked the President.

"'Anywhere, so long as it is out of your presence,' responded d'Épinay.

"'Have a care, monsieur,' responded the President, 'you are no longer in the midst of an assembly, you have now only individuals before you. Do not insult them, or you may be held responsible for such insults.'

"Instead of taking this warning to heart, Monsieur d'Épinay said: 'You are as brave in your carriage as in your club, monsieur, and with good reason, for four men are always stronger than one.'

"The President stopped the carriage. They had just reached the entrance to the Quai des Ormes, where steps lead down to the river.

"'Why do you stop here?' Monsieur d'Épinay asked.

"'Because you have insulted a man, monsieur,' said the President, 'and that man refuses to go a step farther without honourable reparation.'

"'A different form of assassination,' said the General, shrugging his shoulders.

"'No fuss, if you please, monsieur,' replied the President, 'unless you wish me to regard you as one of those you designated just now as cowards, using their weakness as a shield. You are alone, and one only shall answer you. You have a sword at your side, and I have one in my cane. You have no second, but one of these gentlemen is at your service. If these arrangements meet with your approval, you may now remove the bandage.'

"The General instantly tore the kerchief from his eyes, saying: 'At last I shall know with whom I have to deal!'

"The carriage door was opened and the four men alighted."

Franz stopped once more and wiped away the cold sweat that stood out on his brow. There was something awe-inspiring in hearing the pale and trembling son read aloud the hitherto unknown details of his father's death.

Valentine clasped her hands as though in prayer; Noirtier looked at Villefort with an almost sublime expression of contempt and pride. Franz continued:

"It was, as we have said, the fifth of February. For three days there had been five or six degrees of frost and the steps were covered with ice. The General was tall and stout, so the President offered him the side with the railing. The two seconds followed at their heels.

"It was a dark night, and the ground from the steps to the river was slippery with snow and hoar-frost; the river looked black and deep, and was covered with drifting ice. One of the seconds fetched a lantern from a coal barge, and by its light the weapons were examined. The President's sword, which, as he had said, was simply one he carried in his cane, was shorter than his adversary's and had no guard. General d'Épinay suggested they should draw lots for the swords, but the President replied that he was the one who had challenged and in so doing had presumed that each one should use his own weapon. The seconds attempted to insist, but the President ordered them to silence.

"The lanterns were placed on the ground; the two adversaries stood opposite one another; the duel started. In the weird light the two swords had the appearance of flashes of lightning, while the men were scarcely visible in the darkness.

"The General had the reputation of being one of the best swordsmen in the army, but he was pressed so closely from the outset that before long he fell from sheer exhaustion. The seconds thought he was dead, but his adversary, who knew he had not hit him, offered him his arm to assist him to rise. Instead of calming the General, this circumstance only irritated him and he again rushed upon his opponent. The latter, however, did not budge an inch and received him on his sword. Finding himself too closely pressed, the General recoiled three times only to renew the attack, and the third time he fell once more. At first they thought he had slipped as before, but when the seconds saw that he did not move they went to him and tried to raise him: in so doing the one that put his arm round his body felt something warm and damp. It was blood.

"The General, who had almost fainted, revived a little and said: 'Ah, they have sent some ruffian, some fencing-master, to fight me.'

"Without replying the President went up to the second who had the lantern and, drawing back his sleeve, showed where his arm had twice been pierced with the sword; then, opening his coat, he unbuttoned his waistcoat, and there in his side was a third wound where his adversary's sword had pierced him. Yet he had not even uttered a sigh.

"General d'Épinay died five minutes later."

Franz read these last words in such a choked voice that they could scarcely be heard, then he stopped and passed his hand across his eyes as if to disperse a cloud. After a moment's silence, he continued:

"After replacing his sword in his cane, the President went up the steps, leaving traces of blood in the snow. He had not reached the top step when he heard a heavy splash in the water. After ascertaining that the General was dead, the seconds had thrown his body into the river.

"Thus the General fell in an honourable duel and not in ambush, as will probably be reported.

"In witness whereof we hereby sign this document to establish the truth of the facts, lest the time should arrive when one of the actors of this terrible scene should be accused of premeditated murder, or of violation of the laws of honour.

"Signed: BEAUREPAIRE, DUCHAMPY,<br>AND LECHARPAL"

When Franz had finished reading this report, truly a terrible ordeal for a son—when Valentine, pale with emotion, had wiped away her tears, and Villefort, trembling in a corner, had attempted to calm the storm by sending appealing looks at the implacable old man, he turned to Noirtier with the following words:

"Since you know this terrible story in all its details, monsieur, and have had it witnessed by honourable signatures; since you seem to take some interest in me, although, until now, that interest has brought me nothing but grief, do not refuse me the satisfaction of making known to me the name of the President of the club, so that I may at least learn who killed my poor father."

Dazed and bewildered, Villefort reached for the door handle. Valentine knew what her grandfather's answer must be, for she had often seen the scars of two sword wounds on his arm, and she drew back a few steps.

"For heaven's sake, mademoiselle," said Franz, turning to his betrothed, "unite your efforts with mine, so that I may know the name of the man who made me an orphan at two years of age."

Valentine remained silent and motionless.

"I pray you, do not prolong this horrible scene," said Villefort. "The names have been concealed intentionally. My father does not know the President, and, even if he did, he would not know how to communicate his name to you; proper names are not to be found in the dictionary."

"Woe is me!" cried Franz, "the only hope that sustained me throughout this report, and gave me the strength to finish reading it, was that I should at least learn the name of him who killed my father." Then turning to Noirtier: "Oh! I entreat you, in the name of all that is holy, do what you can to indicate to me, to make me understand."

"Yes," was Noirtier's reply.

Oh! mademoiselle, mademoiselle," cried Franz, "your grandfather has made a sign that he can indicate to me the name of this man. Help me . . . you understand him . . . give me your aid."

Noirtier looked at the dictionary. Franz took it, trembling nervously, and repeated the letters of the alphabet till he came to M, when the old man made a sign for him to stop.

The young man's finger glided over the words, but at each one Noirtier made a sign in the negative.

Finally he came to the word 'Myself.'

"Yes," motioned the old man.

"You?" cried Franz, his hair standing on end. "You, Monsieur Noirtier? It was you who killed my father?"

"Yes," replied Noirtier, with a majestic look at the young man.

Franz sank lifeless into a chair.

Villefort opened the door and fled, for he was seized with the impulse to choke out of the old man the little life that remained to him.


### CHAPTER XLIX

## THE PROGRESS OF CAVALCANTI JUNIOR

A SHORT time after the events just recorded, Monte Cristo called one evening on M. Danglars. The banker was out, but Mme Danglars would be pleased to receive him.

When the Count entered the boudoir, the Baroness was glancing at some drawings which her daughter had passed to her, after she and M. Cavalcanti Junior had looked at them together. His presence produced its usual effect, and the Baroness received him with a smile though she had been somewhat discomforted when his name was announced.

Monte Cristo took in the whole scene at a glance. The Baroness was reclining on a settee, and seated beside her was Eugénie, while Cavalcanti stood in front of them. The latter, clad in black, like one of

Goethe's heroes, with patent-leather shoes and white silk open-work stockings, passed his white and manicured hand through his fair hair, thus displaying a sparkling diamond which the vain young man could not resist wearing on his finger. This gesture was accompanied by killing glances at Mlle Danglars and sighs meant for the same lady.

Mlle Danglars was still the same—cold, scornful, and beautiful. Not one of Andrea's looks or sighs escaped her. She greeted the Count coldly, and took advantage of the first opportunity to escape to her studio. Soon two laughing, noisy voices were mingled with a piano, which told Monte Cristo that Mlle Danglars preferred the society of her singing-mistress, Mlle Louise d'Armilly, to either his or M. Cavalcanti's.

While conversing with Mme Danglars, and appearing absorbed by the charm of the conversation, the Count watched M. Andrea's solicitude; how he listened to the music at the door he dared not pass, and how he manifested his admiration.

The Baron soon came in. His first glance was for Monte Cristo, it is true, but the second was for Andrea.

"Have the young ladies not invited you to join them at the piano?" Danglars asked Andrea.

"I am sorry to say they have not," replied Andrea with a deeper sigh than ever.

Danglars went to the communicating door and opened it.

"Well! Are we all to be excluded?" he asked his daughter.

Then he took the young man into the room, and, whether by chance or dexterity, the door was closed behind Andrea in such a way that from where they were sitting, the Baroness and Monte Cristo could not see into the room, but, as the banker had followed Andrea, Mme Danglars did not appear to notice this circumstance.

Shortly afterward, the Count heard Andrea's voice singing a Corsican song to the accompaniment of the piano.

In the meantime, Mme Danglars began boasting to Monte Cristo of the strength of character of her husband, who, that very morning, had lost three or four hundred thousand francs by a business failure in Milan. The praise was certainly well merited, for, if the Count had not known of this fresh piece of ill-luck from the Baroness, or perhaps by one of the means he had of learning everything, the Baron's face would have told him nothing.

"Ha!" thought he, "he is already beginning to hide his losses: a month ago he boasted of them." Then aloud he said:

"But Monsieur Danglars has so much experience on the Exchange, that what he has lost in one way, he will soon make up in another."

"I see you are under a misapprehension, along wi'h every one else. Monsieur Danglars never speculates."

"Oh, yes, that's true. I remember now, Monsieur Debray told me . . . By the way, what has become of Monsieur Debray? I have not seen him for three or four days."

"Neither have I," said Madame Danglars, with miraculous self-possession. "But you commenced a sentence you did not finish."

"Oh, yes. I was saying Monsieur Debray told me it was you who had made sacrifices to the demon of speculation."

"I will own that I was fond of speculating at one time," replied Mme Danglars, "but I do not care for it any more. But we have talked enough about the Exchange, let us change the conversation to the Villeforts. Have you heard how fate is pursuing them? After losing Monsieur de Saint-Méran within three or four days of his departure for Paris, the Marquise died a few days after her arrival. But that is not all. You know their daughter was going to marry Monsieur Franz d'Épinay?"

"Do you mean to say their engagement is broken off?"

"Franz declined the honour yesterday morning."

"Really! Is the reason known?"

"No."

"That is strange. How does Monsieur de Villefort take all this misfortune?"

"As always, quite philosophically."

Just then Danglars re-entered the room alone.

"Well, have you left Monsieur Cavalcanti with your daughter?" asked the Baroness.

"And Mademoiselle d'Armilly," said the banker. "Is she no one?" Turning to Monte Cristo he said: "Prince Cavalcanti is a charming young man, is he not? Is he really a prince, though?"

"I cannot answer for that," said Monte Cristo.

"Do you realize what you are risking?" said the Baroness. "If Monsieur de Morcerf should happen to come, he will find Monsieur Cavalcanti in a room where he, Eugénie's intended, has never had permission to enter."

"Oh, he will not do us the honour of being jealous of his betrothed. He does not care enough for her. Besides, what do I mind if he is vexed or not."

"The Viscount of Morcerf," announced the valet.

The Baroness rose quickly. She was going to tell her daughter when Danglars stopped her.

"Let her be!" he said.

She looked at him in astonishment.

Monte Cristo pretended he had not seen this little comedy.

Albert entered, looking handsome and very cheerful. He greeted the Baroness with ease, Danglars with familiarity, and Monte Cristo with affection; then turning toward the Baroness he said: "May I ask how mademoiselle is?"

"Very well," replied Danglars hastily; "at the present moment she is at the piano with Monsieur Cavalcanti."

Albert remained calm and indifferent; perhaps he felt some annoyance, but he knew that Monte Cristo's eye was on him.

"The fact is, the Prince and my daughter get on very well together. They were the object of general admiration yesterday. How was it we did not see you, Monsieur de Morcerf?"

"What Prince?" asked Albert.

"Prince Cavalcanti," replied Danglars, who persisted in giving the young man this title.

"Oh, pardon, I was unaware that he was a Prince. I was unable to accept your invitation, as I was compelled to accompany Madame de Morcerf to a German concert given by the Countess of Château-Renaud."

After a moment's silence he asked: "May I be permitted to pay my respects to Mademoiselle Danglars?"

"Just one moment, please," said the banker, stopping the young man. "Do you hear that delightful *cavatina? Ta, ti, ta, ti, ta, ti, ta, ta*, it is charming. It will be finished in a second! Splendid! Bravo! Bravo!"

With these words the banker began applauding enthusiastically.

"Yes, indeed, it is charming," said Albert. "No one could understand the music of his country better than Cavalcanti does. You did say Prince, did you not? In any case, if he is not a Prince now, they will make him one. It is a very easy matter in Italy. But to return to the charming musicians. You should ask them to give us the pleasure of another song, without letting them know there is a stranger here."

This time it was Danglars who was vexed by the young man's indifference. He took Monte Cristo aside.

"What do you think of our lover now?"

"He is decidedly very cool. But what can you do? You have given your word."

"I have certainly given my word to bestow my daughter on a man who loves her, but not on a man who does not love her. Look at this one, as cold as marble, as proud as his father; if he were rich, if he had a fortune like the Cavalcantis, one would overlook it. I have not consulted my daughter, but, do you know, if I thought she cared . . ."

"I do not know whether it is my friendship that blinds me," said Monte Cristo, "but I assure you, I find Monsieur de Morcerf a charming young man. He should make your daughter happy and sooner or later he will achieve much, for his father has an excellent position."

"Humph!" was Danglars' reply.

"Why do you doubt?"

"I am thinking of his past . . . his mysterious past."

"But the father's past has nothing to do with the son. You cannot break off the engagement thus. The Morcerfs look upon this marriage as certain."

"Well, then, let them explain themselves. You might give the father a hint to that effect, Count, you are on such an intimate footing there."

"Certainly, if you wish it."

A servant came up to Danglars and said something to him in a low voice.

"I shall be back in a minute," said the banker to Monte Cristo. "Wait for me, I may have something interesting to tell you."

Indeed not many minutes had elapsed before Monsieur Danglars returned visibly agitated.

"Well," said he, "my courier has returned from Greece!"

"And how is King Otto?" asked Albert in a playful tone.

Danglars looked at him slyly without answering; Monte Cristo turned away his head to hide the momentary expression of pity that had found its way to his face.

"Shall we go together?" said Albert to the Count.

"Yes, if you like," replied the latter.

Albert could not understand the banker's look and, turning to Monte Cristo, who understood only too well, he said:

"Did you notice how he looked at me?"

"Yes," replied the Count. "Do you think he meant anything by that look?"

"I am sure of it. What can he have meant by his news from Greece?"

"How can you expect me to know."

"I thought perhaps you had some correspondents in the country."

Monte Cristo smiled in the way one always does when trying to avoid giving an answer.

"Here he is coming towards you," said Albert. "I will go and compliment Mademoiselle Danglars upon her performance, and in the meanwhile you will have an opportunity of speaking to her father."

Albert went up to Eugénie with a smile on his lips. Danglars whispered into the Count's ear: "You gave me excellent advice. There is a long and terrible history connected with the two words Fernand and Janina."

"Nonsense," was Monte Cristo's reply.

"Yes, there is. I will tell you about it. But now take the young man away. It is too embarrassing for me to be together with him at this moment."

"That is just what I was going to do. Do you still wish me to send his father to you?"

"More than ever."

The Count made a sign to Albert. They took their leave of the ladies and went away, and M. Cavalcanti remained master of the field.

## CHAPTER L

## HAYDEE'S STORY

SCARCELY had the horses turned the corner of the boulevard when Albert looked at the Count and burst into a loud fit of laughter, so loud that it was obviously forced.

"Well," said he, "I will ask you the same question King Charles put to Catherine de' Medici after the massacre of St. Bartholomew. How do you think I played my part?"

"In what respect?" asked Monte Cristo.

"Why, with regard to the reception of my rival and your *protégé*, Monsieur Andrea Cavalcanti, in the bosom of the Danglars family."

"None of your poor jokes, Viscount! Monsieur Andrea is no *protégé* of mine, at any rate not so far as Monsieur Danglars is concerned."

"That is just what I should reproach you with if the young man had any need of protection. Happily for me, he can dispense with it."

"What, do you think he is paying her attentions?"

"I am sure of it. He makes eyes at her, sighs and speaks to her in amorous tones. He aspires to the hand of the proud Eugénie!"

"What does that matter so long as they favour you?"

"Don't say that, Count. I am being repulsed from two sides: Mademoiselle Eugénie scarcely answered me to-day, while Mademoiselle d'Armilly, her confidante, did not answer me at all. As to the father, I will warrant that within a week he will shut the door in my face."

"You are quite mistaken, my dear Viscount."

"Have you proofs?"

"Do you want one?"

"Yes."

"Well, then, I have been requested to ask the Count of Morcerf to come to some definite arrangement with the Baron."

"Who requested you?"

"The Baron himself."

"Oh, you surely will not do that, will you?" said Albert coaxingly.

"Oh, yes, I shall since I have promised to."

"Come now," said Albert with a sigh. "You are absolutely determined to make me marry."

"I only wish to be on good terms with every one."

The carriage stopped.

"Here we are," said Monte Cristo. "It is only half-past ten. Will you come in with me?"

"With pleasure."

They both entered the house. The salon was lit up.

"Give us some tea, Baptistin," said the Count.

Baptistin went out without saying a word. Two minutes later he reappeared with a tray laden with all his master's requirements as though, like the supper tables in fairy plays, it had sprung up from the earth.

"Really, Count," said Morcerf, "what I admire in you is not your wealth, for there are perhaps others richer than you; it is not your wit—Beaumarchais had no more, but he had as much as you; no, what I admire is your way of being served without a question, to the minute, to the second, as though your servant guessed what you desired by your manner of sounding the gong, and as though everything were ready and waiting upon your desire."

"What you say is more or less true. My servants know my habits. I will give you an instance. Is there nothing you would like to have with your tea?"

"Indeed there is, I should dearly love a smoke."

Monte Cristo went up to the gong and sounded it once. Within a second a private door opened, and Ali appeared with two chibouques filled with excellent Latakia.

"It is wonderful," said Morcerf.

"Oh, no, it is quite simple," said Monte Cristo. "Ali knows that I generally smoke when I am drinking tea or coffee; he knows I have asked for tea, also that you came in with me. On hearing the gong he guessed my desire, and, coming from a country where the chibouque plays an essential part in hospitality, he brings in two of them."

"That is certainly quite a simple explanation, but it is nevertheless true that you alone . . . Ah, but what is that I hear!" he added, bending his ear toward a door through which sounds were issuing similar to those of a guitar.

"You are doomed to have music this evening, Viscount. You have only just escaped from Mademoiselle Danglars' piano and must now submit to Haydee's *guzla*."

"Haydee! What a charming name. Are there really women elsewhere than in Byron's poems with the name of Haydee?"

"Certainly. It may be an uncommon name in France, but it is common enough in Albania and Epirus; it is as though you said, for instance, Chastity, Modesty, Innocence: it is a baptismal name, as you Parisians call it."

"How very charming! How I should like to hear our French girls called Mademoiselle Goodness, Mademoiselle Silence, Mademoiselle Christian Charity. I say, supposing Mademoiselle Claire Marie Eugénie Danglars were called Mademoiselle Chastity Modesty Innocence Danglars, what a fine effect it would have when the banns of marriage were published!"

"You are mad," said the Count. "Do not joke so loud, Haydee might hear you."

"Would she be annoyed?"

"Certainly not," said the Count. "A slave has no right to be annoyed with her master."

"Now it is you who are joking. There are no slaves now!"

"Since Haydee is my slave there must be."

"Really, Count, you have nothing and do nothing, like other people. Monte Cristo's slave! What a position in France! To judge from the lavish way in which you spend your money, it must be worth a hundred thousand crowns a year."

"A hundred thousand crowns! The poor child possesses a great deal more than that. She came into the world to a cradle lined with treasures compared with which those in *A Thousand and One Nights* are as nought."

"Is she a real princess then?"

"She is; one of the greatest in her country."

"I thought as much. But tell me, how did such a princess become your slave?"

"You are one of my friends and will not chatter. Do you promise to keep a secret?"

"On my word of honour."

"Do you know the history of the Pasha of Janina?"

"Of Ali Tebelin? Surely, since my father made his fortune in his service."

"True, I had forgotten that."

"Well, what has Haydee to do with Ali Tebelin?"

"She is merely his daughter!"

"What! The daughter of Ali Pasha your slave!"

"Oh, dear me, yes."

"But how comes it?"

"Simply that I was passing through the market at Constantinople one fine day and bought her."

"Wonderful! With you, Count, life becomes a dream. Now, listen, I am going to ask you something very indiscreet."

"Say on."

"Since you go out with her and take her to the Opera . . ."

"Well?"

"Will you introduce me to your princess?"

"With pleasure, but on two conditions."

"I accept them in advance."

"The first is that you never tell anyone of this introduction; the second is that you do not tell her that your father served under her father."

"Very well." Morcerf held up his hand. "I swear I will not."

The Count again struck the gong, whereupon Ali appeared and Monte Cristo said to him: "Inform your mistress that I am coming to take my coffee with her, and give her to understand that I ask permission to introduce one of my friends to her."

Ali bowed and retired.

"Then it is understood that you will not ask her any direct questions. If you wish to know anything, tell me and I will ask her."

"Agreed!"

Ali reappeared for the third time and held up the door curtain as an indication to his master and Albert that they were welcome.

"Let us go," said Monte Cristo.

Albert passed his hand through his hair and curled his moustache, while the Count took his hat, put on his gloves, and preceded Albert into the room which was guarded by Ali as advance guard, and defended by three French maids under his command.

Haydee was awaiting them in her salon, her eyes wide open with surprise. This was the first time that any other man than Monte Cristo had found his way to her room. She was seated in a corner of a sofa with her legs crossed under her, thus making, as it were, a nest of the richly embroidered striped Eastern material that fell in soft folds around her. Beside her was the instrument whose sounds had revealed her presence. Altogether she made a charming picture.

"Whom do you bring me?" the girl asked of Monte Cristo in Romaic. "A brother, a friend, a simple acquaintance, or an enemy?"

"A friend," replied Monte Cristo in the same language.

"His name?"

"Count Albert. It is he whom I delivered from the hands of the bandits at Rome."

"In what tongue do you wish me to speak to him?"

Monte Cristo turned toward Albert with the question: "Do you speak modern Greek?"

"Alas! not even ancient Greek," said Albert. "Never have Homer and Plato had a more unworthy, I might almost say contemptuous, scholar than myself."

"Then I shall use the French or Italian tongue if my lord wishes me to speak at all," responded Haydee, showing by this remark that she had understood the Count's question and Albert's answer.

Monte Cristo thought for a moment. "You will speak in Italian," said he at last. Then turning toward Albert: "It is a pity you do not speak either modern or ancient Greek. Haydee speaks both to perfection, and the poor girl may give you a wrong impression of herself by being forced to speak in Italian."

He made a sign to Haydee.

"Welcome, my friend, who have come hither with my lord and master," said the girl in excellent Tuscan with the soft Roman accent which makes the language of Dante as sonorous as that of Homer. "Ali, bring coffee and pipes," she then added.

Ali went to execute his young mistress's order, while Monte Cristo and Albert drew their seats up to a table which contained a narghile as its centre-piece, and on which were arranged flowers, drawings, and music albums. Ali returned with the coffee and chibouques, but Albert refused the pipe the Nubian offered him.

"Take it, take it," said Monte Cristo, "Haydee is almost as civilized as a Parisian. Havanas are distasteful to her because she does not like their strong odour, but Eastern tobacco is a perfume, you must know."

Haydee put out her hand and, encircling the cup of Japanese china with her dainty pink fingers, carried it to her lips with the simple pleasure of a child drinking or eating something it likes.

At the same time two women entered carrying trays laden with ices and sherbet, which they placed on two small tables intended for that purpose.

"Pray excuse my amazement," said Albert in Italian. "I am quite bewildered, and it could not be well otherwise. But a few moments ago I heard the rumbling of the omnibuses and the tinkling of the lemonade-sellers' bells, yet here I am transported to the East, the true East, not as I have seen it, unfortunately, but as I have pictured it to myself in the dreams I have dreamt in the heart of Paris. O, signora! if only I could speak Greek, your conversation, coupled with these fairylike surroundings, would afford an evening that would ever remain in my memory!"

"I speak Italian well enough to converse with you, monsieur," said Haydee calmly. "If you love the East, I will do my best to bring its atmosphere to you."

Albert turned toward Haydee, saying: "At what age did you leave Greece, signora?"

"When I was five years old," responded Haydee.

"Do you remember your country?"

"When I close my eyes, I seem to see once more all that I have ever seen. We have a twofold power of vision, that of the body and that of the mind. Whereas the body may sometimes forget the impressions it has received, the mind never does."

"How far back does your memory go?"

"To the time when I could scarcely walk."

"How old were you at the time?"

"Three years," said Haydee.

"Do you then remember everything that happened around you from the time you were three years of age?"

"Everything."

"Count," said Morcerf to Monte Cristo, "you should let the signora tell us something of her sad history. You have forbidden me to mention my father to her, but perhaps she may speak of him herself, and you have no idea what happiness it would give me to hear his name pronounced by those beautiful lips."

Monte Cristo turned toward Haydee and, making a sign to her to pay great attention to the injunction he was about to impose on her, said in Greek: "Tell us your father's fate, but mention not the treason nor the name of the traitor."

Haydee sighed deeply, and a dark cloud passed over her beautiful brow.

"You are still young, signora," said Albert, taking refuge in banality in spite of himself, "what sufferings can you have experienced?"

Haydee looked at Monte Cristo, who made an almost imperceptible sign to her, murmuring: "Tell it all!"

"Nothing makes such a deep impression on our minds as our earliest memories, and all those of my childhood are mingled with sadness. Do you really wish me to relate them?"

"I implore you to tell them!" said Albert.

"Well, I was four years old when I was awakened one evening by my mother. We were at the palace at Janina. She snatched me up with the cushions on which I was lying, and when I opened my eyes I perceived that hers were filled with big tears. She carried me away without a word. On seeing her weeping, I began to cry too. 'Be quiet, child!' she said.

"At any other time, no matter what my mother might do to console me, or what threats she held out to me, I should have continued to cry, but this time there was such a note of terror in her voice that I stopped instantly. She bore me rapidly away. Then I perceived that we were going down a wide staircase and rushing on in front of us were my mother's women, carrying trunks, bags, clothing, jewellery, and purses filled with gold. Behind the women came a guard of twenty men armed with long rifles and pistols and clad in the uniform which must be familiar to you in France now that Greece has once more become independent. Believe me," continued Haydee, shaking her head and turning pale at the thought of the scene, "there was something ominous in this long line of slaves and women all heavy with sleep, or at least I thought they were, though perhaps it may only have been that as I was only half awake myself, I imagined they were still as sleepy as I. Gigantic shadows thrown by the flickering light of the pine torches chased each other along the walls of the staircase and descended to the very vaults.

"'Quickly, quickly!' said a voice from the end of the gallery, and every one bent forward like a field of corn bowed down by the passing wind. It was my father's voice. He marched in the rearmost clad in his most splendid robes and holding in his hand the carbine your Emperor gave him. Leaning on his favourite Selim, he drove us on before him as a shepherd drives his straggling flock. My father," continued Haydee, raising her head, "was an illustrious man known in Europe under the name of Ali Tebelin, Pasha of Janina, before whom all Turkey trembled."

Without any apparent reason, Albert shuddered on hearing these words uttered with such unspeakable pride and dignity. There seemed to be something terrifying and sombre lurking in the maiden's eyes.

"Soon we came to a halt; we had reached the bottom of the staircase and were on the borders of a lake. My mother pressed me to her heaving bosom, and two paces from us I saw my father looking anxiously round him. Before us were four marble steps, at the bottom of which was a small boat. In the middle of the lake a black object was discernible; it was the kiosk to which we were going. It looked to me to be very far away, but that was probably owing to the darkness of the night.

"We stepped into the boat. I remember noticing that there was no sound as the oars skimmed the water, and I leaned over to look for the cause: they were muffled with the sashes of our Palikars. Besides the oarsmen there was no one in the boat but some women, my father, my mother, Selim, and myself. The Palikars had remained on the edge of the lake to protect us in case of pursuit. Our bark sped like the wind.

"'Why is our boat going so fast?' I asked my mother.

"'Hush, child, hush!' she said. 'It is because we are fleeing.'

"I did not understand. Why should my father, the all-powerful one, flee? He before whom others were accustomed to flee? He who had taken as his device: 'They hate me, therefore they fear me.'

"My father was indeed fleeing across the lake. He told me later that the garrison of the Janina Castle, tired of long service . . ."

Here Haydee cast a questioning look at Monte Cristo, who had never taken his eyes off her. She then continued slowly as though inventing or suppressing some part of her narrative.

"You were saying, signora," returned Albert, who was paying the utmost attention to the recital, "that the garrison of Janina tired of long service . . ."

"Had treated with the Seraskier Kourschid sent by the Sultan to seize my father. Upon learning this Ali Tebelin sent to the Sultan a French officer in whom he placed entire confidence, and then resolved to retire to the place of retreat he had since long prepared for himself, to which he had given the name of *kataphygion,* which means his refuge."

"Do you recollect the officer's name, signora?" Albert asked.

Monte Cristo exchanged a lightning-like glance with the girl which was unobserved by Morcerf.

"No, I do not recollect his name," she said, "but it may come to my mind later on."

Albert was about to mention his father's name when Monte Cristo quietly held up his finger enjoining silence, and, remembering his oath, the young man obeyed.

"It was towards this kiosk that we were making our way. From the outside the kiosk appeared to consist of nothing more than a ground floor ornamented with arabesques with a terrace leading down to the water, and another storey overlooking the lake. Under the ground floor, however, was a vast subterranean cave extending the whole length of the island, whither my mother and myself together with our womenfolk were taken, and where sixty thousand bags and two hundred casks were piled up in a heap. The bags contained twenty-five millions in gold, and the casks were filled with thirty thousand pounds of powder.

"Near these casks stood Selim, my father's favourite slave, whom I mentioned just now. Night and day he stood on guard, holding a lance at the tip of which was a lighted match. His orders were that directly my father gave him the signal, he was to blow up everything, kiosk, guards, women, gold, and the Pasha himself. I still see before me the pale-faced, black-eyed young soldier, and when the angel of Death comes to fetch me I am sure I shall recognize Selim.

"I cannot tell you how long we remained thus, for at that period I was too ignorant of the meaning of time. Sometimes, though rarely, my father would summon my mother and me to the terrace of the palace. Those were hours of real pleasure to me, for in the cave I heard nothing but the wailing of the slaves, and saw nothing but Selim's fiery lance. Seated before a large aperture my father would try to pierce the black horizon; he examined every tiny speck that appeared in the lake, whilst my mother reclined at his side with her head upon his shoulder and I played at his feet.

"One morning my father sent for us; we found him quite calm but paler than usual.

"'Have courage, Vasiliki,' he said to my mother. 'To-day my lord's firman arrives, and my fate will be decided. If I am pardoned, we shall return to Janina in triumph, but if the news is bad, we shall flee to-night.'

"'But what if they do not let us flee?'

"'Set your mind at rest on that score,' replied Ali with a smile. 'Selim and his fiery lance will settle them. They want my death, but they will not want to die with me.'

"My mother's sighs were her only answer to this poor consolation. She prepared some iced water which he drank incessantly, for since his retreat to the kiosk he had been the victim of a burning fever; then she anointed his beard and lighted his chibouque. Sometimes he would sit for hours together pulling at his chibouque abstractedly, and watching the smoke ascend and dwindle into nothingness.

"All of a sudden, he started up abruptly. Without taking his eyes from the object which was attracting his attention, he asked for his telescope, and my mother, whiter than the stucco against which she was leaning, gave it him. I saw my father's hands trembling.

"'A ship ...! two ...! three ...! four!' he murmured.

"With that he rose, and as I sit here I can still see him priming his pistols.

"'Vasiliki,' he said to my mother, visibly trembling, 'the time has now come when our fate will be decided, for in half an hour we shall learn the Sublime Sultan's answer. Go to the cave with Haydee.'

"'I will not leave you,' said Vasiliki. 'If you die, my master, I will die with you.'

"'Go and stay with Selim!' cried my father.

"'Farewell, my lord!' murmured my mother, obedient to the end and bowed down by the near approach of death.

"'Take Vasiliki away,' he said to one of the Palikars.

"But I, whom they had forgotten, ran up to him and held out my arms to him. He saw me, and, bending down, pressed his lips to my forehead.

"All this time twenty Palikars, hidden by the carved woodwork, were seated at my father's feet watching with bloodshot eyes the arrival of the boats. Their long guns, inlaid with mother-of-pearl and silver, were ready to hand and a large number of cartridges were strewn about the floor. My father looked at his watch and began pacing up and down with a look of anguish on his face. This was the scene which impressed itself on my mind when I left my father after he had given me that last kiss.

"My mother and I went down to the cave. Selim was still at his post and gave us a sad smile. We fetched some cushions from the other side of the cave and seated ourselves beside him. Devoted hearts seek one another in time of danger, and, child though I was, I instinctively sensed that some great danger was hanging over our heads."

These sad reminiscences appeared for a single instant to have deprived Haydee of the power of speech. Her head fell into her hands like a flower bowed down by the force of the storm, and her eyes glazed into vacancy as though she were conjuring up before her mind the verdant summit of Pindus and the blue waters of the Lake of Janina, which reflected like a magic mirror the grim picture she was sketching.

Monte Cristo looked at her with an indefinable expression of interest and pity.

"Continue, my child," he said to her in Romaic.

Haydee raised her head as though the sonorous words uttered by Monte Cristo had awakened her from a dream, and she resumed her narrative.

"It was four o'clock in the afternoon, but whereas the day was brilliant and bright outside, we in the cave were plunged in darkness. One single light shone in our cave like a solitary star twinkling in a dark and cloud-covered sky; it was Selim's match.

"From time to time Selim repeated the sacred words: 'Allah is great!' My mother was a Christian, and she prayed incessantly, but she still had a ray of hope. When she was leaving the terrace she had thought she recognized the Frenchman who had been sent to Constantinople and in whom my father placed implicit confidence, for he well knew that the soldiers of the French King are generally noble and generous. She advanced towards the staircase and listened. 'They are drawing near,' she said. 'If only they bring life and peace to us!'

"'What do you fear, Vasiliki?' replied Selim in a voice so gentle and at the same time so proud. 'If they do not bring peace, we will give them death.' And he revived the flame of his lance.

"But I, who was only an unsophisticated child, was frightened by this courage, which appeared to me both ferocious and insensate, and I was filled with alarm by the atmosphere of death I seemed to feel all round me and to see in Selim's flame. My mother must have had the same impression for I felt her shudder.

"'Oh, Mama, Mama!' I cried, 'are we going to die?'

"'May God preserve you, my child, from ever desiring the death you fear to-day!' said my mother. Then in a low voice to Selim: 'What are my master's orders?'

"'If he sends me his poniard, it signifies that the Sultan has refused his pardon and I am to apply the match; if he sends me his ring, it means that the Sultan pardons him and I am to hand over the powder.'

"'Friend,' said my mother, 'when the master's order arrives and if it be the poniard he sends, we will both bare our throats to you and do you kill us with the same poniard instead of dispatching us by that terrible death we both fear.'

"'I will, Vasiliki,' was Selim's calm reply.

"All of a sudden we heard loud shouts. We listened. They were shouts of joy. The name of the French officer who had been sent to Constantinople burst from the throats of the Palikars on all sides. It was evident he had brought the Sultan's answer and that the answer was a favourable one."

"Do you not recollect the name?" said Morcerf, ready to aid the narrator's memory.

Monte Cristo made a sign to her.

"I do not remember it," responded Haydee. "The noise increased; there was the sound of approaching footsteps; they were descending the steps to the cave. Selim made ready his lance. Soon a figure appeared in the grey twilight created by the rays of day which penetrated to the entrance of the cave.

"'Who goes there?' cried Selim. 'Whosoever it may be, advance no farther!'

"'Glory be to the Sultan!' said the figure. 'He has granted full pardon to the Vizier Ali and not only grants him his life, but restores to him his fortune and all his possessions.'

"My mother uttered a cry of joy and pressed me to her heart.

"'Stop!' cried Selim on perceiving that she was about to rush out of the cave. 'You know I must have the ring.'

"'You are right,' replied my mother, and she fell on her knees holding me up towards Heaven as though, while praying to God for me, she wished to lift me up towards Him!"

For the second time Haydee paused, overcome by an emotion which made the perspiration break out in drops upon her forehead and her words choke in her parched throat. Monte Cristo poured a little iced water into a glass and handed it to her, saying with a tenderness in which was mingled a suspicion of command: "Take courage, my child!"

Haydee wiped her eyes and forehead and continued:

"By this time our eyes had become accustomed to the darkness and we recognized the Pasha's envoy: he was a friend. Selim too recognized him, but the brave young man had one duty to fulfil—that was, to obey.

"'In whose name do you come?' said he.

"'I come in the name of our master, Ali Tebelin.'

"'If you come in the name of Ali, do you know what you have to hand me?'

"'Yes,' said the messenger. 'I bring the ring.'

"So saying he held his hand above his head, but from where we were it was too dark and he too far away for Selim to distinguish and recognize the object he held up.

"'I see not what you have there,' said Selim.

"'Come nearer, or if you so wish, I will come nearer to you,' replied the messenger.

"'Neither the one nor the other,' replied the young soldier. 'On the spot where you now stand, so that the rays of this light may fall on it, set down the object you wish to show me and retire till I have seen it.'

"'It shall be done,' answered the messenger. Placing the symbol on the spot indicated, he withdrew.

"Our hearts beat fast, for the object was actually a ring, but was it my father's ring? Still holding in his hand the lighted match, Selim went to the entrance, bent down and picked up the token. 'The master's ring!' he exclaimed, kissing it. 'All is well!' Throwing the match on the ground, he trampled on it till it was extinguished.

"The messenger uttered a cry of joy and clapped his hands. At this signal, four of the Seraskier Kourschid's soldiers rushed in, and Selim fell pierced by the dagger of each of the men. Intoxicated by their crime, though still pale with fear, they then rushed into the cave and made for the bags of gold.

"By this time my mother had seized me in her arms and running nimbly along windings known only to ourselves, reached some secret stairs, where reigned a frightful tumult and confusion. The lower halls were filled with the armed ruffians of Kourschid, our enemies. My mother glued her eyes to a chink in the boards; there happened to be an aperture in front of me, and I looked through it.

"'What do you want?' we heard my father saying to some men who held in their hands a piece of paper inscribed with letters of gold.

"'We wish to communicate to you the will of His Highness. Do you see this firman?'

"'I do,' was my father's reply.

"'Well, read it. It demands your head.'

"My father burst into laughter, more terrible to hear than the wildest threats, and he had not ceased when two pistol shots rang out and the two men were dead.

"The Palikars, who were lying face downward all round my father, rose and began firing. The room became filled with noise, flames, and smoke. At the same time firing started on the other side of the hall, and the boards all around us were soon riddle with shot.

"Oh, how handsome, how noble was the Vizier Ali Tebelin, my father, as he stood there in the midst of the shot, his scimitar in his hand, his face black with powder! How his enemies fled before him! "'Selim! Selim!' cried he. 'Guardian of the fire, do your duty!'

"'Selim is dead,' replied a voice which seemed to come from the depths of the kiosk, 'and you, my lord Ali, are lost!' At the same moment a dull report was heard, and the flooring was shattered to atoms all around my father.

"Twenty shots were fired from underneath through the gap thus created, and flames rushed up as from the crater of a volcano and, gaining the hangings, quickly devoured them.

"In the midst of this frightful tumult two reports more distinct than the others, and two cries more heartrending than all the rest, petrified me with terror. These two shots had mortally wounded my father, and it was he who had uttered the two cries. Nevertheless he would not fall but stood clinging to a window. My mother shook the door in her efforts to force it open to go and die beside him, but the door was locked from the inside. All round him the Palikars were writhing in agony; two or three who were only slightly or not at all wounded leaped through the windows. The floor gave way entirely. My father fell on one knee; instantly twenty hands were stretched out, and twenty blows were dealt simultaneously at one man. My father disappeared in a blaze of fire stirred by these roaring demons as though hell had opened under his feet. I felt myself roll to the ground: my mother had fainted."

Haydee's arms fell to her side, and, uttering a groan, she looked at the Count as though to ask him whether he was satisfied with her obedience. Monte Cristo went up to her, and taking her hand said to her in Romaic: "Calm yourself, dear child, and console yourself in the thought that there is a God who punishes traitors."

"It is a frightful story, Count," said Albert, alarmed at Haydee's paleness, "and I reproach myself with having been so cruelly indiscreet."

"It is nothing," replied Monte Cristo. Then, placing his hand on the maiden's shoulder, he continued: "Haydee is a courageous girl and she sometimes finds solace in recounting her troubles."

"Because my sufferings remind me of your kindness, my lord," was the girl's eager response.

Albert looked at her with curiosity, for she had not yet told him what he was anxious to know, namely, how she had become the

Count's slave. She saw this desire expressed both in the Count's and in Albert's eyes and continued:

"When my mother recovered consciousness we were before the Seraskier. 'Kill me,' she said to him, 'but preserve the honour of Ali's widow.'

"'It is not to me that you have to address yourself,' Kourschid said.

"'Then to whom?'

"'To your new master.'

"'Who is my new master?'

"'Here he is,' said Kourschid, pointing to one of those who had most contributed to my father's death."

"Then you became that man's property?" asked Albert.

"No," responded Haydee. "He did not dare keep us; he sold us to some slave merchants who were going to Constantinople. We crossed over Greece and arrived at the imperial gates in a dying condition surrounded by a curious crowd, who made way for us to pass. My mother followed the direction of their eyes and with a cry suddenly fell to the ground, pointing to a head on a spike of the gate. Above this head were written the words:

"THIS IS THE HEAD OF ALI TEBELIN, PASHA OF JANINA."

"Weeping, I tried to raise my mother. She was dead!

"I was taken to the bazaar; a rich American bought me, had me educated, and, when I was thirteen years of age, he sold me to the Sultan Mahommed."

"From whom I bought her, as I told you, Albert, for an emerald similar to the one in which I keep my hashish pills," said the Count.

"You are good, you are great, my lord," said Haydee, kissing Monte Cristo's hand. "I am very happy to belong to you."

Albert was quite bewildered by all he had heard.

"Finish your coffee," said the Count. "The story is ended."

## CHAPTER LI

# THE REPORT FROM JANINA

FRANZ left Noirtier's room so distraught that even Valentine felt pity for him. Villefort only muttered some incoherent words and took refuge in his study. Two hours later he received the following letter:

"After all that has been disclosed this morning, Monsieur Noirtier de Villefort will appreciate the impossibility of an alliance between his family and that of Monsieur Franz d'Épinay. Monsieur Franz d'Épinay is sorry to think that Monsieur de Villefort, who appeared to be cognizant of the incidents related, should not have anticipated him in the expression of this view."

This outspoken letter from a young man who had always shown so much respect toward him was a deadly blow to the pride of a man like Villefort. He had not been in his study long when his wife entered. The fact that Franz had been called away by M. Noirtier at such a moment had caused so much amazement that Mme de Villefort's position, left alone with the lawyer and the witnesses, had become most embarrassing. At length she determined to stay no longer, and she too took her leave, saying she was going to make inquiries as to the cause of the interruption.

M. de Villefort merely told her that as the result of an explanation between M. Noirtier, M. d'Épinay, and himself, Valentine's engagement was broken off. This was a very awkward answer to have to give to those awaiting her return, so she contented herself with saying that M. Noirtier had been taken with a slight fit of apoplexy at the beginning of their discussion, in consequence of which the signing of the contract would be postponed for a few days. This news, false though it was, came so singularly in the train of the two other similar misfortunes, that her auditors looked at each other in amazement and withdrew without saying a word.

In the meantime Valentine, happy though at the same time terrified at all she had heard, embraced the feeble old man in loving gratitude for having broken a tie she had considered indissoluble, and asked his permission to go to her room for a while to recover her composure. Instead of going to her room, however, Valentine went into the garden. Maximilian was waiting in his customary place ready for any emergency, and convinced that Valentine would run to him the first moment she was free to do so.

He was not mistaken. With his eyes glued to the cracks in the palings he saw her running toward him and throwing her usual precaution to the winds. The first word she uttered filled his heart with joy.

"Saved!" she cried.

"Saved?" repeated Morrel, unable to believe such happiness. "Who has saved us?"

"My grandfather. You should really love him, Morrel!"

Morrel swore to love him with his whole heart; the oath cost him nothing, for at that moment he felt it was not sufficient to love him as a father or a friend, he almost adored him as a god.

"How did he manage it?" he asked. "What means did he use?"

Valentine was about to recount everything when she remembered that at the root of all was a secret which did not belong wholly to her grandfather.

"I will tell you all about it later," she said.

"When?"

"When I am your wife."

The turn the conversation was taking was so pleasing to Morrel that he was quite content to leave the matter at that and be satisfied with the one all-important piece of news for that day. He would not leave her, however, till she had given her promise that she would see him the next evening. This Valentine was ready to do. Her outlook had undergone a complete change, and it was certainly less difficult for her now to believe that she would marry Maximilian than it was for her to believe an hour back that she would not marry Franz.

In the meantime Mme de Villefort went up to Noirtier's room, where she was received with the habitual cold and forbidding look.

"There is no need for me to tell you, monsieur," said she, "that Valentine's engagement is broken off since it is here that the rupture took place; but what you do not know is that I have always been opposed to this marriage and that it was being contracted against my will."

Noirtier looked at his daughter-in-law as though demanding an explanation.

"Now that this marriage, which I know did not meet with your approval, has been stopped, I have come to speak to you of something which neither Monsieur de Villefort nor Valentine could mention."

Noirtier's eyes bade her proceed.

"As the only one disinterested and therefore the only one who has the right to speak on the matter," she continued, "I come to ask you to restore, not your love, for that she has always had, but your fortune to your grandchild."

For an instant Noirtier's eyes hesitated; evidently he was trying to find a motive for this request, but was unable to do so.

"May I hope, monsieur," said Mme de Villefort, "that your intentions coincide with my request?"

"Yes," signalled Noirtier.

"In that case, I leave you a grateful and happy woman, monsieur," she said, and, bowing to Noirtier, she withdrew.

True to his word, M. Noirtier sent for the notary the next day: the first will was torn up and a new one made in which he left the whole of his fortune to Valentine on condition that she should not separate herself from him.

It was then noised abroad that Mlle de Villefort, the heiress of the Marquis and Marquise de Saint-Méran, had been restored to her grandfather's good graces, and that one day she would have an income of over three hundred thousand francs.

While the events recorded above were taking place in the house of

Monsieur de Villefort, the Count of Morcerf had received Monte Cristo's visit, ordered his carriage and driven to the Rue de la Chaussée d'Antin. Danglars was making his monthly balance, and it was certainly not the best time to find him in a good humour; as a matter of fact, it had not been so for the past few months. On seeing his old friend, he assumed his most commanding air and seated himself squarely in his chair. Morcerf, on the other hand, laid aside his habitual stiffness of manner and was almost jovial and affable. Feeling sure that his overtures would be well received, he lost no time in coming to the point.

"Well, here I am, Baron. We have made no headway in our plans since our former conversation."

"What plans, Count?" Danglars asked as though vainly trying to discover some explanation of the General's words.

"Since you are such a stickler, my dear Baron, and since you desire to remind me that the ceremony is to be carried out in all due form, I will comply with your wishes." With a forced smile he rose, made a deep bow to Danglars, and said: "I have the honour, Baron, to ask the hand of Mademoiselle Eugénie Danglars, your daughter, for my son the Viscount Albert de Morcerf."

But instead of welcoming these words as Morcerf had every right to expect, Danglars knit his brows and, without even inviting the Count to take a seat, replied:

"Before giving you an answer, Count, I must think the matter over."

"Think the matter over?" exclaimed Morcerf more and more astonished. "Have you not had time enough for reflection during the eight years that have elapsed since we first spoke of this marriage?"

"Every day things happen, Count, which call for reconsideration of questions which we believed exhaustively considered," was Danglars' reply.

"What do you mean?" asked Morcerf. "I do not understand you."

"What I mean is that during the last fortnight unforeseen circumstances . . ."

"Excuse me, but is this a play we are acting?"

"A play?"

"Yes. Pray let us be more explicit."

"I should be delighted."

"Have you seen the Count of Monte Christo lately?"

"I see him very often. He is a friend of mine."

"When you saw him the other day did you not tell him that I appeared to you to be irresolute and forgetful in regard to this marriage? You see that I am neither the one nor the other since I have come to bid you keep your promise."

Danglars made no reply.

"Have you changed your mind so soon?" continued Morcerf. "Or have you but egged me on to make this proposal in order to see me humiliated?"

Danglars understood that if he continued the conversation in the same strain as that in which he had begun it, he might be taken at a disadvantage, so he said: "I quite comprehend that you are amazed at my reserve, Count. Believe me, I am the first one to regret that painful circumstances compel me to act thus."

"These are but so many empty words," replied the Count. "They might perhaps satisfy an ordinary man, but not the Count of Mercerf. When a man of his position comes to another man to remind him of his plighted word, and that man breaks his word, he is at least justified in demanding from him a good reason for his conduct."

Danglars was a coward but did not wish to appear one; besides he was annoyed at the tone Morcerf had adopted.

"I do not break my word without good reason," he retorted.

"What do you mean by that?"

"That my reason is good enough, but it is not an easy one to tell."

"You must understand, however, that I cannot be put off by such cryptic remarks. In any case, it is quite clear that you reject my proposal."

"Not altogether," replied Danglars, "I merely suspend my decision."

"But surely you do not presume to think that I am going to submit to your whims, and wait patiently and humbly until such time as I shall be restored to your favour again?"

"Then, Count, if you will not wait, we must consider our plan null and void."

The Count bit his lips till they bled in his effort to suppress the outburst which was so natural to his proud and irritable temper. He realized, however, that in this case, a scene would only make him look ridiculous, and had reached the door when he changed his mind and turned back. A cloud had gathered on his brow, which showed that his pride had given way to uneasiness.

"Come now, my dear Danglars," said he, "we have known each other for many long years and should, therefore, have some consideration for one another. You owe me an explanation, and the least you can do is to inform me what unfortunate occurrence has deprived my son of your favour."

"I bear the Viscount personally no ill-will, that is all I can tell you, monsieur," replied Danglars, adopting his insolent attitude once more now that the Count had become calmer.

"Then against whom is your ill-will directed?" asked Morcerf, his uneasiness showing itself in his changed voice and pale face.

Danglars did not let any of these symptoms escape him, and, fixing a look of greater assurance on the Count than was his wont, said: "You may be thankful I do not give a more detailed explanation."

A nervous trembling caused by repressed anger shook Morcerf's whole frame, but pulling himself together with a violent effort, he said: "I have the right to insist on an explanation. Have you anything against Madame de Morcerf? Is my fortune too small for you? Is it because my opinions differ from yours?"

"Nothing of the kind, monsieur," said Danglars. "If it were so, I should be at fault, for I was fully informed on these matters at the time of the engagement. Seek no more for a reason, I pray. I am really quite ashamed to see you indulging in such self-examination. Let us leave the matter as it stands and agree to a postponement. Surely, monsieur, there is no hurry. My daughter is but seventeen and your son twenty-one. In the meanwhile, time follows its course carrying events with it; what is obscure one evening, is often revealed the next, and the vilest calumnies ofttimes die in one day."

"Calumnies, did you say?" exclaimed Morcerf, turning livid. "Can anyone be slandering me?"

"As I already said, monsieur, we will not go into details. I assure you this is more painful for me than for you, for I had reckoned on the honour of an alliance with you, and the breaking off of a marriage proposal always injures the lady more than the gentleman."

"Enough, monsieur, we will drop the subject," said Morcerf, as, crumpling his gloves up in his rage, he left the room.

Danglars noticed that not once had Morcerf dared to ask whether it was on his own account that he, Danglars, had broken his word.

That same evening the banker had a long conference with several friends, and M. Cavalcanti, who had remained in the salon with the ladies, was the last to leave the house.

As soon as he awoke the next morning, Danglars asked for the newspapers. He flung three or four on one side till he came to the *Impartial,* of which Beauchamp was the chief editor. He hastily tore off the wrapper and opened it nervously. Disdainfully passing over the leading article, he came to the miscellaneous news column, and, with a malicious smile, stopped at a paragraph which read as follows:

> A correspondent at Janina writes: A fact hitherto unknown, or at any rate unpublished, has just come to my knowledge. The castles defending this town were given up to the Turks by a French officer in whom the Vizier Ali Tebelin had placed entire confidence. This French officer who was in the service of Ali, Pasha of Janina,

and who not only surrendered the Castle of Janina, but also sold his benefactor to the Turks, at that time was called Fernand, but he has since added to his Christian name a title of nobility and a family name. He is now styled the Count of Morcerf and ranks among the peers.

"Good!" Danglars observed after having read the paragraph; "here is a nice little article on Colonel Fernand which will, methinks, relieve me of the necessity of giving any explanation to the Count of Morcerf."

## CHAPTER LII

## THE LEMONADE

MORREL was, indeed, very happy. M. Noirtier had sent for him, and he was in such haste to learn the reason that, trusting to his own two legs more than to the four legs of a cab-horse, he started off from the Rue Meslay at a rapid pace and ran all the way to the Faubourg Saint-Honoré, while Barrois followed as well he might. Morrel was thirty-one years of age and was urged on by love; Barrois was sixty and parched with the heat. On arriving at the house, Morrel was not even out of breath, for love lends wings; but Barrois had not been in love for many long years and was bathed in perspiration.

The old servant let Morrel in by a private door, and before long the rustling of a dress on the parquet floor announced the arrival of Valentine. She looked adorable in her mourning, in fact so charming that Morrel could almost have dispensed with his interview with Noirtier; but the old man's chair was soon heard being wheeled along to the room in which they were awaiting him.

Noirtier acknowledged with a kind look Morrel's effusive thanks for his marvellous intervention which had saved Valentine and himself from despair. Then, in view of the new favour accorded him, Maximilian sought Valentine's eyes; she was sitting in the far corner timidly waiting till she was forced to speak. Noirtier fixed his eyes on her.

"Am I to say what you told me?" she asked.

"Yes," was Noirtier's reply.

"Grandpapa Noirtier had a great many things to say to you, Monsieur Morrel," said Valentine to the young man, who was devouring her with his eyes. "These he told me three days ago, and he has sent for you to-day that I may repeat them all to you. Since he has chosen me as his interpreter, I will repeat everything in the light of his intentions."

"I am listening with the greatest impatience," replied the young man. "Pray speak, mademoiselle."

"My grandfather wishes to leave this house," she continued. "Barrois is now looking for a suitable flat for him."

"But what will become of you, mademoiselle, who are so dear and so necessary to Monsieur Noirtier?"

"Me?" replied Valentine. "It is quite agreed that I shall not leave my grandfather. I shall live with him. Then I shall be free and have an independent income, and with my grandfather's consent I shall keep the promise I made you."

Valentine said these last words in such a low voice that nothing but Morrel's great interest in them made them audible to him.

"When I am with my grandfather," continued Valentine, "Monsieur Morrel can come and see me in the presence of my good and worthy protector, and if we still feel that our future happiness lies in a union with each other, he can come and claim me. I shall be waiting for him."

"Oh!" cried Morrel. "What have I done to deserve such happiness?"

Noirtier looked at the lovers with ineffable tenderness. Barrois, before whom there were no secrets, had remained at the far end of the room and smiled happily as he wiped away the last drops of perspiration that were rolling down his bald forehead.

"How hot poor old Barrois is!" said Valentine.

"That is because I have been running fast, mademoiselle, but I must give Monsieur Morrel the credit for running still faster."

Noirtier indicated by a look a tray on which were standing a decanter of lemonade and a tumbler. Noirtier himself had drunk some of the lemonade half an hour before.

"Have some of this lemonade, Barrois," the girl said. "I can see you are looking at it with envious eyes."

"The fact is, mademoiselle, I am dying of thirst, and I shall be only too glad to drink your health in a glass of lemonade."

Barrois took the tray and was hardly outside the door, which he had forgotten to close, when they saw him throw back his head to empty the tumbler Valentine had filled for him. Valentine and Morrel were bidding each other good-bye; they heard a bell ringing on Villefort's staircase. It was the signal that a visitor had called. Valentine looked at the clock.

"It is noon," said she, "and as it is Saturday, it is doubtless the doctor. He will come here, so Monsieur Morrel had better go, do you not think so, Grandpapa?"

"Yes," replied the old man.

"Barrois!" called Valentine, "Barrois, come!"

The voice of the old servant was heard to reply: "I am coming, mademoiselle."

"Barrois will conduct you to the door," Valentine said to Morrel. "And now, remember, Monsieur l'Officier, Grandpapa does not wish us to risk anything that might compromise our happiness."

"I have promised to wait, and wait I shall," said Morrel.

At that moment Barrois entered.

"Who rang?" asked Valentine.

"Doctor d'Avrigny," said Barrois, staggering.

"What is the matter, Barrois?" Valentine asked him.

The servant did not answer; he looked at his master with wildly staring eyes, while his cramped hand groped for some support to prevent himself from falling.

"He is going to fall!" cried Morrel.

In fact, the trembling fit which had come over Barrois gradually increased, and the twitching of his facial muscles announced a very grave nervous attack. Seeing his old servant in this state, Noirtier looked at him affectionately, and in those intelligent eyes was expressed every emotion that moves the human heart.

Barrois went a few steps toward his master.

"Oh, my God! My God! Lord have pity on me!" he cried. "What is the matter with me? I am ill. I cannot see. A thousand darts of fire are piercing my brain. Oh, don't touch me! Don't touch me!"

His haggard eyes started out of their sockets, his head fell back, and the rest of his body stiffened. Valentine uttered a cry of horror, and Morrel took her in his arms as though to defend her against some unknown danger.

"Monsieur d'Avrigny! Monsieur d'Avrigny!" the girl called out in a choking voice. "Help! help!"

Barrois turned round, walked a few steps, stumbled and fell at his master's feet with his hand on his knee, and cried out: "My master! my good master!"

Attracted by the screams, Villefort rushed into the room. Morrel instantly relaxed his hold of Valentine, who was now in a half-fainting condition, and going to a far corner of the room, hid behind a curtain. As pale as if he had seen a snake start up to attack him, he gazed in horror on the agonized sufferer. Noirtier was burning with impatience and terror, his soul went out to help the poor old man who was his friend rather than his servant. The terrible struggle between life and death that was going on within him made his veins stand out and the few remaining live muscles round his eyes contract.

With convulsed features, bloodshot eyes, and head thrown back, Barrois lay beating the floor with his hands, whilst his legs had become so stiff that they looked more ready to break than to bend. He was foaming at the mouth and his breathing was laboured. Stupefied, Villefort stood still for an instant, gazing on the spectacle which had met his eyes directly he entered the room. He had not seen Morrel. After a second's dumb contemplation of the scene, during which his face had turned deathly pale and his hair appeared to stand on end, he rushed to the door crying out: "Doctor! Doctor! Come! come!"

"Madame de Villefort, come! Oh, come quickly, and bring your smelling-salts!" Valentine called, running up the stairs.

"What is the matter?" Mme de Villefort asked in a metallic and constrained voice.

"Oh, come quickly."

"But where is the doctor?" cried Villefort. "Where can he have gone?"

The stairs were heard to creak as Mme de Villefort slowly came down them, holding in one hand a handkerchief, with which she was wiping her face, and in the other a bottle of smelling-salts. When she entered the room, her first glance was for Noirtier, who, save for the emotion he naturally felt in the circumstances, appeared to be in his usual state of health; then her eyes fell on the dying man. She turned pale as she saw him, and her eyes, as it were, leaped from the servant to his master.

"For pity's sake, where is the doctor, madame?" exclaimed Valentine.

"He went into your room. Barrois has an attack of apoplexy, as you see, and he may be saved if he is bled."

"Has he eaten anything lately?" asked Mme de Villefort, evading the question.

"He has not yet had his breakfast," replied Valentine, "but he was running very fast this morning on an errand for my grandfather, and when he came back he drank a glass of lemonade."

"Why did he not have some wine? Lemonade is very bad."

"The lemonade was near at hand in Grandpapa's decanter. Poor Barrois was thirsty, and he drank what he could get."

Mme de Villefort started; M. Noirtier watched her with the closest scrutiny.

"He has such a short neck!" said she.

"I ask you once more, madame, where is the doctor?" said Villefort. "For heaven's sake, answer!"

"He is with Edward, who is poorly," replied Mme de Villefort, seeing she could no longer evade the question.

Villefort rushed up the stairs to fetch him.

"Here," said the young woman, giving the smelling salts to Valentine. "The doctor will doubtless bleed him, so I will return to my room. I cannot bear the sight of blood."

With which she followed her husband.

Morrel emerged from his dark corner where he had remained unseen throughout the general consternation.

"Go quickly, Maximilian, and wait till I call you," said Valentine to him.

Morrel cast a questioning glance at Noirtier, and the old man, who had not lost his composure, made a sign of approval. The young man pressed Valentine's hand to his heart and left by the deserted landing just as Villefort and the doctor came in together by the opposite door.

Barrois was returning to consciousness; the attack had passed. He began to groan and raised himself on one knee. D'Avrigny and Villefort carried him on to a sofa.

"What do you prescribe, Doctor?" asked Villefort.

"Get me some water and ether, and send for some oil of turpentine and tartaric acid. And now let every one retire."

"Must I go too?" Valentine asked timidly.

"Yes, mademoiselle, you particularly," said the doctor abruptly.

Valentine looked at d'Avrigny in astonishment, but, after kissing her grandfather, left the room. The doctor shut the door behind her with a look of grim determination.

"See, Doctor, he is coming round. It was only a slight attack after all."

M. d'Avrigny smiled grimly.

"How do you feel?" he asked Barrois.

"A little better, Doctor."

"Can you drink this glass of ether and water?"

"I will try, but do not touch me."

"Why not?"

"I feel that if you touch me, if only with the tip of your fingers, the attack will return."

Barrois took the glass, put it to his lips, and drank about half of its contents.

"Where have you pain?" the doctor asked.

"Everywhere. It is as though I had frightful cramp everywhere."

"What have you eaten to-day?"

"Nothing at all. All I have taken is a glass of my master's lemonade," Barrois replied, making a sign with his head toward Noirtier, who was sitting motionless in his chair, contemplating this dreadful scene without letting a movement or a word escape him.

"Where is the lemonade?" asked the doctor eagerly.

"In the decanter in the kitchen."

"Shall I fetch it, Doctor?" Villefort asked.

"No, stay here and try to make the patient drink the rest of this ether and water."

"But the lemonade . . ."

"I will fetch it myself."

D'Avrigny bounded toward the door, and, rushing down the servants' staircase, nearly knocked over Mme de Villefort, who was also going into the kitchen. She screamed, but the doctor did not even take any notice of her. Obsessed with the one idea, he jumped down the last three or four stairs and flew into the kitchen. Seeing the decanter three parts empty, he pounced upon it like an eagle upon its prey, and with it returned to the sick-room quite out of breath. Mme de Villefort was slowly going up the stairs leading to her room.

"Is this the decanter?" Monsieur d'Avrigny asked Barrois.

"Yes, Doctor."

"Is this some of the same lemonade you drank?"

"I believe so."

"What did it taste like?"

"It had a bitter taste."

The doctor poured several drops of the lemonade into the palm of his hand, sucked it up with his lips, and, after rinsing his mouth with it as one does when tasting wine, he spat it out into the fireplace.

"It is the same right enough," he said. "Did you drink some too, Noirtier?"

"Yes," looked the old man.

"Did you notice the bitter taste?"

"Yes."

"Oh, Doctor, the fit is coming on again! Oh, God, have pity on me!"

The doctor ran to his patient.

"The tartar emetic, Villefort, see if it has come!"

Villefort rushed out shouting: "The emetic! Has it not been brought yet?"

"If I had some means of injecting air into his lungs," said d'Avrigny, looking around him, "I might possibly be able to prevent asphyxiation. But there is nothing, nothing!"

"Are you going to let me die without help, Doctor? Oh, I am dying! Have pity on me, I am dying!"

Barrois was seized with a nervous attack which was more acute than the first one. He had slipped from the sofa on to the floor and lay stretched out stiff and rolling in pain. The doctor left him, for he could do nothing to help him. Going over to Noirtier, he asked him in a low voice:

"How do you feel? Well?"

"Yes."

"Does your stomach feel light or heavy? Light?"

"Yes."

"The same as when you have taken the pills I ordered you to take every Sunday?"

"Yes."

"Did Barrois make the lemonade?"

"Yes."

"Did you invite him to drink it?"

"No."

"Monsieur de Villefort?"

"No."

"Madame de Villefort?"

"No."

"It was Valentine, then?"

"Yes."

A sigh from Barrois, and a yawn which made his jaw-bones crack, attracted the attention of d'Avrigny, who hastened to his side.

"Can you speak, Barrois?"

Barrois uttered a few inaudible words.

"Make an effort, my friend."

Barrois opened his bloodshot eyes.

"Who made the lemonade?"

"I did."

"Did you take it to your master as soon as it was made?"

"No."

"Did you leave it somewhere, then?"

"In the pantry, because I was called away."

"Who brought it into this room?"

"Mademoiselle Valentine."

"Oh, again!" exclaimed d'Avrigny, striking his forehead.

"Doctor! Doctor!" cried Barrois, who felt a third attack approaching.

"Are they never going to bring the emetic?" cried the doctor.

"Here is a glass with one already prepared by the chemist himself, who has come back with me," said Villefort.

"Drink!" said the doctor to Barrois.

"Impossible, Doctor. It is too late. My throat is closing up. I am suffocating. Oh, my heart! My head! Oh, what agony! Am I going to suffer like this for long?"

"No, no, my friend," said the doctor. "You will soon be suffering no more."

"Oh, I understand," said the poor wretch. "My God, have pity on me." With a cry he fell back as though struck by lightning. D'Avrigny placed his hand to his heart and put a mirror to his mouth.

"Well?" said Villefort.

"Go to the kitchen quickly and ask for some syrup of violets." Villefort went immediately.

"Do not be alarmed, Monsieur Noirtier," said the doctor. "I am taking my patient into another room to bleed him; such an attack is truly ghastly to behold."

Taking Barrois under the arms, he dragged him into an adjoining room, but returned at once for the remainder of the lemonade.

Noirtier closed his right eye.

"You want Valentine? I will have her sent to you."

Villefort came back with the syrup of violets and met d'Avrigny on the landing.

"Come with me," said the doctor, taking him into the room where the dead man lay.

"Is he still unconscious?" asked Villefort.

"He is dead."

Villefort started back, clasped his hands to his head, and, looking at the dead man, exclaimed in tones of infinite pity: "Dead so soon!"

"Yes, it was very quick, was it not?" said d'Avrigny, "but that should not astonish you. Monsieur and Madame de Saint-Méran died just as suddenly. Death makes a very sudden appearance in your house, Monsieur de Villefort."

"What!" cried the magistrate in a tone of horror and consternation, "are you still harping on that terrible idea?"

"I am, monsieur, and the thought has not left me for one instant," said d'Avrigny solemnly. "Furthermore, that you may be convinced that I have made no mistake this time, listen to what I have to say."

Villefort trembled convulsively.

"There is a poison which destroys life without leaving any traces after it. I know the poison well. I have made a deep study of it. I recognized the presence of this poison in poor Barrois just as I did in Madame de Saint-Méran. There is one means of detecting its presence. It restores the blue colour of litmus paper which has been dyed red by an acid, and it turns syrup of violets green. We have no litmus paper, but we have syrup of violets. If the lemonade is pure and inoffensive, the syrup will retain its colour; on the other hand, if it contains poison, the syrup will turn green. Watch closely!"

The doctor slowly poured a few drops of lemonade into the cup, and a cloudy sediment was immediately formed at the bottom. First of all this sediment took on a blue hue, then it changed from sapphire to the colour of opal, and again to emerald—to change no more. The experiment left no room for doubt.

"The unfortunate Barrois has been poisoned," said d'Avrigny, "and I am ready to answer for this statement before God and man."

Villefort made no reply; he raised his arms heavenward, opened wide his haggard eyes and sank back into a chair horror-stricken.

## CHAPTER LIII

## THE ACCUSATION

M. D'AVRIGNY soon brought the magistrate round, though he still looked like another corpse in this chamber of death.

"Death is in my house!" he exclaimed.

"Say rather crime," replied the doctor, "for the time has now come when we must act. We must put an end to these incessant deaths. So far as I am concerned, I feel I can no longer conscientiously hold such secrets unless I have the hope of soon seeing the victims, and through them society, avenged."

Villefort cast a melancholy look around him. "Do you, then, suspect anyone?"

"I do not suspect anyone. Death knocks at your door—it enters and goes not blindly, but with circumspection, from room to room. Ah, well! I follow its track, I know its passage and adopt the wisdom of the ancients; I grope about in the dark, for my respect for you and my friendship for your family are like two bandages before my eyes."

"Speak, Doctor, speak. I have courage."

"Well, then, you have in your house, perhaps in the midst of your family, one of those terrible phenomena every century produces."

Villefort wrung his hands and cast a pleading look on the doctor, but the latter continued pitilessly:

"An axiom of jurisprudence says: 'Seek whom the crime would profit!'"

"Alas! Doctor, how many times has not justice been deceived by those fateful words!" exclaimed Villefort. "I know why, but I think this crime . . ."

"Ah, you admit at last that it is a crime?"

"Yes, I acknowledge it. What else can I do? But let me continue. It seems to me this crime is directed against me alone and not against the victims. I sense some calamity for myself at the root of all these strange disasters."

"Oh, Man," muttered d'Avrigny. "The most selfish of all creatures, who believes that the earth turns, the sun shines, and the scythe of death reaps for him alone. And have those who have lost their lives lost nothing? Monsieur de Saint-Méran, Madame de Saint-Méran, Monsieur Noirtier . . ."

"Monsieur Noirtier?"

"Certainly. Do you think it was the unfortunate servant's life they wanted? No, no, like Shakespeare's Polonius, he died for another. Noirtier was intended to drink the lemonade; the other one only drank it by accident."

"How was it my father did not succumb?"

"As I told you one evening in the garden after the death of Madame de Saint-Méran, his system has become accustomed to this very poison; no one, not even the murderer himself, knows that for the past year I have been treating Monsieur Noirtier with brucine for his paralysis, whereas the murderer knows, and has proved by experience, that brucine is a virulent poison."

"Stop! For heaven's sake, have pity on me!" cried Villefort, wringing his hands.

"Let us follow the criminal's course. He kills Monsieur de Saint-Méran, then Madame de Saint-Méran; a double inheritance to look forward to."

Villefort wiped away the perspiration that was streaming down his forehead.

"Listen! Monsieur Noirtier willed his fortune away from you and your family," continued M. d'Avrigny pitilessly, "so he is spared. But he has no sooner destroyed his first will and made a second one than he becomes the victim, no doubt lest he should make a third will. The will was made the day before yesterday, I believe. You see there was no time lost."

"Have mercy, Doctor!"

"No mercy, monsieur! A doctor has a sacred mission on earth, and to fulfil it he has to start at the source of life and descend to the mysterious darkness of the tomb. When a crime has been committed, and God, doubtless horrified, turns away His head, it is for the doctor to say: 'Here is the culprit!'"

"Have mercy on my daughter!" murmured Villefort.

"You see it is you yourself who have named her, you, her father!"

"Have mercy on Valentine. I say, it is impossible! I would sooner accuse myself. Valentine, who is as pure as a lily and whose heart is of gold!"

"No mercy! It is a flagrant crime. Mademoiselle de Villefort herself packed the medicines that were sent to Monsieur de Saint-Méran, and he is dead. She prepared the cooling draughts for Madame de Saint-

Méran, and she is dead. Mademoiselle de Villefort took from Barrois, who was sent out, the decanter with the lemonade her grandfather generally drinks in the morning, and he escapes but by a miracle. Mademoiselle de Villefort is the guilty one! She is the poisoner, and I denounce her as such. Now, do your duty, Monsieur le Procureur du Roi!"

"Doctor, I can hold out no longer. I no longer defend myself. I believe you. But for pity's sake, spare my life, my honour!"

"Monsieur de Villefort, there are times when I overstep the limits of foolish human circumspection," said the doctor with increasing vehemence, "if your daughter had only committed one crime and I saw her meditating a second one, I should say to you: 'Warn her, punish her. Send her to some convent to pass the rest of her days in weeping and praying.' If she had committed two, I should say: 'Monsieur de Villefort, this is a poison for which there is no known antidote; its action is as quick as thought, as rapid as lightning, and as deadly as a thunderbolt. Recommend her soul to God and give her this poison; thus only will you save your honour and your life, for you are her target. I see her coming towards your pillow with her hypocritical smiles and her sweet exhortations! Woe to you if you do not strike first!' This is what I should have said had she killed two persons, but she has witnessed three death agonies, she has watched three people die, she has knelt by three corpses! To the scaffold with the poisoner! To the scaffold!"

Villefort fell on his knees.

"Listen to me!" he cried. "Pity me, help me No, my daughter is not guilty. You may drag us before a tribunal, but I shall still say: 'My daughter is not guilty. There is no crime in this house,' ... Do you understand, I will have no crime in this house, for, like death, crime comes not alone. What does it signify to you if I am murdered? Are you my friend? Are you a man? No, you are a physician. ... Well, then, I say to you: 'I will not drag my daughter into the hands of the executioner.' Ah, the very thought of it would drive me mad! I should tear my heart out with my fingernails. And if you were mistaken, doctor? If it were another than my daughter? If I came to you one day like a ghost and said to you: 'Murderer! you have killed my daughter!' If that were to happen, Monsieur d'Avrigny, Christian though I am, I should take my life!"

"Very well," said the doctor after a moment's silence. "I will wait."

Villefort looked at him as though he still doubted his words.

"But remember this," continued M. d'Avrigny solemnly and slowly. "If some one falls ill in your house, if you yourself are stricken, do not send for me—I shall not come. I will share this terrible secret with you, but I will not let shame and remorse eat into my conscience like a worm, just as misfortune and crime will undermine the foundations of your house."

"Do you forsake me then, Doctor?"

"Yes, for I can follow you no further, and I will only stop at the foot of the scaffold. Another revelation will be made which will bring this terrible tragedy to a close. Good-bye!"

That evening all Villefort's servants, who had assembled in the kitchen to discuss the matter, came in a body to M. de Villefort to give notice. No entreaties, no promises of higher wages could persuade them to stay. To everything they said: "We wish to go, because death is in your house." And in spite of all persuasions, they left, expressing their regret at leaving such a good master and mistress, above all Mademoiselle Valentine, who was so good, so kind-hearted, so gentle.

On hearing what the servants said, Villefort looked at Valentine. She was weeping, and the sight of her in tears filled him with deep emotion. He looked at Mme de Villefort, too, and, strange to say, he seemed to see a fleeting but grim smile pass over her lips like a meteor passing ominously between two clouds in a stormy sky.

## CHAPTER LIV

## THE TRIAL

THE paragraph which appeared in the papers regarding the part Morcerf had played in the surrender of Janina caused great excitement in the Chamber of Peers among the usually calm groups of that high assembly. That day almost every member had arrived before the usual hour to discuss with his compeers the sinister event that was to fix public attention on one of the best-known names in that illustrious body.

Some were reading the article in a subdued voice, others making comments or exchanging reminiscences which substantiated the charges still more. The Count of Morcerf was not popular with his colleagues. In order to maintain his position, he had, like all upstarts, adopted a very haughty manner. The aristocrat smiled at him, the man of talent disclaimed him, and the justly proud instinctively despised him.

The Count of Morcerf alone was ignorant of the news. He did not receive the newspaper containing the defamatory information and had spent the morning writing letters and trying a new horse. He arrived at the Chamber at his usual hour, and with proud step and haughty mien alighted from his carriage and passed along the corridors into the hall without remarking the hesitation of the doorkeepers, or the coldness of his colleagues. The sitting had been in progress about half an hour when he entered.

Every one had the accusing paper before him, and it was evident that all were aching to start the debate, but, as is generally the case, no one wished to take upon himself the responsibility of opening the attack. At length, one of the peers, an open enemy of Morcerf's, ascended the tribune with such solemnity that all felt that the desired moment had arrived.

There was an awe-inspiring silence. Morecerf alone was ignorant of the cause of the deep attention given to an orator they were accustomed to hear with indifference. The Count paid little heed to the preamble in which the speaker announced that he was about to touch upon a subject so grave, so sacred, and at the same time of such vital importance to the Senate, that he demanded the undivided attention of all his colleagues. When Janina and Colonel Fernand were mentioned, the Count of Mercerf turned so horribly pale that a shudder went through the whole assembly and all eyes were turned toward him.

The article was read during this painful silence, and then the speaker declared his reluctance to open the subject, and the difficulty of his task, but it was the honour of M. de Morcerf and of the whole Chamber he proposed to defend by introducing a debate on these personal and ever-pressing questions. He concluded by demanding a speedy inquiry into the matter before the calumny had time to spread, so that M. de Morcerf might be reinstated in the position in public opinion he had so long held.

Morcerf was so completely overwhelmed by this enormous and unexpected attack that it was almost more than he could do to stammer a few words in reply, staring the while at his colleagues with wide-open eyes. This nervousness, which might have been due to the astonishment of innocence as much as to shame of guilt, evoked some sympathy in his favour. An inquiry was voted for, and the Count was asked what time he required to prepare his defence. On realizing that this terrible blow had still left him alive, Morcerf's courage returned to him.

"My brother peers," he replied, "it is not with time that one repulses an attack of this kind that has been made on me by some unknown enemies. I must answer this flash of lightning, which for a moment overpowered me, by a thunderbolt. Instead of defending myself in this way, would that I could shed my blood to prove to my colleagues that I am worthy to be their equal!"

These words made a favourable impression.

"I therefore request that the inquiry be instituted as soon as possible," he continued, " and I undertake to furnish the Chamber with all the necessary evidence."

"Is the Chamber of opinion that the inquiry should take place this very day?" asked the President.

"Yes!" was the unanimous reply.

A Committee of twelve members was appointed to examine the evidence supplied by Morcerf, and the first session was fixed for eight o'clock that evening in the committee room. This decision arrived at, Morcerf asked permission to retire; he had to collect the evidence he had long since prepared against such a storm, which his cunning and indomitable character had foreseen.

The evening arrived; all Paris was agog with expectation. Many believed that Morcerf had only to show himself to overthrow the charge; on the other hand some asserted he would not make an appearance. There were a few who said they had seen him leave for Brussels, and one or two even went to the police station to inquire whether it was true that he had taken out a passport.

Every one arrived punctually at eight o'clock. M. de Morcerf entered the hall at the last stroke of the clock. In his hand he carried some papers. He was carefully but simply dressed, and, according to the ancient military custom, wore his coat buttoned up to the chin. Outwardly he was calm, and, contrary to habit, walked with an unaffected gait.

His presence produced a most favourable effect, and the Committee was far from being ill-disposed toward him. Several of the members went forward to shake hands with him. One of the doorkeepers handed a letter to the President.

"You are now at liberty to speak," said the President, unsealing his letter.

The Count commenced his defence in a most eloquent and skilful manner. He produced evidence to show that the Visier of Janina had honoured him with entire confidence up to his last hour, the best proof being that he had entrusted him with a mission to the Sultan himself, the result of which meant life or death to him. He showed the ring with which Ali Pasha generally sealed his letters, and which he had given him as a token of authority so that upon his return he might gain access to him at any hour of the day or night. He said his mission had unfortunately failed, and, when he returned to defend his benefactor, he found him dead. So great was Ali Pasha's confidence in him, however, that before he died he had entrusted his favourite wife and his daughter to his care.

In the meantime, the President carelessly glanced at the letter that had been given him, but the very first lines aroused his attention; he read the missive again and again, then, fixing his eyes on Morcerf, said:

"You say, Count, that the Vizier of Janina confided his wife and daughter to your care."

"Yes, Monsieur le Président," replied Morcerf. "But in that, as in all else, misfortune dogged my steps. Upon my return, Vasiliki and her daughter Haydee had disappeared."

"Do you know them?"

"Thanks to my intimacy with the Pasha and his great confidence in me, I saw them more than twenty times."

"Have you any idea what has become of them?"

"I have been told that they succumbed to their grief, and maybe to their privation. I was not rich, my life was in constant danger, and, much to my regret, I could not go in search of them."

The President frowned almost imperceptibly as he said: "Messieurs, you have heard Monsieur de Morcerf's defence. Now, Count, can you produce any witnesses to support the truth of what you say?"

"Alas, I cannot," replied the Count. "All those who were at the Pasha's Court, and who knew me there, are either scattered or dead. I believe I am the only one of my compatriots who survived that terrible war. I have only Ali Tebelin's letters, which I have laid before you, and the ring, the token of his goodwill. The most convincing evidence I can put forward is the complete absence of testimony against my honour, and the clean record of my military career."

A murmur of approbation went through the assembly, and at this moment, M. de Morcerf's cause was gained; it only needed to be put to the vote when the President rose and said: "Messieurs, you and the Count will, I presume, not be averse to hearing a witness who claims to hold important evidence and has come forward of his own accord. He is doubtless come to prove the perfect innocence of our colleague. Here is the letter I have just received on the matter." The President read as follows:

"MONSIEUR LE PRÉSIDENT,

"I can furnish the Committee of Inquiry appointed to examine the conduct in Epirus and Macedonia of a certain Lieutenant-General the Count of Morcerf with important facts."

The President made a short pause. The Count of Morcerf turned deathly pale, and the tightly clenched papers that he held in his hand audibly crackled.

The President resumed:

"I was present at Ali Pasha's death and know what became of Vasiliki and Haydee. I hold myself at the disposal of the Committee, and even claim the honour of being heard. I shall be waiting in the corridor when this note is handed to you."

"Who is this witness, or rather enemy?" said the Count, in a very changed voice.

"We shall learn in a moment, monsieur. Is the committee agreed to hear this witness?"

"Yes, yes," was the unanimous reply.

The President called the doorkeeper, and inquired of him whether anyone was waiting in the corridors.

"A woman, accompanied by her attendant," said the doorkeeper.

The members looked at each other in amazement.

"Let this woman enter," said the President.

All eyes were turned toward the door, and five minutes later the doorkeeper reappeared. Behind him came a woman enveloped in a large veil which completely covered her, but the form outlined, and the perfume which exhaled from her, denoted that she was a young and elegant woman. The President requested her to lay aside her veil, and it was seen that she was dressed in Grecian attire and was a remarkably beautiful woman.

M. de Morcerf looked at her in amazement mingled with terror, for this woman held his life in her hands. To the rest of the assembly, however, it was a turn of events so strange and interesting that Morcerf's welfare became but a secondary consideration.

The President offered the young woman a seat, but she made a sign that she would rather stand. The Count, on the other hand, had sunk into his chair, for his legs refused to support him.

"Madame," began the President. "You state in your letter to the Committee that you have important information on the Janina affair, and that you were an eyewitness of the events. Permit me to remark that you must have been very young then."

"I was four years old, but as the events so peculiarly concerned me not a detail has escaped my memory."

"How did these events so concern you? Who are you that this tragedy should have made so deep an impression on you?"

"My name is Haydee," replied the young woman. "I am the daughter of Ali Tebelin, Pasha of Janina, and of Vasiliki, his much-beloved wife."

The modest and at the same time proud blush that suffused the young woman's cheeks, the fire in her eye and the majestic way in which she revealed her identity, made an indescribable impression on the assembly. The Count, on the other hand, could not have been more abashed if a thunderbolt had fallen and opened a chasm at his feet.

"Madame," resumed the President, making a respectful bow, "permit me a simple question. Can you prove the authenticity of what you say?"

"I can, monsieur," said Haydee, taking a perfumed satin bag from her veil. "Here is my birth certificate, drawn up by my father and signed by his principal officers, also my certificate of baptism, my father having allowed me to be brought up in my mother's religion. This latter bears the seal of the Grand Primate of Macedonia and Epirus. Lastly, and this is perhaps the most important, I have the document pertaining to the sale of my person and that of my mother to an Armenian merchant, named El Kobbir, effected by the French officer who, in his infamous treaty with the Porte, had reserved for his share of the booty the wife and daughter of his benefactor. These he sold for the sum of four hundred thousand francs."

A ghastly pallor spread over the Count's cheeks and his eyes became bloodshot when he heard these terrible imputations, which were received by the assembly in grim silence.

Haydee, still calm, but more dangerous in her very calmness than another would have been in anger, handed to the President the record of her sale, drawn up in the Arab tongue.

As it was thought likely that a testimony might be forthcoming in the Arabic, Romaic, or Turkish language, the interpreter of the Chamber had been advised that his presence might be needed, and he was now summoned. One of the peers, to whom the Arabic tongue was familiar, followed closely the original text as the translator read:

"I, El Kobbir, slave merchant and purveyor to the harem of His Highness, acknowledge having received for transmission to the Sublime Sultan from the Count of Monte Cristo an emerald valued at eight hundred thousand francs as purchase money for a young Christian slave, aged eleven years, of the name of Haydee, a recognized daughter of the late Ali Tebelin, Pasha of Janina, and of Vasiliki, his favourite, she having been sold to me seven years ago together with her mother, who died on her arrival at Constantinople, by a French Colonel in the service of the Vizier Ali Tebelin of the name of Fernand Mondego.

"The aforesaid purchase was made on behalf of His Highness, whose mandate I had, for the sum of four hundred thousand francs.

"Given at Constantinople with the authorization of His Highness in the year twelve-forty-seven of the Hegira.

"Signed: EL KOBBIR

"In order to give this document due credence and authority, it will be vested with the imperial seal, which the vendor consents to have affixed."

Beside the merchant's signature was the seal of the Sublime Sultan. A dreadful silence followed. The Count was speechless; his eyes instinctively sought Haydee, and he fixed her with a frenzied stare.

"Is it permitted, madame, to interrogate the Count of Monte Cristo, who, I believe, is staying in Paris just now?" asked the President.

"The Count of Monte Cristo, my second father, has been in Normandy for the past three days, monsieur."

"Then who advised you to take this step, for which this Committee is indebted to you, and which was the natural proceeding in view of your birth and misfortunes?"

"This step was urged upon me by my grief and respect. May God forgive me! Though I am a Christian, my one thought has always been to avenge my illustrious father's death. Therefore as soon as I set foot in France and learned that the traitor lived in Paris, I have ever watched for this opportunity. I live a retired life in my noble protector's house; I wish it so because I like retirement and silence, so that I may live in the thoughts and memories of the past. The Count of Monte Cristo surrounds me with every paternal care, and in the silence of my apartments I receive each day all newspapers and periodicals. From them I glean all information concerning what is going on in the world; from them I learned what transpired in the Chamber this morning and what was to take place this evening."

"Then the Count of Monte Cristo knows nothing of this action on your part?" asked the President.

"He is in absolute ignorance of it, monsieur, and my only fear is that he may disapprove of what I have done. Nevertheless, this is a glorious day for me," continued the young woman, raising her eager eyes heavenward, "the day when I at last have the opportunity of avenging my father."

During all this time the Count had not uttered a single word; his colleagues looked at him, no doubt commiserating with him on this calamity which had been wrought on him by a woman. The ever-increasing lines and wrinkles on his face betrayed his misery.

"Monsieur de Morcerf, do you recognize this lady as the daughter of Ali Tebelin, Pasha of Janina?"

"No," said Morcerf, making an effort to rise. "This is nothing but a plot woven against me by my enemies."

Haydee was looking at the door as though she expected someone, and at these words she turned round sharply, and seeing the Count standing there, uttered a fearful cry.

"You do not recognize me!" she cried. "Fortunately I recognize you! You are Fernand Mondego, the French officer who instructed my father's troops. It was you who surrendered the castle of Janina! It was you who, having been sent to Constantinople by my father to treat directly with the Sultan for the life or death of your benefactor, brought back a falsified firman granting full pardon! It was you who obtained with this same firman the Pasha's ring which would secure for you the obedience of Selim, the guardian of the fire! It was you who stabbed Selim! It was you who sold my mother and myself to El Kobbir! Murderer! Murderer! Your master's blood is still on your brow! Look at him, all of you!"

These words were spoken with such vehemence and with such force of truth that every one looked at the Count's forehead, and he himself put his hand up as though he felt Ali's blood still warm upon his forehead.

"You positively recognize Monsieur de Morcerf as this same officer, Fernand Mondego?"

"Do I recognize him?" cried Haydee. "Oh, Mother! You said to me: 'You are free. You had a father whom you loved; you were destined to be almost a queen. Look well at this man who has made you a slave; it is he who has placed your father's head on the pike, it is he who has sold us, it is he who has betrayed us! Look at his right hand with its large scar. If you forget his face, you will recognize this hand into which El Kobbir's gold fell, piece by piece!' Oh, yes, I know him! Let him tell you himself whether he does not recognize me now!"

Each word cut Morcerf like a knife, and broke down his determination. At the last words he instinctively hid his hand in his bosom, for as a matter of fact it bore the mark of a wound, and once more he sank back into his chair.

This scene had set the opinions of the assembly in a veritable turmoil, like leaves torn from their branches by the violence of a north wind.

"Do not lose courage, Count," said the President. "The justice of this court, like that of God, is supreme and equal to all; it will not permit you to be crushed by your enemies without giving you the means of defending yourself. Do you wish to have further investigations made? Do you wish me to send two members of the Chamber to Janina? Speak!"

Morcerf made no reply.

All the members of the Committee looked at one another in horror. They knew the Count's energetic and violent temper, and realized it must have needed a terrible blow to break down this man's defence; they could but think that this sleeplike silence would be followed by an awakening resembling thunder in its force.

"What have you decided?" the President asked.

"Nothing," said the Count, in a toneless voice.

"Then Ali Tebelin's daughter has spoken the truth? She is indeed the dreaded witness in face of whose evidence the guilty one dares not answer: 'Not guilty?' You have actually committed the crimes of which she accuses you?"

The Count cast around him a look of despair such as would have elicited mercy from a tiger, but it could not disarm his judges; then he raised his eyes toward the roof but instantly turned them away again, as though fearful lest it should open and he should find himself before that other tribunal they call Heaven, and face to face with that other judge whom they call God. He tore at the buttons that fastened the coat which was choking him and walked out of the room like one demented. For an instant his weary steps echoed dolefully, but the sound was soon followed by the rattling of his carriage wheels as he was borne away at a gallop.

"Messieurs," said the President when silence was restored, "is the Count of Morcerf guilty of felony, treason, and dishonour?"

"Yes," was the unanimous reply of all the members.

Haydee was present to the end of the meeting; she heard the verdict passed on the Count, but neither pity nor joy was depicted on her features. Covering her face with her veil, she bowed to the councillors and left the room with queenly tread.

## CHAPTER LV

## THE CHALLENGE

ALBERT was resolved to kill the unknown person who had struck this blow at his father. He had discovered that Danglars was making inquiries through his correspondents concerning the surrender of the castle of Janina, and he now proposed to his friend Beauchamp to accompany him to an interview with the banker, since, in his view, it was unfitting that such a solemn occasion should be unmarked by the presence of a witness.

When they reached Danglar's house they perceived the phaeton and the servant of M. Andrea Cavalcanti at the door.

"Ah, that is all the better," said Albert grimly. "If Monsieur Danglars will not fight with me, I will kill his son-in-law. A Cavalcanti should not shirk a duel."

The young man was announced, but, on hearing Albert's name, the banker, cognizant of what had taken place the previous evening, refused to see him. It was too late, however; he had followed the footman and, hearing the instructions given, pushed open the door and entered the room, followed by Beauchamp.

"Pray, monsieur, is one not at liberty to receive whom one

chooses?" cried the banker. "You appear to have forgotten yourself sadly."

"No, monsieur," said Albert coldly; "there are certain circumstances, such as the present one, when one is compelled to be at home to certain persons, at least if one is not a coward—I offer you that refuge."

"Then what do you want of me?"

"All I want of you," said Albert, going up to him and pretending not to notice Cavalcanti, who was standing with his back to the fireplace, "is to propose a meeting in some secluded spot where we shall not be disturbed for ten minutes; where, of the two men who meet, one will be left under the leaves."

Danglars turned pale. Cavalcanti took a step forward. Albert turned round to the young man and said:

"Oh, certainly! Come too, if you wish, Count. You have a right to be present since you are almost one of the family. I am willing to give this kind of appointment to as many as will accept."

Cavalcanti looked with a stupefied air at Danglars, who rose with an effort and stepped between the two men. This attack on Cavalcanti led him to hope that Albert's visit was due to a different reason from the one he had at first supposed.

"If you have come here, monsieur," said he to Albert, "to pick a quarrel with this gentleman because I preferred him to you, I shall bring the matter before the court."

"You are under a misapprehension, monsieur," said Morcerf with a grim smile. "The appointment I ask for has nothing at all to do with matrimony. I merely addressed Monsieur Cavalcanti, because, for a moment, he appeared inclined to interfere in our discussion."

"I warn you, monsieur, that when I have the misfortune to meet a mad dog, I kill it," said Danglars, white with fear and rage, "and far from thinking myself guilty of a crime, I should consider I had rendered a service to society. Therefore, if you are mad and try to bite me, I shall kill you without mercy. Is it my fault that your father is dishonoured?"

"Yes, it is your fault, you scoundrel," replied Morcerf.

"My fault! Mine?" cried Danglars. "You are mad! Do I know anything about the history of Greece? Have I travelled in those parts? Was it upon my advice that your father sold the castle of Janina and betrayed . . ."

"Silence!" roared Albert. "You did not bring this calamity on us directly, but you hypocritically led up to it. Who wrote to Janina for information concerning my father?"

"It seems to me that anyone and every one can write to Janina."

"Nevertheless, only one person wrote, and you were that person."

"I certainly wrote. If a man's daughter is about to marry a young man, it is surely permissible for him to make inquiries about the young man's family. It is not only a right, it is a duty."

"You wrote knowing full well what answer you would receive," said Albert.

"I assure you," cried Danglars with a confidence and security which emanated perhaps less from fear than from his feeling for the unhappy young man. "I solemnly declare that I should never have thought of writing to Janina. What do I know of Ali Pasha's adversities?"

"Then some one persuaded you to write?"

"Certainly. I was speaking about your father's past history to some one and mentioned that the source of his wealth was still a mystery. He asked where your father had made his fortune. I replied: 'In Greece.' So he said: 'Well, write to Janina.'"

"Who gave you this advice?"

"Why, none other than your friend, the Count of Monte Cristo. Would you like to see the correspondence? I can show it you."

"Does the Count of Monte Cristo know what answer you received?"

"Yes, I showed it him."

"Did he know that my father's Christian name was Fernand, and his family name Mondego?"

"Yes, I told him a long time ago. After all, I have not done more than anyone else would have done in my place, perhaps less. The day after I received the answer, your father, acting on Monte Cristo's advice, asked me officially for my daughter's hand for you. I refused him definitely, but without giving any reason. In what way does the honour or dishonour of Monsieur de Morcerf concern me?"

Albert felt the flush rise to his cheeks. There was no doubt that Danglars was defending himself with the baseness, but at the same time with the assurance of a man speaking at any rate the partial truth, not for conscience' sake, it is true, but through fear. Besides, what did Morcerf seek? It certainly was not to know whether Danglars or Monte Cristo was more to blame. What he sought was a man who would acknowledge the charge, whether venial or grave, a man who would fight, and it was evident that Danglars would not do so.

Then many a detail forgotten or unobserved presented itself to his mind. Monte Cristo knew all since he had bought Ali Pasha's daughter, yet, knowing all, he had advised Danglars to write to Janina. After the answer had been received, he had yielded to Albert's desire to be introduced to Haydee; he had allowed the conversation to turn on the death of Ali, and had not opposed the recital of her story (doubtless after giving her instructions in the few Romaic sentences he spoke, not to let Morcerf recognize his father); besides, had he not begged Morcerf not to mention his father's name before Haydee? There could be no doubt that it was all a premeditated plan and that Monte Cristo was in league with his father's enemies.

Albert took Beauchamp aside and expounded these views to him.

"You are right," his friend said. "In all that has happened Monsieur Danglars has only done the dirty work. You must demand satisfaction of Monsieur de Monte Cristo."

Albert turned to Danglars with the words: "You must understand, monsieur, I am not taking definite leave of you. I must first ascertain from the Count of Monte Cristo that your accusations against him are justified."

Bowing to the banker, he went out with Beauchamp, without taking any further notice of Cavalcanti. Danglars accompanied them to the door, renewing his assurance that he had not been actuated by any motive of personal hatred against the Count of Morcerf.

## CHAPTER LVI

## THE INSULT

They drove to No. 30, Avenue des Champs-Élysées, but the Count was in his bath and could not see anyone. Albert ascertained from Baptistin, however, that he would be going to the Opera that evening.

Retracing his steps, he said to Beauchamp: "If you have anything to do, Beauchamp, do it at once. I count upon you to go to the Opera with me this evening and if you can bring Château-Renaud with you, do so."

On his return home, Albert sent a message to Franz, Debray, and Morrel that he would like to see them at the Opera that evening. Then he went to his mother, who, since the events of the previous evening, had kept her room and refused to see anyone. He found her in bed overwhelmed with grief at their public humiliation. On seeing Albert, she clasped his hand and burst into tears. For a moment he stood silently looking on. It was evident from his pale face and knit brows that his determination for revenge was gaining in force.

"Mother, do you know whether Monsieur de Morcerf has any enemies?" Albert asked.

Mercédès started; she noticed the young man did not say 'my father.'

"My son," she replied, "people in the Count's position always have many secret enemies. Furthermore, the enemies one is cognizant of are not always the most dangerous."

"I know that, and for that reason, I appeal to your perspicacity. You are so observant that nothing escapes you. You remarked, for instance, that at the ball we gave Monsieur de Monte Cristo refused to partake of anything in our house."

Mercédès raised herself on her arm. "What has Monte Cristo to do with the question you asked me?"

"You know, Mother, Monsieur de Monte Cristo is almost an Oriental, and in order to reserve for themselves the liberty of revenge, Orientals never eat or drink in the house of an enemy."

"Do you wish to imply that Monte Cristo is our enemy, Albert?" cried Mercédès. "Who told you so? Why, you are mad, Albert! Monsieur de Monte Cristo has only shown us kindness. He saved your life and you yourself presented him to us. Oh, I entreat you, my son, if you entertain such an idea, dispel it, and I advise you, nay I beg of you, to keep on good terms with him."

"Mother, you have some reason for wishing me to be friendly with this man," replied the young man with a black look.

"I?" said Mercédès.

"Yes, you," replied the young man. "Is it because he has the power to do us some harm?"

Mercédès shuddered, and, casting on him a searching glance, said: "You speak strangely and appear to have singular prejudices. What has the Count done to you?"

An ironical smile passed over Albert's lips. Mercédès saw it with the double instinct of a woman and a mother and guessed all, but, being prudent and strong, she hid both her sorrows and her fears.

Albert dropped the conversation, but after a moment or two the Countess resumed:

"You inquired just now after my health. I will tell you frankly that I do not feel at all well. Stay with me and keep me company. I do not wish to be alone."

"Mother, you know how happy I should be to comply with your wishes, but important and urgent business compels me to be away from you the whole evening."

"Very well," replied Mercédès, with a sigh. "Go, Albert. I will not make you a slave to your filial affection."

Albert feigned not to hear; he took leave of his mother and went to his room to dress. At ten minutes to eight Beauchamp appeared; he had seen Château-Renaud, who promised to be at the Opera before the curtain rose. The two men got into Albert's brougham, and, having no reason to hide whither he was going, Albert said in a loud voice: "To the Opera!"

It was not until the end of the second act that Albert sought Monte Cristo in his box. The Count, whose companion was Maximilian Morrel, had been watching the young man all the evening, so that when he turned round on hearing his door open, he was quite prepared to see Albert before him, accompanied by Beauchamp and Château-Renaud.

"A welcome visit!" said the Count, with that cordiality which distinguished his form of salutation from the ordinary civilities of the social world. "So you have reached your goal at last! Good evening, Monsieur de Morcerf."

"We have not come here to exchange banalities or to make false professions of friendship," returned Albert. "We have come to demand an explanation of you, Count."

The quivering voice of the young man was scarcely louder than a whisper.

"An explanation at the Opera?" said the Count, with the calm tone and penetrating look which characterize the man who has complete confidence in himself. "Unfamiliar as I am with the customs of Paris, I should not have thought this was the place to demand an explanation."

"Nevertheless, when people shut themselves up and will not be seen, on the pretext that they are in the bath, we must not miss the opportunity when we happen to meet them elsewhere."

"I am not difficult of access, monsieur," said Monte Cristo. "If I mistake not, it was but yesterday that you saw me in my house."

"Yesterday I was at your house, monsieur, because I knew not who you were."

Albert had raised his voice to such a pitch when saying these last words that every one in the adjoining boxes and in the corridors heard him.

"Where have you come from, monsieur?" said Monte Cristo, outwardly quite calm. "You do not appear to be in your right senses."

"So long as I understand your perfidies and make you realize that I will be revenged, I am reasonable enough," said Albert in a fury.

"I do not understand you, and even if I did, there is no reason for you to speak in such a loud voice. I am at home here, and I alone have the right to raise my voice. Leave the box, Monsieur de Morcerf!" said the Count of Monte Cristo, as he pointed toward the door with an admirable gesture of command.

Albert understood the allusion to his name in a moment, and was about to throw his glove in the Count's face when Morrel seized his hand. Leaning forward in his chair, Monte Cristo stretched out his hand and took the young man's glove, saying in a terrible voice:

"I consider your glove as having been thrown, monsieur, and I will return it wrapt round a bullet. Now leave me, or I shall call my servants to throw you out!"

Utterly beside himself with anger, and with wild and bloodshot eyes, Albert stepped back; Morrel seized the opportunity to shut the door. Monte Cristo took up his glasses again as though nothing out of the ordinary had happened. The man had, indeed, a heart of iron and a face of marble.

"How have you offended him?" whispered Morrel.

"I? I have not offended him—at least not personally."

"But there must be some reason for this strange scene."

"The Count of Morcerf's adventures have exasperated the young man."

"What shall you do about it?"

"What shall I do? As true as you are here I shall have killed him before the clock strikes ten to-morrow morning. That is what I shall do."

Morrel took the Count's hands in his; they were so cold and steady that they sent a shudder through him.

"Ah, Count," said he, "his father loves him so."

"Tell me not such things!" cried Monte Cristo, with the first signs of anger that he had yet shown. "I would make him suffer!"

Morrel let Monte Cristo's hand fall in amazement.

"Count! Count!" said he.

"My dear Maximilian," interrupted the Count, "listen to the charming manner in which Duprez sings this line:

"Matilda! idol of my heart!

"I was the first to discover Duprez at Naples and the first to applaud him. Bravo! Bravo!"

Morrel saw it was useless to say anything more. The curtain, which had been raised at the conclusion of the scene with Albert, was dropped once more, and a knock was heard at the door.

"Come in," said Monte Cristo, in a voice devoid of all emotion.

Beauchamp entered.

"Good evening, Monsieur Beauchamp," said Monte Cristo, as though this was the first time he had seen the journalist that evening. "Pray be seated."

Beauchamp bowed, and, taking a seat, said: "As you saw, monsieur, I accompanied Monsieur de Morcerf just now."

"Which in all probability means that you had dined together," replied Monte Cristo, laughing. "I am glad to see you are more sober than he was."

"I will own that Albert was wrong in losing his temper, monsieur," said Beauchamp, "and I have come on my own account to apologize for him. Now that I have made my apologies, mine you understand, I should like to add that I consider you too gentlemanly to refuse me some explanation on the subject of your connexion with the people of Janina; then, Count . . ."

"Monsieur Beauchamp," interrupted this extraordinary man, "the Count of Monte Cristo is responsible only to the Count of Monte Cristo. Therefore not a word on this subject, if you please. I do as I please, Monsieur Beauchamp, and believe me, what I do is always well done."

"Honest men are not to be paid with such coin, Count. You must give honourable guarantees."

"I am a living guarantee, monsieur," replied the Count, unmoved, but with a threatening look in his eyes. "Both of us have blood in our veins that we are anxious to shed, and that is our mutual guarantee. Deliver this answer to the Viscount, and tell him that before ten o'clock to-morrow I shall have seen the colour of his blood."

"Then all that remains for me to do is to make the necessary arrangements for the duel," said Beauchamp.

"I am quite indifferent on that score," replied the Count of Monte Cristo. "It was unnecessary to disturb me in the middle of an opera for such a trifling matter. Tell the Viscount that, although I am the one insulted, I will give him the choice of arms and will accept everything without discussion or dispute. Do you understand me? Everything, even combat by drawing lots, which is always very stupid. With me it is different, I am sure of winning."

"Sure of winning?" said Beauchamp, looking at the Count in amazement.

"Certainly," said the Count, slightly shrugging his shoulders. "Otherwise I should not fight with Monsieur de Morcerf. I shall kill him; I cannot help myself. Send me word this evening to my house, indicating the weapon and the hour. I do not like to be kept waiting."

"Pistols the weapon, eight o'clock the hour in the Bois de Vincennes," said Beauchamp somewhat disconcerted, for he could not make up his mind whether he had to deal with an arrogant *braggadocio* or a supernatural being.

"Very well," said Monte Cristo. "Now that is all arranged, pray let me listen to the opera and tell your friend Albert not to return this evening. Tell him to go home and sleep."

Beauchamp left the box perfectly amazed.

"Now," said Monte Cristo, turning toward Morrel. "I may reckon on you, may I not? The young man is acting blindfolded and knows not the true cause of this duel, which is known only to God and to me; but I give you my word, Morrel, that God, Who knows it, will be on our side."

"Enough," said Morrel. "Who is your second witness?"

"I do not know anyone in Paris on whom I could confer the honour except you, Morrel, and your brother-in-law. Do you think Emmanuel will render me this service?"

"I can answer for him as for myself, Count."

"Very well, that is all I require. You will be with me at seven o'clock in the morning?"

"We shall be there."

"Hush! the curtain is rising. Let us listen. I would not lose a note of this opera; the music of *Wilhelm Tell* is charming!"

## CHAPTER LVII

## THE NIGHT

MONTE CRISTO waited, as he usually did, until Duprez had sung his famous *Follow me,* then he rose and went out, followed by Morrel, who left him at the door, renewing his promise to be at his house, together with Emmanuel, at seven o'clock the next morning. Still calm and smiling, the Count entered his brougham and was home in five minutes. On entering the house, he said to Ali: "Ali, my pistols inlaid with ivory!" and no one who knew him could have mistaken the tone in which he said it.

Ali brought the box to his master, who was beginning to examine them when the study door opened to admit Baptistin. Before the latter could say a word, a veiled woman who was following behind him, and who through the open door caught sight of a pistol in the Count's hand and two swords on the table, rushed into the room. Baptistin cast a bewildered look on his master, but upon a sign from the Count, he went out, shutting the door behind him.

"Who are you, madame?" the Count asked of the veiled woman.

The stranger looked round her to make sure they were alone, then, throwing herself on to one knee and clasping her hands, she cried out in a voice of despair:

"Edmond, you will not kill my son!"

The Count started, and, dropping the weapon he held in his hand, uttered a feeble cry.

"What name did you pronounce then, Madame de Morcerf?" said he.

"Yours!" she cried, throwing back her veil. "Your name, which I alone, perhaps, have not forgotten. Edmond, it is not Madame de Morcerf who has come to you. It is Mercédès."

"Mercédès is dead, madame. I know no one now of that name."

"Mercédès lives, and not only lives, but remembers. She alone recognized you when she saw you, and even without seeing you, Edmond, she knew you by the very tone of your voice. From that moment she has followed your every step, watched you, feared you. She has no need to seek the hand that has dealt Monsieur de Morcerf this blow."

"Fernand, you mean, madame," returned Monte Cristo, with bitter irony. "Since we are recalling names, let us remember them all."

He pronounced the name of Fernand with such an expression of venomous hatred that Mercédès was stricken with fear.

"You see, Edmond, I am not mistaken. I have every reason to say: 'Spare my son!'"

"Who told you, madame, that I have evil designs against your son?"

"No one, but alas! a mother is gifted with double sight. I have guessed everything. I followed him to the opera this evening, and, hiding in another box, I saw all that occurred."

"If you saw everything, madame, you also saw that Fernand's son insulted me in public," said Monte Cristo with terrible calmness. "You must also have seen," he continued, "that he would have thrown his glove in my face but that one of my friends held back his arm."

"Listen to me. My son has discovered your identity; he attributes all his father's misfortune to you."

"Madame, you are under a misapprehension. His father is suffering no misfortune; it is a punishment, and it is not inflicted by me, it is the work of Providence."

"Why should you take the place of Providence? Why should you remember when He forgets? In what way do Janina and the Vizier concern you, Edmond? What wrong has Fernand Mondego done you by betraying Ali Tebelin?"

"As you infer, madame, that is all a matter as between the French officer and Vasiliki's daughter and does not concern me. But if I have sworn to take revenge, it is not on the French officer or on the Count of Morcerf; it is on Fernand, the fisherman, the husband of Mercédès the Catalan."

"What terrible vengeance for a fault for which fate alone is responsible! I am the guilty one, Edmond, and if you take revenge on some one, it should be on me, who lacked the strength to bear your absence and my solitude."

"But do you know why I was absent? Do you know why you were left solitary and alone?"

"Because you were arrested and imprisoned, Edmond."

"Why was I arrested? Why was I imprisoned?"

"I know not," said Mercédès.

"'Tis true, you do not know; at least, I hope you do not. Well then, I will tell you. I was arrested and imprisoned because on the eve of the very day on which I was to be married, a man named Danglars wrote this letter in the arbour of La Réserve, and Fernand, the fisherman, posted it."

Going to a writing-desk, Monte Cristo opened a drawer and took out a discoloured piece of paper and laid it before Mercédès. It was Danglars' letter to the Procureur du Roi which the Count of Monte Cristo had taken from the dossier of Edmond Dantès the day he, disguised as an agent of Messrs Thomson and French, paid M. de Boville the sum of two hundred thousand francs.

Filled with dismay, Mercédès read the following lines:

"The Procureur du Roi is herewith informed by a friend to the throne and to religion that a certain Edmond Dantès, mate on the *Pharaon* which arrived this morning from Smyrna after having touched at Naples and Porto Ferrajo, has been entrusted by Murat with a letter for the usurper and by the usurper with a letter for the Bonapartist party in Paris. Corroboration of this crime can be found either on him, or at his father's house, or in his cabin on board the *Pharaon*."

"Good God!" exclaimed Mercédès, passing her hand across her forehead wet with perspiration. "This letter . . ."

"I bought it for two hundred thousand francs, madame," said Monte Cristo. "But it is cheap at the price since it to-day enables me to justify myself in your eyes."

"What was the result of this letter?"

"You know it, madame. It led to my arrest. But what you do not know is how long my imprisonment lasted. You do not know that I lay in a dungeon of the Château d'If, but a quarter of a league from you, for fourteen long years. On each day of those fourteen years, I renewed the vow of vengeance I had taken the first day, though I was unaware that you had married Fernand, and that my father had died of hunger."

"Merciful heavens!" cried Mercédès, utterly crushed.

"That is what I learned on leaving my prison fourteen years after I had been taken there. I have sworn to revenge myself on Fernand because of the living Mercédès and my deceased father, and revenge myself I will!"

"Are you sure this unhappy Fernand did what you say?"

"On my oath it is so. In any case it is not much more odious than that, being a Frenchman by adoption, he passed over to the English; a Spaniard by birth, he fought against the Spanish; a hireling of Ali's, he betrayed and assassinated Ali. In the face of all this, what is that letter you have just read? The French have not avenged themselves on the traitor, the Spaniards have not shot him, and Ali in his tomb has let him go unpunished; but I, betrayed, assassinated, cast into a tomb, have risen from that tomb by the grace of God, and it is my duty to God to punish this man. He has sent me for that purpose and here I am."

"Then take your revenge, Edmond," cried the heartbroken mother, falling on her knees, "but let your vengeance fall on the culprits, on him, on me, but not on my son!"

"I must have my revenge, Mercédès! For fourteen years have I suffered, for fourteen years wept and cursed, and now I must avenge myself."

"Edmond," continued Mercédès, her arms stretched out toward the Count, "ever since I knew you, I have adored your name, have respected your memory. Oh, my friend, do not compel me to tarnish the noble and pure image that is ever reflected in my heart! If you knew how I have prayed for you, both when I thought you living and later when I believed you dead. Yes, dead, alas! I imagined that your dead body had been laid in its shroud in the depths of some gloomy tower or hurled into the bottom of an abyss where gaolers fling their dead prisoners, and I wept. What else could I do, Edmond, but weep and pray? Every night for ten long years I dreamed the same dream. It was reported you had endeavoured to escape, that you had taken the place of another prisoner; that you had slipped into the winding-sheet of a dead man, that your living body had been flung from the top of the Chateau d'If, and that the scream you gave as you were dashed against the rocks first revealed to the men, now become your murderers, what had taken place. Well, Edmond, I swear to you by the son for whose life I now plead, that every night for ten years I have seen these men swinging a shapeless and indistinguishable object on the top of a rock; every night for ten years have I heard a terrible scream that has awakened me trembling and cold. Oh, believe me, Edmond, guilty as I am, I too have suffered much!"

"Have you seen your father die in your absence?" cried Monte

Cristo, thrusting his hands into his hair. "Have you seen the woman you loved give her hand to your rival while you were pining away in the depths of a dungeon? . . ."

"No, but I have seen him whom I loved about to become my son's murderer!"

Mercédès said these words with such infinite sadness and in such tones of despair that they wrung a sob from the Count's throat. The lion was tamed, the avenger was overcome!

"What do you ask of me?" he said. "Your son's life? Well then, he shall live!"

Mercédès uttered a cry which forced two tears into Monte Cristo's eyes, but they disappeared again immediately; doubtless God had sent some angel to collect them, for they were far more precious in his eyes than the richest pearls of Guzerat or Ophir.

"Oh, Edmond, I thank you!" cried Mercédès, taking the Count's hand and pressing it to her lips. "Now you are the man of my dreams, the man I have always loved! I can own it now."

"It is just as well, for poor Edmond will not have long to enjoy your love," replied Monte Cristo. "Death will return to its tomb, the phantom to darkness!"

"What is that you say, Edmond?"

"I say that since you so command me, I must die!"

"Die! Who said that? Who told you to die? Whence come these strange ideas of death?"

"You cannot suppose I have the least desire to live after I have been publicly insulted, before a theatre full of people, in the presence of your friends and those of your son, challenged by a mere child who will glory in my pardon as in a victory? What I have loved most after you, Mercédès, has been myself, that means to say, my dignity, the force that made me superior to all others. This force was life to me. You have broken it, and I must die!"

"But the duel will not take place, Edmond, since you pardon my son."

"It will take place," said Monte Cristo solemnly, "but it will be my blood instead of your son's that will stain the ground."

Mercédès screamed and rushed up to Monte Cristo, but suddenly she came to a halt.

"Edmond," said she, "I know there is a God above, for you still live and I have seen you. I put my whole trust in Him to help me, and in the meantime I depend upon your word. You said my son would live and you mean it, do you not?"

"Yes, madame, he shall live," said Monte Cristo.

Mercédès held out her hand to him, her eyes filling with tears as she said: "Edmond, how noble it is of you, how great, how sublime to have taken pity on a poor woman who appealed to you without daring to hope for mercy. Alas! I have grown old through sorrow rather than years, and I cannot remind my Edmond by a smile or a look of the Mercédès who has been so many years in his thoughts. Believe me, Edmond, I too have suffered as I said before. Ah, it is sad to see one's life pass without having a single joy to recall, without preserving a single hope. I repeat once more, Edmond, it is noble, beautiful, sublime, to forgive as you have done."

"You say that now, Mercédès, but what would you say if you knew how great is the sacrifice I have made?"

Mercédès looked at the Count with eyes full of admiration and gratitude. Without answering his question she said:

"You see that, though my cheeks have become pale and my eyes dull and I have lost all my beauty, that, though Mercédès is no longer like her former self, her heart has remained the same. Farewell, Edmond, I have nothing more to ask of Heaven; I have seen you, and you are as noble and as great as in the days long past. Farewell, Edmond, farewell, and thank you."

The Count made no reply. Mercédès opened the door, and had disappeared before he had woken from his painful and deep reverie into which his thwarted vengeance had plunged him. The clock on the Invalides struck one as the rumbling of the carriage which bore Mme de Morcerf away brought the Count of Monte Cristo back to realities.

"Fool that I am," said he, "that I did not tear out my heart the day I resolved to revenge myself!"

## CHAPTER LVIII

## THE DUEL

THE night wore on. The Count of Monte Cristo knew not how the hours passed, for his mental tortures could only be compared to those he had suffered when, as Edmond Dantès, he had lain in the dungeon of the Château d'If. History was repeating itself once more, only the external circumstances were changed. Then his plans were frustrated at the eleventh hour through no action on his part; now, just as his schemes for revenge were materializing, he must relinquish them for ever, solely because he had not reckoned with one factor—his love for Mercédès!

At length as the clock struck six he roused himself from his dismal meditations, and made his final preparations before going out to meet his voluntary death. When Morrel and Emmanuel called to accompany him to the ground, he was quite ready, and, outwardly at least, calm. They were the first to arrive, but Franz and Debray soon followed. It was not until ten minutes past eight, however, that they saw Albert coming along on horseback at full gallop, followed by a servant.

"How imprudent to come on horseback when about to fight with pistols! And after all the instructions I gave him!" said Château-Renaud.

"And just look at his collar and tie, his open coat and white waistcoat!" said Beauchamp. "He might just as well have marked the exact position of his heart—it would have been simpler and would have ensured a speedier ending."

In the meantime, Albert had arrived within ten paces of the group of five young men; he pulled up his horse, jumped down, and, throwing the bridle to the servant, walked up to the others. He was pale and his eyes red and swollen; it was easily seen he had not slept all night. There was about his whole demeanour an unaccustomed sadness.

"Thank you, messieurs, for having granted my request!" he said. "Believe me, I am most grateful for this token of friendship." Noticing that Morrel had stepped back as he approached he continued: "Draw nearer, Monsieur Morrel, to you especially are my thanks due!"

"I think you must be unaware that I am Monsieur de Monte Cristo's second," replied Morrel.

"I was not certain, but I thought you were. All the better; the more honourable men there are here, the better pleased shall I be."

"Monsieur Morrel, you may inform the Count of Monte Cristo that Monsieur de Morcerf has arrived," said Château-Renaud. "We are at his service."

"Wait, messieurs, I should like a few words with the Count of Monte Cristo," said Albert.

"In private?" Morrel asked.

"No, before every one."

Albert's seconds looked at one another in surprise. Franz and Debray began whispering to one another, while Morrel, overjoyed at this unexpected incident, went in search of the Count, who was walking with Emmanuel a short distance away.

"What does he want?" asked Monte Cristo.

"I only know that he wishes to speak to you."

"I hope he is not going to tempt me with fresh insults?"

"I do not think that is his intention," was Morrel's reply.

The Count approached, accompanied by Maximilian and Emmanuel, his calm and serene mien forming a strange contrast with the grief-stricken face of Albert, who also advanced toward his adversary. When three paces from each other they stopped. "Messieurs, come nearer," Albert said. "I do not want you to lose a word of what I have to say to the Count of Monte Cristo, for strange as it may seem to you, you must repeat it to all who will listen to you."

"I am all attention, monsieur," said the Count.

"I reproached you, monsieur, with having made known Monsieur de Morcerf's conduct in Epirus," began Albert in a tremulous voice, which became firmer as he went on. "I did not consider you had the right to punish him, however guilty he might be. Yet to-day I know better. It is not Fernand Mondego's treachery towards Ali Pasha that makes me so ready to forgive you, it is the treachery of Fernand the fisherman towards you, and the untold sufferings his conduct has caused you. I therefore say to you, and proclaim it aloud, that you were justified in revenging yourself on my father, and I, his son, thank you for not having done more."

Had a thunderbolt fallen in the midst of his listeners, it would not have astonished them more than did Albert's declaration. Monte Cristo slowly raised his eyes to heaven with an expression of gratitude; he could not comprehend how Albert's proud nature could have submitted to this sudden humiliation. He recognized in it Mercédès' influence, and understood now why the noble woman had not refused the sacrifice which she knew would not be necessary.

"Now, monsieur," continued Albert, "if you consider this apology sufficient, give me your hand. In my opinion the quality of recognizing one's faults ranks next to the rare one of infallibility, which you appear to possess. But this confession concerns me alone. I have acted well in the eyes of man, but you have acted well in the eyes of God. An angel alone could have saved one of us from death, and that angel has appeared, not to make us friends, perhaps, but at least to make us esteem one another."

With moistened eyes and heaving bosom, Monte Cristo extended his hand to Albert, who pressed it with respectful awe as he said: "Messieurs! Monsieur de Monte Cristo accepts my apology. I was guilty of a rash act, but have now made reparation for my fault. I trust the world will not look upon me as a coward because I have followed the dictates of my conscience."

"What has happened?" Beauchamp asked Château-Renaud. "Methinks we make a very sorry figure here."

"In truth, Albert's action is either most despicable or else very noble," replied the Baron.

"What does all this mean?" Debray asked Franz. "The Count of

Monte Cristo brings dishonour on Monsieur de Morcerf, and his son acknowledges that he is justified in doing so. In his place, I should consider myself bound to fight at least ten duels." As for Monte Cristo, his head was bowed, his arms hung listless. He was crushed under the weight of twenty-four years' memories. He was not thinking of Albert, Beauchamp, or Château-Renaud, nor yet of anyone around him; he was thinking of the courageous woman who had come to him to crave her son's life. He had offered her his, and now she had saved it by confessing a terrible family secret, capable of killing for ever the young man's love for her.

## CHAPTER LIX

## REVENGE

THE Count of Monte Cristo bowed to the five young men with a sad smile, and, getting into his carriage, drove away with Maximilian and Emmanuel. Albert stood wrapt in deep and melancholy thought for a few moments, then suddenly loosing his horse from the tree around which his servant had tied the bridle, he sprang lightly into the saddle and returned to Paris at a gallop. A quarter of an hour later he entered his house in the Rue du Helder. As he dismounted from his horse, he thought he saw his father's pale face peeping from behind the curtain of his bedroom. Albert turned away his head with a sigh and went to his own apartments. Once there, he cast a last lingering look at all the luxuries that had made his life so easy and happy from his childhood. He looked once more at the pictures; the faces seemed to smile at him and the landscapes to be animated with brighter colours. Taking from its oak frame the portrait of his mother, he rolled it up, leaving empty and bare the gilt frame that had surrounded it. Then he put all his precious knick-knacks in order; went to the cupboards and placed the key in each door; threw into a drawer of his writing-desk all the money he had about him; gathered together all the countless pieces of jewellery that were lying about in cups, in jewel-cases, and on brackets, and made an exact inventory of all, placing it in a conspicuous place on a table from which he first removed all the books and papers which encumbered it.

While he was in the midst of this work and in spite of the instructions Albert had given that he was not to be disturbed, his servant entered.

"What do you want?" Morcerf asked him in a sad, rather than an annoyed, tone of voice.

"Excuse me, monsieur," said the valet. "I know you forbade me to disturb you, but the Count of Morcerf has sent for me."

"Well?"

"I did not wish to go to him before I had received your instructions."

"Why?"

"Because the Count doubtless knows that I accompanied you to the Bois de Vincennes."

"No doubt."

"And if he asks me what happened, what reply shall I make?"

"Tell the truth."

"Then I am to say that the duel did not take place?"

"Say that I apologized to the Count of Monte Cristo. Go!"

The valet bowed and went out, and Albert returned to his inventory. When he had finished, his thoughts turned to his mother, and as no one was there to announce him, he went straight to her bedroom, but, distressed by what he saw and still more by what he guessed, he paused on the threshold.

As though one mind animated these two beings, Mercédès was doing in her room what Albert had been doing in his. Everything was in disorder; lace, clothing, jewellery, money, all was carefully placed in the drawers, and the Countess was just collecting the keys. Albert saw all these preparations and understood; calling out "Mother!" he threw his arms around her neck. The painter who could have caught the expression on those two faces just then would certainly have made a beautiful picture!

All these signs of a firm decision which gave him no cause for fear where he himself was concerned alarmed him for his mother.

"What are you doing, Mother dear?" he asked.

"What have you been doing?" was her reply.

"Oh, Mother!" cried Albert, almost too overwhelmed to speak. "It does not affect you as it does me. No, you surely cannot have taken the same resolution as I have! I am come to inform you that I am leaving this house . . . and you?"

"I am leaving it, too, Albert," replied Mercédès. "I must confess, I had reckoned on being accompanied by my son. Was I mistaken?"

"Mother, I cannot let you share the life I have chosen. I must live henceforth without name and without fortune; to start my apprenticeship, I must borrow from a friend my daily bread till I can earn it myself. So I am going from here, Mother, to Franz, to ask him to lend me the small sum of money I think will be necessary."

"You are going to suffer hunger, poverty, my son?" exclaimed Mercédès. "Oh, say not so or you will break all my resolution."

"But not mine, Mother dear," replied Albert. "I am young and strong and I think I am brave, and I have also learned since yesterday what force of will means. Alas! Mother, there are those who have suffered so much and yet have not succumbed to their sufferings, but instead have built up a new fortune on the ruins of their former happiness. I have learnt this, Mother, and I have seen such men; I know that they have risen with such vigour and glory from the abyss into which their enemies had cast them that they have overthrown their former conquerors. No, Mother, from to-day I have done with the past, and I will accept nothing from it, not even my name, for you understand, do you not, Mother, that your son could not bear the name of a man who should blush before every other man?"

"Albert, my son, had I been stronger, that is the advice I should have given you," said Mercédès. "Your conscience has spoken to you when my enfeebled voice was still; follow its dictates, my son. You had friends, Albert, break with them, but, for your mother's sake, do not despair. Life still has its charms at your age, for you can barely count the twenty-two summers, and as a noble character such as yours must carry with it a name without blemish, take my father's. It was Herrara. Whatever career you pursue, you will soon make this name illustrious. When you have accomplished this, my son, make your appearance again in a world rendered more beautiful by your past sufferings. But, even though the golden future I foresee for you should not come to pass, let me at least cherish the hope. I have nothing else left to me; for me there is no future, and when I leave this house, I go towards my tomb."

"I shall do as you wish, Mother," the young man said. "Your hopes are mine. God's anger cannot follow us, you who are so noble and I who am so innocent. But since we have taken our resolution, let us act with all speed. Monsieur de Morcerf left the house about an hour ago. The opportunity is therefore propitious, and we shall be relieved of the necessity of giving any explanations."

"I am ready," said Mercédès.

Albert ran into the boulevard for a cab to take them away. He thought of a nice little furnished house in the Rue des Saints-Pères where his mother would find a humble, but comfortable lodging. As the cab drew up at the door and Albert alighted, a man approached and handed him a letter. Albert recognized the Count of Monte Cristo's steward.

"From the Count," said Bertuccio.

Albert took the letter and read it; then, with tears in his eyes and his breast heaving with emotion, he went in to find Mercédès and handed it to her without a word.

Mercédès read:

ALBERT,

While showing you that I have discovered the plans you are contemplating, I hope to prove to you also that I have a sense of what is right. You are free, you are leaving the Count's house, taking with you your mother. But remember, Albert, you owe her more than your poor noble heart can give her. Keep the struggle to yourself, bear all the suffering alone and save her the misery that must inevitably accompany your first efforts, for she has not deserved even one fraction of the misfortune that has this day befallen her.

I know you are both leaving the Rue du Helder without taking anything with you. Do not try to discover how I know it; it is enough that I do know it.

Listen, Albert, to what I have to say. Twenty-four years ago, I returned to my country a proud and happy man. I had a sweetheart, Albert, a noble young girl whom I adored, and I was bringing to her a hundred and fifty louis which I had painfully amassed by ceaseless toil. This money was for her, and, knowing how treacherous the sea is, I buried the treasure in the little garden behind the house in Marseilles which your mother knows so well.

Recently I passed through Marseilles on my way from Paris. I went to see this house of sad memories. In the evening I took a spade and dug in the corner where I had buried my treasure. The iron chest was still in the same place: no one had touched it. It is in the corner that is shaded by a beautiful fig tree my father planted on the day of my birth.

By a strange and sad coincidence this money, which was to have contributed to the comfort of the woman I adored, will to-day serve the same purpose. Oh! understand well my meaning. You are a generous man, Albert, but maybe you are blinded by pride or resentment. If you refuse me, if you ask another for what I have the right to offer you, I can but say it is ungenerous of you to refuse what is offered to your mother by one whose father was made to suffer the horrors of hunger and despair by your father.

Albert waited in silence for his mother's decision after she had finished reading the letter.

"I accept," said she. "He has the right to pay the dowry I shall take with me to the convent."

Placing the letter against her heart, she took her son's arm and went down the stairs with a step that surprised her by its firmness.

Meanwhile Monte Cristo had also returned to town with Emmanuel and Maximilian, and was sitting wrapt in thought when the door suddenly opened. The Count frowned.

"Monsieur le Comte de Morcerf," announced Baptistin, as though this name was excuse enough for his admittance.

"Ask Monsieur de Morcerf into the salon."

When Monte Cristo joined the General, he was pacing the length of the floor for the third time.

"Ah, it is really you, Monsieur de Morcerf," said Monte Cristo calmly. "I thought I had not heard aright."

"Yes, it is I," said the Count, with a frightful contraction of the lips which prevented him from articulating clearly.

"I only require to know now to what I owe the pleasure of seeing the Count of Morcerf at such an early hour," continued Monte Cristo.

"You had a meeting with my son this morning, monsieur?"

"You knew about it?"

"I also know that my son had very good reason to fight you and to do his utmost to kill you."

"He had, but you see that, notwithstanding these reasons, he did not kill me; in fact he did not fight."

"Yet he looked upon you as the cause of his father's dishonour and the terrible calamity that has now befallen my house."

"That is true, monsieur," said Monte Cristo, with dreadful calmness; "the secondary cause, but not the principal one."

"No doubt you made some sort of apology or gave some explanation?"

"I gave him no explanation, and it was he who apologized."

"But to what do you attribute such conduct?"

"To conviction; probably he discovered there was one more guilty than I."

"Who is that man?"

"His father!"

"That may be," said the Count, "but you know the guilty do not like to hear themselves convicted of their guilt."

"I know, and I expected all this."

"You expected my son to be a coward?" cried the Count.

"Monsieur Albert de Morcerf is not a coward!" said Monte Cristo.

"A man who holds a sword in his hand, with an enemy within reach of it, is a coward if he does not strike. Ah, that he were here that I might tell him so!"

"I presume you have not come here to tell me your little family affairs," replied Monte Cristo coldly. "Go and say that to Monsieur Albert, perhaps he will know what answer to give you."

"No, no, I have not come for that!" replied the General, with a smile which disappeared immediately. "I came to tell you that I, too, look upon you as my enemy. I have come to tell you that I instinctively hate you, that I seem to have known and hated you always! As the young men of this generation no longer fight, it is for us to do so. Are you of this opinion?"

"Certainly. But let me tell you that when I said I was expecting this, I was referring to your visit."

"All the better. Your preparations are made?"

"I am always ready, monsieur."

"You understand that we shall fight till one of us drops?" said the General, clenching his teeth in rage.

"Till one of us drops," repeated the Count of Monte Cristo, slowly nodding his head.

"Let us go, then; we have no need of seconds."

"Indeed, it were useless," replied Monte Cristo. "We know each other so well."

"On the contrary, it is because we do not know each other."

"Bah!" said Monte Cristo, with the same exasperating coolness. "Are you not the soldier Fernand who deserted on the eve of the battle of Waterloo? Are you not the Lieutenant Fernand who served the French army as guide and spy in Spain? Are you not the Colonel Fernand who betrayed, sold, and assassinated his benefactor, Ali? And have not all these Fernands combined made Lieutenant-General Count of Morcerf, Peer of France?"

"Villain! to reproach me with my shame when you are perhaps about to kill me!" cried the General, as though struck by a red-hot iron. "I did not say I was unknown to you. I know well that, demon that you are, you have penetrated the obscurity of my past and have read, by the light of what torch I know not, every page of my life. But perhaps there is more honour in my shame than in all your outward pomp. No, no, I am known to you, but I do not know you, adventurer sewn up in gold and precious stones! In Paris you call yourself the Count of Monte Cristo, in Italy Sinbad the Sailor, in Malta—who knows? I have forgotten. It is your real name I now ask and wish to know, so that I may pronounce it in the field when I plunge my sword into your heart."

The Count of Monte Cristo turned a ghastly colour; his wild eyes were burning with a devouring flame; he bounded into the adjoining room, and, within a second, tearing off his tie, his coat , and his waistcoat, had put on a small sailor's blouse and a sailor's hat, from under which his long black hair flowed.

He returned thus attired, and, with his arms crossed, walked up to the General, who had wondered at his sudden disappearance. On seeing him again his teeth chattered, his legs gave way under him, and he stepped back until he found a table against which to lay his clenched hand for support.

"Fernand!" cried Monte Cristo, "I need but mention one of my many names to strike terror into your heart. But you guess this name, or rather you remember it, do you not? For, in spite of all my grief and tortures, I show you to-day a face made young by the joy of vengeance, a face that you must often have seen in your dreams since your marriage with—Mercédès."

With head thrown back and hands stretched out, the General stared at this terrible apparition in silence; then, leaning against the wall for support, he glided slowly along it to the door through which he went out backward, uttering but the one distressing and piercing cry: "Edmond Dantès!"

With a moan that can be compared with no human sound, he dragged himself to the yard, staggering like a drunken man, and fell into his valet's arms. "Home! home!" he muttered.

The fresh air and the shame he felt at having given way before his servant made him pull himself together, but the drive was a short one, and the nearer he got to his house the greater was his anguish.

A few paces from his door, the carriage stopped, and the Count alighted. The door of the house was wide open; a cab, whose driver looked his surprise at being called to this magnificent residence, was stationed in the middle of the yard. The Count looked at it in terror, and, not daring to question anyone, fled to his room.

Two people were coming down the staircase, and he had only just time to hide himself in a room near by. It was Mercédès, leaning on her son's arm. They were both leaving the house. They passed quite close to the unhappy man, who, hidden behind a door-curtain, felt Mercédès' silk dress brush past him and the warm breath of his son on his face, as he said:

"Have courage, Mother! Come away, this is no longer our home."

The words died away and the steps were lost in the distance. The General drew himself up, clinging to the curtains with clenched hands, and the most terrible sob escaped him that ever came from the bosom of a father abandoned at the same time by his wife and his son.

Soon he heard the door of the cab closed and the voice of the coachman, followed by the rumbling of the lumbersome vehicle as it shook the window-panes. He rushed into his bedroom to see once more all that he had loved on earth; the cab passed, and neither Mercédès' nor Albert's heads appeared at the door to take a last farewell of the deserted house, or to cast on the abandoned husband and father a last look of farewell and regret.

At the very moment when the wheels of that cab passed under the arched gate, a report was heard, and dark smoke issued through the glass of the bedroom window, which had been broken by the force of the explosion.

## CHAPTER LX

## VALENTINE

ON leaving Monte Cristo, Morrel walked slowly toward Villefort's house. Noirtier and Valentine had allowed him two visits a week, and he was now going to take advantage of his rights. Valentine was waiting for him. Almost beside herself with anxiety, she seized his hand and led him to her grandfather. She had heard of the affair at the Opera and its consequences, and, with her woman's instinct, had guessed that Morrel would be Monte Cristo's second, and, knowing the young man's courage and his affection for the Count, she feared he would not be satisfied with the impassive part assigned to him.

One can understand with what eagerness all details were asked, given, and received, and the expression of indescribable joy that appeared in Valentine's eyes when she learned the happy issue of the terrible affair.

"Now, let us speak of our own affairs," said Valentine, making a sign to Morrel to take a seat beside her grandfather while she sat on a hassock at his feet. "You know Grandpapa wants to leave this house? Do you know what reason he has given?"

Noirtier looked at his granddaughter to impose silence on her, but she was not looking at him; her eyes and smiles were all for Morrel.

"Whatever the reason may be that Monsieur Noirtier has given, I am sure it is a good one!" exclaimed Maximilian.

"He pretends that the air of the Faubourg Saint-Honoré does not suit me!"

"Monsieur Noirtier may be right too," said Morrel. "You have not looked at all well for the past fortnight."

"Perhaps not," replied Valentine, "but my grandfather has become my physician, and, as he knows everything, I have the greatest confidence that he will soon cure me."

"Then you are really ill, Valentine?" Morrel asked anxiously.

"Oh, not really ill; I only feel a little unwell, nothing more."

Noirtier did not let one of Valentine's words escape him.

"What treatment are you following for this strange illness?"

"A very simple one," said Valentine. "Every morning I take a spoonful of my grandfather's medicine; that is, I commenced with one spoonful, but now I take four. Grandfather says it is a panacea."

Valentine smiled, yet her smile was a sad one. Maximilian looked at her in silence, but his eyes looked his love. She was very beautiful, but her paleness had become more marked, her eyes shone more brilliantly than usual, and her hands, which were generally of the whiteness of mother-of-pearl, now resembled wax turned yellow with age.

"But I thought this medicine was made up especially for Monsieur Noirtier?" said Morrel.

"I know it is, and it is very bitter," replied Valentine. "Everything I drink afterwards seems to have the same taste."

Noirtier looked at his granddaughter questioningly.

"Yes, Grandpapa, it is so," she replied. "Just now before coming to you I drank some sugared water; it tasted so bitter that I left half of it."

Noirtier made a sign that he wished to say something. Valentine at once got up to fetch the dictionary, her grandfather following her all the while with visible anguish. As a matter of fact, the blood was rushing to the girl's head, and her cheeks became red.

"Well, this is singular," she said, without losing any of her gaiety. "I have become giddy again. It is the sun shining in my eyes." And she leaned against the window.

"There is no sun," replied Morrel, more concerned by the expression on Noirtier's face than by Valentine's indisposition. He ran toward her.

"Do not be alarmed," she said with a smile. "It is nothing and has already passed. But listen! Do I not hear a carriage in the courtyard?" She opened Noirtier's door, ran to a window in the passage and returned quickly.

"Yes," she said. "It is Madame Danglars and her daughter, who have come to call on us. Good-bye, I must run away, otherwise they will come to look for me here. Stay with Grandpapa, Max. I promise you to come back very soon."

With that she ran out, but she had scarcely gone down three stairs when a cloud passed before her eyes, her legs became stiff, her hands lost the power of holding the baluster, and she rolled down to the bottom.

Morrel started up, and, opening the door, found Valentine stretched out on the landing. Quick as lightning he picked her up in his arms, and, carrying her back into the room, seated her on a chair. Valentine opened her eyes and looked round her. She saw the deepest terror depicted on her grandfather's features, and, trying to smile, said: "Do not be alarmed, Grandpapa. It is nothing at all. I only went giddy."

"Giddy again!" exclaimed Morrel alarmed. "I beg of you, Valentine, take care of yourself."

"But it has passed now, and I am quite myself again. Now let me give you some news. Eugénie Danglars is going to be married in a week and in three days her mother is going to give a sort of betrothal festival. We are all invited, my father, Madame de Villefort, and myself—at least I understand so."

"When will it be our turn to think of these things? Oh, Valentine, you can do so much with your grandfather. Try to persuade him to say it will be soon! Do something quickly. So long as you are not really mine, I am always afraid I may lose you."

"Really, Maximilian, you are too timid for an officer, a soldier who, they say, knows not what fear is," said Valentine with a spasmodic movement of pain, and she burst into harsh, painful laughter. Her arms stiffened, her head fell back on her chair, and she remained motionless.

The cry of terror which was imprisoned in Noirtier's throat found expression in his eyes. Morrel understood he was to call for help. The young man pulled at the bell; the maid, who was in Valentine's room, and the servant who had taken Barrois's place came rushing in immediately.

Valentine was so cold, pale, and inanimate that the fear that prevailed in this accursed house took possession of them, and they flew out of the room shouting for help. At the same moment, Villefort's voice was heard calling from his study: "What is the matter?"

Morrel looked questioningly at Noirtier, who had now regained his composure, and indicated by a look the little room where Morrel had already taken refuge on a similar occasion. He was only just in time, for Villefort's footsteps were heard approaching. He rushed into the room, ran up to Valentine and took her in his arms for an instant, calling out the while: "A doctor! Monsieur d'Avrigny! No, I will go for him myself," and he flew out of the room.

Morrel went out by the other door. A dreadful recollection chilled his heart; the conversation between Villefort and the doctor which he had overheard the night Mme de Saint-Méran died came back to his mind. These were the same symptoms, though less acute, that had preceded Barrois's death. On the other hand Monte Cristo's words seemed to resound in his ears: "If you have need of anything, Morrel, come to me. I can do much," and, quicker than thought, he sped from the Faubourg Saint-Honoré to the Champs Élysées.

In the meantime, Villefort arrived at the doctor's house in a hired cabriolet, and rang the bell so violently that the porter became quite alarmed and hastened to open the door. Without saying a word, Villefort ran up the stairs. The porter knew him and let him pass, calling after him: "In his study, monsieur, in his study!" Villefort pushed open the door.

"Doctor," cried Villefort, shutting the door behind him, "there is a curse on my house!"

"What!" cried d'Avrigny, outwardly calm though inwardly deeply moved. "Is there some one ill again?"

"Yes, Doctor," said Villefort, clutching at his hair.

D'Avrigny's look said: "I told you so," but his lips slowly articulated the words: "Who is dying in your house now? What new victim is going to accuse us of weakness before God?"

A painful sob broke from Villefort's lips. He went up to the doctor and, seizing his arm, said: "Valentine! It is Valentine's turn!"

"Your daughter!" cried the doctor with grief and surprise.

"You see you were mistaken," said the magistrate. "Come and see her on her bed of torture and ask her for forgiveness for having harboured suspicion against her."

"Each time you have summoned me, it has been too late," said d'Avrigny. "No matter, I will come. But let us hasten. You have no time to lose in fighting against your enemies."

"Oh, this time you shall not reproach me with weakness, Doctor. This time I shall seek out the murderer and give him his deserts."

"Let us try to save the victim before thinking of vengeance," said d'Avrigny. The cabriolet which had brought Villefort took them both back at a gallop just as Morrel knocked at the Count of Monte Cristo's door.

The Count was in his study, and, with a worried look, was reading a note Bertuccio had just brought him. On hearing Morrel, who had left him barely two hours before, announced, he raised his head. Doubtless the last two hours had held much for him as well as for the Count, for, whereas he had left him with a smile on his face, he now returned with a troubled mien.

"What is the matter, Maximilian?" the Count asked. "You are quite white, and the perspiration is rolling down your forehead."

"I need your help, or rather, fool that I am, I thought you could help me where God alone can help!"

"In any case tell me what it is."

"I really do not know whether I should reveal this secret to any human ears, Count, but misfortune urges me to it, necessity constrains me to do so."

Morrel hesitated a moment.

"Do you believe in my affection for you?" said Monte Cristo, taking the young man's hands affectionately in his.

"There, you give me courage, and something tells me here"— Morrel laid his hand on his heart "that I must withhold no secrets from you."

"You are right, Morrel. God speaks to your heart and your heart speaks to you. Tell me what it says."

"Count, will you allow me to send Baptistin to inquire after some one you know?"

"I have placed myself at your service and with me my servants."

"I could not live if I did not know she was better!"

Morrel went out, and, calling Baptistin, said a few words to him in a low voice, whereupon the valet ran to do the young man's errand.

"Well, have you sent him?" said Monte Cristo, when he made his appearance again.

"Yes, and I shall be a little calmer now."

"I am all attention," said the Count, smiling.

"Well, then, I will begin. One evening I was in a certain garden. I was hidden behind a clump of trees so that no one was aware of my presence. Two people passed close to me—allow me to conceal their names for the present. They were talking in a low voice, but I was so interested in all they said that I did not lose a word of their conversation. Some one had just died in the house to which this garden belonged. One of the two persons thus conversing was the owner of the garden, the other was the doctor. The former was confiding his fears and troubles to the latter, for it was the second time in a month that death had dealt such a sudden and unexpected blow in this house."

"What reply did the doctor make?" asked Monte Cristo.

"He replied . . . he replied that it was not a natural death, and that it could only be attributed to . . ."

"To what?"

"To poison."

"Really!" said Monte Cristo with a slight cough, "did you really hear that?"

"Yes, I did, and the doctor added that if a similar case occurred again, he would be compelled to appeal to justice. Well, death knocked a third time, yet neither the master of the house nor the doctor said anything. In all probability it is going to knock for the fourth time. In what way do you think the possession of this secret obliges me to act?"

"My dear friend," said Monte Cristo, "you are telling me something that every one of us knows by heart. Look at me; I have not overheard any confidence, but I know it all as well as you do, and yet I have no scruples. If God's justice has fallen on this house, turn away your face, Maximilian, and let His hand hold sway. God has condemned them, and they must submit to their sentence. Three months ago it was Monsieur de Saint-Méran, two months ago it was Madame de Saint-Méran, to-day it is old Noirtier or young Valentine."

"You knew about it then?" cried Morrel in a paroxysm of terror that made Monte Cristo shudder. "You knew it and said nothing?"

"What is it to me?" replied Monte Cristo, shrugging his shoulders. "Do I know these people? Must I lose the one to save the other? Indeed not, for I have no preference between the guilty one and the victim."

"But I . . . I love her!" cried Morrel piteously.

"You love whom?" exclaimed Monte Cristo, jumping on to his feet and seizing Morrel's hands.

"I love her dearly, madly; I love her so much that I would shed all my blood to save her one tear. I love Valentine de Villefort, whom they are killing, do you hear? I love her, and I beseech you to tell me how I can save her."

Monte Cristo uttered a wild cry, which only those can conceive who have heard the roar of a wounded lion.

Never had Morrel beheld such an expression; never had such a dreadful eye flashed before his face, never had the genius of terror, which he had so often seen either on the field of battle or in the murder-infested nights of Algeria, shed round him such sinister fires! He shrunk back in terror. As for Monte Cristo, he closed his eyes for a moment after this outburst, and, during these few seconds, he restrained the tempestuous heaving of his breast as turbulent and foamy waves sink after a shower under the influence of the sun.

This silence and inward struggle lasted about twenty seconds, and then the Count raised his pale face.

"Behold, my dear friend, how God punishes the most boastful and unfeeling for their indifference in the face of terrible disasters," he said. "I looked on unmoved and curious. I watched this grim tragedy developing, and, like one of those fallen angels, laughed at the evil committed by men under the screen of secrecy. And now my turn has come, and I am bitten by the serpent whose tortuous course I have been watching—bitten to the core."

A groan escaped Morrel's lips.

"Come, come, lamenting will not help us. Be a man, be strong and full of hope, for I am here, I am watching over you. I tell you to hope! Know once and for all that I never lie and never make a mistake. It is but midday and you can be grateful, Morrel, that you have come to me now instead of this evening or to-morrow morning. Listen to what I am going to tell you. It is midday, and, if Valentine is not dead now, she will not die!"

"How can you say that when I left her dying!"

Monte Cristo pressed his hand to his forehead. What was passing through that mind heavy with terrible secrets? What was the angel of

light, or the angel of darkness, saying to that implacable human mind?
God alone knows.

Monte Cristo raised his head once more, and this time his face was
as calm as that of a sleeping child.

"Maximilian, return quietly to your home," he said. "I command
you to do nothing, to take no steps, to let no shadow of sorrow be
seen on your face. I will send you tidings. Go!"

"Count, you frighten me with your calm. Have you any power over
death? Are you more than man? Are you an angel?"

The young man who would shrink from no danger now shrank
from Monte Cristo in unutterable terror. Monte Cristo only looked
at him with a smile mingled with sadness which brought the tears to
Morrel's eyes.

"I can do much, my friend," replied the Count. "Go, I need to be
alone . . ."

Conquered by the prodigious ascendancy Monte Cristo exercised
on all around him, Morrel did not even attempt to resist. He shook
the Count's hand and went out, but waited at the door for Baptistin,
whom he saw running toward him.

In the meantime Villefort and d'Avrigny had made all possible
haste. When they returned Valentine was still unconscious, and the
doctor examined her with the care called for by the circumstances and
in the light of the secret he had discovered. Villefort awaited the result
of the examination, watching every movement of the doctor's eyes
and lips. Noirtier, more eager for a verdict than Villefort himself, was
also waiting, and all in him became alert and sensitive.

At last d'Avrigny slowly said: "She still lives!"

"Still!" cried Villefort. "Oh, Doctor, what a terrible word."

"Yes," said the doctor. "I repeat my words; she is still living, and I
am surprised to find it is so."

"She is saved?" asked her father.

"Since she still lives, she is."

At this moment d'Avrigny met Noirtier's eyes, which sparkled with
such extraordinary joy that he was startled and stood for a moment
motionless, looking at the old man, who, on his part, seemed to anticipate and commend all he did.

The door laid the girl back on her chair; her lips were so pale and
bloodless that they were scarcely outlined against the rest of her pallid face.

"Call Mademoiselle de Villefort's maid, if you please," he said to
Villefort.

Villefort left his daughter's side and himself went in search of the maid.
Directly the door was shut behind him, the doctor approached Noirtier.

"You have something to say to me?" he asked.

The old man blinked expressively.

"To me alone?"

"Yes."

"Very well, I will stay with you."

Villefort returned, followed by the maid, and after them came Mme de Villefort.

"What ails the dear child?" she exclaimed with tears in her eyes, and affecting every proof of maternal love as she went up to Valentine and took her hand.

D'Avrigny continued to watch Noirtier; he saw the eyes of the old man dilate and grow large, his cheeks turn pale, and the perspiration break out on his forehead.

"Ah," said he involuntarily as he followed the direction of Noirtier's eyes and fixed his own gaze on Mme de Villefort, who said: "The poor child would be better in bed. Come and help me, Fanny."

M. d'Avrigny saw an opportunity of being alone with M. Noirtier and nodded his assent, but forbade anyone to give her to eat or drink except what he prescribed. Valentine had returned to consciousness, but her whole frame was so shattered by the attack that she was unable to move and scarcely able to speak. She had the strength, however, to throw a farewell glance to her grandfather, and it seemed almost as though in carrying her away, they were taking away part of himself. D'Avrigny followed the invalid, wrote his prescriptions, and told Villefort to take a cab and go himself to the chemist's, have the prescriptions made up before his eyes, and wait for him in the girl's room. After renewing his instructions that Valentine was not to partake of anything, he returned to Noirtier and carefully closed the doors. Ascertaining that no one was listening, he said: "Come now, you know something about your granddaughter's illness."

"Yes," motioned the old man.

"We have no time to lose. I will question you, and you will answer." Noirtier made a sign that he agreed.

"Did you anticipate the accident that has occurred to Valentine to-day?"

"Yes."

D'Avrigny thought for a moment, then, drawing closer to Noirtier, said: "Forgive me what I am going to say, but no stone must be left unturned in this terrible predicament. You saw Barrois die. Do you know what he died of?"

"Yes," was the reply.

"Do you think he died a natural death?"

Something like a smile showed itself on Noirtier's immovable lips.

"Then the idea occurred to you that Barrois had been poisoned?"

"Yes."

"Do you think the poison was intended for him?"

"No."

"Now do you think that the same hand that struck Barrois in mistake for some one else has to-day struck Valentine?"

"Yes."

"Then she will also succumb to it?" d'Avrigny asked, looking attentively at Noirtier to mark the effect these words would have on him.

"No," he replied with an air of triumph which would have bewildered the cleverest of diviners.

"You hope, then? What do you hope?" said the doctor with surprise.

The old man gave him to understand that he could not answer.

"Ah, yes, it is true," murmured d'Avrigny, and turning to Noirtier again: "You hope that the murderer will grow weary of his attempts?"

"No."

"Then do you hope that the poison will not take effect on Valentine?"

"Yes."

"Then in what way do you think Valentine will escape?"

Noirtier fixed his gaze obstinately on one spot; d'Avrigny followed the direction of his eyes and saw that they were fixed on a bottle containing his medicine.

"Ha, ha," said d'Avrigny, struck by a sudden thought. "You conceived the idea of preparing her system against this poison?"

"Yes."

"By accustoming her to it little by little?"

"Yes, yes, yes!" replied Noirtier, delighted at being understood.

"In fact, you heard me say there was brucine in your medicine, and wished to neutralize the effects of the poison by getting her system accustomed to it?"

Noirtier showed the same triumphant joy.

"And you have achieved it, too!" exclaimed the doctor. "Without this precaution Valentine would have died this day, and no one could have helped her. As it is her system has suffered a violent shock, but this time, at any rate, she will not die."

A supernatural joy shone in the old man's eyes as he raised them to Heaven with an expression of infinite gratitude. Just then Villefort returned.

"Here is what you asked for, Doctor," said he.

"Was this medicine made up before you? It has not left your hands?"

"Just so."

D'Avrigny took the bottle, poured a few drops of its contents into the palm of his hand, and swallowed them.

"It is all right," said he. "Now let us go to Valentine. I shall give my instructions to every one, and you must see that no one disregards them."

At the time that d'Avrigny returned to Valentine's room, accompanied by Villefort, an Italian priest, with dignified gait and a calm but decided manner, rented for his use the house adjoining that inhabited by M. de Villefort. It is not known what was done to induce the former occupiers to move out of it, but it was reported that the foundations were unsafe; however, this did not prevent the new tenant from moving in with his humble furniture at about five o'clock in the afternoon of the same day. The new tenant's name was Signor Giacomo Busoni.

Workmen were summoned at once, and the same night the few passers-by were astonished to find carpenters and masons at work repairing the foundations of this tottering house.

## CHAPTER LXI

## THE SECRET DOOR

VALENTINE was confined to her bed; she was very weak and completely exhausted by the severe attack. During the night her sick brain wove vague and strange ideas and fleeting phantoms, while confused forms passed before her eyes, but in the day-time she was brought back to normal reality by her grandfather's presence. The old man had himself carried into his granddaughter's room every morning and watched over her with paternal care. Villefort would spend an hour or two with his father and child when he returned from the Law Courts. At six o'clock Villefort retired to his study, and at eight o'clock Monsieur d'Avrigny arrived, bringing with him the night draught for his young patient. Then Noirtier was taken back to his room, and a nurse, of the doctor's choice, succeeded them. She did not leave the bedside until ten or eleven o'clock, when Valentine had dropped off to sleep, and gave the keys of the room to M de Villefort, so that no one could enter the room except through that occupied by Mme de Villefort and little Edward.

Morrel called on Noirtier every morning for news of Valentine, and, extraordinary as it seemed, each day found him less anxious. For one thing, though she showed signs of great nervous excitement,

Valentine's improvement was more marked each day; then, again, had not Monte Cristo already told him that if she was not dead in two hours, she would be saved? Four days had elapsed, and she still lived! The nervous excitement we mentioned even pursued Valentine in her sleep, or rather in that state of somnolence which succeeded her waking hours. It was in the silence of the night, when the darkness of the room was relieved by a night-light burning in its alabaster receptacle on the chimneypiece, that she saw the shadows pass which come to the rooms of the sick, fanning their fever with their quivering wings. At one time she would see her stepmother threatening her, at another time Morrel was holding his arms out to her, or again she was visited by beings who were almost strangers to her, such as the Count of Monte Cristo; during these moments of delirium even the furniture appeared to become animated. This lasted until about two or three o'clock, when she fell into a deep sleep from which she did not wake until the morning.

One evening after Villefort, d'Avrigny, and Noirtier had successively left her room, and the nurse, after placing within her reach the draught the doctors had prepared for her, had also retired, carefully locking the door after her, an unexpected incident occurred.

Ten minutes had elapsed since the nurse left. For the past hour Valentine had been a prey to the fever which returned every night, and she gave herself up to the active and monotonous workings of her unruly brain, which repeatedly reproduced the same thoughts and conjured up the same images. The nightlight threw out countless rays, each one assuming some weird shape. All at once Valentine dimly saw the door of the library, which was beside the fireplace in a hollow of the wall, slowly open without making the least sound. At any other time she would have seized the bell-pull to call for help, but nothing astonished her in her present state. She was aware that all the visions that surrounded her were the children of her delirium, for in the morning there was no trace of all these phantoms of the night.

A human figure emerged from behind the door. Valentine had become too familiar with such apparitions to be alarmed; she simply stared, hoping to see Morrel. The figure continued to approach her bed, then it stopped and appeared to listen with great attention. Just then a reflection from the night-light played on the face of her nocturnal visitor. "It is not he," she murmured, and waited, convinced that she was dreaming and that the man would disappear or turn into some other person. She noticed the rapid beating of her pulse, and remembered that the best means of dispelling these importunate visions was to take a drink of the draught which had been prescribed by the doctor to calm these agitations. It was so refreshing that, while allaying the fever, it seemed to cause a reaction of the brain and for a moment she suffered less. She, therefore, reached out her hand for the glass, but as she did so the apparition made two big strides to her bed and came so close to her that she thought she heard his breathing and felt the pressure of his hand. This time the illusion, or rather the reality, surpassed anything she had yet experienced. She began to believe herself fully awake and alive, and the knowledge that she was in full possession of her senses made her shudder.

Then the figure, from whom she could not divert her eyes and who appeared desirous of protecting rather than threatening her, took the glass, went over to the light and looked at the draught as though wishing to test its transparency and purity. But this elementary test did not satisfy him, and the man, or rather phantom, for he trod so gently that the carpet deadened the sound of his steps, took a spoonful of the beverage and swallowed it. Valentine watched all this with a feeling of stupefaction. She felt that it must all disappear to give place to another picture, but, instead of vanishing like a shadow, the man came alongside the bed, and, holding the glass to her, he said in an agitated voice: "Now drink!"

Valentine started. It was the first time any of her visions had spoken to her in a living voice. She opened her mouth to scream: the man put his finger to his lips.

"The Count of Monte Cristo!" she murmured.

"Do not call anyone and do not be alarmed," said the Count. "You need not have the slightest shadow of suspicion or uneasiness in your mind. The man you see before you (for you are right this time, Valentine, it is not an illusion), is as tender a father and as respectful a friend as could ever appear to you in your dreams. Listen to me," he went on, "or rather, look at me. Do you see my red-rimmed eyes and my pale face, paler than usual? That is because I have not closed my eyes for an instant during the last four nights; for the last four nights have I been watching over you to protect and preserve you for our friend Maximilian."

The sick girl's cheeks flushed with joy. "Maximilian," she repeated, for the sound of the name was very sweet to her. "Maximilian! He has told you all then!"

"Everything. He has told me that you are his, and I have promised him that you shall live."

"You have promised him that I shall live? Are you a doctor, then?"

"Yes, and believe me, the best one Heaven could send just now."

"You say you have been watching over me?" Valentine asked uneasily. "Where? I have not seen you."

"I have been hidden behind that door," he said. "It leads to an adjoining house which I have rented. "

Valentine bashfully turned her eyes away and said with some indignation: "I think you have been guilty of an unparalleled indiscretion, and what you call protection I look upon as an insult."

"Valentine, during this long vigil over you," the Count said, "all that I have seen has been what people have come to visit you, what food was prepared for you, and what was given you to drink. When I thought there was danger in the drink served to you, I entered as I have done now and emptied your glass, substituting a health-giving potion for the poison. Instead of producing death, as was intended, this drink made the blood circulate in your veins."

"Poison! Death!" cried Valentine, believing that she was again under the influence of some feverish hallucination. "What is that you say?"

"Hush, my child," said Monte Cristo, placing his finger to his lips. "I said poison and I also said death, but drink this." The Count took from his pocket a phial containing a red liquid, of which he poured a few drops into a glass. "When you have drunk that, take nothing more to-night."

Valentine put out her hand but immediately drew it back in fear. Monte Cristo took the glass, drank half of its contents and handed it back to Valentine, who smiled at him and swallowed the rest.

"Oh, yes," said she, "I recognize the flavour of my nightly drinks— the liquid which refreshed and calmed me. Thank you."

"This has saved your life during the last four nights, Valentine," said the Count. "But how have I lived? Oh, the horrible nights I have gone through! The terrible tortures I have suffered when I saw the deadly poison poured into your glass and feared you would drink it before I could pour it away!"

"You say you suffered tortures when you saw the deadly poison poured into my glass?" replied Valentine, terror-stricken. "If you saw the poison poured into my glass, you must have seen the person who poured it?"

"Yes, I did."

Valentine sat up, pulling over her snow-white bosom the embroidered sheet still moist with the dews of fever, to which were now added those of terror.

"Oh, horrible! You are trying to make me believe that something diabolical is taking place; that they are continuing their attempts to murder me in my father's house; on my bed of sickness even! Oh no, it cannot be, it is impossible!"

"Are you the first one this hand has struck, Valentine? Have you not seen Monsieur de Saint-Méran, Madame de Saint-Méran, and Barrois fall under this blow? Would not Monsieur Noirtier have been another victim but for the treatment they have been giving him for nearly three years which has accustomed his system to this poison?"

"Then that is why Grandpapa has been making me share all his beverages for the past month?"

"Had they a bitter flavour, like half-dried orange-peel?"

"Oh, yes, they had."

"That explains all," said Monte Cristo. "He also knows there is some one administering poison here, perhaps he even knows who the person is. He has been protecting you, his beloved child, against this evil. That is why you are still alive after having partaken of this poison, which is as a rule unmerciful."

"But who is this . . . this murderer?"

"Have you never seen anyone enter your room at night?"

"Indeed I have. I have frequently seen shadows pass close to me and then disappear, and even when you came in just now I believed for a long time that I was either delirious or dreaming."

"Then you do not know who is aiming at your life?"

"No. Why should anyone desire my death?"

"You will see this person," said Monte Cristo, listening.

"How?" asked Valentine, looking round her in terror.

"Because you are not delirious or feverish to-night, you are wide awake. Midnight is just striking; this is the hour murderers choose. Summon all your courage to your assistance; still the beatings of your heart; let no sound escape your lips, feign sleep, and you will see, you will see!"

Valentine seized the Count's hand. "I hear a noise," said she. "Go quickly."

"*Au revoir*," replied the Count, as with a sad smile he tiptoed to the door of the library. Before closing the door, he turned round once more and said: "Not a movement, not a word; pretend you are asleep." With this fearful injunction, the Count disappeared behind the door, which he closed noiselessly after him.

## CHAPTER LXII

## THE APPARITION AGAIN

Valentine was alone. Except for the rumbling of distant carriages, all was still. Valentine's attention was concentrated on the clock in the room, which marked the seconds, and noticed that they were twice as slow as the beatings of her heart. Yet she was in a maze of doubt. She, who never did harm to anyone, could not imagine that anyone should desire her death. Why? To what purpose? What harm had she done that she should have an enemy? There was no fear of her falling asleep. A terrible thought kept her mind alert: there existed a person in the world who had attempted to murder her, and was going to make another attempt. What if the Count had not the time to run to her help! What if her last moment were approaching, and she would see Morrel no more!

This train of thought nearly compelled her to ring the bell for help, but she fancied she saw the Count's eye peering through the door, and at the thought of it her mind was overwhelmed with such shame that she did not know whether her feeling of gratitude toward him could be large enough to efface the painful effect of his indiscreet attention.

Thirty minutes, which seemed like an eternity, passed thus, and at length the clock struck the half-hour; at the same moment a slight scratching of fingernails on the door of the library apprised Valentine that the Count was still watching.

Then Valentine seemed to hear the floor creaking on the opposite side, that is to say, in Edward's room. She listened with bated breath; the latch grated, and the door swung on its hinges. Valentine had raised herself upon her elbow, and she only just had time to lay herself down again and cover her eyes with her arms. Then trembling, agitated, and her heart heavy with indescribable terror, she waited.

Some one approached her bed and touched the curtains. Valentine summoned all her strength and breathed with the regular respiration which proclaims tranquil sleep.

"Valentine," said a low voice.

A shudder went through the girl's whole frame, but she made no reply.

"Valentine," the same voice repeated.

The same silence: Valentine had promised not to waken. Then all was still except for the almost noiseless sound of liquid being poured into the tumbler she had just emptied. Then from the vantage ground of her arm she risked opening her eyes a little and saw a woman in a white dressing-gown emptying some liquid from a phial into her tumbler. Perhaps Valentine held her breath for an instant, or made a slight movement, for the woman became uneasy, paused in her devilish work and leaned over the bed to see if Valentine was really asleep. It was Mme de Villefort!

When Valentine recognized her stepmother she trembled so violently that the whole bed shook. Mme de Villefort instantly stepped close to the wall, and from there, herself hidden behind the bed-hangings, watched attentively and silently for the slightest movement on Valentine's part. Summoning all her will power to her assistance, the sick girl forced herself to close her eyes, but so strong was the feeling of curiosity which prompted her to keep her eyes open and learn the truth that this function of the most delicate of our organs, which is generally such a simple action, became almost impossible of achievement at that moment.

However, hearing Valentine's even breathing once more and reassured thereby that she was asleep, Mme de Villefort stretched out her arm once more, and, hidden as she was behind the curtains at the head of the bed, emptied the contents of the phial into Valentine's tumbler. Then she withdrew, but so quietly that not the least sound told Valentine that she had gone.

It is impossible to describe what Valentine went through during the minute and a half that Mme de Villefort was in the room. The scratching of the fingernails on the library door roused the poor girl from the stupor into which she had fallen, and she raised her head with an effort. The door noiselessly turned on its hinges, and the Count of Monte Cristo appeared again.

"Well?" he asked, "do you still doubt?"

"Alas!"

"Did you recognize her?"

Valentine groaned as she answered: "I did, but I still cannot believe it! What am I to do? Can I not leave the house? . . . Can I not escape?"

"Valentine, the hand that pursues you now will follow you everywhere; your servants will be seduced with gold, and death will face you disguised in every shape and form; in the water you drink from the well, in the fruit you pluck from the tree."

"But did you not say my grandfather's precautions had made me immune from poisoning?"

"From one kind of poisoning, but, even then, not large doses. The poison will be changed or the dose increased."

He took the tumbler and put his lips to it.

"You see, it has already been done. She is no longer trying to poison you with brucine but with a simple narcotic. I can recognize the taste of the alcohol in which it has been dissolved. If you had drunk what Mme de Villefort has just poured into this tumbler, you would have been lost."

"Oh, dear!" cried the young girl. "Why does she pursue me thus? I cannot understand. I have never done her any harm!"

"But you are rich, Valentine; you have an income of two hundred thousand francs; what is more, you are keeping her son from getting this money."

"Edward? Poor child! Is it for his sake that all these crimes are committed?"

"Ah, you understand at last."

"Heaven grant that he may not suffer for this!"

"You are an angel, Valentine."

"But why is my grandfather allowed to live?"

"Because she thought that if once you were dead, the money would naturally revert to your brother; unless, of course, he were disinherited, and that after all it would be running a useless risk to commit this crime."

"Has such a plan really been conceived in the mind of a woman? 'Tis too horrible!"

"Do you remember the vine arbour of the Hôtel de la Poste at Perugia and the man in the brown mantle whom your mother questioned about *aqua tofana?* Well, this infernal plan has been maturing in her brain ever since that period!"

"Then if it is so, I see that I am doomed to die!" cried the girl, bursting into tears.

"No, Valentine, for I have foreseen all her plots, and so your enemy is beaten. You will live, Valentine, you will live to love and be loved; you will live to be happy and make a noble heart happy. But to attain this, you must have confidence in me. You must take blindly what I give you. You must trust no one, not even your father."

"My father is not a party to this frightful plot, is he?" cried Valentine, wringing her hands.

"No, and yet your father, who is accustomed to juridical accusations, must know that all these people who have died in your house have not died natural deaths. Your father should have watched over you; he should be where I am now; he should have emptied this tumbler, and he should have risen up against this murderer."

"I shall do all I can to live, for there are two persons in the world who love me so much that my death would mean their death—my grandfather and Maximilian."

"I shall watch over them as I have watched over you," said Monte Cristo. Then he went on: "Whatever happens to you, Valentine, do not be alarmed. Though you suffer and lose your sight and hearing, do not be afraid; though you awaken and know not where you are, fear not; even though on awakening you find yourself in some sepulchral vault or coffin; collect your thoughts quickly and say to yourself: 'At this moment a friend is watching over me, a father, a man who desires our happiness, mine and Maximilian's.'"

"Alas! alas! To think that I have to go through all that!"

"Valentine, would you prefer to denounce your stepmother?"

"I would sooner die a hundred times."

"No, you shall not die, but promise me that whatever happens, you will not complain or lose hope?"

"I shall think of Maximilian."

"You are my darling child, Valentine! I alone can save you, and save you I will! My daughter, believe in my devotion to you, as you believe in the goodness of God and in Maximilian's love for you," said the Count with an affectionate smile.

Valentine gave him a grateful look and became submissive as a little child. Then the Count took from his waistcoat pocket the little emerald box, and, taking off the lid, put into Valentine's right hand a pill about the size of a pea. Valentine took it into her other hand and looked earnestly at the Count. There was a look of grandeur almost divine in the features of her sure protector. He answered her mute inquiry with a nod of assent.

She placed the pill in her mouth and swallowed it.

"Now good-bye, my child," said he. "I shall try to gain a little sleep, for you are saved!"

Monte Cristo looked long at the dear child, as she gradually dropped off to sleep, overcome by the powerful narcotic he had given her. Taking the tumbler, he emptied three-quarters of its contents into the fireplace, so that it might be believed Valentine had drunk it, and replaced it on the table. Then, regaining the door of his retreat he disappeared after casting one more look on Valentine, who was sleeping with the confidence and innocence of an angel at the feet of the Lord.

## CHAPTER LXIII

## THE SERPENT

THE night-light continued to burn on the mantelpiece; all noise in the streets had ceased and the silence of the room was oppressive. The door of Edward's room opened, and a head we have already seen appeared in the mirror opposite: it was Mme de Villefort, who had come to see the effects of her draught. She paused on the threshold and listened; then she slowly approached the night-table to see whether Valentine's tumbler was empty.

It was still a quarter full, as we know. Mme de Villefort took it and emptied the rest of the draught on to the embers, which she disturbed to facilitate the absorption of the liquid; then she carefully washed the tumbler, and drying it with her handkerchief, placed it on the table. Anyone looking into the room at that moment would have observed

Mme de Villefort's reluctance to turn her eyes toward Valentine, or to go up to the bed. The dim light, the silence and the heaviness of the night no doubt combined with the frightful heaviness of her conscience; the poisoner stood in fear of her work!

At length she gained courage, drew aside the curtain, and, leaning over the head of the bed, looked at Valentine. The girl breathed no more; her white lips had ceased to quiver, her eyes appeared to float in a bluish vapour and her long black eyelashes veiled a cheek as white as wax. Mme de Villefort contemplated this face with an expression eloquent in its impassivity. Lowering the quilt, she ventured to place her hand on the young girl's heart. It was still and cold. The only pulsation she felt was that in her own hand. She withdrew her hand with a shudder.

One of Valentine's arms was hanging out of the bed. It was a beautiful arm, but the forearm was slightly contorted, and the delicately shaped wrist was resting with fingers outspread on the mahogany woodwork of the bed. The nails were turning blue. Mme de Villefort could not doubt that all was over. This terrible work was done; the poisoner had nothing more to do in the room. She retired with great precaution, fearing even to hear the sound of her own footsteps.

The hours passed, until a wan light began to filter through the blinds. It gradually grew brighter and brighter, till at length every object in the room was distinguishable. About this time the nurse's cough was heard on the staircase, and she entered the room with a cup in her hand.

One glance would have sufficed to convince a father or a lover that Valentine was dead, but this mercenary woman thought she slept.

"That is good," she said, going up to the night-table; "she has drunk some of her draught, the tumbler is three-quarters empty." Then she went to the fireplace, rekindled the fire, made herself comfortable in an armchair and, though she had but just left her bed, took advantage of the opportunity to snatch a few minutes' sleep.

She was awakened by the clock striking eight. Astonished to find the girl still asleep, and alarmed at seeing her arm still hanging out of bed, she drew nearer. It was not until then that she noticed the cold lips and still bosom. She tried to place the arm alongside the body, and its terrible stiffness could not deceive a nurse. With a horrified scream, she rushed to the door, crying out: "Help! help!"

"Help? For whom?" asked the doctor from the bottom of the stairs, it being the hour he usually called.

"What is the matter?" cried Villefort, rushing out of his room. "Do you not hear the cry for help, Doctor?"

"Yes, let us go quickly to Valentine," replied d'Avrigny.

But before the father and the doctor could reach the room, all the servants who were on the same story had rushed in, and, seeing Valentine pale and motionless on the bed, raised their hands heavenward and stood rooted to the spot with terror.

"Call Mme de Villefort! Wake Mme de Villefort!" shouted the Procureur du Roi from the door, for he seemed almost afraid to enter the room. But, instead of obeying, the servants simply stared at d'Avrigny, who had run to Valentine and taken her in his arms.

"This one too!" he murmured, letting her fall back on to the pillow again. "My God! My God! When will it cease!"

Villefort rushed in. "What do you say, Doctor?" he called out. "Oh, Doctor . . . Doctor . . ."

"I say that Valentine is dead!" replied d'Avrigny in a voice that was terrible in its gravity.

M. de Villefort staggered as though his legs had given way under him, and he fell with his head on Valentine's bed.

On hearing the doctor's words and the father's cries, the servants fled terrified, muttering imprecations as they went. They were heard running down the stairs and the passages, there was a great stir in the courtyards, and all was silence again. The servants had, one and all, deserted the accursed house!

Just then Mme de Villefort, with her dressing-gown half on, appeared. For a moment she stood on the threshold and seemed to be interrogating those present, at the same time endeavouring to summon up a few rebellious tears. Suddenly she stepped, or rather bounded, toward the table, with outstretched hands. She had seen d'Avrigny bend curiously over the table and take the tumbler she was sure she had emptied during the night. The tumbler was one quarter full, just as it had been when she threw its contents on to the embers. Had Valentine's ghost suddenly confronted her, she would not have been more alarmed. The liquid was actually of the same colour as that which she had poured into the tumbler and which the girl had drunk; it was certainly the poison, and it could not deceive M. d'Avrigny, who was now examining it closely. It must have been a miracle worked by the Almighty, that, notwithstanding all her precautions, there should be some trace left, some proof to denounce the crime.

While Mme de Villefort remained as though rooted to the spot, looking like a statue of terror, and Villefort lay with his head hidden in the bedclothes oblivious to everything, d'Avrigny went to the window in order to examine more closely the contents of the tumbler. Dipping his finger into it, he tasted it.

"Ah!" he murmured, "it is no longer brucine, let me see what it is!"

He went to one of the cupboards, which was used as a medicine-chest, and, taking some nitric acid, poured a few drops into the liquid, which instantly turned blood-red.

"Ah!" said d'Avrigny in a tone which combined the horror of a judge to whom the truth has been revealed and the joy of the student who has solved a problem.

For an instant Mme de Villefort was beside herself; her eyes flared up and then dulled again; she staggered toward the door and disappeared. An instant later the distant thud was heard of a body falling. Nobody paid any attention to it, however. The nurse was intent on watching the chemical analysis, and Villefort was still prostrate. Only M. d'Avrigny had watched her and had noticed her departure. He raised the door-curtain, and, looking through Edward's room, perceived her stretched unconscious on the floor of her own room.

"Go and attend to Madame de Villefort, she is not well," he said to the nurse.

"But Mademoiselle de Villefort?" stammered the nurse.

"Mademoiselle de Villefort has no further need of help: she is dead!"

"Dead! dead!" moaned Villefort in a paroxysm of grief which the novelty of such a feeling in this heart of stone made all the more terrible.

"Dead, did you say?" cried a third voice. "Who says that Valentine is dead?"

The two men turned round and perceived Morrel standing at the door, pale and terrible in his grief.

This is what had happened. Morrel had called at his usual hour to obtain tidings of Valentine. Contrary to custom, he found the side door open, and, having no occasion to ring, entered. He waited in the hall for a moment, calling a servant to announce him to M. de Noirtier, but there was no answer, for, as we know, the servants had all fled. Morrel had no particular reason for anxiety that day; he had Monte Cristo's promise that Valentine should live, and so far this promise had held good. The Count had given him a good report each evening which was confirmed by Noirtier the next day. There was something strange about this silence, however; he called a second and a third time, but still there was no sound. In a turmoil of doubt and fear he flew up the stairs and through several deserted rooms until he reached Valentine's chamber. The door was open, and the first sound he heard was a sob. As through a mist, he saw a black figure on his knees and lost in a mass of white drapery. Fear, a terrible fear, rooted him to the spot.

It was at this moment that he heard a voice say: "She is dead!" and a second voice repeat like an echo: "Dead! dead!"

## CHAPTER LXIV

## MAXIMILIAN

VILLEFORT rose, almost ashamed at being surprised in such a paroxysm of grief. The terrible office he had held for twenty-five years had placed him far outside the range of any human feeling. He looked at Morrel in a half-dazed manner.

"Who are you," said he, "that you are unaware that one does not enter a house where death reigns? Go, go!"

Morrel stood still; he could not take his eyes from the disordered bed and the pale figure lying on it.

"Do you hear me, go!" cried Villefort, while d'Avrigny advanced toward Morrel to persuade him to leave.

Dazed, the young man looked at the corpse, the two men, and the room; then he hesitated for a moment and opened his mouth to reply, but could not give utterance to any of the thoughts that crowded in his brain; he thrust his hand in his hair and turned on his heels. D'Avrigny and Villefort, distracted for a moment from their morbid thoughts, looked at one another as though to say: "He is mad."

But in less than five minutes they heard the stairs creaking under a heavy weight and perceived Morrel carrying Noirtier in his chair up the stairs with almost superhuman strength. Arrived at the top, Morrel set the chair down and wheeled it rapidly into Valentine's room. Noirtier's face was dreadful to behold as Morrel pushed him toward the bed: all the resources at the disposal of his intelligence were displayed therein, and all his power was concentrated in his eyes, which had to do duty for the other faculties. This pale face with its glaring eyes seemed to Villefort like a terrible apparition. Every time he had come in contact with his father something disastrous had happened.

"Look what they have done!" cried Morrel, resting one hand on the arm of the chair he had just wheeled up to the bedside, and with the other one pointing to Valentine. "Look, Father, look!"

Villefort started back and looked with amazement on this young man, almost unknown to him, who called M. Noirtier "Father."

In response to Morrel's words, the old man's whole soul seemed to show itself in his eyes, which became bloodshot; the veins of his throat swelled, and his neck, cheeks, and temples assumed a bluish hue. Nothing, indeed, was needed to put the finishing touch to this internal ebullition in his whole being but the utterance of a cry. And in truth a mute cry issued from him, if we may use the expression, which was terrifying and heartrending because of its very silence. D'Avrigny rushed up to the old man and made him inhale a strong restorative.

"They ask me who I am, monsieur, and what right I have to be here!" cried Morrel, seizing the inert hand of the paralytic. "Oh, you know! Tell them! Tell them!" And the young man's voice was choked with sobs. "Tell them that I was betrothed to her; tell them she was my darling, the only one I love on earth." And looking like the personification of broken strength, he fell heavily on his knees before the bed which his hands grasped convulsively. His grief was such that d'Avrigny turned his head away to hide his emotion, and Villefort, attracted by the magnetism which draws us toward such as have loved those we mourn, gave his hand to the young man without asking any further explanations.

For some time nothing was heard in the room but sobs, imprecations and prayers. Yet one sound gained the mastery over all the rest; it was the harsh and heartrending breathing of Noirtier. With each intake it seemed as though his very lungs must burst asunder. At length Villefort, who had, so to say, yielded his place to Morrel and was now the most composed of them all, said to Maximilian: "You say that you loved Valentine and that you were betrothed to her. I was unaware of your love for her, as also of your engagement. Yet I, her father, forgive you, for I see that your grief is deep and true. Besides, my own grief is too great for anger to find a place in my heart. But, as you see, the angel you hoped to possess, has left us. Take your farewell of her sad remains: Valentine has now no further need of anyone but the priest and the doctor."

"You are mistaken, monsieur," cried Morrel, rising on to one knee, and his heart was pierced with a pang sharper than any he had yet felt. "You are quite wrong. Valentine, as I judge from the manner of her death, not only needs a priest but also an avenger. Send for the priest, Monsieur de Villefort; I will be her avenger!"

"What do you mean, monsieur?" murmured Villefort, trembling before this new idea of Morrel's.

"What I mean is that there are two personalities in you: the father has done enough weeping, it is now time that the magistrate bethought him of his duty."

Noirtier's eyes gleamed, and d'Avrigny drew nearer.

"I know what I am saying," continued Morrel, reading the thoughts that were revealed on the faces of those present, "and you all know as well as I do what I am going to say. Valentine has been murdered!"

Villefort hung his head; d'Avrigny advanced a step farther, and Noirtier made a sign of assent.

"You know, monsieur," continued Morrel, "that nowadays a girl does not suddenly disappear without inquiries being made as to her disappearance, even though she be not so young, beautiful, and adorable as Valentine was. Show no mercy, Monsieur le Procureur!" he cried with increasing vehemence. "I denounce the crime; it is now your duty to find the murderer."

"You are mistaken, monsieur," replied Villefort. "No crimes are committed in my house. Fate is against me, God is trying me. It is a horrible thought, but no one has been murdered."

"I tell you that murder has been committed here!" cried the young man, lowering his voice but speaking in a very decided tone. "This is the fourth victim during the past four months. I declare that they attempted to poison Valentine four days ago but failed owing to Monsieur Noirtier's precautions. I declare that the dose has now been doubled or else the poison changed, so that their dastardly work has succeeded. You know all this as well as I do, for this gentleman warned you, both as a friend and a doctor."

"You are raving, monsieur," said Villefort, vainly endeavouring to escape from the trap into which he felt he had fallen.

"I raving!" cried Morrel. "Well, then, I appeal to Monsieur d'Avrigny himself. Ask him, Doctor, whether he remembers his words to you in your garden on the evening of Madame de Saint-Méran's death when you and he thought you were alone! You were conversing about her tragic death, and, as now, you unjustly blamed fate, but the only blame that can attach to fate is that by her decree the murderer was created who has poisoned Valentine. Yes, yes," he continued, "recall those words that you thought were spoken in silence and solitude, whereas every one of them fell on my ear. On seeing Monsieur de Villefort's culpable indifference towards his relatives that evening, I certainly ought to have revealed everything to the authorities. Then I should not have been an accomplice to your death, Valentine, my darling Valentine! But the accomplice shall become the avenger. I swear to you, Valentine, that if your father forsake you, I, yes I, shall pursue the murderer!"

And then it was d'Avrigny's turn.

"I, too, join Monsieur Morrel in demanding justice for the crime," said he. "My blood boils at the thought that my cowardly indifference has encouraged the murderer."

"Have mercy! Oh, my God, have mercy!" murmured Villefort, beside himself.

Morrel raised his head, and, seeing that Noirtier's eyes were shining with an almost supernatural light, he said: "Wait a moment, Monsieur Noirtier wishes to speak. Do you know the murderer?" he continued, turning to the old man.

"Yes," replied Noirtier.

"And you will help us to find him?" cried the young man. "Listen, Monsieur d'Avrigny, listen!"

Noirtier threw the unhappy Morrel a sad smile, one of those smiles expressed in his eyes which had so often made Valentine happy, and demanded his attention. Then having, so to say, riveted his questioner's eyes on his own, he looked toward the door.

"Do you wish me to leave the room?" asked Morrel sadly.

"Yes," looked Noirtier.

"Alas! Alas! Have pity on me!"

The old man's eyes remained relentlessly fixed on the door.

"May I at least come back again?"

"Yes."

"Am I to go alone?"

"No."

"Whom shall I take with me? The doctor?"

"Yes."

"But will Monsieur de Villefort understand you?"

"Yes."

"Have no fear, I understand my father very well," said Villefort, overjoyed that the inquiries between him and his father were to be made privately.

D'Avrigny took the young man's arm and led him into the adjoining room. At length, after a quarter of an hour had elapsed, a faltering footstep was heard, and Villefort appeared on the threshold. "Come," said he, leading them back to Noirtier.

Morrel looked fixedly at Villefort. His face was livid; large drops of perspiration rolled down his face; between his teeth was a pen twisted out of shape and bitten to half its natural length.

"Messieurs," said he in a voice choked with emotion, turning to d'Avrigny and Morrel. "Give me your word of honour that this terrible secret shall remain buried for ever amongst ourselves."

The two men stirred uneasily.

"I entreat you! . . ." continued Villefort.

"But the culprit! . . . the murderer! . . ." cried Morrel.

"Fear not, justice shall be done," said Villefort. "My father has revealed to me the name of the culprit, and, though he is as anxious for revenge as you are, he entreats you even as I do to keep the crime a secret. Oh! if my father makes this request, it is only because he knows that Valentine will be terribly avenged. He knows me, and I have given him my word. I only ask three days. Within three days the vengeance I shall have taken for the murderer of my child will be such as to make the most indifferent of men shudder." As he said these words, he ground his teeth and grasped the lifeless hand of his old father.

"Will this promise be fulfilled, Monsieur Noirtier?" Morrel asked, while d'Avrigny questioned him with his eyes.

"Yes," signalled Noirtier with a look of sinister joy.

"Then swear," said Villefort, joining d'Avrigny's and Morrel's hands, "swear that you will spare the honour of my house and leave it to me to avenge my child!"

D'Avrigny turned round and gave a faint "Yes" in reply, but Morrel pulled his hand away and rushed toward the bed. Pressing his lips to Valentine's mouth, he fled out of the room with a long groan of despair.

As we have said, all the servants had disappeared. M. de Villefort was therefore obliged to request M. d'Avrigny to take charge of the numerous arrangements consequent upon a death, above all upon a death of such a suspicious nature. This he consented to do, and went in search of the official registrar.

The registrar duly gave the death certificate without having the least suspicion of the real cause of death, and, when he had gone, d'Avrigny asked Villefort whether he desired any particular priest to pray over Valentine.

"No," was Villefort's reply. "Fetch the nearest one."

"The nearest one is an Italian priest who lives in the house next to your own," replied the doctor. "Shall I summon him?"

"Pray do so."

"Do you wish to speak to him?"

"All I desire is to be left alone. Make my excuse to him. Being a priest, he will understand my grief."

D'Avrigny found the priest standing at his door and went up to him saying: "Would you be good enough to render a great service to an unhappy father who has lost his daughter? I mean Monsieur de Villefort, the Procureur du Roi."

"Ah, yes, I know that death is rife in that house," replied the priest in a very pronounced Italian accent.

"Then I need not tell you what service it is that he ventures to ask of you?"

"I was just coming to offer myself, monsieur," said the priest. "It is our mission to forestall our duties."

"It is a young girl who has died."

"Yes, I know, I learnt that from the servants whom I saw fleeing from the house. I know that she was called Valentine, and I have already prayed for her."

"Thank you, monsieur, thank you," said d'Avrigny. "Since you have commenced your sacred office, continue it. Come and watch beside the dead girl, and all her mourning relatives will be grateful to you."

"I am coming, monsieur," replied the priest, "and I venture to say that no prayers will be more fervent than mine."

D'Avrigny led the priest into Valentine's room without meeting M. de Villefort, who was closeted in his study. As soon as they entered the room Noirtier's eyes met those of the priest, and no doubt something particular attracted him, for his gaze never left him. D'Avrigny recommended the living as well as the dead to the priest's care, and he promised to devote his prayers to Valentine and his attentions to Noirtier.

The abbé set to his task in all seriousness, and as soon as d'Avrigny had left the room, he not only bolted the door through which the doctor had passed, but also the one leading to Mme de Villefort's room—doubtless that he might not be disturbed in his prayers or Noirtier in his grief.

The Abbé Busoni watched by the corpse until daylight, when he returned to his house without disturbing anyone. When M. de Villefort and the doctor went to see how M. Noirtier had spent the night, they were greatly amazed to find him sitting in his big armchair, which served him as a bed, in a peaceful sleep, with something approaching a smile on his face.

## CHAPTER LXV

# DANGLARS' SIGNATURE

BEFORE paying his last respects to Valentine, Monte Cristo called on Danglars. From his window the banker saw the Count's carriage enter the courtyard, and went to meet him with a sad though affable smile.

"Well, Count," said he, holding out his hand. "Have you come to offer me your condolence? Ill-fortune is certainly dogging my steps. I was beginning to ask myself whether I had not wished bad luck to those poor Morcerfs, thus proving the truth of the proverb: 'He who wishes harm to others shall himself suffer misfortune.' But, on my word, I have wished no harm to Morcerf. He was perhaps a little proud, considering he was a man who had risen from nothing, like myself, and, like myself, owed everything he had to his own wits. But we all have our faults. Have you noticed, Count, that people of our generation—pardon me, you are not of our generation, for you are still young—people of my generation are not lucky this year. For example, look at our puritan, the Procureur du Roi, whose whole family are dying in a most mysterious fashion, the latest victim being his daughter. Then again there is Morcerf, who is dishonoured and killed by his own hand, while I not only am covered with ridicule by that scoundrel Cavalcanti, but have lost my daughter as well.

"Your daughter?"

"Yes, she has gone away with her mother, and, knowing her as I do, I am sure she will never return to France again. She could not endure the shame brought on her by that impostor. Ah! he played his part well! To think that we had been entertaining a murderer, a thief, and an impostor; and that he so nearly became my daughter's husband! The only piece of good fortune in the whole affair was that he was arrested before the contract was signed."

"Still, my dear Baron," said Monte Cristo, "such family griefs, which would crush a poor man whose child was his only fortune, are endurable to a millionaire. Philosophers may say what they like, a practical man will always give them the lie: money compensates for a great deal, and if you recognize the sovereignty of this sovereign balm you should be easily consoled, you who are the kins of finance."

Danglars looked at the Count out of the corner of his eye; he wondered whether he was mocking him or whether he meant it seriously. "Yes," he said, "it is a fact; if wealth brings consolation, I should be consoled, for I am certainly rich."

"So rich, my dear Baron, that your wealth is like the Pyramids; if you wanted to demolish them, you would not dare, and if you dared, you would not be able to do so."

Danglars smiled at this good-natured pleasantry of the Count's.

"That reminds me," said he, "when you came in, I was drawing up five little bills; I have already signed two, will you excuse me while I sign the other three?"

"Certainly, Baron."

There was a moment's silence broken only by the scratching of the banker's pen.

"Are they Spanish, Hayti, or Neapolitan bonds?" said Monte Cristo.

"Neither the one nor the other," replied Danglars with a self-satisfied smile. "They are bearer bonds on the Bank of France. Look there," he added, "if I am the king, you are the emperor of finance, but have you seen many scraps of paper of this size each worth a million?"

The Count took the scraps of paper which the banker proudly handed him and read:

> To the Governor of the Bank of France.
>     Please pay to my order from the deposit placed by me with you the sum of one million in present currency.
>                                        BARON DANGLARS

"One, two, three, four, five!" counted Monte Cristo. "Five millions! Why, you are a regular Croesus! It is marvellous, especially if, as I suppose, the amount is paid in cash."

"It will be."

"It is truly a fine thing to have such credit and could only happen in France. Five scraps of paper worth five millions: it must be seen to be believed."

"Do you discredit it?"

"No."

"You say it in such a tone . . . But wait, if it gives you pleasure, accompany my clerk to the bank, and you will see him leave with treasury bills to that amount."

"No," said Monte Cristo, folding the five notes, "indeed not. It is so interesting that I will make the experiment myself. My credit with you amounted to six millions: I have had nine hundred thousand, so that I still have a balance of five million, one hundred thousand francs. I will accept the five scraps of paper that I now hold as bonds, on the strength of your signature alone; here is a general receipt for six millions which will settle our account. I made it out beforehand because, I must confess, I am greatly in need of money to-day."

With one hand Monte Cristo put the notes into his pocket, and with the other presented the receipt to the banker.

Danglars was terrorstricken.

"What!" he stammered. "Do you intend taking that money, Count? Excuse me, it is a deposit I hold for the hospitals, and I promised to pay it this morning."

"That is a different matter," said Monte Cristo. "I do not care particularly about these five notes. Pay me in some other way. It was only to satisfy my curiosity that I took these, so that I might tell every one that, without any advice or even asking for five minutes' grace, Danglars' bank had paid me five millions in cash. It would have been so remarkable! Here are your bonds, however. Now give me bills of some other sort."

He held out the five bonds to Danglars, who, livid to the lips, stretched out his hand as the vulture stretches out its claw through the bars of its cage to seize the piece of meat that is being snatched from it. All of a sudden he changed his mind, and with a great effort restrained himself. A smile passed over his face and gradually his countenance became serene.

"Just as you like," he said, "your receipt is money."

"Oh, dear, yes; if you were at Rome, Messrs Thomson and French would make no more difficulty about paying you on my receipt than you have done yourself. I can keep this money, then?"

"Yes," said Danglars, wiping his forehead. "Yes, yes."

Monte Cristo put the five bills into his pocket again.

"Yes," said Danglars. "Certainly keep my signatures. But you know no one sticks to formalities more than a financier does, and as I had destined that money for the hospitals it appeared to me, for a moment, that I should be robbing them by not giving them just those five bonds: as though one franc were not as good as another." And he began to laugh, loudly but nervously. "But there is still a sum of one hundred thousand francs?"

"Oh, that is a mere trifle. The commission must come to nearly that much. Keep it and we shall be quits."

"Are you speaking seriously, Count?" asked Danglars.

"I never joke with bankers," replied Monte Cristo with such a serious air that it was tantamount to impertinence, and he turned toward the door just as the footman announced M. de Boville, Treasurer General of Hospitals.

"Upon my word," said Monte Cristo, "it appears I was only just in time for your signatures—another minute and I should have had a rival claimant."

The Count of Monte Cristo exchanged a ceremonious bow with M. de Boville, who was standing in the waiting-room and was at once shown into M. Danglars' room. The Count's stern face was illuminated by a fleeting smile as he caught sight of the portfolio the Treasurer General carried in his hand. He found his carriage at the door and drove to the bank.

In the meantime the banker advanced to meet the Treasurer General with a forced smile on his lips.

"Good morning, my dear creditor," he said, "for I am sure it is the creditor."

"You are quite right, Baron," said M. de Boville. "I come in the name of the hospitals; through me the widows and orphans have come to ask you for an alms of five millions!"

"Yet they say orphans are to be pitied!" said Danglars, gaining time by joking. "Poor children!"

"Well, I have come in their name," said M. de Boville. "Did you receive my letter yesterday?"

"Yes."

"Here is my receipt."

"My dear Monsieur de Boville," began Danglars, "if you so permit, your widows and orphans will be good enough to wait twenty-four hours, as Monsieur de Monte Cristo, who has just left me . . . You saw him, I think, did you not?"

"I did. Well?"

"Well, Monsieur de Monte Cristo took with him their five millions."

"How is that?"

"The Count had unlimited credit upon me opened by Messrs. Thomson and French, of Rome. He came to ask me for five millions right away, and I gave him cheques on the bank. You can well understand that if I draw ten millions on one and the same day, the Governor will think it rather strange. Two separate days will be quite a different matter," he added with a smile.

"What!" cried M. de Boville in an incredulous tone. "You paid five millions to the gentleman who just left the house! Five millions!"

"Yes, here is his receipt."

M. de Boville took the paper Danglars handed him and read:

Received from Baron Danglars the sum of five million francs, which he will redeem at will from Messrs Thomson and French of Rome.

"It is really true then," he said. "Why, this Count of Monte Cristo must be a nabob! I must call on him, and get a pious grant from him."

"You have as good as received it. His alms alone amount to more than twenty thousand francs a month."

"How magnificent! I shall set before him the example of Madame de Morcerf and her son."

"What is that?"

"They have given their whole fortune to the hospitals. They say they do not want money obtained by unclean means."

"What are they to live on?"

"The mother has retired to the provinces, and the son is going to enlist. I registered the deed of gift yesterday."

"How much did they possess?"

"Oh, not very much. Twelve to thirteen thousand francs. But let us return to our millions."

"Willingly," said Danglars, as naturally as possible. "Do you require this money urgently?"

"Yes, our accounts are to be audited to-morrow."

"To-morrow? Why did you not tell me so at once. To-morrow is a long time hence. At what time does the auditing take place?"

"At two o'clock."

"Send round at midday, then," said Danglars with a smile.

"I will come myself."

"Better still, as it will give me the pleasure of seeing you again."

With which they shook hands.

"By the way," said M. de Boville, "are you not going to the funeral of poor Mademoiselle de Villefort, which I met on the way here?"

"No," said the banker, "that Cavalcanti affair has made me look rather ridiculous, and when one bears a name as irreproachable as mine, one is rather sensitive. I shall keep out of sight for a while."

M. de Boville left expressing great sympathy with the banker in his trouble. He was no sooner outside than Danglars called after him with great force, "Fool!" Then, putting Monte Cristo's receipt into his pocket, he added: "Yes, yes, come at noon; I shall be far from here."

Then he double-locked the door, emptied all the cash drawers, collected about fifty thousand francs in banknotes, burnt several papers, placed others in conspicuous parts of the room, and finally wrote a letter which he sealed and addressed to Baroness Danglars.

Taking a passport from his drawer, he looked at it, muttering: "Good! It is valid for another two months!"

## CHAPTER LXVI

## CONSOLATION

M. DE BOVILLE had indeed met the funeral procession which was accompanying Valentine to her last resting-place in the cemetery of Père-Lachaise. As the *cortège* was leaving Paris, a carriage drawn by four horses came along at full speed and suddenly stopped. Monte Cristo alighted and mingled in the crowd who were following the hearse on foot. When Château-Renaud and Beauchamp perceived him, they also alighted from their carriages and joined him. The Count's eager eyes searched the crowd; it was obvious that he was looking for some one. At length he could restrain himself no longer.

"Where is Morrel?" he asked. "Do either of you gentlemen know?"

"We have already asked ourselves that question. No one seems to have seen him."

The Count remained silent but continued to look around him.

They arrived at the cemetery. Monte Cristo peered into every clump of yew and pine, and was at length relieved of all anxiety: he saw a shadow glide along the dark bushes and recognized him whom he sought. This shadow crossed rapidly but unseen to the hearse and walked beside the coffin-bearers to the spot selected for the grave. Every one's attention was occupied, but Monte Cristo saw only the shadow, which was otherwise unobserved by all around him. Twice did the Count leave the ranks to see whether the man had not some weapon hidden under his clothes. When the procession stopped, the shadow was recognized as Morrel. His coat was buttoned up to his chin, his cheeks were hollow and livid, and he nervously clasped and unclasped his hands. He took his place against a tree on a hillock overlooking the grave, so that he might not miss one detail of the service.

Everything was conducted in the usual manner, though Monte Cristo heard and saw nothing; or rather, he saw nothing but Morrel, whose calmness and motionlessness were alarming to him, who could read what was passing through the young man's mind.

The funeral over, the guests returned to Paris. When every one had gone, Maximilian left his place against the tree and spent a few minutes in silent prayer beside Valentine's grave; then he got up, and, without looking back once, turned down the Rue de la Roquette. Monte Cristo had been hiding behind a large tomb, watching Morrel's every movement. Dismissing his carriage, he now followed the young man on foot as he crossed the canal and entered the Rue Meslay by the boulevards.

Five minutes after the door had been closed on Morrel, it was opened again for Monte Cristo. Julie was in the garden watching Penelon, who, taking his position as gardener very seriously, was grafting some Bengal roses.

"Ah, is that you, Count!" she cried with the delight each member of the family generally manifested every time he made his appearance there.

"Maximilian has just come in, has he not?" asked the Count.

"I think I saw him come in," replied the young woman, "but pray call Emmanuel."

"Excuse me a minute, madame, I must go up to Maximilian at once. I have something of the greatest importance to tell him."

"Go along, then," she said, giving him a charming smile.

Monte Cristo soon ran up the two flights of stairs that separated Maximilian's room from the ground floor; he stood on the landing for a moment and listened; there was not a sound. As is the case in most old houses, the door of the chamber was panelled with glass. Maximilian had shut himself inside, and it was impossible to see through the glass what was happening in the room as a red silk curtain was drawn across. The Count's anxiety was manifested by his high colour, an unusual sign of emotion in this impassive man.

"What am I to do?" he murmured, as he reflected for a moment. "Shall I ring? Oh, no, the sound of a bell announcing a visitor often hastens the resolution of those in the position in which Maximilian must now be; then the tinkling of the bell will be accompanied by another sound." He was trembling from head to foot, and, with his usual lightning-like rapidity in coming to a decision, he suddenly pushed his elbow through one of the panes of the door, which broke into a thousand pieces. Raising the curtain, he saw Morrel at his desk with a pen in his hand. He started up with a jump when he heard the noise made by the broken glass.

"I am so sorry," said the Count. "It is nothing; I slipped, and in doing so pushed my elbow through your door. However, I will now take the opportunity of paying you a visit. Pray, do not let me disturb you." Putting his hand through the broken glass, he opened the door.

Obviously annoyed, Morrel came forward to meet the Count, not so much with the intention of welcoming him as of barring his way.

"It is your servant's fault," said Monte Cristo, rubbing his elbow. "Your floors are as slippery as glass."

"Have you cut yourself?" Morrel asked coldly.

"I do not know. But what were you doing? Were you writing with those ink-stained fingers?"

"Yes, I was writing," replied Morrel. "I do sometimes, though I am a soldier."

Monte Cristo went farther into the room, and Morrel was compelled to let him pass.

"You were writing?" inquired Monte Cristo, with an annoyingly searching look.

"I have already had the honour of telling you that I was."

The Count looked around him.

"Your pistols on your desk beside you?" said he, pointing to the two weapons.

"I am going on a journey."

"My friend!" said Monte Cristo with infinite tenderness, "my good friend, make no hasty resolution, I beg of you!"

"I make a hasty resolution?" exclaimed Morrel. "In what way can a journey be deemed a hasty resolution?"

"Maximilian," resumed Monte Cristo, "let us lay aside our masks. You can no more deceive me with your exterior calmness than I can mislead you with my frivolous solicitude. You no doubt understand that to have acted as I have done, to have broken a pane of glass, intruded on the privacy of a friend, I must have been actuated by a terrible conviction. Morrel, you intend to take your life!"

Morrel started. "Whence do you get that idea, Count?" he said.

"I declare that you intend taking your life. Here is my proof!" said Monte Cristo, in the same tone of voice; going to the desk, he removed the blank piece of paper with which the young man had covered a half-finished letter and picked it up. Morrel reached forward to wrest it from him, but Monte Cristo had anticipated this and forestalled him by seizing his wrist.

"You must confess that you intended to kill yourself, for it is written here," said the Count.

"Well, and if I have decided to turn this pistol against myself, who shall prevent me?" cried Morrel, passing from his momentary appearance of calmness to an expression of violence. "When I say that all my hopes are frustrated, my heart broken, and my life worthless, since the world holds no more charms for me, nothing but grief and mourning; when I say that it would be a mercy to let me die, for, if you do not, I shall lose my reason and become mad; when I tell you all this with tears of heartfelt anguish, who can say to me: 'You are wrong?' Who would prevent me from putting an end to such a miserable existence? Tell me, Count, would you have the courage?"

"Yes, Morrel," said Monte Cristo, in a voice which contrasted strangely with the young man's excitement. "Yes, I would."

"You!" cried Morrel with an angry and reproachful expression. "You who deceived me with absurd hopes! You who cheered me, solaced and soothed me with vain promises when I could have saved her life by some swift and drastic step, or at least could have seen her die in my arms! You who pretended to have all the resources of science at your disposal and all power over matter, yet could not administer an antidote to a poisoned girl! In truth, Count, if it were not that you inspire me with horror, I should feel pity for you!"

"Morrel . . . !"

"You told me to lay aside my mask, and rest assured I will do so. When you followed me here, I allowed you to enter, for I am softhearted, but since you abuse my confidence and defy me in my own room, where I had enclosed myself as in my tomb, since you bring me new tortures when I thought all were exhausted, then, Count of Monte Cristo, my false benefactor, the universal saviour, be satisfied, you shall see your friend die . . ."

With a maniacal laugh, he rushed toward the pistols again. Pale as a ghost, his eyes darting fire, Monte Cristo put his hand over the weapons saying: "And I repeat once more that you shall not take your life!"

"And who are you that you should take upon yourself such an authority over a free and rational being?"

"Who am I?" repeated Monte Cristo. "I will tell you. I am the only man who has the right to say to you: 'Morrel, I do not wish your father's son to die to-day!'

Morrel, involuntarily acknowledging the Count's ascendency over him, gave way a step.

"Why do you speak of my father?" he stammered. "Why bring my father's memory into what I am going to do to-day?"

"Because I am the man who saved your father's life when he

wanted to take it as you do to-day! Because I am the man who sent the purse to your sister and the *Pharaon* to old Monsieur Morrel! Because I am Edmond Dantès!"

Morrel staggered, choking and crushed; his strength failed him, and with a cry he fell prostrate at Monte Cristo's feet. Then all of a sudden his true nature completely reasserted itself; he rose and flew out of the room, calling out at the top of his voice:

"Julie! Julie! Emmanuel! Emmanuel!"

Monte Cristo also attempted to rush out, but Maximilian would sooner have let himself be killed than leave go of the handle of the door, which he shut against him. Upon hearing Maximilian's shouts, Julie, Emmanuel, Penelon, and several servants came running up the stairs in alarm. Morrel seized Julie by the hand, and, opening the door, called out in a voice stifled with sobs: "On your knees! on your knees! This is our benefactor, this is the man who saved our father, this is . . ."

He was going to say "Edmond Dantès," but the Count restrained him. Julie threw herself into the Count's arms, Emmanuel embraced him, and Morrel once more fell on to his knees. Then this man of iron felt his heart swelling within him, a burning flame seemed to rise in his throat, and from thence rush to his eyes; he bowed his head and wept. For a while nothing was heard in the room but weeping and sobbing; a sound that must have been sweet to the angels in Heaven!

Julie had scarcely recovered from the deep emotion that had overcome her when she rushed down to the salon and, with a childlike joy, raised the glass case that protected the purse given by the unknown man of the Allées de Meilhan. Meanwhile, Emmanuel said to the Count in a broken voice:

"Oh, Count, when you heard us speak so often of our unknown benefactor and perceived with what gratitude and homage we clothed his memory, how could you wait until to-day to make yourself known to us? It was cruel to us, and, I almost venture to say, to yourself too, Count!"

"Listen, my friend," said the Count. "I may call you thus, for, without knowing it, you have been my friend for eleven years. The discovery of this secret has been torn from me by a great event of which you must ever remain in ignorance. God is my witness that I intended to bury it for ever in the depths of my heart, but your brother Maximilian has wrested it from me by a violence which, I am sure, he now regrets." Then, seeing that Maximilian had thrown himself on to a chair apart from the others, he added in a low voice: "Watch over him."

"Why?" asked the young man amazed.

"I cannot give you the reason, but watch over him."

Emmanuel looked round the room and caught sight of the pistols.

With a frightened look, he slowly raised his hand and pointed to them. Monte Cristo nodded his head. Emmanuel went to take the pistols.

"Leave them!" said the Count, and, going to Maximilian, took his hand. The tumultuous emotions that had for a moment shaken the young man's heart had now given way to profound stupor.

Julie returned, holding in her hand the red silk purse; two bright tears of joy coursed down her cheeks like two drops of morning dew.

"Here is the relic," she said, "but do not imagine it will be less dear to us because our benefactor has been revealed to us."

"Permit me to take back that purse," responded Monte Cristo, turning a deep red. "Since you know the features of my face, I only wish to be remembered by the affection I ask you to give me."

"Oh, no! no!" said Julie, pressing the purse to her heart. "I entreat you not to take it away, for unfortunately you might be leaving us one day. Is that not so?"

"You have guessed rightly," replied Monte Cristo with a smile. "In a week I shall have left this country where so many people who merit the vengeance of Heaven live happily, whilst my father died of grief and hunger."

Then, realizing that he must make one final struggle against his friend's grief, he took Julie and Emmanuel's hands in his, and said to them with the gentle authority of a father: "My good friends, I pray you, leave me alone with Maximilian."

Julie saw a means of carrying away her precious relic, which Monte Cristo had forgotten to mention again, so she drew her husband away, saying: "Let us leave them."

The Count stayed behind with Morrel, who remained as still as a statue.

"Come, come!" said the Count, tapping him on the shoulder with his burning fingers. "Are you going to be a man again."

"Yes, since I am again beginning to suffer."

The Count's forehead wrinkled in apparent indecision. "Maximilian! Maximilian," said he. "The ideas to which you are giving way are unworthy of a Christian."

"Oh, do not be afraid!" said Morrel, raising his head and smiling at the Count with a smile of ineffable sadness. "I shall make no attempt on my life."

"Then we shall have no more weapons and no more despair!"

"No, for I have a better remedy for my grief than a bullet or the point of a knife."

"You poor, foolish fellow! What is this remedy?"

"My grief itself will kill me!"

"Listen to me, my friend," said Monte Cristo. "One day, in a moment of despair as deep as yours, since it evoked a similar resolution, I, like you, wished to take my life; one day your father, equally desperate, wanted to kill himself. If anyone had said to your father at the moment when he put the muzzle of the pistol to his forehead—if anyone had said to me when I pushed from me the prison bread I had not tasted for three days—if anyone had said to us both at those critical moments: 'Live! The day will come when you will be happy and will bless your life!'—no matter whence the voice had come, we should have welcomed it with a doubtful smile or with agonizing incredulity. Yet how many times has your father not blessed his life when he embraced you—how many times have I myself . . ."

"Ah! you only lost your liberty," interrupted Morrel. "My father only lost his fortune, but I have lost Valentine!"

"Look at me, Morrel," said Monte Cristo with that air of solemnity which, on certain occasions, made him so grand and persuasive. "I have neither tears in my eyes nor fever in my veins, yet I see you suffer, Maximilian, you whom I love as a son! Does that not tell you that in grief as in life there is always a hidden future? And if I entreat, nay, command you to live, Morrel, it is because I am convinced that the day will come when you will thank me for having saved your life!"

"Good God!" cried the young man. "What are you telling me, Count? Take care. But perhaps you have never loved?"

"Child!" was the sole reply.

"I mean as I love. You see I have been a soldier ever since I was a boy, and was twenty-nine before I fell in love, for none of the feelings I experienced before that time were worthy of the name of love. Well, when I was twenty-nine years of age, I met Valentine, and have loved her for the past two years, and during that time I have observed in her all the virtues that make a true daughter and wife. To have possessed Valentine, Count, would have been an infinite and immense happiness, too complete and divine for this world. Since this happiness has been denied me, there is nothing left for me on earth but despair and desolation."

"I tell you to hope, Morrel," repeated the Count.

"Ah! you are trying to persuade me, you are trying to inspire me with the belief that I shall see Valentine again."

The Count smiled.

"My friend, my father!" cried Morrel excitedly. "The ascendancy you hold over me alarms me. Weigh your words carefully, for my eyes lighten up again and my heart takes on a fresh lease of life. I should obey you though you commanded me to raise the stone which once more covers the sepulchre of the daughter of Jairus; I should walk upon the waves like the apostle if you made a sign to me to do so; so have a care, I should obey in all."

"Hope, my dear friend!" repeated the Count.

"Ah, you are playing with me," said Morrel, falling from the heights of exaltation to the abyss of despair. "You are doing the same as those good, or rather selfish, mothers who calm their children's sorrow with honeyed words because their cries annoy them. No, my friend. I will bury my grief so deep down in my heart and shall guard it so carefully from the eyes of man that you will need have no sympathy for me. Good-bye, my friend, good-bye!"

"On the contrary," said the Count. "From now onward, you will live with me and not leave me. In a week we shall have left France behind us."

"Do you still bid me hope?"

"I do, for I know of a remedy for you."

"You are only prolonging my agony, Count!"

"Are you so feeble-hearted that you cannot give your friend a few days' trial? I have great faith in my promise, so let me make the experiment. Do you know what the Count of Monte Cristo is capable of? Do you know that he has faith enough in God to obtain miracles from Him Who said that with faith one would remove mountains? Well, wait for the miracle for which I hope, or . . ."

"Or . . ." repeated Morrel.

"Or take care, Morrel, lest I call you ungrateful."

"Have pity on me, Count!"

"I feel so much pity for you that if I do not cure you in a month to the very day, mark my words, Morrel, I myself will place before you two loaded pistols and a cup of the deadliest poison—a poison which is more potent and prompt of action than that which killed Valentine."

"Do you promise me this?"

"I not only promise it, I swear it," said Monte Cristo, giving him his hand.

"Then on your word of honour, if I am not consoled in a month, you leave me free to take my life, and, whatever I may do, you will not call me ungrateful?"

"In a month to the day, and it is a date that is sacred to us. I do not remember whether you remember that to-day is the fifth of September? It is ten years ago to-day that I saved your father when he wanted to take his life."

Morrel seized the Count's hands and kissed them, and the Count suffered him to do it, for he felt that this homage was due to him.

"In a month," continued Monte Cristo, "you will have before you on the table at which we shall both be seated, two trusty weapons and a gentle death-giving potion, but in return you must promise me to wait until then and live."

"I swear it!" exclaimed Morrel.

Monte Cristo drew the young man toward him and held him for a few minutes in close embrace.

"Well, then, from to-day you will live with me; you can occupy Haydee's rooms, and my daughter will be replaced by my son."

"Haydee?" said Morrel. "What has happened to Haydee?"

"She left last night."

"To leave you for ever?"

"To wait for me . . . Make ready to join me at Rue des Champs-Élysées and now let me out without anyone seeing me."

## CHAPTER LXVII

## SEPARATION

IN the house in the Rue Saint-Germain-des-Prés that Albert de Morcerf had chosen for his mother, the first floor was let to a very mysterious person. The porter himself had never seen this man's face, for in the winter he buried his chin in one of those red kerchiefs worn by coachmen of the nobility, and in the summer he always blew his nose when he passed the porter's lodge. Contrary to custom, he was not watched, and it was reported that he was a man of high standing with a great deal of influence, so that his incognito was respected. His visits were generally regular. At four o'clock, winter and summer, he would arrive, and twenty minutes later a carriage drew up at the house. A woman dressed in black or dark blue, and always thickly veiled, would alight, and, passing by the lodge like a shadow, run up the stairs so gently that not a stair creaked under the pressure of her light foot. No one ever asked her whither she was going, and no one ever saw her face. Needless to say, she never went higher than the first floor. She tapped at the door in a peculiar way; it was opened to her and then fastened again. They left the house in the same way; the woman went first and was followed twenty minutes later by the unknown man.

The day after that on which the Count of Monte Cristo had called on M. Danglars, the day of Valentine's funeral, the mysterious tenant entered his flat at ten o'clock in the morning, instead of his usual hour. Almost immediately afterward, without the usual interval, a hired cab arrived, and the veiled lady quickly ran up the stairs. The door was opened, and before it could be closed again, she called out: "Oh, Lucien, oh, my dear!"

In this way the porter who had overheard the exclamation, learned for the first time that his tenant was named Lucien, but as he was a model porter he decided not even to tell his wife.

"Well, what is the matter, dear?" asked he whose name either trouble or eagerness had forced from the veiled lady's lips. "Tell me quickly." "Can I depend upon you?"

"You know you can. But what is the matter? Your note of this morning, so hastily and untidily written, has made me feel very anxious."

"A great event has happened," said the lady. "Monsieur Danglars left last night."

"Left! Monsieur Danglars left! Where has he gone to?"

"I do not know."

"How do you mean, you do not know? Has he gone away for good?"

"No doubt. At ten o'clock last night his horses took him to the Charenton gate, where he found a post-chaise waiting for him. He stepped into it with his valet, telling his coachman that he was going to Fontainebleau. He left me a letter."

"A letter?"

"Yes, read it." And the Baroness took from her pocket an unsealed letter, which she handed to Debray.

Before reading it he hesitated a moment as though trying to guess its contents, or rather, as though knowing its contents, he was making up his mind what action to take. He had no doubt come to a decision after a second or two, for he read the note which had caused Mme Danglars so much anxiety and which ran as follows:

MADAME AND MOST FAITHFUL WIFE . . .

Debray involuntarily paused and looked at the Baroness, who blushed to the roots of her hair.

"Read," she said; and Debray continued:

When you receive this letter, you will no longer have a husband. Oh, you need not be alarmed, you will only have lost him in the same way in which you have lost your daughter, that is to say, I shall be travelling along one of the thirty or forty roads which lead out of France.

I owe you an explanation, and, as you are a woman of quick comprehension, I will give it to you. A bill of five million francs was unexpectedly presented to me for repayment this morning, which I effected. This was immediately followed by another bill for the same amount; I postponed this payment until to-morrow, and I am going away in order to escape that to-morrow, which would be too unpleasant for me to endure. You understand me, do you not, my most precious wife? I say you understand because you are as conversant with my business affairs as I am myself, in fact more so, for if I had to say what had become of a good half of my fortune, which until recently was quite a considerable one, I should be unable to do so, whereas I am certain that you, on the contrary, would be able to give a very fair answer. Women have infallible instincts, and, by means of an algebra unknown to man, they can explain the most marvellous things. I only understand my figures: from the day these figures fail me, I know nothing.

I am leaving you, madame and most prudent wife, and my conscience does not reproach me in the least at doing so. You have your friends, and, to complete your happiness, the liberty I hasten to restore to you.

There is one more observation I should like to make. As long as I hoped you were working for the good of our firm and the fortune of our daughter, I philosophically closed my eyes to all, but since you have brought about the ruin of our firm, I do not wish to serve as a foundation for another's fortune. You were rich when I married you, though little respected. Pardon me for speaking with such frankness, but as this is in all likelihood only between ourselves, I do not see why I should choose my words.

I augmented our fortune, and it continued to increase for fifteen years until unexpected and incomprehensible disasters overtook me, and, through no fault of my own, I find myself a ruined man. You, madame, have only sought to increase your own fortune, and I am convinced you have been successful.

I leave you then as you were when I married you, rich, though with little honour. Farewell! From to-day I also shall work for myself. Accept my gratitude for the example which you have set me and which I intend following.

Your very devoted husband,
BARON DANGLARS

The Baroness watched Debray as he read this long and painful letter, and saw that in spite of his self-command the young man had changed colour once or twice. When he had finished reading the letter, he folded it up slowly and reassumed his pensive attitude.

"Well?" asked Mme Danglars, with very comprehensible anxiety.

"Well, madame?" repeated Debray mechanically.

"What do you think of that letter?"

"It is quite simple, madame. Monsieur Danglars has gone away full of suspicion."

"Undoubtedly. But is that all you have to say to me?"

"I do not understand you," said Debray, with freezing coolness.

"He has gone! Gone, never to return."

"Oh, do not believe that, Baroness."

"I tell you he will never return. Had he thought I should be useful to him, he would have taken me with him. He has left me at Paris because our separation would serve his purpose. It is therefore irrevocable, and I am free for ever," added Madame Danglars, with the same tone of entreaty.

But, instead of replying, Debray left her in suspense.

"What!" she said at last. "You have no answer?"

"I have but one question to put to you. What do you intend to do?"

"That is what I was going to ask you," replied the Baroness, with wildly beating heart. "I ask you to advise me."

"Then I advise you to travel," replied the young man coldly.

"To travel!" murmured Mme Danglars.

"Certainly. As Monsieur Danglars says, you are rich and perfectly free. It is absolutely necessary for you to leave Paris, at least I think so, after the double scandal of your daughter's rejected marriage and your husband's disappearance. The world must be led to think that you are poor, for opulence in a bankrupt's wife is an unforgivable sin. You have only to remain in Paris for a fortnight, telling every one that you have been deserted; relate to your best friends how it all happened, and they will soon spread it abroad. Then you can quit your home, leaving your jewels behind you, and giving up your jointure, and then every one will be singing your praises because of your disinterestedness. It will be known that your husband has deserted you, and it will be thought that you are poor. I alone know your financial position, and am ready to render you an account as an honest partner."

Pale with amazement, the Baroness listened to this discourse with as much despair and terror as Debray had manifested indifference in pronouncing it.

"Deserted!" she repeated. "Ah, yes, utterly deserted. You are right, monsieur, every one will know that."

"But you are rich, nay, very rich," continued Debray, taking from his pocket-book some papers which he spread on the table. Mme Danglars suffered him to give her the details of their joint financial transactions, but she did not heed his words. She was fully occupied in stilling the turbulent beating of her heart and in keeping back the tears which she felt rising to the surface. At length her dignity conquered, and, though she may not have succeeded in restraining her heart, she at least prevented the fall of a single tear. It was with indifference that she listened as he recounted how he had multiplied their money, for all she wanted was a tender word to console her for being so rich. But she waited in vain for that word.

"Now, madame," Debray continued, "your share amounts to one million three hundred and forty thousand francs, so that you have a fine income, something like sixty thousand francs, which is enormous for a woman who cannot keep up an appearance of wealth, at least not for a year or so. Nevertheless, if this should prove insufficient for your needs, for the sake of the past, I am disposed to offer you a loan of all I possess, that is, one million sixty thousand francs."

"Thank you," replied the Baroness. "You have already handed over to me far more than is required by a poor woman who intends to live in retirement for some time to come."

Debray was astonished for a moment, but he quickly recovered himself and made a gesture which in the most polite manner possible seemed to imply: "Just as you please."

Until that moment, Mme Danglars had hoped for something more; but when she saw Debray's gesture of indifference and the sidelong glance which accompanied it, as well as the profound and significant silence which followed it, she raised her head, opened the door, and calmly and unhesitatingly descended the stairs without even a farewell look at one who could let her leave him in this manner.

Debray quietly waited until Mme Danglars had been gone twenty minutes before he made up his mind to leave, and during all this interval he occupied himself with calculations, his watch by his side.

Above the room where Debray had been dividing his two and a half million francs with Mme Danglars, there was another room in which we shall find friends who have played important parts in the incidents related, friends whose reappearance will cause us pleasure. Mercédès and Albert were there. Mercédès was very much changed in the last few days, not that even in the height of her fortune she had ever dressed with that display of ostentatious magnificence which renders a woman unrecognizable as soon as she appears in simple attire; not that she had lapsed into that state of depression in which one feels constrained to put on again the garments of poverty; no, Mercédès had changed because her eyes had lost their sparkle, her mouth its smile, and to complete all, abashment and perplexity ever arrested on her lips that flow of speech which had issued so easily in former days from her ever ready wit. Poverty had not broken her spirit, and want of courage had not made her poverty appear unendurable to her. Descended from the high position in which she had been living, lost in the new sphere she had chosen like some one passing suddenly from a brilliantly lighted room to utter darkness, Mercédès was like a queen who had stepped from her palace into a hut and could not accustom herself to the earthenware vessels she was obliged to place on the table herself, nor the pallet which had succeeded her bed.

In truth, the beautiful Catalan and noble Countess had lost both her proud look and her charming smile, for her eyes saw nothing but what was distasteful and distressing to her. The walls of her room were hung with a dull grey paper chosen by economical landlords because it would not show the dirt; the floor was uncarpeted; the furniture attracted attention by its poor attempt at magnificence; in fact, everything was so gaudy that it was a continual eyesore to anyone accustomed to refinement and elegance. Mme de Morcerf had lived here ever since she left her magnificent house. The perpetual silence oppressed her, but she knew that Albert was secretly watching her to discover the state of her mind, and this forced her lips into the appearance of an empty smile, which, deprived of the warmth infused into it by her eyes, appeared only like a simple ray of light, that is to say, light without heat.

Albert, too, was very moody and ill at ease. The results of a luxurious life hampered him in his present position. When he wanted to go out without gloves, his hands appeared too white; when he wished to go about the town on foot, his boots appeared too elegant. Yet these two noble and intelligent beings, united by the indissoluble ties of maternal and filial love, had succeeded in tacitly understanding one another. Thus they could face bitter facts without their being preceded by softening words. Albert had been able to say: "Mother, we have no more money," without evoking any visible agitation.

Mercédès had never known what real want was; in her youth she had often spoken of poverty, but it was not the same thing, for between want and necessity there is a wide gulf. When she was at the Catalans, Mercédès wanted a number of things, but she was never in need of the necessaries of life. As long as the nets were good, they caught fish, and as long as they sold fish, they could mend their nets. Devoid of all friendship and having but one great affection which did not enter into her material life, she thought of no one but herself and of nothing but herself. She had managed very well on the little she had, but to-day there were two to manage for and she had nothing with which to do it.

Winter approached. Mercédès, who had been accustomed to a house heated from the hall to her boudoir, had no fire in her cold, bare room; she whose house had been one conservatory of costly exotic plants, had not one humble little flower! But she had her son!

Hitherto the excitement of fulfilling a duty, an exaggerated one perhaps, had sustained them, but their enthusiasm had worn off, and they had been compelled to descend from their world of dreams to face stern realities.

"Mother, let us count our wealth, if you please," Albert was saying at the precise moment that Mme Danglars was descending the staircase. "I must know what it totals before I make my plans."

"Total: nothing," said Mercédès with a sad smile.

"Oh, yes it is, Mother! Total: three thousand francs to begin with, and I dare to hope that with this amount we two shall have a very happy time."

"Child!" said Mercédès.

"Alas, Mother," said the young man, "I have unfortunately spent too much of your money not to know the value of it. Look you, three thousand francs is an enormous sum, and with it I have planned a secure and wonderful future."

"You may well say that, my son, but in the first place are we going to accept this money?" said Mercédès, blushing.

"But I thought we had agreed to that," said Albert, in a firm tone.

"We will accept it all the more readily since we have not got it, for as you know it is buried in the little garden in the Allées de Meilhan at Marseilles. Two hundred francs will take the two of us to Marseilles."

"Two hundred francs? Have you thought it out, Albert?"

"Oh, yes, I have made inquiries with regard to diligences and steamboats, and have made all my calculations. An inside seat in the diligence to Chalon will cost you thirty-five francs. You see, Mother, I am treating you like a queen!"

Albert took his pen and wrote:

| | |
|---|---|
| Diligence to Chalon . . . . . . . . . . . . . . . . . | 35 francs |
| From Chalon to Lyons by steamboat . . . . . . | 6  ,, |
| From Lyons to Avignon by steamboat . . . . . | 16  ,, |
| From Avignon to Marseilles . . . . . . . . . . . | 7  ,, |
| Incidental expenses . . . . . . . . . . . . . . . . . | 50  ,, |
| | 114  ,, |

"Let us say a hundred and twenty," added Albert, smiling. "Am I not generous, Mother?"

"But what about you, my son?"

"Don't you see that I have reserved eighty francs for myself? A young man does not need too much comfort, besides, I am used to travelling."

"Do as you like. But where are the two hundred francs coming from?"

"Here they are, and two hundred more as well. I have sold my watch for a hundred francs and the seals for three hundred. How fortunate that the seals fetched more than the watch! The same story of superfluities again! See how rich we are! Instead of the necessary hundred and fourteen francs for the journey you have two hundred and fifty."

"But we owe something here."

"Thirty francs, which I shall pay out of my hundred and fifty. With care I shall only need eighty francs for my journey, so you see I am wallowing in riches. And it does not end with this. What do you think of this, Mother?"

He took out a small pocket-book with gold clasps and from it a note for one thousand francs.

"What is that?" asked Mercédès.

"A thousand francs, Mother! Oh, it is perfectly genuine."

"But whence have you obtained them?"

"Listen to what I have to say, Mother, and do not get too agitated." He went up to his mother and kissed her on both cheeks, then he paused a moment to look at her.

"You have no idea how beautiful you are to me!" said the young man with deep feelings of filial love. "You are truly the most beautiful and the noblest woman I have ever seen!"

"And I shall never be unhappy so long as I have my son," replied Mercédès, vainly endeavouring to keep back the tears which would rise to her eyes.

"Just so, but this is where our trial begins," said Albert. "Mother, do you know what we have decided?"

"Have we decided anything?"

"Yes, we have agreed that you shall live at Marseilles while I go to Africa, where I shall win the right to the name I have adopted in the place of the one I have cast aside. I joined the Spahis yesterday, or rather, I thought that as my body was my own, I could sell it. Yesterday I took the place of another. And I sold myself for more than I thought I was worth," he continued, trying to smile, "that is to say, for two thousand francs."

"So these thousand francs . . .?" inquired Mercédès, trembling.

"It is half the amount, Mother. I shall receive the other half in a year."

Mercédès raised her eyes to Heaven with an expression which it would be impossible to describe, and the tears lurking in her eyes overflowed with the power of her emotion and silently ran down her cheeks.

"The price of his blood!" she murmured.

"Yes, if I am killed, Mother," said he laughing. "But I assure you I shall sell my life dearly, for never has it been so precious to me as now. Besides, why should I be killed? Has Lamouricière been killed? Or Changarnier? Or yet again, Morrel, whom we know? Think of your joy, Mother, when I come back dressed in my embroidered uniform! I must own that I shall look splendid in it, and that I chose this regiment from pure vanity!"

Though Mercédès attempted to smile she could not repress a sigh. This devoted mother felt it was wrong of her to let the whole weight of the sacrifice fall upon her son.

"Well, Mother, you understand that this means that you have a sure four thousand francs," continued Albert, "and you can live on that for two years at least."

"Do you think so?" said Mercédès mechanically, but in tones of such deep sorrow that the real sense of the words did not escape Albert; he felt his heart grow heavy, and, taking his mother's hand, he said tenderly: "Oh, yes, you will live!"

"Then you must not leave me, my son."

"Mother, I must go," said Albert, in a calm but firm voice. "You love me too much to let me stay idle and useless with you. Besides, I have signed the agreement."

"Do as you will, my son. I shall do God's will."

"It is not as I will, Mother, but according to the dictates of common sense and necessity. We are two despairing creatures, are we not? What is life to you to-day? Nothing! What is it to me? Worth very little without you, Mother, I assure you. But I will live if you promise not to give up hope, and in permitting me to care for your future you give me double strength. Out there in Algeria, I shall go to the Governor, who is a noble-hearted man and essentially a soldier, and shall tell him my story and entreat him to interest himself in me. Then, Mother, I shall either be an officer within six months or else dead. If I am an officer, your future is assured, for I shall have money enough for you and for me, and in addition a name of which we shall both be proud, for it will be your own name. If I am killed . . . then, Mother dear, you also will die, and our misfortunes and sorrows will have an end."

"As you wish," replied Mercédès, with a noble and eloquent glance.

"But you must have no morbid thoughts, Mother," exclaimed the young man. "I assure you we can be very happy. Then it is settled that we separate? We can even begin from to-day; I will go and procure your ticket."

"But what about yours."

"I must stay on here two or three days longer. It will accustom us to our separation, and I have to gather some information on Africa, and also, I want some introductions before I join you at Marseilles."

"Well, then, let us go!" said Mercédès, wrapping round her the only shawl she had taken away with her, which happened to be a valuable black cashmere one. "Let us go."

Albert quickly gathered up his papers, rang for the proprietor, and paid him the thirty francs owing. Then he gave his arm to his mother, and they descended the stairs. Some one was going down in front of them, who, on hearing the rustling of a silk dress against the balustrade, turned round.

"Debray!" murmured Albert.

"You, Moncerf!" replied the minister's secretary, standing still.

Then, noticing in the semi-darkness the veiled and still youthful figure of Mme de Morcerf: "Oh, pardon," he said with a smile. "I will leave you, Albert."

Albert understood his thoughts.

"Mother," said he, turning towards Mercédès, "this is Monsieur Debray, secretary to the Minister of the Interior, and a former friend of mine."

"Former?" stammered Debray. "Why do you say that?"

"I say that, Monsieur Debray, because to-day I have no more friends and must not have any," replied Albert. "I thank you, monsieur, for having acknowledged me."

Debray went up two stairs and cordially shook Albert's hand as he said with all the feeling of which he was capable: "Believe me, I have felt deep sympathy with you in the misfortune that has befallen you, and if I can serve you in any way, pray call on me to do so."

"Thank you, monsieur," said Albert smiling, "but in the midst of our misfortune we are still rich enough to require no outside help. We are leaving Paris, and, after our travelling expenses are paid, we shall still have five thousand francs."

The colour rose to Debray's cheeks at the thought of the million francs he had in his pocket-book, and, unimaginative though he was, he could not help reflecting that a few minutes back there were in that house two women: the one, justly dishonoured, had left with 1,500,000 francs under her cloak, while the other one, unjustly smitten, yet superb in her misfortune, considered herself rich with a few francs. This parallel disturbed his usual politeness, the philosophy of the example overwhelmed him; he stammered a few words of general courtesy and quickly ran down the stairs. The minister's clerks, his subordinates, had to suffer from his ill-humour the rest of the day. In the evening however, he consoled himself by becoming the owner of a splendid house in the Boulevard de la Madeleine, yielding an income of fifty thousand francs.

About five o'clock the next evening, at the very moment when Debray was signing the agreement, Mme de Morcerf entered the diligence after tenderly kissing her son and being as tenderly embraced by him, and was driven away.

A man was hidden behind an arched window of Laffitte's offices. He saw Mercédès enter the diligence, watched the conveyance drive away, and saw Albert turn back. Then he passed his hand across his wrinkled forehead, saying to himself: "Alas! by what means can I restore to these two innocent beings the happiness I have snatched from them? God will help me."

## CHAPTER LXVIII

# THE JUDGE

IT will be remembered that the Abbé Busoni stayed alone with
Noirtier in the chamber of death. Perhaps it was the abbé's Christian
exhortations, perhaps his tender compassion, or, maybe, his persuasive
words, that gave Noirtier courage; whatever it may have been, certain
it is that ever since the day on which he had conversed with the priest,
his despair had given way to complete resignation, to the great astonishment of all who knew his deep affection for Valentine.

M. de Villefort had not seen his father since the morning of the
tragedy. The whole household had undergone a complete change;
another valet had been engaged for himself, a new servant for
Noirtier; two women had entered the service of Mme de Villefort:
everywhere there were new faces.

The assizes were to be opened in three days, and Villefort spent
most of his day closeted in his study preparing his cases, which
afforded him the only distraction from his sorrow. Once only had he
seen his father. Harassed and fatigued, he had gone into the garden
and, deep in gloomy thought, he paced the avenues, lopping off with
his cane the long, withering stalks of the hollyhocks, which stood on
either side of the path like the ghosts of the brilliantly coloured flowers that had bloomed in the season just passed. More than once had
he reached the bottom of the garden where the famous paling separated it from the deserted enclosure, but he always returned by the
selfsame path, and at the same pace. All of a sudden his eyes were
involuntarily attracted toward the house, where he heard the noisy
play of Edward, who had come home from school to spend the
Sunday and Monday with his mother. At the same time he perceived
Noirtier at one of the open windows, to which he had had his chair
wheeled so that he might enjoy the last warm rays of the sun as they
took leave of the red leaves of the Virginia creeper round the balcony.

The old man's eyes were riveted on a spot which Villefort could
only imperfectly distinguish, but their expression was so full of hatred,
venom, and impatience that the Procureur du Roi, ever quick to read
the impressions on that face that he knew so well, turned out of his
path to discover the object of that dark look. He saw Mme de
Villefort seated under a clump of lime-trees nearly divested of their
foliage. She had a book in her hand which she laid aside from time to
time to smile at her son or to return to him his ball, which he persisted in throwing into the garden of the salon. Villefort turned pale,
for he understood what was passing through his father's mind.

Noirtier continued to look at the same object, but suddenly his eyes were turned from the wife to the husband, and Villefort himself had to submit to the gaze of those piercing eyes, which, while changing their objective, had also changed their language, but without losing their menacing expression.

Drawn by an irresistible attraction, as a bird is attracted by a snake, Villefort approached the house. Noirtier's eyes followed him all the while, and the fire they emitted was so fierce that it seemed to pierce him to the very core. Indeed, the look held a deep reproach, and at the same time a terrible menace. He raised his eyes to Heaven as though reminding his son of an unfulfilled promise.

"Yes, yes!" Villefort replied from below. "Have patience for one day more; what I have said shall be done!"

These words seemed to calm Noirtier, for he turned away his eyes. Villefort, on the other hand, tore open his coat, for it was choking him, and, passing his hand over his brow, returned to his study.

The night was cold and calm; everybody in the house had gone to bed as usual, only Villefort once more remained up and worked till five o'clock in the morning. The first sitting of the assizes was to take place the next day, which was a Monday. Villefort saw that day dawn pale and gloomy. He dropped off to sleep for a moment or two when the lamp was at its last flicker; its flickering awakened him, and he found his fingers damp and red as though they had been dipped in blood.

He opened his window; a red streak traversed the sky in the distance, and seemed to cut in two the slender poplars which stood out in black relief against the horizon. In the lucerne-field beyond the chestnut-trees, a lark rose to the sky, pouring out its clear morning song. The dews bathed Villefort's head and refreshed his memory. "To-day," said he with an effort, "the man who wields the knife of justice must strike wherever there is guilt!"

Involuntarily his glance fell on the window where he had seen Noirtier the previous evening. The curtains were drawn, yet his father's image was so vividly impressed on his mind that he addressed himself to the closed window, as though it were open and he still beheld the menacing old man.

"Yes," he muttered, "yes, it shall be done!"

His head dropped upon his chest, and, with his head thus bowed, he paced his room several times till at last he threw himself on a settee, not so much because he wanted to sleep as to rest his tired and cold limbs. By degrees everybody in the house began to stir. From his room Villefort heard all the noises that constitute the life of a house: the opening and shutting of doors, the tinkle of Mme de Villefort's bell summoning her maid, and the shouts of his boy, who

woke fully alive to the enjoyments of life, as children at that age generally do.

Villefort rang his bell. His new valet entered, bringing the newspapers, and with them a cup of chocolate.

"What have you there?" asked Villefort.

"A cup of chocolate, monsieur."

"I did not ask for it. Who has so kindly sent it me?"

"Madame; she said you would doubtless have to do much speaking
at the assizes to-day and needed to fortify yourself," said the valet, as
he placed the cup on the paper-bestrewn table near the sofa. Then he
went out.

For a moment Villefort looked at the cup with a gloomy expression, then he suddenly seized it in a nervous grasp and swallowed the
whole of its contents at a single draught. It appeared almost as though
he hoped that the beverage was poisoned, and that he sought death to
deliver him from a duty which demanded of him something which
was more difficult of accomplishment than it would be to die. He rose
and began walking up and down the room with a smile which would
have been terrible to behold, if anyone had been there to see it. The
chocolate was harmless, and M. de Villefort felt no ill effects from it.

The breakfast-hour arrived, but M. de Villefort did not make his
appearance. The valet entered his room.

"Madame desires me to remind you that it has struck eleven
o'clock, monsieur, and that the sitting begins at noon," he said.

"Well, what else?"

"Madame is ready to accompany you, Monsieur."

"Whither?"

"To the Law Courts."

"Does she really wish to go?" said Villefort in terrifying tones.

The servant started back.

"If you wish to go alone, monsieur, I will inform madame."

For a moment Villefort remained silent, digging his fingernails into
his cheek, the paleness of which was accentuated by his ebony black
hair.

"Tell madame that I wish to speak to her," he said at length, "and that
I request her to wait for me in her room. Then come and shave me."

"Yes, monsieur."

The valet returned almost immediately, and, after having shaved
Villefort, helped him into a sombre black suit. When he had finished,
he said: "Madame said she would expect you, monsieur, as soon as you
were dressed."

"I am going to her."

With his papers under his arm and his hat in his hand, he went to his wife's room. He paused outside for a moment to wipe his clammy forehead. Then he pushed open the door.

Mme de Villefort was sitting on an ottoman impatiently turning over the leaves of a newspaper which Edward, by way of amusing himself, was tearing to pieces before his mother had time to finish reading it. She was dressed ready to go out; her hat was lying on a chair, her gloves were on her hands.

"Ah, here you are," she said, with a calm and natural voice. "But you are very pale! Have you been working all through the night again? Why did you not come and breakfast with us? Well, are you going to take me or shall I go alone with Edward?"

Mme de Villefort had asked one question after another in order to elicit one single answer, but to all her inquiries M. de Villefort remained as cold and mute as a statue.

"Edward, go and play in the salon," he said, looking sternly at the child. "I wish to speak to your mother."

Mme de Villefort trembled as she beheld his cold countenance and heard his resolute tone, which presaged some new disaster. Edward raised his head and looked at his mother, and, seeing she did not confirm his father's orders, proceeded to cut off the heads of his lead soldiers.

"Edward, do you hear me? Go!" cried M. de Villefort, so harshly that the child jumped.

Unaccustomed to such treatment, he rose, pale and trembling, but whether from fear or anger it were difficult to say. His father went up to him, took him in his arms and, kissing him, said: "Go, my child, go!"

Edward went out, and M. de Villefort locked the door behind him.

"Oh, heavens! what is the matter?" cried the young woman, endeavouring to read her husband's inmost thoughts, and forcing a smile which froze M. de Villefort's impassibility.

"Madame, where do you keep the poison you generally use?" the magistrate said slowly without any preamble, as he placed himself between his wife and the door.

Madame's feelings were those of the lark when it sees the kite over its head making ready to swoop down upon it. A harsh, stifled sound, which was neither a cry nor a sigh, escaped from her lips, and she turned deathly white.

"I . . . I do not understand," she said, sinking back on to her cushions.

"I asked you," continued Villefort in a perfectly calm voice, "where you hide the poison by means of which you have killed my father-in-law, my mother-in-law, Barrois, and my daughter Valentine."

"Whatever are you saying?" cried Mme de Villefort, clasping her hands.

"It is not for you to question, but to answer."

"My husband, or the judge?" stammered Mme de Villefort.

"The judge, madame, the judge."

The pallor of the woman, the anguish in her look, and the trembling of her whole frame, were frightful to behold.

"You do not answer, madame?" cried her terrible examiner. Then, with a smile which was more terrifying than his anger, he added: "It must be true since you do not deny it."

She made a movement.

"And you cannot deny it," added Villefort, extending his hand toward her as though to arrest her in the name of the law. "You have accomplished these crimes with impudent skill, nevertheless, you have only been able to deceive those who were blinded by their affection for you. Ever since the death of Madame de Saint-Méran have I known that there was a poisoner in my house—Monsieur d'Avrigny warned me of it. After the death of Barrois—may God forgive me!—my suspicions fell on some one, an angel, for I am ever suspicious, even where there is no crime. But since the death of Valentine there has been no doubt in my mind, madame, or in that of others. Thus your crime, known by two persons and suspected by many, will be made public. Moreover, as I told you just now, I do not speak to you as your husband, but as your judge!"

The young woman hid her face in her hands.

"Oh, I beg of you, do not trust to appearances," she stammered.

"Are you a coward?" cried Villefort in a contemptuous tone. "Indeed, I have always remarked that poisoners are cowards. Is it possible, though, that you are a coward, you who have had the awful courage to watch the death agony of three old people and a young girl, your victims? Is it possible that you are a coward, you who have counted the minutes while four people were slowly done to death? Is it possible that you, who were able to lay your plans so admirably, forgot to reckon on one thing, namely, where the discovery of your crimes would lead you? No, it is impossible! You must have kept some poison, more potent, subtle, and deadly than all the rest, to save you from the punishment you deserve! At all events I hope so!"

Mme de Villefort wrung her hands and fell on her knees.

"I understand, oh yes! I understand that you own your guilt," he continued. "But a confession made to your judges at the eleventh hour when it is impossible to deny the crime in no way diminishes the punishment they inflict on the guilty one."

"Punishment!" cried Mme de Villefort, "Punishment! Twice have you said that word!"

"Yes, twice. Did you think you would escape because you had been guilty four times? Did you think that because you were the wife of him who demands retribution it would be withheld you? No, madame, no! The poisoner shall go to the scaffold whoever she may be, unless, as I said just now, she was cautious enough to keep for herself a few drops of the deadliest poison."

Mme de Villefort uttered a wild scream, and a hideous and invincible terror laid hold of her distorted features.

"Oh, do not fear the scaffold, madame," resumed the magistrate. "I do not wish to dishonour you, for in doing so, I should bring dishonour on myself. On the contrary, if you have heard me correctly, you must understand that you are not to die on the scaffold!"

"No, I do not understand. What do you mean?" stammered the unhappy woman, completely overwhelmed.

"I mean that the wife of the first magistrate will not, by her infamy, sully an unblemished name and, with one blow, bring dishonour on her husband and her child."

"No . . . Oh, no . . .!"

"Well, madame, it will be a kind action on your part, and I thank you for it."

"You thank me? For what?"

"For what you have just told me."

"What did I say? My head is in a whirl, and I can understand nothing. Oh, my God! My God!"

She rose from her seat, foaming at the mouth and her hair all dishevelled.

"You have not answered the question that I put to you when I came in, madame. Where is the poison you generally use, madame?"

She raised her arms to Heaven, and wringing her hands in despair, exclaimed: "No, no! You could not wish that!"

"What I do not wish, madame, is that you should perish on the scaffold, do you understand?" replied Villefort.

"Have mercy!"

"What I demand, madame, is that justice shall be done. My mission on earth is to punish," he added with a fierce look in his eyes. "I should send the executioner to any other woman were she the Queen herself, but to you I am merciful! To you I say: 'Madame, have you not put aside a few drops of the most potent, the swiftest, and deadliest poison?'"

"Oh, forgive me! Let me live! Remember that I am your wife!"

"You are a poisoner."

"For heaven's sake . . . ! for the sake of the love you once bore me! for our child's sake! Oh, let me live for our child's sake!"

"No! no! no! I tell you. If I let you live, you will perhaps kill him like the rest."

"I kill my son!" cried the desperate mother, throwing herself upon Villefort. "I kill my Edward! Ha! ha!" She finished the sentence with a frightful laugh, a mad, demoniacal laugh, which ended in a terrible rattle. She had fallen at her husband's feet! Villefort bent down to her.

"Remember, madame," he said, "if justice has not been done when I return, I shall denounce you with my own lips and arrest you with my own hands!"

She listened panting, overwhelmed, crushed; only her eyes had any life in them, and they glared horribly.

"Remember what I say," said Villefort. "I am going to the Courts to pass sentence of death upon a murderer. . . . If I find you alive upon my return, you will spend the night in a prison cell."

Mme de Villefort groaned, her nerves relaxed, and she sank upon the floor exhausted.

For a moment the magistrate appeared to feel pity for her; he looked at her less sternly, and, slightly bending toward her, he said: "Good-bye, madame, good-bye!"

This farewell fell upon Mme de Villefort like the knife of an executioner, and she fainted.

The judge went out and double-locked the door behind him.

## CHAPTER LXIX

## EXPIATION

THE Court had risen, and as the Procureur du Roi drove home through the crowded streets, the tumultuous thoughts of the morning surged through and through his weary brain. His wife a murderess! Doubtless she was at this moment recalling all her crimes to her memory and imploring God's mercy; perhaps she was writing a letter asking her virtuous husband's forgiveness. Suddenly he said to himself: "That woman must live. She must repent and bring up my son, my poor son, the sole survivor of my unfortunate family except the indestructible old man. She loved him. It was for him that she committed the crimes. One must never despair of the heart of a mother who loves her child. She will repent, and no one shall know of her guilt. She shall take her son and her treasurers far away from here, and she will be happy, for all her happiness is centred round her love for her son, and her son will never leave her. I shall have done a good deed, and that will ease my mind."

The carriage stopped in the yard. He stepped out and ran into the house. When passing Noirtier's door, which was half open, he saw

two men, but he did not trouble himself about who was with his
father, his thoughts were elsewhere. He went into the salon—it was
empty!

He rushed up to her bedroom. The door was locked. A shudder
went through him, and he stood still.

"Héloïse!" he cried, and he thought he heard some furniture move.

"Héloïse!" he repeated.

"Who is there?" asked a voice.

"Open quickly!" called Villefort. "It is I."

But, notwithstanding the request and the tones of anguish in which
it was made, the door remained closed, and he broke it open with a
violent kick.

Mme de Villefort was standing at the entrance to the room which
led to her boudoir. She was pale and her face was contracted; she
looked at him with a terrifying glare.

"Héloïse! Héloïse!" he cried. "What ails you? Speak!"

The young woman stretched out her stiff and lifeless hand.

"It is done, monsieur," she said with a rattling which seemed to tear
at her very throat. "What more do you want?" And with that she fell
her full length on the carpet. Villefort ran up to her and seized her
hand, which held in a convulsive grasp a glass bottle with a gold stop-
per. Mme de Villefort was dead!

Frantic with horror, Villefort started back to the door and contemplated the corpse.

"My son!" he called out. "Where is my son? Edward! Edward!"

He rushed out of the room calling out, "Edward! Edward!" in
tones of such anguish that the servants came crowding round him in
alarm.

"My son—where is my son?" asked Villefort. "Send him out of the
house! Do not let me him see . . ."

"Monsieur Edward is not downstairs, monsieur," said the valet.

"He is probably playing in the garden. Go and see quickly."

"Madame called her son in nearly half an hour ago, monsieur.
Monsieur Edward came to madame and has not been down since."

A cold sweat broke out on Villefort's forehead; his legs gave way
under him, and thoughts began to chase each other across his mind
like the uncontrollable wheels of a broken clock.

"He came into Madame de Villefort's room?" he murmured, as he
slowly retraced his steps, wiping his forehead with one hand and supporting himself against the wall with the other.

"Edward! Edward!" he muttered. There was no answer. Villefort went
farther. Mme de Villefort's body was lying across the doorway leading to
the boudoir in which Edward must be; the corpse seemed to guard the

threshold with wide staring eyes, while the lips held an expression of terrible and mysterious irony. Behind the body the raised curtain permitted one to see into part of the boudoir: an upright piano and the end of a blue satin sofa. Villefort advanced two or three steps, and on the sofa—no doubt asleep—he perceived his child lying. The unhappy man had a feeling of inexpressible joy; a ray of pure light descended into the depths in which he was struggling. All he had to do was to step across the dead body, take the child in his arms, and flee far, far away.

He was no longer the exquisite degenerate typified by the man of modern civilization; he had become like a tiger wounded unto death. It was not prejudice he now feared, but phantoms. He jumped over his wife's body as though it were a yawning furnace of red-hot coals. Taking the boy in his arms, he pressed him to his heart, called him, shook him, but the child made no response. He pressed his eager lips to the child's cheeks—they were cold and livid; he felt the stiffened limbs; he placed his hand over his heart—it beat no more. The child was dead.

Terror-stricken, Villefort dropped upon his knees; the child fell from his arms and rolled beside his mother. A folded paper fell from his breast; Villefort picked it up and recognized his wife's handwriting, and eagerly read the following:

> You know that I have been a good mother, since it was for my son's sake that I became a criminal. A good mother never leaves her son!

Villefort could not believe his eyes, and thought he must be losing his reason. He dragged himself toward Edward's body, examined it once more with the careful attention of a lioness contemplating its cub.

Then a heartrending cry escaped his breast. "God!" he murmured. "It is the hand of God!"

Villefort rose from his knees, his head bowed under the weight of grief. He, who had never felt compassion for anyone, decided to go to his father so that in his weakness he would have some one to whom he could relate his sufferings, some one with whom he could weep. He descended the little stairs with which we are acquainted, and entered Noirtier's room.

As he entered, Noirtier appeared to be listening attentively, and as affectionately as his paralysed body would permit, to Abbé Busoni, who was as calm and cold as usual. On seeing the abbé, Villefort drew his hand across his forehead. The past all came back to him, and he recollected the visit the abbé had paid him on the day of Valentine's death.

"You here?" he said. "Do you never appear except hand in hand with Death?"

Busoni started up. "I came to pray over the body of your daughter," replied Busoni.

"And why have you come to-day?"

"I have come to-day to tell you that you have made abundant retribution to me and from to-day I shall pray God to forgive you."

"Good heavens!" cried Villefort, starting back with a look of terror in his eyes. "That is not Abbé Busoni's voice!"

"No," said the abbé, and as he tore off his false tonsure his long black hair fell around his manly face.

"That is the face of Monte Cristo!" cried Villefort, a haggard look in his eyes.

"You are not right yet. You must go still further back."

"That voice! That voice! Where have I heard it before?"

"You first heard it at Marseilles twenty-three years ago, on the day of your betrothal to Mademoiselle de Saint-Méran."

"You are not Busoni? Nor yet Monte Cristo? My God! you are my secret, implacable, mortal enemy. I must have wronged you in some way at Marseilles. Ah! woe is me!"

"You are right, it is so," said the Count, crossing his arms over his broad chest. "Think! Think!"

"But what did I do to you?" cried Villefort, whose mind was struggling on the borders between reason and insanity and had sunk into that state which is neither dreaming nor reality. "What have I done? Tell me! Speak!"

"You condemned me to a slow and hideous death; you killed my father; you robbed me of liberty, love, and happiness!"

"Who are you then? Who can you be?"

"I am the ghost of an unhappy wretch you buried in the dungeons of the Château d'If. At length this ghost left his tomb under the disguise of the Count of Monte Cristo, and loaded himself with gold and diamonds that you might not recognize him until to-day."

"Ah! I recognize you! I recognize you!" cried the Procureur du Roi. "You are . . ."

"I am Edmond Dantès!"

"You are Edmond Dantès!" cried the magistrate, seizing the Count by the wrist. "Then come with me!" He dragged him up the stairs, and the astonished Monte Cristo followed him, not knowing where he was leading him, though he had a presentiment of some fresh disaster.

"Look, Edmond Dantès!" said Villefort, pointing to the dead bodies of his wife and son. "Are you satisfied with your vengeance?"

Monte Cristo turned pale at the frightful sight. Realizing that he had passed beyond the bounds of vengeance, he felt he could no longer say: "God is for me and with me." With an expression of indescribable anguish, he threw himself on the child's body, opened his eyes, felt his pulse, and, rushing with him into Valentine's room, locked the door.

"My child!" de Villefort called out. "He has taken the body of my dead child! Oh, curse you! Curses on you in life and death!"

He wanted to run after Monte Cristo, but his feet seemed rooted to the spot, and his eyes looked ready to start out of their sockets; he dug his nails into chest his until his fingers were covered with blood; the veins of his temples swelled and seemed about to burst through their narrow limits and flood his brain with a deluge of boiling fire. Then with a shrill cry followed by a loud burst of laughter, he ran down the stairs.

A quarter of an hour later the door of Valentine's room opened, and the Count of Monte Cristo reappeared. Pale, sad of eye, and heavy of heart, all the noble features of that usually calm face were distorted with grief. He held in his arms the child whom no skill had been able to recall to life. Bending his knee, he reverently placed him beside his mother with his head upon her breast. Then, rising, he went out of the room and, meeting a servant on the staircase, asked: "Where is Monsieur de Villefort?"

Instead of replying, the servant pointed to the garden. Monte Cristo went down the steps, and, approaching the spot indicated, saw Villefort in the midst of his servants with a spade in his hand digging the earth in a fury and wildly calling out: "Oh, I shall find him. You may pretend he is not here, but I shall find him, even if I have to dig until the day of the Last Judgment."

Monte Cristo recoiled in terror. "He is mad!" he cried.

And as though fearing that the walls of the accursed house would fall and crush him, he rushed into the street, doubting for the first time whether he had the right to do what he had done.

"Oh, enough, enough of all this!" he said. "Let me save the last one!

On arriving home he met Morrel, who was wandering about the house in the Champs Élysées like a ghost waiting for its appointed time to enter the tomb.

"Get yourself ready, Maximilian," he said to him with a smile. "We leave Paris to-morrow."

"Have you nothing more to do here?" asked Morrel.

"No," replied Monte Cristo, "and God grant that I have not already done too much!"


## CHAPTER LXX

## THE DEPARTURE

THE events just recorded were the talk of all Paris. Emmanuel and his wife were recounting them with very natural astonishment in their little salon in the Rue Meslay, and comparing the three sudden and unexpected calamities that had overtaken Morcerf, Danglars, and de Villefort. Morrel, who had come to pay them a visit, listened to them, or rather was present in his usual state of apathy.

"Really, Emmanuel," said Julie, "one could almost imagine that when all these rich people, who were so happy but yesterday, laid the foundations of their wealth, happiness, and prestige, they forgot the part played by their evil genius; and like the wicked fairy of our childhood days who had not received an invitation to some christening or wedding, this genius has suddenly appeared to take his vengeance for the neglect."

"What disasters!" said Emmanuel, thinking of Morcerf and Danglars.

"What suffering!" said Julie, whose sympathy tuned toward Valentine but whose name she, with her womanly delicacy of feeling, would not mention before her brother.

"If it is God's hand that has overtaken them," continued Emmanuel, "it must be that He Who is goodness itself has found nothing in the past life of these people which merited mitigation of their suffering."

"Is that not a very rash judgment, Emmanuel?" said Julie. "If anyone had said, 'This man deserves his punishment' when my father held his pistol to his head, would that person not have been mistaken?"

"Yes, but God did not permit him to die just as He did not permit Abraham to sacrifice his son. To the patriarch and to us He sent an angel at the last moment to stay the hand of Death."

He had scarcely finished speaking when the bell rang, and almost at the same moment the door opened to admit Monte Cristo. There was a cry of joy from the two young people, but Maximilian only raised his head to let it drop again.

"Maximilian, I have come to fetch you," said the Count, without appearing to notice the different impressions his presence had produced on his hosts.

"To fetch me?" said Morrel, as though waking from a dream.

"Yes," said Monte Cristo. "Is it not agreed that I should take you away? And did I not tell you to be ready?"

"I am quite ready. I have come to bid them farewell."

"Whither are you going, Count?" asked Julie.

"In the first instance to Marseilles, and I am taking your brother with me."

"Oh, Count, bring him back to us cured of his melancholy!" said Julie.

"Have you then noticed that he is unhappy?" said the Count.

"Yes, and I am afraid he finds it very dull with us."

"I shall divert him," said the Count.

"I am ready," said Maximilian. "Good-bye, Emmanuel! Good-bye, Julie!"

"What! Good-bye?" cried Julie. "You are not going away without any preparations and without a passport?"

"Delays only double grief when one has to part," said Monte Cristo, "and I am sure Maximilian has provided himself with everything; at all events I asked him to do so."

"I have my passports, and my trunks are packed," said Morrel in a lifeless tone of voice. "Good-bye, sister! Good-bye, Emmanuel!"

"Let us be off," said the Count.

"Before you go, Count, permit me to tell you what the other day . . ."

"Madame," replied the Count, taking her two hands, "all that you can tell me in words can never express what I read in your eyes, or the feelings awakened in your heart, as also in mine. Like the benefactors of romances, I would have left without revealing myself to you, but this virtue was beyond me, because I am but a weak and vain man, and because I feel a better man for seeing a look of gratitude, joy and affection in the eyes of my fellow beings. I will leave you now, and I carry my egoism so far as to say: 'Do not forget me, my friends, for you will probably never see me again!'"

"Never see you again!" exclaimed Emmanuel, while the tears rolled down Julie's cheeks.

He pressed his lips to Julie's hand and tore himself away from this home where happiness was the host; he made a sign to Morrel, who followed him with all the indifference he had manifested since Valentine's death.

"Restore my brother to happiness again," Julie whispered to Monte Cristo.

He pressed her hand as he had done eleven years ago on the staircase leading to Morrel's study.

"Do you still trust Sindbad the Sailor?" he asked with a smile.

"Oh, yes."

"Well, then, sleep in the peace and confidence of the Lord."

The post-chaise was waiting; four vigorous horses were shaking their manes and pawing the ground in their impatience. Ali was waiting at the bottom of the steps, his face bathed in perspiration as though he had been running.

"Well, did you see the old gentleman?" the Count asked him in Arabic.

Ali made a sign in the affirmative.

"And did you unfold the letter before him as I instructed you to do?"

The slave again made a sign in the affirmative.

"What did he say to you, or rather, what did he do?"

Ali placed himself under the light so that his master might see him, and in his intelligent manner he imitated the expression on the old man's face when he closed his eyes in token of assent.

"It is well, he accepts," said Monte Cristo. "Let us start!"

Half an hour passed, and the carriage suddenly stopped; the Count had pulled the silken cord that was attached to Ali's finger. The Nubian alighted and opened the door.

It was a lovely starlit night. They were on top of the Villejuif hill, whence Paris appeared like a dark sea, and her millions of lights like phosphorescent waves; waves which were more clamorous, more passionate, more greedy than those of the tempestuous ocean; waves which are ever raging, foaming, and ever ready to devour what comes in their way.

At a sign from the Count, the carriage went on, leaving him alone. Then, with arms crossed, he contemplated for a long time this modern Babylon which inspires the poet, the religious enthusiast, and the materialist alike. Bowing his head and joining his hands as though in prayer, he murmured:

"Oh, great city! In thy palpitating bosom have I found what I sought; like a patient miner have I dug out thy very entrails to root out the evil. My work is accomplished, my mission ended, and now thou canst hold neither pleasure nor pain for me. Farewell, Paris! Farewell!"

His eyes wandered over the vast plain like that of a genius of the night, then passing his hand across his brow, he once more entered his carriage, which disappeared over the hill in a cloud of dust.

They travelled thus for ten leagues in complete silence, Morrel wrapt in dreams and Monte Cristo watching him dream.

"Morrel," said the Count at length, "do you regret having come with me?"

"No, Count, but in leaving Paris . . ."

"If I had thought your happiness was to be found in Paris, I should have left you there."

"Valentine is laid at rest in Paris, and I feel as though I were losing her for a second time."

"Maximilian, the friends we have lost do not repose under the ground," said the Count; "they are buried deep in our hearts. It has been thus ordained that they may always accompany us. I have two such friends. The one is he who gave me being, and the other is he who brought my intelligence to life. Their spirits are ever with me. When in doubt I consult them, and if I ever do anything that is good, I owe it to them. Consult the voice of your heart, Morrel, and ask it whether you should continue this behaviour towards me."

"The voice of my heart is a very sad one," said Maximilian, "and promises nothing but unhappiness."

The journey was made with extraordinary rapidity; villages fled past them like shadows; trees, shaken by the first autumn winds, seemed like dishevelled giants rushing up only to flee as soon as they had reached them. They arrived at Chalon the next morning, where the Count's steamboat awaited them. Without loss of time the two travellers embarked, and their carriage was taken aboard.

The boat was almost like an Indian canoe, and was specially built for racing. Her two paddle-wheels were like two wings with which she skimmed the water like a bird. Even Morrel seemed intoxicated with the rapidity of their motion, and at times it almost seemed as though the wind, in blowing his hair back from his forehead, also momentarily dispelled the dark clouds that were gathered there. Marseilles was soon reached. As they stood on the Cannebière a boat was leaving for Algiers. Passengers were crowded on the decks, relatives and friends were bidding farewell, some weeping silently, others crying aloud in their grief. It was a touching sight even to those accustomed to witnessing it every day, yet it had not the power to distract Morrel from the one thought that had occupied his mind ever since he set foot on the broad stones of the quay.

"Here is the very spot where my father stood when the *Pharaon* entered the port," he said to the Count. "It was here that the honest man whom you saved from death and dishonour threw himself into my arms; I still feel his tears on my face."

Monte Cristo smiled. "I was there," he said, pointing to a corner of the street. As he spoke a heartrending sob was heard issuing from the very spot indicated by the Count, and they saw a woman making signs to a passenger on the departing boat. The woman was veiled. Monte Cristo watched her with an emotion which must have been evident to Morrel had his eyes not been fixed on the boat.

"Good heavens!" cried Morrel. "Surely I am not mistaken. That young man waving his hand, the one in uniform, is Albert de Morcerf."

"Yes," said Monte Cristo. "I recognized him."

"How can you have done? You were looking the other way."

The Count smiled in the way he had when he did not wish to answer. His eyes turned again to the veiled woman, who soon disappeared round the corner of the street. Then, turning to Maximilian, he said: "Have you nothing to do in the town?"

"Yes, I wish to pay a visit to my father's grave," replied Morrel in a lifeless voice.

"Very well, go and wait for me; I will join you there."

"You are leaving me?"

"Yes . . . I have also a visit of devotion to make."

Morrel let his hand fall into the one the Count held out to him; then, with an inexpressibly melancholy nod of the head, he took his leave of the Count and directed his steps toward the east of the town.

Monte Cristo stayed where he was until Maximilian was out of sight, then he wended his way to the Allées de Meilhan in search of a little house that was made familiar to our readers at the beginning of this story.

In spite of its age the little house, once inhabited by Dantès' father, still looked charming and not even its obvious poverty could deprive it of its cheerful aspect. It was to this little house that the veiled woman repaired when Monte Cristo saw her leaving the departing ship. She was just closing the gate when he turned the corner of the street, so that she disappeared from his vision almost as soon as he had found her again. The worn steps were old acquaintances of his; he knew better than anyone how to open the old gate with its large-headed nail, which raised the latch from the inside.

He entered without knocking or announcing himself in any way. At the end of a paved path was a little garden that caught all the sunshine and light, and its trees could be seen from the front door. It was here Mercédès had found, in the spot indicated, the sum of money which the Count's delicacy of feeling had led him to say had been deposited in this little garden for twenty-four years.

Monte Cristo heard a deep sigh and, looking in the direction whence it came, he beheld Mercédès sitting in an arbour covered with jasmine with thick foliage and slender purple flowers; her head was bowed, and she was weeping bitterly. She had partly raised her veil and being alone, was giving full vent to the sighs and sobs which had so long been repressed by the presence of her son.

Monte Cristo advanced a few steps, crunching the gravel under his feet as he trod. Mercédès raised her head and gave a cry of fear at seeing a man before her.

"Madame, it is no longer in my power to bring you happiness," said the Count, "but I offer you consolation. Will you deign to accept it from a friend?"

"In truth I am a most unhappy woman, and all alone in the world," replied Mercédès. "My son was all I had, and he too has left me."

"He has acted rightly, madame," replied the Count. "He is a noble-hearted soul who realizes that every man owes a tribute to his country; some their talents, others their industry, others their blood. Had he remained beside you, he would have led a useless life. In struggling against adversity, he will become great and powerful and will change his adversity into prosperity. Let him remake a future for himself and for you, madame, and I venture to say you are leaving it in safe hands."

"I shall never enjoy the prosperity of which you speak," said the poor woman, shaking her head sadly, "but from the bottom of my heart I pray God to grant it to my son. There has been so much sorrow in my life that I feel my grave is not far distant. You have done well, Count, in bringing me back to the spot where I was once so happy. One should wait for death there, where one has found happiness."

"Alas!" said Monte Cristo, "your words fall heavily on my heart, and they are all the more bitter and cutting since you have every reason to hate me. It is I who am the cause of all your misfortunes; why do you pity me instead of reproaching me?"

"Hate you! Reproach you, Edmond! Hate and reproach the man who save my son's life, for I know it was your intention to kill the son of whom Monsieur de Morcerf was so proud, was it not? Look at me and you will see whether I bear the semblance of a reproach against you."

The Count looked up and fixed his gaze on Mercédès, who, half rising from her seat, stretched her hands toward him.

"Oh, look at me," she continued in tones of deep melancholy. "My eyes are no longer bright, as in the days when I smiled upon Edmond Dantès, who was waiting for me at the window of this garret where his father lived. Since then many sorrowful days have passed and made a gulf between that time and now. Reproach you! Hate you, Edmond! my friend! No, it is myself that I hate and reproach!" she cried, wringing her hands and raising her eyes to heaven. "Ah, but I have been sorely punished. . . . I had faith, innocence, and love—everything that makes for supreme happiness, yet, unhappy wretch that I am, I doubted God's goodness!"

Monte Cristo silently took her hand.

"No, my friend, do not touch me," she said, gently withdrawing it. "You have spared me, yet of all I am the most to blame. All the others were prompted by hatred, cupidity, or selfishness, but cowardice was at the root of all my actions. No, do not take my hand, Edmond; you wish to say some kind and affectionate words, I know, but keep them for some one else. I am not worthy of them. See—see how misfortune has silvered my hair. I have shed so many tears that dark rings encircle my eyes; my forehead is covered with wrinkles. You, on the contrary, are still young, Edmond; you are still handsome and dignified. That is because you have preserved your faith and your strength: you trusted in God, and He has sustained you. I was a coward; I denied Him, and He has forsaken me."

Mercédès burst into tears; her woman's heart was breaking in the clash of her memories. Monte Cristo took her hand and kissed it respectfully, but she knew that it was a kiss without feeling, such as he would have imprinted on the marble statue of a saint.

"No, Mercédès," said he, "you must form a better opinion of yourself. You are a good and noble woman, and you disarmed me by your sorrow; but behind me there was concealed an invisible and offended God, Whose agent I was and Who did not choose to withhold the blow I had aimed. I call God to witness, at Whose feet I have prostrated myself every day for the last ten years, that I have offered the sacrifice of my life and my lifelong projects to you. But, and I say it with pride, Mercédès, God had need of me and my life was spared. The first part of my life passed away amid terrible misfortunes, cruel sufferings, desertion on the part of those who loved me, persecution by those who did not know me. Then after captivity, solitude, and tribulation, I was suddenly restored to fresh air and liberty, and I became the possessor of a large fortune, so dazzling and fabulous, that I could only conclude that God had sent it me for some great purpose. I looked upon this wealth as a sacred charge. From that time I did not experience a single hour's peace: I felt myself pushed onward like a cloud of fire sent from Heaven to burn the cities of the wicked. I habituated my body to the most violent exercise, and my spirit to the severest trials. I taught my arm to slay, my eyes to behold suffering, my lips to smile at the most terrible sights. From being a kind and confiding nature, I made myself into a vindictive, treacherous and wicked man. Then I set forth on the path that was opened up to me; I conquered space and I have reached my goal: woe to those I encountered on my way!"

"Enough, Edmond, enough," said Mercédès. "Now bid me farewell, Edmond. We must part."

"Before I leave you, Mercédès, is there nothing I can do for you?" asked Monte Cristo.

"I have but one desire, Edmond—my son's happiness."

"Pray to God, who alone disposes over life and death, to spare his life, and I will do the rest. And for yourself, Mercédès?"

"I need nothing for myself. I live, as it were, between two graves. The one is that of Edmond Dantès, who died many years ago. Ah! how I loved him! The other grave belongs to the man Edmond Dantès killed; I approve of the deed, but I must pray for the dead man."

"Your son shall be happy, madame," the count repeated.

"Then I also shall be as happy as it is possible for me to be."

"But . . . what are you going to do?"

"All I am fit for now is to pray. I do not need to work; I have the little treasure you buried and which has been found in the spot you indicated. There will be much gossip as to who I am, what I do, and how I subsist, but what does that matter? Those are questions which concern but God, you, and me."

"Mercédès," said the Count, "I do not wish to reproach you, but you have taken an exaggerated view as to your sacrifice of the fortune amassed by Monsieur de Morcerf. By rights half of it was yours in virtue of your vigilance and economy."

"I know what you are going to propose. I cannot accept it, Edmond; my son would not permit it."

"I will not do anything without Albert's approval. I will make myself acquainted with his intentions and shall submit to them. But if he agrees to what I propose, will you follow his example?"

"You know, Edmond, that I have no longer any reasoning powers, and no will, unless it be the will not to take any decision. My will has been swept away by the storms that have raged over my head. I am as helpless in God's hands as a sparrow in the talons of an eagle. Since He does not wish me to die, I live; if He sends me help, it is because He so desires, and I shall accept it."

Monte Cristo bowed his head under the vehemence of her grief. "Will you not say *au revoir* to me?" he said, holding out his hand.

"On the contrary, I do say *au revoir*," Mercédès replied, solemnly pointing to heaven, "and that is a proof that I still hope."

She touched the Count's hand with her own trembling fingers, ran up the stairs, and disappeared from his sight. Monte Cristo left the house with heavy steps. But Mercédès did not see him; her eyes were searching in the far distance for the ship that was carrying her son toward the vast ocean. Nevertheless her voice almost involuntarily murmured softly: "Edmond! Edmond!"

The Count went with a heavy heart from the house where he had taken leave of Mercédès, in all probability never to see her again, and turned his steps toward the cemetery where Morrel was awaiting him.

Ten years previously, he had also sought piously for a grave in this same cemetery, but he had sought in vain. He who had returned to France with millions of money had been unable to find the grave of his father, who had died of hunger. Morrel had had a cross erected, but it had fallen down, and the sexton had burnt it with the rubbish. The worthy merchant had been more fortunate. He had died in the arms of his children, and by them had been laid beside his wife, who had preceded him into eternity by two years.

Two large marble slabs, on which were engraved their names, were standing side by side in a little railed-in enclosure shaded by four cypresses.

Maximilian was leaning against one of these trees staring at the two graves with unseeing eyes. He was obviously deeply affected.

"Maximilian, it is not on those graves you should look, but there!" said the Count, pointing to the sky.

"The dead are everywhere," said Morrel. "Did you not tell me so yourself when you made me leave Paris?"

"On the journey, Maximilian, you asked me to let you stay a few days at Marseilles. Is that still your wish?"

"I have no longer any wishes, Count, but I think the time of waiting would pass less painfully here than anywhere."

"All the better, Maximilian, for I must leave you, but I have your word, have I not?"

"I shall forget it, Count, I know I shall."

"No, you will not forget it, for you are, above all things, a man of honour, Morrel; you have sworn to wait and will now renew your oath."

"Have pity on me, Count, I am so unhappy!"

"I have known a man unhappier than you, Morrel."

"What man is there unhappier than he who has lost the only being he loved on earth?"

"Listen, Morrel, and fix your whole mind on what I am going to tell you. I once knew a man who, like you, had set all his hopes of happiness upon a woman. He was young; he had an old father whom he loved, and a sweetheart whom he adored. He was about to marry her, when suddenly he was overtaken by one of those caprices of fate which would make us doubt in the goodness of God, if He did not reveal Himself later by showing us that all is but a means to an end. This man was deprived of his liberty, of the woman he loved, of the future of which he had dreamed and which he believed was his, and plunged into the depths of a dungeon. He stayed there fourteen years, Morrel. Fourteen years!" repeated the Count. "And during those fourteen years he suffered many an hour of despair. Like you, Morrel, he also thought he was the unhappiest of men, and sought to take his life."

"Well?" asked Morrel.

"Well, when he was at the height of his despair, God revealed Himself to him through another human being. It takes a long time for eyes that are swollen with weeping to see clearly, and at first, perhaps, he did not comprehend this infinite mercy, but at length he took patience and waited. One day he miraculously left his tomb, transfigured, rich and powerful. His first cry was for his father, but his father was dead! When his son sought his grave, ten years after his death, even that had disappeared, and no one could say to him: 'There rests in the Lord the father who so dearly loved you!' That man, therefore, was unhappier than you, for he did not even know where to look for his father's grave."

"But then he still had the woman he loved."

"You are wrong, Morrel. This woman was faithless. She married one of the persecutors of her betrothed. You see, Morrel, that in this again he was unhappier than you."

"And did this man find consolation?"

"At all events he found peace."

"Is it possible for this man ever to be happy again?"

"He hopes so."

The young man bowed his head, and after a moment's silence he gave Monte Cristo his hand, saying: "You have my promise, Count, but remember . . ."

"I shall expect you on the Isle of Monte Cristo on the fifth of October, Morrel. On the fourth, a yacht named the *Eurus* will be waiting for you in the Port of Bastia. Give your name to the captain, and he will bring you to me. That is quite definite, is it not?"

"It is, Count, and I shall do as you say. You are leaving me?"

"Yes, I have business in Italy. I am leaving you alone with your grief."

"When are you going?"

"At once. The steamboat is waiting for me, and in an hour I shall be far from you. Will you go with me as far as the harbour?"

"I am entirely at your service."

Morrel accompanied the Count to the harbour. The smoke was already issuing from the black funnel like an immense plume. The boat got under weigh, and an hour later, as Monte Cristo had said, the same feather of white smoke was scarcely discernible on the horizon as it mingled with the first mists of the night.

## CHAPTER LXXI

## THE FIFTH OF OCTOBER

IT was about six o'clock in the evening; an opalescent light through which the autumn sun shed a golden ray descended on the sea. The heat of the day had gradually diminished into that delicious freshness which seems like nature's breathing after the burning siesta of the afternoon, and a light breeze was bringing to the shores of the Mediterranean the sweet perfume of trees and plants mingled with the salt smell of the sea.

A small yacht, elegant in shape, was drifting in the evening air over this immense lake, like some swan opening its wings to the wind and gliding through the water. It advanced rapidly, although there seemed hardly sufficient wind to ruffle the curls of a young maiden.

Standing on the prow, a tall dark man was watching the approach of land, a cone-shaped mass, which appeared to rise out of the water like a huge Catalan hat.

"Is that Monte Cristo?" he asked of the skipper in a voice full of sadness.

"Yes, Your Excellency," replied the latter. "We are there."

Ten minutes later, with sails furled, they anchored a hundred feet from the little harbour. The cutter was ready with four oarsmen and the pilot. The eight oars dipped together without a splash, and the boat glided rapidly onward. A moment later they found themselves in a small natural creek and ran aground on fine sand.

"If Your Excellency will get on to the shoulders of two of our men they will carry you to dry land," said the pilot. The young man's answer was a shrug of complete indifference as he swung himself out of the boat into the water.

"Ah, Excellency!" cried the pilot. "That is wrong of you! The master will scold us."

The young man continued to follow the two sailors, and after about thirty steps reached the shore, where he stood and peered into the darkness. Then he felt a hand on his shoulder, and a voice startled him by saying: "Good evening, Maximilian. You are very punctual."

"It is you, Count!" cried the young man, delightedly pressing Monte Cristo's two hands in his.

"Yes, and, as you see, as punctual as you are. But you are drenched, my friend; come, there is a house prepared for you, where you will forget cold and fatigue."

The sailors were dismissed, and the two friends proceeded on their way. They walked for some time in silence, each busy with his own thoughts. Presently Morrel, with a sigh, turned to his companion: "I am come," said he, "to say to you as the gladiator would say to the Roman Emperor: 'He who is about to die salutes you.'"

"You have not found consolation then?" Monte Cristo asked, with a strange look.

"Did you really think I could?" Morrel said with great bitterness. "Listen to me, Count, as to one whose spirit lives in heaven while his body still walks on the earth. I am come to die in the arms of a friend. It is true there are those I love, my sister and her husband, Emmanuel, but I have need of strong arms and one who will smile on me during my last moments. I have your word, Count. You will conduct me to the gates of death by pleasant paths, will you not? Oh, Count, how peacefully and contentedly I shall sleep in the arms of death!"

Morrel said the last words with such determination that the Count trembled.

Seeing that Monte Cristo was silent, Morrel continued: "My friend, you named the fifth of October as the day on which my trial should end. It is to-day the fifth of October. . . . I have but a short while to live."

"So be it," said Monte Cristo. "Come with me."

Morrel followed the Count mechanically, and they had entered the grotto before he perceived it. There was a carpet under his feet; a door opened, exhaling fragrant perfumes, and a bright light dazzled his eyes. Morrel paused, not venturing to advance. He mistrusted the enervating delights that surrounded him. Monte Cristo gently drew him in.

He sat down, and Morrel took a seat opposite him.

They were in a wonderful dining-room, where the marble statues bore baskets on their heads laden with flowers and fruit. Morrel looked at everything in a vague way, though it is even possible he did not see anything.

"Count, you are the essence of all human knowledge," he resumed, "and you make me think you have descended from a more advanced and wiser world than ours. Tell me, is it painful to die?"

Monte Cristo looked at Morrel with indescribable tenderness.

"Yes, it is undoubtedly painful when you violently break this mortal coil that obstinately demands to live. According as we have lived, death is either a friend who rocks us as gently as a nurse, or an enemy who violently tears the soul from the body."

"I understand now why you have brought me here to this deserted isle in the middle of an ocean; to this subterranean palace, which is a sepulchre such as would awaken envy in the heart of a Pharaoh. It is because you love me, is it not, Count? Because you love me well enough to give me a death without agony; a death which will permit me to glide away, holding your hand and murmuring the name of Valentine."

"Yes, yes, you have guess aright, Morrel," said the Count simply. "That is what I intended. Now," he said to himself, "I must bring this young man back to happiness; he has passed through enough sorrow to merit happiness at last." Then aloud he added: "Listen to me, Morrel; I see that your grief is overwhelming. As you know, I have no one in the world to call my own. I have learned to regard you as my son, and to save that son I would sacrifice my life, nay, even my fortune."

"What do you mean?"

"I mean that you wish to leave this world because you do not know all the pleasures a large fortune can give. Morrel, I have nearly a hundred millions; I give them to you. With such a fortune nothing is denied you. Have you ambitions? Every career is opened to you. Turn the world upside down, change its character, let no mad scheme be too mad for you, become a criminal if it is necessary—but live!"

"I have your word, Count," said Morrel coldly. Taking out his watch, he added: "It is half-past eleven."

"Morrel, consider. You would do this thing before my eyes? In my house?"

"Then let me go hence," replied Maximilian gloomily. "Otherwise I shall think that you do not love me for myself but for yourself."

"It is well," said the Count, whose face had brightened at these words. "You wish it, and you are firmly resolved on death. You are certainly most unhappy, and, as you say, a miracle alone could save you. Sit down and wait."

Morrel obeyed. Monte Cristo rose and went to a cupboard, and unlocking it with a key which he wore on a gold chain, took out a small silver casket wonderfully carved; the corners represented four bending women symbolical of angels aspiring to heaven.

He placed the casket on the table, and, opening it, took out a small gold box, the lid of which opened by the pressure of a secret spring. This box contained an unctuous, half-solid substance of an indefinable colour. It was like an iridescence of blue, purple, and gold.

The Count took a small quantity of this substance with a gold spoon and offered it to Morrel while fixing a long and steadfast glance upon him. It was then seen that the substance was of a greenish hue.

"This is what you asked for and what I promised to give you," said the Count.

Taking the spoon from the Count's hand, the young man said:

"I thank you from the bottom of my heart. Farewell, my noble and generous friend. I am going to Valentine and shall tell her all that you have done for me."

Slowly, but without any hesitation, and waiting only to press the Count's hand, Morrel swallowed, or rather tasted, the mysterious substance the Count offered him.

The lamps gradually became dim in the hands of the marble statues that held them, and the perfumes seemed to become less potent. Seated opposite to Morrel, Monte Cristo watched him in the shadow, and Morrel saw nothing but the Count's bright eyes. An immense sadness overtook the young man.

"My friend, I feel that I am dying."

Then he seemed to see Monte Cristo smile, no longer the strange, frightening smile that had several times revealed to him the mysteries of that profound mind, but with the benevolent compassion of a father toward an unreasonable child. At the same time the Count appeared to increase in stature. Nearly double his height he was outlined against the red hangings, and, as he stood there erect and proud, he looked like one of those angels with which the wicked are threatened on the Day of Judgment. Depressed and overcome, Morrel threw himself back in his chair, and a delicious torpor crept into his veins; he seemed to be entering upon the vague delirium that precedes the unknown thing they call death. He endeavoured once more to give his hand to the Count, but it would not move; he wished to articulate a last farewell, but his tongue lay heavy in his mouth like a stone at the mouth of a sepulchre. His languid eyes involuntarily closed, yet through his closed eyelids he perceived a form moving which he recognized in spite of the darkness that seemed to envelop him.

It was the Count, who was opening a door. Immediately a brilliant light from the adjoining room inundated the one where Morrel was gently passing into oblivion. Then he saw a woman of marvellous beauty standing on the threshold. She seemed like a pale and sweetly smiling angel of mercy come to conjure the angel of vengeance.

"Is heaven opening before me?" the dying man thought to himself. "This angel resembles the one I have lost!"

Monte Cristo pointed to the sofa where Morrel was reclining. The young woman advanced toward it with clasped hands and a smile on he lips.

"Valentine! Valentine!" Morrel's soul went out to her, but he uttered no sound; only a sigh escaped his lips and he closed his eyes.

Valentine ran up to him, and his lips opened as though in speech.

"He is calling you," said the Count. "He is calling you in his sleep, he to whom you have entrusted your life is calling you. Death would have separated you, but by good fortune I was near and I have overcome death! Valentine, henceforth you must never leave him, for, in order to rejoin you, he courted death. Without me you would both have died; I give you to one another. May God give me credit for the two lives I have saved!"

Valentine seized Monte Cristo's hand, and in a transport of irresistible joy carried it to her lips.

"Oh, yes, yes, I do thank you, and with all my heart," said she. "If you doubt the sincerity of my gratitude, ask Haydee, ask my dear sister Haydee, who, since our departure from France, has helped me to await this happy day that has dawned for me."

"Do you love Haydee?" asked Monte Cristo, vainly endeavouring to hide his agitation.

"With my whole heart."

"Well, then, I have a favour to ask of you, Valentine," said the Count.

"Of me? Are you really giving me that happiness?"

"Yes, you called Haydee your sister; be a real sister to her, Valentine; give to her all that you believe you owe to me. Protect her, both Morrel and you, for henceforth she will be alone in the world."

"Alone in the world?" repeated a voice behind the Count. "Why?" Monte Cristo turned round.

Haydee was standing there pale and motionless, looking at the Count in mortal dread.

"To-morrow, you will be free, my daughter," answered the Count. "You will then assume your proper place in society; I do not wish my fate to overcloud yours. Daughter of a prince! I bestow on you the wealth and the name of your father!"

Haydee turned pale, and, in a voice choking with emotion, she said: "Then you are leaving me, my lord?"

"Haydee! Haydee! You are young and beautiful. Forget even my name and be happy!"

"So be it!" said Haydee. "Your orders shall be obeyed, my lord. I shall even forget your name and be happy!" and stepping back she sought to retire.

The Count shuddered as he caught the tones of her voice which penetrated to the inmost recesses of his heart. His eyes encountered the maiden's, and he could not bear their brilliancy.

"My God!" cried he. "Is it possible that my suspicions are correct? Haydee, would you be happy never to leave me again."

"I am young," she replied. "I love the life you made so sweet to me, and I should regret to die!"

"Does that mean to say that if I were to leave you . . .?"

"I should die? Yes, my lord."

"Do you love me, then?"

"Oh, Valentine, he asks me whether I love him! Valentine, tell him whether you love Maximilian!"

The Count felt his heart swelling within him; he opened his arms, and Haydee threw herself into them with a cry.

"Oh, yes, I love you!" she said. "I love you as one loves a father, a brother, a husband! I love you as I love my life, for to me you are the noblest, the best, and the greatest of all created beings!"

"Let it be as you wish, my sweet angel," said the Count. "God has sustained me against my enemies and I see now He does not wish me to end my triumph with repentance. I intended punishing myself, but God has pardoned me! Love me, Haydee! Who knows? Perhaps your love will help me to forget all I do not wish to remember!"

"What do you mean, my lord?" asked she.

"What I mean is that one word from you, Haydee, has enlightened me more than twenty years of bitter experience. I have but you in the world, Haydee. Through you I come back to life, through you I can suffer, and through you I can be happy."

"Do you hear him, Valentine?" Haydee cried out. "He says he can suffer through me! Through me, who would give my life for him!"

The Count reflected for a moment.

"Have I caught a glimpse of the truth?" he said. "But, whether it be for recompense or punishment, I accept this fate. Come, Haydee!"

Throwing his arms round the young girl, he shook Valentine by the hand and disappeared.

An hour or so elapsed, and Valentine still stood beside Morrel breathless, voiceless, with her eyes fixed on him. At length she felt his heart beat, his lips parted to emit a slight breath, and the shudder which announces a return to life ran through his whole frame. Finally his eyes opened, though with an expressionless stare at first; then his vision returned and with it the power of feeling and grief.

"Oh, I still live!" he cried in accents of despair. "The Count has deceived me!" Extending his hand toward the table, he seized a knife.

"My dear one!" said Valentine with her sweet smile. "Awake and look at me!"

With a loud cry, frantic, doubting, and dazzled as by a celestial vision, Morrel fell upon his knees.

At daybreak the next day Morrel and Valentine were walking arm in arm along the seashore, while Valentine related how Monte Cristo had appeared in her room, how he had disclosed everything and pointed to the crime, and finally how he had miraculously saved her from death by making believe that she was dead.

They had found the door of the grotto open and had gone out whilst the last stars of the night were still shining in the morning sky. After a time, Morrel perceived a man standing amongst the rocks waiting for permission to advance, and pointed him out to Valentine.

"It is Jacopo, the captain of the yacht!" she said, making signs for him to approach.

"Have you something to tell us?" Morrel asked.

"I have a letter from the Count for you."

"From the Count!" they exclaimed together.

"Yes, read it."

Morrel opened the letter and read:

MY DEAR MAXIMILIAN,

There is a felucca waiting for you. Jacopo will take you to Leghorn, where Monsieur Noirtier is awaiting his granddaughter to give her his blessing before you conduct her to the altar. All that is in the grotto, my house in the Champs Élysées, and my little château at Tréport are the wedding present of Edmond Dantès to the son of his old master,

Morrel. Ask Mademoiselle de Villefort to accept one half, for I beseech her to give to the poor of Paris all the money which she inherits from her father, who is now insane, as also from her brother, who died last September with her stepmother.

Tell the angel who is going to watch over you, Morrel, to pray for a man who, like Satan, believed for one moment he was the equal of God, but who now acknowledges in all Christian humility that in God alone is supreme power and infinite wisdom. Her prayers will perhaps soothe the remorse in the depths of his heart.

Live and be happy, beloved children of my heart, and never forget that, until the day comes when God will deign to reveal the future to man, all human wisdom is contained in these words: Wait and hope!

Your friend,
EDMOND DANTÈS,
Count of Monte Cristo

During the perusal of this letter, which informed Valentine for the first time of the fate of her father and her brother, she turned pale, a painful sigh escaped from her bosom, and silent tears coursed down her cheeks; her happiness had cost her dear.

Morrel looked around him uneasily.

"Where is the Count, my friend?" said he. "Take me to him."

Jacopo raised his hand toward the horizon.

"What do you mean?" asked Valentine. "Where is the Count? Where is Haydee?"

"Look!" said Jacopo.

The eyes of the two young people followed the direction of the sailor's hand, and there, on the blue horizon separating the sky from the Mediterranean they perceived a sail, which loomed large and white like a seagull.

"Gone!" cried Morrel. "Farewell, my friend, my father!"

"Gone!" murmured Valentine. "Good-bye, my friend, my sister!"

"Who knows whether we shall ever see them again," said Morrel, wiping away a tear.

"My dear," replied Valentine, "has not the Count just told us that all human wisdom is contained in the words 'Wait and hope!'"

A CATALOG OF SELECTED
**DOVER BOOKS**
IN ALL FIELDS OF INTEREST

# A CATALOG OF SELECTED DOVER
# BOOKS IN ALL FIELDS OF INTEREST

100 BEST-LOVED POEMS, Edited by Philip Smith. "The Passionate Shepherd to His Love," "Shall I compare thee to a summer's day?" "Death, be not proud," "The Raven," "The Road Not Taken," plus works by Blake, Wordsworth, Byron, Shelley, Keats, many others. 96pp. 5³⁄₁₆ x 8¼.                 0-486-28553-7

100 SMALL HOUSES OF THE THIRTIES, Brown-Blodgett Company. Exterior photographs and floor plans for 100 charming structures. Illustrations of models accompanied by descriptions of interiors, color schemes, closet space, and other amenities. 200 illustrations. 112pp. 8⅜ x 11.              0-486-44131-8

1000 TURN-OF-THE-CENTURY HOUSES: With Illustrations and Floor Plans, Herbert C. Chivers. Reproduced from a rare edition, this showcase of homes ranges from cottages and bungalows to sprawling mansions. Each house is meticulously illustrated and accompanied by complete floor plans. 256pp. 9⅜ x 12¼.
                                             0-486-45596-3

101 GREAT AMERICAN POEMS, Edited by The American Poetry & Literacy Project. Rich treasury of verse from the 19th and 20th centuries includes works by Edgar Allan Poe, Robert Frost, Walt Whitman, Langston Hughes, Emily Dickinson, T. S. Eliot, other notables. 96pp. 5³⁄₁₆ x 8¼.            0-486-40158-8

101 GREAT SAMURAI PRINTS, Utagawa Kuniyoshi. Kuniyoshi was a master of the warrior woodblock print — and these 18th-century illustrations represent the pinnacle of his craft. Full-color portraits of renowned Japanese samurais pulse with movement, passion, and remarkably fine detail. 112pp. 8⅜ x 11.     0-486-46523-3

ABC OF BALLET, Janet Grosser. Clearly worded, abundantly illustrated little guide defines basic ballet-related terms: arabesque, battement, pas de chat, relevé, sissonne, many others. Pronunciation guide included. Excellent primer. 48pp. 4³⁄₁₆ x 5¾.
                                             0-486-40871-X

ACCESSORIES OF DRESS: An Illustrated Encyclopedia, Katherine Lester and Bess Viola Oerke. Illustrations of hats, veils, wigs, cravats, shawls, shoes, gloves, and other accessories enhance an engaging commentary that reveals the humor and charm of the many-sided story of accessorized apparel. 644 figures and 59 plates. 608pp. 6⅛ x 9¼.
                                             0-486-43378-1

ADVENTURES OF HUCKLEBERRY FINN, Mark Twain. Join Huck and Jim as their boyhood adventures along the Mississippi River lead them into a world of excitement, danger, and self-discovery. Humorous narrative, lyrical descriptions of the Mississippi valley, and memorable characters. 224pp. 5³⁄₁₆ x 8¼.     0-486-28061-6

ALICE STARMORE'S BOOK OF FAIR ISLE KNITTING, Alice Starmore. A noted designer from the region of Scotland's Fair Isle explores the history and techniques of this distinctive, stranded-color knitting style and provides copious illustrated instructions for 14 original knitwear designs. 208pp. 8⅜ x 10⅞.    0-486-47218-3

ALICE'S ADVENTURES IN WONDERLAND, Lewis Carroll. Beloved classic about a little girl lost in a topsy-turvy land and her encounters with the White Rabbit, March Hare, Mad Hatter, Cheshire Cat, and other delightfully improbable characters. 42 illustrations by Sir John Tenniel. 96pp. 5³⁄₁₆ x 8¼. 0-486-27543-4

AMERICA'S LIGHTHOUSES: An Illustrated History, Francis Ross Holland. Profusely illustrated fact-filled survey of American lighthouses since 1716. Over 200 stations — East, Gulf, and West coasts, Great Lakes, Hawaii, Alaska, Puerto Rico, the Virgin Islands, and the Mississippi and St. Lawrence Rivers. 240pp. 8 x 10¾. 0-486-25576-X

AN ENCYCLOPEDIA OF THE VIOLIN, Alberto Bachmann. Translated by Frederick H. Martens. Introduction by Eugene Ysaye. First published in 1925, this renowned reference remains unsurpassed as a source of essential information, from construction and evolution to repertoire and technique. Includes a glossary and 73 illustrations. 496pp. 6⅛ x 9¼. 0-486-46618-3

ANIMALS: 1,419 Copyright-Free Illustrations of Mammals, Birds, Fish, Insects, etc., Selected by Jim Harter. Selected for its visual impact and ease of use, this outstanding collection of wood engravings presents over 1,000 species of animals in extremely lifelike poses. Includes mammals, birds, reptiles, amphibians, fish, insects, and other invertebrates. 284pp. 9 x 12. 0-486-23766-4

THE ANNALS, Tacitus. Translated by Alfred John Church and William Jackson Brodribb. This vital chronicle of Imperial Rome, written by the era's great historian, spans A.D. 14-68 and paints incisive psychological portraits of major figures, from Tiberius to Nero. 416pp. 5³⁄₁₆ x 8¼. 0-486-45236-0

ANTIGONE, Sophocles. Filled with passionate speeches and sensitive probing of moral and philosophical issues, this powerful and often-performed Greek drama reveals the grim fate that befalls the children of Oedipus. Footnotes. 64pp. 5³⁄₁₆ x 8 ¼. 0-486-27804-2

ART DECO DECORATIVE PATTERNS IN FULL COLOR, Christian Stoll. Reprinted from a rare 1910 portfolio, 160 sensuous and exotic images depict a breathtaking array of florals, geometrics, and abstracts — all elegant in their stark simplicity. 64pp. 8⅜ x 11. 0-486-44862-2

THE ARTHUR RACKHAM TREASURY: 86 Full-Color Illustrations, Arthur Rackham. Selected and Edited by Jeff A. Menges. A stunning treasury of 86 full-page plates span the famed English artist's career, from *Rip Van Winkle* (1905) to masterworks such as *Undine, A Midsummer Night's Dream,* and *Wind in the Willows* (1939). 96pp. 8⅜ x 11. 0-486-44685-9

THE AUTHENTIC GILBERT & SULLIVAN SONGBOOK, W. S. Gilbert and A. S. Sullivan. The most comprehensive collection available, this songbook includes selections from every one of Gilbert and Sullivan's light operas. Ninety-two numbers are presented uncut and unedited, and in their original keys. 410pp. 9 x 12. 0-486-23482-7

THE AWAKENING, Kate Chopin. First published in 1899, this controversial novel of a New Orleans wife's search for love outside a stifling marriage shocked readers. Today, it remains a first-rate narrative with superb characterization. New introductory Note. 128pp. 5³⁄₁₆ x 8¼. 0-486-27786-0

BASIC DRAWING, Louis Priscilla. Beginning with perspective, this commonsense manual progresses to the figure in movement, light and shade, anatomy, drapery, composition, trees and landscape, and outdoor sketching. Black-and-white illustrations throughout. 128pp. 8⅜ x 11. 0-486-45815-6

CATALOG OF DOVER BOOKS

THE BATTLES THAT CHANGED HISTORY, Fletcher Pratt. Historian profiles 16 crucial conflicts, ancient to modern, that changed the course of Western civilization. Gripping accounts of battles led by Alexander the Great, Joan of Arc, Ulysses S. Grant, other commanders. 27 maps. 352pp. 5⅜ x 8½. 0-486-41129-X

BEETHOVEN'S LETTERS, Ludwig van Beethoven. Edited by Dr. A. C. Kalischer. Features 457 letters to fellow musicians, friends, greats, patrons, and literary men. Reveals musical thoughts, quirks of personality, insights, and daily events. Includes 15 plates. 410pp. 5⅜ x 8½. 0-486-22769-3

BERNICE BOBS HER HAIR AND OTHER STORIES, F. Scott Fitzgerald. This brilliant anthology includes 6 of Fitzgerald's most popular stories: "The Diamond as Big as the Ritz," the title tale, "The Offshore Pirate," "The Ice Palace," "The Jelly Bean," and "May Day." 176pp. 5⅜ x 8½. 0-486-47049-0

BESLER'S BOOK OF FLOWERS AND PLANTS: 73 Full-Color Plates from Hortus Eystettensis, 1613, Basilius Besler. Here is a selection of magnificent plates from the *Hortus Eystettensis*, which vividly illustrated and identified the plants, flowers, and trees that thrived in the legendary German garden at Eichstätt. 80pp. 8⅜ x 11. 0-486-46005-3

THE BOOK OF KELLS, Edited by Blanche Cirker. Painstakingly reproduced from a rare facsimile edition, this volume contains full-page decorations, portraits, illustrations, plus a sampling of textual leaves with exquisite calligraphy and ornamentation. 32 full-color illustrations. 32pp. 9⅜ x 12¼. 0-486-24345-1

THE BOOK OF THE CROSSBOW: With an Additional Section on Catapults and Other Siege Engines, Ralph Payne-Gallwey. Fascinating study traces history and use of crossbow as military and sporting weapon, from Middle Ages to modern times. Also covers related weapons: balistas, catapults, Turkish bows, more. Over 240 illustrations. 400pp. 7¼ x 10⅛. 0-486-28720-3

THE BUNGALOW BOOK: Floor Plans and Photos of 112 Houses, 1910, Henry L. Wilson. Here are 112 of the most popular and economic blueprints of the early 20th century — plus an illustration or photograph of each completed house. A wonderful time capsule that still offers a wealth of valuable insights. 160pp. 8⅜ x 11. 0-486-45104-6

THE CALL OF THE WILD, Jack London. A classic novel of adventure, drawn from London's own experiences as a Klondike adventurer, relating the story of a heroic dog caught in the brutal life of the Alaska Gold Rush. Note. 64pp. 5³⁄₁₆ x 8¼. 0-486-26472-6

CANDIDE, Voltaire. Edited by Francois-Marie Arouet. One of the world's great satires since its first publication in 1759. Witty, caustic skewering of romance, science, philosophy, religion, government — nearly all human ideals and institutions. 112pp. 5³⁄₁₆ x 8¼. 0-486-26689-3

CELEBRATED IN THEIR TIME: Photographic Portraits from the George Grantham Bain Collection, Edited by Amy Pastan. With an Introduction by Michael Carlebach. Remarkable portrait gallery features 112 rare images of Albert Einstein, Charlie Chaplin, the Wright Brothers, Henry Ford, and other luminaries from the worlds of politics, art, entertainment, and industry. 128pp. 8⅜ x 11. 0-486-46754-6

CHARIOTS FOR APOLLO: The NASA History of Manned Lunar Spacecraft to 1969, Courtney G. Brooks, James M. Grimwood, and Loyd S. Swenson, Jr. This illustrated history by a trio of experts is the definitive reference on the Apollo spacecraft and lunar modules. It traces the vehicles' design, development, and operation in space. More than 100 photographs and illustrations. 576pp. 6¾ x 9¼. 0-486-46756-2

Browse over 9,000 books at www.doverpublications.com

A CHRISTMAS CAROL, Charles Dickens. This engrossing tale relates Ebenezer Scrooge's ghostly journeys through Christmases past, present, and future and his ultimate transformation from a harsh and grasping old miser to a charitable and compassionate human being. 80pp. 5³⁄₁₆ x 8¼. 0-486-26865-9

COMMON SENSE, Thomas Paine. First published in January of 1776, this highly influential landmark document clearly and persuasively argued for American separation from Great Britain and paved the way for the Declaration of Independence. 64pp. 5³⁄₁₆ x 8¼. 0-486-29602-4

THE COMPLETE SHORT STORIES OF OSCAR WILDE, Oscar Wilde. Complete texts of "The Happy Prince and Other Tales," "A House of Pomegranates," "Lord Arthur Savile's Crime and Other Stories," "Poems in Prose," and "The Portrait of Mr. W. H." 208pp. 5³⁄₁₆ x 8¼. 0-486-45216-6

COMPLETE SONNETS, William Shakespeare. Over 150 exquisite poems deal with love, friendship, the tyranny of time, beauty's evanescence, death, and other themes in language of remarkable power, precision, and beauty. Glossary of archaic terms. 80pp. 5³⁄₁₆ x 8¼. 0-486-26686-9

THE COUNT OF MONTE CRISTO: Abridged Edition, Alexandre Dumas. Falsely accused of treason, Edmond Dantès is imprisoned in the bleak Chateau d'If. After a hair-raising escape, he launches an elaborate plot to extract a bitter revenge against those who betrayed him. 448pp. 5³⁄₁₆ x 8¼. 0-486-45643-9

CRAFTSMAN BUNGALOWS: Designs from the Pacific Northwest, Yoho & Merritt. This reprint of a rare catalog, showcasing the charming simplicity and cozy style of Craftsman bungalows, is filled with photos of completed homes, plus floor plans and estimated costs. An indispensable resource for architects, historians, and illustrators. 112pp. 10 x 7. 0-486-46875-5

CRAFTSMAN BUNGALOWS: 59 Homes from "The Craftsman," Edited by Gustav Stickley. Best and most attractive designs from Arts and Crafts Movement publication — 1903–1916 — includes sketches, photographs of homes, floor plans, descriptive text. 128pp. 8¼ x 11. 0-486-25829-7

CRIME AND PUNISHMENT, Fyodor Dostoyevsky. Translated by Constance Garnett. Supreme masterpiece tells the story of Raskolnikov, a student tormented by his own thoughts after he murders an old woman. Overwhelmed by guilt and terror, he confesses and goes to prison. 480pp. 5³⁄₁₆ x 8¼. 0-486-41587-2

THE DECLARATION OF INDEPENDENCE AND OTHER GREAT DOCUMENTS OF AMERICAN HISTORY: 1775-1865, Edited by John Grafton. Thirteen compelling and influential documents: Henry's "Give Me Liberty or Give Me Death," Declaration of Independence, The Constitution, Washington's First Inaugural Address, The Monroe Doctrine, The Emancipation Proclamation, Gettysburg Address, more. 64pp. 5³⁄₁₆ x 8¼. 0-486-41124-9

THE DESERT AND THE SOWN: Travels in Palestine and Syria, Gertrude Bell. "The female Lawrence of Arabia," Gertrude Bell wrote captivating, perceptive accounts of her travels in the Middle East. This intriguing narrative, accompanied by 160 photos, traces her 1905 sojourn in Lebanon, Syria, and Palestine. 368pp. 5⅜ x 8½.
0-486-46876-3

A DOLL'S HOUSE, Henrik Ibsen. Ibsen's best-known play displays his genius for realistic prose drama. An expression of women's rights, the play climaxes when the central character, Nora, rejects a smothering marriage and life in "a doll's house." 80pp. 5³⁄₁₆ x 8¼. 0-486-27062-9

DOOMED SHIPS: Great Ocean Liner Disasters, William H. Miller, Jr. Nearly 200 photographs, many from private collections, highlight tales of some of the vessels whose pleasure cruises ended in catastrophe: the *Morro Castle, Normandie, Andrea Doria, Europa,* and many others. 128pp. 8⅞ x 11¼. 0-486-45366-9

THE DORÉ BIBLE ILLUSTRATIONS, Gustave Doré. Detailed plates from the Bible: the Creation scenes, Adam and Eve, horrifying visions of the Flood, the battle sequences with their monumental crowds, depictions of the life of Jesus, 241 plates in all. 241pp. 9 x 12. 0-486-23004-X

DRAWING DRAPERY FROM HEAD TO TOE, Cliff Young. Expert guidance on how to draw shirts, pants, skirts, gloves, hats, and coats on the human figure, including folds in relation to the body, pull and crush, action folds, creases, more. Over 200 drawings. 48pp. 8¼ x 11. 0-486-45591-2

DUBLINERS, James Joyce. A fine and accessible introduction to the work of one of the 20th century's most influential writers, this collection features 15 tales, including a masterpiece of the short-story genre, "The Dead." 160pp. 5³⁄₁₆ x 8¼. 0-486-26870-5

EASY-TO-MAKE POP-UPS, Joan Irvine. Illustrated by Barbara Reid. Dozens of wonderful ideas for three-dimensional paper fun — from holiday greeting cards with moving parts to a pop-up menagerie. Easy-to-follow, illustrated instructions for more than 30 projects. 299 black-and-white illustrations. 96pp. 8⅜ x 11. 0-486-44622-0

EASY-TO-MAKE STORYBOOK DOLLS: A "Novel" Approach to Cloth Dollmaking, Sherralyn St. Clair. Favorite fictional characters come alive in this unique beginner's dollmaking guide. Includes patterns for Pollyanna, Dorothy from *The Wonderful Wizard of Oz,* Mary of *The Secret Garden,* plus easy-to-follow instructions, 263 black-and-white illustrations, and an 8-page color insert. 112pp. 8¼ x 11. 0-486-47360-0

EINSTEIN'S ESSAYS IN SCIENCE, Albert Einstein. Speeches and essays in accessible, everyday language profile influential physicists such as Niels Bohr and Isaac Newton. They also explore areas of physics to which the author made major contributions. 128pp. 5 x 8. 0-486-47011-3

EL DORADO: Further Adventures of the Scarlet Pimpernel, Baroness Orczy. A popular sequel to *The Scarlet Pimpernel,* this suspenseful story recounts the Pimpernel's attempts to rescue the Dauphin from imprisonment during the French Revolution. An irresistible blend of intrigue, period detail, and vibrant characterizations. 352pp. 5³⁄₁₆ x 8¼. 0-486-44026-5

ELEGANT SMALL HOMES OF THE TWENTIES: 99 Designs from a Competition, Chicago Tribune. Nearly 100 designs for five- and six-room houses feature New England and Southern colonials, Normandy cottages, stately Italianate dwellings, and other fascinating snapshots of American domestic architecture of the 1920s. 112pp. 9 x 12. 0-486-46910-7

THE ELEMENTS OF STYLE: The Original Edition, William Strunk, Jr. This is the book that generations of writers have relied upon for timeless advice on grammar, diction, syntax, and other essentials. In concise terms, it identifies the principal requirements of proper style and common errors. 64pp. 5⅜ x 8½. 0-486-44798-7

THE ELUSIVE PIMPERNEL, Baroness Orczy. Robespierre's revolutionaries find their wicked schemes thwarted by the heroic Pimpernel — Sir Percival Blakeney. In this thrilling sequel, Chauvelin devises a plot to eliminate the Pimpernel and his wife. 272pp. 5³⁄₁₆ x 8¼. 0-486-45464-9

AN ENCYCLOPEDIA OF BATTLES: Accounts of Over 1,560 Battles from 1479 B.C. to the Present, David Eggenberger. Essential details of every major battle in recorded history from the first battle of Megiddo in 1479 B.C. to Grenada in 1984. List of battle maps. 99 illustrations. 544pp. 6½ x 9¼. 0-486-24913-1

ENCYCLOPEDIA OF EMBROIDERY STITCHES, INCLUDING CREWEL, Marion Nichols. Precise explanations and instructions, clearly illustrated, on how to work chain, back, cross, knotted, woven stitches, and many more — 178 in all, including Cable Outline, Whipped Satin, and Eyelet Buttonhole. Over 1400 illustrations. 219pp. 8⅜ x 11¼. 0-486-22929-7

ENTER JEEVES: 15 Early Stories, P. G. Wodehouse. Splendid collection contains first 8 stories featuring Bertie Wooster, the deliciously dim aristocrat and Jeeves, his brainy, imperturbable manservant. Also, the complete Reggie Pepper (Bertie's prototype) series. 288pp. 5⅜ x 8½. 0-486-29717-9

ERIC SLOANE'S AMERICA: Paintings in Oil, Michael Wigley. With a Foreword by Mimi Sloane. Eric Sloane's evocative oils of America's landscape and material culture shimmer with immense historical and nostalgic appeal. This original hardcover collection gathers nearly a hundred of his finest paintings, with subjects ranging from New England to the American Southwest. 128pp. 10⅝ x 9. 0-486-46525-X

ETHAN FROME, Edith Wharton. Classic story of wasted lives, set against a bleak New England background. Superbly delineated characters in a hauntingly grim tale of thwarted love. Considered by many to be Wharton's masterpiece. 96pp. 5³⁄₁₆ x 8¼. 0-486-26690-7

THE EVERLASTING MAN, G. K. Chesterton. Chesterton's view of Christianity — as a blend of philosophy and mythology, satisfying intellect and spirit — applies to his brilliant book, which appeals to readers' heads as well as their hearts. 288pp. 5⅜ x 8½. 0-486-46036-3

THE FIELD AND FOREST HANDY BOOK, Daniel Beard. Written by a co-founder of the Boy Scouts, this appealing guide offers illustrated instructions for building kites, birdhouses, boats, igloos, and other fun projects, plus numerous helpful tips for campers. 448pp. 5³⁄₁₆ x 8¼. 0-486-46191-2

FINDING YOUR WAY WITHOUT MAP OR COMPASS, Harold Gatty. Useful, instructive manual shows would-be explorers, hikers, bikers, scouts, sailors, and survivalists how to find their way outdoors by observing animals, weather patterns, shifting sands, and other elements of nature. 288pp. 5⅜ x 8½. 0-486-40613-X

FIRST FRENCH READER: A Beginner's Dual-Language Book, Edited and Translated by Stanley Appelbaum. This anthology introduces 50 legendary writers — Voltaire, Balzac, Baudelaire, Proust, more — through passages from *The Red and the Black*, *Les Misérables, Madame Bovary*, and other classics. Original French text plus English translation on facing pages. 240pp. 5⅜ x 8½. 0-486-46178-5

FIRST GERMAN READER: A Beginner's Dual-Language Book, Edited by Harry Steinhauer. Specially chosen for their power to evoke German life and culture, these short, simple readings include poems, stories, essays, and anecdotes by Goethe, Hesse, Heine, Schiller, and others. 224pp. 5⅜ x 8½. 0-486-46179-3

FIRST SPANISH READER: A Beginner's Dual-Language Book, Angel Flores. Delightful stories, other material based on works of Don Juan Manuel, Luis Taboada, Ricardo Palma, other noted writers. Complete faithful English translations on facing pages. Exercises. 176pp. 5⅜ x 8½. 0-486-25810-6

# CATALOG OF DOVER BOOKS

FIVE ACRES AND INDEPENDENCE, Maurice G. Kains. Great back-to-the-land classic explains basics of self-sufficient farming. The one book to get. 95 illustrations. 397pp. 5⅜ x 8½.　　　　　　　　　　　　　　　　　0-486-20974-1

FLAGG'S SMALL HOUSES: Their Economic Design and Construction, 1922, Ernest Flagg. Although most famous for his skyscrapers, Flagg was also a proponent of the well-designed single-family dwelling. His classic treatise features innovations that save space, materials, and cost. 526 illustrations. 160pp. 9⅜ x 12¼.
0-486-45197-6

FLATLAND: A Romance of Many Dimensions, Edwin A. Abbott. Classic of science (and mathematical) fiction — charmingly illustrated by the author — describes the adventures of A. Square, a resident of Flatland, in Spaceland (three dimensions), Lineland (one dimension), and Pointland (no dimensions). 96pp. 5³⁄₁₆ x 8¼.
0-486-27263-X

FRANKENSTEIN, Mary Shelley. The story of Victor Frankenstein's monstrous creation and the havoc it caused has enthralled generations of readers and inspired countless writers of horror and suspense. With the author's own 1831 introduction. 176pp. 5³⁄₁₆ x 8¼.　　　　　　　　　　　　　　　　0-486-28211-2

THE GARGOYLE BOOK: 572 Examples from Gothic Architecture, Lester Burbank Bridaham. Dispelling the conventional wisdom that French Gothic architectural flourishes were born of despair or gloom, Bridaham reveals the whimsical nature of these creations and the ingenious artisans who made them. 572 illustrations. 224pp. 8⅜ x 11.　　　　　　　　　　　　　　　　　　　　　0-486-44754-5

THE GIFT OF THE MAGI AND OTHER SHORT STORIES, O. Henry. Sixteen captivating stories by one of America's most popular storytellers. Included are such classics as "The Gift of the Magi," "The Last Leaf," and "The Ransom of Red Chief." Publisher's Note. 96pp. 5³⁄₁₆ x 8¼.　　　　　　　　　　　0-486-27061-0

THE GOETHE TREASURY: Selected Prose and Poetry, Johann Wolfgang von Goethe. Edited, Selected, and with an Introduction by Thomas Mann. In addition to his lyric poetry, Goethe wrote travel sketches, autobiographical studies, essays, letters, and proverbs in rhyme and prose. This collection presents outstanding examples from each genre. 368pp. 5⅜ x 8½.　　　　　　　0-486-44780-4

GREAT EXPECTATIONS, Charles Dickens. Orphaned Pip is apprenticed to the dirty work of the forge but dreams of becoming a gentleman — and one day finds himself in possession of "great expectations." Dickens' finest novel. 400pp. 5³⁄₁₆ x 8¼.
0-486-41586-4

GREAT WRITERS ON THE ART OF FICTION: From Mark Twain to Joyce Carol Oates, Edited by James Daley. An indispensable source of advice and inspiration, this anthology features essays by Henry James, Kate Chopin, Willa Cather, Sinclair Lewis, Jack London, Raymond Chandler, Raymond Carver, Eudora Welty, and Kurt Vonnegut, Jr. 192pp. 5⅜ x 8½.　　　　　　　　　　　　0-486-45128-3

HAMLET, William Shakespeare. The quintessential Shakespearean tragedy, whose highly charged confrontations and anguished soliloquies probe depths of human feeling rarely sounded in any art. Reprinted from an authoritative British edition complete with illuminating footnotes. 128pp. 5³⁄₁₆ x 8¼.　　　0-486-27278-8

THE HAUNTED HOUSE, Charles Dickens. A Yuletide gathering in an eerie country retreat provides the backdrop for Dickens and his friends — including Elizabeth Gaskell and Wilkie Collins — who take turns spinning supernatural yarns. 144pp. 5⅜ x 8½.　　　　　　　　　　　　　　　　　　　　　0-486-46309-5

HEART OF DARKNESS, Joseph Conrad. Dark allegory of a journey up the Congo River and the narrator's encounter with the mysterious Mr. Kurtz. Masterly blend of adventure, character study, psychological penetration. For many, Conrad's finest, most enigmatic story. 80pp. 5³⁄₁₆ x 8¼. 0-486-26464-5

HENSON AT THE NORTH POLE, Matthew A. Henson. This thrilling memoir by the heroic African-American who was Peary's companion through two decades of Arctic exploration recounts a tale of danger, courage, and determination. "Fascinating and exciting." — *Commonweal.* 128pp. 5⅜ x 8½. 0-486-45472-X

HISTORIC COSTUMES AND HOW TO MAKE THEM, Mary Fernald and E. Shenton. Practical, informative guidebook shows how to create everything from short tunics worn by Saxon men in the fifth century to a lady's bustle dress of the late 1800s. 81 illustrations. 176pp. 5⅜ x 8½. 0-486-44906-8

THE HOUND OF THE BASKERVILLES, Arthur Conan Doyle. A deadly curse in the form of a legendary ferocious beast continues to claim its victims from the Baskerville family until Holmes and Watson intervene. Often called the best detective story ever written. 128pp. 5³⁄₁₆ x 8¼. 0-486-28214-7

THE HOUSE BEHIND THE CEDARS, Charles W. Chesnutt. Originally published in 1900, this groundbreaking novel by a distinguished African-American author recounts the drama of a brother and sister who "pass for white" during the dangerous days of Reconstruction. 208pp. 5⅜ x 8½. 0-486-46144-0

THE HUMAN FIGURE IN MOTION, Eadweard Muybridge. The 4,789 photographs in this definitive selection show the human figure — models almost all undraped — engaged in over 160 different types of action: running, climbing stairs, etc. 390pp. 7⅞ x 10⅝. 0-486-20204-6

THE IMPORTANCE OF BEING EARNEST, Oscar Wilde. Wilde's witty and buoyant comedy of manners, filled with some of literature's most famous epigrams, reprinted from an authoritative British edition. Considered Wilde's most perfect work. 64pp. 5³⁄₁₆ x 8¼. 0-486-26478-5

THE INFERNO, Dante Alighieri. Translated and with notes by Henry Wadsworth Longfellow. The first stop on Dante's famous journey from Hell to Purgatory to Paradise, this 14th-century allegorical poem blends vivid and shocking imagery with graceful lyricism. Translated by the beloved 19th-century poet, Henry Wadsworth Longfellow. 256pp. 5³⁄₁₆ x 8¼. 0-486-44288-8

JANE EYRE, Charlotte Brontë. Written in 1847, *Jane Eyre* tells the tale of an orphan girl's progress from the custody of cruel relatives to an oppressive boarding school and its culmination in a troubled career as a governess. 448pp. 5³⁄₁₆ x 8¼. 0-486-42449-9

JAPANESE WOODBLOCK FLOWER PRINTS, Tanigami Kônan. Extraordinary collection of Japanese woodblock prints by a well-known artist features 120 plates in brilliant color. Realistic images from a rare edition include daffodils, tulips, and other familiar and unusual flowers. 128pp. 11 x 8¼. 0-486-46442-3

JEWELRY MAKING AND DESIGN, Augustus F. Rose and Antonio Cirino. Professional secrets of jewelry making are revealed in a thorough, practical guide. Over 200 illustrations. 306pp. 5⅜ x 8½. 0-486-21750-7

JULIUS CAESAR, William Shakespeare. Great tragedy based on Plutarch's account of the lives of Brutus, Julius Caesar and Mark Antony. Evil plotting, ringing oratory, high tragedy with Shakespeare's incomparable insight, dramatic power. Explanatory footnotes. 96pp. 5³⁄₁₆ x 8¼. 0-486-26876-4

THE JUNGLE, Upton Sinclair. 1906 bestseller shockingly reveals intolerable labor practices and working conditions in the Chicago stockyards as it tells the grim story of a Slavic family that emigrates to America full of optimism but soon faces despair. 320pp. 5³⁄₁₆ x 8¼. 0-486-41923-1

THE KINGDOM OF GOD IS WITHIN YOU, Leo Tolstoy. The soul-searching book that inspired Gandhi to embrace the concept of passive resistance, Tolstoy's 1894 polemic clearly outlines a radical, well-reasoned revision of traditional Christian thinking. 352pp. 5³⁄₁₆ x 8¼. 0-486-45138-0

THE LADY OR THE TIGER?: and Other Logic Puzzles, Raymond M. Smullyan. Created by a renowned puzzle master, these whimsically themed challenges involve paradoxes about probability, time, and change; metapuzzles; and self-referentiality. Nineteen chapters advance in difficulty from relatively simple to highly complex. 1982 edition. 240pp. 5⅜ x 8½. 0-486-47027-X

LEAVES OF GRASS: The Original 1855 Edition, Walt Whitman. Whitman's immortal collection includes some of the greatest poems of modern times, including his masterpiece, "Song of Myself." Shattering standard conventions, it stands as an unabashed celebration of body and nature. 128pp. 5³⁄₁₆ x 8¼. 0-486-45676-5

LES MISÉRABLES, Victor Hugo. Translated by Charles E. Wilbour. Abridged by James K. Robinson. A convict's heroic struggle for justice and redemption plays out against a fiery backdrop of the Napoleonic wars. This edition features the excellent original translation and a sensitive abridgment. 304pp. 6⅛ x 9¼. 0-486-45789-3

LILITH: A Romance, George MacDonald. In this novel by the father of fantasy literature, a man travels through time to meet Adam and Eve and to explore humanity's fall from grace and ultimate redemption. 240pp. 5⅜ x 8½. 0-486-46818-6

THE LOST LANGUAGE OF SYMBOLISM, Harold Bayley. This remarkable book reveals the hidden meaning behind familiar images and words, from the origins of Santa Claus to the fleur-de-lys, drawing from mythology, folklore, religious texts, and fairy tales. 1,418 illustrations. 784pp. 5⅜ x 8½. 0-486-44787-1

MACBETH, William Shakespeare. A Scottish nobleman murders the king in order to succeed to the throne. Tortured by his conscience and fearful of discovery, he becomes tangled in a web of treachery and deceit that ultimately spells his doom. 96pp. 5³⁄₁₆ x 8¼. 0-486-27802-6

MAKING AUTHENTIC CRAFTSMAN FURNITURE: Instructions and Plans for 62 Projects, Gustav Stickley. Make authentic reproductions of handsome, functional, durable furniture: tables, chairs, wall cabinets, desks, a hall tree, and more. Construction plans with drawings, schematics, dimensions, and lumber specs reprinted from 1900s *The Craftsman* magazine. 128pp. 8⅛ x 11. 0-486-25000-8

MATHEMATICS FOR THE NONMATHEMATICIAN, Morris Kline. Erudite and entertaining overview follows development of mathematics from ancient Greeks to present. Topics include logic and mathematics, the fundamental concept, differential calculus, probability theory, much more. Exercises and problems. 641pp. 5⅜ x 8½. 0-486-24823-2

MEMOIRS OF AN ARABIAN PRINCESS FROM ZANZIBAR, Emily Ruete. This 19th-century autobiography offers a rare inside look at the society surrounding a sultan's palace. A real-life princess in exile recalls her vanished world of harems, slave trading, and court intrigues. 288pp. 5⅜ x 8½. 0-486-47121-7

**Browse over 9,000 books at www.doverpublications.com**